SHORT STORIES
Classic, Modern, Contemporary

Short Stories

Classic,
Modern,
Contemporary

Edited by

MARCUS KLEIN
State University of New York at Buffalo

ROBERT PACK
Middlebury College

Little, Brown and Company • Boston

LIBRARY OF CONGRESS CATALOG CARD NO. 67–17093

FIRST PRINTING

Published simultaneously in Canada
by Little, Brown & Company (Canada) Limited

PRINTED IN THE UNITED STATES OF AMERICA

"A Passion in the Desert" by Honoré de Balzac as translated by Raymond Federman was prepared especially for inclusion in this volume.

"The Nose," copyright © 1957 by David Magarshack, from the book *Tales of Good and Evil* by Nikolai Gogol, translated by David Magarshack, is reprinted by permission of Doubleday & Company, Inc.

"The Legend of St Julian Hospitator," translated by Robert Baldick, is reprinted from *Three Tales* by Gustave Flaubert by permission of Penguin Books Ltd.

"How Much Land Does a Man Need?" from *Twenty-Three Tales* by Leo Tolstoy, translated by Louise and Aylmer Maude, is reprinted by permission of the publishers, Oxford University Press (London).

"The Jolly Corner" is reprinted with the permission of Charles Scribner's Sons from Volume XVII, *The Novels and Tales of Henry James*. Copyright 1909 Charles Scribner's Sons; renewal copyright 1937 Henry James.

"Prince Roman" from *Tales of Hearsay* by Joseph Conrad is reprinted by permission of J. M. Dent & Sons Ltd. (London) and the Trustees of the Joseph Conrad Estate.

"At Sea — A Sailor's Story" from *Anton Chekhov Selected Stories,* translated by Ann Dunnigan, copyright © 1960 by Ann Dunnigan, is reprinted by permission of The New American Library, Inc. (New York).

"The Black Monk" from Anton Chekhov's *Collected Works,* translated by Jessie Coulson, is published by Oxford University Press (London) in their World's Classics Series (1963) and is reprinted with their permission.

"Twilight and Nocturnal Storm," translated by Tania and James Stern, is reprinted from *Selected Prose* of Hugo von Hofmannsthal, Bollingen Series XXXIII, Pantheon Books, pp. 215–219.

"The Fight Between Jappe and Do Escobar," translated by H. T. Lowe-Porter, copyright 1936 by Alfred A. Knopf, Inc., is reprinted from

*Special acknowledgment to
Patricia Pack for much
editorial and research
assistance*

Table of Contents

Introduction

The editors have attempted to bring together in this anthology a group of stories and writers which would indicate what might be called the contemporary tradition. Certain writers have come to be acknowledged as masters of the short story. It has been our task to discover which of the masters are now most compelling to our contemporary sensibilities, and in them we have sought the center of the contemporary tradition. Some of the masters have been given an emphasis in this anthology which is not customary. Not so long ago, Herman Melville's stories — except for the novella "Billy Budd" — were ambiguous oddities, important but not central. In the case of Edgar Allan Poe, for instance, we have selected his generally underestimated tale, "The Man of the Crowd," rather than one of his ghoul-haunted stories. In the case of Joseph Conrad, we have selected the serenely accomplished and seldom-read "Prince Roman."

Those masters whose immediacy seems to have diminished for the contemporary student have been excluded. European and Russian writers, on the other hand, who are particularly relevant to modern literature have been included. It has been a complementary part of our effort in defining the axis of the contemporary tradition in the short story to select some new stories by new writers which we think, by reason of their technical achievement, depth, and comprehension, belong with the works of the acknowledged masters.

We have tried to guide the student to the contemporary tradition with the feeling that it involves him personally, and that in studying these stories he is exploring his own heritage and its present sensibility. The short stories in this anthology have come from a variety of historical moments from the beginning of the modern period to our own time. Stories, however, are not merely documents, and history is not their prime subject. Rather, they are events in the lives of particular men living in specific times and, therefore, exist within a context of lives and times. They are events that take place in the human imagination as other imaginations have affected it, and this is the continuity and the heritage that concerns us here.

In assembling these stories, the editors also wanted to provide the student with a text which would introduce him to the technical possibilities of the short story and to the accomplishments of some of its greatest practitioners. We have not made another attempt to define the short story, and we state only that it is a prose work whose form demands a concentration of narrative in the presentation of conflict, climax, and denouement. The short story never follows a rigid prescription.

We have hoped in our selections to make the student aware of the vast possibilities of form, technical literary devices, thematic content, mood, style, and the uses of language. These stories contain differences in effect and meaning as viewed from various vantage points; within these differences, additional distinctions, nuances, and ingenuities are still to be discovered. The student may find it instructive, for instance, to compare the omniscient narrators in Balzac's "A Passion in the Desert" and Stephen Crane's "The Blue Hotel." Or, the student may find it instructive to analyze the kinds of meaning inherent in the epistolary form of Nabokov's "That in Aleppo Once . . ." and in the circumscribed perspective of Henry James's "The Jolly Corner."

With its infinite possibilities of technique, the short story is, above all, the form most appropriate for the sudden reversal, the epiphany, and the transforming revelation. It should be the curious ambition of the student to be both satisfied and surprised and thereby perceive, in full, the insight achieved by the storyteller, over and above that anticipated by the reader.

HONORÉ DE BALZAC (1799–1850) Balzac was born in Tours, France. His mother was a beautiful heiress and his father served in various army departments. Balzac had little family life. He was boarded out to nurse until the age of four and sent to the *Collège de Vendôme* from the ages of seven to thirteen. After being tutored in Paris, he studied law and obtained his degree. He decided to give up law, however, and since his father left him with little support, he began writing in a Paris garret. Although Balzac always fancied himself a great businessman, his first business venture as a publisher, printer, and type-founder incurred debts which plagued him for ten years until his mother paid them.

Balzac's life was filled with debts, rich women, and volumes of writing; his novels contain more than two thousand characters. His literary career actually began in 1829 with the publication of *Les Chouans* and *Physiologie du mariage*. Two of Balzac's most famous novels, *Eugénie Grandet* (1833) and *Le Père Goriot* (1834), concern the human condition. "Passion in the Desert" also deals with the human condition, here seen fundamentally as man contrasted with beast, conscious of the possibilities of friendship and trust.

Balzac is considered to be the father of the realistic novel in France. His tome on French society, *La Comédie Humaine,* was written in forty-seven volumes and remained unfinished. In a letter of 1884 he compares his ambition with the accomplishments of Napoleon, Cuvier, and O'Connell: "The first lived the life of Europe, he inoculated himself with armies! The second took the round earth itself in marriage! The third embodied a nation! I shall have carried an entire society in my head." Balzac's France, like Faulkner's Yoknapatawpha County, is a complete world.

A PASSION IN THE DESERT

Honoré de Balzac

"This spectacle is frightening!" she cried, coming out of Mr. Martin's menagerie. She had just watched the daring trainer "*work* with his hyena," to use the language of the posters.

"By what means," she went on, "can he have tamed these animals to the point of being sure of their affection so that . . ."

"This fact which seems a problem to you," I answered, interrupting her, "is nevertheless quite natural . . ."

"Oh!" she exclaimed, allowing an incredulous smile to wander across her lips.

"Do you believe, then, that animals are entirely deprived of passions?" I asked. "It might surprise you to learn that we can give them all the vices that result from our state of civilization."

She looked astonished.

"But," I went on, "when I first saw Mr. Martin, I must admit, I too gave vent to an exclamation of surprise. I was standing next to an old soldier whose right leg had been amputated. We had walked in together, and his face had struck me. It was one of those heroic faces marked by the seal of war and on which are written the battles of Napoleon. This old soldier had a particular air of frankness and good-humor which always impresses me favorably. He was no doubt one of these troopers who are surprised at nothing, who find something to laugh at in the last grimace of a dying friend, who bury or plunder him light-heartedly, who challenge bullets with authority, whose deliberations finally are brief, and who would fraternize with the Devil himself. After having watched, quite attentively, the owner of the menagerie as he came out of the dressing-room, my companion pursed his lips to show mocking disdain by this significant pouting which superior men use when they want to distinguish themselves from the dupes. Thus, when I showed amazement at

3

the courage of Mr. Martin, he smiled and told me with a knowing look, shaking his head: "Nothing new!"

"What do you mean, 'Nothing new'?" I said. "If you could
explain this mystery to me, I would be most obliged."

After a few moments during which we became acquainted, we
went to dine at the first restaurant which caught our eyes. At
dessert, a bottle of champagne helped this old soldier's memory
to regain its clarity. He told me his story, and I saw that he had
been right in saying: *"Nothing new!"*

Once we were back in her house, she teased me so much, made
so many promises, that I agreed to write down for her the soldier's confidences. The next day, she received this episode of an
epic which could be entitled: "The French in Egypt."

*   *   *

During the expedition in Upper Egypt undertaken by General
Desaix, a Provençal soldier was captured by the Maugrabins and
was taken by these Arabs to the desert beyond the cataracts of
the Nile. In order to put as much distance as possible between
them and the French army for their tranquility, the Maugrabins
force-marched, and stopped only at night-fall. They set up camp
around a well hidden by palm trees near which they had previously buried some provisions. Not thinking that their prisoner
would attempt to escape, they merely tied his hands, and all went
to sleep after having eaten a few dates and given their horses
some oats. When the brave Provençal saw that his enemies were
no longer watching him, he used his teeth to take hold of a scimitar, and using his knees to fix the blade firmly, he cut the ropes
from his hands and freed himself. He quickly grabbed a rifle and
a dagger, took the precaution to supply himself with a provision
of dry dates, a little bag of oats, some gun powder and bullets.
The scimitar in his belt, he leaped to a horse and spurred on
vigorously in the direction where he assumed to find the French
army. So anxious was he of seeing a bivouac again that he pressed
the already tired horse so much that the poor animal died, his
flanks torn open, leaving the Frenchman in the middle of the
desert.

After walking for some time in the sand with all the courage
of an escaped convict, the soldier was forced to stop, as the day
was almost ended. In spite of the beauty of an Oriental sky at
night, he did not have the strength to continue. Fortunately, he

managed to reach the top of a hill where a few palm trees shot up in the air and whose foliage stared at for a long time in the distance had awakened sweet hopes in his heart. His fatigue was so great that he lay down on a granite rock capriciously carved like a soldier's cot; there he fell asleep without taking any precautions for his security. He had made the sacrifice of his life. His last thought was one of regret. He was sorry to have left the Maugrabins whose nomadic life was beginning to smile on him now that he was far from them and without help. He was awakened by the sun whose pitiless rays fell directly downward on the granite and produced an unbearable heat. It so happened that the Provençal had had the stupidity of placing himself on the wrong side of the shadows projected by the green and majestic heads of the palm trees. . . . He looked at these solitary trees, and shuddered! They reminded him of the elegant shafts crowned by long leaves peculiar to the Saracen columns of the cathedral of Arles. But when, after having counted the palm trees, he looked around him, the most frightful despair fell upon his soul. He saw an ocean without end. The somber sands of the desert stretched out of sight in all directions, and glittered like a steel blade under a bright light. It might have been a sea of ice or a lake polished like a mirror. Carried by waves, a vapor of fire whirled above the moving earth. The sky had an Oriental reflection of insupportable purity, leaving nothing to desire to the imagination. The sky and the earth were on fire. The silence was frightening by its savage and terrible majesty. Infinity, immensity pressed the soul from all sides: not a cloud in the sky, not a breath of wind in the air, not a rise on the bosom of the sand, ever flowing with minute waves. The horizon ended, as on the sea on a clear day, with a line of light as sharp as the edge of a sword.

The Provençal clutched the trunk of a palm tree, as though it were the body of a friend; then, hiding in the straight and slender shadow which the tree cast on the granite, he wept. He remained seated there contemplating with deep sadness the implacable scene before his eyes. Suddenly, he shouted as if to tempt the solitude. His voice, lost in the hollows of the hill, resounded faintly in the distance and aroused no echo; the echo was in his heart. The Provençal was twenty-two years old — he loaded his gun.

"There'll always be time enough!" he said to himself as he placed on the ground the gun which was his only hope for deliverance.

Looking in turn at the dark expanse of the desert and the blue expanse of the sky, the soldier dreamt of France. He smelled with delight the gutters of Paris; he remembered the towns through which he had passed, the faces of his friends, and the smallest details of his life. Finally, in the play of the heat which undulated above the stretch of desert, his Southern imagination soon showed him the stones of his beloved Provence. Fearing all the dangers of this cruel mirage, he went down the opposite side of the hill where he had climbed the night before. His joy was great when he discovered a sort of grotto, naturally carved into the immense fragments of granite which formed the base of this hill. The torn pieces of a mat announced that this refuge had been at one time inhabited. Then a few steps further he saw palm trees loaded with dates. Immediately the instinct which binds us to life awoke in his heart. He hoped to live long enough to await the passage of some Maugrabins, or perhaps he would soon hear the sound of the cannons, for at this very moment Bonaparte was crossing Egypt. Revived by this thought, the Frenchman shook a few clusters of ripe fruit under the weight of which the palm trees were bending, and he assured himself, in tasting this unhoped-for manna, that the inhabitant of the cave had cultivated the palm trees. In fact, the fresh and tasty meat of the dates were proof of the care of his predecessor.

He passed suddenly from a dark despair to an almost insane joy. He climbed the hill again, and busied himself for the rest of the day in cutting down one of the barren palm trees which, the night before, had served him as shelter. A vague memory made him think of the wild animals of the desert, and anticipating that they might come to drink at the spring lost in the sand but visible at the foot of the rock, he decided to protect himself from their visits by building a barrier at the entrance of his hermitage. In spite of his ardor, in spite of the strength which the fear of being devoured during his sleep gave him, he was unable to cut the tree in pieces, though he managed to cut it down. Towards evening, when this king of the desert fell, the noise of its fall resounded in the distance, and it was like a moan from the solitude. The soldier shuddered as though he had heard a voice predicting woe. But, like an heir who does not long bewail the death of a relative, he stripped this beautiful tree of its tall broad green leaves which are its poetic adornment, and used these to mend the mat on which he was to sleep.

Tired from the heat and his work, he fell asleep under the red vault of his damp cave. In the middle of the night his sleep was disturbed by an extraordinary noise. He sat up, and the deep silence around him permitted him to recognize the alternative accents of a respiration whose savage energy could not belong to a human creature. A profound fear, reinforced by the darkness, the silence, and the waking fantasies, froze his heart. He almost felt his hair stand on end, when, straining to dilate the pupils of his eyes, he perceived in the dark two faint yellow lights. At first he attributed these lights to the reflection of his own pupils, but soon, the bright glare of the night helped him to distinguish the objects around him in the cave, and he saw an enormous animal lying but a few steps away from him. Was it a lion, a tiger, or a crocodile? The Provençal was not educated enough to know under what species his enemy ought to be classified, but his terror was all the more pronounced as his ignorance made him imagine all sorts of misfortunes. He endured the cruel torture of listening, of grasping the whims of this respiration, without losing a thing, and without daring the least movement. A smell as strong as that exhaled by a fox, but more penetrating, heavier, so to speak, filled the cave, and when the Provençal had snifted it, his terror reached its limit, for he could no longer doubt the existence of his terrible companion whose royal dwelling served him as a shelter. Presently, the reflection of the moon which was rushing toward the horizon lit the den, rendering gradually visible and resplendent the spotted pelt of a panther.

This Egyptian lion slept, curled up like a big dog, the peaceful owner of a sumptuous niche at the entrance of an hotel. Its eyes opened for a moment, and closed again. Its face was turned toward the Frenchman. A thousand confused thoughts passed through the mind of the panther's prisoner. First he thought of killing it with his rifle, but he saw there was not enough room to take proper aim — the muzzle would have reached beyond the animal. And what if it were to awaken? This thought made him rigid with fear. He listened to his heart beat in the depth of silence, and cursed the too loud pulsations of his rushing blood

which might disturb that sleep which allowed him to seek a
means of escape. Twice he placed his hand on his scimitar, intending to cut off the head of his enemy; but the difficulty of
slashing the stiff short hair forced him to abandon his wild project. "What if I should miss? It would mean certain death," he
thought. He preferred the chances of a fight, and decided to wait
for daylight. The morning was not long in coming. The Frenchman was then able to examine the panther; its muzzle was stained
with blood. "She has eaten well," he thought, without concerning
himself if the feast had been human flesh. "She won't be hungry
when she awakes."

It was a female. The fur on her belly and thighs glistened
white. Several little spots, like velvet, formed pretty bracelets
around her legs. The muscular tail was also white, but ending
with black rings. The upper part of her dress, yellow like burnished gold, smooth and soft, had these characteristic spots, in
the form of roses, which distinguishes panthers from all other
feline species. This tranquil and formidable hostess snored in a
pose as graceful as that of a cat sleeping on the cushion of an
Ottoman. Her blood-stained paws, nervous and well armed, were
stretched in front of her head which rested upon them, and from
which darted her sparse and straight whiskers, like silver threads.
If she had been like that in a cage, the Provençal would certainly
have admired the gracefulness of this beast and the vigorous contrasts of vivid colors which gave her robe an imperial splendor;
but just then his sight was troubled by her sinister appearance.
The presence of the panther, even asleep, made him feel the
effect which the magnetic eyes of a snake are said to have on a
nightingale. The soldier's courage began to wane for a moment
before this danger, though, no doubt, it would have risen at the
mouth of a canon vomiting shrapnels. Nevertheless, a daring
thought brought daylight to his soul, and the source of cold sweat
which poured from his brow dried up. Acting like a man who,
driven to the last resort, succeeds in defying death and offers himself to her blows, he saw without recognizing it a tragedy in this
adventure, and therefore resolved to play his role with honor to
the last.

"The day before yesterday, the Arabs would have killed me,
perhaps," he said to himself. Considering himself as good as dead
already, he waited bravely with restless curiosity the awakening

of his enemy. When the sun rose, the panther suddenly opened her eyes, then she thrust out her paws violently, as if to stretch and get rid of cramps. At last she yawned, showing the formidable apparatus of her teeth and her pronged tongue rough as a file. "Just like a little mistress!" thought the Frenchman, watching her roll about so softly and coquettishly. She licked off the blood which stained her paws, her muzzle, and scratched her head with repeated movements full of gracefulness. "Very good! Make your little *toilette*," said the Frenchman to himself, beginning to regain his gaiety and courage. "We'll say good morning to each other in a moment." And he seized the short dagger he had taken from the Maugrabins.

Just then the panther turned her head toward the man and stared at him without moving. The rigidity of her metallic eyes and their unbearable clarity made him shudder, particularly when the beast moved toward him; but he contemplated her caressingly, and peered into her eyes as if to hypnotize her, and let her come close to him. Then with a movement as soft and loving as though he were caressing the most beautiful woman, he passed his hand over her body, from the head to the tail, scratching the flexible vertebras which divided the panther's yellow back. The animal curled her tail voluptuously, her eyes softened, and when for the third time the Frenchman performed this interested flattery, she began to purr the same as our cats when they express pleasure, but this murmur issued from a throat so powerful and so deep that it resounded through the cave like the last vibrations of an organ in a church. The Provençal, realizing the importance of his caresses, redoubled them in order to stun and stupefy this imperious courtesan. When he felt sure of having extinguished the ferocity of this capricious companion, whose hunger had so fortunately been satisfied the night before, he got up to walk out of the cave. The panther let him go out, but when he had climbed the hill, she sprang after him with the lightness of a sparrow hopping from branch to branch, and rubbed herself against the soldier's legs with her back hunched like that of a cat. Then looking at her host with eyes whose sparkle had softened a little, she gave vent to that savage cry which naturalists compare to the grating of a saw.

"She is demanding!" said the Frenchman, smiling. He was daring enough to play with her ears, caress her belly and scratch her head hard with his nails. And when he saw his success, he tickled her skull with the point of his dagger, waiting for the right moment to kill her; but the hardness of her bones made him tremble at the thought of failure.

The sultana of the desert approved the talents of her slave by raising her head, stretching her neck, expressing pleasure by the tranquility of her attitude. It suddenly occurred to the Frenchman that to kill this fierce princess with a single blow he would have to stab her in the throat. He raised his blade, when the panther, satisfied, no doubt, laid herself gracefully at his feet, and looked up at him with glances touched with kindness, in spite of the natural rigor of her eyes. The poor Provençal ate his dates, leaning against a palm tree, and casting his eyes alternately on the desert, hoping for some liberator, and on his terrible companion, spying her uncertain clemency. The panther kept staring at the spot where the pits from the dates fell, and every time he threw one down her eyes expressed an incredible mistrust. She examined the Frenchman with a commercial prudence; however, this examination was favorable to him, for when he had finished his meager meal, she came and licked his shoes, and her powerful rough tongue brushed off miraculously the dust incrusted in the creases.

"But what will happen when she'll be hungry?" thought the Provençal. In spite of the shudder this thought caused him, the soldier began to measure curiously the panther's proportions, certainly one of the most beautiful specimens of its race, for she was three feet high and four feet long, without counting the tail. This powerful weapon, rounded like a club, was nearly three feet long. The head, large as that of a lioness, had a rare expression of refinement. The cold cruelty of a tiger was the dominating feature, but there was also a vague resemblance to the face of a cunning woman. Indeed, the face of this solitary queen revealed at this moment the gaiety of a drunken Nero: she had quenched her thirst with blood, and now she wanted to play.

The soldier tried to pace back and forth, and the panther let him free, merely following him with her eyes, less like a faithful dog than a big Angora cat, watchful of everything, even his master's movements. When he turned around, he saw by the spring the remains of his horse whose carcass the panther had dragged there. About two-thirds of it was devoured. This sight reassured him. It was easy now to explain the panther's absence, and the respect she had had for him while he slept. This first piece of luck encouraged him to tempt the future, and he conceived the wild hope of living happily with the panther at least for the rest of the day, neglecting no means of taming her and of gaining her good graces. He returned to her and had the unspeakable joy of seeing her wag her tail with an almost imperceptible movement as he came near. He then sat next to her without fear, and they began to play together; he took her paws and muzzle, pulled her ears gently, rolled her on her back, and scratched hard her warm and silky flanks. She let him do whatever he wanted, and when he began to smooth the hair on her paws, she carefully withdrew her curved claws. The Frenchman, keeping one hand on the dagger, thought of plunging it into the belly of the too confident panther; but he was afraid that he would be strangled in the animal's last convulsions. Besides, he heard in his heart a kind of remorse which shouted to him to respect an inoffensive creature. He seemed to have found a friend in this endless desert. Unconsciously he thought of his first mistress, whom he had nicknamed "Mignonne," because she was so atrociously jealous that during the whole time of their liaison he always feared the knife with which she repeatedly threatened him. This memory of his youth suggested to him this name for the young panther, whose agility, grace, and softness he now admired with less terror.

Towards the end of the day, having become familiar with his perilous predicament, he now almost liked its anguish. At last, his companion had taken the habit of looking up at him whenever he cried in a falsetto voice: "Mignonne." At sundown, Mignonne let out several deep and melancholic cries. "She is well-bred," thought the happy soldier, "she says her prayers!" But this mental joke occurred to him only when he noticed the peaceful attitude in which his friend was resting. "Come, my little blonde, I'll let you go to bed first," he told her, counting on the speed of his legs to escape when she would be asleep, and seek another refuge for the night. The soldier awaited with impatience the hour of his flight, and when it had arrived, he walked vigorously in the direction of the Nile. But hardly had he gone half a mile in the sand when he heard the panther bounding after him, crying with that saw-like shriek, more frightening yet than the sound of her leaping.

"Well," he said to himself, "she has taken a liking to me. This young panther has never met anyone before, and I should be flattered to be her first love!" At that very moment, the Frenchman fell into one of these quicksands so terrible to travelers, and from where it is impossible to save oneself. Feeling himself caught, he let out a cry of alarm; the panther grabbed him with her teeth by the collar, and springing vigorously backward, she pulled him out, as if by magic, of this abyss. "Ah, Mignonne," cried the soldier, caressing her enthusiastically, "it's life and death between us now. But no jokes, you hear!" And he retraced his steps.

As of that moment the desert seemed inhabited. It contained a being to whom the Frenchman could talk, and whose ferocity had softened for him, though he could not explain the reasons for this strange friendship. However strong the soldier's desire was to remain standing on guard, he fell asleep. When he awoke, he did not see Mignonne. He climbed the hill, and in the distance saw her springing towards him, as these animals do because of the extreme flexibility of their vertebral column. Mignonne arrived, blood on her pendulous lips. She received the wonted caresses of her companion, showing with several grave purrs how happy she was. Her eyes full of languor, even more gently than the night before, turned towards the Provençal, who talked to her as one would to a tame animal.

"Ah, Mademoiselle, you are a nice girl, aren't you? Just look at that . . . So we like to be appreciated? Aren't you ashamed? Have you devoured some Maugrabin? And yet, they are animals just like you. But don't start eating Frenchmen . . . Or else, I'll stop loving you."

She played like a puppy dog plays with his master, letting herself be rolled on the ground, knocked around and stroked in turn; and sometimes, she herself would provoke the soldier by stretching her paw toward him in a soliciting gesture.

A few days passed this way. This companionship allowed the Provençal to admire the sublime beauty of the desert. From the moment when he found hours of fear and tranquility, food, and a creature to occupy his thoughts, his soul became filled with contrasts. It was a life of opposites. Solitude revealed all its secrets to him, surrounded him with its charm. He discovered in the rising and setting of the sun spectacles unknown to the world. He learned to tremble on hearing overhead the soft hiss of a bird's wings — rare occurrence — on seeing clouds gather together — colorful changing travelers. During the night, he studied the reflection of the moon on the ocean of sand, where the simoon made quick changes of waves and undulations. He lived the life of the Eastern day, admiring its splendid pomp, and often, after having enjoyed the terrible spectacle of a hurricane over the plain, where the whirling sand raised red dry fog, deadly clouds, he would see the night come with delight, for then fell the comforting freshness of the stars. He listened to imaginary music from the skies. Then solitude taught him to unfold the treasures of dreams. He spent whole hours remembering mere nothings, comparing his past life to the present. Finally, he became passionately fond of his panther, for he needed affection. Whether because the soldier's will, forcefully projected, had modified the character of his companion, or whether she found enough nourishment from the dead soldiers in the desert, she respected the Frenchman's life, who finally no longer distrusted her, seeing her so well tamed.

He spent most of his time sleeping; but he was forced to keep watch, like a spider in the center of its web, not to miss the moment of deliverance, if anyone should pass within the sphere marked by the horizon. He had sacrificed his shirt to make a flag, which he hoisted to the top of a palm tree barren of leaves. Guided by necessity, he even found a way to keep it spread out with sticks, for the wind might not be blowing at the moment when the passing traveler would look across the desert.

It was during the long hours when he had abandoned hope that he played with the panther. He had come to learn the different inflections of her voice, the expressions of her eyes; he had studied the whims of all the spots which shaded the gold of her dress. Mignonne would no longer growl even when he would grab the tuft at the end of her formidable tail to count the black and white rings, those graceful ornaments which glittered like jewels in the sun. It gave him pleasure to contemplate the supple lines of her body, the whiteness of her belly, the gracefulness of her head. But it was particularly when she frolicked that he felt most pleasure; the agility and youthful movements always surprised him. He admired the suppleness with which she leaped, crawled, glided, crouched, rolled, cuddled, or darted about. However swift her spring, however smooth the block of granite, she would always stop short at the word "Mignonne."

One day, the sun burning bright, an immense bird hovered in the air. The Provençal left the panther to examine this new guest; but after waiting a while, the neglected sultana growled deeply. "By God! I believe that she is jealous," he exclaimed, seeing her eyes rigid again. "The soul of Virginia has passed in her body, it's certain . . ." The eagle disappeared into the air while the soldier admired the rounded rump of the panther. But there was so much grace, so much youth in her form! She was beautiful as a woman. The blond fur of her dress mingled well with the shades of faint white of the thighs. The profuse light of the sun made this living gold, these russet spots, shine with indefinable charm. The Provençal and the panther looked at each other with a look full of meaning. The coquette trembled when she felt the nails of her friend scratching her scalp; her eyes flashed like lightning, and then she closed them tightly.

"She has a soul . . .," he said, studying the stillness of this queen of the sand, golden like the sand, white like the sand, solitary and burning like the sand.

*   *   *

"Well," my lady-friend said to me, "I have read your plea in favor of animals. But how did two persons so well suited to understand each other end?"

"Ah! You see, they ended as all great passions do, by a misunderstanding. Each believes the other to have betrayed him, pride prevents any explanation, and stubbornness brings parting."

"Yet, sometimes in the best moments," she said, "a look, an exclamation suffice . . . Oh well, go on with your story."

"It is horribly difficult, but you will understand what the old grumbler told me, when, while finishing his bottle of champagne, he suddenly cried: 'I don't know what pain I caused her, but she turned around as though enraged, and with her sharp teeth bit my leg, gently I admit. But I, thinking she would devour me, plunged my knife into her throat. She rolled over with a wild cry which froze my heart, and I saw her dying, still looking at me without anger. I would have given anything in the world, even my cross which I did not yet have, to have brought her back to life. It was as though I had murdered a real person. And the soldiers who at last had seen my flag, and who rushed to my help, found me in tears. . . .' "

"Well, Sir," he went on after a moment of silence, "since then I have fought the war in Germany, Spain, Russia, France; I have certainly dragged my carcass a great deal, but I have never seen anything like that desert . . . Ah, how beautiful it is."

"What did you feel there?" I asked.

"Oh! It cannot be told, young man. Besides, I don't always regret my cluster of palm trees and my panther. Only when I am sad. You see, in the desert there is everything, and nothing."

"But, can't you explain?"

"Well," he continued with a gesture of impatience, "it's God without mankind."

(Translated by Raymond Federman)

NATHANIEL HAWTHORNE (1804–1864) Hawthorne was born on July 4th in Salem, Massachusetts where his parents' families had lived for six generations. He was the son of a sea captain and a descendant of John Hathorne, one of the judges at the Salem witch trials. His boyhood was a solitary one, spent virtually by himself in Salem, Massachusetts and Raymond, Maine, reading, walking, and telling stories to himself and his sisters who remained unmarried.

After graduating from Bowdoin College in 1825 where he was a classmate of Longfellow and Franklin Pierce, Hawthorne retired to Salem to write. Although he did travel to some extent, he was for the most part a recluse for the next twelve years: "I sat down by the wayside of life, like a man under enchantment, and a shrubbery sprung up around me, and the bushes grew to be saplings, and the saplings became trees, until no exit appeared possible, through the tangling depths of my obscurity." Hawthorne's self-imposed isolation remained the well from which he wrote; many of his characters, however, are isolated men seeking to re-enter society.

In 1837 he published *Twice-Told Tales* and, in 1842, he married and took his bride to the Old Manse, Emerson's former house in Concord. Here, the Hawthornes knew Emerson, Thoreau, and Alcott. From 1846–1849, he was Surveyor of Customs at Salem. During the next four years he published *The Scarlet Letter* (1850), *The House of the Seven Gables* (1851), *The Blithedale Romance* (1852), and *Tanglewood Tales* (1853).

Hawthorne wrote a campaign biography for Franklin Pierce, and when Pierce became President, Hawthorne was appointed U.S. Consul at Liverpool from 1853–1857. After resigning his consulship, Hawthorne and his family traveled in France and Italy; he began *The Marble Faun* (1860) in Rome. For the last four years of his life Hawthorne was unwell, tired, and unproductive. He died in his sleep in Plymouth, New Hampshire and was buried in Sleepy Hollow Cemetery in Concord, Massachusetts.

THE MAYPOLE OF MERRY MOUNT

Nathaniel Hawthorne

There is an admirable foundation for a philosophic romance in the curious history of the early settlement of Mount Wollaston, or Merry Mount. In the slight sketch here attempted, the facts, recorded on the grave pages of our New England annalists, have wrought themselves, almost spontaneously, into a sort of allegory. The masques, mummeries, and festive customs, described in the text, are in accordance with the manners of the age. Authority on these points may be found in Strutt's Book of English Sports and Pastimes.

Bright were the days at Merry Mount, when the Maypole was the banner staff of that gay colony! They who reared it, should their banner be triumphant, were to pour sunshine over New England's rugged hills, and scatter flower seeds throughout the soil. Jollity and gloom were contending for an empire. Midsummer eve had come, bringing deep verdure to the forest, and roses in her lap, of a more vivid hue than the tender buds of Spring. But May, or her mirthful spirit, dwelt all the year round at Merry Mount, sporting with the Summer months, and revelling with Autumn, and basking in the glow of Winter's fireside. Through a world of toil and care she flitted with a dreamlike smile, and came hither to find a home among the lightsome hearts of Merry Mount.

Never had the Maypole been so gayly decked as at sunset on midsummer eve. This venerated emblem was a pine-tree, which had preserved the slender grace of youth, while it equalled the loftiest height of the old wood monarchs. From its top streamed a silken banner, colored like the rainbow. Down nearly to the ground the pole was dressed with birchen boughs, and others of the liveliest green, and some with silvery leaves, fastened by ribbons that fluttered in fantastic knots of twenty different colors, but no sad ones. Garden flowers, and blossoms of the wilderness,

laughed gladly forth amid the verdure, so fresh and dewy that
they must have grown by magic on that happy pine-tree. Where
this green and flowery splendor terminated, the shaft of the Maypole was stained with the seven brilliant hues of the banner at
its top. On the lowest green bough hung an abundant wreath of
roses, some that had been gathered in the sunniest spots of the
forest, and others, of still richer blush, which the colonists had
reared from English seed. O, people of the Golden Age, the chief
of your husbandry was to raise flowers!

But what was the wild throng that stood hand in hand about
the Maypole? It could not be that the fauns and nymphs, when
driven from their classic groves and homes of ancient fable, had
sought refuge, as all the persecuted did, in the fresh woods of the
West. These were Gothic monsters, though perhaps of Grecian
ancestry. On the shoulders of a comely youth uprose the head
and branching antlers of a stag; a second, human in all other
points, had the grim visage of a wolf; a third, still with the trunk
and limbs of a mortal man, showed the beard and horns of a
venerable he-goat. There was the likeness of a bear erect, brute
in all but his hind legs, which were adorned with pink silk stockings. And here again, almost as wondrous, stood a real bear of the
dark forest, lending each of his fore paws to the grasp of a human
hand, and as ready for the dance as any in that circle. His inferior
nature rose half way, to meet his companions as they stooped.
Other faces wore the similitude of man or woman, but distorted
or extravagant, with red noses pendulous before their mouths,
which seemed of awful depth, and stretched from ear to ear in
an eternal fit of laughter. Here might be seen the Salvage Man,
well known in heraldry, hairy as a baboon, and girdled with
green leaves. By his side, a noble figure, but still a counterfeit,
appeared an Indian hunter, with feathery crest and wampum
belt. Many of this strange company wore foolscaps, and had little
bells appended to their garments, tinkling with a silvery sound,
responsive to the inaudible music of their gleesome spirits. Some
youths and maidens were of soberer garb, yet well maintained
their places in the irregular throng by the expression of wild
revelry upon their features. Such were the colonists of Merry
Mount, as they stood in the broad smile of sunset round their
venerated Maypole.

Had a wanderer, bewildered in the melancholy forest, heard their mirth, and stolen a half-affrighted glance, he might have fancied them the crew of Comus, some already transformed to brutes, some midway between man and beast, and the others rioting in the flow of tipsy jollity that foreran the change. But a band of Puritans, who watched the scene, invisible themselves, compared the masques to those devils and ruined souls with whom their superstition peopled the black wilderness.

Within the ring of monsters appeared the two airiest forms that had ever trodden on any more solid footing than a purple and golden cloud. One was a youth in glistening apparel, with a scarf of the rainbow pattern crosswise on his breast. His right hand held a gilded staff, the ensign of high dignity among the revellers, and his left grasped the slender fingers of a fair maiden, not less gayly decorated than himself. Bright roses glowed in contrast with the dark and glossy curls of each, and were scattered round their feet, or had sprung up spontaneously there. Behind this lightsome couple, so close to the Maypole that its boughs shaded his jovial face, stood the figure of an English priest, canonically dressed, yet decked with flowers, in heathen fashion, and wearing a chaplet of the native vine leaves. By the riot of his rolling eye, and the pagan decorations of his holy garb, he seemed the wildest monster there, and the very Comus of the crew.

"Votaries of the Maypole," cried the flower-decked priest, "merrily, all day long, have the woods echoed to your mirth. But be this your merriest hour, my hearts! Lo, here stand the Lord and Lady of the May, whom I, a clerk of Oxford, and high priest of Merry Mount, am presently to join in holy matrimony. Up with your nimble spirits, ye morris-dancers, green men, and glee maidens, bears and wolves, and horned gentlemen! Come; a chorus now, rich with the old mirth of Merry England, and the wilder glee of this fresh forest; and then a dance, to show the youthful pair what life is made of, and how airily they should go through it! All ye that love the Maypole, lend your voices to the nuptial song of the Lord and Lady of the May!"

This wedlock was more serious than most affairs of Merry Mount, where jest and delusion, trick and fantasy, kept up a continual carnival. The Lord and Lady of the May, though their titles must be laid down at sunset, were really and truly to be

partners for the dance of life, beginning the measure that same
bright eve. The wreath of roses, that hung from the lowest green
bough of the Maypole, had been twined for them, and would be
thrown over both their heads, in symbol of their flowery union.
When the priest had spoken, therefore, a riotous uproar burst
from the rout of monstrous figures.

"Begin you the stave, reverend Sir," cried they all; "and never
did the woods ring to such a merry peal as we of the Maypole
shall send up!"

Immediately a prelude of pipe, cithern, and viol, touched with
practised minstrelsy, began to play from a neighboring thicket,
in such a mirthful cadence that the boughs of the Maypole
quivered to the sound. But the May Lord, he of the gilded staff,
chancing to look into his Lady's eyes, was wonder struck at the
almost pensive glance that met his own.

"Edith, sweet Lady of the May," whispered he reproachfully,
"is yon wreath of roses a garland to hang above our graves, that
you look so sad? O, Edith, this is our golden time! Tarnish it not
by any pensive shadow of the mind; for it may be that nothing of
futurity will be brighter than the mere remembrance of what is
now passing."

"That was the very thought that saddened me! How came it in
your mind too?" said Edith, in a still lower tone than he, for it
was high treason to be sad at Merry Mount. "Therefore do I sigh
amid this festive music. And besides, dear Edgar, I struggle as
with a dream, and fancy that these shapes of our jovial friends are
visionary, and their mirth unreal, and that we are no true Lord
and Lady of the May. What is the mystery in my heart?"

Just then, as if a spell had loosened them, down came a little
shower of withering rose leaves from the Maypole. Alas, for the
young lovers! No sooner had their hearts glowed with real passion
than they were sensible of something vague and unsubstantial in
their former pleasures, and felt a dreary presentiment of inevitable change. From the moment that they truly loved, they had
subjected themselves to earth's doom of care and sorrow, and
troubled joy, and had no more a home at Merry Mount. That
was Edith's mystery. Now leave we the priest to marry them, and
the masquers to sport round the Maypole, till the last sunbeam
be withdrawn from its summit, and the shadows of the forest

mingle gloomily in the dance. Meanwhile, we may discover who
these gay people were.

Two hundred years ago, and more, the old world and its in-
habitants became mutually weary of each other. Men voyaged
by thousands to the West: some to barter glass beads, and such
like jewels, for the furs of the Indian hunter; some to conquer
virgin empires; and one stern band to pray. But none of these
motives had much weight with the colonists of Merry Mount.
Their leaders were men who had sported so long with life, that
when Thought and Wisdom came, even these unwelcome guests
were led astray by the crowd of vanities which they should have
put to flight. Erring Thought and perverted Wisdom were made
to put on masques, and play the fool. The men of whom we
speak, after losing the heart's fresh gayety, imagined a wild
philosophy of pleasure, and came hither to act out their latest
day-dream. They gathered followers from all that giddy tribe
whose whole life is like the festal days of soberer men. In their
train were minstrels, not unknown in London streets: wandering
players, whose theatres had been the halls of noblemen; mum-
mers, rope-dancers, and mounte-banks, who would long be missed
at wakes, church ales, and fairs; in a word, mirth makers of every
sort, such as abounded in that age, but now began to be dis-
countenanced by the rapid growth of Puritanism. Light had their
footsteps been on land, and as lightly they came across the sea.
Many had been maddened by their previous troubles into a gay
despair; others were as madly gay in the flush of youth, like the
May Lord and his Lady; but whatever might be the quality of
their mirth, old and young were gay at Merry Mount. The young
deemed themselves happy. The elder spirits, if they knew that
mirth was but the counterfeit of happiness, yet followed the
false shadow wilfully, because at least her garments glittered
brightest. Sworn triflers of a lifetime, they would not venture
among the sober truths of life not even to be truly blest.

All the hereditary pastimes of Old England were transplanted
hither. The King of Christmas was duly crowned, and the Lord of
Misrule bore potent sway. On the Eve of St. John, they felled
whole acres of the forest to make bonfires, and danced by the
blaze all night, crowned with garlands, and throwing flowers into
the flame. At harvest time, though their crop was of the smallest,

they made an image with the sheaves of Indian corn, and wreathed it with autumnal garlands, and bore it home triumphantly. But what chiefly characterized the colonists of Merry Mount was their veneration for the Maypole. It has made their true history a poet's tale. Spring decked the hallowed emblem with young blossoms and fresh green boughs; Summer brought roses of the deepest blush, and the perfected foliage of the forest; Autumn enriched it with that red and yellow gorgeousness which converts each wildwood leaf into a painted flower; and Winter silvered it with sleet, and hung it round with icicles, till it flashed in the cold sunshine, itself a frozen sunbeam. Thus each alternate season did homage to the Maypole, and paid it a tribute of its own richest splendor. Its votaries danced round it, once, at least, in every month; sometimes they called it their religion, or their altar; but always, it was the banner staff of Merry Mount.

Unfortunately, there were men in the new world of a sterner faith than these Maypole worshippers. Not far from Merry Mount was a settlement of Puritans, most dismal wretches, who said their prayers before daylight, and then wrought in the forest or the cornfield till evening made it prayer time again. Their weapons were always at hand to shoot down the straggling savage. When they met in conclave, it was never to keep up the old English mirth, but to hear sermons three hours long, or to proclaim bounties on the heads of wolves and the scalps of Indians. Their festivals were fast days, and their chief pastime the singing of psalms. Woe to the youth or maiden who did but dream of a dance! The selectman nodded to the constable; and there sat the light-heeled reprobate in the stocks; or if he danced, it was round the whipping-post, which might be termed the Puritan Maypole.

A party of these grim Puritans, toiling through the difficult woods, each with a horseload of iron armor to burden his footsteps, would sometimes draw near the sunny precincts of Merry Mount. There were the silken colonists, sporting round their Maypole; perhaps teaching a bear to dance, or striving to communicate their mirth to the grave Indian; or masquerading in the skins of deer and wolves, which they had hunted for that especial purpose. Often, the whole colony were playing at blindman's bluff, magistrates and all, with their eyes bandaged, except a single scapegoat, whom the blinded sinners pursued by the tinkling of the bells at his garments. Once, it is said, they were seen following a flower-decked corpse, with merriment and festive music, to his grave. But did the dead man laugh? In the quietest times, they sang ballads and told tales, for the edification of their pious visitors; or perplexed them with juggling tricks; or grinned at them through horse collars; and when sport itself grew wearisome, they made game of their own stupidity, and began a yawning match. At the very least of these enormities, the men of iron shook their heads and frowned so darkly that the revellers looked up, imagining that a momentary cloud had over-cast the sunshine, which was to be perpetual there. On the other hand, the Puritans affirmed that, when a psalm was pealing from their place of worship, the echo which the forest sent them back seemed often like the chorus of a jolly catch, closing with a roar of laughter. Who but the fiend, and his bond slaves, the crew of Merry Mount, had thus disturbed them? In due time, a feud arose, stern and bitter on one side, and as serious on the other as anything could be among such light spirits as had sworn allegiance to the Maypole. The future complexion of · New England was involved in this important quarrel. Should the grizzly saints establish their jurisdiction over the gay sinners, then would their spirits darken all the clime, and make it a land of clouded visages, of hard toil, of sermon and psalm forever. But should the banner staff of Merry Mount be fortunate, sunshine would break upon the hills, and flowers would beautify the forest, and late posterity do homage to the Maypole.

After these authentic passages from history, we return to the nuptials of the Lord and Lady of the May. Alas! we have delayed too long, and must darken our tale too suddenly. As we glance again at the Maypole, a solitary sunbeam is fading from the summit, and leaves only a faint, golden tinge blended with the hues of the rainbow banner. Even that dim light is now withdrawn, relinquishing the whole domain of Merry Mount to the evening gloom, which has rushed so instantaneously from the black surrounding woods. But some of these black shadows have rushed forth in human shape.

Yes, with the setting sun, the last day of mirth had passed from Merry Mount. The ring of gay masquers was disordered and broken; the stag lowered his antlers in dismay; the wolf grew weaker than a lamb; the bells of the morris-dancers tinkled with tremulous affright. The Puritans had played a characteristic part

in the Maypole mummeries. Their darksome figures were inter-
mixed with the wild shapes of their foes, and made the scene a
picture of the moment, when waking thoughts start up amid the
scattered fantasies of a dream. The leader of the hostile party
stood in the centre of the circle, while the route of monsters
cowered around him, like evil spirits in the presence of a dread
magician. No fantastic foolery could look him in the face. So
stern was the energy of his aspect, that the whole man, visage,
frame, and soul, seemed wrought of iron, gifted with life and
thought, yet all of one substance with his headpiece and breast-
plate. It was the Puritan of Puritans; it was Endicott himself!

"Stand off, priest of Baal!" said he, with a grim frown, and
laying no reverent hand upon the surplice. "I know thee, Blackstone![1] Thou art the man who couldst not abide the rule even
of thine own corrupted church, and hast come hither to preach
iniquity, and to give example of it in thy life. But now shall it be
seen that the Lord hath sanctified this wilderness for his peculiar
people. Woe unto them that would defile it! And first, for this
flower-decked abomination, the altar of thy worship!"

And with his keen sword Endicott assaulted the hallowed Maypole. Nor long did it resist his arm. It groaned with a dismal
sound; it showered leaves and rosebuds upon the remorseless
enthusiast; and finally, with all its green boughs and ribbons and
flowers, symbolic of departed pleasures, down fell the banner
staff of Merry Mount. As it sank, tradition says, the evening sky
grew darker, and the woods threw forth a more sombre shadow.

"There," cried Endicott, looking triumphantly on his work,
"there lies the only Maypole in New England! The thought is
strong within me that, by its fall, is shadowed forth the fate of
light and idle mirth makers, amongst us and our posterity. Amen,
saith John Endicott."

"Amen!" echoed his followers.

But the votaries of the Maypole gave one groan for their idol.
At the sound, the Puritan leader glanced at the crew of Comus,
each a figure of broad mirth, yet, at this moment, strangely expressive of sorrow and dismay.

[1] Did Governor Endicott speak less positively, we should suspect a
mistake here. The Rev. Mr. Blackstone, though an eccentric, is not
known to have been an immoral man. We rather doubt his identity
with the priest of Merry Mount.

"Valiant captain," quoth Peter Palfrey, the Ancient of the band, "what order shall be taken with the prisoners?"

"I thought not to repent me of cutting down a Maypole," replied Endicott, "yet now I could find in my heart to plant it again, and give each of these bestial pagans one other dance round their idol. It would have served rarely for a whipping-post!"

"But there are pine-trees enow," suggested the lieutenant.

"True, good Ancient," said the leader. "Wherefore, bind the heathen crew, and bestow on them a small matter of stripes apiece, as earnest of our future justice. Set some of the rogues in the stocks to rest themselves, so soon as Providence shall bring us to one of our own well-ordered settlements, where such accommodations may be found. Further penalties, such as branding and cropping of ears, shall be thought of hereafter."

"How many stripes for the priest?" inquired Ancient Palfrey.

"None as yet," answered Endicott, bending his iron frown upon the culprit. "It must be for the Great and General Court to determine, whether stripes and long imprisonment, and other grievous penalty, may atone for his transgressions. Let him look to himself! For such as violate our civil order, it may be permitted us to show mercy. But woe to the wretch that troubleth our religion!"

"And this dancing bear," resumed the officer. "Must he share the stripes of his fellows?"

"Shoot him through the head!" said the energetic Puritan. "I suspect witchcraft in the beast."

"Here be a couple of shining ones," continued Peter Palfrey, pointing his weapon at the Lord and Lady of the May. "They seem to be of high station among these misdoers. Methinks their dignity will not be fitted with less than a double share of stripes."

Endicott rested on his sword, and closely surveyed the dress and aspect of the hapless pair. There they stood, pale, downcast, and apprehensive. Yet there was an air of mutual support, and of pure affection, seeking aid and giving it, that showed them to be man and wife, with the sanction of a priest upon their love. The youth, in the peril of the moment, had dropped his gilded staff, and thrown his arm about the Lady of the May, who leaned against his breast, too lightly to burden him, but with weight enough to express that their destinies were linked together, for good or evil. They looked first at each other, and then into the grim captain's face. There they stood, in the first hour of wedlock, while the idle pleasures, of which their companions were the emblems, had given place to the sternest cares of life, personified by the dark Puritans. But never had their youthful beauty seemed so pure and high as when its glow was chastened by adversity.

"Youth," said Endicott, "ye stand in an evil case thou and thy maiden wife. Make ready presently, for I am minded that ye shall both have a token to remember your wedding day!"

"Stern man," cried the May Lord, "how can I move thee? Were the means at hand, I would resist to the death. Being powerless, I entreat! Do with me as thou wilt, but let Edith go untouched!"

"Not so," replied the immitigable zealot. "We are not wont to show an idle courtesy to that sex, which requireth the stricter discipline. What sayest thou, maid? Shall thy silken bridegroom suffer thy share of the penalty, besides his own?"

"Be it death," said Edith, "and lay it all on me!"

Truly, as Endicott had said, the poor lovers stood in a woeful case. Their foes were triumphant, their friends captive and abased, their home desolate, the benighted wilderness around them, and a rigorous destiny, in the shape of the Puritan leader, their only guide. Yet the deepening twilight could not altogether conceal that the iron man was softened; he smiled at the fair spectacle of early love; he almost sighed for the inevitable blight of early hopes.

"The troubles of life have come hastily on this young couple," observed Endicott. "We will see how they comport themselves under their present trials ere we burden them with greater. If, among the spoil, there be any garments of a more decent fashion, let them be put upon this May Lord and his Lady, instead of their glistening vanities. Look to it, some of you."

"And shall not the youth's hair be cut?" asked Peter Palfrey, looking with abhorrence at the lovelock and long glossy curls of the young man.

"Crop it forthwith, and that in the true pumpkin-shell fashion," answered the captain. "Then bring them along with us, but more gently than their fellows. There be qualities in the youth, which may make him valiant to fight, and sober to toil, and pious to pray; and in the maiden, that may fit her to become a mother in our Israel, bringing up babes in better nurture than her own hath been. Nor think ye, young ones, that they are the happiest, even in our lifetime of a moment, who misspend it in dancing round a Maypole!"

And Endicott, the severest Puritan of all who laid the rock foundation of New England, lifted the wreath of roses from the ruin of the Maypole, and threw it, with his own gauntleted hand, over the heads of the Lord and Lady of the May. It was a deed of prophecy. As the moral gloom of the world overpowers all systematic gayety, even so was their home of wild mirth made desolate amid the sad forest. They returned to it no more. But as their flowery garland was wreathed of the brightest roses that had grown there, so, in the tie that united them, were intertwined all the purest and best of their early joys. They went heavenward, supporting each other along the difficult path which it was their lot to tread, and never wasted one regretful thought on the vanities of Merry Mount.

EDGAR ALLAN POE (1809–1849) Poe, the son of a professional actor and actress, was born in Boston, Massachusetts. Orphaned before he was three years old, he was taken into the home of a wealthy merchant in Richmond, Virginia where he was raised and educated in prosperous circumstances. As he came of age, however, his relationship to his foster parents grew more and more uncertain and, at the age of eighteen after a quarrel, he left home and enlisted in the United States Army. The same year his first collection of poems was published.

After his discharge, he held a series of positions as a magazine editor and supplemented his income with much literary hackwork. His most serious literary efforts were now largely devoted to the short story although it was with the publication of his poem "The Raven," in 1845, that he finally secured a measure of fame as a writer. Unfortunately by this time, after years of dreary poverty and hard work, he was an exhausted man.

Poe's ideas about the writing of fiction may be found in his review of Hawthorne's *Twice-Told Tales*. His best-known stories are "Ligeia," "The Fall of the House of Usher," "The Masque of the Red Death," "The Pit and the Pendulum," and "The Tell-Tale Heart."

THE MAN OF THE CROWD

Edgar Allan Poe

Ce grand malheur, de ne pouvoir être seul. — LA BRUYÈRE.

It was well said of a certain German book that *"es lässt sich nicht lesen"* — it does not permit itself to be read. There are some secrets which do not permit themselves to be told. Men die nightly in their beds, wringing the hands of ghostly confessors, and looking them piteously in the eyes — die with despair of heart and convulsion of throat, on account of the hideousness of mysteries which will not *suffer themselves* to be revealed. Now and then, alas, the conscience of man takes up a burthen so heavy in horror that it can be thrown down only into the grave. And thus the essence of all crime is undivulged.

Not long ago, about the closing in of an evening in autumn, I sat at the large bow window of the D—— Coffee-House in London. For some months I had been ill in health, but was now convalescent, and, with returning strength, found myself in one of those happy moods which are so precisely the converse of *ennui* — moods of the keenest appetency, when the film from the mental vision departs — the ἀχλὺς ἣ πρὶν ἐπῆεν — and the intellect, electrified, surpasses as greatly its everyday condition, as does the vivid yet candid reason of Leibnitz, the mad and flimsy rhetoric of Gorgias. Merely to breathe was enjoyment; and I derived positive pleasure even from many of the legitimate sources of pain. I felt a calm but inquisitive interest in every thing. With a cigar in my mouth and a newspaper in my lap, I had been amusing myself for the greater part of the afternoon, now in poring over advertisements, now in observing the promiscuous company in the room, and now in peering through the smoky panes into the street.

This latter is one of the principal thoroughfares of the city, and had been very much crowded during the whole day. But, as

29

the darkness came on, the throng momently increased; and, by the time the lamps were well lighted, two dense and continuous tides of population were rushing past the door. At this particular period of the evening I had never before been in a similar situation, and the tumultuous sea of human heads filled me, therefore, with a delicious novelty of emotion. I gave up, at length, all care of things within the hotel, and became absorbed in contemplation of the scene without.

At first my observations took an abstract and generalizing turn. I looked at the passengers in masses, and thought of them in their aggregrate relations. Soon however, I descended to details, and regarded with minute interest the innumerable varieties of figure, dress, air, gait, visage, and expression of countenance.

By far the greater number of those who went by had a satisfied business-like demeanour, and seemed to be thinking only of making their way through the press. Their brows were knit, and their eyes rolled quickly; when pushed against by fellow-wayfarers they evinced no symptom of impatience, but adjusted their clothes and hurried on. Others, still a numerous class, were restless in their movements, had flushed faces, and talked and gesticulated to themselves, as if feeling in solitude on account of the very denseness of the company around. When impeded in their progress, these people suddenly ceased muttering, but redoubled their gesticulations, and awaited, with an absent and overdone smile upon the lips, the course of the persons impeding them. If jostled, they bowed profusely to the jostlers, and appeared overwhelmed with confusion. — There was nothing very distinctive about these two large classes beyond what I have noted. Their habiliments belonged to that order which is pointedly termed the decent. They were undoubtedly noblemen, merchants, attorneys, tradesmen, stock-jobbers — the Eupatrids and the commonplaces of society — men of leisure and men actively engaged in affairs of their own — conducting business upon their own responsibility. They did not greatly excite my attention.

The tribe of clerks was an obvious one; and here I discerned two remarkable divisions. There were the junior clerks of flash houses — young gentlemen with tight coats, bright boots, well-oiled hair, and supercilious lips. Setting aside a certain dapperness of carriage, which may be termed *deskism* for want of a better word, the manner of these persons seemed to me an exact facsimile of what had been the perfection of *bon ton* about twelve or eighteen months before. They wore the cast-off graces of the gentry; — and this, I believe, involves the best definition of the class.

The division of the upper clerks of staunch firms, or of the "steady old fellows," it was not possible to mistake. These were known by their coats and pantaloons of black or brown, made to sit comfortably, with white cravats and waistcoats, broad solid-looking shoes, and thick hose or gaiters. — They had all slightly bald heads, from which the right ears, long used to pen-holding, had an odd habit of standing off on end. I observed that they always removed or settled their hats with both hands, and wore watches, with short gold chains of a substantial and ancient pattern. Theirs was the affectation of respectability; — if indeed there be an affectation so honourable.

There were many individuals of dashing appearance, whom I easily understood as belonging to the race of swell pick-pockets, with which all great cities are infested. I watched these gentry with much inquisitiveness, and found it difficult to imagine how they should ever be mistaken for gentlemen by gentlemen themselves. Their voluminousness of wristband, with an air of excessive frankness, should betray them at once.

The gamblers, of whom I descried not a few, were still more easily recognizable. They wore every variety of dress, from that of the desperate thimble-rig bully, with velvet waistcoat, fancy neckerchief, gilt chains, and filigreed buttons, to that of the scrupulously inornate clergyman than which nothing could be less liable to suspicion. Still all were distinguished by a certain sodden swarthiness of complexion, a filmy dimness of eye, and pallor and compression of lip. There were two other traits, moreover, by which I could always detect them; — a guarded lowness of tone in conversation, and a more than ordinary extension of the thumb in a direction at right angles with the fingers. — Very often, in company with these sharpers, I observed an order of men somewhat different in habits, but still birds of a kindred feather. They may be defined as the gentlemen who live by their wits. They seem to prey upon the public in two battalions — that of the dandies and that of the military men. Of the first grade the leading features are long locks and smiles; of the second frogged coats and frowns.

Descending in the scale of what is termed gentility, I found darker and deeper themes for speculation. I saw Jew pedlars, with hawk eyes flashing from countenances whose every other feature wore only an expression of abject humility; sturdy professional street beggars scowling upon mendicants of a better stamp, whom despair alone had driven forth into the night for charity; feeble and ghastly invalids, upon whom death had placed a sure hand, and who sidled and tottered through the mob, looking every one beseechingly in the face, as if in search of some chance consolation, some lost hope; modest young girls returning from long and late labour to a cheerless home, and shrinking more tearfully than indignantly from the glances of ruffians, whose direct contact, even, could not be avoided; women of the town of all kinds and of all ages — the unequivocal beauty in the prime of her womanhood, putting one in mind of the statue in Lucian, with the surface of Parian marble, and the interior filled with filth — the loathsome and utterly lost leper in rags — the wrinkled, bejewelled and paint-begrimed beldame, making a last effort at youth — the mere child of immature form, yet, from long association, an adept in the dreadful coquetries of her trade, and burning with a rabid ambition to be ranked the equal of her elders in vice; drunkards innumerable and indescribable — some in shreds and patches, reeling, inarticulate, with bruised visage and lack-lustre eyes — some in whole although filthy garments, with a slightly-unsteady swagger, thick sensual lips, and hearty-looking rubicund faces — others clothed in materials which had once been good, and which even now were scrupulously well brushed — men who walked with a more than naturally firm and springy step, but whose countenances were fearfully pale, whose eyes hideously wild and red, and who clutched with quivering fingers, as they strode through the crowd, at every object which came within their reach; beside these, piemen, porters, coal-heavers, sweeps; organ-grinders, monkey-exhibitors and ballad-mongers, those who vended with those who sang; ragged artisans and exhausted labourers of every description, and all full of a noisy and inordinate vivacity which jarred discordantly upon the ear, and gave an aching sensation to the eye.

As the night deepened, so deepened to me the interest of the scene; for not only did the general character of the crowd ma-

terially alter (its gentler features retiring in the gradual with-
drawal of the more orderly portion of the people, and its harsher
ones coming out into bolder relief, as the late hour brought forth
every species of infamy from its den), but the rays of the gas-
lamps, feeble at first in their struggle with the dying day, had now
at length gained ascendancy, and threw over every thing a fitful
and garish lustre. All was dark yet spendid — as that ebony to
which has been likened the style of Tertullian.

The wild effects of the light enchained me to an examination
of individual faces; and although the rapidity with which the
world of light flitted before the window, prevented me from
casting more than a glance upon each visage, still it seemed that,
in my then peculiar mental state, I could frequently read, even
in that brief interval of a glance, the history of long years.

With my brow to the glass, I was thus occupied in scrutinizing
the mob, when suddenly there came into view a countenance (that
of a decrepit old man, some sixty-five or seventy years of age) —
a countenance which at once arrested and absorbed my whole
attention, on account of the absolute idiosyncrasy of its expression. Any thing even remotely resembling that expression I had
never seen before. I well remember that my first thought, upon
beholding it, was that Retzsch, had he viewed it, would have
greatly preferred it to his own pictural incarnations of the fiend.
As I endeavoured, during the brief minute of my original survey,
to form some analysis of the meaning conveyed, there arose con-
fusedly and paradoxically within my mind, the ideas of vast
mental power, of caution, of penuriousness, of avarice, of cool-
ness, of malice, of blood-thirstiness, of triumph, of merriment, of
excessive terror, of intense — of extreme despair. I felt singularly
aroused, startled, fascinated. "How wild a history," I said to myself, "is written within that bosom!" Then came a craving desire
to keep the man in view — to know more of him. Hurriedly putting on an overcoat, and seizing my hat and cane, I made my
way into the street, and pushed through the crowd in the direction which I had seen him take; for he had already disappeared.
With some little difficulty I at length came within sight of him,
approached, and followed him closely, yet cautiously, so as not
to attract his attention.

I had now a good opportunity of examining his person. He was
short in stature, very thin, and apparently very feeble. His

clothes, generally, were filthy and ragged; but as he came, now and then, within the strong glare of a lamp, I perceived that his linen, although dirty, was of beautiful texture: and my vision deceived me, or, through a rent in a closely-buttoned and evidently second-handed *roquelaure* which enveloped him, I caught a glimpse both of a diamond and of a dagger. These observations heightened my curiosity, and I resolved to follow the stranger whithersoever he should go.

It was now fully nightfall, and a thick humid fog hung over the city, soon ending in a settled and heavy rain. This change of weather had an odd effect upon the crowd, the whole of which was at once put into new commotion, and overshadowed by a world of umbrellas. The waver, the jostle, and the hum increased in a tenfold degree. For my own part I did not much regard the rain — the lurking of an old fever in my system rendering the moisture somewhat too dangerously pleasant. Tying a handkerchief about my mouth, I kept on. For half an hour the old man held his way with difficulty along the great thoroughfare; and I here walked close at his elbow through fear of losing sight of him. Never once turning his head to look back, he did not observe me. By and bye he passed into a cross street, which, although densely filled with people, was not quite so much thronged as the main one he had quitted. Here a change in his demeanour became evident. He walked more slowly and with less object than before — more hesitatingly. He crossed and re-crossed the way repeatedly without apparent aim; and the press was still so thick, that, at every such movement, I was obliged to follow him closely. The street was a narrow and long one, and his course lay within it for nearly an hour, during which the passengers had gradually diminished to about that number which is ordinarily seen at noon in Broadway near the Park — so vast a difference is there between a London populace and that of the most frequented American city. A second turn brought us into a square, brilliantly lighted, and overflowing with life. The old manner of the stranger reappeared. His chin fell upon his breast, while his eyes rolled wildly from under his knit brows, in every direction, upon those who hemmed him in. He urged his way steadily and perseveringly. I was surprised, however, to find, upon his having made the circuit of the square, that he turned and retraced his steps. Still more was I astonished to see him repeat the same walk several times — once nearly detecting me as he came round with a sudden movement.

In this exercise he spent another hour, at the end of which we met with far less interruption from passengers than at first. The rain fell fast; the air grew cool; and the people were retiring to their homes. With a gesture of impatience, the wanderer passed into a by-street comparatively deserted. Down this, some quarter of a mile long, he rushed with an activity I could not have dreamed of seeing in one so aged, and which put me to much trouble in pursuit. A few minutes brought us to a large and busy bazaar, with the localities of which the stranger appeared well acquainted, and where his original demeanour again became apparent, as he forced his way to and fro, without aim, among the host of buyers and sellers.

During the hour and a half, or thereabouts, which we passed in this place, it required much caution on my part to keep him within reach without attracting his observation. Luckily I wore a pair of caoutchouc over-shoes, and could move about in perfect silence. At no moment did he see that I watched him. He entered shop after shop, priced nothing, spoke no word, and looked at all objects with a wild and vacant stare. I was now utterly amazed at his behaviour, and firmly resolved that we should not part until I had satisfied myself in some measure respecting him.

A loud-toned clock struck eleven, and the company were fast deserting the bazaar. A shop-keeper, in putting up a shutter, jostled the old man, and at the instant I saw a strong shudder come over his frame. He hurried into the street, looked anxiously around him for an instant, and then ran with incredible swiftness through many crooked and people-less lanes, until we emerged once more upon the great thoroughfare whence we had started — the street of the D—— Hotel. It no longer wore, however, the same aspect. It was still brilliant with gas; but the rain fell fiercely, and there were few persons to be seen. The stranger grew pale. He walked moodily some paces up the once populous avenue, then, with a heavy sigh, turned in the direction of the river, and, plunging through a great variety of devious ways, came out, at length, in view of one of the principal theatres. It was about being closed, and the audience were thronging from the doors. I saw the old man gasp as if for breath while he threw himself amid the crowd; but I thought that the intense agony

of his countenance had, in some measure, abated. His head again
fell upon his breast; he appeared as I had seen him at first. I
observed that he now took the course in which had gone the
greater number of the audience — but, upon the whole, I was at
a loss to comprehend the waywardness of his actions.

As he proceeded, the company grew more scattered, and his
old uneasiness and vacillation were resumed. For some time he
followed closely a party of some ten or twelve roisterers; but from
this number one by one dropped off, until three only remained
together, in a narrow and gloomy lane little frequented. The
stranger paused, and, for a moment, seemed lost in thought; then,
with every mark of agitation, pursued rapidly a route which
brought us to the verge of the city, amid regions very different
from those we had hitherto traversed. It was the most noisome
quarter of London, where every thing wore the worst impress
of the most deplorable poverty, and of the most desperate crime.
By the dim light of an accidental lamp, tall, antique, worm-eaten,
wooden tenements were seen tottering to their fall, in directions
so many and capricious that scarce the semblance of a passage was discernible between them. The paving-stones lay at
random, displaced from their beds by the rankly-growing
grass. Horrible filth festered in the damned-up gutters. The
whole atmosphere teemed with desolation. Yet, as we proceeded,
the sounds of human life revived by sure degrees, and at length
large bands of the most abandoned of a London populace were
seen reeling to and fro. The spirits of the old man again flickered
up, as a lamp which is near its death-hour. Once more he strode
onward with elastic tread. Suddenly a corner was turned, a blaze
of light burst upon our sight, and we stood before one of the
huge suburban temples of Intemperance — one of the palaces of
the fiend, Gin.

It was now nearly day-break; but a number of wretched ine-
briates still pressed in and out of the flaunting entrance. With a
half shriek of joy the old man forced a passage within, resumed
at once his original bearing, and stalked backward and forward,
without apparent object, among the throng. He had not been
thus long occupied, however, before a rush to the doors gave
token that the host was closing them for the night. It was something even more intense than despair that I then observed upon
the countenance of the singular being whom I had watched so

pertinaciously. Yet he did not hesitate in his career, but, with a mad energy, retraced his steps at once, to the heart of the mighty London. Long and swiftly he fled, while I followed him in the wildest amazement, resolute not to abandon a scrutiny in which I now felt an interest all-absorbing. The sun arose while we proceeded, and, when we had once again reached that most thronged mart of the populous town, the street of the D———— Hotel, it presented an appearance of human bustle and activity scarcely inferior to what I had seen on the evening before. And here, long, amid the momently increasing confusion, did I persist in my pursuit of the stranger. But, as usual, he walked to and fro, and during the day did not pass from out the turmoil of that street. And, as the shades of the second evening came on, I grew wearied unto death, and, stopping fully in front of the wanderer, gazed at him steadfastly in the face. He noticed me not, but resumed his solemn walk, while I, ceasing to follow, remained absorbed in contemplation. "This old man," I said at length, "is the type and the genius of deep crime. He refuses to be alone. *He is the man of the crowd.* It will be in vain to follow; for I shall learn no more of him, nor of his deeds. The worst heart of the world is a grosser book than the 'Hortulus Animæ,' and perhaps it is but one of the great mercies of God that *es lässt sich nicht lesen.*"

NIKOLAI GOGOL (1809–1852)   Gogol, the son of a small Ukrainian landowner, was born in Poltava Province, Russia. Gogol's father, an amateur writer of Ukrainian comic plays, died when Gogol was sixteen. After finishing grammar school at the age of nineteen, Gogol left the Ukraine for St. Petersburg. His first poem, published under a pseudonym in 1829, elicited a brief unfavorable review causing Gogol to buy and burn all the copies he could find and to flee Russia. On his return to St. Petersburg he worked in the Civil Service and taught history at the Patriotic Institute for Young Ladies. His group of Ukrainian short stories, *Evenings on a Farm near Dikanka* (1831), brought him recognition as a literary figure. From 1834–1835, he was an Assistant Professor of Medieval History at the University of Petersburg. From 1835–1836, Gogol published two short story collections, *Arabesques* and *Mirogorod,* and also "The Nose." Gogol was proud of his abnormally long nose and bragged it could "penetrate personally without the assistance of fingers into the smallest snuff-box." The motif of "the nose" recurs frequently in Gogol's works. Nabokov in his biography of Gogol asserts that "Gogol's long sensitive nose had discovered new smells in literature . . . As a Russian saying goes 'the man with the longest nose sees further'; and Gogol saw with his nostrils . . . When he destroyed his own genius by trying to become a preacher, he lost his nose just as Kovalev lost his."

The controversy provoked by *The Government Inspector* (1836) and *Dead Souls* (1842) drove Gogol abroad where he lived for twelve years, mostly in Rome, visiting Russia only occasionally. Gogol was confused by the situation which raged about him since he was not a social reformer as the liberals proclaimed, but a conservative who did not want to disturb the patriarchal system. He did feel, however, that his moral purpose was to regenerate Russia and "to portray national defects and national virtues in such a manner as to help readers to persevere in the latter and rid themselves of the former."

The last ten years of Gogol's life were fraught with melancholy and religious despair. He made a pilgrimage to the Holy Land. On his return to Russia he fell under the influence of the fanatical ascetic, Father Matthew Konstantinovsky, who told him to renounce literature and enter a monastery. Shortly before he died as the result of starvation due to asceticism and self-mortification, Gogol burned the second part of *Dead Souls.*

THE NOSE

Nikolai Gogol

I

A most extraordinary thing happened in Petersburg on the twenty-fifth of March. The barber, Ivan Yakovlevich, who lives on the Voznessensky Avenue (his surname is lost, and even on his sign-board, depicting a gentleman with a lathered face and bearing the inscription: "Also lets blood," no surname appears) — the barber Ivan Yakovlevich woke up rather early and inhaled the smell of hot bread. Raising himself a little in bed, he saw that his wife, a highly respectable lady who was very fond of a cup of coffee, was taking out of the oven some freshly baked bread.

"I won't have coffee today, my dear," said Ivan Yakovlevich. "Instead I'd like some hot bread with onions."

(That is to say, Ivan Yakovlevich would have liked both, but he knew that it was absolutely impossible to ask for two things at once; for his wife disliked such absurd whims.)

"Let the fool eat bread," his wife thought to herself. "All the better for me: there'll be an extra cup of coffee left." And she flung a loaf on the table.

After putting on, for propriety's sake, his frock coat over his shirt, Ivan Yakovlevich sat down at the table, sprinkled some salt, peeled two onions, picked up a knife, and, assuming a solemn expression, began cutting the bread. Having cut it in two, he had a look into the middle of one of the halves and, to his astonishment, noticed some white object there. Ivan Yakovlevich prodded it carefully with the knife and felt it with a finger. "It's solid," he said to himself. "What on earth can it be?"

He dug his fingers into the bread and pulled out — a nose! Ivan Yakovlevich's heart sank: he rubbed his eyes and felt it again: a nose! There could be no doubt about it: it was a nose! And a familiar nose, too, apparently. Ivan Yakovlevich looked

39

horrified. But his horror was nothing compared to the indignation with which his wife was overcome.

"Where have you cut off that nose, you monster?" she screamed
angrily. "Blackguard! Drunkard! I shall inform the police against
you myself. What a cutthroat! Three gentlemen have told me
already that when you are shaving them you pull so violently at
their noses that it is a wonder they still remain on their faces!"

But Ivan Yakovlevich was more dead than alive. He recognised
the nose as belonging to no other person than the Collegiate
Assessor Kovalyov, whom he shaved every Wednesday and every
Sunday.

"Wait, my dear, I'll wrap it in a rag and put it in a corner:
let it stay there for a bit and then I'll take it out."

"I won't hear of it! What do you take me for? Keep a cut-off
nose in my room? You heartless villain, you! All you know is to
strop your razor. Soon you won't be fit to carry out your duties
at all, you whoremonger, you scoundrel, you! You don't expect
me to answer to the police for you, do you? Oh, you filthy wretch,
you blockhead, you! Out with it! Out! Take it where you like,
only don't let me see it here again!"

Ivan Yakovlevich stood there looking utterly crushed. He
thought and thought and did not know what to think.

"Damned if I know how it happened," he said at last, scratching behind his ear. "Did I come home drunk last night? I'm sure
I don't know. And yet the whole thing is quite impossible — it
can't be true however you look at it: for bread is something you
bake, and a nose is something quite different. Can't make head
or tail of it!"

Ivan Yakovlevich fell silent. The thought that the police might
find the nose at his place and charge him with having cut it off
made him feel utterly dejected. He could already see the scarlet
collar, beautifully embroidered with silver, the sabre — and he
trembled all over. At last he got his trousers and boots, pulled on
these sorry objects, and, accompanied by his wife's execrations,
wrapped the nose in a rag and went out into the street.

He wanted to shove it under something, either under the seat
by the gates or drop it, as it were, by accident and then turn off
into a side street. But as ill luck would have it, he kept coming
across people he knew, who at once addressed him with the question: "Where are you off to?" or "Who are you going to shave

so early in the morning?" — so that he could not find a right moment for getting rid of it. On one occasion he did succeed in dropping it, but a policeman shouted to him from the distance, pointing to it with his halberd: "Hey, you, pick it up! You've dropped something!" And Ivan Yakovlevich had to pick up the nose and put it in his pocket. He was overcome by despair, particularly as the number of people in the streets was continually increasing with the opening of the stores and the small shops.

He decided to go to the Issakiyevsky Bridge, for it occurred to him that he might be able to throw it into the Neva. But I'm afraid I am perhaps a little to blame for not having so far said something more about Ivan Yakovlevich, an estimable man in many respects.

Ivan Yakovlevich, like every other Russian working man, was a terrible drunkard. And though every day he shaved other people's chins, he never bothered to shave his own. Ivan Yakovlevich's frock coat (he never wore an ordinary coat) was piebald; that is to say, it was black, but covered all over with large brown, yellow, and grey spots; his collar was shiny; and instead of three buttons only bits of thread dangled from his coat. Ivan Yakovlevich was a great cynic, and every time the Collegiate Assessor Kovalyov said to him: "Your hands always stink, Ivan Yakovlevich," he would reply with the question: "Why should they stink, sir?" "I don't know why, my dear fellow," the Collegiate Assessor would say, "only they do stink." And after taking a pinch of snuff, Ivan Yakovlevich would lather him for that all over his cheeks, under the nose, behind his ears, and under his beard, in short, wherever he fancied.

This worthy citizen had in the meantime reached Issakiyevsky Bridge. First of all he looked round cautiously, then he leaned over the parapet, as though anxious to see whether there were a great many fishes swimming by, and as he did so he stealthily threw the rag with the nose into the river. He felt as though a heavy weight had been lifted from his shoulders: Ivan Yakovlevich even grinned. Instead of going to shave the chins of civil servants, he set off towards an establishment which bore the inscription: "Tea and Victuals," intending to ask for a glass of punch, when he suddenly noticed at the end of the bridge a police inspector of noble exterior, with large whiskers, with a three-cornered hat, and with a sabre. He stood rooted to the spot; meanwhile the police officer beckoned to him and said: "Come here, my man!"

Knowing the rules, Ivan Yakovlevich took off his cap some way off and, coming up promptly, said: "I hope your honour is well."

"No, no, my good man, not 'your honour.' Tell me, what were you doing there on the bridge?"

"Why, sir, I was going to shave one of my customers and I just stopped to have a look how fast the current was running."

"You're lying, sir, you're lying! You won't get off with that. Answer my question, please!"

"I'm ready to shave you two or even three times a week, sir, with no conditions attached," replied Ivan Yakovlevich.

"No, my dear sir, that's nothing! I have three barbers who shave me and they consider it a great honour, too. You'd better tell me what you were doing there!"

Ivan Yakovlevich turned pale. . . . But here the incident is completely shrouded in a fog and absolutely nothing is known of what happened next.

II

Collegiate Assessor Kovalyov woke up fairly early and muttered, "Brr . . ." with his lips, which he always did when he woke up, though he could not say himself why he did so. Kovalyov stretched and asked for the little looking glass standing on the table. He wanted to look at the pimple which had appeared on his nose the previous evening, but to his great astonishment, instead of his nose, he saw a completely empty, flat place! Frightened, Kovalyov asked for some water and rubbed his eyes with a towel: there was no nose! He began feeling with his hand and pinched himself to see whether he was still asleep: no, he did not appear to be asleep. The Collegiate Assessor Kovalyov jumped out of bed and shook himself: he had no nose! He immediately told his servant to help him dress and rushed off straight to the Commissioner of Police.

Meanwhile we had better say something about Kovalyov so that the reader may see what sort of a person this Collegiate Assessor was. Collegiate Assessors who receive that title in consequence of their learned diplomas cannot be compared with those

Collegiate Assessors who obtain this rank in the Caucasus. They are two quite different species. Learned Collegiate Assessors . . . But Russia is such a wonderful country that if you say something about one Collegiate Assessor, all the Collegiate Assessors, from Riga to Kamchatka, will most certainly think that you are referring to them. The same, of course, applies to all other callings and ranks. Kovalyov was a Caucasian Collegiate Assessor. He had obtained that rank only two years earlier and that was why he could not forget it for a moment; and to add to his own importance and dignity, he never described himself as a Collegiate Assessor, that is to say, a civil servant of the eighth rank, but always as a major, that is to say, by the corresponding rank in the army. "Look here, my good woman," he used to say when he met a peasant woman selling shirt fronts in the street, "you go to my house — I live on Sadovaya Street — and just ask: Does Major Kovalyov live here? Anyone will show you." But if he met some pretty little minx, he'd give her besides a secret instruction, adding: "You just ask for Major Kovalyov's apartment, darling." And that is why we, too, will in future refer to this Collegiate Assessor as Major Kovalyov.

Major Kovalyov was in the habit of taking a stroll on Nevsky Avenue every day. The collar of his shirt front was always extremely clean and well starched. His whiskers were such as one can still see nowadays on provincial district surveyors, architects, and army doctors, as well as on police officers performing various duties and, in general, on all gallant gentlemen who have full, ruddy cheeks and are very good at a game of boston: these whiskers go right across the middle of the cheek and straight up to the nose. Major Kovalyov wore a great number of cornelian seals, some with crests and others which had engraved on them: Wednesday, Thursday, Monday, and so on. Major Kovalyov came to Petersburg on business, to wit, to look for a post befitting his rank: if he were lucky, the post of a vice-governor, if not, one of an administrative clerk in some important department. Major Kovalyov was not averse to matrimony, either, but only if he could find a girl with a fortune of two hundred thousand. The reader can, therefore, judge for himself the state in which the major was when he saw, instead of a fairly handsome nose of moderate size, a most idiotic, flat, smooth place.

As misfortune would have it, there was not a single cab to be
seen in the street and he had to walk, wrapping himself in his
cloak and covering his face with a handkerchief, as though his
nose were bleeding. "But perhaps I imagined it all," he thought.
"It's impossible that I could have lost my nose without noticing
it!" He went into a pastry cook's for the sole purpose of having
a look at himself in a mirror. Fortunately, there was no one in
the shop: the boys were sweeping the rooms and arranging the
chairs; some of them, sleepy-eyed, were bringing in hot cream
puffs on trays; yesterday's papers, stained with coffee, were lying
about on tables and chairs. "Well, thank God, there's nobody
here," he said. "Now I can have a look." He went timidly up to
the mirror and looked. "Damn it," he said, disgusted, "the whole
thing is too ridiculous for words; If only there'd be something
instead of a nose, but there's just nothing!"

Biting his lips with vexation, Kovalyov went out of the pastry
cook's and made up his mind, contrary to his usual practice, not
to look or smile at anyone. Suddenly he stopped dead in his
tracks at the front doors of a house; a most inexplicable thing
happened before his very eyes: a carriage drew up before the entrance, the carriage door opened, and a gentleman in uniform
jumped out and, stooping, rushed up the steps. Imagine the
horror and, at the same time, amazement of Kovalyov when he
recognised that this was his own nose! At this extraordinary sight
everything went swimming before his eyes. He felt that he could
hardly stand on his feet; but he made up his mind that, come
what may, he would wait for the gentleman's return to the carriage. He was trembling all over as though in a fever. Two
minutes later the nose really did come out. He wore a gold-embroidered uniform with a large stand-up collar, chamois-leather
breeches, and a sword at his side. From his plumed hat it could
be inferred that he was a State Councillor, a civil servant of the
fifth rank. Everything showed that he was going somewhere to
pay a visit. He looked round to the right and to the left, shouted
to his driver, who had driven off a short distance, to come back,
got into the carriage, and drove off.

Poor Kovalyov nearly went out of his mind. He did not know
what to think of such a strange occurrence. And, indeed, how was
it possible for a nose which had only the day before been on his

face and which could neither walk nor drive — to be in a uniform! He ran after the carriage which, luckily, did not go far, stopping before the Kazan Cathedral.

He hastened into the cathedral, pushing his way through the crowd of beggarwomen with bandaged faces and only two slits for the eyes, at whom he used to laugh so much before, and went into the church. There were only a few worshippers inside the church; they were all standing near the entrance. Kovalyov felt so distraught that he was unable to pray and he kept searching with his eyes for the gentleman in the State Councillor's uniform. At last he saw him standing apart from the other worshippers. The nose was hiding his face completely in his large stand-up collar and was saying his prayers with the expression of the utmost piety.

"How am I to approach him?" thought Kovalyov. "It is clear from everything, from his uniform, from his hat, that he is a State Councillor. I'm damned if I know how to do it!"

He went up to him and began clearing his throat; but the nose did not change his devout attitude for a moment and carried on with his genuflections.

"Sir," said Kovalyov, inwardly forcing himself to take courage, "Sir — "

"What do you want?" answered the nose, turning round.

"I find it strange, sir, I — I believe you ought to know your proper place. And all of a sudden I find you in church of all places! You — you must admit that — "

"I'm sorry but I can't understand what you are talking about. . . . Explain yourself."

"How can I explain it to him?" thought Kovalyov and, plucking up courage, began: "Of course — er — you see — I — I am a major and — and you must admit that it isn't right for — er — a man of my rank to walk about without a nose. I mean — er — a tradeswoman selling peeled oranges on Voskressensky Bridge can sit there without a nose; but for a man like me who expects to obtain the post of a governor, which without a doubt he will obtain and — er — besides, being received in many houses by ladies of good position, such as Mrs. Chekhtaryov, the widow of a State Councillor, sir, and many others — er — Judge for yourself, sir, I mean, I — I don't know" — Major Kovalyov shrugged his shoulders — "I am sorry but if one were to look upon it according to the rules of honour and duty — er — you can understand yourself, sir — "

"I don't understand anything sir," replied the nose. "Please explain yourself more clearly."

"Sir," said Kovalyov with a consciousness of his own dignity, "I don't know how to understand your words. It seems to me the whole thing is perfectly obvious. Or do you wish — I mean, you are my own nose, sir!"

The nose looked at the major and frowned slightly.

"You are mistaken, sir. I am *myself*. Besides, there can be no question of any intimate relationship between us. I see, sir, from the buttons of your uniform that you are serving in a different department."

Having said this, the nose turned away and went on praying.

Kovalyov was utterly confounded, not knowing what to do or even what to think. At that moment he heard the agreeable rustle of a lady's dress; an elderly lady, her dress richly trimmed with lace, walked up to them, accompanied by a slim girl in a white dress, which looked very charming on her slender figure, and in a straw-coloured hat, as light as a pastry puff. Behind them, opening a snuffbox, stood a tall flunkey with enormous whiskers and quite a dozen collars on his Cossack coat.

Kovalyov came nearer, pulled out the cambric collar of his shirt front, straightened the seals hanging on his gold watch chain and, turning his head this way and that and smiling, turned his attention to the ethereal young lady who, like a spring flower, bent forward a little, as she prayed, and put her little white hand with its semi-transparent fingers to her forehead to cross herself. The smile on Kovalyov's face distended a little more when he caught sight under her pretty hat of a chin of dazzling whiteness and part of her cheek, suffused with the colour of the first spring rose. But suddenly he sprang back as though he had burnt himself. He recollected that, instead of a nose, he had absolutely nothing on his face, and tears started to his eyes. He turned round, intending to tell the gentleman in uniform plainly that he was merely pretending to be a State Councillor, that he was a rogue and an impostor and nothing else than his own nose. . . . But the nose was no longer there: he had managed to gallop off, no doubt to pay another visit. . . .

That plunged Kovalyov into despair. He left the church and stopped for a moment under the colonnade, carefully looking in all directions to see whether he could catch sight of the nose anywhere. He remembered very well that he wore a hat with a plume and a gold-embroidered uniform; but he had not noticed his cloak, nor the colour of his carriage, nor his horses, nor even whether he had a footman behind him and, if so, in what livery. Besides, there were so many carriages careening backwards and forwards that it was difficult to distinguish one from another. But even if he had been able to distinguish any of them, there was no way of stopping it. It was a lovely, sunny day. There were hundreds of people on Nevsky Avenue. A whole flowery cascade of ladies was pouring all over the pavement from the Police Bridge to the Anichkin Bridge. There he saw coming a good acquaintance of his, a civil servant of the seventh rank, whom he always addressed as lieutenant colonel, especially in the presence of strangers. And there was Yaryzhkin, the head clerk in the Senate, a great friend of his, who always lost points when he went eight at boston. And here was another major, who had received the eighth rank of Collegiate Assessor in the Caucasus, waving to him to come up. . . .

"Oh, hell!" said Kovalyov. "Hey, cabby, take me straight to the Commissioner of Police!"

Kovalyov got into the cab and kept shouting to the driver: "Faster! Faster!"

"Is the Police Commissioner at home?" he asked, entering the hall.

"No, sir," replied the janitor. "He's just gone out."

"Well, of all things!"

"Yes, sir," the janitor added, "he's not been gone so long, but he's gone all right. If you'd come a minute earlier, you'd probably have found him at home."

Without taking his handkerchief off his face, Kovalyov got into the cab and shouted in an anguished voice:

"Drive on!"

"Where to, sir?" asked the cabman.

"Straight ahead!"

"Straight ahead, sir? But there's a turning here: to right or to left?"

This question stumped Kovalyov and made him think again.

A man in his position ought first of all apply to the City Police Headquarters, not because they dealt with matters of this kind there, but because instructions coming from there might be complied with much more quickly than those coming from any other place; to seek satisfaction from the authorities of the department in which the nose claimed to be serving would have been unreasonable, for from the nose's replies he perceived that nothing was sacred to that individual and that he was quite capable of telling a lie just as he had lied in denying that he had ever seen him. Kovalyov was, therefore, about to tell the cabman to drive him to Police Headquarters, when it again occurred to him that this rogue and impostor, who had treated him in such a contumelious way, might take advantage of the first favourable opportunity and slip out of town, and then all his searches would be in vain or, which God forbid, might go on for a whole month. At last it seemed that Heaven itself had suggested a plan of action to him. He decided to go straight to a newspaper office and, while there was still time, put in an advertisement with a circumstantial description of the nose so that anyone meeting it might bring it to him at once or, at any rate, let him know where it was. And so, having made up his mind, he told the cabman to drive him to the nearest newspaper office and all the way there he kept hitting the cabman on the back with his fist, repeating, "Faster, you rogue! Faster, you scoundrel!" "Good Lord, sir, what are you hitting me for?" said the cabman, shaking his head and flicking with the rein at the horse, whose coat was as long as a lap dog's. At last the cab came to a stop and Kovalyov ran panting into a small reception room where a grey-haired clerk, in an old frock coat and wearing spectacles, sat at a table, with a pen between his teeth, counting some coppers.

"Who receives advertisements here?" cried Kovalyov. "Oh, good morning!"

"How do you do?" said the clerk, raising his eyes for a moment and dropping them again on the carefully laid out heaps of coppers before him.

"I should like to insert — "

"One moment, sir, I must ask you to wait a little," said the clerk, writing down a figure on a piece of paper with one hand and moving two beads on his abacus with the other.

A footman with galloons on his livery and a personal appearance which showed that he came from an aristocratic house, was
standing beside the clerk with a note in his hand. He thought it
an opportune moment for displaying his knowledge of the world.

"Would you believe it, sir," he said, "the little bitch isn't worth
eighty copecks, and indeed I shouldn't give even eight copecks
for her, but the countess dotes on her, sir, she simply dotes on
her, and that's why she's offering a hundred roubles to anyone
who finds her! Now, to put it politely, sir, just as you and me
are speaking now, you can never tell what people's tastes may be.
What I mean is that if you are a sportsman, then keep a pointer
or a poodle, don't mind spending five hundred or even a thousand roubles, so long as your dog is a good one."

The worthy clerk listened to this with a grave air and at the
same time kept counting the number of letters in the advertisement the footman had brought. The room was full of old women,
shop assistants, and house porters — all with bits of paper in their
hands. In one a coachman of sober habits was advertised as being
let out on hire; in another an almost new, secondhand carriage,
brought from Paris in 1814, was offered for sale; in still others
were offered for sale: a serf girl of nineteen, experienced in laundry work and suitable for other work, a well-built open carriage
with only one spring broken, a young, dappled-grey, mettlesome
horse of seventeen years of age, a new consignment of turnip and
radish seed from London, a summer residence with all the con-
veniences, including two boxes for horses and a piece of land on
which an excellent birchwood or pinewood could be planted;
there was also an advertisement containing a challenge to those
who wished to purchase old boot soles with an invitation to come
to the auction rooms every day from eight o'clock in the morning
to three o'clock in the afternoon. The room, in which all these
people were crowded, was very small and the air extremely thick;
but the Collegiate Assessor Kovalyov did not notice the bad smell
because he kept the handkerchief over his face and also because
his nose was at the time goodness knows where.

"Excuse me, sir," he said at last with impatience, "it's very
urgent. . . ."

"Presently, presently," said the grey-haired gentleman, flinging
their notes back to the old women and the house porters. "Two

roubles forty copecks! One moment, sir! One rouble sixty-four copecks! What can I do for you?" he said at last, turning to Kovalyov.

"Thank you, sir," said Kovalyov. "You see, I've been robbed or swindled, I can't so far say which, but I should like you to put in an advertisement that anyone who brings the scoundrel to me will receive a handsome reward."

"What is your name, sir?"

"What do you want my name for? I'm sorry I can't give it to you. I have a large circle of friends: Mrs. Chekhtaryov, the widow of a State Councillor, Pelageya Grigoryevna Podtochin, the widow of a first lieutenant. . . . God forbid that they should suddenly find out! You can simply say: a Collegiate Assessor or, better still, a gentleman of the rank of major."

"And is the runaway your house serf?"

"My house serf? Good Lord, no! That wouldn't have been so bad! You see, it's my — er — nose that has run away from me. . . ."

"Dear me, what a strange name! And has this Mr. Nosov robbed you of a large sum of money?"

"I said nose, sir, nose! You're thinking of something else! It is my nose, my own nose that has disappeared I don't know where. The devil himself must have played a joke on me!"

"But how did it disappear? I'm afraid I don't quite understand it."

"I can't tell you how it happened. The worst of it is that now it is driving about all over the town under the guise of a State Councillor. That's why I should like you to insert an advertisement that anyone who catches him should bring him at once to me. You can see for yourself, sir, that I cannot possibly carry on without such a conspicuous part of myself. It's not like some little toe which no one can see whether it is missing or not once I'm wearing my boots. I call on Thursdays on Mrs. Chekhtaryov, the widow of a State Councillor. Mrs. Podtochin, the widow of a first lieutenant, and her pretty daughter are also good friends of mine, and you can judge for yourself the position I am in now. I can't go and see them now, can I?"

The clerk pursed his lips tightly which meant that he was thinking hard.

"I'm sorry, sir," he said at last, after a long pause, "but I can't possibly insert such an advertisement in the paper."

"What? Why not?"

"Well, you see, sir, the paper might lose its reputation. If everyone were to write that his nose had run away, why — As it is, people are already saying that we are publishing a lot of absurd stories and false rumours."

"But why is it so absurd? I don't see anything absurd in it."

"It only seems so to you. Last week, for instance, a similar thing happened. A civil servant came to see me just as you have now. He brought an advertisement, it came to two roubles and seventy-three copecks, but all it was about was that a poodle with a black coat had run away. You wouldn't think there was anything in that, would you? And yet it turned out to be a libellous statement. You see, the poodle was the treasurer of some institution or other. I don't remember which."

"But I am not asking you to publish an advertisement about a poodle, but about my own nose, which is the same as about myself."

"No, sir, I cannot possibly insert such an advertisement."

"Not even if my own nose really has disappeared?"

"If it's lost, then it's a matter for a doctor. I'm told there are people who can fit you with a nose of any shape you like. But I can't help observing, sir, that you are a gentleman of a merry disposition and are fond of pulling a person's leg."

"I swear to you by all that is holy! Why, if it has come to that, I don't mind showing you."

"Don't bother, sir," said the clerk, taking a pinch of snuff. "Still," he added, unable to suppress his curiosity, "if it's no bother, I'd like to have a look."

The Collegiate Assessor removed the handkerchief from his face.

"It is very strange, indeed!" said the clerk. "The place is perfectly flat, just like a pancake from a frying pan. Yes, quite incredibly flat."

"Well, you won't dispute it now, will you? You can see for yourself that you simply must insert it. I shall be infinitely grateful to you and very glad this incident has given me the pleasure of making your acquaintance. . . ."

It may be seen from that that the major decided to lay it on a bit thick this time.

"Well, of course, it's easy enough to insert an advertisement," said the clerk, "but I don't see that it will do you any good. If you really want to publish a thing like that, you'd better put it in the hands of someone skilful with his pen and let him describe it as a rare natural phenomenon and publish it in *The Northern Bee*" — here he took another pinch of snuff — "for the benefit of youth" — here he wiped his nose — "or just as a matter of general interest."

The Collegiate Assessor was utterly discouraged. He dropped his eyes and glanced at the bottom of the newpaper where the theatrical announcements were published; his face was ready to break into a smile as he read the name of a very pretty actress, and his hand went automatically to his pocket to feel whether he had a five-rouble note there, for, in Kovalyov's opinion, officers of the higher ranks ought to have a seat in the stalls — but the thought of his nose spoilt it all!

The clerk himself appeared to be touched by Kovalyov's embarrassing position. Wishing to relieve his distress a little, he thought it proper to express his sympathy in a few words.

"I'm very sorry indeed, sir," he said, "that such a thing should have happened to you. Would you like a pinch of snuff? It relieves headaches, dispels melancholy moods, and it is even a good remedy against haemorrhoids."

Saying this, the clerk offered his snuffbox to Kovalyov, very deftly opening the lid with the portrait of a lady in a hat on it.

This unintentional action made Kovalyov lose his patience.

"I can't understand, sir," he said angrily, "how you can joke in a matter like this! Don't you see I haven't got the thing with which to take a pinch of snuff? To hell with your snuff! I can't bear the sight of it now, and not only your rotten beresina brand, but even if you were to offer me rappee itself!"

Having said this, he walked out of the newspaper office, greatly vexed, and went to see the police inspector of his district, a man who had a great liking for sugar. At his home, the entire hall, which was also the dining room, was stacked with sugar loaves with which local tradesmen had presented him out of friendship. When Kovalyov arrived, the police inspector's cook was helping him off with his regulation top boots; his sabre and the rest of his martial armour were already hung peaceably in the corners of the room, and his three-year-old son was playing with his awe-inspiring three-cornered hat. He himself was getting ready to partake of the pleasures of peace after his gallant, warlike exploits.

Kovalyov walked in at the time when he stretched, cleared his throat, and said: "Oh, for a couple of hours of sleep!" It could, therefore, be foreseen that the Collegiate Assessor could have hardly chosen a worse time to arrive; indeed, I am not sure whether he would have got a more cordial reception even if he had brought the police inspector several pounds of sugar or a piece of cloth. The inspector was a great patron of the arts and manufactures, but he preferred a bank note to everything else. "This is something," he used to say. "There is nothing better than that: it doesn't ask for food, it doesn't take up a lot of space, there's always room for it in the pocket, and when you drop it, it doesn't break."

The inspector received Kovalyov rather coldly and said that after dinner was not the time to carry out investigations and that nature herself had fixed it so that after a good meal a man had to take a nap (from which the Collegiate Assessor could deduce that the inspector was not unfamiliar with the sayings of the ancient sages), and that a respectable man would not have his nose pulled off.

A bull's eye! . . . It must be observed that Kovalyov was extremely quick to take offence. He could forgive anything people said about himself, but he could never forgive an insult to his rank or his calling. He was even of the opinion that any reference in plays to army officers or civil servants of low rank was admissible, but that the censorship ought not to pass any attack on persons of higher rank. The reception given him by the police inspector disconcerted him so much that he tossed his head and said with an air of dignity, with his hands slightly parted in a gesture of surprise: "I must say that after such offensive remarks, I have nothing more to say. . . ." and went out.

He arrived home hardly able to stand on his feet. By now it was dusk. After all these unsuccessful quests his rooms looked melancholy or rather extremely disgusting to him. On entering the hall, he saw his valet Ivan lying on his back on the dirty leather sofa and spitting on the ceiling and rather successfully aiming at the same spot. Such an indifference on the part of his servant maddened him; he hit him on the forehead with his hat, saying: "You pig, you're always doing something stupid!"

Ivan jumped up and rushed to help him off with his cloak.

On entering his room, the major, tired and dejected, threw himself into an armchair and, at last, after several sighs, said:

"Lord, oh Lord, why should I have such bad luck? If I had lost an arm or a leg, it would not be so bad; if I had lost my ears, it would be bad enough, but still bearable; but without a nose a man is goodness knows what, neither fish, nor flesh, nor good red herring — he isn't a respectable citizen at all! He is simply something to take and chuck out of the window! If I had had it cut off in battle or in a duel or had been the cause of its loss myself, but to lose it without any reason whatever, for nothing, for absolutely nothing! . . . But no," he added after a brief reflection, "it can't be. It's inconceivable that a nose should be lost, absolutely inconceivable. I must be simply dreaming or just imagining it all. Perhaps by some mistake I drank, instead of water, the spirits which I rub on my face after shaving. Ivan, the blithering fool, did not take it away and I must have swallowed it by mistake."

To convince himself that he was not drunk, the major pinched himself so painfully that he cried out. The pain completely convinced him that he was fully awake and that everything had actually happened to him. He went up slowly to the looking glass and at first screwed up his eyes with the idea that perhaps he would see his nose in its proper place; but almost at the same moment he jumped back, saying: "What a horrible sight!"

And, indeed, the whole thing was quite inexplicable. If he had lost a button, a silver spoon, his watch, or something of the kind, but to lose — and in his own apartment, too! Taking all the circumstances into consideration, Major Kovalyov decided that he would not be far wrong in assuming that the whole thing was the fault of no other person than Mrs. Podtochin, who wanted him to marry her daughter. He was not himself averse to flirting with her, but he avoided a final decision. But when Mrs. Podtochin told him plainly that she would like her daughter to marry him, he quietly hung back with his compliments, declaring that he was still too young, that he had to serve another five years, as he had decided not to marry till he was exactly forty-two. That was why Mrs. Podtochin, out of revenge no doubt, had made up her mind to disfigure him and engaged some old witch to do the foul deed, for he simply refused to believe that his nose had been cut off; no one had entered the room, and his barber, Ivan Yakovlevich, had shaved him on Wednesday, and during the whole of that day and even on Thursday his nose was intact — he remembered that, he knew that for certain; besides, he would have felt pain and the wound could not possibly have healed so quickly and become as smooth as a pancake. He made all sorts of plans in his head: to issue a court summons against her or to go to see her and confront her with the undeniable proof of her crime. His thoughts were interrupted by a gleam of light through all the cracks of the door, which let him know that Ivan had lighted a candle in the hall. Soon Ivan himself appeared, carrying the candle in front of him and lighting the whole room brightly. Kovalyov instinctively seized his handkerchief and covered the place where his nose had been only the day before so that the stupid fellow should not stand there gaping, seeing his master so strangely transformed.

Ivan had scarcely had time to go back to his cubbyhole when an unfamiliar voice was heard in the hall, saying:

"Does the Collegiate Assessor Kovalyov live here?"

"Come in," said Kovalyov, jumping up quickly and opening the door. "Major Kovalyov is here."

A police officer of a handsome appearance, with whiskers that were neither too dark nor too light and with fairly full cheeks, came in. It was, in fact, the same police officer who, at the beginning of this story, had been standing at the end of Issakiyevsky Bridge.

"Did you lose your nose, sir?"

"That's right."

"It's been found now."

"What are you saying?" cried Major Kovalyov.

He was bereft of speech with joy. He stared fixedly at the police officer who was standing before him and whose full lips and cheeks reflected the flickering light of the candle.

"How was it found?"

"By a most extraordinary piece of luck, sir. It was intercepted just before he was leaving town. It was about to get into the stage-coach and leave for Riga. He even had a passport made out in the name of a certain civil servant. And the funny thing is that at first I was myself inclined to take him for a gentleman. But luckily I was wearing my glasses at the time and I saw at once that it was a nose. You see, sir, I am shortsighted, and if you were to stand in front of me I would just see that you have a face, but would not be able to make out either your nose or your beard or anything else for that matter. My mother-in-law, that is to say, my wife's mother, can't see anything, either."

Kovalyov was beside himself with excitement.

"Where is it? Where? I'll go at once!"

"Don't trouble, sir. Realising how much you must want it, I brought it with me. And the funny part about it is that the chief acccomplice in this affair is the scoundrel of a barber on Voznessensky Avenue, who is now locked up in a cell at the police station. I've suspected him for a long time of theft and drunkenness and, as a matter of fact, he stole a dozen buttons from a shop only the other day. Your nose, sir, is just as it was."

At these words, the police officer put his hand in his pocket and pulled out the nose wrapped in a piece of paper.

"Yes, yes, it's my nose!" cried Kovalyov. "It's my nose all right! Won't you have a cup of tea with me, sir?"

"I'd be very glad to, sir, but I'm afraid I'm rather in a hurry. I have to go to the House of Correction from here. Food prices have risen a great deal, sir. . . . I have my mother-in-law, that is to say, my wife's mother, living with me and, of course, there are the children. My eldest, in particular, is a very promising lad, sir. A very clever boy he is, sir, but I haven't the means to provide a good education for him — none at all. . . ."

Kovalyov took the hint and, snatching up a ten-rouble note from the table, thrust it into the hand of the police officer, who bowed and left the room, and almost at the same moment Kovalyov heard his voice raised in the street, where he was boxing the ears of a foolish peasant who had happened to drive with his cart on to the boulevard.

After the departure of the police officer, the Collegiate Assessor remained for a time in a sort of daze, and it was only after several minutes that he was able to recover his senses, so overwhelmed was he by his joy at the unexpected recovery of his nose. He took the newly found nose very carefully in both his cupped hands and examined it attentively once more.

"Yes, it's my nose all right!" said Major Kovalyov. "There's the pimple on the left side which I only got the other day."

The major almost laughed with joy. But nothing lasts very long in the world, and that is why even joy is not so poignant after the first moment. A moment later it grows weaker still and at last it merges imperceptibly into one's ordinary mood, just as a circle made in the water by a pebble at last merges into its smooth surface. Kovalyov began to ponder and he realised that the matter was not at an end: the nose had been found, but it had still to be affixed, to be put back in its place.

"And what if it doesn't stick?"

At this question that he had put to himself the major turned pale.

With a feeling of indescribable panic he rushed up to the table and drew the looking glass closer to make sure that he did not stick his nose on crookedly. His hands trembled. Carefully and with the utmost circumspection he put it back on its former place. Oh horror! The nose did not stick! . . . He put it to his mouth, breathed on it to warm it a little, and once more put it back on the smooth place between his two cheeks; but, try as he might, the nose refused to stick.

"Come on, come on! Stick, you idiot!" he kept saying to it.

But the nose, as though made of wood, kept falling down on the table with so strange a sound that it might have been cork. The major's face contorted spasmodically. "Won't it adhere?" he asked himself in a panic. But though he kept putting it back on its own place a great many times, his efforts were as unavailing as ever.

He called Ivan and sent him for the doctor, who occupied the best flat on the ground floor of the same house. The doctor was a fine figure of a man; he had wonderful pitch-black whiskers, a fresh, healthy wife, he ate fresh apples in the morning and kept his mouth quite extraordinarily clean, rinsing it every morning for nearly three quarters of an hour and brushing his teeth with five different kinds of toothbrushes. The doctor came at once. After asking how long it was since the accident, he lifted up Major Kovalyov's face by the chin and gave a fillip with his thumb, on the spot where the nose had been, with such force that the major threw back his head so violently that he hit the wall. The doctor said that it was nothing and, after advising him

to move away from the wall a little, told him to bend his head
to the right. After feeling the place where the nose had been,
he said: "H'm!" Then he told him to bend his head to the left,
and again said: "H'm!" In conclusion he gave him another fillip
with the thumb so that the major tossed his head like a horse
whose teeth are being examined. Having carried out this experi-
ment, the doctor shook his head and said:

"No, I'm afraid it can't be done! You'd better remain like this,
for it might be much worse. It is, of course, quite possible to affix
your nose. In fact, I could do it right now. But I assure you that
it might be the worse for you."

"How do you like that! How am I to remain without a nose?"
said Kovalyov. "It can't possibly be worse than now. It's — it's
goodness only knows what! How can I show myself with such a
horrible face? I know lots of people of good social position. Why,
today I have been invited to two parties. I have a large circle
of friends: Mrs. Chekhtaryov, the widow of a State Councillor,
Mrs. Podtochin, the widow of an army officer — though after
what she did to me now I shall have no further dealings with her
except through the police. Do me a favour, Doctor," said Kovalyov in an imploring voice. "Is there no way at all? Stick it on
somehow. It may not be quite satisfactory, but so long as it sticks
I don't mind. I could even support it with a hand in an emergency. Besides, I don't dance, so that I could hardly do any harm
to it by some inadvertent movement. As for my gratitude for your
visits, you may be sure that I will recompense you as much as
I can. . . ."

"Believe me, sir," said the doctor neither in too loud nor in too
soft a voice, but in a very persuasive and magnetic one, "I never
allow any selfish motives to interfere with the treatment of my
patients. This is against my principles and my art. It is true I
charge for my visits, but that is only because I hate to offend by my
refusal. Of course, I could put your nose back, but I assure you
on my honour, if you won't believe my words, that it will be
much worse. You'd better leave it to nature. Wash it often with
cold water, and I assure you that without a nose you will be as
healthy as with one. As for your nose, I'd advise you to put it in a
bottle of spirits or, better still, pour two spoonfuls of aqua fortis
and warmed-up vinegar into the bottle, and you'd be able to get

a lot of money for it. I might take it myself even, if you won't ask too much for it."

"No, no," cried the desperate Major Kovalyov, "I'd rather it rotted away!"

"I'm sorry," said the doctor, taking his leave, "I wish I could be of some help to you, but there's nothing I can do! At least you saw how anxious I was to help you."

Having said this, the doctor left the room with a dignified air. Kovalyov did not even notice his face, and in his profound impassivity only caught sight of the cuffs of his spotlessly clean white shirt peeping out of his black frock coat.

On the following day he decided, before lodging his complaint, to write to Mrs. Podtochin a letter with a request to return to him without a fight what she had taken away from him. The letter was as follows:

Dear Mrs. Podtochin,

    I cannot understand your strange treatment of me. I assure you that, by acting like this, you will gain nothing and will certainly not force me to marry your daughter. Believe me, I know perfectly well what happened to my nose and that you, and no one else, are the chief instigator of this affair. Its sudden detachment from its place, its flight, and its disguise, first in the shape of a civil servant and then in its own shape, is nothing more than the result of witchcraft employed by you or by those who engage in the same honourable occupations as yourself. For my part, I deem it my duty to warn you that if the aforementioned nose is not back in its usual place today, I shall be forced to have recourse to the protection and the safeguard of the law.

    However, I have the honour of remaining, madam, with the utmost respect

    Your obedient servant,

                      Platon Kovalyov

Dear Platon Kuzmich,

    Your letter has greatly surprised me. To be quite frank, I never expected it, particularly as regards your unjust reproaches. I wish to inform you that I have never received the civil servant you mention, neither in disguise nor in his own

shape. It is true, Filipp Ivanovich Potachkin used to come to
see me. And though he did ask me for my daughter's hand and
is a man of good and sober habits and of great learning, I have
never held out any hopes to him. You also mention your nose.
If you mean by that that I wished to put your nose out of
joint, that is, to give you a formal refusal, I am surprised that
you should speak of such a thing when, as you know perfectly
well, I was quite of the contrary opinion and if you should
now make a formal proposal to my daughter, I should be ready
to satisfy you immediately, for that has always been my dearest
wish, in the hope of which

    I remain always at your service,

                                                    Pelageya Podtochin

"No," said Kovalyov, after he had read the letter, "she had
certainly nothing to do with it. It's impossible! The letter is not
written as a guilty person would have written it." The Collegiate
Assessor was an expert on such things, for, while serving in the
Caucasus, he had several times been under judicial examination.
"How then, in what way, did it happen? The devil alone can
sort it out!" he said at last, utterly discouraged.

Meanwhile the rumours about this extraordinary affair spread
all over the town and, as usually happens, not without all sorts
of embellishments. At that time people's minds were particularly
susceptible to anything of an extraordinary nature: only a short
time before everybody had shown a great interest in the experi-
ments of magnetism. Besides, the story of the dancing chairs in
Konyushennaya Street was still fresh in people's minds, and it is
therefore not surprising that people soon began talking about
the Collegiate Assessor Kovalyov's nose which, it was alleged,
was taking a walk on Nevsky Avenue at precisely three o'clock in
the afternoon. Thousands of curious people thronged Nevsky
Avenue every day. Someone said that the nose was in Junker's
Stores, and such a crowd of people collected at the stores that
the police had to be called to restore order. One enterprising,
bewhiskered businessman of respectable appearance, who was selling all sorts of dry pasties at the entrance to the theatre, had
purposely made beautiful wooden benches on which it was perfectly safe to stand and invited people to use them for eighty
copecks each. One highly estimable colonel, who had left his

home earlier than usual so that he could see the nose, pushed his
way through the crowd with great difficulty; but, to his great indignation, he saw in the window of the stores, instead of the nose,
an ordinary woollen sweater and a lithograph of a girl pulling
up her stocking and a dandy, with a small beard and an open
waistcoat, peeping at her from behind a tree — a picture that had
hung in the same place for over ten years. On stepping back
from the window, he said with vexation: "One should not be
allowed to create a disturbance among the common people by
such stupid and improbable stories."

Then the rumour spread that Major Kovalyov's nose was not
taking a walk on Nevsky Avenue but in Tavrichesky Gardens and
that he had been there for a long time; in fact, that when the
Persian Prince Khozrev Mirza had lived there he had greatly
marvelled at that curious freak of nature. A few students of the
Surgical Academy set off there. One highly aristocratic lady wrote
a letter to the head keeper of the gardens specially to ask him
to show that rare phenomenon to her children and, if possible,
with instructive and edifying explanations for young boys.

All men about town, without whom no important social gathering is complete, who liked to amuse the ladies and whose stock
of amusing stories had been entirely used up at the time, were
extremely glad of all this affair. A small section of respectable
and well-meaning people were highly dissatisfied. One gentleman
declared indignantly that he failed to understand how in our
enlightened age such absurd stories could be spread abroad and
that he was surprised the government paid no attention to it.
This gentleman evidently was one of those gentlemen who would
like to involve the government in everything, even in his daily
tiffs with his wife. After that — but here again a thick fog descends on the whole incident, and what happened afterwards is
completely unknown.

III

The world is full of all sorts of absurdities. Sometimes there
is not even a semblance of truth: suddenly the very same nose,
which had been driving about disguised as a State Councillor
and had created such an uproar in town, found itself, as if nothing had happened, on its accustomed place again, namely, between the two cheeks of Major Kovalyov. This happened on the
seventh of April. Waking up and looking quite accidentally into

the mirror, he saw — his nose! He grabbed it with his hand — it was his nose all right! . . . "Aha!" said Kovalyov, and nearly went leaping barefoot all over the room in a roisterous dance in his joy. But Ivan, who entered just then, prevented him. He told Ivan to bring in some water for washing at once and, while washing, glanced once again into the mirror: he had a nose! While wiping himself with a towel, he again glanced into the mirror: he had a nose!

"Have a look, Ivan, there seems to be a pimple on my nose," he said, thinking to himself: "Won't it be awful if Ivan were to say, No, sir, there's no pimple and no nose, either!"

But Ivan said: "There's nothing, sir. I can't see no pimple. Nothing at all on your nose, sir."

"That's good, damn it!" said the major to himself, snapping his fingers.

At that moment the barber Ivan Yakovlevich poked his head through the door, but as timidly as a cat which had just been thrashed for the theft of suet.

"Tell me first of all — are your hands clean?" Kovalyov shouted to him from the other end of the room.

"They are clean, sir."

"You're lying!"

"I swear they are clean, sir!"

"Very well, they'd better be!"

Kovalyov sat down. Ivan Yakovlevich put a napkin round him and in a twinkling, with the aid of his brush alone, transformed his whole beard and part of his cheek into the sort of cream that is served in a merchant's home at a name-day party.

"Well, I never!" said Ivan Yakovlevich to himself as he glanced at the nose. Then he bent his head to the other side and looked at the nose sideways. "Well, I'm damned," he went on, looking at the nose for some considerable time. "Dear, oh dear, just think of it!" At last, gently and as cautiously as can only be imagined, he raised two fingers to grasp it by its end. Such was Ivan Yakovlevich's system.

"Mind, mind what you're doing!" cried Kovalyov.

Ivan Yakovlevich was utterly discouraged, perplexed, and confused as he had never been confused before. At last he began carefully titillating him with the razor under the beard, and though he found it difficult and not at all convenient to shave without holding on to the olfactory organ, he did at last overcome all the obstacles by pressing his rough thumb against the cheek and the lower jaw and finished shaving him.

When everything was ready, Kovalyov hastened to dress at once, took a cab, and drove straight to the nearest pastry cook's. On entering, he at once shouted to the boy at the other end of the shop: "Boy, a cup of chocolate!" and immediately went up to the looking glass: he had a nose all right! He turned round gaily and glanced ironically, screwing up one eye a little, at two military gentlemen, one of whom had a nose no bigger than a waistcoat button. After that he set off for the office of the department where he was trying to obtain the post of vice-governor or, if unsuccessful, of an administrative clerk. On passing through the reception room, he glanced into the looking glass: he had a nose all right! Then he went to see another Collegiate Assessor, a man who was very fond of sneering at people, to whom he often used to say in reply to his biting remarks: "Oh, away with you! I know you, Mr. Pinprick!" On the way he thought: "If the major does not split his sides with laughter when he sees me, it's a sure sign that everything is in its proper place." But the Collegiate Assessor showed no signs of merriment. "It's perfect, perfect, damn it!" thought Kovalyov to himself. On the way back he met Mrs. Podtochin and her daughter, greeted them and was met with joyful exclamations, which again proved to him that there was nothing wrong with him. He talked a long time with them and, taking out his snuffbox deliberately, kept stuffing his nose with snuff at both entrances for a great while, saying to himself: "There, I'm putting on this show specially for you, stupid females! And I won't marry your daughter all the same. Flirt with her — by all means, but nothing more!" And Major Kovalyov took his walks after that as if nothing had happened. He was to be seen on Nevsky Avenue, in the theatres — everywhere. And his nose, too, just as if nothing had happened, remained on his face, without as much as a hint that he had been playing truant. And after that Major Kovalyov was always seen in the best of humour, smiling, running after all the pretty ladies, and once even stopping before a little shop in the Arcade and buying himself a ribbon of some order for some mysterious reason, for he had never been a member of any order.

So that is the sort of thing that happened in the northern

capital of our far-flung Empire. Only now, on thinking it all over, we can see that there is a great deal that is improbable in it. Quite apart from the really strange fact of the supernatural displacement of the nose and its appearance in various parts of the town in the guise of a State Councillor, how did Kovalyov fail to realise that he could not advertise about his nose in a newspaper? I am not saying that because I think that advertisement rates are too high — that's nonsense, and I am not at all a mercenary person. But it's improper, awkward, not nice! And again — how did the nose come to be in a loaf of bread and what about Ivan Yakovlevich? No, that I cannot understand, I simply cannot understand it! But what is even stranger and more incomprehensible than anything is that authors should choose such subjects. I confess that is entirely beyond my comprehension. It's like — no, I simply don't understand it. In the first place it's of no benefit whatever to our country, and in the second place — but even in the second place there's no benefit whatever. I simply don't know what to make of it. . . .

And yet, in spite of it all, though, of course, we may take for granted this and that and the other — may even — But then where do you not find all sorts of absurdities? All the same, on second thought, there really is something in it. Say what you like, but such things do happen — not often, but they do happen.

(Translated by David Magarshack)

HERMAN MELVILLE (1819–1891) Born in New York City, Melville entered upon his literary career during his late twenties with two novels based on his own recent adventures. After desultorily pursuing a number of vocations, he ran away to sea. On his second voyage, to the South Seas, he deserted ship and spent some weeks among the natives of the Marquesas and Tahiti. The resulting novels, *Typee* and *Omoo,* were immediately successful.

By the time he wrote his greatest novel, however, *Moby Dick* (1851), he had deliberately turned away from the formula of adventure and exoticism by which he had earlier secured his fame. His writings now were dark, frequently obscure and, like "The Lightning-Rod Man," antagonistic to the progressive rationalism of most of his American contemporaries. Like his Bartleby, Melville chose not to participate and, consequently, rapidly lost his audience. With *The Confidence-Man* (1857), he made his last attempt to support himself as a professional writer. Although he continued to publish some of his poetry, he spent most of his remaining years as a Deputy Inspector for Customs in New York City. As a writer he was all but forgotten when he died; it remained for later generations to recognize his great achievement.

THE LIGHTNING-ROD MAN

Herman Melville

What grand irregular thunder, thought I, standing on my hearth-stone among the Acroceraunian hills, as the scattered bolts boomed overhead, and crashed down among the valleys, every bolt followed by zigzag irradiations, and swift slants of sharp rain, which audibly rang, like a charge of spear-points, on my low shingled roof. I suppose, though, that the mountains here-abouts break and churn up the thunder, so that it is far more glorious here than on the plain. Hark! — some one at the door. Who is this that chooses a time of thunder for making calls? And why don't he, man-fashion, use the knocker, instead of making that doleful undertaker's clatter with his fist against the hollow panel? But let him in. Ah, here he comes. "Good day, sir": an entire stranger. "Pray be seated." What is that strange-looking walking-stick he carries: "A fine thunder-storm, sir."

"Fine? — Awful!"

"You are wet. Stand here on the hearth before the fire."

"Not for worlds!"

The stranger still stood in the exact middle of the cottage, where he had first planted himself. His singularity impelled a closer scrutiny. A lean, gloomy figure. Hair dark and lank, mat-tedly streaked over his brow. His sunken pitfalls of eyes were ringed by indigo halos, and played with an innocuous sort of lightning: the gleam without the bolt. The whole man was dripping. He stood in a puddle on the bare oak floor: his strange walking-stick vertically resting at his side.

It was a polished copper rod, four feet long, lengthwise at-tached to a neat wooden staff, by insertion into two balls of green-ish glass, ringed with copper bands. The metal rod terminated at the top tripodwise, in three keen tines, brightly gilt. He held the thing by the wooden part alone.

"Sir," said I, bowing politely, "have I the honor of a visit from that illustrious god, Jupiter Tonans? So stood he in the Greek statue of old, grasping the lightning-bolt. If you be he, or his vice-roy, I have to thank you for this noble storm you have brewed among our mountains. Listen: That was a glorious peal. Ah, to a lover of the majestic, it is a good thing to have the Thunderer himself in one's cottage. The thunder grows finer for that. But pray be seated. This old rush-bottomed arm-chair, I grant, is a poor substitute for your evergreen throne on Olympus; but, condescend to be seated."

While I thus pleasantly spoke, the stranger eyed me, half in wonder, and half in a strange sort of horror; but did not move a foot.

"Do, sir, be seated; you need to be dried ere going forth again."

I planted the chair invitingly on the broad hearth, where a little fire had been kindled that afternoon to dissipate the damp-ness, not the cold; for it was early in the month of September.

But without heeding my solicitation, and still standing in the middle of the floor, the stranger gazed at me portentously and spoke.

"Sir," said he, "excuse me; but instead of my accepting your invitation to be seated on the hearth there, I solemnly warn *you,* that you had best accept *mine,* and stand with me in the middle of the room. Good heavens!" he cried, starting — "there is an-other of those awful crashes. I warn you, sir, quit the hearth."

"Mr. Jupiter Tonans," said I, quietly rolling my body on the stone, "I stand very well here."

"Are you so horridly ignorant, then," he cried, "as not to know, that by far the most dangerous part of a house, during such a terrific tempest as this, is the fire-place?"

"Nay, I did not know that," involuntarily stepping upon the first board next to the stone.

The stranger now assumed such an unpleasant air of successful admonition, that — quite involuntarily again — I stepped back upon the hearth, and threw myself into the erectest, proudest pos-ture I could command. But I said nothing.

"For Heaven's sake," he cried, with a strange mixture of alarm and intimidation — "for Heaven's sake, get off the hearth! Know you not, that the heated air and soot are conductors; — to say nothing of those immense iron fire-dogs? Quit the spot — I con-jure — I command you."

"Mr. Jupiter Tonans, I am not accustomed to be commanded in my own house."

"Call me not by that pagan name. You are profane in this time of terror."

"Sir, will you be good as to tell me your business? If you seek shelter from the storm, you are welcome, so long as you be civil; but if you come on business, open it forthwith. Who are you?"

"I am a dealer in lightning-rods," said the stranger, softening his tone; "my special business is — Merciful heaven! what a crash! — Have you ever been struck — your premises, I mean? No? It's best to be provided"; — significantly rattling his metallic staff on the floor; — "by nature, there are no castles in thunder-storms; yet, say but the word, and of this cottage I can make a Gibraltar by a few waves of this wand. Hark, what Himalayas of concussions!"

"You interrupted yourself; your special business you were about to speak of."

"My special business is to travel the country for orders for lightning-rods. This is my specimen-rod"; tapping his staff; "I have the best of references" — fumbling in his pockets. "In Criggan last month, I put up three-and-twenty rods on only five buildings."

"Let me see. Was it not at Criggan last week, about midnight on Saturday, that the steeple, the big elm, and the assembly-room cupola were struck? Any of your rods there?"

"Not on the tree and cupola, but the steeple."

"Of what use is your rod, then?"

"Of life-and-death use. But my workman was heedless. In fitting the rod at top to the steeple, he allowed a part of the metal to graze the tin sheeting. Hence the accident. Not my fault, but his. Hark!"

"Never mind. That clap burst quite loud enough to be heard without finger-pointing. Did you hear of the event at Montreal last year? A servant girl struck at her bed-side with a rosary in her hand; the beads being metal. Does your beat extend into the Canadas?"

"No. And I hear that there, iron rods only are in use. They should have *mine*, which are copper. Iron is easily fused. Then they draw out the rod so slender, that it has not body enough to conduct the full electric current. The metal melts; the building is destroyed. My copper rods never act so. Those Canadians are fools. Some of them knob the rod at the top, which risks a deadly explosion, instead of imperceptibly carrying down the current into the earth, as this sort of rod does. *Mine* is the only true rod. Look at it. Only one dollar a foot."

"This abuse of your own calling in another might make one distrustful with respect to yourself."

"Hark! The thunder becomes less muttering. It is nearing us, and nearing the earth, too. Hark! One crammed crash! All the vibrations made one by nearness. Another flash. Hold!"

"What do you?" I said, seeing him now, instantaneously relinquishing his staff, lean intently forward towards the window, with his right fore and middle fingers on his left wrist.

But ere the words had well escaped me, another exclamation escaped him.

"Crash! only three pulses — less than a third of a mile off — yonder, somewhere in that wood. I passed three stricken oaks there, ripped out new and glittering. The oak draws lightning more than other timber, having iron in solution in its sap. Your floor here seems oak."

"Heart-of-oak. From the peculiar time of your call upon me, I suppose you purposely select stormy weather for your journeys. When the thunder is roaring, you deem it an hour peculiarly favorable for producing impressions favorable to your trade."

"Hark! — Awful!"

"For one who would arm others with fearlessness, you seem unbeseemingly timorous yourself. Common men choose fair weather for their travels: you choose thunder-storms; and yet — "

"That I travel in thunder-storms, I grant; but not without particular precautions, such as only a lightning-rod man may know. Hark! Quick — look at my specimen rod. Only one dollar a foot."

"A very fine rod, I dare say. But what are these particular precautions of yours? Yet first let me close yonder shutters; the slanting rain is beating through the sash. I will bar up."

"Are you mad? Know you not that yon iron bar is a swift conductor? Desist."

"I will simply close the shutters, then, and call my boy to bring me a wooden bar. Pray, touch the bell-pull there."

"Are you frantic? That bell-wire might blast you. Never

touch bell-wire in a thunder-storm, nor ring a bell of any sort."

"Nor those in belfries? Pray, will you tell me where and how one may be safe in a time like this? Is there any part of my house I may touch with hopes of my life?"

"There is; but not where you now stand. Come away from the wall. The current will sometimes run down a wall, and — a man being a better conductor than a wall — it would leave the wall and run into him. Swoop! *That* must have fallen very nigh. That must have been globular lightning."

"Very probably. Tell me at once, which is, in your opinion, the safest part of this house?"

"This room, and this one spot in it where I stand. Come hither."

"The reasons first."

"Hark! — after the flash the gust — the sashes shiver — the house, the house! — Come hither to me!"

"The reasons, if you please."

"Come hither to me!"

"Thank you again, I think I will try my old stand — the hearth. And now, Mr. Lightning-rod man, in the pauses of the thunder, be so good as to tell me your reasons for esteeming this one room of the house the safest, and your own one stand-point there the safest spot in it."

There was now a little cessation of the storm for a while. The Lightning-rod man seemed relieved and replied:—

"Your house is a one-storied house, with an attic and a cellar; this room is between. Hence its comparative safety. Because lightning sometimes passes from the clouds to the earth, and sometimes from the earth to the clouds. Do you comprehend? — and I choose the middle of the room, because, if the lightning should strike the house at all, it would come down the chimney or walls; so, obviously, the further you are from them, the better. Come hither to me, now."

"Presently. Something you just said, instead of alarming me, has strangely inspired confidence."

"What have I said?"

"You said that sometimes lightning flashes from the earth to the clouds."

"Aye, the returning-stroke, as it is called; when the earth, being overcharged with the fluid, flashes its surplus upward."

"The returning-stroke; that is, from earth to sky. Better and better. But come here on the hearth and dry yourself."

"I am better here, and better wet."

"How?"

"It is the safest thing you can do — Hark, again! — to get yourself thoroughly drenched in a thunder-storm. Wet clothes are better conductors than the body; and so, if the lightning strike, it might pass down the wet clothes without touching the body. The storm deepens again. Have you a rug in the house? Rugs are non-conductors. Get one, that I may stand on it here, and you, too. The skies blacken — it is dusk at noon. Hark! — the rug, the rug!"

I gave him one; while the hooded mountains seemed closing and tumbling into the cottage.

"And now, since our being dumb will not help us," said I, resuming my place, "let me hear your precautions in traveling during thunder-storms."

"Wait till this one is passed."

"Nay, proceed with the precautions. You stand in the safest possible place according to your own account. Go on."

"Briefly, then. I avoid pine-trees, high houses, lonely barns, upland pastures, running water, flocks of cattle and sheep, a crowd of men. If I travel on foot — as to-day — I do not walk fast; if in my buggy, I touch not its back or sides; if on horseback, I dismount and lead the horse. But of all things, I avoid tall men."

"Do I dream? Man avoid man? and in danger-time, too."

"Tall men in a thunder-storm I avoid. Are you so grossly ignorant as not to know, that the height of a six-footer is sufficient to discharge an electric cloud upon him? Are not lonely Kentuckians, ploughing, smit in the unfinished furrow? Nay, if the six-footer stand by running water, the cloud will sometimes *select* him as its conductor to that running water. Hark! Sure, yon black pinnacle is split. Yes, a man is a good conductor. The lightning goes through and through a man, but only peels a tree. But sir, you have kept me so long answering your questions, that I have not yet come to business. Will you order one of my rods? Look at this specimen one? See: it is of the best of copper. Copper's the best conductor. Your house is low; but being upon the mountains, that lowness does not one whit depress it. You mountaineers are most exposed. In mountainous countries the lightning-rod man should have most business. Look at the specimen, sir. One rod will answer for a house so small as this. Look over these recommendations. Only one rod, sir; cost, only twenty dollars. Hark! There go all the granite Taconics and Hoosics dashed together like pebbles. By the sound, that must have struck something. An elevation of five feet above the house, will protect twenty feet radius all about the rod. Only twenty dollars, sir — a dollar a foot. Hark! — Dreadful! — Will you order? Will you buy? Shall I put down your name? Think of being a heap of charred offal, like a haltered horse burnt in his stall; and all in one flash!"

"You pretended envoy extraordinary and minister plenipotentiary to and from Jupiter Tonans," laughed I; "you mere man who come here to put you and your pipestem between clay and sky, do you think that because you can strike a bit of green light from the Leyden jar, that you can thoroughly avert the supernal bolt? Your rod rusts, or breaks, and where are you? Who has empowered you, you Tetzel, to peddle round your indulgences from divine ordinations? The hairs of our heads are numbered, and the days of our lives. In thunder as in sunshine, I stand at ease in the hands of my God. False negotiator, away! see, the scroll of the storm is rolled back; the house is unharmed; and in the blue heavens I read in the rainbow, that the Deity will not, of purpose, make war on man's earth."

"Impious wretch!" foamed the stranger, blackening in the face as the rainbow beamed, "I will publish your infidel notions."

The scowl grew blacker on his face; the indigo-circles enlarged round his eyes as the storm-rings round the midnight moon. He sprang upon me; his tri-forked thing at my heart.

I seized it; I snapped it; I dashed it; I trod it; and dragging the dark lightning-king out of my door, flung his elbowed, copper sceptre after him.

But spite of my treatment, and spite of my dissuasive talk of him to my neighbors, the Lightning-rod man still dwells in the land; still travels in storm time, and drives a brave trade with the fears of man.

BARTLEBY THE SCRIVENER
A Story of Wall Street
Herman Melville

I am a rather elderly man. The nature of my avocations for the last thirty years has brought me into more than ordinary contact with what would seem an interesting and somewhat singular set of men, of whom as yet nothing that I know of has ever been written: — I mean the law-copyists or scriveners. I have known very many of them, professionally and privately, and if I pleased, could relate divers histories, at which good-natured gentlemen might smile, and sentimental souls might weep. But I waive the biographies of all other scriveners for a few passages in the life of Bartleby, who was a scrivener the strangest I ever saw or heard of. While of other law-copyists I might write the complete life, of Bartleby nothing of that sort can be done. I believe that no materials exist for a full and satisfactory biography of this man. It is an irreparable loss to literature. Bartleby was one of those beings of whom nothing is ascertainable, except from the original sources, and in his case those are very small. What my own astonished eyes saw of Bartleby, *that* is all I know of him, except, indeed, one vague report which will appear in the sequel.

Ere introducing the scrivener, as he first appeared to me, it is fit I make some mention of myself, my *employés,* my business, my chambers, and general surroundings; because some such description is indispensable to an adequate understanding of the chief character about to be presented.

Imprimis: I am a man who, from his youth upward, has been filled with a profound conviction that the easiest way of life is the best. Hence, though I belong to a profession proverbially energetic and nervous, even to turbulence, at times, yet nothing of that sort have I ever suffered to invade my peace. I am one of those unambitious lawyers who never addresses a jury, or in any way draws down public applause; but in the cool tranquillity of a snug retreat, do a snug business among rich men's bonds and mortgages and title-deeds. All who know me, consider me an eminently *safe* man. The late John Jacob Astor, a personage little given to poetic enthusiasm, had no hesitation in pronouncing my first grand point to be prudence; my next, method. I do not speak it in vanity, but simply record the fact, that I was not unemployed in my profession by the late John Jacob Astor; a name which, I admit, I love to repeat, for it hath a rounded and orbicular sound to it, and rings like unto bullion. I will freely add, that I was not insensible to the late John Jacob Astor's good opinion.

Some time prior to the period at which this little history begins, my avocations had been largely increased. The good old office, now extinct in the State of New York, of a Master in Chancery, had been conferred upon me. It was not a very arduous office, but very pleasantly remunerative. I seldom lose my temper; much more seldom indulge in dangerous indignation at wrongs and outrages; but I must be permitted to be rash here and declare, that I consider the sudden and violent abrogation of the office of Master in Chancery, by the new Constitution, as a ———— premature act; inasmuch as I had counted upon a life-lease of the profits, whereas I only received those of a few short years. But this is by the way.

My chambers were upstairs at No. ———— Wall Street. At one end they looked upon the white wall of the interior of a spacious sky-light shaft, penetrating the building from top to bottom. This view might have been considered rather tame than otherwise, deficient in what landscape painters call "life." But if so, the view from the other end of my chambers offered, at least, a contrast, if nothing more. In that direction my windows commanded an unobstructed view of a lofty brick wall, black by age and everlasting shade; which wall required no spy-glass to bring out its lurking beauties, but for the benefit of all near-sighted spectators, was pushed up to within ten feet of my window panes. Owing to the great height of the surrounding buildings, and my chambers being on the second floor, the interval between this wall and mine not a little resembled a huge square cistern.

At the period just preceding the advent of Bartleby, I had two persons as copyists in my employment, and a promising lad as an office-boy. First, Turkey; second, Nippers; third, Ginger Nut.

These may seem names, the like of which are not usually found in the Directory. In truth they were nicknames, mutually conferred upon each other by my three clerks, and were deemed expressive of their respective persons or characters. Turkey was a short, pursy Englishman of about my own age, that is, somewhere not far from sixty. In the morning, one might say, his face was of a fine florid hue, but after twelve o'clock, meridian — his dinner hour — it blazed like a grate full of Christmas coals; and continued blazing — but, as it were, with a gradual wane — till 6 o'clock P.M. or thereabouts, after which I saw no more of the proprietor of the face, which, gaining its meridian with the sun, seemed to set with it, to rise, culminate, and decline the following day, with the like regularity and undiminished glory. There are many singular coincidences I have known in the course of my life, not the least among which was the fact, that exactly when Turkey displayed his fullest beams from his red and radiant countenance, just then, too, at that critical moment, began the daily period when I considered his business capacities as seriously disturbed for the remainder of the twenty-four hours. Not that he was absolutely idle, or averse to business then; far from it. The difficulty was, he was apt to be altogether too energetic. There was a strange, inflamed, flurried, flighty recklessness of activity about him. He would be incautious in dipping his pen into his inkstand. All his blots upon my documents, were dropped there after twelve o'clock, meridian. Indeed, not only would he be reckless and sadly given to making blots in the afternoon, but some days he went further, and was rather noisy. At such times, too, his face flamed with augmented blazonry, as if cannel coal had been heaped on anthracite. He made an unpleasant racket with his chair; spilled his sand-box; in mending his pens, impatiently split them all to pieces, and threw them on the floor in a sudden passion; stood up and leaned over his table, boxing his papers about in a most indecorous manner, very sad to behold in an elderly man like him. Nevertheless, as he was in many ways a most valuable person to me, and all the time before twelve o'clock, meridian, was the quickest, steadiest creature, too, accomplishing a great deal of work in a style not easy to be matched — for these reasons, I was willing to overlook his eccentricities, though indeed, occasionally, I remonstrated with him. I did this very gently, however, because, though the civilest, nay, the bland-

est and most reverential of men in the morning, yet in the afternoon he was disposed, upon provocation, to be slightly rash with
his tongue, in fact, insolent. Now, valuing his morning services
as I did, and resolving not to lose them — yet, at the same time,
made uncomfortable by his inflamed ways after twelve o'clock;
and being a man of peace, unwilling by my admonitions to call
forth unseemly retorts from him — I took upon me, one Saturday
noon (he was always worse on Saturdays), to hint to him, very
kindly, that perhaps now that he was growing old, it might be
well to abridge his labours; in short, he need not come to my
chambers after twelve o'clock, but, dinner over, had best go home
to his lodgings and rest himself till tea-time. But no; he insisted
upon his afternoon devotions. His countenance became intolerably fervid, as he oratorically assured me — gesticulating, with
a long ruler, at the other side of the room — that if his services
in the morning were useful, how indispensable, then, in the
afternoon?

"With submission, sir," said Turkey on this occasion, "I consider myself your right-hand man. In the morning I but marshal
and deploy my columns; but in the afternoon I put myself at
their head, and gallantly charge the foe, thus!" — and he made a
violent thrust with the ruler.

"But the blots, Turkey," intimated I.

"True, — but, with submission, sir, behold these hairs! I am
getting old. Surely, sir, a blot or two of a warm afternoon is not
to be severely urged against grey hairs. Old age — even if it blot
the page — is honourable. With submission, sir, we *both* are getting old."

This appeal to my fellow-feeling was hardly to be resisted. At
all events, I saw that go he would not. So I made up my mind
to let him stay, resolving, nevertheless, to see to it, that during the
afternoon he had to do with my less important papers.

Nippers, the second on my list, was a whiskered, sallow, and,
upon the whole, rather piratical-looking young man of about five
and twenty. I always deemed him the victim of two evil powers —
ambition and indigestion. The ambition was evinced by a certain
impatience of the duties of a mere copyist — an unwarrantable
usurpation of strictly professional affairs, such as the original
drawing up of legal documents. The indigestion seemed be-
tokened in an occasional nervous testiness and grinning irritabil-

ity causing the teeth to audibly grind together over mistakes committed in copying; unnecessary maledictions, hissed, rather than spoken, in the heat of business; and especially by a continual discontent with the height of the table where he worked. Though of a very ingenious mechanical turn, Nippers could never get this table to suit him. He put chips under it, blocks of various sorts, bits of pasteboard, and at last went so far as to attempt an exquisite adjustment by final pieces of folded blotting-paper. But no invention would answer. If, for the sake of easing his back, he brought the table lid at a sharp angle well up toward his chin, and wrote there like a man using the steep roof of a Dutch house for his desk — then he declared that it stopped the circulation in his arms. If now he lowered the table to his waistbands, and stooped over it in writing, then there was a sore aching in his back. In short, the truth of the matter was, Nippers knew not what he wanted. Or, if he wanted anything, it was to be rid of a scrivener's table altogether. Among the manifestations of his diseased ambition was a fondness he had for receiving visits from certain ambiguous-looking fellows in seedy coats, whom he called his clients. Indeed I was aware that not only was he, at times, considerable of a ward-politician, but he occasionally did a little business at the Justices' courts, and was not unknown on the steps of the Tombs. I have good reason to believe, however, that one individual who called upon him at my chambers, and who, with a grand air, he insisted was his client, was no other than a dun, and the alleged title-deed, a bill. But with all his failings, and the annoyances he caused me, Nippers, like his compatriot Turkey, was a very useful man to me; wrote a neat, swift hand; and, when he chose, was not deficient in a gentlemanly sort of deportment. Added to this, he always dressed in a gentlemanly sort of way; and so, incidentally, reflected credit upon my chambers. Whereas with respect to Turkey, I had much ado to keep him from being a reproach to me. His clothes were apt to look oily and smell of eating-houses. He wore his pantaloons very loose and baggy in summer. His coats were execrable; his hat not to be handled. But while the hat was a thing of indifference to me, inasmuch as his natural civility and deference, as a dependent Englishman, always led him to doff it the moment he entered the room, yet his coat was another matter. Concerning his coats, I reasoned with him; but with no effect. The truth was, I suppose, that a man with so small an income, could not afford to sport such a lustrous face and a lustrous coat at one and the same time. As Nippers once observed, Turkey's money went chiefly for red ink. One winter day I presented Turkey with a highly-respectable looking coat of my own, a padded grey coat, of a most comfortable warmth, and which buttoned straight up from the knee to the neck. I thought Turkey would appreciate the favour, and abate his rashness and obstreperousness of afternoons. But no. I verily believe that buttoning himself up in so downy and blanket-like a coat had a pernicious effect upon him; upon the same principle that too much oats are bad for horses. In fact, precisely as a rash, restive horse is said to feel his oats, so Turkey felt his coat. It made him insolent. He was a man whom prosperity harmed.

Though concerning the self-indulgent habits of Turkey I had my own private surmises, yet touching Nippers I was well persuaded that whatever might be his faults in other respects, he was, at least, a temperate young man. But, indeed, nature herself seemed to have been his vintner, and at his birth charged him so thoroughly with an irritable, brandy-like disposition, that all subsequent potations were needless. When I consider how, amid the stillness of my chambers, Nippers would sometimes impatiently rise from his seat, and stooping over his table, spread his arms wide apart, seize the whole desk, and move it, and jerk it, with a grim, grinding motion on the floor, as if the table were a perverse voluntary agent, intent on thwarting and vexing him; I plainly perceive that for Nippers, brandy and water were altogether superfluous.

It was fortunate for me that, owing to its peculiar cause — indigestion — the irritability and consequent nervousness of Nippers, were mainly observable in the morning, while in the afternoon he was comparatively mild. So that Turkey's paroxysms only coming on about twelve o'clock, I never had to do with their eccentricities at one time. Their fits relieved each other like guards. When Nippers's was on, Turkey's was off; and *vice versa*. This was a good natural arrangement under the circumstances.

Ginger Nut, the third on my list, was a lad some twelve years old. His father was a carman, ambitious of seeing his son on the bench instead of a cart, before he died. So he sent him to my office as student at law, errand boy, and cleaner and sweeper, at the rate of one dollar a week. He had a little desk to himself,

but he did not use it much. Upon inspection, the drawer ex-
hibited a great array of the shells of various sorts of nuts. Indeed,
to this quick-witted youth the whole noble science of the law
was contained in a nut-shell. Not the least among the employ-
ments of Ginger Nut, as well as one which he discharged with
the most alacrity, was his duty as cake and apple purveyor for
Turkey and Nippers. Copying law papers being proverbially a
dry, husky sort of business, my two scriveners were fain to moisten
their mouths very often with Spitzenbergs to be had at the numerous stalls nigh the Custom House and Post Office. Also, they
sent Ginger Nut very frequently for that peculiar cake — small,
flat, round, and very spicy — after which he had been named by
them. Of a cold morning, when business was but dull, Turkey
would gobble up scores of these cakes, as if they were mere wafers
— indeed they sell them at the rate of six or eight for a penny —
the scrape of his pen blending with the crunching of the crisp
particles in his mouth. Of all the fiery afternoon blunders and
flurried rashness of Turkey, was his once moistening a ginger-
cake between his lips, and clapping it on to a mortgage for a seal.
I came within an ace of dismissing him then. But he molli-
fied me by making an oriental bow and saying — "With submission, sir, it was generous of me to find you in stationery on my
own account."

Now my original business — that of a conveyancer and title
hunter, and drawer-up of recondite documents of all sorts — was
considerably increased by receiving the master's office. There was
now great work for scriveners. Not only must I push the clerks
already with me, but I must have additional help. In answer to
my advertisement, a motionless young man one morning stood
upon my office threshold, the door being open, for it was summer.
I can see that figure now — pallidly neat, pitiably respectable, incurably forlorn! It was Bartleby.

After a few words touching his qualifications, I engaged him,
glad to have among my corps of copyists a man of so singularly
sedate an aspect, which I thought might operate beneficially upon
the flighty temper of Turkey, and the fiery one of Nippers.

I should have stated before that ground glass folding-doors
divided my premises into two parts, one of which was occupied by
my scriveners, the other by myself. According to my humour I
threw open these doors, or closed them. I resolved to assign

Bartleby a corner by the folding-doors, but on my side of them, so as to have this quiet man within easy call, in case any trifling thing was to be done. I placed his desk close up to a small side-window in that part of the room, a window which originally had afforded a lateral view of certain grimy back-yards and bricks, but which, owing to subsequent erections, commanded at present no view at all, though it gave some light. Within three feet of the panes was a wall, and the light came down from far above, between two lofty buildings, as from a very small opening in a dome. Still further to a satisfactory arrangement, I procured a high green folding screen, which might entirely isolate Bartleby from my sight, though not remove him from my voice. And thus, in a manner, privacy and society were conjoined.

At first Bartleby did an extraordinary quantity of writing. As if long famishing for something to copy, he seemed to gorge himself on my documents. There was no pause for digestion. He ran a day and night line, copying by sun-light and by candle-light. I should have been quite delighted with his application, had he been cheerfully industrious. But he wrote on silently, palely, mechanically.

It is, of course, an indispensable part of a scrivener's business to verify the accuracy of his copy, word by word. Where there are two or more scriveners in an office, they assist each other in this examination, one reading from the copy, the other holding the original. It is a very dull, wearisome, and lethargic affair. I can readily imagine that to some sanguine temperaments it would be altogether intolerable. For example, I cannot credit that the mettlesome poet Byron would have contentedly sat down with Bartleby to examine a law document of, say five hundred pages, closely written in a crimpy hand.

Now and then, in the haste of business, it had been my habit to assist in comparing some brief document myself, calling Turkey or Nippers for this purpose. One object I had in placing Bartleby so handy to me behind the screen, was to avail myself of his services on such trivial occasions. It was on the third day, I think, of his being with me, and before any necessity had arisen for having his own writing examined, that, being much hurried to complete a small affair I had in hand, I abruptly called to Bartleby. In my haste and natural expectancy of instant compliance, I sat with my head bent over the original on my desk, and my right hand sideways, and somewhat nervously extended with the copy, so that immediately upon emerging from his retreat, Bartleby might snatch it and proceed to business without the least delay.

In this very attitude did I sit when I called to him, rapidly stating what it was I wanted him to do — namely, to examine a small paper with me. Imagine my surprise, nay, my consternation, when without moving from his privacy, Bartleby in a singularly mild, firm voice, replied, "I would prefer not to."

I sat awhile in perfect silence, rallying my stunned faculties. Immediately it occurred to me that my ears had deceived me, or Bartleby had entirely misunderstood my meaning. I repeated my request in the clearest tone I could assume. But in quite as clear a one came the previous reply, "I would prefer not to."

"Prefer not to," echoed I, rising in high excitement, and crossing the room with a stride. "What do you mean? Are you moonstruck? I want you to help me compare this sheet here — take it," and I thrust it toward him.

"I would prefer not to," said he.

I looked at him steadfastly. His face was leanly composed; his grey eye dimly calm. Not a wrinkle of agitation rippled him. Had there been the least uneasiness, anger, impatience or impertinence in his manner; in other words, had there been anything ordinarily human about him; doubtless I should have violently dismissed him from the premises. But as it was, I should have as soon thought of turning my pale plaster-of-paris bust of Cicero out of doors. I stood gazing at him awhile, as he went on with his own writing, and then reseated myself at my desk. This is very strange, thought I. What had one best do? But my business hurried me. I concluded to forget the matter for the present, reserving it for my future leisure. So calling Nippers from the other room, the paper was speedily examined.

A few days after this, Bartleby concluded four lengthy documents, being quadruplicates of a week's testimony taken before me in my High Court of Chancery. It became necessary to examine them. It was an important suit, and great accuracy was imperative. Having all things arranged, I called Turkey, Nippers and Ginger Nut from the next room, meaning to place the four copies in the hands of my four clerks, while I should read from the original. Accordingly Turkey, Nippers and Ginger Nut had

82   Herman Melville

taken their seats in a row, each with his document in hand, when
I called to Bartleby to join this interesting group.

"Bartleby! quick, I am waiting."

I heard a slow scrape of his chair legs on the uncarpeted floor,
and soon he appeared standing at the entrance of his hermitage.

"What is wanted?" said he mildly.

"The copies, the copies," said I hurriedly. "We are going to
examine them. There" — and I held toward him the fourth
quadruplicate.

"I would prefer not to," he said, and gently disappeared behind
the screen.

For a few moments I was turned into a pillar of salt, standing
at the head of my seated column of clerks. Recovering myself, I
advanced toward the screen, and demanded the reason for such
extraordinary conduct.

"*Why* do you refuse?"

"I would prefer not to."

With any other man I should have flown outright into a dreadful passion, scorned all further words, and thrust him ignominiously from my presence. But there was something about Bartleby
that not only strangely disarmed me, but in a wonderful manner
touched and disconcerted me. I began to reason with him.

"These are your copies we are about to examine. It is labour
saving to you, because one examination will answer for your four
papers. It is common usage. Every copyist is bound to help examine his copy. Is it not so? Will you not speak? Answer!"

"I prefer not to," he replied in a flute-like tone. It seemed to
me that while I had been addressing him, he carefully revolved
every statement that I made; fully comprehended the meaning;
could not gainsay the irresistible conclusion; but, at the same
time, some paramount consideration prevailed with him to reply
as he did.

"You are decided, then, not to comply with my request — a
request made according to common usage and common sense?"

He briefly gave me to understand that on that point my judgment was sound. Yes: his decision was irreversible.

It is not seldom the case that when a man is browbeaten in
some unprecedented and violently unreasonable way, he begins
to stagger in his own plainest faith. He begins, as it were, vaguely
to surmise that, wonderful as it may be, all the justice and all the

reason are on the other side. Accordingly, if any disinterested persons are present, he turns to them for some reinforcement for his own faltering mind.

"Turkey," said I, "what do you think of this? Am I not right?"

"With submission, sir," said Turkey, with his blandest tone, "I think that you are."

"Nippers," said I, "what do *you* think of it?"

"I think I should kick him out of the office."

(The reader of nice perceptions will here perceive that, it being morning, Turkey's answer is couched in polite and tranquil terms but Nippers's reply in ill-tempered ones. Or, to repeat a previous sentence, Nippers's ugly mood was on duty, and Turkey's off.)

"Ginger Nut," said I, willing to enlist the smallest suffrage in my behalf, "what do *you* think of it?"

"I think, sir, he's a little *luny*," replied Ginger Nut, with a grin.

"You hear what they say," said I, turning towards the screen, "come forth and do your duty."

But he vouchsafed no reply. I pondered a moment in sore perplexity. But once more business hurried me. I determined again to postpone the consideration of this dilemma to my future leisure. With a little trouble we made out to examine the papers without Bartleby, though at every page or two, Turkey deferentially dropped his opinion that this proceeding was quite out of the common; while Nippers, twitching in his chair with a dyspeptic nervousness, ground out between his set teeth occasional hissing maledictions against the stubborn oaf behind the screen. And for his (Nippers's) part, this was the first and the last time he would do another man's business without pay.

Meanwhile Bartleby sat in his hermitage, oblivous to everything but his own peculiar business there.

Some days passed, the scrivener being employed upon another lengthy work. His late remarkable conduct led me to regard his ways narrowly. I observed that he never went to dinner; indeed that he never went any where. As yet I had never of my personal knowledge known him to be outside of my office. He was a perpetual sentry in the corner. At about eleven o'clock though, in the morning, I noticed that Ginger Nut would advance towards the opening in Bartleby's screen, as if silently beckoned

thither by a gesture invisible to me where I sat. The boy would
then leave the office jingling a few pence, and reappear with a
handful of ginger-nuts which he delivered in the hermitage,
receiving two of the cakes for his trouble.

He lives, then, on ginger-nuts, thought I; never eats a dinner,
properly speaking; he must be a vegetarian then; but no; he
never eats even vegetables, he eats nothing but ginger-nuts. My
mind then ran on in reveries concerning the probable effects
upon the human constitution of living entirely on ginger-nuts.
Ginger-nuts are so called because they contain ginger as one of
their peculiar constituents, and the final flavouring one. Now
what was ginger? A hot, spicy thing. Was Bartleby hot and spicy?
Not at all. Ginger, then, had no effect upon Bartleby. Probably
he preferred it should have none.

Nothing so aggravates an earnest person as a passive resistance.
If the individual so resisted be of a not inhumane temper, and
the resisting one perfectly harmless in his passivity; then, in the
better moods of the former, he will endeavour charitably to con-
strue to his imagination what proves impossible to be solved by
his judgment. Even so, for the most part, I regarded Bartleby and
his ways. Poor fellow! thought I, he means no mischief; it is plain
he intends no insolence; his aspects sufficiently evinces that his
eccentricities are involuntary. He is useful to me. I can get along
with him. If I turn him away, the chances are he will fall in with
some less indulgent employer, and then he will be rudely treated,
and perhaps driven forth miserably to starve. Yes. Here I can
cheaply purchase a delicious self-approval. To befriend Bartleby;
to humour him in his strange wilfulness, will cost me little or
nothing, while I lay up in my soul what will eventually prove a
sweet morsel for my conscience. But this mood was not invariable
with me. The passiveness of Bartleby sometimes irritated me. I
felt strangely goaded on to encounter him in new opposition, to
elicit some angry spark from him answerable to my own. But
indeed I might as well have essayed to strike fire with my knuckles
against a bit of Windsor soap. But one afternoon the evil impulse
in me mastered me, and the following little scene ensued:

"Bartleby," said I, "when those papers are all copied, I will
compare them with you."

"I would prefer not to."

"How? Surely you do not mean to persist in that mulish vagary?"

No answer.

I threw open the folding-doors near by, and turning upon Turkey and Nippers, exclaimed in an excited manner:

"He says, a second time, he won't examine his papers. What do you think of it, Turkey?"

It was afternoon, be it remembered. Turkey sat glowing like a brass boiler, his bald head steaming, his hands reeling among his blotted papers.

"Think of it?" roared Turkey; "I think I'll just step behind his screen, and black his eyes for him!"

So saying, Turkey rose to his feet and threw his arms into a pugilistic position. He was hurrying away to make good his promise, when I detained him, alarmed at the effect of incautiously rousing Turkey's combativeness after dinner.

"Sit down, Turkey," said I, "and hear what Nippers has to say. What do you think of it, Nippers? Would I not be justified in immediately dismissing Bartleby?"

"Excuse me, that is for you to decide, sir. I think his conduct quite unusual, and indeed unjust, as regards Turkey and myself. But it may only be a passing whim."

"Ah," exclaimed I, "you have strangely changed your mind then — you speak very gently of him now."

"All beer," cried Turkey; "gentleness is effects of beer — Nippers and I dined together to-day. You see how gentle *I* am, sir. Shall I go and black his eyes?"

"You refer to Bartleby, I suppose. No, not to-day, Turkey," I replied; "pray, put up your fists."

I closed the doors, and again advanced towards Bartleby. I felt additional incentives tempting me to my fate. I burned to be rebelled against again. I remembered that Bartleby never left the office.

"Bartleby," said I, "Ginger Nut is away; just step round to the Post Office, won't you? (it was but a three minutes' walk), and see if there is anything for me."

"I would prefer not to."

"You *will* not?"

"I *prefer* not."

I staggered to my desk, and sat there in a deep study. My blind
inveteracy returned. Was there any other thing in which I could
procure myself to be ignominiously repulsed by this lean, penniless wight? — my hired clerk? What added thing is there, perfectly
reasonable, that he will be sure to refuse to do?

"Bartleby!"

No answer.

"Bartleby," in a louder tone.

No answer.

"Bartleby," I roared.

Like a very ghost, agreeably to the laws of magical invocation,
at the third summons, he appeared at the entrance of his hermitage.

"Go to the next room, and tell Nippers to come to me."

"I prefer not to," he respectfully and slowly said, and mildly
disappeared.

"Very good, Bartleby," said I, in a quiet sort of serenely severe
self-possessed tone, intimating the unalterable purpose of some
terrible retribution very close at hand. At the moment I half
intended something of the kind. But upon the whole, as it was
drawing towards my dinner-hour, I thought it best to put on my
hat and walk home for the day, suffering much from perplexity
and distress of mind.

Shall I acknowledge it? The conclusion of this whole business
was, that it soon became a fixed fact of my chambers, that a pale
young scrivener, by the name of Bartleby, had a desk there; that
he copied for me at the usual rate of four cents a folio (one
hundred words); but he was permanently exempt from examining
the work done by him, that duty being transferred to Turkey
and Nippers, out of compliment doubtless to their superior acuteness; moreover, said Bartleby was never on any account to be
despatched on the most trivial errand of any sort; and that even
if entreated to take upon him such a matter, it was generally
understood that he would prefer not to — in other words, that
he would refuse point-blank.

As days passed on, I became considerably reconciled to Bartleby. His steadiness, his freedom from all dissipation, his incessant
industry (except when he chose to throw himself into a standing
revery behind his screen), his great stillness, his unalterableness
of demeanour under all circumstances, made him a valuable

acquisition. One prime thing was this, — *he was always there;* — first in the morning, continually through the day, and the last at night. I had a singular confidence in his honesty. I felt my most precious papers perfectly safe in his hands. Sometimes to be sure I could not, for the very soul of me, avoid falling into sudden spasmodic passions with him. For it was exceeding difficult to bear in mind all the time those strange peculiarities, privileges, and unheard of exemptions, forming the tacit stipulations on Bartleby's part under which he remained in my office. Now and then, in the eagerness of despatching pressing business, I would inadvertently summon Bartleby, in a short, rapid tone, to put his finger, say, on the incipient tie of a bit of red tape with which I was about compressing some papers. Of course, from behind the screen the usual answer, "I prefer not to," was sure to come; and then, how could a human creature with the common infirmities of our nature, refrain from bitterly exclaiming upon such per-verseness — such unreasonableness. However, every added repulse of this sort which I received only tended to lessen the probability of my repeating the inadvertence.

Here it must be said, that according to the custom of most legal gentlemen occupying chambers in densely-populated law buildings, there were several keys to my door. One was kept by a woman residing in the attic, which person weekly scrubbed and daily swept and dusted my apartments. Another was kept by Turkey for convenience sake. The third I sometimes carried in my own pocket. The fourth I knew not who had.

Now, one Sunday morning I happened to go to Trinity Church, to hear a celebrated preacher, and finding myself rather early on the ground, I thought I would walk round to my cham-bers for awhile. Luckily I had my key with me; but upon apply-ing it to the lock, I found it resisted by something inserted from the inside. Quite surprised, I called out; when to my conster-nation a key was turned from within; and thrusting his lean visage at me, and holding the door ajar, the apparition of Bar-tleby appeared, in his shirt sleeves, and otherwise in a strangely tattered dishabille, saying quietly that he was sorry, but he was deeply engaged just then, and — preferred not admitting me at present. In a brief word or two, he moreover added, that perhaps I had better walk round the block two or three times, and by that time he would probably have concluded his affairs.

Now, the utterly unsurmised appearance of Bartleby, tenanting my law-chambers of a Sunday morning, with his cadaverously gentlemanly *nonchalance,* yet withal firm and self-possessed, had such a strange effect upon me, that incontinently I slunk away from my own door, and did as desired. But not without sundry twinges of impotent rebellion against the mild effrontery of this unaccountable scrivener. Indeed, it was his wonderful mildness chiefly, which not only disarmed me, but unmanned me, as it were. For I consider that one, for the time, is in a way unmanned when he tranquilly permits his hired clerk to dictate to him, and order him away from his own premises. Furthermore, I was full of uneasiness as to what Bartleby could possibly be doing in my office in his shirt sleeves, and in an otherwise dismantled condition of a Sunday morning. Was anything amiss going on? Nay, that was out of the question. It was not to be thought of for a moment that Bartleby was an immoral person. But what could he be doing there — copying? Nay again, whatever might be his eccentricities, Bartleby was an eminently decorous person. He would be the last man to sit down to his desk in any state approaching to nudity. Besides, it was Sunday; and there was something about Bartleby that forbade the supposition that he would by any secular occupation violate the proprieties of the day.

Nevertheless, my mind was not pacified; and full of a restless curiosity, at last I returned to the door. Without hindrance I inserted my key, opened it, and entered. Bartleby was not to be seen. I looked round anxiously, peeped behind his screen; but it was very plain that he was gone. Upon more closely examining the place, I surmised that for an indefinite period Bartleby must have ate, dressed, and slept in my office, and that too without plate, mirror, or bed. The cushioned seat of a ricketty old sofa in one corner bore the faint impress of a lean, reclining form. Rolled away under his desk, I found a blanket; under the empty grate, a blacking box and brush; on a chair, a tin basin, with soap and a ragged towel; in a newspaper a few crumbs of ginger-nuts and a morsel of cheese. Yes, thought I, it is evident enough that Bartleby has been making his home here, keeping bachelor's hall all by himself. Immediately then the thought came sweeping across me, What miserable friendlessness and loneliness are here revealed! His poverty is great; but his solitude, how horrible! Think of it. Of a Sunday, Wall street is deserted as Petra; and every night of every day it is an emptiness. This building too, which of week-days hums with industry and life, at nightfall echoes with sheer vacancy, and all through Sunday is forlorn. And here Bartleby makes his home; sole spectator of a solitude which he has seen all populous — a sort of innocent and transformed Marius brooding among the ruins of Carthage!

For the first time in my life a feeling of overpowering stinging melancholy seized me. Before, I had never experienced aught but a not-unpleasing sadness. The bond of a common humanity now drew me irresistibly to gloom. A fraternal melancholy! For both I and Bartleby were sons of Adam. I remembered the bright silks and sparkling faces I had seen that day, in gala trim, swan-like sailing down the Mississippi of Broadway; and I contrasted them with the pallid copyist, and thought to myself, Ah, happiness courts the light, so we deem the world is gay; but misery hides aloof, so we deem that misery there is none. These sad fancyings — chimeras, doubtless, of a sick and silly brain — led on to other and more special thoughts, concerning the eccentricities of Bartleby. Presentiments of strange discoveries hovered round me. The scrivener's pale form appeared to me laid out, among uncaring strangers, in its shivering winding sheet.

Suddenly I was attracted by Bartleby's closed desk, the key in open sight left in the lock.

I mean no mischief, seek the gratification of no heartless curiosity, thought I; besides, the desk is mine, and its contents, too, so I will make bold to look within. Everything was methodically arranged, the papers smoothly placed. The pigeon holes were deep, and, removing the files of documents, I groped into their recesses. Presently I felt something there, and dragged it out. It was an old bandana handkerchief, heavy and knotted. I opened it, and saw it was a savings' bank.

I now recalled all the quiet mysteries which I had noted in the man. I remembered that he never spoke but to answer; that though at intervals he had considerable time to himself, yet I had never seen him reading — no, not even a newspaper; that for long periods he would stand looking out, at his pale window behind the screen, upon the dead brick wall; I was quite sure he never visited any refectory or eating-house; while his pale face clearly indicated that he never drank beer like Turkey, or tea and coffee even, like other men; that he never went anywhere in particular that I could learn; never went out for a walk, unless indeed that was the case at present; that he had declined telling who he was, or whence he came, or whether he had any relatives in the world; that though so thin and pale, he never complained of ill health. And more than all, I remembered a certain unconscious air of pallid — how shall I call it? — of pallid haughtiness, say, or rather an austere reserve about him, which had positively awed me into my tame compliance with his eccentricities, when I had feared to ask him to do the slightest incidental thing for me, even though I might know, from his long-continued motionlessness, that behind his screen he must be standing in one of those dead-wall reveries of his.

Revolving all these things, and coupling them with the recently discovered fact that he made my office his constant abiding place and home, and not forgetful of his morbid moodiness; revolving all these things, a prudential feeling began to steal over me. My first emotions had been those of pure melancholy and sincerest pity; but just in proportion as the forlornness of Bartleby grew and grew to my imagination, did that same melancholy merge into fear, that pity into repulsion. So true it is, and so terrible, too, that up to a certain point the thought or sight of misery enlists our best affections; but, in certain special cases, beyond that point it does not. They err who would assert that invariably this is owing to the inherent selfishness of the human heart. It rather proceeds from a certain hopelessness of remedying excessive and organic ill. To a sensitive being, pity is not seldom pain. And when at last it is perceived that such pity cannot lead to effectual succour, common sense bids the soul be rid of it. What I saw that morning persuaded me that the scrivener was the victim of innate and incurable disorder. I might give alms to his body; but his body did not pain him; it was his soul that suffered, and his soul I could not reach.

I did not accomplish the purpose of going to Trinity Church that morning. Somehow, the things I had seen disqualified me for the time from church-going. I walked homeward, thinking what I would do with Bartleby. Finally, I resolved upon this: — I would put certain calm questions to him the next morning, touching his history, &c., and if he declined to answer them openly and unreservedly (and I supposed he would prefer not), then to give him a twenty dollar bill over and above whatever I might owe him, and tell him his services were no longer required; but that if in any other way I could assist him, I would be happy to do so, especially if he desired to return to his native place, wherever that might be, I would willingly help to defray the expenses. Moreover, if, after reaching home, he found himself at any time in want of aid, a letter from him would be sure of a reply.

The next morning came.

"Bartleby," said I, gently calling to him behind his screen.

No reply.

"Bartleby," said I, in a still gentler tone, "come here; I am not going to ask you to do anything you would prefer not to do — I simply wish to speak to you."

Upon this he noiselessly slid into view.

"Will you tell me, Bartleby, where you were born?"

"I would prefer not to."

"Will you tell me *anything* about yourself?"

"I would prefer not to."

"But what reasonable objection can you have to speak to me? I feel friendly towards you."

He did not look at me while I spoke, but kept his glance fixed upon my bust of Cicero, which, as I then sat, was directly behind me, some six inches above my head.

"What is your answer, Bartleby?" said I, after waiting a considerable time for a reply, during which his countenance remained immovable, only there was the faintest conceivable tremor of the white attenuated mouth.

"At present I prefer to give no answer," he said, and retired into his hermitage.

It was rather weak in me I confess, but his manner on this occasion nettled me. Not only did there seem to lurk in it a certain calm disdain, but his perverseness seemed ungrateful, considering the undeniable good usage and indulgence he had received from me.

Again I sat ruminating what I should do. Mortified as I was at his behaviour, and resolved as I had been to dismiss him when I entered my office, nevertheless I strangely felt something superstitious knocking at my heart, and forbidding me to carry out my purpose, and denouncing me for a villain if I dared to breathe one bitter word against this forlornest of mankind. At last, familiarly drawing my chair behind his screen, I sat down and said: "Bartleby, never mind then about revealing your history; but let me entreat you, as a friend, to comply as far as may be with the usages of this office. Say now you will help to examine papers to-morrow or next day: in short, say now that in a day or two you will begin to be a little reasonable: — say so, Bartleby."

"At present I would prefer not to be a little reasonable," was his mildly cadaverous reply.

Just then the folding-doors opened, and Nippers approached. He seemed suffering from an unusually bad night's rest, induced by severer indigestion than common. He overheard those final words of Bartleby.

"*Prefer not,* eh?" gritted Nippers — "I'd *prefer* him, if I were you, sir," addressing me — "I'd *prefer* him; I'd give him preferences, the stubborn mule! What is it, sir, pray, that he *prefers* not to do now?"

Bartleby moved not a limb.

"Mr. Nippers," said I, "I'd prefer that you would withdraw for the present."

Somehow, of late I had got into the way of involuntarily using this word "prefer" upon all sorts of not exactly suitable occasions. And I trembled to think that my contact with the scrivener had already and seriously affected me in a mental way. And what further and deeper aberration might it not yet produce? This apprehension had not been without efficacy in determining me to summary means.

As Nippers, looking very sour and sulky, was departing, Turkey blandly and deferentially approached.

"With submission, sir," said he, "yesterday I was thinking about Bartleby here, and I think that if he would but prefer to take a quart of good ale every day, it would do much towards mending him, and enabling him to assist in examining his papers."

"So you have got the word, too," said I, slightly excited.

"With submission, what word, sir," asked Turkey, respectfully crowding himself into the contracted space behind the screen, and by so doing, making me jostle the scrivener. "What word, sir?"

"I would prefer to be left alone here," said Bartleby, as if offended at being mobbed in his privacy.

"*That's* the word, Turkey," said I — "*that's* it."

"Oh, *prefer?* oh, yes — queer word. I never use it myself. But, sir, as I was saying, if he would but prefer — "

"Turkey," interrupted I, "you will please withdraw."

"Oh certainly, sir, if you prefer that I should."

As he opened the folding-door to retire, Nippers at his desk caught a glimpse of me, and asked whether I would prefer to have a certain paper copied on blue paper or white. He did not in the least roguishly accent the word prefer. It was plain that it involuntarily rolled from his tongue. I thought to myself, surely I must get rid of a demented man, who already has in some degree turned the tongues, if not the heads, of myself and clerks. But I thought it prudent not to break the dismission at once.

The next day I noticed that Bartleby did nothing but stand at his window in his dead-wall revery. Upon asking him why he did not write, he said that he had decided upon doing no more writing.

"Why, how now? what next?" exclaimed I, "do no more writing?"

"No more."

"And what is the reason?"

"Do you not see the reason for yourself?" he indifferently replied.

I looked steadfastly at him, and perceived that his eyes looked dull and glazed. Instantly it occurred to me, that his unexampled diligence in copying by his dim window for the first few weeks of his stay with me might have temporarily impaired his vision.

I was touched. I said something in condolence with him. I hinted that, of course, he did wisely in abstaining from writing for a while, and urged him to embrace that opportunity of taking wholesome exercise in the open air. This, however, he did not do. A few days after this, my other clerks being absent, and being in a great hurry to despatch certain letters by the mail, I thought that, having nothing else earthly to do, Bartleby would surely be less inflexible than usual, and carry these letters to the Post Office. But he blankly declined. So, much to my inconvenience, I went myself.

Still added days went by. Whether Bartleby's eyes improved or not, I could not say. To all appearance, I thought they did. But when I asked him if they did, he vouchsafed no answer. At all events, he would do no copying. At last, in reply to my urgings, he informed me that he had permanently given up copying.

"What!" exclaimed I; "suppose your eyes should get entirely well — better than ever before — would you not copy then?"

"I have given up copying," he answered and slid aside.

He remained, as ever, a fixture in my chamber. Nay — if that were possible — he became still more of a fixture than before. What was to be done? He would do nothing in the office: why should he stay there? In plain fact, he had now become a millstone to me, not only useless as a necklace, but afflictive to bear. Yet I was sorry for him. I speak less than truth when I say that, on his own account, he occasioned me uneasiness. If he would but have named a single relative or friend, I would instantly have written, and urged their taking the poor fellow away to some convenient retreat. But he seemed alone, absolutely alone in the universe. A bit of wreckage in the mid-Atlantic. At length, necessities connected with my business tyrannized over all other considerations. Decently as I could, I told Bartleby that in six days' time he must unconditionally leave the office. I warned him to take measures, in the interval, for procuring some other abode. I offered to assist him in this endeavour, if he himself would but take the first step towards a removal. "And when you finally quit me, Bartleby," added I, "I shall see that you go away not entirely unprovided. Six days from this hour, remember."

At the expiration of that period, I peeped behind the screen, and lo! Bartleby was there.

I buttoned up my coat, balanced myself; advanced slowly towards him, touched his shoulder, and said, "The time has come; you must quit this place; I am sorry for you; here is money; but you must go."

"I would prefer not," he replied, with his back still towards me.

"You *must*."

He remained silent.

Now I had an unbounded confidence in this man's common honesty. He had frequently restored to me sixpences and shillings carelessly dropped upon the floor, for I am apt to be very reckless in such shirt-button affairs. The proceeding then which followed will not be deemed extraordinary.

"Bartleby," said I, "I owe you twelve dollars on account; here are thirty-two; the odd twenty are yours. — Will you take it?" and I handed the bills towards him.

But he made no motion.

"I will leave them here then," putting them under a weight on the table. Then taking my hat and cane and going to the door, I tranquilly turned and added — "After you have removed your things from these offices, Bartleby, you will of course lock the door — since every one is now gone for the day but you — and if you please, slip your key underneath the mat, so that I may have it in the morning. I shall not see you again; so good-bye to you. If hereafter in your new place of abode I can be of any service to you, do not fail to advise me by letter. Good-bye, Bartleby, and fare you well."

But he answered not a word; like the last column of some ruined temple, he remained standing mute and solitary in the middle of the otherwise deserted room.

As I walked home in a pensive mood, my vanity got the better of my pity. I could not but highly plume myself on my masterly management in getting rid of Bartleby. Masterly I call it, and such it must appear to any dispassionate thinker. The beauty of my procedure seemed to consist in its perfect quietness. There was no vulgar bullying, no bravado of any sort, no choleric hectoring, no striding to and fro across the apartment, jerking out vehement commands for Bartleby to bundle himself off with his beggarly traps. Nothing of the kind. Without loudly bidding Bartleby depart — as an inferior genius might have done — I *assumed* the ground that depart he must; and upon that assumption built all I had to say. The more I thought over my procedure, the more I was charmed with it. Nevertheless, next morning, upon awakening, I had my doubts, — I had somehow slept off the fumes of vanity. One of the coolest and wisest hours a man has, is just after he awakes in the morning. My procedure seemed as sagacious as ever, — but only in theory. How it would prove in practice — there was the rub. It was truly a beautiful thought to have assumed Bartleby's departure; but, after all, that assumption was simply my own, and none of Bartleby's. The great point was, not whether I had assumed that he would quit me, but whether he would prefer so to do. He was more a man of preferences than assumptions.

After breakfast, I walked down town, arguing the probabilities *pro* and *con*. One moment I thought it would prove a miserable failure, and Bartleby would be found all alive at my office as usual; the next moment it seemed certain that I should see his chair empty. And so I kept veering about. At the corner of Broadway and Canal Street, I saw quite an excited group of people standing in earnest conversation.

"I'll take odds he doesn't," said a voice as I passed.

"Doesn't go? — done!" said I, "put up your money."

I was instinctively putting my hand in my pocket to produce my own, when I remembered that this was an election day. The words I had overheard bore no reference to Bartleby, but to the success or non-success of some candidate for the mayoralty. In my intent frame of mind, I had, as it were, imagined that all Broadway shared in my excitement, and were debating the same question with me. I passed on, very thankful that the uproar of the street screened my momentary absent-mindedness.

As I had intended, I was earlier than usual at my office door. I stood listening for a moment. All was still. He must be gone. I tried the knob. The door was locked. Yes, my procedure had worked to a charm; he indeed must be vanished. Yet a certain melancholy mixed with this: I was almost sorry for my brilliant success. I was fumbling under the door mat for the key, which Bartleby was to have left there for me, when accidentally my knee knocked against a panel, producing a summoning sound, and in response a voice came to me from within — "Not yet; I am occupied."

It was Bartleby.

I was thunderstruck. For an instant I stood like the man who, pipe in mouth, was killed one cloudless afternoon long ago in Virginia, by summer lightning; at his own warm open window he was killed, and remained leaning out there upon the dreamy afternoon, till some one touched him, and he fell.

"Not gone!" I murmured at last. But again obeying that wondrous ascendency which the inscrutable scrivener had over me — and from which ascendency, for all my chafing, I could not completely escape — I slowly went down stairs and out into the street, and while walking round the block, considered what I should next do in this unheard-of perplexity. Turn the man out by an actual thrusting I could not; to drive him away by calling him hard names would not do; calling in the police was an unpleasant idea; and yet, permit him to enjoy his cadaverous triumph over me, — this too I could not think of. What was to be done? or, if nothing could be done, was there anything further that I could *assume* in the matter? Yes, as before I had prospectively assumed that Bartleby would depart, so now I might retrospectively assume that departed he was. In the legitimate carrying out of this assumption, I might enter my office in a great hurry, and pretending not to see Bartleby at all, walk straight against him as if he were air. Such a proceeding would in a singular degree have the appearance of a home-thrust. It was hardly possible that Bartleby could withstand such an application of the doctrine of assumptions. But, upon second thought, the success of the plan seemed rather dubious. I resolved to argue the matter over with him again.

"Bartleby," said I, entering the office, with a quietly severe expression, "I am seriously displeased. I am pained, Bartleby. I had thought better of you. I had imagined you of such a gentlemanly organization, that in any delicate dilemma a slight hint would suffice — in short, an assumption; but it appears I am deceived. Why," I added, unaffectedly starting, "you have not even touched that money yet," pointing to it, just where I had left it the evening previous.

He answered nothing.

"Will you, or will you not, quit me?" I now demanded in a sudden passion, advancing close to him.

"I would prefer *not* to quit you," he replied, gently emphasizing the *not*.

"What earthly right have you to stay here? Do you pay any rent? Do you pay my taxes? Or is this property yours?"

He answered nothing.

"Are you ready to go on and write now? Are your eyes recovered? Could you copy a small paper for me this morning? or help examine a few lines? or step round to the Post Office? In a word, will you do any thing at all, to give a colouring to your refusal to depart the premises?"

He silently retired into his hermitage.

I was now in such a state of nervous resentment that I thought it but prudent to check myself, at present, from further demonstrations. Bartleby and I were alone. I remembered the tragedy of the unfortunate Adams and the still more unfortunate Colt in the solitary office of the latter; and how poor Colt, being dreadfully incensed by Adams, and imprudently permitting himself to get wildly excited, was at unawares hurried into his fatal act — an act which certainly no man could possibly deplore more than the actor himself. Often it had occurred to me in my ponderings upon the subject, that had that altercation taken place in the public street, or at a private residence, it would not have terminated as it did. It was the circumstance of being alone in a solitary office, upstairs, of a building entirely unhallowed by humanizing domestic associations — an uncarpeted office, doubtless, of a dusty, haggard sort of appearance; — this it must have been, which greatly helped to enhance the irritable desperation of the hapless Colt.

But when this old Adam of resentment rose in me and tempted me concerning Bartleby, I grappled him and threw him. How? Why, simply by recalling the divine injunction: "A new commandment give I unto you, that ye love one another." Yes, this it was that saved me. Aside from higher considerations, charity often operates as a vastly wise and prudent principle — a great safeguard to its possessor. Men have committed murder for jealousy's sake, and anger's sake, and hatred's sake, and selfishness' sake, and spiritual pride's sake; but no man that ever I heard of, ever committed a diabolical murder for sweet charity's sake. Mere self-interest, then, if no better motive can be enlisted, should, especially with high-tempered men, prompt all beings to charity and philanthropy. At any rate, upon the occasion in question, I strove to drown my exasperated feelings toward the scrivener by benevolently construing his conduct. Poor fellow, poor fellow! thought I, he doesn't mean any thing; and besides, he has seen hard times, and ought to be indulged.

I endeavoured also immediately to occupy myself, and at the same time to comfort my despondency. I tried to fancy that in the course of the morning, at such time as might prove agreeable to him, Bartleby, of his own free accord, would emerge from his hermitage, and take up some decided line of march in the direction of the door. But no. Half-past twelve o'clock came; Turkey began to glow in the face, overturn his inkstand, and become generally obstreperous; Nippers abated down into quietude and courtesy; Ginger Nut munched his noon apple; and Bartleby remained standing at his window in one of his profoundest dead-wall reveries. Will it be credited? Ought I to acknowledge it? That afternoon I left the office without saying one further word to him.

Some days now passed, during which at leisure intervals I looked a little into "Edwards on the Will," and "Priestley on Necessity." Under the circumstances, those books induced a salutary feeling. Gradually I slid into the persuasion that these troubles of mine, touching the scrivener, had been all predestinated from eternity, and Bartleby was billeted upon me for some mysterious purpose of an all-wise Providence, which it was not for a mere mortal like me to fathom. Yes, Bartleby, stay there behind your screen, thought I; I shall persecute you no more; you are harmless and noiseless as any of these old chairs; in short, I never feel so private as when I know you are here. At least I see it, I feel it; I penetrate to the predestinated purpose of my life. I am content. Others may have loftier parts to enact; but my mission in this world, Bartleby, is to furnish you with office room for such period as you may see fit to remain.

I believe that this wise and blessed frame of mind would have continued with me had it not been for the unsolicited and uncharitable remarks obtruded upon me by my professional friends who visited the rooms. But thus it often is, that the constant friction of illiberal minds wears out at last the best resolves of the more generous. Though to be sure, when I reflected upon it, it was not strange that people entering my office should be struck by the peculiar aspect of the unaccountable Bartleby, and so be tempted to throw out some sinister observations concerning him. Sometimes an attorney having business with me, and calling at my office, and finding no one but the scrivener there, would undertake to obtain some sort of precise information from him touching my whereabouts; but without heeding his idle talk, Bartleby would remain standing immovable in the middle of the room. So, after contemplating him in that position for a time, the attorney would depart, no wiser than he came.

Also, when a Reference was going on, and the room full of lawyers and witnesses and business was driving fast, some deeply occupied legal gentleman present, seeing Bartleby wholly unemployed, would request him to run round to his (the legal gentleman's) office and fetch some papers for him. Thereupon,

Bartleby would tranquilly decline, and yet remain idle as before. Then the lawyer would give a great stare, and turn to me. And what could I say? At last I was made aware that all through the circle of my professional acquaintance, a whisper of wonder was running round, having reference to the strange creature I kept at my office. This worried me very much. And as the idea came upon me of his possibly turning out a long-lived man, and keep occupying my chambers, and denying my authority; and perplexing my visitors; and scandalizing my professional reputation; and casting a general gloom over the premises; keeping soul and body together to the last upon his savings (for doubtless he spent but half a dime a day), and in the end perhaps outlive me, and claim possession of my office by right of his perpetual occupancy: as all these dark anticipations crowded upon me more and more, and my friends continually intruded their relentless remarks upon the apparition in my room, a great change was wrought in me. I resolved to gather all my faculties together, and for ever rid me of this intolerable incubus.

Ere revolving any complicated project, however, adapted to this end, I first simply suggested to Bartleby the propriety of his permanent departure. In a calm and serious tone, I commended the idea to his careful and mature consideration. But having taken three days to meditate upon it, he apprised me that his original determination remained the same; in short, that he still preferred to abide with me.

What shall I do? I now said to myself, buttoning up my coat to the last button. What shall I do? what ought I to do? what does conscience say I *should* do with this man, or rather ghost? Rid myself of him, I must; go, he shall. But how? You will not thrust him, the poor, pale, passive mortal, — you will not thrust such a helpless creature out of your door? you will not dishonour yourself by such cruelty? No, I will not, I cannot do that. Rather would I let him live and die here, and then mason up his remains in the wall. What then will you do? For all your coaxing, he will not budge. Bribes he leaves under your own paper-weight on your table; in short, it is quite plain that he prefers to cling to you.

Then something severe, something unusual must be done. What! surely you will not have him collared by a constable, and commit his innocent pallor to the common jail? And upon what ground could you procure such a thing to be done? — a vagrant, is he? What! he a vagrant, a wanderer, who refuses to budge? It is because he will *not* be a vagrant, then, that you seek to count him *as* a vagrant. That is too absurd. No visible means of support: there I have him. Wrong again: for indubitably he *does* support himself, and that is the only unanswerable proof that any man can show of his possessing the means so to do. No more then. Since he will not quit me, I must quit him. I will change my offices; I will move elsewhere; and give him fair notice, that if I find him on my new premises I will then proceed against him as a common trespasser.

Acting accordingly, next day I thus addressed him: "I find these chambers too far from the City Hall; the air is unwholesome. In a word, I propose to remove my offices next week, and shall no longer require your services. I tell you this now, in order that you may seek another place."

He made no reply, and nothing more was said.

On the appointed day I engaged carts and men, proceeded to my chambers, and having but little furniture, everything was removed in a few hours. Throughout all, the scrivener remained standing behind the screen, which I directed to be removed the last thing. It was withdrawn; and being folded up like a huge folio, left him the motionless occupant of a naked room. I stood in the entry watching him a moment, while something from within me upbraided me.

I re-entered, with my hand in my pocket — and — and my heart in my mouth.

"Good-bye, Bartleby; I am going — good-bye, and God some way bless you; and take that," slipping something in his hand. But it dropped upon the floor and then — strange to say — I tore myself from him whom I had so longed to be rid of.

Established in my new quarters, for a day or two I kept the door locked, and started at every footfall in the passages. When I returned to my rooms after any little absence, I would pause at the threshold for an instant, and attentively listen, ere applying my key. But these fears were needless. Bartleby never came nigh me.

I thought all was going well, when a perturbed looking stranger visited me, inquiring whether I was the person who had recently occupied rooms at No. ——— Wall street.

Full of forebodings, I replied that I was.

"Then sir," said the stranger, who proved a lawyer, "you are responsible for the man you left there. He refuses to do any copying, he refuses to do anything; and he says he prefers not to; and he refuses to quit the premises."

"I am very sorry, sir," said I, with assumed tranquillity, but an inward tremor, "but, really, the man you allude to is nothing to me — he is no relation or apprentice of mine, that you should hold me responsible for him."

"In mercy's name, who is he?"

"I certainly cannot inform you. I know nothing about him. Formerly I employed him as a copyist; but he has done nothing for me now for some time past."

"I shall settle him then, — good morning, sir."

Several days passed, and I heard nothing more; and though I often felt a charitable prompting to call at the place and see poor Bartleby, yet a certain squeamishness of I know not what withheld me.

All is over with him, by this time, thought I at last, when through another week no further intelligence reached me. But coming to my room the day after, I found several persons waiting at my door in a high state of nervous excitement.

"That's the man — here he comes," cried the foremost one, whom I recognized as the lawyer who had previously called upon me alone.

"You must take him away, sir, at once," cried a portly person among them, advancing upon me, and whom I knew to be the landlord of No. ——— Wall street. "These gentlemen, my tenants, cannot stand it any longer; Mr. B ———," pointing to the lawyer, "has turned him out of his room, and he now persists in haunting the building generally, sitting upon the banisters of the stairs by day, and sleeping in the entry by night. Everybody here is concerned; clients are leaving the offices; some fears are entertained of a mob; something you must do, and that without delay."

Aghast at this torrent, I fell back before it, and would fain have locked myself in my new quarters. In vain I persisted that Bartleby was nothing to me — no more than to any one else there. In vain: — I was the last person known to have anything

to do with him, and they held me to the terrible account. Fearful
then of being exposed in the papers (as one person present obscurely threatened) I considered the matter, and at length said,
that if the lawyer would give me a confidential interview with
the scrivener, in his (the lawyer's) own room, I would that afternoon strive my best to rid them of the nuisance they complained
of.

Going up stairs to my old haunt, there was Bartleby silently
sitting upon the banister at the landing.

"What are you doing here, Bartleby?" said I.

"Sitting upon the banister," he mildly replied.

I motioned him into the lawyer's room, who then left us.

"Bartleby," said I, "are you aware that you are the cause of
great tribulation to me, by persisting in occupying the entry after
being dismissed from the office?"

No answer.

"Now one of two things must take place. Either you must do
something, or something must be done to you. Now what sort of
business would you like to engage in? Would you like to re-en-
gage in copying for some one?"

"No; I would prefer not to make any change."

"Would you like a clerkship in a dry-goods store?"

"There is too much confinement about that. No, I would not
like a clerkship; but I am not particular."

"Too much confinement," I cried, "why you keep yourself
confined all the time!"

"I would prefer not to take a clerkship," he rejoined, as if to
settle that little item at once.

"How would a bartender's business suit you? There is no trying
of the eyesight in that."

"I would not like it at all; though, as I said before, I am not
particular."

His unwonted wordiness inspirited me. I returned to the
charge.

"Well then, would you like to travel through the country col-
lecting bills for the merchants? That would improve your
health."

"No, I would prefer to be doing something else."

"How then would going as a companion to Europe to entertain

some young gentleman with your conversation, — how would that suit you?"

"Not at all. It does not strike me that there is anything definite about that. I like to be stationary. But I am not particular."

"Stationary you shall be then," I cried, now losing all patience, and for the first time in all my exasperating connection with him fairly flying into a passion. "If you do not go away from these premises before night, I shall feel bound — indeed I *am* bound — to — to — to quit the premises myself!" I rather absurdly concluded, knowing not with what possible threat to try to frighten his immobility into compliance. Despairing of all further efforts, I was precipitately leaving him, when a final thought occurred to me — one which had not been wholly unindulged before.

"Bartleby," said I, in the kindest tone I could assume under such exciting circumstances, "will you go home with me now — not to my office, but my dwelling — and remain there till we can conclude upon some convenient arrangement for you at our leisure? Come, let us start now, right away."

"No: at present I would prefer not to make any change at all."

I answered nothing; but effectually dodging every one by the suddenness and rapidity of my flight, rushed from the building, ran up Wall street toward Broadway, and then jumping into the first omnibus was soon removed from pursuit. As soon as tranquillity returned I distinctly perceived that I had now done all that I possibly could, both in respect to the demands of the landlord and his tenants, and with regard to my own desire and sense of duty, to benefit Bartleby, and shield him from rude persecution. I now strove to be entirely care-free and quiescent; and my conscience justified me in the attempt; though indeed it was not so successful as I could have wished. So fearful was I of being again hunted out by the incensed landlord and his exasperated tenants, that, surrendering my business to Nippers, for a few days I drove about the upper part of the town and through the suburbs, in my rockaway; crossed over to Jersey City and Hoboken, and paid fugitive visits to Manhattanville and Astoria. In fact I almost lived in my rockaway for the time.

When again I entered my office, lo, a note from the landlord lay upon the desk. I opened it with trembling hands. It informed me that the writer had sent to the police, and had Bartleby re-moved to the Tombs as a vagrant. Moreover, since I knew more about him than any one else, he wished me to appear at that place, and make a suitable statement of the facts. These tidings had a conflicting effect upon me. At first I was indignant; but at last almost approved. The landlord's energetic, summary disposi-tion had led him to adopt a procedure which I do not think I would have decided upon myself; and yet as a last resort, under such peculiar circumstances, it seemed the only plan.

As I afterwards learned, the poor scrivener, when told that he must be conducted to the Tombs, offered not the slightest ob-stacle, but in his own pale, unmoving way silently acquiesced.

Some of the compassionate and curious bystanders joined the party; and headed by one of the constables, arm-in-arm with Bartleby the silent procession filed its way through all the noise, and heat, and joy of the roaring thoroughfares at noon.

The same day I received the note I went to the Tombs, or, to speak more properly, the Halls of Justice. Seeking the right officer, I stated the purpose of my call, and was informed that the individual I described was indeed within. I then assured the functionary that Bartleby was a perfectly honest man, and greatly to be a compassionated (however unaccountable) eccentric. I nar-rated all I knew, and closed by suggesting the idea of letting him remain in as indulgent confinement as possible till something less harsh might be done — though indeed I hardly knew what. At all events, if nothing else could be decided upon, the alms-house must receive him. I then begged to have an interview.

Being under no disgraceful charge, and quite serene and harm-less in all his ways, they had permitted him freely to wander about the prison, and especially in the inclosed grass-platted yards thereof. And so I found him there, standing all alone in the quietest of the yards, his face toward a high wall — while all around, from the narrow slits of the jail windows, I thought I saw peering out upon him the eyes of murderers and thieves.

"Bartleby!"

"I know you," he said, without looking round, — "and I want nothing to say to you."

"It was not I that brought you here, Bartleby," said I, keenly pained at his implied suspicion. "And to you, this should not be so vile a place. Nothing reproachful attaches to you by being here. And see, it is not so sad a place as one might think. Look, there is the sky and here is the grass."

"I know where I am," he replied, but would say nothing more, and so I left him.

As I entered the corridor again a broad, meat-like man in an apron accosted me, and jerking his thumb over his shoulder said— "Is that your friend?"

"Yes."

"Does he want to starve? If he does, let him live on the prison fare, that's all."

"Who are you?" asked I, not knowing what to make of such an unofficially speaking person in such a place.

"I am the grub-man. Such gentlemen as have friends here, hire me to provide them with something good to eat."

"Is this so?" said I, turning to the turnkey.

He said it was.

"Well then," said I, slipping some silver into the grub-man's hands (for so they called him), "I want you to give particular attention to my friend there; let him have the best dinner you can get. And you must be as polite to him as possible."

"Introduce me, will you?" said the grub-man, looking at me with an expression which seemed to say he was all impatience for an opportunity to give a specimen of his breeding.

Thinking it would prove of benefit to the scrivener, I acquiesced; and asking the grub-man his name, went up with him to Bartleby.

"Bartleby, this is Mr. Cutlets; you will find him very useful to you."

"Your sarvant, sir, your sarvant," said the grub-man, making a low salutation behind his apron. "Hope you find it pleasant here, sir; — spacious grounds — cool apartments, sir — hope you'll stay with us some time — try to make it agreeable. May Mrs. Cutlets and I have the pleasure of your company to dinner, sir, in Mrs. Cutlets' private room?"

"I prefer not to dine to-day," said Bartley, turning away. "It would disagree with me; I am unused to dinners." So saying, he slowly moved to the other side of the inclosure and took up a position fronting the dead-wall.

"How's this?" said the grub-man, addressing me with a stare of astonishment. "He's odd, ain't he?"

"I think he is a little deranged," said I, sadly.

"Deranged? deranged is it? Well now, upon my word, I thought that friend of yourn was a gentleman forger; they are always pale and genteel-like, them forgers. I can't help pity 'em — can't help it, sir. Did you know Monroe Edwards?" he added touchingly, and paused. Then, laying his hand pityingly on my shoulder, sighed, "he died of the consumption at Sing-Sing. So you weren't acquainted with Monroe?"

"No, I was never socially acquainted with any forgers. But I cannot stop longer. Look to my friend yonder. You will not lose by it. I will see you again."

Some few days after this, I again obtained admission to the Tombs, and went through the corridors in quest of Bartleby; but without finding him.

"I saw him coming from his cell not long ago," said a turnkey, "maybe he's gone to loiter in the yards."

So I went in that direction.

"Are you looking for the silent man?" said another turnkey passing me. "Yonder he lies — sleeping in the yard there. 'Tis not twenty minutes since I saw him lie down."

The yard was entirely quiet. It was not accessible to the common prisoners. The surrounding walls, of amazing thickness, kept off all sounds behind them. The Egyptian character of the masonry weighed upon me with its gloom. But a soft imprisoned turf grew under foot. The heart of the eternal pyramids, it seemed, wherein by some strange magic, through the clefts grass-seed, dropped by birds, had sprung.

Strangely huddled at the base of the wall — his knees drawn up, and lying on his side, his head touching the cold stones — I saw the wasted Bartleby. But nothing stirred. I paused; then went close up to him; stooped over, and saw that his dim eyes were open; otherwise he seemed profoundly sleeping. Something prompted me to touch him. I felt his hand, when a tingling shiver ran up my arm and down my spine to my feet.

The round face of the grub-man peered upon me now. "His dinner is ready. Won't he dine to-day, either? Or does he live without dining?"

"Lives without dining," said I, and closed the eyes.

"Eh! — He's asleep, ain't he?"

"With kings and counsellors," murmured I.

.   .   .   .   .   .

There would seem little need for proceeding further in this history. Imagination will readily supply the meagre recital of poor Bartleby's interment. But ere parting with the reader, let me say, that if this little narrative has sufficiently interested him, to awaken curiosity as to who Bartleby was, and what manner of life he led prior to the present narrator's making his acquaintance, I can only reply, that in such curiosity I fully share — but am wholly unable to gratify it. Yet here I hardly know whether I should divulge one little item of rumour, which came to my ear a few months after the scrivener's decease. Upon what basis it rested, I could never ascertain; and hence, how true it is I cannot now tell. But inasmuch as this vague report has not been without a certain strange suggestive interest to me, however sad, it may prove the same with others; and so I will briefly mention it. The report was this: that Bartleby had been a subordinate clerk in the Dead Letter Office at Washington, from which he had been suddenly removed by a change in the administration. When I think over this rumour I cannot adequately express the emotions which seize me. Dead letters! does it not sound like dead men? Conceive a man by nature and misfortune prone to a pallid hopelessness: can any business seem more fitted to heighten it than that of continually handling these dead letters, and assorting them for the flames? For by the cartload they are annually burned. Sometimes from out the folded paper the pale clerk takes a ring: — the finger it was meant for, perhaps, moulders in the grave; a bank-note sent in swiftest charity: — he whom it would relieve, nor eats nor hungers any more; pardon for those who died despairing; hope for those who died unhoping; good tidings for those who died stifled by unrelieved calamities. On errands of life, these letters speed to death.

Ah Bartleby! Ah humanity!

GUSTAVE FLAUBERT (1821–1880) Flaubert was born in Rouen, France. His father was a surgeon who directed the public hospital Hôtel-Dieu. Flaubert's family lived in the hospital, and he remembered playing in the dissection room as a child. Growing up in a hospital had a profound effect on Flaubert: "I have never seen a child without thinking that he would become an old man, nor a cradle without thinking of a grave. The contemplation of a woman makes me wonder about her skeleton."

Flaubert studied at the *Collège de Rouen* at the time when romanticism first reached the French provinces. He greatly admired Victor Hugo, and his first attempts at writing were romantic. For a while he was an intern for his father; later he studied law in Paris. During his twenties he had severe nervous seizures forcing him to retreat to Croisset, a family property on the Seine where he spent most of his life.

From 1849–1851 he traveled in the East and filled his memory "with a belly-full of colors." After his return he began *Madame Bovary,* a novel of provincial bourgeois life, which marked him as a leading exponent of the naturalistic school of writing. Its publication in 1857 created a scandal, and Flaubert was prosecuted for committing an "outrage to public morals and religion." He regarded the nineteenth century world with disgust, believing that the bourgeois and its products were antipathetic to the real needs of the human mind. *Bouvard and Pécuchet,* an encyclopedic satire of the intellectual life of France (for which Flaubert claimed to have read more than fifteen hundred books) is the culmination of his analysis of bourgeois culture.

In 1877 Flaubert completed work on "The Legend of St Julian Hospitator," an allegorical tale inspired by a stained glass window on Rouen Cathedral. Here he explores the extremity of human violence and repentance in prose as exquisite and serene as a tapestry.

THE LEGEND OF
ST JULIAN HOSPITATOR

Gustave Flaubert

I

Julian's father and mother lived in a castle in the middle of a forest, on the slope of a hill.

The four towers at its corners had pointed roofs covered with lead scales, and the base of the walls rested on blocks of solid rock which fell steeply to the bottom of the moat.

The pavement of the courtyard was as clean as the flagstones of a church. Long gutter-spouts, shaped like dragons hanging head-down, spat all the rain-water into a cistern; and on every window-sill of every storey a basil or a heliotrope flowered in a painted earthenware pot.

Inside a second enclosure, made with stakes, there was first an orchard, then a garden plot in which flowers had been arranged to form figures, after that a pergola for taking the air, and finally an alley where the pages could play mall. On the other side were the kennels, the stables, the bake-house, the press-house, and the barns. All round this there wound a strip of green grazing-ground, itself enclosed by a stout thorn-hedge.

Peace had prevailed for so long that the portcullis was not lowered any more, the moat was full of grass, swallows nested in the look-out slits, and the archer who patrolled the battlements all day retired to his watch-tower when the sun grew too hot and dozed off like a monk.

Inside the castle the ironwork shone brightly everywhere; tapestries lined the walls to keep out the cold; and the cupboards were crammed with linen, the cellars piled high with tuns of wine, and the oak coffers creaking under the weight of money-bags.

In the armoury, between military standards and wild beasts' heads, were to be seen weapons of every age and every nation, from Amalekite slings and Garamantian javelins to Saracen brackmards and Norman coats of mail.

The master-spit in the kitchen could roast an ox. The chapel was as magnificent as a king's oratory. There was even a bath-house of the Roman type tucked away somewhere, but the noble lord made no use of it as he held it to be a heathen institution.

Always wrapped in a mantle of fox pelts, he would stride about his castle, dispensing justice to his vassals and settling his neighbours' quarrels. In winter he watched the snowflakes falling or had stories read to him. When the first fine days came, he rode out on his mule along the by-paths, beside the green corn-fields, talking with the peasants and giving them advice.

After many adventures, he had taken a maiden of noble birth as his wife. She was very fair of skin, and somewhat proud and solemn. The horns of her coif brushed against the lintels of the doors; the train of her cloth dress trailed three paces behind her. Her household was as well-regulated as a monastery. Every morning she gave her serving-women their instructions, inspected the preserves and ointments, span on her distaff, or embroidered an altar-cloth. In answer to her prayers a son was born to her.

Then there was great merry-making, with a torchlight banquet which lasted three days and four nights, to the sound of harps, with green branches strewn on the flagstones. The rarest spices were eaten at this meal, and fowls as fat as sheep. To amuse the guests, a dwarf appeared out of a pie; and as more people kept arriving and there were not enough bowls to go round, they were obliged to drink out of horns and helmets.

The young mother took no part in these festivities, but remained quietly in bed. One night she awoke and, in the moonlight which shone through her window, she saw what appeared to be a shadow moving. It was an old man in a homespun robe, with a rosary at his side and a wallet across his shoulder, looking just like a hermit. He came up to her bed and without opening his lips said:

"Rejoice, mother, for your son shall be a saint!"

She was about to cry out but, gliding along the moonbeam, he rose gently into the air and disappeared. The songs of the guests burst forth louder than ever. She heard the voices of angels, and her head fell back upon the pillow, over which there hung a martyr's bone set in a frame of garnets.

The next day all the servants were questioned, and all denied having seen the hermit. Dream or reality, this was obviously a message from heaven, but she was careful to say nothing about it, for fear that she should be accused of pride.

At dawn the guests departed. Julian's father was standing outside the postern-gate, where he had just taken leave of the last of them, when suddenly a beggar rose up before him out of the mist. The man was a gipsy with a plaited beard, silver bracelets on his arms, and blazing eyes. As though inspired, he stammered out these disconnected words:

"Ah! Ah! Your son! Much bloodshed! Much glory! Always fortunate! An emperor's family!"

And, bending down to pick up his alms, he disappeared in the grass and vanished from sight.

The noble lord looked around and called out with all his might. There was no one there; only the whistling wind, and the morning mists drifting away.

He attributed this vision to weariness from having too little sleep. "If I mention it, they will only laugh at me," he thought. But the glorious destiny promised to his son dazzled him, although the promise was not clear and he was not even certain that he had heard it.

He and his wife kept their secrets from each other. But they both cherished their child equally and, respecting him as one marked out by God, lavished infinite care upon him. His cradle was padded with the finest down; a lamp in the shape of a dove burned continually above it; three nurses rocked him to sleep. Wrapped in his swaddling clothes, with his pink face and blue eyes, his mantle of brocade and his bonnet loaded with pearls, he looked like an Infant Jesus. He cut all his teeth without crying once.

When he was seven his mother taught him to sing, and his father, to give him courage, hoisted him on to a big horse. The boy smiled with pleasure and soon knew all about chargers.

A very learned old monk taught him Holy Scripture, the Arabic numerals, the Latin letters, and the art of painting miniatures on vellum. They used to work together high up in a turret where there was no noise to disturb them. When a lesson was over they would go down into the garden, where they studied the flowers as they walked slowly up and down.

Sometimes a string of pack-animals was seen making its way along the valley below, led by a man on foot in Eastern garb. The lord of the castle, recognizing the man for a merchant, would send a servant out to him, and the stranger would trustfully turn aside from his path. Ushered into the parlour, he would bring out of his chests pieces of velvet and silk, jewels and spices, and curious things of unknown use; and eventually he would take his leave, having made a handsome profit and suffered no violence.

At other times a band of pilgrims would come knocking at the gate. Their wet clothes would steam in front of the fire, and when they had eaten their fill they would tell stories of their travels — of voyages across foaming seas, marshes across burning sands, the cruelty of the heathen, the Syrian caves, the Manger and the Sepulchre. And then they would give the young lord scallop-shells from their cloaks.

Often the lord of the castle gave a feast to his old comrades in arms. As they drank together they talked about the battles they had fought and the fortresses they had stormed, recalling fabulous wounds and the thunderous din of the engines of war. Julian gave cries of delight as he listened to them, and then his father felt sure that one day he would be a conqueror. But every evening, as he came out from the Angelus and passed between rows of poor people bowing before him, he would dip into his purse with such modesty and nobility that his mother was certain that she would live to see him an archbishop.

His place in the chapel was beside his parents, and however long the office might be, he remained kneeling at his stool, his hat on the floor and his hands clasped in prayer.

One day, during Mass, he looked up and noticed a little white mouse coming out of a hole in the wall. It trotted along the first of the altar steps, and after turning right and left two or three times, ran back the way it had come. The following Sunday he was disturbed by the thought that he might see it again. It did come back, and every Sunday he watched for it with growing irritation, until at last he was seized with hatred for the creature and decided to get rid of it.

So, after closing the door and sprinkling some cake crumbs on the altar steps, he stationed himself in front of the hole with a stick in his hand.

After a long time a pink nose appeared, followed by the rest of the mouse. He gave it a light tap, and was astonished to see the little body lie there without moving. A drop of blood showed on the flagstone. He quickly wiped it off with his sleeve, threw the mouse away outside, and said nothing about it to anyone.

All sorts of birds used to peck at the seeds in the garden. He hit upon the idea of shooting peas at them through a hollow reed, and whenever he heard a twittering in the trees, he crept up quietly, raised his pipe, and puffed out his cheeks. The little creatures rained down on his shoulders in such abundance that he could not help laughing, he was so pleased at his cleverness.

One morning, as he was coming back along the battlements, he saw a fat pigeon preening itself in the sunshine on the crest of the wall. He stopped to look at it, and since there was a breach in this part of the wall his fingers happened on a lump of stone. He swung his arm, the stone hit the bird, and it dropped like a plummet into the moat.

He dashed down after it, tearing his skin in the undergrowth and ferreting around everywhere, as nimble as a puppy.

The pigeon, its wings broken and its body quivering, was caught in the branches of a privet.

Its stubborn refusal to die infuriated the child. He set about wringing its neck, and its convulsions made his heart beat wildly, filling him with a savage, passionate delight. When it finally went stiff in his hands he felt he was going to faint.

That evening, during supper, his father declared that he was old enough to begin learning the art of venery, and he went to look for an old copy-book of his which contained, in the form of questions and answers, all there was to be known about the chase. In this book a master explained to his pupil the art of training hounds, taming falcons, and setting snares; how to recognize a stag by its droppings, a fox by its tracks, a wolf by the scratches it left on the ground; the best way of distinguishing their spoor, how to start them, where their lairs were likely to be found, which were the most favourable winds, and what were the calls and rules of the kill.

As soon as Julian could recite all these things by heart, his father got together a pack of hounds for him. It included twenty-four Barbary greyhounds, swifter than gazelles but liable to bolt, and seventeen pairs of Breton dogs, with russet coats and white markings, sure in their judgement, strong in the chest, and mighty bayers. For the attack on the boar and other dangerous situations, there were forty griffon terriers, as shaggy as bears. Then there were some flame-coloured Tartary mastiffs, almost as big as donkeys, with broad backs and long legs, which were intended for hunting the wild ox. The black coats of the spaniels shone like satin; the yelping of the talbots rivalled the chanting of the beagles. In a yard by themselves, growling, shaking their chains, and rolling their eyes, were eight alans, formidable brutes which would fly at a horseman's belly and were not afraid of lions.

All these hounds were fed on wheaten bread, drank out of stone troughs, and bore high-sounding names.

The falcons were perhaps even more remarkable than the hounds, for the noble lord had obtained, at great expense, tercelets from the Caucasus, sakers from Babylon, gerfalcons from Germany, and peregrine falcons captured on cliffs beside icy seas in far-off lands. They were housed in a thatched shed, chained to their perch according to size, with a strip of turf in front of them on which they were placed from time to time to loosen their limbs.

Bag-nets, hooks, wolf-traps, and all kinds of other devices were put together.

Often they took setters out into the country, and it was never long before they came to a point. Then the prickers, creeping slowly forward, carefully spread a huge net over their motionless bodies. At a word of command they started barking, and quail flew up into the net. The ladies of the neighbourhood, invited to the hunt with their husbands, their children, and their hand-maids, all threw themselves upon the birds and caught them easily.

At other times drums were beaten to start hares, foxes fell into pits, or the spring of a trap uncoiled and caught a wolf by its paw.

But Julian despised these facile contrivances and preferred to go hunting on his own, with his horse and his falcon. This was nearly always a great Scythian tartar as white as snow. Its leather hood was topped with a plume, golden bells jingled on its blue feet and it stood fast on its master's arm while the horse galloped along and the plains unfolded before them. Slipping its jesses, Julian would suddenly let it go; the fearless bird would soar into the air as straight as an arrow; and soon two specks of unequal size would be seen circling, meeting, and disappearing in the blue skies above. Then the falcon would come down, tearing some bird to pieces, and return to settle on the gauntlet with its wings quivering.

In this way Julian flew herons, kites, crows, and vultures.

He loved to sound his horn and follow his hounds as they coursed along the hill slopes, jumped the streams, and climbed up to the woods again; and when the stag began to groan under their bites, he would kill it quickly and then watch with delight as the mastiffs frantically devoured the carcass, chopped in pieces on its reeking hide.

On misty days he plunged deep into a marsh to lie in wait for geese, otters, and young wild-duck.

At dawn every day three squires used to wait for him at the foot of the steps; and although the old monk, leaning out of his window, might beckon him back, he never turned round. He went off in the heat of the sun, in pouring rain, or at the height of a storm, drinking spring-water from the hollow of his hand, eating wild apples as he jogged along, and resting under an oak if he was tired; and he came home in the middle of the night, covered with blood and mud, with thorns in his hair and the smell of wild beasts all about him. He grew to resemble them. When his mother kissed him, he submitted coldly to her embrace and seemed to be pondering over weighty matters.

He killed bears with a knife, bulls with an axe, and boars with a spear; and once he even made do with a stick, the only weapon he had, to defend himself against some wolves which were gnawing the corpses at the foot of a gibbet.

One winter morning he set off before dawn, well equipped, with a cross-bow on his shoulder and a quiver of arrows at his saddle-bow.

His Danish jennet, followed by a pair of basset hounds, trotted along at a steady pace, making the ground ring with the sound of its hoofs. Drops of rime clung to his cloak and a stiff breeze was blowing. One side of the horizon cleared, and in the pale morning twilight he noticed some rabbits hopping about outside their burrows. The two basset hounds promptly rushed at them and swiftly broke a few backs.

Soon afterwards he entered a forest. A wood-grouse, numbed by the cold, was asleep on the end of a branch with its head under its wing. With a backward sweep of his sword, Julian lopped its feet off, and went on his way without stopping to pick it up.

Three hours later he found himself on the peak of a mountain so high that the sky seemed almost black. Sloping away in front of him was a rock like a long wall which hung over an abyss, and at the far end two wild goats were looking into the chasm beneath. Not having any arrows with him, for he had left his horse further back, he decided to go down to where they were. Bent nearly double and barefooted, he finally reached the first of the two goats and plunged a dagger between its ribs. The other animal, seized with panic, leapt into the void. Julian sprang forward to stab it, his right foot slipped, and he fell on top of the first goat's carcass, with his arms outspread and his head hanging over the abyss.

Going down into the plain again, he followed a line of willows growing alongside a river. From time to time cranes, flying very low, passed over his head. He struck them down with his whip and never once missed his aim.

Meanwhile the milder air had melted the hoar frost, trails of mist were swirling around and at last the sun appeared. In the distance Julian saw a gleaming lake, so still that it looked like lead. In the middle of it was an animal he did not recognize, a black-nosed beaver. In spite of the distance an arrow killed it, and he was annoyed at not being able to carry off its skin.

Then he went along an avenue of great trees, whose tops formed a kind of triumphal arch leading into a forest. A roe bounded out of a covert, a buck appeared at a cross-way, a badger came out of a hole, and a peacock spread its tail on the grass. And when he had killed them all, more roes came forward, more bucks, more badgers, more peacocks, together with blackbirds, jays, polecats, foxes, hedgehogs and lynxes — an endless succession of birds and beasts, growing more numerous at every step. They circled round him, all trembling and gazing at him with gentle, supplicating eyes. But Julian did not tire of killing,

first drawing his cross-bow, then unsheathing his sword and after
that thrusting with his knife. He had no thought or recollection
of anything at all. Only the fact of his being alive told him that
he had been hunting for an indefinite time in some indetermi-
nate place, for everything happened with dreamlike ease.

An extraordinary sight brought him to a halt. Before him lay
a valley shaped like an amphitheatre and filled with stags. They
were crowded close together, warming each other with their
breath, which he could see steaming in the mist.

For a few minutes the prospect of such carnage as this left
him breathless with delight. Then he dismounted, rolled up his
sleeves, and began shooting.

As the first arrow whistled through the air, all the stags turned
their heads at once. Gaps appeared in their midst, plaintive cries
arose, and a great tremor went through the herd.

The lip of the valley was too high to climb, and they bounded
about in the enclosure, looking for a means of escape. Julian
went on taking aim and shooting, and his arrows fell like shafts
of rain in a heavy storm. The maddened stags fought, reared up
in the air, and climbed on each other's backs, their bodies and
tangled antlers making a broad mound which kept shifting and
crumbling.

At last they died, stretched out on the sand, their nostrils foaming, their entrails gushing out, and the heaving of their bellies
gradually subsiding. Then all was still.

Night was drawing on, and behind the forest, through the
spaces in the branches, the sky showed red like a sheet of blood.

Julian leant back against a tree, considering with wide-eyed
wonderment the magnitude of the slaughter, unable to understand how he could have carried it out.

Then, on the far side of the valley, at the edge of the forest,
he saw a stag with a doe and its fawn.

The stag was a huge black beast, a sixteen-pointer with a white
beard. The doe, as light in colour as a dead leaf, was cropping
the grass, while the dappled fawn, without impeding her movements, pulled at her dugs.

Once again the cross-bow twanged. The fawn was killed instantly. Then its mother, looking up at the sky, gave a deep,
heart-rending, human cry. Julian, exasperated, stretched her on
the ground with a shot full in the breast.

The great stag had seen him and bounded forward. Julian sent his last arrow at him. It struck him in the forehead and remained planted there.

The great stag did not seem to feel it. Striding over the dead bodies, it came steadily nearer, apparently bent on attacking and disembowelling him. Julian fell back in unspeakable terror. The huge beast stopped; and with blazing eyes, solemn as a patriarch or a judge, and to the accompaniment of a bell tolling in the distance, it said three times:

"Accursed, accursed, accursed! One day, cruel heart, you will kill your father and mother!"

The stag's knees gave way, its eyes gently closed, and it died.

Julian was dumbfounded, and then suddenly overwhelmed with fatigue; disgust and a feeling of infinite sadness took hold of him. He wept for a long time, his face buried in his hands.

His horse was lost, his hounds had left him, and the solitude which surrounded him seemed pregnant with indefinable perils. Filled with fear, he set off across country, choosing a path at random, and found himself almost at once at the castle gate.

He could not sleep that night. By the flickering light of the hanging lamp he kept seeing the great black stag. He was obsessed by the animal's prophecy and tried to fight against it. "No, no, no!" he told himself. "I cannot possibly kill them!" Then he thought: "But what if I wanted to?" And he was afraid that the Devil might inspire him with that desire.

For three whole months his anguished mother prayed by his bedside, and his father paced up and down the corridors groaning. He sent for the most famous doctors, who prescribed innumerable drugs. Julian's illness, they said, was caused by some noxious wind or some amorous desire. But the young man shook his head in answer to all the questions that were asked him.

His strength revived and he was taken for walks round the courtyard, the old monk and the noble lord each supporting him with an arm.

When he had completely recovered he stubbornly refused to go hunting.

His father, wanting to make him happy, made him a present of a great Saracen sword. It hung with other weapons at the top of a pillar, and a ladder was needed to reach it. Julian climbed up.

The sword was too heavy and slipped out of his grasp, falling so close to the noble lord that it cut his surcoat. Julian thought that he had killed his father, and fainted.

From then on he had a dread of weapons. The sight of a naked blade made him turn pale. This weakness caused his parents great distress, and at last the old monk ordered him in the name of God, of honour and his ancestors, to take up a nobleman's pursuits once more.

Every day the squires used to amuse themselves by practising with the javelin. Julian very soon excelled at this sport. He could throw his javelin into the neck of a bottle, break the pointers of a weather-vane, and hit the nails in a door at a hundred paces.

One summer evening, at the hour when mist makes things indistinct, he was standing under the pergola in the garden and saw at the far end two white wings fluttering along the top of the wall. He was sure that this was a stork, and he threw his javelin.

A piercing shriek rang out.

It was his mother, whose coif with its long flaps remained nailed to the wall.

Julian fled from the castle and never came back.

II

He enlisted in a troop of soldiers of fortune which was passing by.

He came to know hunger and thirst, fever and vermin. He grew accustomed to the noise of battle and the sight of death. The wind tanned his skin; the wearing of armour toughened his limbs; and as he was strong, courageous, temperate, and intelligent, he was soon given command of a company.

At the start of a battle he would urge his men forward with a great flourish of his sword. With the aid of a knotted rope he would scale the walls of citadels by night, swinging to and fro in the gale, while flakes of Greek fire stuck to his cuirass and boiling resin and molten lead poured from the battlements. Often a falling stone shattered his buckler. Bridges overladen with men gave way under him. Swinging his mace, he disposed of fourteen horsemen. He defeated every challenger who entered the lists against him. Over a score of times he was left for dead.

Thanks to divine providence he always escaped with his life, for he protected churchmen, orphans, widows, and, most particularly, old men. When he saw an old man walking ahead of him, he would call out to him to show his face, as if he were afraid of killing him by mistake.

Runaway serfs, rebellious peasants, penniless bastards, and all manner of brave fellows flocked to his flag, and he formed an army of his own.

It grew. He became famous and sought after.

One after the other, he helped the Dauphin of France and the King of England, the Templars of Jerusalem and the Surena of the Parthians, the Negus of Abyssinia and the Emperor of Calicut. He fought against Scandinavians covered with fishscales, Negroes carrying roundels of hippopotamus hide and mounted on red asses, and golden-skinned Indians brandishing broadswords brighter than mirrors above their diadems. He conquered the Troglodytes and the Anthropophagi. He travelled across lands so hot that men's hair caught fire like torches in the burning sun, others so cold that their arms dropped off and fell to the ground, and yet others so foggy that they walked about surrounded by phantoms.

Republics in difficulties consulted him. At interviews with ambassadors he obtained unhoped-for terms. If a monarch behaved too badly, Julian would suddenly arrive and remonstrate with him. He liberated subject peoples. He freed queens shut up in prison towers. It was he and no other who slew the Viper of Milan and the Dragon of Oberbirbach.

Now the Emperor of Occitania, having defeated the Spanish Moors, had taken the sister of the Caliph of Córdoba as his concubine, and he had a daughter by her whom he had brought up as a Christian. But the Caliph, pretending that he wished to be converted, visited him with a great escort, massacred his entire garrison, and threw him into the deepest of dungeons, where he was treated very harshly in the hope of extorting his treasures from him.

Julian rushed to his aid, destroyed the infidel army, laid siege to the city, killed the Caliph, cut off his head, and tossed it over the ramparts like a ball. Then he released the Emperor from his prison and set him on his throne again in the presence of his assembled court.

As a reward for so great a service, the Emperor presented him with a number of baskets containing an immense fortune. Julian would not take them. Thinking that he wanted more money, the Emperor offered him three-quarters of his wealth. Again Julian refused. Then he offered to share his kingdom with him, and once more Julian declined. The Emperor was weeping with vexation, not knowing how to show his gratitude, when suddenly he slapped his forehead and whispered in a courtier's ear. The arras curtains were drawn aside and a girl appeared.

Her great dark eyes shone like two soft lights and her lips were parted in a delightful smile. The ringlets of her hair had caught on the jewels of her open-necked robe, and her transparent tunic hinted at the youthfulness of her body. She was dainty, round-cheeked, and slender-waisted.

Julian was dazzled with love for her, the more so because till then he had lead a very chaste life.

So he took the Emperor's daughter in marriage, together with a castle which she had from her mother; and when the wedding festivities were over, and countless courtesies had been exchanged, bride and groom set off for their new home.

It was a palace of white marble in the Moorish style, built on a promontory in a grove of orange-trees. Terraces covered with flowers went down to the edge of a bay, where pink shells crackled underfoot. Behind the castle there stretched a forest in the shape of a fan. The sky was forever blue, and the trees swayed gently in the sea breeze or in the wind from the mountains which bounded the distant horizon.

The rooms were full of shadow, but received some light from the inlaid decoration of the walls. Tall columns, as slender as reeds, supported the domes, which were adorned with reliefs imitating the stalactites which are to be found in grottoes.

There were fountains in the main rooms, mosaics in the courtyards, festooned walls, countless architectural refinements, and everywhere a silence so profound that one could hear the rustle of a scarf or the echo of a sigh.

Julian went no more to war. He rested in the midst of a people at peace, and every day a crowd passed before him, genuflecting and kissing his hands in the Eastern fashion.

Dressed in purple, he would remain for hours in a window-recess, leaning on the ledge and calling to mind his hunting days.

He would have liked to be racing across the desert after the ga-
zelle and the ostrich, stalking the leopard through the bamboo-
canes, crossing forests teeming with rhinoceros, climbing the most
inaccessible peaks to take better aim at the eagle, or fighting the
white bear on drift-ice floating in the sea.

Sometimes, in a dream, he would see himself like our father
Adam in the middle of Paradise, with all the birds and beasts
around him; and stretching out his arm, he would put them to
death. Or else they would file past him, two by two, according
to size, from the elephants and lions down to the stoats and
ducks, as they did on the day they entered Noah's ark. From the
shadow of a cave he would hurl javelins at them which never
missed their aim, but others would follow them, there would be
no end to the slaughter, and he would wake up with his eyes
rolling wildly.

Some princes among his friends invited him to go hunting with
them. He always refused, in the belief that by this kind of pen-
ance he would avert his evil destiny, for it seemed to him that
the fate of his parents was bound up with the killing of animals.
But it grieved him not to see anything of them, and this other
longing of his became well-nigh unbearable.

His wife sent for jugglers and dancers to amuse him. She
would go out with him into the country in an open litter; at
other times they would lie in a boat, watching the fish darting
about in water as clear as the sky. Often she would throw flowers
in his face, or crouch at his feet drawing melodies from a three-
stringed mandolin. Then, laying her clasped hand on his shoulder, she would ask shyly: "What ails you, my dear lord?"

He would not answer, or would burst out sobbing. But at last
one day he told her of his dreadful fear.

She fought against it, reasoning very soundly: his father and
mother were probably dead, but if he were ever to see them
again, what chance or purpose could possibly lead him to commit such a horrible crime? His fear was completely groundless,
and he ought to take up hunting again.

Julian smiled as he listened to her, but could not make up his
mind to satisfy his desire.

One evening in August when they were in their room, she had
just got into bed, and he was kneeling down to say his prayers,
when he heard the bark of a fox, followed by some light foot-

steps under the window. In the half-light he saw what appeared to be animal forms. The temptation was too strong for him and he took down his quiver from the wall.

She looked surprised.

"I am obeying your orders," he said. "I shall be back at sunrise."

However, she feared some disaster. He reassured her and went out, astonished at her inconsistency.

Shortly afterwards a page came to tell her that two strangers, in the absence of the lord of the castle, were asking to see the lady.

And soon an old man and an old woman came into the room, bowed and dusty, dressed in coarse linen, and each leaning on a stick.

Plucking up courage, they explained that they brought Julian news of his parents.

She bent down to hear what they had to tell, but after exchanging glances they asked her if he still loved them and if he ever spoke of them.

"Oh, yes!" she said.

"Well, we are they!" they cried, and they sat down, being very tired and weary.

The young wife was far from being convinced that her husband was their son, but they gave her proof by describing certain special marks on his skin.

She jumped out of bed, called her page, and had a meal set before them.

Although they were very hungry, they could scarcely eat anything; and watching them, she noticed how their bony hands shook as they lifted their goblets.

They asked her countless questions about Julian. She answered every one, but careful not to mention the gloomy obsession in which they were concerned.

When he had shown no sign of returning home, they had left their castle and they had been travelling now for several years, following up vague clues without ever losing hope. So much money had been required for river tolls and hostelry charges, to settle the dues of princes and satisfy the demands of robbers, that their purses were quite empty and they were now reduced to beggary. But what did that matter, when soon they would be embracing their son? They extolled his good fortune in having such a charming wife, and never tired of gazing at her and kissing her.

The sumptuousness of the room greatly astonished them, and the old man, after examining the walls, asked why they were decorated with the coat of arms of the Emperor of Occitania.

"He is my father," she replied.

At that he started, remembering the gipsy's prophecy, while the old woman thought of the hermit's words. No doubt her son's high estate was only a foretaste of the eternal glory that lay before him. And both parents sat open-mouthed in the light of the candelabrum on the table.

They must have been very handsome in their youth. The mother had not lost any of her hair, which hung in thin tresses to the bottom of her cheeks, like strips of snow. The father, with his tall build and his great beard, looked like a statue in a church.

Julian's wife advised them not to wait up for him. She installed them in her own bed and shut the window. They fell asleep. Day was about to dawn, and the little birds had begun singing outside.

Julian had crossed the park and was walking through the forest with a springy step, enjoying the softness of the turf and the mildness of the air.

The shadows of the trees lay across the moss. Here and there the moon made white patches in the clearings, and he would pause, thinking he saw a pool of water, or else the surface of still ponds blending with the colour of the grass. Everywhere there was a great silence, and he could see none of the animals which a few minutes earlier had been prowling round his castle.

The forest became thicker and the darkness deeper. Puffs of warm air, heavy with enervating scents, went by him. He kept sinking into heaps of dead leaves, and leant against an oak to get his breath back.

Suddenly, from behind his back, a darker shape leapt forward —a wild boar. Julian had no time to take hold of his bow, and he was as distressed by this as if he had suffered some misfortune.

Then, when he had come out of the forest, he saw a wolf moving along beside a hedge. He shot an arrow at it. The wolf stopped, turned its head to look at him, and went on its way. It trotted on, always at the same distance, stopping from time to time and then, as soon as he took aim, continuing its flight.

In this way Julian crossed an endless plain and then some sandhills, and finally found himself on a plateau dominating a great stretch of country. Flat stones were strewn about among ruined burial vaults. He kept stumbling over dead men's bones; here and there worm-eaten crosses leaned over in a pitiful way. But suddenly something moved in the vague shadows around the tombs, and some hyenas sprang out, frightened and panting. Their claws tapped on the stones as they came up close to sniff at him, baring their fangs and showing their gums. He drew his sword, and at once they scattered in all directions, keeping up their headlong, limping gallop until they disappeared from view in a cloud of dust.

An hour later he met a mad bull in a ravine. Its horns were lowered and it was pawing the sand. Julian thrust his lance at it under the dewlap. The lance was shivered to pieces, as if the animal were made of bronze; and he closed his eyes, expecting to be killed. When he opened them again, the bull had vanished.

Then his very soul was overcome with shame. Realizing that some higher power was rendering his strength ineffective, he went back into the forest to make his way home.

His path was choked with creepers, and he was cutting them with his sword when a marten suddenly slipped between his legs, a panther leapt over his shoulder, and a snake wound its way up an ash-tree.

Among the leaves was a huge jackdaw, looking down at Julian, and here and there between the branches there appeared a host of gleaming lights, as if the sky had rained down all its stars into the forest. They were the eyes of animals — wild cats, squirrels, owls, parrots, monkeys.

Julian shot his arrows at them, and the feathered shafts settled on the leaves like white butterflies. He threw stones at them, and the stones fell to the ground without touching anything. He cursed out loud, spoiling for a fight, howling imprecations, choking with rage.

And all the animals he had hunted reappeared and formed a narrow ring around him. Some sat on their haunches; the others stood erect. He remained in the middle, numb with terror, incapable of making the slightest movement. By a supreme effort of will he took one step forward. The creatures in the trees spread their wings, those on the ground stirred their limbs, and all accompanied him.

The hyenas went in front, the wolf and the wild boar behind. The bull, on his right, swung its head from side to side, and on his left the snake slithered through the grass, while the panther, arching its back, advanced with great velvet-footed strides. He walked as slowly as possible so as not to irritate them, and as he went he saw porcupines, foxes, vipers, jackals, and bears emerging from the depths of the undergrowth.

He broke into a run, and they ran too. The snake hissed, and the foul beasts slavered. The wild boar prodded his heels with its tusks, and the wolf pushed its hairy muzzle into the palms of his hands. The monkeys pinched him and made faces at him; the marten rolled on his feet. A bear knocked his hat off with its paw, and the panther disdainfully dropped an arrow it was carrying in its mouth.

A certain irony was discernible in their sly behaviour; and as they watched him out of the corner of their eyes, they seemed to be thinking out a plan of revenge. Deafened by the insects' buzzing, bruised by the birds' tails, and suffocated by the animals' breath, he walked on with his arms outstretched and his eyes shut, like a blind man, without even the strength to cry for mercy.

The crow of a cock rang through the air and other cocks answered. It was day; and beyond the orange-trees he recognized the roof of his palace.

Then, at the edge of a field, only three paces away, he saw some red partridges fluttering about in the stubble. He unfastened his cloak and threw it over them like a net. When he uncovered them he found only one there, and that had been dead a long time and was decomposing.

This disappointment exasperated him more than all the others. His lust for blood took hold of him again, and since animals were lacking he would gladly have slaughtered men.

He climbed the three terraces and burst open the door with a blow of his fist, but at the foot of the stairs the thought of his beloved wife softened his heart. She was probably asleep. He decided to take her by surprise.

Removing his sandals, he turned the lock gently and went in.

The leaded window-panes dimmed the pale light of dawn.
Julian's feet caught in some clothes lying on the floor, and a
little farther on he knocked against a side-table which was still
laden with dishes. "She must have had something to eat," he
thought, and he went on towards the bed, which was hidden in
darkness at the far end of the room. He came up beside it, and
to kiss his wife, bent down over the pillow where the two heads
were lying side by side. Then he felt the touch of a beard against
his mouth.

He started back, thinking he was going mad, but returned to
the bedside, groping about until his fingers came across some
long tresses of hair. To convince himself he was mistaken, he
passed his hand slowly over the pillow again. This time there was
no doubt it was a beard, and a man — a man sleeping with his
wife!

In a burst of uncontrollable rage he plunged his dagger into
their bodies, stamping his feet, foaming at the mouth, and roaring like a wild beast. Then he stopped. The two victims, pierced
through the heart, had not even moved. He listened closely to the
rattle of their dying breath, which came almost in unison, and
as it grew fainter another in the distance took it up. Vague at
first, this plaintive, long-drawn voice came nearer, grew louder,
took on a cruel note; and to his horror he recognized the belling
of the great black stag.

As he turned round, he thought he saw his wife's ghost framed
in the doorway, with a light in her hand.

The noise of the murder had brought her to the spot. With
one all-embracing glance she took everything in, and fled in
horror, dropping her torch.

He picked it up.

His father and mother lay before him, stretched out on their
backs with holes in their breasts; and their faces, serene and
majestic, looked as though they were keeping some eternal secret.
There were splashes and pools of blood on their white skin, on
the bedclothes and the floor, and trickling down an ivory crucifix
which hung in the alcove. The sun caught the stained-glass
window at that moment, casting a crimson glow over the red
splashes and multiplying them all over the room.

Julian went up to the two bodies, telling himself, and trying to
believe, that this could not be true, that he must be mistaken,

that one sometimes came across remarkable likenesses. Finally
he bent forward slightly to look at the old man at close quarters,
and between the half-closed eyelids he saw a glazed pupil which
burnt through him like fire. Then he went to the other side of
the bed where the other body lay, its white hair covering part of
the face. Julian slipped his fingers under the tresses of hair and
raised the head. He gazed at it, supporting it at arm's length
with one hand and holding up the torch in the other. Drops of
blood were oozing from the mattress and falling one by one on
the floor.

At the end of the day he appeared before his wife, and in a
voice quite unlike his own commanded her first of all not to
answer him, come near him, or even look at him, but to carry
out under pain of damnation all his orders, which were irre-
vocable.

The funeral rites were to be performed in accordance with
the written instructions he had left on a *prie-dieu* in the mor-
tuary chamber. He made over to her his palace, his vassals, and
all his possessions, not excepting even his clothes or his sandals,
which would be found at the head of the stairs.

She had done God's will in providing the occasion of his
crime, and now she should pray for his soul, since from that day
onwards he ceased to exist.

The dead were buried with great pomp in a monastery church
three days' journey from the castle. A monk whose cowl was
pulled down over his face followed the procession, but he stayed
at some distance from the others, and no one dared to speak to
him.

During the Mass he remained prone in the centre of the doorway, his arms stretched out in the form of a cross, and his forehead in the dust.

After the burial he was seen to take the road leading to the
mountains. He turned to look back several times, and finally
disappeared.

III

He went his way, begging for his daily bread all over the world.

He would hold out his hand to riders on the high roads, bend
his knee before harvesters, or stand motionless at courtyard gates,
and his face was so sad that no one ever refused him alms.

In a spirit of humility he would tell his story, and then everyone would flee from him, making the sign of the cross. In the villages he had passed through before, he was no sooner recognized than people shut their doors, shouted threats, or threw stones at him. The most charitable of them would put a bowl of soup on their window-sills and then close the shutters so as not to see him.

Rebuffed on all sides, he shunned mankind, and fed on roots, plants, wild fruit, and shell-fish which he looked for along the seashore.

Sometimes, rounding a hill, he saw beneath him a jumble of roofs crowded together, with stone spires, bridges, towers, and a network of dark streets from which a continual murmur rose to his ears.

The craving to take part in the life of other men impelled him to go down into the city. But the bestial faces of the people he met, the noise of their work, and the triviality of their conversation froze his heart. On feast-days, when the sound of the great cathedral bells filled everyone with joy from daybreak onwards, he would watch the townspeople coming out of their houses, the dancing in the squares, the beer-fountains at the crossroads, the damask awnings in front of princely homes; and in the evening, through ground-floor windows, the long family tables where grandparents dandled little children on their knees. Sobs choked him, and he would turn away back to the open country.

He felt pangs of love as he gazed at foals in the meadows, birds in their nests, and insects on the flowers. But at his approach they all ran farther off, hid in terror, or flew swiftly away.

He sought out lonely places. But the wind would sound in his ears like the rattle of a death-agony. The dew falling on the ground would recall other, heavier drops. The sun, every evening, would splash blood across the clouds, and each night in his dreams the murder of his parents would begin all over again.

He made himself a hair-shirt with iron spikes. He climbed on his knees every hill which had a chapel at the top. But the pitiless thought dimmed the glory of the shrines, and tortured him even in his acts of mortification.

He did not rebel against God for having imposed this deed on him, and yet the idea that he could have committed it reduced him to despair.

His own body was so repulsive to him that in the hope of freeing himself from it, he risked it in perilous enterprises. He saved paralytics from fires and children from yawning chasms. The abyss cast him up; the flames spared him.

Time did not ease his suffering. It became so intolerable that he resolved to die.

And one day when he was standing beside a pool, bending over it to gauge the depth of the water, he saw before him a gaunt old man, with a white beard and a face so sad that Julian could not restrain his tears. The other wept too. Without recognizing his own reflection, he vaguely remembered having seen a face like this before. Then he gave a cry — it was his father; and he thought no more of killing himself.

So, bearing the burden of his memories, he travelled through many lands, until he came to a river which was dangerous to cross because of the strong current and the great stretch of mud along its banks. No one for a long time past had dared to try to cross it.

An old boat had been left among the reeds, with its stern buried in the mud and its bows up in the air. Julian examined it and found a pair of oars, and he was struck by the thought of spending his life in the service of others.

He began by making a kind of causeway on the bank so that people could get down to the stream. He broke his nails moving the huge stones, carried them pressed against his belly, slipped in the mud, sank into it, and several times came near to death. Next he mended the boat with bits of wreckage, and built himself a hut out of tree-trunks and clay.

Once the ferry became known, travellers appeared. They signalled to him from the other side by waving flags, and Julian promptly jumped into his boat. It was very heavy, and they overloaded it with all sorts of packs and bundles, not to mention the beasts of burden, which added to the confusion by lashing out in fright. Julian asked nothing for his labour; some gave him scraps of food from their wallets or worn-out clothes they did not want any longer. Some brutish ruffians would shout curses at him. Julian remonstrated gently with them, only to be answered with abuse. He contented himself with giving them his blessing.

A little table, a stool, a bed of dead leaves, and three clay cups were all the furniture he had. Two holes in the wall served as windows. On one side, as far as the eye could see, stretched barren plains dotted here and there with pale meres, while in front of him the greenish waters of the great river rolled by. In spring the damp earth gave out an odour of decay. Then a blustering wind would raise clouds of dust which penetrated everywhere, muddying the water and leaving grit in his mouth. A little later it was the turn of clouds of mosquitoes, whose humming and stinging went on night and day. And after that came dreadful frosts which made everything as hard as stone and inspired a frantic craving for meat.

Months went by when Julian saw no one. Often he would close his eyes and try to recapture his youth in memory. The courtyard of the castle would appear before him, with greyhounds on the steps, pages in the armoury, and a fair-haired boy under a vine-covered arbour, between an old man wrapped in furs and a lady with a great coif. And suddenly the two corpses were there. He would throw himself flat on his bed, weeping and crying: "Ah, poor father! Poor mother, poor mother!" And he would fall into a fitful slumber in which these funeral visions continued to haunt him.

One night, while he was asleep, he thought he heard someone calling him. He strained his ears, but could make out nothing but the roar of the waves.

But again the same voice called out:

"Julian!"

It came from the far bank, and this struck him as extraordinary, considering the width of the river.

A third time the summons came:

"Julian!"

And this penetrating voice had the sound of a church bell.

Lighting his lantern, Julian left the hut. A raging tempest was blowing through the night. The darkness was profound, broken only here and there by the whiteness of the leaping waves.

After a moment's hesitation Julian cast off the painter. At once the water became calm, and the boat glided across it to the other bank, where a man was waiting.

He was wrapped in a ragged cloth, his face like a plaster mask and his two eyes redder than burning coals. Holding the lantern up to him, Julian saw that he was covered with a hideous leprosy, and yet there was something kingly in his bearing.

As soon as he got into the boat, it went a long way down in the water, under the weight of his body; then it rose again with a jolt, and Julian started rowing.

At every stroke the surf lifted the bows up in the air. The water, looking blacker than ink, streamed furiously past on either side. It hollowed out abysses and built up mountains, and the boat leapt up before sinking again into the depths, where it spun round, tossed by the wind.

Julian bent his body, stretched his arms out, and arched himself backwards from his feet to get more power. The hail lashed his hands, the rain ran down his back, the violence of the wind took his breath away, and at last he stopped. The boat then began drifting away downstream. But realizing that this was a matter of the first importance, a trust he must on no account desert, he took up his oars again, and the rattle of the rowlocks cut through the clamour of the storm.

The little lantern was shining in front of him. Birds fluttering past it hid it from time to time. But all the while he could see the eyes of the Leper, who stood in the stern of the boat, motionless as a pillar.

And this went on for a long, long time.

When they reached the hut, Julian shut the door and saw the Leper sitting on the stool. The shroud-like garment which covered him had slipped down to his hips, and his shoulders, his chest, and his scrawny arms were hidden under patches of scaly pustules. His brow was furrowed with enormous wrinkles. Like a skeleton he had a hole where the nose should have been, and from his bluish lips came a nauseous breath as thick as a fog.

"I am hungry," he said.

Julian gave him what he had: an old gammon of bacon and the crust from a loaf of black bread.

When he had finished eating, the table, the bowl, and the handle of the knife bore the same marks that could be seen on his body.

Next he said: "I am thirsty."

Julian went to get his pitcher, and as he picked it up, there arose from it a scent which made his heart and nostrils expand.

It was wine. What a wonderful find this was, he thought. But the Leper stretched out his hand and emptied the whole pitcher at one draught.

Then he said: "I am cold."

With his candle Julian set light to a bundle of bracken in the middle of the hut.

The Leper came near to warm himself. Squatting on his heels, he began trembling all over. His strength was flagging, his eyes had stopped shining, his sores were running, and in an almost inaudible voice he murmured: "Your bed!"

Julian tenderly helped him to drag himself to it, even spreading the sail of his boat over him to cover him.

The Leper lay there groaning. His teeth showed at the corners of his mouth, his chest heaved as his dying breath came more and more quickly, and at every gasp his belly was sucked in as far as his backbone.

Then he closed his eyes.

"My bones are like ice. Come here beside me!"

And Julian, lifting the sail, lay down side by side with him on the dead leaves.

The Leper turned his head.

"Take off your clothes so that I may feel the warmth of your body!"

Julian stripped, and then, naked as on the day he was born, he lay down on the bed again. And against his thigh he felt the Leper's skin, colder than a snake and as rough as a file.

He spoke encouragingly to him, and the other gasped out in reply:

"Ah, I am dying! Come closer and warm me! No, not with your hands, with your whole body!"

Julian stretched himself out on top of him, mouth to mouth, breast to breast.

Then the Leper clasped him in his arms. And all at once his eyes took on the brightness of the stars, his hair spread out like the rays of the sun, and the breath of his nostrils had the sweetness of roses. A cloud of incense rose from the hearth and the waves outside began to sing.

Meanwhile an abundance of delight, a superhuman joy swept like a flood into Julian's soul as he lay there in a swoon. And the one whose arms still held him tight grew and grew, until his head and his feet touched the walls of the hut. The roof flew off, the heavens unfolded — and Julian rose towards the blue, face to face with Our Lord Jesus Christ, who bore him up to Heaven.

And that is the story of St Julian Hospitator, more or less as it is depicted on a stained-glass window in a church in my part of the world.

(Translated by Robert Baldick)

LEO TOLSTOY (1828–1910) Tolstoy, next to the youngest of five sons, was born at his aristocratic parents' estate in the Tula province of Russia. Orphaned at the age of nine (his mother had died when he was three), he was raised by elderly aunts, and his early education was supervised by French tutors. For three years he studied at Kazan University but left without a degree and with a contempt for academicism. In 1847 Tolstoy began his self-critical Diary. After serving in the Caucasus and the Crimean War from 1851–1857, he retired to his ancestral estate Yasnaya Polyana where he emancipated his serfs and instituted a school for peasant children. At the age of thirty-four, while managing his estate in good fortune, he married a girl sixteen years younger than himself, and they had nine children.

Tolstoy was a man of enormous vitality and energy; Gorky saw him as "a titan roaming the earth in antique majesty." Philip Rahv has described the Tolstoian novel in these terms: "It is never the division but always the unity of art and life which makes the illumination . . . in a sense there are no plots in Tolstoy but simply the unquestioned and unalterable process of life itself."

War and Peace and *Anna Karenina* belong to the period before Tolstoy's religious conversion of 1876. His religious conversion and espousal of a "new Christianity" based on non-resistance to evil brought an immense change in his life and works. He renounced the Russian Orthodox Church and condemned the State and the possession of property. He became a vegetarian, repudiated his possessions, and lived as a peasant. Yasnaya Polyana became a retreat for Tolstoyites. Tolstoy's later works — *The Memoirs of a Madman* (1884), *The Death of Ivan Ilyich* (1886), and *Master and Man* (1895) — are marked by a despair through which glimmered a hope for redemption, symbolically represented. At the age of eighty-two, Tolstoy and his daughter fled his embittered wife; shortly thereafter, he died. He was buried at Yasnaya Polyana.

HOW MUCH LAND
DOES A MAN NEED?

Leo Tolstoy

An elder sister came to visit her younger sister in the country. The elder was married to a tradesman in town, the younger to a peasant in the village. As the sisters sat over their tea talking, the elder began to boast of the advantages of town life: saying how comfortably they lived there, how well they dressed, what fine clothes her children wore, what good things they ate and drank, and how she went to the theatre, promenades, and entertainments.

The younger sister was piqued, and in turn disparaged the life of a tradesman, and stood up for that of a peasant.

"I would not change my way of life for yours," said she. "We may live roughly, but at least we are free from anxiety. You live in better style than we do, but though you often earn more than you need, you are very likely to lose all you have. You know the proverb, 'Loss and gain are brothers twain.' It often happens that people who are wealthy one day are begging their bread the next. Our way is safer. Though a peasant's life is not a fat one, it is a long one. We shall never grow rich, but we shall always have enough to eat."

The elder sister said sneeringly:

"Enough? Yes, if you like to share with the pigs and the calves! What do you know of elegance or manners! However much your goodman may slave, you will die as you are living — on a dung heap — and your children the same."

"Well, what of that?" replied the younger. "Of course our work is rough and coarse. But, on the other hand, it is sure, and we need not bow to anyone. But you, in your towns, are surrounded by temptations; to-day all may be right, but to-morrow the Evil One may tempt your husband with cards, wine, or

women, and all will go to ruin. Don't such things happen often
enough?"

Pahóm, the master of the house, was lying on the top of the
stove and he listened to the women's chatter.

"It is perfectly true," thought he. "Busy as we are from childhood tilling mother earth, we peasants have no time to let any
nonsense settle in our heads. Our only trouble is that we haven't
land enough. If I had plenty of land, I shouldn't fear the Devil
himself!"

The women finished their tea, chatted a while about dress,
and then cleared away the tea-things and lay down to sleep.

But the Devil had been sitting behind the stove, and had heard
all that was said. He was pleased that the peasant's wife had led
her husband into boasting, and that he had said that if he had
plenty of land he would not fear the Devil himself.

"All right," thought the Devil. "We will have a tussle. I'll give
you land enough; and by means of that land I will get you into
my power."

II

Close to the village there lived a lady, a small landowner who
had an estate of about three hundred acres.[1] She had always
lived on good terms with the peasants until she engaged as her
steward an old soldier, who took to burdening the people with
fines. However careful Pahóm tried to be, it happened again
and again that now a horse of his got among the lady's oats, now
a cow strayed into her garden, now his calves found their way
into her meadows — and he always had to pay a fine.

Pahóm paid up, but grumbled and, going home in a temper,
was rough with his family. All through that summer, Pahóm had
much trouble because of this steward, and he was even glad when
winter came and the cattle had to be stabled. Though he grudged
the fodder when they could no longer graze on the pasture-land,
at least he was free from anxiety about them.

In the winter the news got about that the lady was going to
sell her land and that the keeper of the inn on the high road
was bargaining for it. When the peasants heard this they were
very much alarmed.

[1] 120 desyatíns. The desyatína is properly 2.7 acres; but in this story
round numbers are used.

"Well," thought they, "if the innkeeper gets the land, he will worry us with fines worse than the lady's steward. We all depend on that estate."

So the peasants went on behalf of their Commune, and asked the lady not to sell the land to the innkeeper, offering her a better price for it themselves. The lady agreed to let them have it. Then the peasants tried to arrange for the Commune to buy the whole estate, so that it might be held by them all in common. They met twice to discuss it, but could not settle the matter; the Evil One sowed discord among them and they could not agree. So they decided to buy the land individually, each according to his means; and the lady agreed to this plan as she had to the other.

Presently Pahóm heard that a neighbor of his was buying fifty acres, and that the lady had consented to accept one half in cash and to wait a year for the other half. Pahóm felt envious.

"Look at that," thought he, "the land is all being sold, and I shall get none of it." So he spoke to his wife.

"Other people are buying," said he, "and we must also buy twenty acres or so. Life is becoming impossible. That steward is simply crushing us with his fines."

So they put their heads together and considered how they could manage to buy it. They had one hundred rúbles laid by. They sold a colt and one half of their bees, hired out one of their sons as a laborer and took his wages in advance; borrowed the rest from a brother-in-law, and so scraped together half the purchase money.

Having done this, Pahóm chose out a farm of forty acres, some of it wooded, and went to the lady to bargain for it. They came to an agreement, and he shook hands with her upon it and paid her a deposit in advance. Then they went to town and signed the deeds; he paying half the price down, and undertaking to pay the remainder within two years.

So now Pahóm had land of his own. He borrowed seed, and sowed it on the land he had bought. The harvest was a good one, and within a year he had managed to pay off his debts both to the lady and to his brother-in-law. So he became a landowner, ploughing and sowing his own land, making hay on his own land, cutting his own trees, and feeding his cattle on his own pasture. When he went out to plough his fields, or to look at his growing corn, or at his grass-meadows, his heart would fill with joy. The grass that grew and the flowers that bloomed there seemed to him unlike any that grew elsewhere. Formerly, when he had passed by that land, it had appeared the same as any other land, but now it seemed quite different.

III

So Pahóm was well-contented, and everything would have been right if the neighboring peasants would only not have trespassed on his corn-fields and meadows. He appealed to them most civilly, but they still went on: now the Communal herdsmen would let the village cows stray into his meadows, then horses from the night pasture would get among his corn. Pahóm turned them out again and again, and forgave their owners, and for a long time he forbore to prosecute any one. But at last he lost patience and complained to the District Court. He knew it was the peasants' want of land, and no evil intent on their part, that caused the trouble, but he thought:

"I cannot go on overlooking it or they will destroy all I have. They must be taught a lesson."

So he had them up, gave them one lesson, and then another, and two or three of the peasants were fined. After a time Pahóm's neighbors began to bear him a grudge for this, and would now and then let their cattle on to his land on purpose. One peasant even got into Pahóm's wood at night and cut down five young lime trees for their bark. Pahóm passing through the wood one day noticed something white. He came nearer and saw the stripped trunks lying on the ground, and close by stood the stumps where the trees had been. Pahóm was furious.

"If he had only cut one here and there it would have been bad enough," thought Pahóm, "but the rascal has actually cut down a whole clump. If I could only find out who did this, I would pay him out."

He racked his brain as to who it could be. Finally he decided: "It must be Simon — no one else could have done it." So he went to Simon's homestead to have a look round, but he found nothing, and only had an angry scene. However, he now felt more certain than ever that Simon had done it, and he lodged a complaint. Simon was summoned. The case was tried, and retried, and at the end of it all Simon was acquitted, there being no evidence against him. Pahóm felt still more aggrieved, and let his anger loose upon the Elder and the Judges.

"You let thieves grease your palms," said he. "If you were honest folk yourselves you would not let a thief go free."

So Pahóm quarrelled with the Judges and with his neighbors. Threats to burn his buildings began to be uttered. So though Pahóm had more land, his place in the Commune was much worse than before.

About this time a rumor got about that many people were moving to new parts.

"There's no need for me to leave my land," thought Pahóm. "But some of the others might leave our village and then there would be more room for us. I would take over their land myself and make my estate a bit bigger. I could then live more at ease. As it is, I am still too cramped to be comfortable."

One day Pahóm was sitting at home when a peasant, passing through the village, happened to call in. He was allowed to stay the night, and supper was given him. Pahóm had a talk with this peasant and asked him where he came from. The stranger answered that he came from beyond the Vólga, where he had been working. One word led to another, and the man went on to say that many people were settling in those parts. He told how some people from his village had settled there. They had joined the Commune, and had had twenty-five acres per man granted them. The land was so good, he said, that the rye sown on it grew as high as a horse, and so thick that five cuts of a sickle made a sheaf. One peasant, he said, had brought nothing with him but his bare hands, and now he had six horses and two cows of his own.

Pahóm's heart kindled with desire. He thought:

"Why should I suffer in this narrow hole, if one can live so well elsewhere? I will sell my land and my homestead here, and with the money I will start afresh over there and get everything new. In this crowded place one is always having trouble. But I must first go and find out all about it myself."

Towards summer he got ready and started. He went down the Vólga on a steamer to Samára, then walked another three hundred miles on foot, and at last reached the place. It was just as the stranger had said. The peasants had plenty of land: every man had twenty-five acres of Communal land given him for his use, and any one who had money could buy, besides, at a rúble an acre as much good freehold land as he wanted.

Having found out all he wished to know, Pahóm returned home as autumn came on, and began selling off his belongings. He sold his land at a profit, sold his homestead and all his cattle, and withdrew from membership in the Commune. He only waited till the spring, and then started with his family for the new settlement.

IV

As soon as Pahóm and his family reached their new abode, he applied for admission into the Commune of a large village. He stood treat to the Elders and obtained the necessary documents. Five shares of Communal land were given him for his own and his sons' use: that is to say — 125 acres (not all together, but in different fields) besides the use of the Communal pasture. Pahóm put up the buildings he needed, and bought cattle. Of the Communal land alone he had three times as much as at his former home, and the land was good corn-land. He was ten times better off than he had been. He had plenty of arable land and pasturage, and could keep as many head of cattle as he liked.

At first, in the bustle of building and settling down, Pahóm was pleased with it all, but when he got used to it he began to think that even here he had not enough land. The first year, he sowed wheat on his share of the Communal land and had a good crop. He wanted to go on sowing wheat, but had not enough Communal land for the purpose, and what he had already used was not available; for in those parts wheat is only sown on virgin soil or on fallow land. It is sown for one or two years, and then the land lies fallow till it is again overgrown with prairie grass. There were many who wanted such land and there was not enough for all; so that people quarreled about it. Those who were better off wanted it for growing wheat, and those who were poor wanted it to let to dealers, so that they might raise money to pay their taxes. Pahóm wanted to sow more wheat, so he rented land from a dealer for a year. He sowed much wheat and had a fine crop, but the land was too far from the village — the wheat had to be carted more than ten miles. After a time Pahóm noticed that some peasant-dealers were living on separate farms and were growing wealthy; and he thought:

"If I were to buy some freehold land and have a homestead on it, it would be a different thing altogether. Then it would all be nice and compact."

The question of buying freehold land recurred to him again and again.

He went on in the same way for three years, renting land and sowing wheat. The seasons turned out well and the crops were good, so that he began to lay money by. He might have gone on living contentedly, but he grew tired of having to rent other people's land every year, and having to scramble for it. Wherever there was good land to be had, the peasants would rush for it and it was taken up at once, so that unless you were sharp about it you got none. It happened in the third year that he and a dealer together rented a piece of pasture-land from some peasants; and they had already ploughed it up, when there was some dispute and the peasants went to law about it, and things fell out so that the labor was all lost.

"If it were my own land," thought Pahóm, "I should be independent, and there would not be all this unpleasantness."

So Pahóm began looking out for land which he could buy; and he came across a peasant who had bought thirteen hundred acres, but having got into difficulties was willing to sell again cheap. Pahóm bargained and haggled with him, and at last they settled the price at 1,500 rúbles, part in cash and part to be paid later. They had all but clinched the matter when a passing dealer happened to stop at Pahóm's one day to get a feed for his horses. He drank tea with Pahóm and they had a talk. The dealer said that he was just returning from the land of the Bashkírs, far away, where he had bought thirteen thousand acres of land, all for 1,000 rúbles. Pahóm questioned him further, and the tradesman said:

"All one need do is to make friends with the chiefs. I gave away about one hundred rúbles' worth of silk robes and carpets, besides a case of tea, and I gave wine to those who would drink it: and I got the land for less than a penny an acre."[2] And he showed Pahóm the title-deeds, saying:

"The land lies near a river, and the whole prairie is virgin soil."

Pahóm plied him with questions, and the tradesman said:

[2] Five kopéks for a desyatína.

"There is more land there than you could cover if you walked
a year, and it all belongs to the Bashkírs. They are as simple as
sheep, and land can be got almost for nothing."

"There now," thought Pahóm, "with my one thousand rúbles,
why should I get only thirteen hundred acres, and saddle myself
with a debt besides? If I take it out there, I can get more than
ten times as much for the money."

V

Pahóm inquired how to get to the place, and as soon as the
tradesman had left him, he prepared to go there himself. He left
his wife to look after the homestead, and started on his journey
taking his man with him. They stopped at a town on their way
and bought a case of tea, some wine, and other presents, as the
tradesman had advised. On and on they went until they had gone
more than three hundred miles, and on the seventh day they
came to a place where the Bashkírs had pitched their tents. It
was all just as the tradesman had said. The people lived on the
steppes, by a river, in felt-covered tents.[3] They neither tilled the
ground, nor ate bread. Their cattle and horses grazed in herds
on the steppe. The colts were tethered behind the tents, and the
mares were driven to them twice a day. The mares were milked,
and from the milk kumiss was made. It was the women who prepared kumiss, and they also made cheese. As far as the men were
concerned, drinking kumiss and tea, eating mutton, and playing
on their pipes, was all they cared about. They were all stout and
merry, and all the summer long they never thought of doing any
work. They were quite ignorant, and knew no Russian, but were
good-natured enough.

As soon as they saw Pahóm, they came out of their tents and
gathered round their visitor. An interpreter was found, and
Pahóm told them he had come about some land. The Bashkírs
seemed very glad; they took Pahóm and led him into one of the
best tents, where they made him sit on some down cushions
placed on a carpet, while they sat round him. They gave him
some tea and kumiss, and had a sheep killed, and gave him mutton to eat. Pahóm took presents out of his cart and distributed
them among the Bashkírs, and divided the tea amongst them.

[3] A kibítka is a movable dwelling, made up of detachable wooden
frames, forming a round, and covered over with felt.

The Bashkírs were delighted. They talked a great deal among themselves, and then told the interpreter to translate.

"They wish to tell you," said the interpreter, "that they like you, and that it is our custom to do all we can to please a guest and to repay him for his gifts. You have given us presents, now tell us which of the things we possess please you best, that we may present them to you."

"What pleases me best here," answered Pahóm, "is your land. Our land is crowded and the soil is exhausted; but you have plenty of land and it is good land. I never saw the like of it."

The interpreter translated. The Bashkírs talked among themselves for a while. Pahóm could not understand what they were saying, but saw that they were much amused and that they shouted and laughed. Then they were silent and looked at Pahóm while the interpreter said:

"They wish me to tell you that in return for your presents they will gladly give you as much land as you want. You have only to point it out with your hand and it is yours."

The Bashkírs talked again for a while and began to dispute. Pahóm asked what they were disputing about, and the interpreter told him that some of them thought they ought to ask their Chief about the land and not act in his absence, while others thought there was no need to wait for his return.

VI

While the Bashkírs were disputing, a man in a large fox-fur cap appeared on the scene. They all became silent and rose to their feet. The interpreter said, "This is our Chief himself."

Pahóm immediately fetched the best dressing-gown and five pounds of tea, and offered these to the Chief. The Chief accepted them, and seated himself in the place of honor. The Bashkírs at once began telling him something. The Chief listened for a while, then made a sign with his head for them to be silent, and addressing himself to Pahóm, said in Russian:

"Well, let it be so. Choose whatever piece of land you like; we have plenty of it."

"How can I take as much as I like?" thought Pahóm. "I must get a deed to make it secure, or else they may say, 'It is yours,' and afterwards may take it away again."

"Thank you for your kind words," he said aloud. "You have

much land, and I only want a little. But I should like to be sure which bit is mine. Could it not be measured and made over to me? Life and death are in God's hands. You good people give it to me, but your children might wish to take it away again."

"You are quite right," said the Chief. "We will make it over to you."

"I heard that a dealer had been here," continued Pahóm, "and that you gave him a little land, too, and signed title-deeds to that effect. I should like to have it done in the same way."

The Chief understood.

"Yes," replied he, "that can be done quite easily. We have a scribe, and we will go to town with you and have the deed properly sealed."

"And what will be the price?" asked Pahóm.

"Our price is always the same: one thousand rúbles a day."

Pahóm did not understand.

"A day? What measure is that? How many acres would that be?"

"We do not know how to reckon it out," said the Chief. "We sell it by the day. As much as you can go round on your feet in a day is yours, and the price is one thousand rúbles a day."

Pahóm was surprised.

"But in a day you can get round a large tract of land," he said.

The Chief laughed.

"It will all be yours!" said he. "But there is one condition: If you don't return on the same day to the spot whence you started, your money is lost."

"But how am I to mark the way that I have gone?"

"Why, we shall go to any spot you like, and stay there. You must start from that spot and make your round, taking a spade with you. Wherever you think necessary, make a mark. At every turning, dig a hole and pile up the turf; then afterwards we will go round with a plough from hole to hole. You may make as large a circuit as you please, but before the sun sets you must return to the place you started from. All the land you cover will be yours."

Pahóm was delighted. It was decided to start early next morning. They talked a while, and after drinking some more kumiss and eating some more mutton, they had tea again, and then the night came on. They gave Pahóm a feather-bed to sleep on, and the Bashkírs dispersed for the night, promising to assemble the next morning at daybreak and ride out before sunrise to the appointed spot.

VII

Pahóm lay on the feather-bed, but could not sleep. He kept thinking about the land.

"What a large tract I will mark off!" thought he. "I can easily do thirty-five miles in a day. The days are long now, and within a circuit of thirty-five miles what a lot of land there will be! I will sell the poorer land, or let it to peasants, but I'll pick out the best and farm it. I will buy two oxteams, and hire two more laborers. About a hundred and fifty acres shall be ploughland, and I will pasture cattle on the rest."

Pahóm lay awake all night, and dozed off only just before dawn. Hardly were his eyes closed when he had a dream. He thought he was lying in that same tent and heard somebody chuckling outside. He wondered who it could be, and rose and went out, and he saw the Bashkír Chief sitting in front of the tent holding his sides and rolling about with laughter. Going nearer to the Chief, Pahóm asked: "What are you laughing at?" But he saw that it was no longer the Chief, but the dealer who had recently stopped at his house and had told him about the land. Just as Pahóm was going to ask, "Have you been here long?" he saw that it was not the dealer, but the peasant who had come up from the Vólga, long ago, to Pahóm's old home. Then he saw that it was not the peasant either, but the Devil himself with hoofs and horns, sitting there and chuckling, and before him lay a man barefoot, prostrate on the ground, with only trousers and a shirt on. And Pahóm dreamt that he looked more attentively to see what sort of a man it was that was lying there, and he saw that the man was dead, and that it was himself! He awoke horror-struck.

"What things one does dream," thought he.

Looking round he saw through the open door that the dawn was breaking.

"It's time to wake them up," thought he. "We ought to be starting."

He got up, roused his man (who was sleeping in his cart), bade him harness; and went to call the Bashkírs.

"It's time to go to the steppe to measure the land," he said.

The Bashkírs rose and assembled, and the Chief came too. Then they began drinking kumiss again, and offered Pahóm some tea, but he would not wait.

"If we are to go, let us go. It is high time," said he.

VIII

The Bashkírs got ready and they all started: some mounted on horses, and some in carts. Pahóm drove in his own small cart with his servant and took a spade with him. When they reached the steppe, the morning red was beginning to kindle. They ascended a hillock (called by the Bashkírs a *shikhan*) and dismounting from their carts and their horses, gathered in one spot. The Chief came up to Pahóm and stretching out his arm towards the plain:

"See," said he, "all this, as far as your eye can reach, is ours. You may have any part of it you like."

Pahóm's eyes glistened: it was all virgin soil, as flat as the palm of your hand, as black as the seed of a poppy, and in the hollows different kinds of grasses grew breast high.

The Chief took off his fox-fur cap, placed it on the ground and said:

"This will be the mark. Start from here, and return here again. All the land you go round shall be yours."

Pahóm took out his money and put it on the cap. Then he took off his outer coat, remaining in his sleeveless under-coat. He unfastened his girdle and tied it tight below his stomach, put a little bag of bread into the breast of his coat, and tying a flask of water to his girdle, he drew up the tops of his boots, took the spade from his man, and stood ready to start. He considered for some moments which way he had better go — it was tempting everywhere.

"No matter," he concluded, "I will go towards the rising sun."

He turned his face to the east, stretched himself, and waited for the sun to appear above the rim.

"I must lose no time," he thought, "and it is easier walking while it is still cool."

The sun's rays had hardly flashed above the horizon, before Pahóm, carrying the spade over his shoulder, went down into the steppe.

Pahóm started walking neither slowly nor quickly. After having gone a thousand yards he stopped, dug a hole, and placed pieces of turf one on another to make it more visible. Then he went on; and now that he had walked off his stiffness he quickened his pace. After a while he dug another hole.

Pahóm looked back. The hillock could be distinctly seen in the sunlight, with the people on it, and the glittering tires of the cart-wheels. At a rough guess Pahóm concluded that he had walked three miles. It was growing warmer; he took off his undercoat, flung it across his shoulder, and went on again. It had grown quite warm now; he looked at the sun, it was time to think of breakfast.

"The first shift is done, but there are four in a day, and it is too soon yet to turn. But I will just take off my boots," said he to himself.

He sat down, took off his boots, stuck them into his girdle, and went on. It was easy walking now.

"I will go on for another three miles," thought he, "and then turn to the left. The spot is so fine, that it would be a pity to lose it. The further one goes, the better the land seems."

He went straight on for a while, and when he looked round, the hillock was scarcely visible and the people on it looked like black ants, and he could just see something glistening there in the sun.

"Ah," thought Pahóm, "I have gone far enough in this direction, it is time to turn. Besides I am in a regular sweat, and very thirsty."

He stopped, dug a large hole, and heaped up pieces of turf. Next he untied his flask, had a drink, and then turned sharply to the left. He went on and on; the grass was high, and it was very hot.

Pahóm began to grow tired: he looked at the sun and saw that it was noon.

"Well," he thought, "I must have a rest."

He sat down, and ate some bread and drank some water; but he did not lie down, thinking that if he did he might fall asleep. After sitting a little while, he went on again. At first he walked easily: the food had strengthened him; but it had become terribly hot and he felt sleepy, still he went on, thinking: "An hour to suffer, a life-time to live."

He went a long way in this direction also, and was about to

turn to the left again, when he perceived a damp hollow: "It would be a pity to leave that out," he thought. "Flax would do well there." So he went on past the hollow, and dug a hole on the other side of it before he turned the corner. Pahóm looked towards the hillock. The heat made the air hazy: it seemed to be quivering, and through the haze the people on the hillock could scarcely be seen.

"Ah!" thought Pahóm, "I have made the sides too long; I must make this one shorter." And he went along the third side, stepping faster. He looked at the sun: it was nearly half-way to the horizon, and he had not yet done two miles of the third side of the square. He was still ten miles from the goal.

"No," he thought, "though it will make my land lop-sided, I must hurry back in a straight line now. I might go too far, and as it is I have a great deal of land."

So Pahóm hurriedly dug a hole, and turned straight towards the hillock.

IX

Pahóm went straight towards the hillock, but he now walked with difficulty. He was done up with the heat, his bare feet were cut and bruised, and his legs began to fail. He longed to rest, but it was impossible if he meant to get back before sunset. The sun waits for no man, and it was sinking lower and lower.

"Oh dear," he thought, "if only I have not blundered trying for too much! What if I am too late?"

He looked towards the hillock and at the sun. He was still far from his goal, and the sun was already near the rim.

Pahóm walked on and on; it was very hard walking. but he went quicker and quicker. He pressed on, but was still far from the place. He began running, threw away his coat, his boots, his flask, and his cap, and kept only the spade which he used as a support.

"What shall I do," he thought again, "I have grasped too much and ruined the whole affair. I can't get there before the sun sets."

And this fear made him still more breathless. Pahóm went on running, his soaking shirt and trousers stuck to him and his mouth was parched. His breast was working like a blacksmith's bellows, his heart was beating like a hammer, and his legs were giving way as if they did not belong to him. Pahóm was seized with terror lest he should die of the strain.

Though afraid of death, he could not stop. "After having run all that way they will call me a fool if I stop now," thought he. And he ran on and on, and drew near and heard the Bashkírs yelling and shouting to him, and their cries inflamed his heart still more. He gathered his last strength and ran on.

The sun was close to the rim, and cloaked in mist looked large, and red as blood. Now, yes now, it was about to set! The sun was quite low, but he was also quite near his aim. Pahóm could already see the people on the hillock waving their arms to hurry him up. He could see the fox-fur cap on the ground and the money on it, and the Chief sitting on the ground holding his sides. And Pahóm remembered his dream.

"There is plenty of land," thought he, "but will God let me live on it? I have lost my life, I have lost my life! I shall never reach that spot!"

Pahóm looked at the sun, which had reached the earth: one side of it had already disappeared. With all his remaining strength he rushed on, bending his body forward so that his legs could hardly follow fast enough to keep from falling. Just as he reached the hillock it suddenly grew dark. He looked up — the sun had already set! He gave a cry: "All my labor has been in vain," thought he, and was about to stop, but he heard the Bashkírs still shouting, and remembered that though to him, from below, the sun seemed to have set, they on the hillock could still see it. He took a long breath and ran up the hillock. It was still light there. He reached the top and saw the cap. Before it sat the Chief laughing and holding his sides. Again Pahóm remembered his dream, and he uttered a cry: his legs gave way beneath him, he fell forward and reached the cap with his hands.

"Ah, that's a fine fellow!" exclaimed the Chief. "He has gained much land!"

Pahóm's servant came running up and tried to raise him, but he saw that blood was flowing from his mouth. Pahóm was dead!

The Bashkírs clicked their tongues to show their pity.

His servant picked up the spade and dug a grave long enough for Pahóm to lie in, and buried him in it. Six feet from his head to his heels was all he needed.

(Translated by Louise and Aylmer Maude)

HENRY JAMES (1843–1916) James was born in New York City of a wealthy family and was educated both in America and Europe. When, in his late twenties, he decided to devote his life to the writing of fiction, he settled first in Paris where he was friendly with the literary group which included Flaubert, Zola, and Turgenev. He settled finally in England but remained an American citizen until the year before his death.

Probably no American writer of fiction has had such far-reaching influence as Henry James. More than any writer of English of his time, he conceived of fiction as an art and dedicated his life to discovering its techniques. During his lifetime he was the "master" to many writers in America, England, and France; it is not too much to say that all serious writers in English in the twentieth century are to some extent indebted to James. His most important criticism is to be found in the essay "The Art of Fiction" and in the prefaces to his own fiction collected in *The Art of the Novel,* edited by R. P. Blackmur. Among his greatest novels are: *The American* (1877), *The Portrait of a Lady* (1881), *The Wings of the Dove* (1902), *The Ambassadors* (1903), and *The Golden Bowl* (1904).

In the years after the turn of the century, James's novels and stories achieved an unparalleled subtlety and complexity of style, organization, and theme. At the same time he was concerned with the subject which commanded his attention during the earliest years of his career — the so-called "international theme," focused upon the differences in manners and morals between Americans and Europeans. "The Jolly Corner" (1908) reflects this concern and demonstrates the highest development of James's craft.

THE JOLLY CORNER

Henry James

I

"Every one asks me what I 'think' of everything," said Spencer Brydon; "and I make answer as I can — begging or dodging the question, putting them off with any nonsense. It wouldn't matter to any of them really," he went on, "for, even were it possible to meet in that stand-and-deliver way so silly a demand on so big a subject, my 'thoughts' would still be almost altogether about something that concerns only myself." He was talking to Miss Staverton, with whom for a couple of months now he had availed himself of every possible occasion to talk; this disposition and this resource, this comfort and support, as the situation in fact presented itself, having promptly enough taken the first place in the considerable array of rather unattenuated surprises attending his so strangely belated return to America. Everything was somehow a surprise; and that might be natural when one had so long and so consistently neglected everything, taken pains to give surprises so much margin for play. He had given them more than thirty years — thirty-three, to be exact; and they now seemed to him to have organised their performance quite on the scale of that licence. He had been twenty-three on leaving New York — he was fifty-six today: unless indeed he were to reckon as he had sometimes, since his repatriation, found himself feeling; in which case he would have lived longer than is often allotted to man. It would have taken a century, he repeatedly said to himself, and said also to Alice Staverton, it would have taken a longer absence and a more averted mind than those even of which he had been guilty, to pile up the differences, the newnesses, the queernesses, above all the bignesses, for the better or the worse, that at present assaulted his vision wherever he looked.

The great fact all the while however had been the incalculability; since he *had* supposed himself, from decade to decade, to be allowing, and in the most liberal and intelligent manner, for brilliancy of change. He actually saw that he had allowed for nothing; he missed what he would have been sure of finding, he found what he would never have imagined. Proportions and values were upside-down; the ugly things he had expected, the ugly things of his far-away youth, when he had too promptly waked up to a sense of the ugly — these uncanny phenomena placed him rather, as it happened, under the charm; whereas the "swagger" things, the modern, the monstrous, the famous things, those he had more particularly, like thousands of ingenuous en- quirers every year, come over to see, were exactly his sources of dismay. They were as so many set traps for displeasure, above all for reaction, of which his restless tread was constantly pressing the spring. It was interesting, doubtless, the whole show, but it would have been too disconcerting hadn't a certain finer truth saved the situation. He had distinctly not, in this steadier light, come over *all* for the monstrosities; he had come, not only in the last analysis but quite on the face of the act, under an impulse with which they had nothing to do. He had come — putting the thing pompously — to look at his "property," which he had thus for a third of a century not been within four thousand miles of; or, expressing it less sordidly, he had yielded to the humour of seeing again his house on the jolly corner, as he usually, and quite fondly, described it — the one in which he had first seen the light, in which various members of his family had lived and had died, in which the holidays of his overschooled boyhood had been passed and the few social flowers of his chilled adolescence gathered, and which, alienated then for so long a period, had, through the successive deaths of his two brothers and the ter- mination of old arrangements, come wholly into his hands. He was the owner of another, not quite so "good" — the jolly corner having been, from far back, superlatively extended and conse- crated; and the value of the pair represented his main capital, with an income consisting, in these later years, of their respective rents which (thanks precisely to their original excellent type) had never been depressingly low. He could live in "Europe," as he had been in the habit of living, on the product of these flourish- ing New York leases, and all the better since, that of the second structure, the mere number in its long row, having within a twelvemonth fallen in, renovation at a high advance had proved beautifully possible.

These were items of property indeed, but he had found himself since his arrival distinguishing more than ever between them. The house within the street, two bristling blocks westward, was already in course of reconstruction as a tall mass of flats; he had acceded, some time before, to overtures for this conversion — in which, now that it was going forward, it had been not the least of his astonishments to find himself able, on the spot, and though without a previous ounce of such experience, to participate with a certain intelligence, almost with a certain authority. He had lived his life with his back so turned to such concerns and his face addressed to those of so different an order that he scarce knew what to make of this lively stir, in a compartment of his mind never yet penetrated, of a capacity for business and a sense for construction. These virtues, so common all round him now, had been dormant in his own organism — where it might be said of them perhaps that they had slept the sleep of the just. At present, in the splendid autumn weather — the autumn at least was a pure boon in the terrible place — he loafed about his "work" undeterred, secretly agitated; not in the least "minding" that the whole proposition, as they said, was vulgar and sordid, and ready to climb ladders, to walk the plank, to handle materials and look wise about them, to ask questions, in fine, and challenge explanations and really "go into" figures.

It amused, it verily quite charmed him; and, by the same stroke, it amused, and even more, Alice Staverton, though perhaps charming her perceptibly less. She wasn't however going to be better off for it, as *he* was — and so astonishingly much: nothing was now likely, he knew, ever to make her better off than she found herself, in the afternoon of life, as the delicately frugal possessor and tenant of the small house in Irving Place to which she had subtly managed to cling through her almost unbroken New York career. If he knew the way to it now better than to any other address among the dreadful multiplied numberings which seemed to him to reduce the whole place to some vast ledger-page, overgrown, fantastic, of ruled and criss-crossed lines and figures — if he had formed, for his consolation, that habit, it was really not a little because of the charm of his having encountered and recognised, in the vast wilderness of the wholesale, breaking through the mere gross generalisation of wealth and force and success, a small still scene where items and shades, all delicate things, kept the sharpness of the notes of a high voice perfectly trained, and where economy hung about like the scent of a garden. His old friend lived with one maid and herself, dusted her relics and trimmed her lamps and polished her silver; she stood off, in the awful modern crush, when she could, but she sallied forth and did battle when the challenge was really to "spirit," the spirit she after all confessed to, proudly and a little shyly, as to that of the better time, that of *their* common, their quite far-away and antediluvian social period and order. She made use of the street-cars when need be, the terrible things that people scrambled for as the panic-stricken at sea scramble for the boats; she affronted, inscrutably, under stress, all the public concussions and ordeals; and yet, with that slim mystifying grace of her appearance, which defied you to say if she were a fair young woman who looked older through trouble, or a fine smooth older one who looked young through successful indifference; with her precious reference, above all, to memories and histories into which he could enter, she was as exquisite for him as some pale pressed flower (a rarity to begin with), and, failing other sweetnesses, she was a sufficient reward of his effort. They had communities of knowledge, "their" knowledge (this discriminating possessive was always on her lips) of presences of the other age, presences all overlaid, in his case, by the experience of a man and the freedom of a wanderer, overlaid by pleasure, by infidelity, by passages of life that were strange and dim to her, just by "Europe" in short, but still unobscured, still exposed and cherished, under that pious visitation of the spirit from which she had never been diverted.

She had come with him one day to see how his "apartment-house" was rising; he had helped her over gaps and explained to her plans, and while they were there had happened to have, before her, a brief but lively discussion with the man in charge, the representative of the building-firm that had undertaken his work. He had found himself quite "standing-up" to this person-age over a failure on the latter's part to observe some detail of one of their noted conditions, and had so lucidly argued his case that, besides ever so prettily flushing, at the time, for sympathy in his triumph, she had afterwards said to him (though to a slightly greater effect of irony) that he had clearly for too many years neglected a real gift. If he had but stayed at home he would have anticipated the inventor of the sky-scraper. If he had but stayed at home he would have discovered his genius in time really to start some new variety of awful architectural hare and run it till it burrowed in a gold-mine. He was to remember these words, while the weeks elapsed, for the small silver ring they had sounded over the queerest and deepest of his own lately most disguised and most muffled vibrations.

It had begun to be present to him after the first fortnight, it had broken out with the oddest abruptness, this particular wanton wonderment: it met him there — and this was the image under which he himself judged the matter, or at least, not a little, thrilled and flushed with it — very much as he might have been met by some strange figure, some unexpected occupant, at a turn of one of the dim passages of an empty house. The quaint analogy quite hauntingly remained with him, when he didn't indeed rather improve it by a still intenser form: that of his opening a door behind which he would have made sure of finding nothing, a door into a room shuttered and void, and yet so coming, with a great suppressed start, on some quite erect confronting presence, something planted in the middle of the place and facing him through the dusk. After that visit to the house in construction he walked with his companion to see the other and always so much the better one, which in the eastward direction formed one of the corners, the "jolly" one precisely, of the street now so generally dishonoured and disfigured in its westward reaches, and of the comparatively conservative Avenue. The Avenue still had pretensions, as Miss Staverton said, to decency; the old people had mostly gone, the old names were unknown, and here and there an old association seemed to stray, all vaguely, like some very aged person, out too late, whom you might meet and feel the impulse to watch or follow, in kindness, for safe restoration to shelter.

They went in together, our friends; he admitted himself with his key, as he kept no one there, he explained, preferring, for his reasons, to leave the place empty, under a simple arrangement with a good woman living in the neighbourhood and who came for a daily hour to open windows and dust and sweep. Spencer

Brydon had his reasons and was growingly aware of them; they
seemed to him better each time he was there, though he didn't
name them all to his companion, any more than he told her as
yet how often, how quite absurdly often, he himself came. He
only let her see for the present, while they walked through the
great blank rooms, that absolute vacancy reigned and that, from
top to bottom, there was nothing but Mrs. Muldoon's broom-
stick, in a corner, to tempt the burglar. Mrs. Muldoon was then
on the premises, and she loquaciously attended the visitors, preceding them from room to room and pushing back shutters and
throwing up sashes — all to show them, as she remarked, how little there was to see. There was little indeed to see in the great
gaunt shell where the main dispositions and the general appor-
tionment of space, the style of an age of ampler allowances, had
nevertheless for its master their honest pleading message, affecting him as some good old servant's, some lifelong retainer's appeal for a character, or even for a retiring-pension; yet it was also
a remark of Mrs. Muldoon's that, glad as she was to oblige him
by her noonday round, there was a request she greatly hoped he
would never make of her. If he should wish her for any reason to
come in after dark she would just tell him, if he "plased," that he
must ask it of somebody else.

The fact that there was nothing to see didn't militate for the
worthy woman against what one *might* see, and she put it frankly
to Miss Staverton that no lady could be expected to like, could
she? "scraping up to thim top storeys in the ayvil hours." The
gas and the electric light were off the house, and she fairly evoked
a gruesome vision of her march through the great grey rooms —
so many of them as there were too! — with her glimmering taper.
Miss Staverton met her honest glare with a smile and the profession that she herself certainly would recoil from such an
adventure. Spencer Brydon meanwhile held his peace — for the
moment; the question of the "evil" hours in his old home had
already become too grave for him. He had begun some time
since to "crape," and he knew just why a packet of candles addressed to that pursuit had been stowed by his own hand, three
weeks before, at the back of a drawer of the fine old sideboard
that occupied, as a "fixture," the deep recess in the dining-room.
Just now he laughed at his companions — quickly however
changing the subject; for the reason that, in the first place, his

laugh struck him even at that moment as starting the odd echo, the conscious human resonance (he scarce knew how to qualify it) that sounds made while he was there alone sent back to his ear or his fancy; and that, in the second, he imagined Alice Staverton for the instant on the point of asking him, with a divination, if he ever so prowled. There were divinations he was unprepared for, and he had at all events averted enquiry by the time Mrs. Muldoon had left them, passing on to other parts.

There was happily enough to say, on so consecrated a spot, that could be said freely and fairly; so that a whole train of declarations was precipitated by his friend's having herself broken out, after a yearning look round: "But I hope you don't mean they want you to pull *this* to pieces!" His answer came, promptly, with his re-awakened wrath: it was of course exactly what they wanted, and what they were "at" him for, daily, with the iteration of people who couldn't for their life understand a man's liability to decent feelings. He had found the place, just as it stood and beyond what he could express, an interest and a joy. There were values other than the beastly rent-values, and in short, in short — ! But it was thus Miss Staverton took him up. "In short you're to make so good a thing of your sky-scraper that, living in luxury on *those* ill-gotten gains, you can afford for a while to be sentimental here!" Her smile had for him, with the words, the particular mild irony with which he found half her talk suffused; an irony without bitterness and that came, exactly, from her having so much imagination — not, like the cheap sarcasms with which one heard most people, about the world of "society," bid for the reputation of cleverness, from nobody's really having any. It was agreeable to him at this very moment to be sure that when he had answered, after a brief demur, "Well yes: so, precisely, you may put it!" her imagination would still do him justice. He explained that even if never a dollar were to come to him from the other house he would nevertheless cherish this one; and he dwelt, further, while they lingered and wandered, on the fact of the stupefaction he was already exciting, the positive mystification he felt himself create.

He spoke of the value of all he read into it, into the mere sight of the walls, mere shapes of the rooms, mere sound of the floors, mere feel, in his hand, of the old silver-plated knobs of the several mahogany doors, which suggested the pressure of the palms of the dead; the seventy years of the past in fine that these things represented, the annals of nearly three generations, counting his grandfather's, the one that had ended there, and the impalpable ashes of his long-extinct youth, afloat in the very air like microscopic motes. She listened to everything; she was a woman who answered intimately but who utterly didn't chatter. She scattered abroad therefore no cloud of words; she could assent, she could agree, above all she could encourage, without doing that. Only at the last she went a little further than he had done himself. "And then how do you know? You may still, after all, want to live here." It rather indeed pulled him up, for it wasn't what he had been thinking, at least in her sense of the words. "You mean I may decide to stay on for the sake of it?"

"Well, *with* such a home — !" But, quite beautifully, she had too much tact to dot so monstrous an *i*, and it was precisely an illustration of the way she didn't rattle. How could any one — of any wit — insist on any one else's "wanting" to live in New York?

"Oh," he said, "I *might* have lived here (since I had my opportunity early in life); I might have put in here all these years. Then everything would have been different enough — and, I dare say, 'funny' enough. But that's another matter. And then the beauty of it — I mean of my perversity, of my refusal to agree to a 'deal' — is just in the total absence of a reason. Don't you see that if I had a reason about the matter at all it would *have* to be the other way, and would then be inevitably a reason of dollars? There are no reasons here *but* of dollars. Let us therefore have none whatever — not the ghost of one."

They were back in the hall then for departure, but from where they stood the vista was large, through an open door, into the great square main saloon, with its almost antique felicity of brave spaces between windows. Her eyes came back from that reach and met his own a moment. "Are you very sure the 'ghost' of one doesn't, much rather, serve — ?"

He had a positive sense of turning pale. But it was as near as they were then to come. For he made answer, he believed, between a glare and a grin: "Oh ghosts — of course the place must swarm with them! I should be ashamed of it if it didn't. Poor Mrs. Muldoon's right, and it's why I haven't asked her to do more than look in."

Miss Staverton's gaze again lost itself, and things she didn't utter, it was clear, came and went in her mind. She might even for the minute, off there in the fine room, have imagined some element dimly gathering. Simplified like the death-mask of a handsome face, it perhaps produced for her just then an effect akin to the stir of an expression in the "set" commemorative plaster. Yet whatever her impression may have been she produced instead a vague platitude. "Well, if it were only furnished and lived in — !"

She appeared to imply that in case of its being still furnished he might have been a little less opposed to the idea of a return. But she passed straight into the vestibule, as if to leave her words behind her, and the next moment he had opened the house-door and was standing with her on the steps. He closed the door and, while he re-pocketed his key, looking up and down, they took in the comparatively harsh actuality of the Avenue, which reminded him of the assault of the outer light of the Desert on the traveller emerging from an Egyptian tomb. But he risked before they stepped into the street his gathered answer to her speech. "For me it *is* lived in. For me it *is* furnished." At which it was easy for her to sigh "Ah yes — !" all vaguely and discreetly; since his parents and his favourite sister, to say nothing of other kin, in numbers, had run their course and met their end there. That represented, within the walls, ineffaceable life.

It was a few days after this that, during an hour passed with her again, he had expressed his impatience of the too flattering curiosity — among the people he met — about his appreciation of New York. He had arrived at none at all that was socially producible, and as for that matter of his "thinking" (thinking the better or the worse of anything there) he was wholly taken up with one subject of thought. It was mere vain egoism, and it was moreover, if she liked, a morbid obsession. He found all things come back to the question of what he personally might have been, how he might have led his life and "turned out," if he had not so, at the outset, given it up. And confessing for the first time to the intensity within him of this absurd speculation — which but proved also, no doubt, the habit of too selfishly thinking — he affirmed the impotence there of any other source of interest, any other native appeal. "What would it have made of me, what would it have made of me? I keep for ever wondering, all idiot-

ically; as if I could possibly know! I see what it has made of
dozens of others, those I meet, and it positively aches within me,
to the point of exasperation, that it would have made something
of me as well. Only I can't make out *what,* and the worry of it,
the small rage of curiosity never to be satisfied, brings back what
I remember to have felt, once or twice, after judging best, for
reasons, to burn some important letter unopened. I've been sorry,
I've hated it — I've never known what was in the letter. You may
of course say it's a trifle — !"

"I don't say it's a trifle," Miss Staverton gravely interrupted.
She was seated by her fire, and before her, on his feet and restless, he turned to and fro between this intensity of his idea and
a fitful and unseeing inspection, through his single eyeglass, of
the dear little old objects on her chimney-piece. Her interruption
made him for an instant look at her harder. "I shouldn't care
if you did!" he laughed, however; "and it's only a figure, at any
rate, for the way I now feel. *Not* to have followed my perverse
young course — and almost in the teeth of my father's curse, as
I may say; not to have kept it up, so, 'over there,' from that day
to this, without a doubt or a pang; not, above all, to have liked
it, to have loved it, so much, loved it, no doubt, with such an
abysmal conceit of my own preference: some variation from *that,*
I say, must have produced some different effect for my life and
for my 'form.' I should have stuck here — if it had been possible;
and I was too young, at twenty-three, to judge, *pour deux sous,*
whether it *were* possible. If I had waited I might have seen it
was, and then I might have been, by staying here, something
nearer to one of these types who have been hammered so hard
and made so keen by their conditions. It isn't that I admire them
so much — the question of any charm in them, or of any charm,
beyond that of the rank money-passion, exerted by their conditions *for* them, has nothing to do with the matter: it's only a
question of what fantastic, yet perfectly possible, development of
my own nature I mayn't have missed. It comes over me that I
had then a strange *alter ego* deep down somewhere within me, as
the full-blown flower is in the small tight bud, and that I just
took the course, I just transferred him to the climate, that
blighted him for once and for ever."

"And you wonder about the flower," Miss Staverton said. "So
do I, if you want to know; and so I've been wondering these

several weeks. I believe in the flower," she continued, "I feel it would have been quite splendid, quite huge and monstrous."

"Monstrous above all!" her visitor echoed; "and I imagine, by the same stroke, quite hideous and offensive."

"You don't believe that," she returned; "if you did you wouldn't wonder. You'd know, and that would be enough for you. What you feel — and what I feel *for* you — is that you'd have had power."

"You'd have liked me that way?" he asked.

She barely hung fire. "How should I not have liked you?"

"I see. You'd have liked me, have preferred me, a billionaire!"

"How should I not have liked you?" she simply again asked.

He stood before her still — her question kept him motionless. He took it in, so much there was of it; and indeed his not otherwise meeting it testified to that. "I know at least what I am," he simply went on; "the other side of the medal's clear enough. I've not been edifying — I believe I'm thought in a hundred quarters to have been barely decent. I've followed strange paths and worshipped strange gods; it must have come to you again and again — in fact you've admitted to me as much — that I was leading, at any time these thirty years, a selfish frivolous scandalous life. And you see what it has made of me."

She just waited, smiling at him. "You see what it has made of *me*."

"Oh you're a person whom nothing can have altered. You were born to be what you are, anywhere, anyway: you've the perfection nothing else could have blighted. And don't you see how, without my exile, I shouldn't have been waiting till now — ?" But he pulled up for the strange pang.

"The great thing to see," she presently said, "seems to me to be that it has spoiled nothing. It hasn't spoiled your being here at last. It hasn't spoiled this. It hasn't spoiled your speaking — " She also however faltered.

He wondered at everything her controlled emotion might mean. "Do you believe then — too dreadfully! — that I *am* as good as I might ever have been?"

"Oh no! Far from it!" With which she got up from her chair and was nearer to him. "But I don't care," she smiled.

"You mean I'm good enough?"

She considered a little. "Will you believe it if I say so? I mean

will you let that settle your question for you?" And then as if
making out in his face that he drew back from this, that he had
some idea which, however absurd, he couldn't yet bargain away:
"Oh you don't care either — but very differently: you don't care
for anything but yourself."

Spencer Brydon recognised it — it was in fact what he had
absolutely professed. Yet he importantly qualified. "*He* isn't
myself. He's the just so totally other person. But I do want to
see him," he added. "And I can. And I shall."

Their eyes met for a minute while he guessed from something
in hers that she divined his strange sense. But neither of them
otherwise expressed it, and her apparent understanding, with no
protesting shock, no easy derision, touched him more deeply than
anything yet, constituting for his stifled perversity, on the spot,
an element that was like breathable air. What she said however
was unexpected. "Well, *I've* seen him."

"You — ?"

"I've seen him in a dream."

"Oh a 'dream' — !" It let him down.

"But twice over," she continued. "I saw him as I see you now."

"You've dreamed the same dream — ?"

"Twice over," she repeated. "The very same."

This did somehow a little speak to him, as it also gratified
him. "You dream about me at that rate?"

"Ah about *him!*" she smiled.

His eyes again sounded her. "Then you know all about him."
And as she said nothing more: "What's the wretch like?"

She hesitated, and it was as if he were pressing her so hard that,
resisting for reasons of her own, she had to turn away. "I'll tell
you some other time!"

II

It was after this that there was most of a virtue for him, most
of a cultivated charm, most of a preposterous secret thrill, in
the particular form of surrender to his obsession and of address
to what he more and more believed to be his privilege. It was
what in these weeks he was living for — since he really felt life
to begin but after Mrs. Muldoon had retired from the scene
and, visiting the ample house from attic to cellar, making sure
he was alone, he knew himself in safe possession and, as he tacitly
expressed it, let himself go. He sometimes came twice in the

twenty-four hours; the moments he liked best were those of gathering dusk, of the short autumn twilight; this was the time of which, again and again, he found himself hoping most. Then he could, as seemed to him, most intimately wander and wait, linger and listen, feel his fine attention, never in his life before so fine, on the pulse of the great vague place: he preferred the lampless hour and only wished he might have prolonged each day the deep crepuscular spell. Later — rarely much before midnight, but then for a considerable vigil — he watched with his glimmering light; moving slowly, holding it high, playing it far, rejoicing above all, as much as he might, in open vistas, reaches of communication between rooms and by passages; the long straight chance or show, as he would have called it, for the revelation he pretended to invite. It was a practice he found he could perfectly "work" without exciting remark; no one was in the least the wiser for it; even Alice Staverton, who was moreover a well of discretion, didn't quite fully imagine.

He let himself in and let himself out with the assurance of calm proprietorship; and accident so far favoured him that, if a fat Avenue "officer" had happened on occasion to see him entering at eleven-thirty, he had never yet, to the best of his belief, been noticed as emerging at two. He walked there on the crisp November nights, arrived regularly at the evening's end; it was as easy to do this after dining out as to take his way to a club or to his hotel. When he left his club, if he hadn't been dining out, it was ostensibly to go to his hotel; and when he left his hotel, if he had spent a part of the evening there, it was ostensibly to go to his club. Everything was easy in fine; everything conspired and promoted: there was truly even in the strain of his experience something that glossed over, something that salved and simplified, all the rest of consciousness. He circulated, talked, renewed, loosely and pleasantly, old relations — met indeed, so far as he could, new expectations and seemed to make out on the whole that in spite of the career, of such different contacts, which he had spoken of to Miss Staverton as ministering so little, for those who might have watched it, to edification, he was positively rather liked than not. He was a dim secondary social success — and all with people who had truly not an idea of him. It was all mere surface sound, this murmur of their welcome, this popping of their corks — just as his gestures of response were the extravagant shadows, emphatic in proportion as they meant little, of some game of *ombres chinoises*. He projected himself all day, in thought, straight over the bristling line of hard unconscious heads and into the other, the real, the waiting life; the life that, as soon as he had heard behind him the click of his great house-door, began for him, on the jolly corner, as beguilingly as the slow opening bars of some rich music follows the tap of the conductor's wand.

He always caught the first effect of the steel point of his stick on the old marble of the hall pavement, large black-and-white squares that he remembered as the admiration of his childhood and that had then made in him, as he now saw, for the growth of an early conception of style. This effect was the dim reverber-ating tinkle as of some far-off bell hung who should say where? — in the depths of the house, of the past, of that mystical other world that might have flourished for him had he not, for weal or woe, abandoned it. On this impression he did ever the same thing; he put his stick noiselessly away in a corner — feeling the place once more in the likeness of some great glass bowl, all pre-cious concave crystal, set delicately humming by the play of a moist finger round its edge. The concave crystal held, as it were, this mystical other world, and the indescribably fine murmur of its rim was the sigh there, the scarce audible pathetic wail to his strained ear, of all the old baffled forsworn possibilities. What he did therefore by this appeal of his hushed presence was to wake them into such measure of ghostly life as they might still enjoy. They were shy, all but unappeasably shy, but they weren't really sinister; at least they weren't as he had hitherto felt them — before they had taken the Form he so yearned to make them take, the Form he at moments saw himself in the light of fairly hunting on tiptoe, the points of his evening-shoes, from room to room and from storey to storey.

That was the essence of his vision — which was all rank folly, if one would, while he was out of the house and otherwise occu-pied, but which took on the last verisimilitude as soon as he was placed and posted. He knew what he meant and what he wanted; it was as clear as the figure on a cheque presented in demand for cash. His *alter ego* "walked" — that was the note of his image of him, while his image of his motive for his own odd pastime was the desire to waylay him and meet him. He roamed, slowly, warily, but all restlessly, he himself did — Mrs. Muldoon had been right, absolutely, with her figure of their "craping"; and the presence he watched for would roam restlessly too. But it would be as cautious and as shifty; the conviction of its probable, in fact its already quite sensible, quite audible evasion of pursuit grew for him from night to night, laying on him finally a rigour to which nothing in his life had been comparable. It had been the theory of many superficially-judging persons, he knew, that he was wasting that life in a surrender to sensations, but he had tasted of no pleasure so fine as his actual tension, had been introduced to no sport that demanded at once the patience and the nerve of this stalking of a creature more subtle, yet at bay perhaps more formidable, than any beast of the forest. The terms, the comparisons, the very practices of the chase positively came again into play; there were even moments when passages of his occasional experience as a sportsman, stirred memories, from his younger time, of moor and mountain and desert, revived for him — and to the increase of his keenness — by the tremendous force of analogy. He found himself at moments — once he had placed his single light on some mantel-shelf or in some recess — stepping back into shelter or shade, effacing himself behind a door or in an embrasure, as he had sought of old the vantage of rock and tree; he found himself holding his breath and living in the joy of the instant, the supreme suspense created by big game alone.

He wasn't afraid (though putting himself the question as he believed gentlemen on Bengal tiger-shoots or in close quarters with the great bear of the Rockies had been known to confess to having put it); and this indeed — since here at least he might be frank! — because of the impression, so intimate and so strange, that he himself produced as yet a dread, produced certainly a strain, beyond the liveliest he was likely to feel. They fell for him into categories, they fairly became familiar, the signs, for his own perception, of the alarm his presence and his vigilance created; though leaving him always to remark, portentously, on his probably having formed a relation, his probably enjoying a consciousness, unique in the experience of man. People enough, first and last, had been in terror of apparitions, but who had ever before so turned the tables and become himself, in the apparitional world, an incalculable terror? He might have found this sublime had he quite dared to think of it; but he didn't too much insist, truly, on that side of his privilege. With habit and repetition he gained to an extraordinary degree the power to penetrate the dusk of distances and the darkness of corners, to resolve back into their innocence the treacheries of uncertain light, the evil-looking forms taken in the gloom by mere shadows, by accidents of the air, by shifting effects of perspective; putting down his dim luminary he could still wander on without it, pass into other rooms and, only knowing it was there behind him in case of need, see his way about, visually project for his purpose a comparative clearness. It made him feel, this acquired faculty, like some monstrous stealthy cat; he wondered if he would have glared at these moments with large shining yellow eyes, and what it mightn't verily be, for the poor hard-pressed *alter ego,* to be confronted with such a type.

He liked however the open shutters; he opened everywhere those Mrs. Muldoon had closed, closing them as carefully afterwards, so that she shouldn't notice: he liked — oh this he did like, and above all in the upper rooms! — the sense of the hard silver of the autumn stars through the window-panes, and scarcely less the flare of the street-lamps below, the white electric lustre which it would have taken curtains to keep out. This was human actual social; this was of the world he had lived in, and he was more at his ease certainly for the countenance, coldly general and impersonal, that all the while and in spite of his detachment it seemed to give him. He had support of course mostly in the rooms at the wide front and the prolonged side; it failed him considerably in the central shades and the parts at the back. But if he sometimes, on his rounds, was glad of his optical reach, so none the less often the rear of the house affected him as the very jungle of his prey. The place was there more subdivided; a large "extension" in particular, where small rooms for servants had been multiplied, abounded in nooks and corners, in closets and passages, in the ramifications especially of an ample back staircase over which he leaned, many a time, to look far down — not deterred from his gravity even while aware that he might, for a spectator, have figured some solemn simpleton playing at hide-and-seek. Outside in fact he might himself make that ironic *rapprochement;* but within the walls, and in spite of the clear windows, his consistency was proof against the cynical light of New York.

It had belonged to that idea of the exasperated consciousness of his victim to become a real test for him; since he had quite put it to himself from the first that, oh distinctly! he could "cultivate" his whole perception. He had felt it as above all open to cultivation — which indeed was but another name for his manner of spending his time. He was bringing it on, bringing it to perfection, by practice; in consequence of which it had grown so fine that he was now aware of impressions, attestations of his general postulate, that couldn't have broken upon him at once. This was the case more specifically with a phenomenon at last quite frequent for him in the upper rooms, the recognition — absolutely unmistakable, and by a turn dating from a particular hour, his resumption of his campaign after a diplomatic drop, a calculated absence of three nights — of his being definitely followed, tracked at a distance carefully taken and to the express end that he should the less confidently, less arrogantly, appear to himself merely to pursue. It worried, it finally quite broke him up, for it proved, of all the conceivable impressions, the one least suited to his book. He was kept in sight while remaining himself — as regards the essence of his position — sightless, and his only recourse then was in abrupt turns, rapid recoveries of ground. He wheeled about, retracing his steps, as if he might so catch in his face at least the stirred air of some other quick revolution. It was indeed true that his fully dislocalised thought of these manœuvres recalled to him Pantaloon, at the Christmas farce, buffeted and tricked from behind by ubiquitous Harlequin; but it left intact the influence of the conditions themselves each time he was re-exposed to them, so that in fact this association, had he suffered it to become constant, would on a certain side have but ministered to his intenser gravity. He had made, as I have said, to create on the premises the baseless sense of a reprieve, his three absences; and the result of the third was to confirm the after-effect of the second.

On his return, that night — the night succeeding his last intermission — he stood in the hall and looked up the staircase with a certainty more intimate than any he had yet known. "He's *there*, at the top, and waiting — not, as in general, falling back

for disappearance. He's holding his ground, and it's the first time
— which is a proof, isn't it? that something has happened for
him." So Brydon argued with his hand on the banister and his
foot on the lowest stair; in which position he felt as never before
the air chilled by his logic. He himself turned cold in it, for he
seemed of a sudden to know what now was involved. "Harder
pressed? — yes, he takes it in, with its thus making clear to him
that I've come, as they say, 'to stay.' He finally doesn't like and
can't bear it, in the sense, I mean, that his wrath, his menaced
interest, now balances with his dread. I've hunted him till he has
'turned': that, up there, is what has happened — he's the fanged
or the antlered animal brought at last to bay." There came to
him, as I say — but determined by an influence beyond my no-
tation! — the acuteness of this certainty; under which however
the next moment he had broken into a sweat that he would as
little have consented to attribute to fear as he would have dared
immediately to act upon it for enterprise. It marked none the
less a prodigious thrill, a thrill that represented sudden dismay,
no doubt, but also represented, and with the selfsame throb, the
strangest, the most joyous, possibly the next minute almost the
proudest, duplication of consciousness.

"He has been dodging, retreating, hiding, but now, worked up
to anger, he'll fight!" — this intense impression made a single
mouthful, as it were, of terror and applause. But what was wondrous was that the applause, for the felt fact, was so eager, since,
if it was his other self he was running to earth, this ineffable
identity was thus in the last resort not unworthy of him. It
bristled there — somewhere near at hand, however unseen still
— as the hunted thing, even as the trodden worm of the adage
must at last bristle; and Brydon at this instant tasted probably
of a sensation more complex than had ever before found itself
consistent with sanity. It was as if it would have shamed him
that a character so associated with his own should triumphantly
succeed in just skulking, should to the end not risk the open, so
that the drop of this danger was, on the spot, a great lift of the
whole situation. Yet with another rare shift of the same subtlety
he was already trying to measure by how much more he himself
might now be in peril of fear; so rejoicing that he could, in another form, actively inspire that fear, and simultaneously quak-
ing for the form in which he might passively know it.

The apprehension of knowing it must after a little have grown in him, and the strangest moment of his adventure perhaps, the most memorable or really most interesting, afterwards, of his crisis, was the lapse of certain instants of concentrated conscious *combat*, the sense of a need to hold on to something, even after the manner of a man slipping and slipping on some awful incline; the vivid impulse, above all, to move, to act, to charge, somehow and upon something — to show himself, in a word, that he wasn't afraid. The state of "holding-on" was thus the state to which he was momentarily reduced; if there had been anything, in the great vacancy, to seize, he would presently have been aware of having clutched it as he might under a shock at home have clutched the nearest chair-back. He had been surprised at any rate — of this he *was* aware — into something unprecedented since his original appropriation of the place; he had closed his eyes, held them tight, for a long minute, as with that instinct of dismay and that terror of vision. When he opened them the room, the other contiguous rooms, extraordinarily, seemed lighter — so light, almost, that at first he took the change for day. He stood firm, however that might be, just where he had paused; his resistance had helped him — it was as if there were something he had tided over. He knew after a little what this was — it had been in the imminent danger of flight. He had stiffened his will against going; without this he would have made for the stairs, and it seemed to him that, still with his eyes closed, he would have descended them, would have known how, straight and swiftly, to the bottom.

Well, as he had held out, here he was — still at the top, among the more intricate upper rooms and with the gauntlet of the others, of all the rest of the house, still to run when it should be his time to go. He would go at his time — only at his time: didn't he go every night very much at the same hour? He took out his watch — there was light for that: it was scarcely a quarter past one, and he had never withdrawn so soon. He reached his lodgings for the most part at two — with his walk of a quarter of an hour. He would wait for the last quarter — he wouldn't stir till then; and he kept his watch there with his eye on it, reflecting while he held it that this deliberate wait, a wait with an effort, which he recognised, would serve perfectly for the attestation he desired to make. It would prove his courage — unless

indeed the latter might most be proved by his budging at last
from his place. What he mainly felt now was that, since he hadn't
originally scuttled, he had his dignities — which had never in his
life seemed so many — all to preserve and to carry aloft. This
was before him in truth as a physical image, an image almost
worthy of an age of greater romance. That remark indeed glimmered for him only to glow the next instant with a finer light;
since what age of romance, after all, could have matched either
the state of his mind or, "objectively," as they said, the wonder
of his situation? The only difference would have been that,
brandishing his dignities over his head as in a parchment scroll,
he might then — that is in the heroic time — have proceeded
downstairs with a drawn sword in his other grasp.

At present, really, the light he had set down on the mantel
of the next room would have to figure his sword; which utensil,
in the course of a minute, he had taken the requisite number of
steps to possess himself of. The door between the rooms was
open, and from the second another door opened to a third.
These rooms, as he remembered, gave all three upon a common
corridor as well, but there was a fourth, beyond them, without
issue save through the preceding. To have moved, to have heard
his step again, was appreciably a help; though even in recognis-
ing this he lingered once more a little by the chimney-piece on
which his light had rested. When he next moved, just hesitating
where to turn, he found himself considering a circumstance that,
after his first and comparatively vague apprehension of it, produced in him the start that often attends some pang of recollection, the violent shock of having ceased happily to forget. He
had come into sight of the door in which the brief chain of communication ended and which he now surveyed from the nearer
threshold, the one not directly facing it. Placed at some distance
to the left of this point, it would have admitted him to the last
room of the four, the room without other approach or egress,
had it not, to his intimate conviction, been closed *since* his
former visitation, the matter probably of a quarter of an hour
before. He stared with all his eyes at the wonder of the fact,
arrested again where he stood and again holding his breath while
he sounded its sense. Surely it had been *subsequently* closed —
that is it had been on his previous passage indubitably open!

He took it full in the face that something had happened between — that he couldn't not have noticed before (by which he
meant on his original tour of all the rooms that evening) that
such a barrier had exceptionally presented itself. He had indeed
since that moment undergone an agitation so extraordinary that
it might have muddled for him any earlier view; and he tried to
convince himself that he might perhaps then have gone into the
room and, inadvertently, automatically, on coming out, have
drawn the door after him. The difficulty was that this exactly
was what he never did; it was against his whole policy, as he
might have said, the essence of which was to keep vistas clear.
He had them from the first, as he was well aware, quite on the
brain: the strange apparition, at the far end of one of them, of
his baffled "prey" (which had become by so sharp an irony so little the term now to apply!) was the form of success his imagination had most cherished, projecting into it always a refinement
of beauty. He had known fifty times the start of perception that
had afterwards dropped; had fifty times gasped to himself
"There!" under some fond brief hallucination. The house, as the
case stood, admirably lent itself; he might wonder at the taste,
the native architecture of the particular time, which could rejoice
so in the multiplication of doors — the opposite extreme to the
modern, the actual almost complete proscription of them; but it
had fairly contributed to provoke this obsession of the presence
encountered telescopically, as he might say, focussed and studied
in diminishing perspective and as by a rest for the elbow.

It was with these considerations that his present attention was
charged — they perfectly availed to make what he saw porten-
tous. He *couldn't,* by any lapse, have blocked that aperture; and
if he hadn't, if it was unthinkable, why what else was clear but
that there had been another agent? Another agent? — he had
been catching, as he felt, a moment back, the very breath of him;
but when had he been so close as in this simple, this logical, this
completely personal act? It was so logical, that is, that one might
have *taken* it for personal; yet for what did Brydon take it, he
asked himself, while, softly panting, he felt his eyes almost leave
their sockets. Ah this time at last they *were,* the two, the opposed
projections of him, in presence; and this time, as much as one
would, the question of danger loomed. With it rose, as not be-

fore, the question of courage — for what he knew the blank
face of the door to say to him was "Show us how much you
have!" It stared, it glared back at him with that challenge; it put
to him the two alternatives: should he just push it open or not?
Oh to have this consciousness was to *think* — and to think, Brydon knew, as he stood there, was, with the lapsing moments, not
to have acted! Not to have acted — that was the misery and the
pang — was even still not to act; was in fact *all* to feel the thing
in another, in a new and terrible way. How long did he pause
and how long did he debate? There was presently nothing to
measure it; for his vibration had already changed — as just by
the effect of its intensity. Shut up there, at bay, defiant, and with
the prodigy of the thing palpably proveably *done,* thus giving
notice like some stark signboard — under that accession of accent the situation itself had turned; and Brydon at last remarkably made up his mind on what it had turned to.

It had turned altogether to a different admonition; to a supreme hint, for him, of the value of Discretion! This slowly
dawned, no doubt — for it could take its time; so perfectly, on
his threshold, had he been stayed, so little as yet had he either
advanced or retreated. It was the strangest of all things that now
when, by his taking ten steps and applying his hand to a latch,
or even his shoulder and his knee, if necessary, to a panel, all
the hunger of his prime need might have been met, his high
curiosity crowned, his unrest assuaged — it was amazing, but it
was also exquisite and rare, that insistence should have, at a
touch, quite dropped from him. Discretion — he jumped at that;
and yet not, verily, at such a pitch, because it saved his nerves or
his skin, but because, much more valuably, it saved the situation.
When I say he "jumped" at it I feel the consonance of this term
with the fact that — at the end indeed of I know not how long
— he did move again, he crossed straight to the door. He
wouldn't touch it — it seemed now that he might *if* he would:
he would only just wait there a little, to show, to prove, that he
wouldn't. He had thus another station, close to the thin partition by which revelation was denied him; but with his eyes bent
and his hands held off in a mere intensity of stillness. He listened
as if there had been something to hear, but this attitude, while
it lasted, was his own communication. "If you won't then —
good: I spare you and I give up. You affect me as by the appeal

positively for pity: you convince me that for reasons rigid and sublime — what do I know? — we both of us should have suffered. I respect them then, and, though moved and privileged as, I believe, it has never been given to man, I retire, I renounce — never, on my honour, to try again. So rest for ever — and let *me!*"

That, for Brydon was the deep sense of this last demonstration — solemn, measured, directed, as he felt it to be. He brought it to a close, he turned away; and now verily he knew how deeply he had been stirred. He retraced his steps, taking up his candle, burnt, he observed, well-nigh to the socket, and marking again, lighten it as he would, the distinctness of his footfall; after which, in a moment, he knew himself at the other side of the house. He did here what he had not yet done at these hours — he opened half a casement, one of those in the front, and let in the air of the night; a thing he would have taken at any time previous for a sharp rupture of his spell. His spell was broken now, and it didn't matter — broken by his concession and his surrender, which made it idle henceforth that he should ever come back. The empty street — its other life so marked even by the great lamplit vacancy — was within call, within touch; he stayed there as to be in it again, high above it though he was still perched; he watched as for some comforting common fact, some vulgar human note, the passage of a scavenger or a thief, some night-bird however base. He would have blessed that sign of life; he would have welcomed positively the slow approach of his friend the policeman, whom he had hitherto only sought to avoid, and was not sure that if the patrol had come into sight he mightn't have felt the impulse to get into relation with it, to hail it, on some pretext, from his fourth floor.

The pretext that wouldn't have been too silly or too compromising, the explanation that would have saved his dignity and kept his name, in such a case, out of the papers, was not definite to him: he was so occupied with the thought of recording his Discretion — as an effect of the vow he had just uttered to his intimate adversary — that the importance of this loomed large and something had overtaken all ironically his sense of proportion. If there had been a ladder applied to the front of the house, even one of the vertiginous perpendiculars employed by painters and roofers and sometimes left standing overnight, he would have managed somehow, astride of the window-sill, to compass

by outstretched leg and arm that mode of descent. If there had
been some such uncanny thing as he had found in his room at
hotels, a workable fire-escape in the form of notched cable or a
canvas shoot, he would have availed himself of it as a proof —
well, of his present delicacy. He nursed that sentiment, as the
question stood, a little in vain, and even — at the end of he
scarce knew, once more, how long — found it, as by the action
on his mind of the failure of response of the outer world,
sinking back to vague anguish. It seemed to him he had waited
an age for some stir of the great grim hush; the life of the town
was itself under a spell — so unnaturally, up and down the whole
prospect of known and rather ugly objects, the blankness and
the silence lasted. Had they ever, he asked himself, the hard-
faced houses, which had begun to look livid in the dim dawn,
had they ever spoken so little to any need of his spirit? Great
builded voids, great crowded stillnesses put on, often, in the
heart of cities, for the small hours, a sort of sinister mask, and it
was of this large collective negation that Brydon presently became conscious — all the more that the break of day was, almost
incredibly, now at hand, proving to him what a night he had
made of it.

He looked again at his watch, saw what had become of his
time-values (he had taken hours for minutes — not, as in other
tense situations, minutes for hours) and the strange air of the
streets was but the weak, the sullen flush of a dawn in which
everything was still locked up. His choked appeal from his own
open window had been the sole note of life, and he could but
break off at last as for a worse despair. Yet while so deeply de-
moralised he was capable again of an impulse denoting — at least
by his present measure — extraordinary resolution; of retracing
his steps to the spot where he had turned cold with the extinction
of his last pulse of doubt as to there being in the place another
presence than his own. This required an effort strong enough to
sicken him; but he had his reason, which over-mastered for the
moment everything else. There was the whole of the rest of the
house to traverse, and how should he screw himself to that if the
door he had seen closed were at present open? He could hold to
the idea that the closing had practically been for him an act of
mercy, a chance offered him to descend, depart, get off the ground

and never again profane it. This conception held together, it worked; but what it meant for him depended now clearly on the amount of forbearance his recent action, or rather his recent inaction, had engendered. The image of the "presence," whatever it was, waiting there for him to go — this image had not yet been so concrete for his nerves as when he stopped short of the point at which certainty would have come to him. For, with all his resolution, or more exactly with all his dread, he did stop short — he hung back from really seeing. The risk was too great and his fear too definite: it took at this moment an awful specific form.

He knew — yes, as he had never known anything — that, *should* he see the door open, it would all too abjectly be the end of him. It would mean that the agent of his shame — for his shame was the deep abjection — was once more at large and in general possession; and what glared him thus in the face was the act that this would determine for him. It would send him straight about to the window he had left open, and by that window, be long ladder and dangling rope as absent as they would, he saw himself uncontrollably insanely fatally take his way to the street. The hideous chance of this he at least could avert; but he could only avert it by recoiling in time from assurance. He had the whole house to deal with, this fact was still there; only he now knew that uncertainty alone could start him. He stole back from where he had checked himself — merely to do so was suddenly like safety — and, making blindly for the greater staircase, left gaping rooms and sounding passages behind. Here was the top of the stairs, with a fine large dim descent and three spacious landings to mark off. His instinct was all for mildness, but his feet were harsh on the floors, and, strangely, when he had in a couple of minutes become aware of this, it counted somehow for help. He couldn't have spoken, the tone of his voice would have scared him, and the common conceit or resource of "whistling in the dark" (whether literally or figuratively) have appeared basely vulgar; yet he liked none the less to hear himself go, and when he had reached his first landing — taking it all with no rush, but quite steadily — that stage of success drew from him a gasp of relief.

The house, withal, seemed immense, the scale of space again

inordinate; the open rooms, to no one of which his eyes deflected, gloomed in their shuttered state like mouths of caverns; only the high skylight that formed the crown of the deep well created for him a medium in which he could advance, but which might have been, for queerness of colour, some watery under-world. He tried to think of something noble, as that his property was really grand, a splendid possession; but this nobleness took the form too of the clear delight with which he was finally to sacrifice it. They might come in now, the builders, the destroyers — they might come as soon as they would. At the end of two flights he had dropped to another zone, and from the middle of the third, with only one more left, he recognised the influence of the lower windows, of half-drawn blinds, of the occasional gleam of street-lamps, of the glazed spaces of the vestibule. This was the bottom of the sea, which showed an illumination of its own and which he even saw paved — when at a given moment he drew up to sink a long look over the banisters — with the marble squares of his childhood. By that time indubitably he felt, as he might have said in a commoner cause, better; it had allowed him to stop and draw breath, and the ease increased with the sight of the old black-and-white slabs. But what he most felt was that now surely, with the element of impunity pulling him as by hard firm hands, the case was settled for what he might have seen above had he dared that last look. The closed door, blessedly re-mote now, was still closed — and he had only in short to reach that of the house.

He came down further, he crossed the passage forming the access to the last flight; and if here again he stopped an instant it was almost for the sharpness of the thrill of assured escape. It made him shut his eyes — which opened again to the straight slope of the remainder of the stairs. Here was impunity still, but impunity almost excessive; inasmuch as the side-lights and the high fan-tracery of the entrance were glimmering straight into the hall; an appearance produced, he the next instant saw, by the fact that the vestibule gaped wide, that the hinged halves of the inner door had been thrown far back. Out of that again the *question* sprang at him, making his eyes, as he felt, half-start from his head, as they had done, at the top of the house, before the sign of the other door. If he had left that one open, hadn't he left this one closed, and wasn't he now in *most* immediate presence of some inconceivable occult activity? It was as sharp, the question, as a knife in his side, but the answer hung fire still and seemed to lose itself in the vague darkness to which the thin admitted dawn, glimmering archwise over the whole outer door, made a semicircular margin, a cold silvery nimbus that seemed to play a little as he looked — to shift and expand and contract.

It was as if there had been something within it, protected by indistinctness and corresponding in extent with the opaque surface behind, the painted panels of the last barrier to his escape, of which the key was in his pocket. The indistinctness mocked him even while he stared, affected him as somehow shrouding or challenging certitude, so that after faltering an instant on his step he let himself go with the sense that here *was* at last something to meet, to touch, to take, to know — something all unnatural and dreadful, but to advance upon which was the condition for him either of liberation or of supreme defeat. The penumbra, dense and dark, was the virtual screen of a figure which stood in it as still as some image erect in a niche or as some black-vizored sentinel guarding a treasure. Brydon was to know afterwards, was to recall and make out, the particular thing he had believed during the rest of his descent. He saw, in its great grey glimmering margin, the central vagueness diminish, and he felt it to be taking the very form toward which, for so many days, the passion of his curiosity had yearned. It gloomed, it loomed, it was something, it was somebody, the prodigy of a personal presence.

Rigid and conscious, spectral yet human, a man of his own substance and stature waited there to measure himself with his power to dismay. This only could it be — this only till he recognised, with his advance, that what made the face dim was the pair of raised hands that covered it and in which, so far from being offered in defiance, it was buried as for dark deprecation. So Brydon, before him, took him in; with every fact of him now, in the higher light, hard and acute — his planted stillness, his vivid truth, his grizzled bent head and white masking hands, his queer actuality of evening-dress, of dangling double eye-glass, of gleaming silk lappet and white linen, of pearl button and gold watch-guard and polished shoe. No portrait by a great modern

master could have presented him with more intensity, thrust
him out of his frame with more art, as if there had been "treatment," of the consummate sort, in his every shade and salience.
The revulsion, for our friend, had become, before he knew it,
immense — this drop, in the act of apprehension, to the sense of
his adversary's inscrutable manœuvre. That meaning at least,
while he gaped, it offered him; for he could but gape at his other
self in this other anguish, gape as a proof that *he,* standing there
for the achieved, the enjoyed, the triumphant life, couldn't be
faced in his triumph. Wasn't the proof in the splendid covering
hands, strong and completely spread? — so spread and so inten-
tional that, in spite of a special verity that surpassed every other,
the fact that one of these hands had lost two fingers, which were
reduced to stumps, as if accidentally shot away, the face was effectually guarded and saved.

"Saved," though, *would* it be? — Brydon breathed his wonder
till the very impunity of his attitude and the very insistence of
his eyes produced, as he felt, a sudden stir which showed the next
instant as a deeper portent, while the head raised itself, the betrayal of a braver purpose. The hands, as he looked, began to
move, to open; then, as if deciding in a flash, dropped from the
face and left it uncovered and presented. Horror, with the sight,
had leaped into Brydon's throat, gasping there in a sound he
couldn't utter; for the bared identity was too hideous as *his,* and
his glare was the passion of his protest. The face, *that* face,
Spencer Brydon's? — he searched it still, but looking away from
it in dismay and denial, falling straight from his height of sub-
limity. It was unknown, inconceivable, awful, disconnected from
any possibility — ! He had been "sold," he inwardly moaned,
stalking such game as this: the presence before him was a presence, the horror within him a horror, but the waste of his nights
had been only grotesque and the success of his adventure an
irony. Such an identity fitted his at *no* point, made its alternative
monstrous. A thousand times yes, as it came upon him nearer
now — the face was the face of a stranger. It came upon him
nearer now, quite as one of those expanding fantastic images
projected by the magic lantern of childhood; for the stranger,
whoever he might be, evil, odious, blatant, vulgar, had advanced as for aggression, and he knew himself give ground. Then

harder pressed still, sick with the force of his shock, and falling back as under the hot breath and the roused passion of a life larger than his own, a rage of personality before which his own collapsed, he felt the whole vision turn to darkness and his very feet give way. His head went round; he was going; he had gone.

III

What had next brought him back, clearly — though after how long? — was Mrs. Muldoon's voice, coming to him from quite near, from so near that he seemed presently to see her as kneeling on the ground before him while he lay looking up at her; himself not wholly on the ground, but half-raised and upheld — conscious, yes, of tenderness of support and, more particularly, of a head pillowed in extraordinary softness and faintly refreshing fragrance. He considered, he wondered, his wit but half at his service; then another face intervened, bending more directly over him, and he finally knew that Alice Staverton had made her lap an ample and perfect cushion to him, and that she had to this end seated herself on the lowest degree of the staircase, the rest of his long person remaining stretched on his old black-and-white slabs. They were cold, these marble squares of his youth; but *he* somehow was not, in this rich return of consciousness — the most wonderful hour, little by little, that he had ever known, leaving him, as it did, so gratefully, so abysmally passive, and yet as with a treasure of intelligence waiting all round him for quiet appropriation; dissolved, he might call it, in the air of the place and producing the golden glow of a late autumn afternoon. He had come back, yes — come back from further away than any man but himself had ever travelled; but it was strange how with this sense what he had come back *to* seemed really the great thing, and as if his prodigious journey had been all for the sake of it. Slowly but surely his consciousness grew, his vision of his state thus completing itself: he had been miraculously *carried* back — lifted and carefully borne as from where he had been picked up, the uttermost end of an interminable grey passage. Even with this he was suffered to rest, and what had now brought him to knowledge was the break in the long mild motion.

It had brought him to knowledge, to knowledge — yes, this was the beauty of his state; which came to resemble more and more that of a man who has gone to sleep on some news of a great inheritance, and then, after dreaming it away, after profaning it with matters strange to it, has waked up again to serenity of certitude and has only to lie and watch it grow. This was the drift of his patience — that he had only to let it shine on him. He must moreover, with intermissions, still have been lifted and borne; since why and how else should he have known himself, later on, with the afternoon glow intenser, no longer at the foot of his stairs — situated as these now seemed at that dark other end of his tunnel — but on a deep window-bench of his high saloon, over which had been spread, couch-fashion, a mantle of soft stuff lined with grey fur that was familiar to his eyes and that one of his hands kept fondly feeling as for its pledge of truth. Mrs. Muldoon's face had gone, but the other, the second he had recognised, hung over him in a way that showed how he was still propped and pillowed. He took it all in, and the more he took it the more it seemed to suffice: he was as much at peace as if he had had food and drink. It was the two women who had found him, on Mrs. Muldoon's having plied, at her usual hour, her latch-key — and on her having above all arrived while Miss Staverton still lingered near the house. She had been turning away, all anxiety, from worrying the vain bell-handle — her calculation having been of the hour of the good woman's visit; but the latter, blessedly, had come up while she was still there, and they had entered together. He had then lain, beyond the vestibule, very much as he was lying now — quite, that is, as he appeared to have fallen, but all so wondrously without bruise or gash; only in a depth of stupor. What he most took in, however, at present, with the steadier clearance, was that Alice Staverton had for a long unspeakable moment not doubted he was dead.

"It must have been that I *was*." He made it out as she held him. "Yes — I can only have died. You brought me literally to life. Only," he wondered, his eyes rising to her, "only, in the name of all the benedictions, how?"

It took her but an instant to bend her face and kiss him, and something in the manner of it, and in the way her hands clasped and locked his head while he felt the cool charity and virtue of her lips, something in all this beatitude somehow answered everything. "And now I keep you," she said.

"Oh keep me, keep me!" he pleaded while her face still hung over him: in response to which it dropped again and stayed close, clingingly close. It was the seal of their situation — of which he tasted the impress for a long blissful moment in silence. But he came back. "Yet how did you know — ?"

"I was uneasy. You were to have come, you remember — and you had sent no word."

"Yes, I remember — I was to have gone to you at one today." It caught on to their "old" life and relation — which were so near and so far. "I was still out there in my strange darkness — where was it, what was it? I must have stayed there so long." He could but wonder at the depth and the duration of his swoon.

"Since last night?" she asked with a shade of fear for her possible indiscretion.

"Since this morning — it must have been: the cold dim dawn of today. Where have I been," he vaguely wailed, "where have I been?" He felt her hold him close, and it was as if this helped him now to make in all security his mild moan. "What a long dark day!"

All in her tenderness she had waited a moment. "In the cold dim dawn?" she quavered.

But he had already gone on piecing together the parts of the whole prodigy. "As I didn't turn up you came straight — ?"

She barely cast about. "I went first to your hotel — where they told me of your absence. You had dined out last evening and hadn't been back since. But they appeared to know you had been at your club."

"So you had the idea of *this* — ?"

"Of what?" she asked in a moment.

"Well — of what has happened."

"I believed at least you'd have been here. I've known, all along," she said, "that you've been coming."

" 'Known' it — ?"

"Well, I've believed it. I said nothing to you after that talk we had a month ago — but I felt sure. I knew you *would*," she declared.

"That I'd persist, you mean?"

"That you'd see him."

"Ah but I didn't!" cried Brydon with his long wail. "There's somebody — an awful beast; whom I brought, too horribly, to bay. But it's not me."

At this she bent over him again, and her eyes were in his eyes. "No — it's not you." And it was as if, while her face hovered, he might have made out in it, hadn't it been so near, some particular meaning blurred by a smile. "No, thank heaven," she repeated — "it's not you! Of course it wasn't to have been."

"Ah but it *was*," he gently insisted. And he stared before him now as he had been staring for so many weeks. "I was to have known myself."

"You couldn't!" she returned consolingly. And then reverting, and as if to account further for what she had herself done, "But it wasn't only *that*, that you hadn't been at home," she went on. "I waited till the hour at which we had found Mrs. Muldoon that day of my going with you; and she arrived, as I've told you, while, failing to bring any one to the door, I lingered in my despair on the steps. After a little, if she hadn't come, by such a mercy, I should have found means to hunt her up. But it wasn't," said Alice Staverton, as if once more with her fine intention — "it wasn't only that."

His eyes, as he lay turned back to her. "What more then?"

She met it, the wonder she had stirred. "In the cold dim dawn, you say? Well, in the cold dim dawn of this morning I too saw you."

"Saw *me* — ?"

"Saw *him*," said Alice Staverton. "It must have been at the same moment."

He lay an instant taking it in — as if he wished to be quite reasonable. "At the same moment?"

"Yes — in my dream again, the same one I've named to you. He came back to me. Then I knew it for a sign. He had come to you."

At this Brydon raised himself; he had to see her better. She helped him when she understood his movement, and he sat up, steadying himself beside her there on the window-bench and with his right hand grasping her left. "*He* didn't come to me."

"You came to yourself," she beautifully smiled.

"Ah I've come to myself now — thanks to you, dearest. But this brute, with his awful face — this brute's a black stranger.

He's none of *me, even* as I *might* have been," Brydon sturdily declared.

But she kept the clearness that was like the breath of infallibility. "Isn't the whole point that you'd have been different?"

He almost scowled for it. "As different as *that* — ?"

Her look again was more beautiful to him than the things of this world. "Haven't you exactly wanted to know *how* different? So this morning," she said, "you appeared to me."

"Like *him?*"

"A black stranger!"

"Then how did you know it was I?"

"Because, as I told you weeks ago, my mind, my imagination, had worked so over what you might, what you mightn't have been — to show you, you see, how I've thought of you. In the midst of that you came to me — that my wonder might be answered. So I knew," she went on; "and believed that, since the question held you too so fast, as you told me that day, you too would see for yourself. And when this morning I again saw I knew it would be because you had — and also then, from the first moment, because you somehow wanted me. *He* seemed to tell me of that. So why," she strangely smiled, "shouldn't I like him?"

It brought Spencer Brydon to his feet. "You 'like' that horror — ?"

"I *could* have liked him. And to me," she said, "he was no horror. I had accepted him."

" 'Accepted' — ?" Brydon oddly sounded.

"Before, for the interest of his difference — yes. And as *I* didn't disown him, as *I* knew him — which you at last, confronted with him in his difference, so cruelly didn't, my dear — well, he must have been, you see, less dreadful to me. And it may have pleased him that I pitied him."

She was beside him on her feet, but still holding his hand — still with her arm supporting him. But though it all brought for him thus a dim light, "You 'pitied' him?" he grudgingly, resentfully asked.

"He has been unhappy; he has been ravaged," she said.

"And haven't I been unhappy? Am not I — you've only to look at me! — ravaged?"

"Ah I don't say I like him *better*," she granted after a thought. "But he's grim, he's worn — and things have happened to him. He doesn't make shift, for sight, with your charming monocle."

"No" — it struck Brydon: "I couldn't have sported mine 'downtown.' They'd have guyed me there."

"His great convex pince-nez — I saw it, I recognised the kind — is for his poor ruined sight. And his poor right hand — !"

"Ah!" Brydon winced — whether for his proved identity or for his lost fingers. Then, "He has a million a year," he lucidly added. "But he hasn't you."

"And he isn't — no, he isn't — *you!*" she murmured as he drew her to his breast.

JOSEPH CONRAD (1857–1924) Josef Konrad Korzeniowski was born of Polish gentry near Morilow, Poland. The romantic material of Conrad's novels and short stories came from a life of exile and adventure. His aristocratic parents, resisting Czarism, were exiled to Russia when he was five. At seventeen, not long after the death of his parents in exile, he joined the French merchant marine and, during the next four years, sailed to the West Indies and ran arms to revolutions in Mexico and Spain. When he was twenty-one, he joined the British merchant marine which he left in 1894 in order to write. Conrad's twenty years spent on remote rivers and seas became the intimate source from which he derived his stories of men in isolation, of outcasts whose dangers lay equally outside in the world and within their own psychologies.

His first novel, *Almayer's Folly* (1895), was begun on a Congo river trip during which he narrowly escaped death both from drowning and from a severe tropical fever which periodically affected his health thereafter. Conrad's fascination with the problem of moral guilt was perhaps initiated by this Congo experience. "Before the Congo I was just a mere animal." Even his doomed and dying characters acknowledge a responsibility — if only to their unsalvaged souls, if only to the final image they have of themselves.

Conrad married an Englishwoman and became a naturalized British subject in 1886. A polyglot, Conrad wrote in English yet he did not learn English until he was twenty-one, claiming that it was the most complex language. The year he died, he refused to be knighted.

"Prince Roman," written in 1911, was published in a posthumous volume, *Tales of Hearsay,* a title Conrad had chosen before his death. It is the only story that directly evokes the history of his native Poland.

Conrad's major novels include *Outcast of the Islands* (1896), *Nigger of the Narcissus* (1897), *Lord Jim* (1900), *Nostromo* (1904), *The Secret Agent* (1907), *Chance* (1913), and *Victory* (1915). *Youth* (1902), *Typhoon* (1903), and *'Twixt Land and Sea* (1912) are collections of his short stories.

PRINCE ROMAN

Joseph Conrad

"Events which happened seventy years ago are perhaps rather too far off to be dragged aptly into a mere conversation. Of course the year 1831 is for us an historical date, one of these fatal years when in the presence of the world's passive indignation and eloquent sympathies we had once more to murmur 'Vae Victis' and count the cost in sorrow. Not that we were ever very good at calculating, either in prosperity or in adversity. That's a lesson we could never learn, to the great exasperation of our enemies who have bestowed upon us the epithet of Incorrigible. . . ."

The speaker was of Polish nationality, that nationality not so much alive as surviving, which persists in thinking, breathing, speaking, hoping and suffering in its grave, railed in by a million of bayonets and triple-sealed with the seals of three great empires.

The conversation was about aristocracy. How did this, nowadays discredited, subject come up? It is some years ago now and the precise recollection has faded. But I remember that it was not considered practically as an ingredient in the social mixture; and I verily believed that we arrived at that subject through some exchange of ideas about patriotism — a somewhat discredited sentiment, because the delicacy of our humanitarians regards it as a relic of barbarism. Yet neither the great Florentine painter who closed his eyes in death thinking of his city, nor St. Francis blessing with his last breath the town of Assisi were barbarians. It requires a certain greatness of soul to interpret patriotism worthily — or else a sincerity of feeling denied to the vulgar refinement of modern thought which cannot understand the august simplicity of a sentiment proceeding from the very nature of things and men.

The aristocracy we were talking about was the very highest, the great families of Europe, not impoverished, not converted, not liberalized, the most distinctive and specialized class of all classes, for which even ambition itself does not exist among the usual incentives to activity and regulators of conduct.

The undisputed right of leadership having passed away from them we judged that their great fortunes, their cosmopolitanism, brought about by wide alliances, their elevated station, in which there is so little to gain and so much to lose, must make their position difficult in times of political commotion or national upheaval. No longer born to command — which is the very essence of aristocracy — it becomes difficult for them to do ought else but hold aloof from the great movements of popular passion.

We had reached that conclusion when the remark about far off events was made and the date of 1831 mentioned. And the speaker continued:—

I don't mean to say that I knew Prince Roman at that remote time. I begin to feel pretty ancient, but I am not so ancient as that. In fact Prince Roman was married the very year my father was born. It was in 1828; the nineteenth century was young yet and the Prince was even younger than the century, but I don't know exactly by how much. In any case his was an early marriage. It was an ideal alliance from every point of view. The girl was young and beautiful, an orphan heiress of a great name and of a great fortune. The Prince, then an officer in the Guards and distinguished amongst his fellows by something reserved and reflective in his character, had fallen headlong in love with her beauty, her charm and the serious qualities of her mind and heart. He was a rather silent young man; but his glances, his bearing, his whole person expressed his absolute devotion to the woman of his choice, a devotion which she returned in her own frank and fascinating manner.

The flame of this pure young passion promised to burn for ever; and for a season it lit up the dry, cynical atmosphere of the great world of St. Petersburg. The Emperor Nicholas himself, the grandfather of the present man, the one who died from the Crimean war, the last perhaps of the Autocrats with a mystical belief in the Divine character of his mission, showed some interest in this pair of married lovers. It is true that Nicholas kept a watchful eye on all the doings of the great Polish nobles. The young people leading a life appropriate to their station were obviously wrapped up in each other; and society, fascinated by the sincerity of a feeling moving serenely among the artificialities of its anxious and fastidious agitation, watched them with benevolent indulgence and an amused tenderness.

The marriage was the social event of 1828 in the capital. Just forty years afterwards I was staying in the country house of my mother's brother in our southern provinces.

It was the dead of winter. The great lawn in front was as pure and smooth as an Alpine snowfield, a white and feathery level sparkling under the sun as if sprinkled with diamond-dust, declining gently to the lake — a long, sinuous piece of frozen water looking bluish and more solid than the earth. A cold brilliant sun glided low above an undulating horizon of great folds of snow in which the villages of Ukrainian peasants remained out of sight, like clusters of boats hidden in the hollows of a running sea. And everything was very still.

I don't know now how I had managed to escape at eleven o'clock in the morning from the school-room. I was a boy of eight, the little girl, my cousin, a few months younger than myself, though hereditarily more quick-tempered, was less adventurous. So I had escaped alone; and presently I found myself in the great stone-paved hall, warmed by a monumental stove of white tiles, a much more pleasant locality than the school-room which for some reason or other, perhaps hygienic, was always kept at a low temperature.

We children were aware that there was a guest staying in the house. He had arrived the night before just as we were being driven off to bed. We broke back through the line of beaters to rush and flatten our noses against the dark window panes; but we were too late to see him alight. We had only watched in a ruddy glare the big travelling carriage on sleigh-runners harnessed with six horses, a black mass against the snow, going off to the stables, preceded by a horseman carrying a blazing ball of tow and resin in an iron basket at the end of a long stick swung from his saddle bow. Two stable boys had been sent out early in the afternoon along the snow-tracks to meet the expected guest at dusk and light his way with these road torches. At that time, you must remember, there was not a single mile of railways in our southern provinces. My little cousin and I had no knowledge of trains and engines, except from picture-books, as of things rather vague, extremely remote, and not particularly interesting unless to grown-ups who travelled abroad.

Our notion of princes, perhaps a little more precise, was mainly literary and had a glamour reflected from the light of fairy tales, in which princes always appear young, charming, heroic and fortunate. Yet, as well as any other children, we could draw a firm line between the real and the ideal. We knew that princes were historical personages. And, there was some glamour in that fact too. But what had driven me to roam cautiously over the house like an escaped prisoner, was the hope of snatching an interview with a special friend of mine, the head forester, who generally came to make his report at that time of the day. I yearned for news of a certain wolf. You know, in a country where wolves are to be found, every winter almost brings forward an individual eminent by the audacity of his misdeeds, by his more perfect wolfishness, so to speak. I wanted to hear some new thrilling tale of that wolf — perhaps the dramatic story of his death. . . .

But there was no one in the hall.

Deceived in my hopes I became suddenly very much depressed. Unable to slip back in triumph to my studies I elected to stroll spiritlessly into the billiard-room where certainly I had no business. There was no one there either, and I felt very lost and desolate under its high ceiling, all alone with the massive English billiard-table which seemed, in heavy, rectilinear silence, to disapprove of that small boy's intrusion.

As I began to think of retreat I heard footsteps in the adjoining drawing-room; and, before I could turn tail and flee, my uncle and his guest appeared in the doorway. To run away after having been seen would have been highly improper, so I stood my ground. My uncle looked surprised to see me; the guest by his side was a spare man, of average stature, buttoned up in a black frock coat and holding himself very erect with a stiffly soldier-like carriage. From the folds of a soft white cambric neckcloth peeped the points of a collar close against each shaven cheek. A few wisps of thin grey hair were brushed smoothly across the top of his bald head. His face, which must have been beautiful in its day, had preserved in age the harmonious simplicity of its lines. What amazed me was its even, almost deathlike pallor. He seemed to me to be prodigiously old, a faint smile, a mere mo-

mentary alteration in the set of his thin lips acknowledged my
blushing confusion; and I became greatly interested to see him
reach into the inside breastpocket of his coat. He extracted there-
from a lead pencil and a block of detachable pages, which he
handed to my uncle with an almost imperceptible bow.

I was very much astonished, but my uncle received it as a
matter of course. He wrote something at which the other glanced
and nodded slightly. A thin wrinkled hand — the hand was older
than the face — patted my cheek and then rested on my head
lightly. An unringing voice, a voice as colourless as the face itself,
issued from his sunken lips, while the eyes, dark and still, looked
down at me kindly.

"And how old is this shy little boy?"

Before I could answer my uncle wrote down my age on the
pad. I was deeply impressed. What was this ceremony? Was this
personage too great to be spoken to? Again he glanced at the pad,
and again gave a nod, and again that impersonal, mechanical
voice was heard — "He resembles his grandfather."

I remembered my paternal grandfather. He had died not long
before. He, too, was prodigiously old. And to me it seemed perfectly natural that two such ancient and venerable persons should
have known each other in the dim ages of creation before my
birth. But my uncle obviously had not been aware of the fact.
So obviously that the mechanical voice explained.

— "Yes, yes. Comrades in '31. He was one of those who knew.
Old times, my dear sir, old times. . . ."

He made a gesture as if to put aside an importunate ghost.
And now they were both looking down at me. I wondered
whether anything was expected from me. To my round, question-
ing eyes my uncle remarked, "He's completely deaf." And the
unrelated, inexpressive voice said — "Give me your hand."

Acutely conscious of inky fingers I put it out timidly. I had
never seen a deaf person before and was rather startled. He
pressed it firmly and then gave me a final pat on the head.

My uncle addressed me weightily.

— "You have shaken hands with Prince Roman S———. It's
something for you to remember when you grow up."

I was impressed by his tone. I had enough historical information to know vaguely that the Princes S——— counted amongst

the sovereign Princes of Ruthenia till the union of all Ruthenian lands to the kingdom of Poland, when they became great Polish magnates, sometime at the beginning of the fifteenth century. But what concerned me most was the failure of the fairy-tale glamour. It was shocking to discover a prince who was deaf, bald, meagre, and so prodigiously old. It never occurred to me that this imposing and disappointing man had been young, rich, beautiful. I could not know that he had been happy in the felicity of an ideal marriage uniting two young hearts, two great names and two great fortunes; happy with a happiness which, as in fairy tales, seemed destined to last for ever. . . .

But it did not last for ever. It was fated not to last very long even by the measure of the days allotted to men's passage on this earth, where enduring happiness is only found in the conclusion of fairy tales. A daughter was born to them and shortly afterwards the health of the young princess began to fail. For a time she bore up with smiling intrepidity, sustained by the feeling that now her existence was necessary for the happiness of two lives. But at last the husband, thoroughly alarmed by the rapid changes in her appearance, obtained an unlimited leave and took her away from the capital, to his parents in the country.

The old prince and princess were extremely frightened at the state of their beloved daughter-in-law. Preparations were at once made for a journey abroad. But it seemed as if it were already too late; and the invalid herself opposed the project with gentle obstinacy. Thin and pale in the great armchair, where the insidious and obscure nervous malady made her appear smaller and more frail every day without effacing the smile of her eyes or the charming grace of her wasted face, she clung to her native land and wished to breathe her native air. Nowhere else could she expect to get well so quickly, nowhere else would it be so easy for her to die.

She died before her little girl was two years old. The grief of the husband was terrible and the more alarming to his parents because perfectly silent and dry-eyed. After the funeral, while the immense bareheaded crowd of peasants surrounding the private chapel in the grounds was dispersing, the Prince, waving away his friends and relations, remained alone to watch the masons of the estate closing the family vault. When the last stone was in position he uttered a groan, the first sound of pain which had escaped from him for days, and walking away with lowered head shut himself up again in his apartments.

His father and mother feared for his reason. His outward tranquillity was appalling to them. They had nothing to trust to but that very youth which made his despair so self-absorbed and so intense. Old Prince John, fretful and anxious, repeated, "Poor Roman should be roused somehow. He's so young." But they could find nothing to rouse him with. And the old princess, wiping her eyes, wished in her heart he were young enough to come and cry at her knee.

In time Prince Roman making an effort would join now and again the family circle. But it was as if his heart and his mind had been buried in the family vault with the wife he had lost. He took to wandering in the woods with a gun, watched over secretly by one of the keepers, who would report in the evening that "His Serenity has never fired a shot all day." Sometimes walking to the stables in the morning he would order in subdued tones a horse to be saddled, wait switching his boot till it was led up to him, then mount without a word and ride out of the gates at a walking pace. He would be gone all day. People saw him on the roads looking neither to the right nor to the left, white-faced, sitting rigidly in the saddle like a horseman of stone on a living mount.

The peasants working in the fields, the great unhedged fields, looked after him from the distance; and sometimes some sympathetic old woman on the threshold of a low, thatched hut, was moved to make the sign of the cross in the air behind his back; as though he were one of themselves, a simple village soul struck by a sore affliction.

He rode looking straight ahead, seeing no one, as if the earth were empty and all mankind buried in that grave which had opened so suddenly in his path to swallow up his happiness. What were men to him with their sorrows, joys, labours and passions, from which she who had been all the world to him had been cut off so early?

They did not exist; and he would have felt as completely lonely and abandoned as a man in the toils of a cruel nightmare if it had not been for this countryside where he had been born and had spent his happy boyish years. He knew it well — every slight rise crowned with trees amongst the ploughed fields, every dell concealing a village. The dammed streams made a chain of lakes set in the green meadows. Far away to the north the great Lithuanian forest faced the sun, no higher than a hedge; and to the south, the way to the plains, the vast brown spaces of the earth touched the blue sky.

And this familiar landscape associated with the days without thought and without sorrow, this land the charm of which he felt without even looking at it, soothed his pain, like the presence of an old friend who sits silent and disregarded by one in some dark hour of life.

One afternoon, it happened that the Prince, after turning his horse's head for home, remarked a low dense cloud of dark dust cutting off slantwise a part of the view. He reined in on a knoll and peered. There were slender gleams of steel here and there in that cloud, and it contained moving forms which revealed themselves at last as a long line of peasant carts full of soldiers, moving slowly in double file under the escort of mounted Cossacks.

It was like an immense reptile creeping over the fields; its head dipped out of sight in a slight hollow and its tail went on writhing and growing shorter as though the monster were eating its way slowly into the very heart of the land.

The Prince directed his way through a village lying a little off the track. The roadside inn with its stable, byre and barn under one enormous thatched roof, resembled a deformed, hunchbacked, ragged giant, sprawling amongst the small huts of the peasants. The innkeeper, a portly, dignified Jew, clad in a black satin coat reaching down to his heels and girt with a red sash, stood at the door stroking his long silvery beard.

He watched the Prince approach and bowed gravely from the waist, not expecting to be noticed even, since it was well known that their young lord had no eyes for anything or anybody in his grief. It was quite a shock for him when the Prince pulled up and asked: — "What's all this, Yankel?" — "That is, please your Serenity, that is a convoy of footsoldiers; they are hurrying down to the south."

He glanced right and left cautiously, but as there was no one near but some children playing in the dust of the village street, he came up close to the stirrup.

— "Doesn't your Serenity know? It has begun already down there. All the landowners great and small are out in arms, and even the common people have risen. Only yesterday the saddler from Grodek (it was a tiny market-town near by) went through here with his two apprentices on his way to join. He left even his cart with me. I gave him a guide through our neighbourhood. You know, your Serenity, our people they travel a lot and they see all that's going on, and they know all the roads."

He tried to keep down his excitement, for the Jew Yankel, innkeeper and tenant of all the mills on the estate, was a Polish patriot. And in a still lower voice:

— "I was already a married man when the French and all the other nations passed this way with Napoleon. Tse! Tse! That was a great harvest for death, Nu! Perhaps this time God will help."

The Prince nodded. "Perhaps" — and falling into deep meditation he let his horse take him home.

That night he wrote a letter and early in the morning sent a mounted express to the post town. During the day he came out of his taciturnity, to the great joy of the family circle, and conversed with his father of recent events — the revolt in Warsaw, the flight of the Grand Duke Constantine, the first slight successes of the Polish army (at that time there was a Polish army), the risings in the provinces. Old Prince John, moved and uneasy, speaking from a purely aristocratic point of view, mistrusted the popular origins of the movement, regretted its democratic tendencies, and did not believe in the possibility of success.

He was sad, inwardly agitated.

— "I am judging all this calmly. There are secular principles of legitimacy and order which have been violated in this reckless enterprise for the sake of most subversive illusions. Though of course the patriotic impulses of the heart. . . ."

Prince Roman had listened in a thoughtful attitude. He took advantage of the pause to tell his father quietly that he had sent that morning a letter to St. Petersburg resigning his commission in the Guards.

The old prince remained silent. He thought that he ought to have been consulted. His son was also ordnance officer to the Emperor and he knew that the Tzar would never forget this appearance of defection in a Polish noble. In a discontented tone he pointed out to his son that as it was he had an unlimited leave. The right thing would have been to keep quiet. They had too much tact at Court to recall a man of his name. Or at worst some distant mission might have been asked for — to the Caucasus for instance — away from this unhappy struggle which was wrong in principle and therefore destined to fail.

"Presently you shall find yourself without any interest in life and with no occupation. And you shall need something to occupy you, my poor boy. You have acted rashly, I fear."

Prince Roman murmured.

"I thought it better."

His father faltered under his steady gaze.

— "Well, well — perhaps! But as ordnance officer to the Emperor and in favour with all the Imperial family . . ."

— "Those people had never been heard of when our house was already illustrious," the young man let fall disdainfully.

This was the sort of remark to which the old prince was sensible. — "Well — perhaps it is better," he conceded at last.

The father and son parted affectionately for the night. The next day Prince Roman seemed to have fallen back into the depths of his indifference. He rode out as usual. He remembered that the day before he had seen a reptile-like convoy of soldiery bristling with bayonets crawling over the face of that land which was his. The woman he loved had been his too. Death had robbed him of her. Her loss had been to him a moral shock. It had opened his heart to a greater sorrow, his mind to a vaster thought, his eyes to all the past, and to the existence of another love fraught with pain but as mysteriously imperative as that lost one to which he had entrusted his happiness.

That evening he retired earlier than usual and rang for his personal servant.

— "Go and see if there is light yet in the quarters of the Master-of-the-Horse. If he is still up ask him to come and speak to me."

While the servant was absent on this errand the Prince tore up hastily some papers, locked the drawers of his desk, and hung a medallion containing the miniature of his wife round his neck against his breast.

The man the Prince was expecting belonged to that past which the death of his love had called to life. He was of a family of small nobles who for generations had been adherents, servants

and friends of the Princes S———. He remembered the times
before the last partition, and had taken part in the struggles of
the last hour. He was a typical old Pole of that class, with a great
capacity for emotion, for blind enthusiasm; with martial instincts
and simple beliefs; and even with the old-time habit of larding
his speech with Latin words. And his kindly shrewd eyes, his
ruddy face, his lofty brow and his thick, grey, pendent moustache
were also very typical of his kind.

— "Listen, Master Francis," the Prince said familiarly and
without preliminaries. "Listen, old friend. I am going to vanish
from here quietly. I go where something louder than my grief
and yet something with a voice very like it calls me. I confide
in you alone. You will say what's necessary when the time comes."

The old man understood. His extended hands trembled ex-
ceedingly. But as soon as he found his voice he thanked God
aloud for letting him live long enough to see the descendant of
the illustrious family in its youngest generation give an example
coram Gentibus, of the love of his country and of valour in the
field. He doubted not of his dear Prince attaining a place in
council and in war worthy of his high birth; he saw already that
in fulgore of family glory *affulget patride serenitas.* At the end
of the speech he burst into tears and fell into the Prince's arms.

The Prince quieted the old man, and when he had him seated
in an armchair and comparatively composed he said:

— "Don't misunderstand me, Master Francis. You know how
I loved my wife. A loss like that opens one's eyes to unsuspected
truths. There is no question here of leadership and glory. I
mean to go alone and to fight obscurely in the ranks. I am going
to offer my country what is mine to offer, that is my life, as simply
as the saddler from Grodek who went through yesterday with his
apprentices. . . ."

The old man cried out at this. That could never be. He could
not allow it. But he had to give way before the arguments and
the express will of the Prince.

— "Ha! If you say that it is a matter of feeling and conscience
— so be it. But you cannot go utterly alone. Alas! that I am too
old to be of any use. *Cripit verba dolor,* my dear Prince, at the
thought that I am over seventy and of no more account in the
world than a cripple in the church porch. It seems that to sit at
home and pray to God for the nation and for you is all I am fit

for. But there is my son, my youngest boy, Peter. He will make a worthy companion for you. And as it happens he's staying with me here. There has not been for ages a Prince S——— hazarding his life without a companion of our name to ride by his side. You must have by you somebody who knows who you are if only to let your parents and your old servant hear what is happening to you. And when does your Princely Mightiness mean to start?"

— "In an hour," said the Prince; and the old man hurried off to warn his son.

Prince Roman took up a candlestick and walked quietly along a dark corridor in the silent house. The head-nurse said afterwards that waking up suddenly she saw the Prince looking at his child, one hand shading the light from its eyes. He stood and gazed at her for some time, and then putting the candlestick on the floor bent over the cot and kissed lightly the little girl, who did not wake. He went out noiselessly taking the light away with him. She saw his face perfectly well, but she could read nothing of his purpose in it. It was pale but perfectly calm, and after he turned away from the cot he never looked back at it once.

The only other trusted person, besides the old man and his son Peter, was the Jew Yankel. When he asked the Prince where precisely he wanted to be guided the Prince answered, "To the nearest party." A grandson of the Jew, a lanky youth, conducted the two young men by little known paths, across woods and morasses, and led them in sight of the few fires of a small detachment camped in a hollow. Some invisible horses neighed, a voice in the dark cried "Who goes there?" . . . and the young Jew departed hurriedly, explaining that he must make haste home to be in time for keeping the Sabbath.

Thus humbly and in accord with the simplicity of the vision of duty he saw when death had removed the brilliant bandage of happiness from his eyes, did Prince Roman bring his offering to his country. His companion made himself known as the son of the Master-of-the-Horse to the Princes S——— and declared him to be a relation, a distant cousin from the same parts as himself and, as people presumed, of the same name. In truth no one inquired much. Two more young men, clearly of the right sort, had joined. Nothing more natural.

Prince Roman did not remain long in the south. One day

while scouting with several others, they were ambushed near the entrance of a village by some Russian infantry. The first discharge laid low a good many and the rest scattered in all directions. The Russians, too, did not stay, being afraid of a return in force. After some time, the peasants coming to view the scene extricated Prince Roman from under his dead horse. He was unhurt but his faithful companion had been one of the first to fall. The Prince helped the peasants to bury him and the other dead.

Then alone, not certain where to find the body of partisans which was constantly moving about in all directions, he resolved to try and join the main Polish army facing the Russians on the borders of Lithuania. Disguised in peasant clothes, in case of meeting some marauding Cossacks, he wandered a couple of weeks before he came upon a village occupied by a regiment of Polish cavalry on outpost duty.

On a bench, before a peasant hut of a better sort, sat an elderly officer whom he took for the Colonel. The Prince approached respectfully, told his story shortly and stated his desire to enlist; and when asked his name by the officer, who had been looking him over carefully, he gave on the spur of the moment the name of his dead companion.

The elderly officer thought to himself: Here's the son of some peasant proprietor of the liberated class. He liked his appearance.
— "And can you read and write, my good fellow?" he asked.
— "Yes, your honour, I can," said the Prince.
— "Good. Come along inside the hut; the regimental adjutant is there. He will enter your name and administer the oath to you."

The adjutant stared very hard at the new-comer but said nothing. When all the forms had been gone through and the recruit gone out, he turned to his superior officer.
— "Do you know who that is?"
— "Who? That Peter? A likely chap."
— "That's Prince Roman S———."
— "Nonsense."

But the adjutant was positive. He had seen the Prince several times, about two years before, in the Castle in Warsaw. He had even spoken to him once at a reception of officers held by the Grand Duke. — "He's changed. He seems much older, but I am certain of my man. I have a good memory for faces."

The two officers looked at each other in silence. "He's sure to be recognized sooner or later," murmured the adjutant. The Colonel shrugged his shoulders.

— "It's no affair of ours — if he has a fancy to serve in the ranks. As to being recognized it's not so likely. All our officers and men come from the other end of Poland."

He meditated gravely for a while, then smiled. "He told me he could read and write. There's nothing to prevent me making him a sergeant at the first opportunity. He's sure to shape all right."

Prince Roman as a non-commissioned officer surpassed the Colonel's expectations. Before long Sergeant Peter became famous for his resourcefulness and courage. It was not the reckless courage of a desperate man; it was a self-possessed, as if conscientious, valour which nothing could dismay; a boundless but equable devotion, unaffected by time, by reverses, by the discouragement of endless retreats, by the bitterness of waning hopes and the horrors of pestilence added to the toils and perils of war. It was in this year that the cholera made its first appearance in Europe. It devastated the camps of both armies, affecting the firmest minds with the terror of a mysterious death stalking silently between the piled up arms and around the bivouac fires.

A sudden shriek would wake up the harassed soldiers and they would see in the glow of embers one of themselves writhe on the ground like a worm trodden on by an invisible foot. And before the dawn broke he would be stiff and cold. Parties so visited have been known to rise like one man, abandon the fire and run off into the night in mute panic. Or a comrade talking to you on the march would stammer suddenly in the middle of a sentence, roll affrighted eyes, and fall down with distorted face and blue lips breaking the ranks with the convulsions of his agony. Men were struck in the saddle, on sentry duty, in the firing line, carrying orders, serving the guns. I have been told that in a battalion forming under fire with perfect steadiness for the assault of a village, three cases occurred within five minutes at the head of the column; and the attack could not be delivered because the leading companies scattered all over the fields like chaff before the wind.

Sergeant Peter, young as he was, had a great influence over his men. It was said that the number of desertions in the squad-

ron in which he served was less than in any other in the whole
of that cavalry division. Such was supposed to be the compelling
example of one man's quiet intrepidity in facing every form of
danger and terror.

However that may be, he was liked and trusted generally.
When the end came and the remnants of that army corps, hard
pressed on all sides, were preparing to cross the Prussian frontier,
Sergeant Peter had enough influence to rally round him a score
of troopers. He managed to escape with them at night from the
hemmed-in army. He led this band through 200 miles of country
covered by numerous Russian detachments and ravaged by the
cholera. But this was not to avoid captivity, to go into hiding and
try to save themselves. No. He led them into a fortress which was
still occupied by the Poles, and where the last stand of the
vanquished revolution was to be made.

This looks like mere fanaticism. But fanaticism is human.
Man has adored ferocious divinities. There is ferocity in every
passion, even in love itself. The religion of undying hope resembles the mad cult of despair, of death, of annihilation. The
difference lies in the moral motive springing from the secret
needs and the unexpressed aspiration of the believers. It is only
to vain men that all is vanity; and all is deception only to those
who have never been sincere with themselves.

It was in the fortress that my grandfather found himself together with Sergeant Peter. My grandfather was a neighbour of
the S—— family in the country, but he did not know Prince
Roman, who, however, knew his name perfectly well. The Prince
introduced himself one night as they both sat on the ramparts,
leaning against a gun carriage.

The service he wished to ask for was, in case of his being killed,
to have the intelligence conveyed to his parents.

They talked in low tones, the other servants of the piece lying
about near them. My grandfather gave the required promise,
and then asked frankly — for he was greatly interested by the
disclosure so unexpectedly made:

— "But tell me, Prince, why this bequest. Have you any evil
forebodings as to yourself?"

— "Not in the least; I was thinking of my people. They have
no idea where I am," answered Prince Roman. "I'll engage to
do as much for you, if you like. It's certain that half of us at

least shall be killed before the end, so there's an even chance of one of us surviving the other."

My grandfather told him where, as he supposed, his wife and children were then. From that moment till the end of the siege the two were much together. On the day of the great assault my grandfather received a severe wound. The town was taken. Next day the citadel itself, its hospital full of dead and dying, its magazines empty, its defenders having burnt their last cartridge, opened its gates.

During all the campaign the Prince, exposing his person conscientiously on every occasion, had not received a scratch. No one had recognized him, or at any rate had betrayed his identity. Till then, as long as he did his duty, it had mattered nothing who he was.

Now, however, the position was changed. As ex-guardsman and as late ordnance officer to the Emperor, this rebel ran a serious risk of being given special attention in the shape of a firing squad at ten paces. For more than a month he remained lost in the miserable crowd of prisoners packed in the casemates of the citadel, with just enough food to keep body and soul together but otherwise allowed to die from wounds, privation and disease at the rate of forty or so a day.

The position of the fortress being central, new parties, captured in the open in the course of a thorough pacification, were being sent in frequently. Amongst such new-comers, there happened to be a young man, a personal friend of the Prince from his school days. He recognized him, and in the extremity of his dismay cried aloud, "My God! Roman, you here!"

It is said that years of life embittered by remorse paid for this momentary lack of self-control. All this happened in the main quadrangle of the citadel. The warning gesture of the Prince came too late. An officer of the gendarmes on guard had heard the exclamation. The incident appeared to him worth inquiring into. The investigation which followed was not very arduous because the Prince, asked categorically for his real name, owned up at once.

The intelligence of the Prince S—— being found amongst the prisoners was sent to St. Petersburg. His parents were already there living in sorrow, incertitude and apprehension. The capital of the Empire was the safest place to reside in for a noble whose

son had disappeared so mysteriously from home in a time of
rebellion. The old people had not heard from him, or of him,
for months. They took care not to contradict the rumours of
suicide from despair circulating in the great world, which remembered the interesting love-match, the charming and frank
happiness brought to an end by death. But they hoped secretly
that their son survived, and that he had been able to cross the
frontier with that part of the army which had surrendered to
the Prussians.

The news of his captivity was a crushing blow. Directly, nothing could be done for him. But the greatness of their name, of
their position, their wide relations and connections in the highest
spheres, enabled his parents to act indirectly; and they moved
heaven and earth, as the saying is, to save their son from the
"consequences of his madness," as poor Prince John did not hesitate to express himself. Great personages were approached by
society leaders, high dignitaries were interviewed, powerful officials were induced to take an interest in that affair. The help of
every possible secret influence was enlisted. Some private secretaries got heavy bribes. The mistress of a certain senator obtained
a large sum of money.

But, as I have said, in such a glaring case no direct appeal
could be made and no open steps taken. All that could be done
was to incline by private representation the mind of the President
of the Military Commission to the side of clemency. He ended
by being impressed by the hints and suggestions, some of them
from very high quarters, which he received from St. Petersburg.
And, after all, the gratitude of such great nobles as the Princes
S—— was something worth having from a worldly point of
view. He was a good Russian, but he was also a good-natured
man. Moreover, the hate of Poles was not at that time a cardinal
article of patriotic creed as it became some thirty years later. He
felt well disposed at first sight towards that young man, bronzed,
thin-faced, worn out by months of hard campaigning, the hard-
ships of the siege and the rigours of captivity.

The Commission was composed of three officers. It sat in the
citadel in a bare, vaulted room behind a long black table. Some
clerks occupied the two ends, and, besides the gendarmes who
brought in the Prince, there was no one else there.

Within those four sinister walls shutting out from him all the sights and sounds of liberty, all hopes of the future, all consoling illusions — alone in the face of his enemies erected for judges — who can tell how much love of life there was in Prince Roman? How much remained in that sense of duty, revealed to him in sorrow? How much of his awakened love for his native country? That country which demands to be loved as no other country has ever been loved, with the mournful affection one bears to the unforgotten dead and with the unextinguishable fire of a hopeless passion which only a living, breathing, warm ideal can kindle in our breasts for our pride, for our weariness, for our exultation, for our undoing.

There is something monstrous in the thought of such an exaction till it stands before us embodied in the shape of a fidelity without fear and without reproach. Nearing the supreme moment of his life the Prince could only have had the feeling that it was about to end. He answered the questions put to him clearly, concisely . . . with the most profound indifference. After all those tense months of action to talk was a weariness to him. But he concealed it, lest his foes should suspect in his manner the apathy of discouragement or the numbness of a crushed spirit. The details of his conduct could have no importance one way or another; with his thoughts these men had nothing to do. He preserved a scrupulously courteous tone. He had refused the permission to sit down.

What happened at this preliminary examination is only known from the Presiding Officer. Pursuing the only possible course in that glaringly bad case he tried from the first to bring to the Prince's mind the line of defence he wished him to take. He absolutely framed his questions so as to put the right answers in the culprit's mouth, going so far as to suggest the very words: — how, distracted by excessive grief after his young wife's death, rendered irresponsible for his conduct by his despair, in a moment of blind recklessness, without realizing the highly reprehensible nature of the act, nor yet its danger and its dishonour, he went off to join the nearest rebels on a sudden impulse. And that now, penitently . . .

But Prince Roman was silent. The military judges looked at him hopefully. In silence he reached for a pen and wrote on a sheet of paper he found under his hand: "I joined the national rising from conviction."

He pushed the paper across the table. The president took it up, showed it in turn to his two colleagues sitting to the right and left, then looking fixedly at Prince Roman let it fall from his hand. And the silence remained unbroken till he spoke to the gendarmes ordering them to remove the prisoner.

Such was the written testimony of Prince Roman in the supreme moment of his life. I have heard that the Princes of the S—— family, in all its branches, adopted the last two words, "from conviction," for the device under the armorial bearings of their house. I don't know whether the report is true. My uncle could not tell me. He remarked only that, naturally, it was not to be seen on Prince Roman's own seal.

He was condemned for life to Siberian mines. Emperor Nicholas, who always took personal cognisance of all sentences on Polish nobility, wrote with his own hand in the margin: "The authorities are severely warned to take care that this convict walks in chains like any other criminal every step of the way."

It was a sentence of deferred death. Very few survived entombment in these mines for more than three years. Yet as he was reported as still alive at the end of that time he was allowed, on a petition of his parents and by way of exceptional grace, to serve as common soldier in the Caucasus. All communication with him was forbidden. He had no civil rights. For all practical purposes except that of suffering he was a dead man. The little child he had been so careful not to wake up when he kissed her in her cot, inherited all the fortune after Prince John's death. Her existence saved those immense estates from confiscation.

It was twenty-five years before Prince Roman, stone deaf, his health broken, was permitted to return to Poland. His daughter, married splendidly to a Polish-Austrian *grand seigneur* and moving in the cosmopolitan sphere of the highest European aristocracy, lived mostly abroad in Nice and Vienna. He, settling down on one of her estates, not the one with the palatial residence but another where there was a modest little house, saw very little of her.

But Prince Roman did not shut himself up as if his work were done. There was hardly anything done in the private and public life of the neighbourhood, in which Prince Roman's advice and assistance were not called upon, and never in vain. It was well said that his days did not belong to himself but to his fellow citizens. And especially he was the particular friend of all returned exiles, helping them with purse and advice, arranging their affairs and finding them means of livelihood.

I heard from my uncle many tales of his devoted activity, in which he was always guided by a simple wisdom, a high sense of honour and the most scrupulous conception of private and public probity. He remains a living figure for me because of that meeting in a billiard-room, when, in my anxiety to hear about a particularly wolfish wolf, I came in momentary contact with a man who was pre-eminently a man amongst all men capable of feeling deeply, of believing steadily, of loving ardently.

I remember to this day the grasp of Prince Roman's bony, wrinkled hand closing on my small inky paw, and my uncle's half-serious, half-amused way of looking down at his trespassing nephew.

They moved on and forgot that little boy. But I did not move; I gazed after them, not so much disappointed as disconcerted by this Prince so utterly unlike a prince in a fairy tale. They moved very slowly across the room. Before reaching the other door the Prince stopped; and I heard him — I seem to hear him now — saying: — "I wish you would write to Vienna about filling up that post. He's a most deserving fellow — and your recommendation would be decisive."

My uncle's face turned to him expressed genuine wonder. It said as plainly as any speech could say: what better recommendation than a father's can be needed? The Prince was quick at reading expressions. Again he spoke with the toneless accent of a man who has not heard his own voice for years, for whom the soundless world is like an abode of silent shades.

And to this day I remember the very words.

— "I ask you because, you see, my daughter and my son-in-law don't believe me to be a good judge of men. They think that I let myself be guided too much by mere sentiment."

ANTON CHEKHOV (1860–1904) Born in Taganrog, Russia, Chekhov was the son of a tradesman and the grandson of a serf who had purchased freedom for his family. When business failed, his family moved to Moscow leaving Chekhov behind to finish his schooling. Three years later Chekhov joined his family and entered the medical school at the University of Moscow. On his arrival in Moscow he began writing sketches and stories for the Moscow comic papers and soon became the main support of his family. After receiving his medical degree, Chekhov relied on his popularity in the comic papers rather than pursuing medicine. Later he commented: "Medicine is my lawful wife and literature is my mistress."

In 1886 his early collection *Particoloured Stories* appeared; their craftsmanship attracted the attention of the influential editor Suvorin who gave Chekhov a special weekly literary supplement in his paper. The transition from writing popular stories of buffoonery to his own particular style and genre came quickly; by 1889, when "A Dreary Story" appeared, his mature style had evolved and "Chekhovian state of mind" became a term in Russian literary jargon. Chekhov claimed that the "aim of fiction is absolute and honest truth." Beneath the trivia of everyday life, Chekhov writes of the sameness of all men and the lack of communication and understanding which keep all men and women isolated.

Chekhov gave generously of the money earned by writing for a museum and library in Taganrog; he also bought land and a home in Melkihovo for himself, his parents, his sister, and brother. His family ties remained steadfast from the time he came to Moscow as a medical student until his death.

Chekhov's social conscience and his humanitarianism led to his study, *Sakhalin Island* (1891), of prison conditions in far-off Sakhalin before the Trans-Siberian railroad. During a cholera epidemic in Melkihovo in 1892 he worked as a doctor. He protested the Dreyfus injustice and resigned his membership to the Russian Academy when, due to government interference, Gorky was suddenly refused admittance just after being elected to the Academy.

In 1897 consumption forced Chekhov to leave Melkihovo; he spent the rest of his life in health resorts on the Crimean Sea, in France, and

Germany. With the production of his play *The Seagull* (1896), his fame as a playwright was established. Performances of *Uncle Vanya* (1899), *The Three Sisters* (1901), and *The Cherry Orchard* (1904) triumphantly followed. In 1901 Chekhov married an actress in the Art Theater and moved to Yalta. On his doctor's advice he went to Badenweiler in the Black Forest in 1904 where he died the same year.

AT SEA
A Sailor's Story

Anton Chekhov

Only the dimming lights of the receding harbor were visible in an ink-black sky. We could feel the heavy storm clouds overhead about to burst into rain, and it was suffocating, in spite of the wind and cold.

Crowded together in the crew's quarters we, the sailors, were casting lots. Loud, drunken laughter filled the air. One of our comrades was playfully crowing like a cock. A slight shiver ran through me from the back of my neck to my heels, as if cold small shot were pouring down my naked body from a hole in the back of my head. I was shivering both from the cold and certain other causes, which I wish to describe.

In my opinion, man is, as a rule, foul; and the sailor can sometimes be the foulest of all the creatures of the earth — fouler than the lowest beast, which has, at least, the excuse of obeying his instincts. It is possible that I may be mistaken, since I do not know life, but it appears to me that a sailor has more occasion than anyone else to despise and curse himself. A man who at any moment may fall headlong from a mast to be forever hidden beneath a wave, a man who may drown, God alone knows when, has need of nothing, and one on dry land feels pity for him. We sailors drink a lot of vodka and are dissolute because we do not know what one needs virtue for at sea. However, I shall continue.

We were casting lots. There were twenty-two of us who, having stood watch, were now at liberty. Out of this number only two were to have the luck of enjoying a rare spectacle. On this particular night the honeymoon cabin was occupied, but the wall of the cabin had only two holes at our disposal. One of them I myself had made with a fine saw, after boring through with a corkscrew; the other had been cut out with a knife by one of my comrades. We had worked at it for more than a week.

"You got one hole!"

"Who?"

They pointed to me. "Who got the other?"

"Your father."

My father, a humpbacked old sailor with a face like a baked apple, came up to me and clapped me on the back. "Today, my boy, we're lucky!" he said. "Do you hear, boy? Luck came to us both at the same time. That means something." Impatiently he asked the time; it was only eleven o'clock.

I went up on deck, lit my pipe and gazed out to sea. It was dark, but it can be assumed that my eyes reflected what was taking place in my soul, as I made out images on the black background of the night, visualizing what was so lacking in my own still young but already ruined life. . . .

At midnight I walked past the saloon and glanced in at the door. The bridegroom, a young pastor with a handsome blond head, sat at a table holding the Gospels in his hands. He was explaining something to a tall, gaunt Englishwoman. The bride, a very beautiful, shapely young woman, sat at her husband's side with her light blue eyes fixed on him. A tall, plump, elderly Englishman, a banker, with a repulsive red face, paced up and down the saloon. He was the husband of the middle-aged lady to whom the pastor was talking.

"Pastors have a habit of talking for hours," I thought. "He won't finish before morning." At one o'clock my father came to me, pulled me by the sleeve and said: "It's time. They've left the saloon."

In the twinkling of an eye I flew down the companionway and approached the familiar wall. Between this wall and the side of the ship there was a space where soot, water, and rats collected. I soon heard the heavy tread of the old man, my father. He cursed as he stumbled over a mat-sack and some kerosene cans. I felt for the hole in the wall and pulled out the square piece of wood I had so painstakingly sawed. I was looking at a thin, transparent muslin through which penetrated a soft, rosy light. Together with the light, my burning face was caressed by a delightful, sultry fragrance; this, no doubt, was the smell of an

aristocratic bedroom. In order to see the room it was necessary to
draw aside the muslin with two fingers, which I hastened to do.
I saw bronze, velvet, lace, all bathed in a pink glow. About ten
feet from my face stood the bed.

"Let me have your place," said my father, impatiently pushing
me aside. "I can see better here." I did not answer him. "Your
eyes are better than mine, boy, and it makes no difference to you
if you look from far or near."

"Be quiet," I said, "they might hear us."

The bride sat on the side of the bed, dangling her little feet
in a foot muff. She was staring at the floor. Before her stood her
husband, the young pastor. He was telling her something, what
I do not know; the noise of the steamer made it impossible for
me to hear. He spoke passionately, with gestures, his eyes flashing. She listened and shook her head in refusal.

"The devil!" my father muttered. "A rat bit me!"

I pressed my chest to the wall, as if fearing my heart would
jump out. My head was burning.

The bride and groom talked at great length. At last he sank
to his knees and held out his arms, imploring her. She shook her
head in refusal. He leaped to his feet, crossed the cabin, and
from the expression on his face and the movements of his arms
I surmised that he was threatening her. The young wife rose and
went slowly towards the wall where I was standing. She stopped
near the opening and stood motionless in thought. I devoured
her face with my eyes. It seemed to me that she was suffering,
struggling with herself, not knowing what to do; but at the same
time her features expressed anger. I did not understand it.

We continued to stand there face to face for about five minutes, then she moved slowly away and, pausing in the middle
of the cabin, nodded to the pastor — a sign of consent, undoubtedly. He smiled happily, kissed her hand and went out.

Within three minutes the door opened and the pastor re-
entered followed by the tall, plump Englishman whom I mentioned above. The Englishman went over to the bed and asked
the beautiful woman a question. Pale, not looking at him, she
nodded her head affirmatively. The banker then took out of his
pocket a packet of some sort — evidently bank notes — and
handed it to the pastor, who examined it, counted it, bowed and
went out. The elderly Englishman locked the door after him.

I sprang away from the wall as if I had been stung. I was frightened. It seemed to me the wind was tearing our ship to pieces, that we were going down. My father, that drunken, debauched old man, took me by the arm and said: "Let's go away from here! You shouldn't see that. You're still a boy."

He was hardly able to stand. I carried him up the steep winding stairs. Above an autumn rain had begun to fall.

(Translated by Ann Dunnigan)

THE BLACK MONK

Anton Chekhov

I

Andrey Vasilyich Kovrin, a postgraduate student, was over-strained and nervy. He was not receiving treatment for his complaint, but he had mentioned it casually over a bottle of wine to a friend who was a doctor, and who advised him to spend the spring and summer in the country. Just at that moment there arrived a long letter from Tanya Pesotskaya, in which she asked him to go down and stay with them at Borisovka. He decided that he really must go away.

First of all — this was in April — he went to his own family estate of Kovrinka, where he spent three weeks in solitude; then, having waited for the fine weather, he travelled by road to visit his former guardian, Pesotsky, well known in Russia as a horti-culturist, who had brought him up. From Kovrinka to Borisovka, where the Pesotskys lived, was not reckoned to be more than seventy versts, and travelling in a comfortable, well-sprung carriage along roads softened by the spring thaw was a real pleasure.

The Pesotskys' was an enormous house, with columns, peeling plaster lions, and a frock-coated manservant at the front door. The ancient park, grim and severe, laid out in the English style, stretched for nearly a verst from the house to the river, where it ended abruptly in a steep earthen bank on which grew pine-trees whose exposed roots looked like hairy paws; below, the water had an inhospitable gleam, snipe drifted past with a melancholy cry and at all times the mood of the place might well have prompted one to sit down and write a woeful ballad. Near the house, on the other hand, in the courtyard and the orchard, which, with the nurseries, covered about eighty acres, it was bright and cheerful even in bad weather. Kovrin had never seen anywhere else such marvellous roses, lilies, camellias, tulips of every conceivable colour from pure white to soot black, and altogether such a

wealth of flowers, as at the Pesotskys'. Spring was as yet only beginning and the real peak of magnificence of the flower gardens
still lay concealed in the greenhouses, but what was already in
bloom along the walks and here and there in the beds was
enough to make one feel, strolling about the garden, that one
was in a kingdom of delicate colour, especially in the early hours
when the dew sparkled on every petal.

This, the ornamental part of the garden, which Pesotsky himself scornfully called a lot of nonsense, had produced on Kovrin
at one time in his childhood the effect of a fairy-tale. Such flights
of fancy, such elegant monstrosities and mockeries of nature!
There were espaliered fruit-trees, a pear in the shape of a Lombardy poplar, spherical oaks and limes, an umbrella made from
an apple-tree, arches, monograms, candelabra and even the figures 1862 — the date when Pesotsky first took up horticulture —
in plum-trees. There were handsome, well-shaped little trees, too,
with trunks as strong and straight as a palm-tree's, and it was
only if you looked closely that you would recognize gooseberry or
currant bushes in these small trees. But the most heartening thing
in the garden, and what gave it its look of animation, was its
constant bustle. From early morning until evening people
swarmed like ants round the trees and shrubs, in the walks and
about the flower-beds, with wheelbarrows, hoes, and watering-
cans . . .

Kovrin reached the Pesotskys' in the evening, between nine and
ten o'clock. He found Tanya and her father, Egor Semenych,
very worried. The clear, starry sky and the thermometer both
presaged frost before morning, and the head gardener, Ivan
Karlych, had gone to the town, so that there was nobody they
could rely on. At supper the talk was all of the early frost, and it
was decided that Tanya would not go to bed, but soon after
midnight would walk through the garden to see whether all was
in order, and Egor Semenych would get up at three o'clock or
even earlier.

Kovrin sat with Tanya all the evening and soon after midnight
went out with her into the garden. It was cold. Outside there
was already a strong smell of burning. In the big orchard, which
was called the Money-maker and brought Egor Semenych a few
thousand roubles clear profit every year, thick black acrid smoke
lay along the ground and enveloped the trees, preserving those

thousands from the frost. The trees here stood in a chessboard pattern, their rows as straight and regular as ranks of soldiers, and this pedantically strict correctness and the fact that all the trees were the same size and had identical crowns and trunks produced a scene of monotony and indeed dullness. Kovrin and Tanya walked along the rows, where fires of dung, straw, and all kinds of refuse smouldered, now and then meeting workmen wandering through the smoke like shadows. Only the cherries, plums, and some sorts of apples were in flower, but the whole orchard was drowned in smoke and it was only near the nurseries that Kovrin could fill his lungs with air.

"When I was a child the smoke here used to make me sneeze," he said, shrugging his shoulders, "but to this day I don't understand how smoke can be a protection against the frost."

"The smoke replaces the clouds when there aren't any," answered Tanya.

"And why are clouds necessary?"

"There are no early morning frosts in dull and cloudy weather."

"So that's it!"

He laughed and took her arm. Her broad, intensely serious face, pinched with cold, her thin black eyebrows, the turned-up collar of her coat which prevented the free movement of her head, her whole slim graceful figure, and her dress tucked up to avoid the dew, all moved him.

"Good Lord, she is grown-up already!" he said. "When I left here last time, about five years ago, you were still quite a child. You were so scraggy and long-legged, with your head bare and a short little frock, and I used to call you the heron . . . What time does!"

"Yes, it is five years!" sighed Tanya. "A lot of water has flowed under the bridges since then. Tell me, Andryusha, honestly," she hurried on, looking into his face, "have you grown away from us? But need I ask? You are a man, you live your own interesting life, you amount to something . . . Some estrangement is so natural! But whatever happens, Andryusha, I want you to think of us as your own family. We have a right to that."

"I do, Tanya."

"Word of honour?"

"Word of honour."

"You were surprised today that we have so many photographs of you. But you know my father adores you. I sometimes think he loves you more than me. He is proud of you. You are a scholar, a distinguished man, you have made a brilliant career for yourself, and he believes that you have turned out the way you have because he brought you up. I don't try to stop him thinking so. Let him."

Dawn was already approaching, and this was particularly noticeable in the distinctness with which the puffs of smoke and the tree tops were beginning to stand out in the air. Nightingales were singing, and the piping of quails was borne in from the fields.

"It's time for bed," said Tanya. "And it is cold." She took his arm. "Thank you for coming, Andryusha. The people we know are uninteresting, and there are not many even of them. With us everything is garden, garden, garden — and nothing else. Standards, half-standards," she laughed, "pippins, rennets, russets, budding, whip-grafts . . . Everything, the whole of our lives, has gone into the garden; I don't even dream of anything but apples and pears. Of course it's very good, it's useful, but sometimes I can't help wishing for something else for a change. I remember when you used to come here for the holidays, or just for a visit, the house seemed somehow fresher and lighter, as though we had taken the covers off the furniture and chandeliers. I was only a little girl then, but I understood."

She went on talking for a long time, with great feeling. For some reason it suddenly came into his head that during the summer he might become attached to this frail little chatterbox, be attracted, fall in love — in their situation it was so possible and so natural! The idea touched and amused him; he bent his head towards the dear worried face and began to sing softly,

> "Onegin, there is no concealing
> That I love Tatyana madly . . ."

When they reached the house, Egor Semenych was already up. Kovrin was not sleepy, and he chatted to the old man and returned with him to the garden. Egor Semenych was tall, broad-shouldered, and big-bellied, and he suffered from asthma, but he always walked so fast that it was difficult to keep up with him. He wore an extremely worried look and was always hurrying, with an expression that seemed to say that if he delayed even for one minute, all would be lost!

"Now here is an odd thing, my dear chap . . ." he began, stopping to get his breath. "On the surface of the ground, as you can see, there is frost, but take a stick and lift the thermometer about fifteen feet above the ground, and it is warm there . . . Why is that?"

"Really, I don't know," said Kovrin, laughing.

"Hm . . . Of course, nobody can know everything . . . However capacious a mind may be, it can't find room for everything. I suppose philosophy would be much more in your line?"

"Yes. I am reading psychology, but I study philosophy in general."

"And doesn't it bore you?"

"On the contrary, it's all I live for."

"Well, please God . . ." said Egor Semenych, thoughtfully stroking his grey whiskers. "Please God . . . I'm very glad for you . . . glad, my dear . . ."

Suddenly he pricked up his ears and, with a terrible grimace, ran off to one side and disappeared behind the trees in clouds of smoke.

"Who has tied a horse to the apple-tree?" he cried in a desperate, heart-rending shriek. "What ruffianly scoundrel has dared to tie a horse to the tree? My God, my God! Spoilt, frozen, destroyed, ruined! The garden's finished! The garden's done for! My God!"

When he returned to Kovrin his face was outraged and worn with emotion.

"What are you to do with these damnable people?" he said in a complaining voice, waving his arms. "During the night Stepka brought a load of dung and tied his horse to an apple-tree! The wretch twisted the reins round as tight as he could, so that the bark got rubbed in three places. A fine thing! I speak to him, but he's a stupid blockhead and only stands and blinks! Hanging's too good for him!"

When he calmed down, he embraced Kovrin and kissed him on the cheek.

"Well, please God . . . please God . . ." he murmured. "I am very glad you have come. Unspeakably glad . . . Thank you."

Then with the same quick gait and worried expression he walked all round the garden and showed his former ward all the orangeries and hot-houses and his two apiaries, which he called the marvels of our age.

While they talked the sun came up and shone brightly on the garden. It grew warm. Anticipating a long, fine, cheerful day, Korvin remembered that it was still only the beginning of May and that the whole summer was still to come, just as long, fine and cheerful, and suddenly the joyful, youthful feeling he had known when he ran about this garden as a child stirred again in his breast. And in his turn he embraced the old man and kissed him tenderly. Both much affected, they returned to the house and sat down to drink tea from antique porcelain cups, with cream and rich, satisfying cracknels — and these little things again reminded Kovrin of his childhood and youth. The wonderful present and the newly awakened memories of the past within it merged together, crowding in upon the mind, but bringing a feeling of well-being.

He waited until Tanya woke up, and drank a great deal of coffee with her, took a stroll and then went to his own room and sat down to work. He read carefully, making notes, occasionally raising his eyes to look at the open windows or the fresh flowers, still wet with dew, that stood in vases on the table, and lowering them again to his book; and every nerve seemed to leap and quiver with pleasure.

II

He continued to lead exactly the same strained and restless life in the country as in the town. He wrote and read a great deal, studied Italian and, when he went for a walk, took pleasure in the thought that he would soon be sitting down to work again. He slept so little that everybody was amazed; if he chanced to doze for half an hour during the day he did not sleep at all the following night, and felt as well and in as good spirits after his sleepless night as if nothing had happened.

He talked a lot, drank wine, and smoked expensive cigars. Frequently, indeed almost every day, young ladies from the neighbouring houses drove over to the Pesotskys', and Tanya sang and played the piano with them; sometimes another neighbour, a young man who played the fiddle very well, came as

well. Kovrin listened so avidly to the music and singing that he
was exhausted by it, an exhaustion expressed physically by closed
eyes and a head sunk on one side.

One evening he was sitting on the balcony after tea, reading.
In the drawing-room Tanya, who was a soprano, and one of the
young ladies, a contralto, were practising Braga's well-known
Serenade with the young violinist. Kovrin listened to the words
— they were in Russian — without being able to grasp their
sense. At last, abandoning his book and giving all his attention
to the song, he understood that a young girl, morbidly imaginative, has heard in the garden at night sounds so beautiful and so
strange that she must recognize that their harmony is heavenly
and not to be understood by us mortals, and that it therefore
mounts again to the skies. Kovrin's eyelids grew heavy. He rose
and walked wearily through the drawing-room and into the big
ballroom. When the singing ceased he took Tanya's arm and
walked out on to the balcony with her.

"I have been thinking about a certain legend ever since this
morning," he said. "I don't remember whether I read it somewhere or was told about it, but it is rather strange and completely absurd. To begin with, it is not notable for clarity. A
thousand years ago a monk, dressed in black, was walking in the
desert, somewhere in Syria or Arabia . . . Some miles away from
where he was walking some fishermen saw another black monk
moving slowly over the surface of a lake. This second monk was
a mirage. Now forget all the laws of optics, which the legend apparently does not acknowledge, and listen further. From the
mirage arose a second mirage, and from the second a third, so
that the image of the black monk began to be transmitted endlessly from one layer of the atmosphere to another. He was seen
now in Africa, now in Spain, now in India, now in the Far
North . . . Finally, he left the limits of the earth's atmosphere
and is now wandering all through the universe, and has still not
encountered the conditions which would allow him to disappear.
Perhaps he can now be seen somewhere on Mars or on one of
the stars of the Southern Cross. But, my dear, the essence, the
whole kernel, of the legend is that exactly a thousand years after
the monk walked in the desert, the mirage will again fall into
the earth's atmosphere and appear to men. And it seems that the
thousand years have almost run out . . . According to the idea of

the legend we may expect to see the black monk any day now."

"A strange sort of mirage," said Tanya, who did not like the legend.

"But the oddest thing," laughed Kovrin, "is that I simply can't remember where I got the legend into my head from. Did I read it somewhere? Was I told it? Or perhaps I dreamed of the black monk? I solemnly swear that I don't remember. But the legend engrosses me. I have been thinking about it all day."

Allowing Tanya to go back to her guests, he left the house and walked thoughtfully among the flower-beds. The flowers, because they had just been watered, gave out a damp and disturbing scent. The singing had begun again in the house, and from a distance the violin produced the effect of a human voice. Kovrin, still racking his brains to remember where he had heard or read the legend, wandered slowly into the park and came by degrees as far as the river.

By a footpath that ran down the steep bank among the exposed tree-roots he descended to the level of the water, disturbing the snipe and frightening two ducks. Here and there on the sombre pines the last rays of the setting sun still shone, but on the level of the river it was already evening. Kovrin crossed to the other side by a foot-bridge. Before him lay a wide field, covered with young rye not yet in flower. The distance held neither a human dwelling nor a living soul, and it seemed that if one followed the path it would lead one to that same mysterious and unknown place where the sun had just sunk and where the sunset now glowed with such imposing grandeur.

"How spacious and free and peaceful it is here!" thought Kovrin, walking along the path. "It seems as though the whole world were watching me, keeping quiet, and waiting for me to understand it . . ."

But now ripples ran over the rye and a faint evening breeze lightly touched his uncovered head. A minute later there was another gust of wind, but stronger — the rye rustled and the dull murmur of the pines sounded from far behind him. Kovrin stood still in astonishment. On the horizon, like a tornado or a cyclone, a tall black pillar rose from earth to heaven. Its outlines were indistinct, but in the first moment it was possible to make out that it was not standing still but moving with terrible speed, moving straight towards Kovrin, and the closer it moved, the smaller and clearer it became. Kovrin flung himself to one side, among the rye, to make way for it, and he was only just in time . . .

Past him sped a black-robed monk, with a grey head and black brows, his arms crossed on his breast . . . His bare feet did not touch the ground. His progress had carried him some yards past when he looked round at Kovrin, nodded his head and smiled graciously and at the same time slyly. But how pale, terribly pale and thin the face was! Once more increasing in stature, he skimmed across the river, noiselessly struck against the clayey bank and the pines and, passing right through them, disappeared like smoke.

"Well, do you see that?" muttered Kovrin. "That means there is truth in the legend."

Without trying to explain the strange apparition to himself, satisfied merely to have seen so close and so distinctly not only the black robe but even the monk's face and eyes, and pleasurably excited, he returned to the house.

In the park and the garden people were moving quietly about, in the house somebody was playing — that meant that only he had seen the monk. He very much wanted to tell Tanya and Egor Semenych all about it, but he reflected that they would probably think he was raving and be frightened; it was better to say nothing. He laughed aloud, sang, danced a mazurka; he was in high spirits, and everybody, Tanya and her guests alike, found something special, radiant, and inspired in his face, and thought him very interesting.

III

After supper, when the visitors had gone, he went to his room and lay down on the sofa: he wanted to think about the monk. But a minute later Tanya came in.

"Here, Andryusha, have a look at father's articles," she said, handing him a packet of pamphlets and offprints. "Wonderful articles. He writes excellently."

"Oh yes, excellently!" said Egor Semenych, coming in after her and laughing constrainedly; he felt embarrassed. "Please don't listen to her, don't read them! However, if you want to send yourself to sleep you might perhaps read them: they are an excellent way of inducing sleep."

"I think they are magnificent articles," said Tanya with profound conviction. "You read them, Andryusha, and persuade papa to write more often. He could write a whole course of horticulture."

Egor Semenych guffawed awkwardly, blushed, and began to make the kind of remark usually produced by bashful authors. At length he yielded.

"In that case read Gauchet's article first, and these Russian articles," he muttered, sorting through the pamphlets with shaking hands, "or you won't be able to understand. Before reading my replies, you must know what I am replying to. Still, they're only bits of nonsense . . . very dull. Besides, I think it's bedtime."

Tanya went out. Egor Semenych sat down beside Kovrin on his sofa and sighed deeply.

"Yes, my dear boy . . ." he began after a silence. "Yes, indeed, my dear young scholar. Here I am writing articles, and exhibiting at shows, and getting medals . . . Pesotsky's apples, they say, are as big as your head, and Pesotsky, they say, has made a fortune out of his garden. In short, rich and famous is Kochubey the Magician. But the question arises: what's it all for? The garden really is marvellous, a showpiece . . . It is not a garden so much as a complete institution, and it possesses immense importance for the State, because it is, so to speak, a step towards the new era of Russian agriculture and Russian industry. But what's it for? What's the object of it all?"

"It speaks for itself."

"That's not what I mean. I want to know what is going to happen to the garden when I die. In the form you see it in at present it won't last for more than a month without me. The whole secret of my success is not that the garden is very big and employs a lot of workmen, but that I love the thing — do you know what I mean? — I love it perhaps more than myself. Look at me — I do everything myself, I work from morning till night. I do all the grafting, all the pruning, all the planting — the whole lot. When anybody helps me I get jealous and irritated and shout at them. The whole secret is love, the master's sharp eye, that is, and the master's hand, and the feeling, when you go out somewhere for a short time, that you may sit there, but your heart isn't in it, you are preoccupied, afraid all the time something has happened in the garden. And when I die, who will look after it? Who will do the work? The head gardener? The workmen? Will they? I can tell you one thing, my very dear friend: the principal enemy in our line of business is not hares, nor insect pests, nor frost, but the indifferent stranger."

"What about Tanya?" asked Kovrin laughing. "She can't possibly do more damage than a hare. She loves gardening and understands it."

"Yes, she loves it and understands it. If she gets the garden after I'm dead and runs it herself, of course I could want nothing better. Well, but if, God forbid, she got married?" whispered Egor Semenych, looking at Kovrin with an expression of alarm. "That's the point! She will get married, children will come along, and then there won't be time to think of the garden. What I am most afraid of is that she will marry some young spark who will be greedy and let the garden to market-women, and the whole place will go to the devil in the very first year. In our business women are the scourge of God!"

Egor Semenych sighed and sat silent for a moment.

"Perhaps it is selfish, but I tell you plainly I don't want Tanya to get married. I'm afraid of it! There is one young fop who comes here and saws away on his violin; I know Tanya would never marry him, I'm quite sure of it, but I can't bear to see him! Altogether, my dear boy, I'm a very odd sort of person, I confess."

Egor Semenych got up and walked restlessly about the room, and it was plain that he wanted to say something very important, but could not bring himself to do so.

At last he made up his mind. "I am very fond of you, and I will speak plainly," he said, thrusting his hands into his pockets. "I take a very simple line with certain ticklish subjects and say straight out what I think; I can't bear so-called mental reservations. I tell you plainly you are the only man I would not be afraid to let my daughter marry. You have a brain and a heart, and you wouldn't let my beloved work go to rack and ruin. But the main reason is that I love you like my own son . . . and I am proud of you. If you and Tanya came to some sort of understanding — well, I should be very pleased and happy. I tell you so straight out, without mincing matters, like an honest man."

Kovrin smiled. Egor Semenych opened the door and paused on the threshold.

"If you and Tanya had a son, I'd make a gardener of him," he said thoughtfully. "But that's all idle dreaming . . . Good night."

Left alone, Kovrin made himself more comfortable and began turning over the articles. One was entitled *Catch-crops;* another *Remarks on Mr. Z's Observations on Double Trenching the Soil of a New Garden;* a third, *Further Considerations on Grafting with Dormant Buds* — and there were more of the same kind. But what a harsh and discordant style, what passionate, almost morbid, feeling! Here was one article with what seemed a most unprovocative title and impersonal subject: it dealt with the golden rennet apple. But Egor Semenych had begun with the words *"Audi alteram partem"* and ended with *"Sapienti sat,"* and in between these two sayings there was an absolute spate of envenomed expressions to the address of the "learned ignorance of our professorial horticultural experts, observing nature from their distant academic heights" or "Mr. Gauchet, whose success has been created by amateurs and ignoramuses," followed by out-of-place, forced, and insincere regrets that it was no longer possible to have peasants flogged for stealing fruit and breaking the trees.

"Gardening is a decorative, good-humoured, and healthy pursuit," thought Kovrin, "but even here we find passions and warfare. It must be because everywhere and in every calling, intellectuals are creatures of nerves and remarkable for heightened sensitivity. It is probably inevitable."

He thought of Tanya, who was so pleased with Egor Semenych's articles. Short, pale, so thin that her collarbones showed; the eyes wide open, dark, intelligent, always gazing somewhere, seeking something; steps short and quick, like her father's. She talked a great deal, loved to argue and, when she did so, underlined every phrase, however insignificant, with gesture and facial expression. She must be in the highest degree a creature of nerves.

Kovrin resumed his reading but found it impossible to follow the thread, and abandoned it. The same enjoyable excitement with which he had recently listened to the music and danced the mazurka now possessed him again and evoked a multiplicity of ideas. He got up and began to walk about the room, thinking about the black monk. It came into his mind that if he alone had seen that strange, supernatural monk it must mean that he was sick and had already reached the stage of hallucination. This consideration frightened him, but not for long.

"But after all I feel all right, and I do nobody any harm; that means there is nothing bad in my hallucinations," he thought, feeling reassured.

He sat down on the sofa and wound his arms round his head, as if to keep in check the incomprehensible joy that filled his whole being, then again walked about the room for a time before sitting down to work. But the ideas he found in his book did not satisfy him. He wanted something vast, immense, stupendous. Towards morning he undressed and went reluctantly to bed: after all, he must sleep!

When he heard the steps of Egor Semenych going into the garden, Kovrin rang and ordered the servant to bring him some wine. He drank several glasses of claret with enjoyment, then covered up his head; his consciousness grew cloudy and he fell asleep.

IV

Egor Semenych and Tanya often quarrelled and exchanged unpleasant remarks.

One morning they had both lost their tempers. Tanya burst into tears and went into her own room. She did not emerge either for dinner or for tea. At first Egor Semenych went about with a pompous, sullen air, as though wishing it to be understood that for him the interests of truth and order ranked above everything else on earth, but he was unable to keep this up for long and soon lost heart. He wandered glumly about the park, sighing constantly. "Ah, dear God, dear God!" — and at dinner did not eat a morsel. At last, with a guilty and conscience-stricken look, he knocked at the locked door and called timidly.

"Tanya! Tanya!"

From the other side of the door a voice, weak and faint with crying, but resolute, answered,

"Leave me alone, I implore you."

The master's trouble was reflected all over the house and even among the people working in the garden. Kovrin was engrossed in the interest of his work, but towards the last even he began to feel bored and uncomfortable. In order to disperse the general ill-humour, he made up his mind to intervene and late in the afternoon knocked at Tanya's door and was admitted.

"Oh, oh, how disgraceful!" he began playfully, gazing with astonishment at Tanya's woebegone face, tear-stained and covered with red blotches. "Is it so serious? Oh, oh!"

"If you knew how he makes me suffer!" she said, and copious bitter tears rained from her big eyes. "He tortures me!" she went on, wringing her hands. "I didn't say anything to him . . . nothing . . . I only said there was no need to keep . . . unnecessary workers on, when . . . when we can get day labourers if we want them. After all . . . after all, the workmen have been doing nothing for a whole week . . . I . . . I only said that, and he began to shout and say a lot . . . of hurtful, terribly insulting things to me. Why?"

"Stop it, stop it," said Kovrin, smoothing her hair. "You've quarrelled, you've had your cry, that's enough. You mustn't go on being angry, it's not nice . . . especially as he loves you very, very dearly."

"He's spoilt . . . spoilt my whole life," Tanya sobbed. "I hear nothing but taunts and . . . and insults from him. He thinks I am in the way in his house. Well, what about it? He's right. I'll leave tomorrow, I'll get work as a telegraph clerk . . . Let him . . ."

"Come, come, come . . . Don't cry, Tanya. You mustn't, my dear . . . You are both hot-tempered and easily upset, and you are both in the wrong. Come along, I'll make it up between you."

Kovrin spoke gently and persuasively, but she went on crying, her shoulders shaking and her hands clenched, as though she really had suffered a terrible misfortune. He was all the more sorry for her because her grievance was not serious, although her suffering was profound. What little things were sufficient to make her unhappy for a whole day and, it might well be, for all her life! While he tried to comfort Tanya, Kovrin was thinking that besides this young girl and her father there were no others to be found in the whole world who loved him like one of themselves, as one of the family; he had lost his mother and father in early childhood and so might never, if it had not been for these two people, have known what sincere affection was, or that simple-hearted uncritical love which is lavished only on near kindred. And he felt that his own ravelled, half-sick nerves responded to the nerves of this quivering weeping girl like iron to a magnet. He could never have loved a strong healthy rosy cheeked woman, but the pale weak unhappy Tanya appealed to him.

Willingly he continued to stroke her hair and shoulders, pressed her hand and wiped away her tears . . . At length she stopped crying. She still went on for a long time complaining of her father and her intolerably difficult life in that house, and begging Kovrin to enter into her situation, then little by little she began to smile and sigh over the fact that God had given her such a bad disposition, and at last, with a loud laugh, called herself a wicked girl and ran out of the room.

When Kovrin went out into the garden a little later, Egor Semenych and Tanya were walking side by side along one of the paths as though nothing had happened, and eating rye-bread and salt as if they were both hungry.

V

Pleased that he had been so successful in the role of peacemaker, Kovrin went into the park. Sitting contemplatively on a bench, he heard carriage wheels and women's voices; visitors were arriving. When the evening shadows fell across the garden, the faint sounds of a violin and of voices singing came to his ears and reminded him of the black monk. Where, through what country, over what planet, was that optical illusion now in motion?

Hardly had he recalled the legend and pictured in his imagination the sombre vision he had seen in the rye-field than from beyond the pines directly opposite there emerged silently, without the slightest rustle, a man of medium height with an uncovered grey head, dressed all in black and with bare feet like a beggar, and on his pale deathly face the black brows stood out sharply. With a nod of greeting the beggar or pilgrim noiselessly approached the bench and sat down, and Kovrin recognized the black monk. For a moment they looked at one another, Kovrin with astonishment, the monk amiably and, as before, somewhat slyly, with the expression of a cunning old fox.

"But you're a mirage, you know," said Kovrin. "How is it that you are here, and sitting still in one place? It doesn't fit in with the legend."

"That does not matter," answered the monk softly, after a

short pause, turning his face towards him. "The legend, the mirage, and I myself are all products of your excited imagination. I am an illusion."

"Then you don't exist?" asked Kovrin.

"Think what you choose," said the monk, smiling faintly. "I exist in your imagination, and your imagination is part of nature, which means that I exist in nature, too."

"You have a very old, intelligent, and remarkably expressive face, as though you really had lived a thousand years," said Kovrin. "I didn't know my imagination was capable of creating such phenomena. But why do you look at me so delightedly? Are you pleased with me?"

"Yes. You are one of the few who are rightly called God's elect. You serve eternal truth. Your thoughts and purposes, your astonishing scholarship and your whole life bear a divine, a heavenly stamp, since they are dedicated to reason and beauty, that is to what is eternal."

"You say eternal truth . . . But is eternal truth attainable by or necessary to men, if there is not eternal life?"

"There is eternal life," said the monk.

"You believe in human immortality?"

"Yes, of course. A great and brilliant future awaits mankind. And the more people there are on earth like you, the sooner that future will come into being. Without you, the servants of the high First Cause, living consciously and freely, humanity would be null; in the natural course of development it would have to wait a long time for the end of its earthly history. But you will lead it several thousand years in advance into the realm of eternal truth — and in this lies your high desert. You are the embodiment of the blessing of God which rests on mankind."

"What is the object of eternal life?" asked Kovrin.

"Like that of all life, delight. True delight is in knowledge; and eternal life presents uncountable and inexhaustible sources of knowledge, and this is the sense in which it is written, 'In my Father's house are many mansions.' "

"If you knew what a pleasure it is to listen to you!" said Kovrin, rubbing his hands with enjoyment.

"I am very glad."

"But I know that when you go away I shall be worried by the

question of your reality. You are an illusion, an hallucination. Does that mean that I am sick in mind, not normal?"

"Even if that is so, why be troubled? You are ill because you are overworked and have exhausted your strength, and that means that you have sacrificed your health to the Idea, and the time is near when you will give it your very life. What could be better? This is the end to which all noble natures, gifted from on high, aspire."

"If I know that I am mentally ill, can I have faith in myself?"

"And how do you know that the men of genius in whom the whole world has faith did not see visions too? Scientists now say that genius is akin to madness. My friend, only the commonplace, the herd, are healthy and normal. Ideas about this being an age of nerves, degeneracy, overwork, and so on can seriously disturb only those for whom the present is the object of life, that is the herd."

"The Romans said: *mens sana in corpore sano.*"

"Not everything the Greeks or Romans said is true. Exaltation, excitement, ecstasy — everything that distinguishes prophets, poets, and martyrs of the Idea from ordinary people, is antagonistic to the animal side of man, that is to his physical health. I repeat: if you want to be healthy and normal, join the herd."

"It is strange — you say the same things as have often come into my own mind," said Kovrin. "It's as if you had spied and eavesdropped on my secret thoughts. But don't let us talk about me. What do you understand by eternal truth?"

The monk did not answer. Kovrin looked at him and could not distinguish his face: his features had grown fluid and hazy. Then the monk's head and hands began to disappear; his body merged into the bench and the twilight, and he vanished completely.

"The hallucination is over!" said Kovrin, and he laughed. "A pity!"

He went back to the house cheerful and happy. The little that the black monk had said to him flattered not his vanity but his whole soul, his whole being. To be one of the elect, to serve eternal truth, to stand in the ranks of those who were trying to make mankind worthy of the kingdom of God several thousand years in advance, that is to spare them several thousand years of strife, sin, and suffering, to sacrifice everything to the Idea — youth, strength, health — to be ready to die for the common good — what an exalted and happy fate! His past, pure, virtuous, laborious, rose before his memory, he remembered what he had learnt and what he had taught to others, and decided that there was no exaggeration in the monk's words.

Tanya was walking towards him through the park. She had already changed her clothes.

"So this is where you are!" she said. "We have been looking for you everywhere . . . But what is the matter with you?" she wondered, looking at his radiant excited face and eyes full of tears. "How strange you seem, Andryusha!"

"I am content, Tanya," said Kovrin, putting his hands on her shoulders. "I am more than content, I am happy! Tanya, dear Tanya, you are an extraordinarily sympathetic person. Dear Tanya, I am so glad, so glad!"

He kissed both her hands warmly and went on,

"I have just experienced some bright, wonderful, celestial moments. But I can't tell you everything, because you will call me mad or not believe me. Let us talk about you. Dear, wonderful Tanya! I love you, and I have grown used to loving you. It has become necessary to my heart to have you near and meet you a dozen times a day. I do not know how I can do without you when I go back home."

"Well!" laughed Tanya. "You will forget about us in two days. We are little people and you are a great man."

"No, we must be serious!" he said. "I will take you with me, Tanya. Shall I? You will come with me? You will be mine?"

"Well!" said Tanya, trying to laugh again, but the laugh would not come, and red patches appeared on her face.

She began to breathe fast and walked quicker and quicker, not towards the house, but further into the park.

"I did not think of this . . . I did not!" she said, clasping her hands as though in despair.

Kovrin went after her, saying with the same radiant, delighted face,

"I want a love which will possess me wholly, and that love only you can give me, Tanya. I am happy! Happy!"

She was stunned; she was stooping and shrunken as though she

had aged ten years in a moment, but he thought her beautiful
and expressed aloud his delight:

"How pretty she is!"

VI

When he learned from Kovrin that there not only was a romance
afoot, but would even be a wedding, Egor Semenych spent a long
time pacing from corner to corner, trying to hide his excitement.
His hands began to shake, his neck swelled and went red, he
ordered out his racing droshky and drove off somewhere. Tanya,
seeing how he lashed the horse and how his cap was pulled down
almost to his ears, understood his mood, shut herself up in her
room and wept all day.

In the orangeries the peaches and plums were already ripe; the
picking and dispatch to Moscow of this capricious and delicate
freight demanded much care, labour, and trouble. Thanks to the
hot dry summer, every tree had to be watered, which took much
time and workers' effort; and a multitude of caterpillars made
their appearance and, to Kovrin's disgust, the workmen and even
Egor Semenych and Tanya crushed them with their bare fingers.
With all this, it was necessary to take orders already for fruit and
trees for the autumn, and conduct a big correspondence. And in
the very busiest time, when nobody seemed to have a moment to
spare, work in the fields began, taking away from the garden
more than half of the labourers; Egor Semenych, deeply sun-
burnt, tired out, bad tempered, galloped from garden to field
and shouted that he was being torn in pieces and would put a
bullet through his head.

On top of this there was the bustle over the trousseau, to which
the Pesotskys attached no small importance; the clashing of scis-
sors, the noise of sewing machines, the fumes from the irons, and
the whims of the dressmaker, a nervous and touchy lady, made
the heads of everybody in the house swim. And as though on
purpose to make matters worse, every day saw the arrival of
visitors who had to be amused, fed, and even put up for the
night. But all this drudgery passed unnoticed, as if in a dream.
Tanya felt as though love and happiness had taken her unawares,
although since the age of fourteen she had somehow been convinced that Kovrin was certain to marry her. She was stunned
and bewildered, she could not believe it . . . Now she was visited

by a sudden access of such joy that she wanted to fly above the clouds to give thanks to God, now she suddenly remembered that in August she would have to leave the nest and part from her father, or the idea would come from God knows where that she was worthless, trivial, and undeserving of the love of such a great man as Kovrin — and she would go off to her room, lock herself in, and weep bitterly for several hours. When there were visitors it would suddenly be borne in upon her that Kovrin was uncommonly handsome and that all the ladies were in love with him and jealous of her, and her heart would fill with pride and rapture, as though she had conquered the whole world, but it was enough for him to smile politely at some young lady for her to tremble with jealousy, go away to her room — and dissolve once more into tears. These new emotions took complete possession of her; she helped her father mechanically and noticed neither the peaches, nor the caterpillars, nor the workmen, nor how quickly the time fled.

Almost the same thing was happening with Egor Semenych. He worked from morning till night, was always hurrying off somewhere, losing his temper, getting beside himself with rage, but all in some enchanted half-dream. It was as if there were two people inside him: one was the real Egor Semenych who listened to the head gardener, Ivan Karlych, reporting that something had gone wrong, and waxed indignant or clutched his head in despair, the other an impostor, who seemed half drunk and would break off a business conversation in mid-sentence, clap the gardener on the shoulder and begin to mutter,

"Whatever you say, blood counts for a lot. His mother was a wonderful person, the best and cleverest of women. It was a pleasure to look at her kind, bright, pure face, like an angel's. She painted beautifully, wrote verses, spoke five foreign languages, sang . . . The poor thing, Heaven rest her soul, died of consumption."

The false Egor Semenych sighed and, after a moment's silence, went on,

"When he was a boy and growing up in my house, he had the same angelic face, bright and good. His look, his movements, and his way of talking were gentle and elegant, like his mother's. And his mind? We were always struck by the quality of his mind. Indeed, he didn't get his master's degree for nothing! Not for nothing! You wait and see, Ivan Karlych, what he will be in ten years! There'll be no touching him!"

But here the true Egor Semenych, recollecting himself, pulled a terrible face, clutched his head and cried,

"Devils! Spoilt, destroyed, frozen! The garden's ruined! The garden's done for!"

Kovrin was working with all his former ardour and did not notice the turmoil. Love had only added fuel to his fires. After every interview with Tanya he returned, exalted and happy, to his room and took up a book or his manuscript with the same passion with which he had just been kissing and declaring his love for her. What the black monk had said about God's elect, eternal truth, the dazzling future of mankind, and so on, had given his work a special and extraordinary significance and filled his soul with pride and the consciousness of his own eminence. Once or twice every week, in the park or the house, he saw the black monk and held long conversations with him, but this did not frighten him, on the contrary it enraptured him, since he was firmly convinced that such visions appear only to the elect, to outstanding people who have dedicated themselves to the service of the Idea.

On one occasion the monk appeared during dinner and sat down by a window in the dining-room. Kovrin was delighted and adroitly led the conversation with Egor Semenych and Tanya to topics with might interest the monk; the black-robed visitor listened and nodded affably, and Egor Semenych also listened and smiled cheerfully, with no suspicion that Kovrin was talking not to them but to his hallucination.

The Feast of the Assumption arrived almost unnoticed, and soon after came the day of the wedding, which was celebrated, on Egor Semenych's insistence, "with a splash," that is with senseless revelry that lasted for forty-eight hours. Something like three thousand people ate and drank, but what with the very bad hired orchestra, the noisy toasts, the hurrying servants, the din, and the crush, nobody could appreciate either the expensive wines or the marvellous food ordered from Moscow.

VII

During one of the long nights of winter Kovrin was lying in bed reading a French novel. Poor Tanya who, unused to town life, always had a headache in the evening, had long been asleep, and occasionally uttered some fragmentary, wandering phrases.

It struck three. Kovrin extinguished the candle and lay down, but he could not sleep because the room was very hot and Tanya was talking in her sleep. At half-past four he lit the candle again and saw as he did so the black monk sitting in an armchair near the bed.

"Good morning," said the monk and after a moment's silence asked, "What are you thinking about?"

"Fame," answered Kovrin. "The French novel I have just been reading depicts a man, a young scholar, who does stupid things and pines away out of longing for fame. It is a longing I cannot understand."

"Because you are sensible. You treat fame with indifference, like a toy which does not interest you."

"Yes, that's true."

"Reputation does not attract you. What is there flattering, or entertaining, or edifying about having your name cut on a tombstone and the inscription with its gilding wiped away afterwards by the hand of time? Besides, there are luckily too many of you for a feeble human memory to be able to retain your names."

"To be sure," agreed Kovrin. "Besides, why should they be remembered? But let us talk about something else. Happiness, for example. What is happiness?"

When the clock struck five he was sitting on the edge of the bed and saying to the monk.

"In antiquity a certain fortunate man grew at length afraid of his luck, it was so great, and in order to appease the gods he sacrificed his favourite ring to them. You remember? And I, like Polycrates, am beginning to be a little worried by my good fortune. It seems strange that I experience nothing from morning to night but gladness; it fills me completely and stifles all other feelings. I don't know what is meant by grief, sadness, or boredom. As you see, I don't sleep, I have insomnia, but I'm not bored. Seriously, it is beginning to worry me."

"But why?" the monk wondered. "Is joy an unnatural feeling? Should it not be a man's normal state? The higher a man's mental and moral development and the freer he is, the more pleasure does life give him. Socrates, Diogenes, and Marcus Aurelius ex-

perienced joy, not sorrow. And the apostle says, 'Rejoice alway.'
Rejoice, then, and be happy."

"And if the gods grow suddenly jealous?" asked Kovrin jest-
ingly, with a laugh. "If they take away my comforts and make me
suffer cold and hunger, it will hardly be to my taste."

Meanwhile Tanya had awakened and was watching her husband with amazement and terror. He was talking, addressing the
armchair, gesticulating and laughing; his eyes glittered and there
was something strange in his laugh.

"Andryusha, who are you talking to?" she asked, seizing the
hand he had stretched towards the monk. "Andryusha! Who is
it?"

"What? Who to?" said Kovrin, disconcerted. "To him . . .
There he is, sitting there," he went on, pointing to the black
monk.

"There is nobody here . . . nobody! Andryusha, you are ill!"

Tanya put her arms round her husband, clinging to him as
though shielding him from the apparition, and covered his eyes
with her hand.

"You're ill," she sobbed, her whole body shaking.

"Forgive me, my dear, but I have seen for a long time that
your mind was disturbed . . . You are ill in mind, Andryusha . . ."

Her trembling communicated itself to him. He looked once
more at the armchair, which was now empty, felt a sudden weakness in his arms and legs, and began to dress in alarm.

"It's nothing, Tanya, it's nothing," he muttered, still shaking.
"I really am a little unwell . . . it is time I recognized it."

"I noticed it long ago . . . and papa noticed," she said, trying to
restrain her sobs. "You talk to yourself, you smile in a strange
sort of way . . . you don't sleep. Oh God, God save us!" she said
in terror. "But don't be afraid, Andryusha, don't be afraid, for
God's sake don't be afraid . . ."

She also began to dress. Only now, looking at her, did Kovrin
understand the full danger of his position, the meaning of the
black monk and his conversations with him. Now it was clear to
him that he was mad.

Both, without knowing why, finished dressing and went into
the drawing-room, she first, he following her. There, awakened
by the sobbing, Egor Semenych, who was on a visit to them,
stood in his dressing-gown and with a candle in his hand.

"Don't be afraid, Andryusha," said Tanya, shaking as though with fever, "don't be afraid . . . Papa, all this will pass . . . it will all pass . . ."

Kovrin could not speak for agitation. He tried to say to his father-in-law in a jesting tone, "Congratulate me, it seems I've gone out of my mind," but he could only move his lips and smile bitterly.

At nine o'clock in the morning they put on his overcoat and fur coat, wrapped him in a shawl, and took him in the carriage to his doctor's. He began to have treatment.

VIII

Summer had come again, and the doctor had ordered him to go into the country. Kovrin was already well again, he had ceased to see the black monk, and it only remained for him to regain his physical strength. Living with his father-in-law in the country he drank a great deal of milk, worked only two hours a day, and did not drink or smoke.

In the middle of July, on the eve of St. Elias's Day, an evening service was held in the house. When the clerk handed the priest the censer, the huge old ballroom began to smell like a cemetery, and Kovrin to feel restless. He went out into the garden. Paying no attention to the rich profusion of flowers, he wandered round the garden, sat for a while on a bench, and then walked through the park; when he came to the river he went down the bank and stood there irresolutely, looking at the water. From the sombre pines with their mossy roots, which had seen him there the year before, so young, fit, and pleased with life, there now came not a whisper; they stood motionless and dumb, as though they did not know him. And indeed, his head had been cropped and the long, beautiful hair had gone, his movements were languid, and his face was fuller and paler than in the previous summer.

He crossed to the other side by the footbridge. There, where there had been rye the year before, the oats had been reaped and left lying in rows. The sun had gone down and a wide red sunset flared on the horizon, promising windy weather for the next day. It was quiet. Gazing in the direction from which the black monk had appeared the year before, Kovrin stood for about twenty minutes, until the red glow had begun to fade . . .

When he returned to the house, weary and dissatisfied, the

service was over. Egor Semenych and Tanya were sitting on the
terrace drinking tea. They were talking about something, but
stopped abruptly when they saw him, and he concluded from
their expressions that the conversation had been about him.

"I think it is time for your milk," said Tanya to her husband.

"No, it's not," he answered, sitting down on the lowest step.
"Drink it yourself. I won't."

Tanya exchanged alarmed glances with her father and said
apologetically,

"You say yourself that the milk is good for you."

"Yes, very good!" Kovrin sneered. "I congratulate you; I have
put on another pound since Friday." Clutching his head tightly
with his hands, he said in anguished tones, "Why, oh why, did
you try to cure me? Bromides, idleness, warm baths, constant
watching, cowardly misgivings over every mouthful and every
step — in the end it will all make a complete idiot of me. I was
going out of my mind, I had delusions of grandeur, but on the
other hand I was cheerful, vigorous, and even happy, I was interesting and original. Now I have become more reasonable and
stable, but on the other hand I'm like everybody else: I'm a
mediocrity, I'm bored with life . . . Oh, how cruel you have been
to me! I did have hallucinations, but what harm did they do
anybody? I ask you, what harm did they do anybody?"

"God knows what you are talking about!" sighed Egor Semenych. "It's tiresome even to listen to you."

"Then don't listen."

The presence of other people, especially Egor Semenych, now
irritated Kovrin; he answered him dryly, coldly, even rudely,
sometimes without looking at him, as though he found him ridiculous or hateful, and Egor Semenych grew confused and coughed
apologetically, although he did not feel guilty in any way. Not
understanding why their pleasant, placid relations had changed
so sharply, Tanya clung to her father and gazed anxiously into
his eyes; she wanted to understand but she could not, and the
only thing that was clear to her was that their relations grew
worse and worse with every day, that her father had recently
aged very much, and that her husband had grown moody, capricious, quarrelsome, and uninteresting. She could no longer laugh
or sing, ate nothing at dinner, lay awake all night long waiting
for something terrible to happen, and was so exhausted that

sometimes she lay in a stupor from dinner-time until evening. During the service she had thought her father was crying, and now when they were all three sitting on the terrace she strove her utmost not to think about it.

"How lucky Buddha and Mahomet and Shakespeare were — they had no kind relatives and doctors to cure them of their ecstasies and inspirations!" said Kovrin. "If Mahomet had taken potassium bromide for his nerves, worked only two hours a day, and drunk milk, as little would have remained of that remarkable man as of his dog. In the long run, the result of what the doctors and the kind relatives do will be that mankind will grow stupid, mediocrity will be considered genius, and civilization will perish. If you only knew how grateful I am to you!" said Kovrin, with venom.

He felt a rush of annoyance, and in order not to say more than he should, stood up quickly and went into the house. The night was still and the scent of tobacco-flowers and jalap was borne in through the open windows from the garden. In the great dark ballroom the moonlight lay in green patches on the floor and the grand piano. Kovrin was reminded of the delights of the previous summer, when the jalap was just as sweet-scented and the moon shone through the windows. In an attempt to bring back the mood of the past summer he hurried to his study, lit a strong cigar and ordered a servant to bring some wine. But the cigar made his mouth taste bitter and disgusting, and the wine did not seem to have the same savour as the year before. And what a difference the loss of habit made! The cigar and two mouthfuls of wine made his head begin to swim and his heart to pound, so that he had to take potassium bromide.

Before she went to bed, Tanya said to him,

"My father adores you. You are annoyed with him over something, and it is killing him. Look, he is ageing not daily but hourly. I implore you, Andryusha, for God's sake, for the sake of your own dead father, for my peace of mind, be kind to him!"

"I can't and I won't."

"But why not?" asked Tanya, her whole body beginning to tremble. "Explain to me."

"Because we are not in sympathy, that's all," Kovrin answered with a careless shrug of the shoulders; "but we won't talk about him, he is your father."

"I can't understand, I can't!" said Tanya, clutching her temples and staring fixedly at one point. "Something incomprehensible and horrible is happening in this house. You have changed, you are not like yourself . . . You, an exceptional and reasonable man, lose your temper over trifles and get involved in petty wrangles . . . Such little things upset you that sometimes we are left gaping and unable to believe this can really be you. Well, don't be angry, don't be angry," she went on, frightened by her own words and kissing his hands. "You are clever and good and noble. You will be fair to my father. He is so good!"

"He's not good, only good-natured. Stage uncles like your father, with well-fed, good-humoured faces and extraordinary hospitality and eccentricity, once used to touch and amuse me in books or music-hall sketches and in real life, but now I find them repulsive. They are egoists to the marrow of their bones. What I most dislike is their good living, and that visceral optimism, like a bull's or a wild boar's."

Tanya sat down on the bed and laid her head on the pillow.

"This is torture," she said, and her voice clearly showed that she was completely worn out and found it difficult to speak. "Not one moment's peace since the winter! . . . My God, it is dreadful! I am in agony . . ."

"Yes, of course, I am Herod and you and your father are the Egyptian innocents. Of course!"

His face looked ugly and unpleasant to Tanya. Hatred and sneering did not suit him. Even earlier she had noticed that his face seemed to lack something, as though it too had lost something when his hair was cropped. She wanted to say something wounding, but the moment she detected a feeling of enmity in herself she took fright and went out of the bedroom.

IX

Kovrin had been given a university chair. His inaugural lecture was arranged for 2 December, and a notice announcing it hung in the university corridor. But on the appointed day he informed the supervisor of students by telegram that illness would prevent him from giving the lecture.

He was suffering from effusions of blood from the throat. He frequently spat blood, and once or twice a month it flowed copiously, and then he felt extremely weak and fell into a lethargic state. The illness did not particularly alarm him, since he knew that his mother had lived ten years or more with exactly the same condition, and the doctors assured him that it was not dangerous; they merely advised him not to get excited, to lead a regular life, and not to talk so much.

In January again the lecture did not take place, for the same reason, and in February it was already too late to start the course. It had to be postponed until the next academic year.

He was no longer living with Tanya, but with another woman, two years older than himself, who looked after him like a child. His mood was peaceful and accommodating; he submitted willingly to everything, and when Varvara Nikolaevna — that was the name of his companion — proposed to take him to the Crimea, he consented, although he foresaw that no good would come of the journey.

They arrived in Sebastopol in the evening and stopped at a hotel to rest before going on the next day to Yalta. Both were weary with travelling. Varvara Nikolaevna had some tea, went to bed and was soon asleep. But Kovrin did not go to bed. At home, an hour before they left for the station, he had received a letter from Tanya, which he had felt unable to open, and now it lay in one of his pockets and the thought of it was unpleasantly exciting. In the depths of his heart he now sincerely believed that his marriage to Tanya had been a mistake, he was pleased to have broken finally with her, and the memory of this woman, who had in the end become a living, walking corpse, in which everything seemed to have died but the great, clever, staring eyes — her memory aroused only his pity and his anger against himself. The handwriting on the envelope reminded him that about two years ago he had been unjust and cruel, had avenged himself on innocent people for his spiritual emptiness, boredom, loneliness, and dissatisfaction with life. He remembered, too, how he had once torn into little pieces his thesis and all the articles he had written during his illness and thrown them out of the window, and how the pieces, carried on the wind, had lodged in the trees and on the flowers; in every line he had seen strange, unfounded pretensions, frivolous rage, insolence, and delusions of grandeur, and this had produced the same effect on him as reading an inventory of his own vices might have done; but when the last notebook had been torn up and vanished out of the

window, he had felt suddenly vexed and bitter, and he had gone
to his wife and assailed her with a flood of disagreeable remarks.
God, how he had tormented her! Once, when he wished to cause
her pain, he had told her that her father's part in their romance
had been unsavoury, since he had asked him to marry her; Egor
Semenych had chanced to overhear this, and had burst into the
room, but desperation made him unable to utter a word and
he could only stamp and produce a strange bellowing, as though
his tongue had been torn out, while Tanya looked at her father,
gave a heart-rending shriek, and fainted. It had been an ugly
scene.

All this passed through his memory as he looked at the familiar
handwriting. Kovrin went out on to the balcony; the weather
was calm and warm and there was a smell of the sea. The glorious bay, reflecting the moon and the lights, had a colour to
which it was difficult to put a name. It was a soft and tender
mingling of blue and green; in places the water looked like blue
copperas and in places it seemed as though the moonlight had
thickened and now filled the bay instead of water; altogether,
what a harmony of colours, what a mood of peace, exaltation,
and tranquillity!

Below the balcony the windows of the floor beneath probably
stood open, and the sound of laughter and women's voices could
be clearly heard. Evidently a party was taking place there.

Kovrin made an effort, opened the letter and, going into the
room read:

"My father has just died. I am indebted to you for this, since
it was you who killed him. Our garden is being ruined, it is
already in the hands of strangers; that is to say that the very thing
my poor father was so afraid of is happening. This also I owe
to you. I hate you with my whole soul, and I hope you will soon
perish. Oh, how I am suffering! My heart burns with unendur-
able pain . . . May you be accursed! I took you for an unusual
being, a genius, I loved you, but you proved to be a madman . . ."

Kovrin could read no more, and he tore up the letter and
threw it away. He was in the grip of an anxiety that was very like
panic. Varvara Nikolaevna was asleep behind the screen and her
breathing was audible; from the lower floor came the sound of
women's voices and laughter, but he felt as though besides himself there was not a living soul in the hotel. Because the unhappy

Tanya, overcome by grief, had cursed him in her letter and wished for his destruction, he was uneasy and glanced at the door as though afraid that the same unknown power that had brought such devastation into his life and the lives of those near to him would enter the hotel room and once again do as it pleased with him.

He knew by experience that when the nerves get out of control, the best remedy is work. He must sit down at his desk and force himself at whatever cost to concentrate his thoughts on one particular idea. From his red portfolio he took out a notebook in which he had sketched out the plan for a short piece of work he had thought of compiling, if he found the Crimea boring with nothing to do. He sat down and began to tackle this plan, and it seemed to him that his old peaceful, resigned, unconcerned, mood was returning. The notebook with its plan even led him to contemplate the vanities of this world. He thought of how much life takes from us in return for the trumpery or very mediocre benefits it is able to bestow. For example, to obtain a university chair, to be a very ordinary professor expounding very ordinary ideas that were not even his own, in lifeless, ponderous, and boring language, to attain, in short, the position of a second-rate scholar, he, Kovrin, had been obliged to study for fifteen years, to work day and night, to suffer from a serious psychological illness, and to commit a great number of such stupidities and wrongs as it would be pleasanter to forget. Kovrin now clearly recognized that he was a mediocrity, and had willingly reconciled himself to the fact, since in his opinion every human being ought to be satisfied with what he is.

His plan would have had complete success in soothing him, but that the torn letter lying on the floor prevented him from concentrating. He got up from the table, picked up the bits of paper and flung them out of the window, but a light breeze was blowing in from the sea and the paper scattered on the windowsill. Again an uneasiness that resembled fear took possession of him, and he began to feel as though except for himself there was not a soul in the whole hotel . . . He went out on to the balcony. The bay, like something alive, looked at him with a multitude of azure, dark blue, turquoise, and fiery-red eyes, and drew him towards itself. It was certainly hot and stuffy and it would not be a bad idea to bathe.

Suddenly a violin began to play on the lower floor, under the balcony, and two sweet women's voices began to sing. It was something familiar. The drawing-room ballad which was being sung down there was about a young girl with a sick imagination, listening in the garden at night to mysterious sounds and deciding that this was a sacred harmony, incomprehensible to mortals like us . . . Kovrin caught his breath, his heart contracted with sorrow, and yet a marvellous sweet joy, which he had long forgotten, quivered in his breast.

A tall black pillar, like a tornado or a typhoon, appeared on the far shore of the bay. With terrible swiftness it moved across the bay towards the hotel, growing steadily darker and smaller, and Kovrin barely had time to move aside to give it passage . . . A monk with a grey uncovered head and black brows, barefooted, his arms crossed on his breast, swept past him and stopped in the middle of the room.

"Why did you not believe me?" he asked reproachfully, looking courteously at Kovrin. "If you had believed me when I said that you were a genius you would not have spent two such sad and barren years."

Kovrin already believed that he was one of God's elect and a genius, he vividly remembered all his former conversations with the black monk and would have spoken, but blood was flowing from his throat and down his breast; he passed his hands helplessly over his breast and his cuffs were wet with blood. He tried to summon Varvara Nikolaevna, sleeping behind the screen, made a great effort and said,

"Tanya!"

He fell to the floor and called again, raising himself on his hands,

"Tanya!"

He was invoking Tanya, invoking the great garden with its wealth of flowers sprinkled with dew, invoking the park, the pines with their mossy roots, the rye-field, his wonderful learning, his youth and fearlessness and his joy, invoking life itself, which had been so beautiful. On the floor near his head he could see a great pool of blood and he was so weak that now he could not speak a word, but a boundless, inexpressible happiness filled his whole being. Downstairs under the balcony they were playing the serenade, and the black monk was whispering to him that he was a genius, and that he was dying only because his weak mortal body had lost its equilibrium and could no longer serve as a sheath for his genius.

When Varvara Nikolaevna woke up and came out from behind the screen, Kovrin was dead, with a fixed smile of beatitude on his face.

(Translated by Jessie Coulson)

STEPHEN CRANE (1871–1900) Born in Newark, New Jersey, Crane was the fourteenth child of a Methodist minister. He died of tuberculosis in Badenweiler, Germany at the age of twenty-eight.

During the second of the two semesters he attended college he wrote *Maggie: A Girl of the Streets* (1893). In the few years of life remaining to him, he wrote fiction, poetry, and journalism which, in the collected edition, fill twelve volumes. During these years he was a New York newspaperman and foreign correspondent and traveled extensively within the United States and Mexico. Once, returning from a filibustering expedition to Cuba, he was shipwrecked. He was commended for bravery under fire when he covered the Greco-Turkish War. Near the end of his life he married and settled in Surrey, England where he secured the devoted friendship of Joseph Conrad, Henry James, and H. G. Wells.

Much of Crane's writing was composed at a furious pace and under financial pressure. In his best work, such as "The Blue Hotel" (1898) and his novel *The Red Badge of Courage* (1895), he created a concentrated narrative which is at once naturalistic, symbolic, and impressionistic.

THE BLUE HOTEL

Stephen Crane

I

The Palace Hotel at Fort Romper was painted a light blue, a shade that is on the legs of a kind of heron, causing the bird to declare its position against any background. The Palace Hotel, then, was always screaming and howling in a way that made the dazzling winter landscape of Nebraska seem only a grey swampish hush. It stood alone on the prairie, and when the snow was falling the town two hundred yards away was not visible. But when the traveller alighted at the railway station he was obliged to pass the Palace Hotel before he could come upon the company of low clapboard houses which composed Fort Romper, and it was not to be thought that any traveller could pass the Palace Hotel without looking at it. Pat Scully, the proprietor, had proved himself a master of strategy when he chose his paints. It is true that on clear days, when the great transcontinental expresses, long lines of swaying Pullmans, swept through Fort Romper, passengers were overcome at the sight, and the cult that knows the brown-reds and the subdivisions of the dark greens of the East expressed shame, pity, horror, in a laugh. But to the citizens of this prairie town and to the people who would naturally stop there, Pat Scully had performed a feat. With this opulence and splendour, these creeds, classes, egotisms, that streamed through Romper on the rails day after day, they had no colour in common.

As if the displayed delights of such a blue hotel were not sufficiently enticing, it was Scully's habit to go every morning and evening to meet the leisurely trains that stopped at Romper and work his seductions upon any man that he might see wavering, gripsack in hand.

One morning, when a snow-crusted engine dragged its long string of freight cars and its one passenger coach to the station, Scully performed the marvel of catching three men. One was a shaky and quick-eyed Swede, with a great shining cheap valise; one was a tall bronzed cowboy, who was on his way to a ranch near the Dakota line; one was a little silent man from the East, who didn't look it, and didn't announce it. Scully practically made them prisoners. He was so nimble and merry and kindly that each probably felt it would be the height of brutality to try to escape. They trudged off over the creaking board sidewalks in the wake of the eager little Irishman. He wore a heavy fur cap squeezed tightly down on his head. It caused his two red ears to stick out stiffly, as if they were made of tin.

At last, Scully, elaborately, with boisterous hospitality, conducted them through the portals of the blue hotel. The room which they entered was small. It seemed to be merely a proper temple for an enormous stove, which, in the centre, was humming with godlike violence. At various points on its surface the iron had become luminous and glowed yellow from the heat. Beside the stove Scully's son Johnnie was playing High-Five with an old farmer who had whiskers both grey and sandy. They were quarrelling. Frequently the old farmer turned his face toward a box of sawdust — coloured brown from tobacco juice — that was behind the stove, and spat with an air of great impatience and irritation. With a loud flourish of words Scully destroyed the game of cards, and bustled his son upstairs with part of the baggage of the new guests. He himself conducted them to three basins of the coldest water in the world. The cowboy and the Easterner burnished themselves fiery red with this water, until it seemed to be some kind of metal-polish. The Swede, however, merely dipped his fingers gingerly and with trepidation. It was notable that throughout this series of small ceremonies the three travellers were made to feel that Scully was very benevolent. He was conferring great favours upon them. He handed the towel from one to another with an air of philanthropic impulse.

Afterward they went to the first room, and, sitting about the stove, listened to Scully's officious clamour at his daughters, who were preparing the midday meal. They reflected in the silence of experienced men who tread carefully amid new people. Nevertheless, the old farmer, stationary, invincible in his chair near the warmest part of the stove, turned his face from the sawdust-box frequently and addressed a glowing commonplace to the strangers. Usually he was answered in short but adequate sentences by either the cowboy or the Easterner. The Swede said nothing. He seemed to be occupied in making furtive estimates of each man in the room. One might have thought that he had the sense of silly suspicion which comes to guilt. He resembled a badly frightened man.

Later, at dinner, he spoke a little, addressing his conversation entirely to Scully. He volunteered that he had come from New York, where for ten years he had worked as a tailor. These facts seemed to strike Scully as fascinating, and afterward he volunteered that he had lived at Romper for fourteen years. The Swede asked about the crops and the price of labour. He seemed barely to listen to Scully's extended replies. His eyes continued to rove from man to man.

Finally, with a laugh and a wink, he said that some of these Western communities were very dangerous; and after his statement he straightened his legs under the table, tilted his head, and laughed again, loudly. It was plain that the demonstration had no meaning to the others. They looked at him wondering and in silence.

II

As the men trooped heavily back into the front room, the two little windows presented views of a turmoiling sea of snow. The huge arms of the wind were making attempts — mighty, circular, futile — to embrace the flakes as they sped. A gate-post like a still man with a blanched face stood aghast amid this profligate fury. In a hearty voice Scully announced the presence of a blizzard. The guests of the blue hotel, lighting their pipes, assented with grunts of lazy masculine contentment. No island of the sea could be exempt in the degree of this little room with its humming stove. Johnnie, son of Scully, in a tone which defined his opinion of his ability as a card-player, challenged the old farmer of both grey and sandy whiskers to a game of High-Five. The farmer agreed with a contemptuous and bitter scoff. They sat close to the stove, and squared their knees under a wide board. The cowboy and the Easterner watched the game with interest. The Swede remained near the window, aloof, but with a countenance that showed signs of an inexplicable excitement.

The play of Johnnie and the grey-beard was suddenly ended by another quarrel. The old man arose while casting a look of heated scorn at his adversary. He slowly buttoned his coat, and then stalked with fabulous dignity from the room. In the discreet silence of all the other men the Swede laughed. His laughter rang somehow childish. Men by this time had begun to look at him askance, as if they wished to inquire what ailed him.

A new game was formed jocosely. The cowboy volunteered to become the partner of Johnnie, and they all then turned to ask the Swede to throw in his lot with the little Easterner. He asked some questions about the game, and, learning that it wore many names, and that he had played it when it was under an alias, he accepted the invitation. He strode toward the men nervously, as if he expected to be assaulted. Finally, seated, he gazed from face to face and laughed shrilly. This laugh was so strange that the Easterner looked up quickly, the cowboy sat intent and with his mouth open, and Johnnie paused, holding the cards with still fingers.

Afterward there was a short silence. Then Johnnie said, "Well, let's get at it. Come on now!" They pulled their chairs forward until their knees were bunched under the board. They began to play, and their interest in the game caused the others to forget the manner of the Swede.

The cowboy was a board-whacker. Each time that he held superior cards he whanged them, one by one, with exceeding force, down upon the improvised table, and took the tricks with a glowing air of prowess and pride that sent thrills of indignation into the hearts of his opponents. A game with a board-whacker in it is sure to become intense. The countenances of the Easterner and the Swede were miserable whenever the cowboy thundered down his aces and kings, while Johnnie, his eyes gleaming with joy, chuckled and chuckled.

Because of the absorbing play none considered the strange ways of the Swede. They paid strict heed to the game. Finally, during a lull caused by a new deal, the Swede suddenly addressed Johnnie: "I suppose there have been a good many men killed in this room." The jaws of the others dropped and they looked at him.

"What in hell are you talking about?" said Johnnie.

The Swede laughed again his blatant laugh, full of a kind of false courage and defiance. "Oh, you know what I mean all right," he answered.

"I'm a liar if I do!" Johnnie protested. The card was halted, and the men stared at the Swede. Johnnie evidently felt that as the son of the proprietor he should make a direct inquiry. "Now, what might you be drivin' at, mister?" he asked. The Swede winked at him. It was a wink full of cunning. His fingers shook on the edge of the board. "Oh, maybe you think I have been to nowheres. Maybe you think I'm a tenderfoot?"

"I don't know nothin' about you," answered Johnnie, "and I don't give a damn where you've been. All I got to say is that I don't know what you're driving at. There hain't never been nobody killed in this room."

The cowboy, who had been steadily gazing at the Swede, then spoke: "What's wrong with you, mister?"

Apparently it seemed to the Swede that he was formidably menaced. He shivered and turned white near the corners of his mouth. He sent an appealing glance in the direction of the little Easterner. During these moments he did not forget to wear his air of advanced pot-valour. "They say they don't know what I mean," he remarked mockingly to the Easterner.

The latter answered after prolonged and cautious reflection. "I don't understand you," he said, impassively.

The Swede made a movement then which announced that he thought he had encountered treachery from the only quarter where he had expected sympathy, if not help. "Oh, I see you are all against me. I see — "

The cowboy was in a state of deep stupefaction. "Say," he cried, as he tumbled the deck violently down upon the board, "say, what are you gittin' at, hey?"

The Swede sprang up with the celerity of a man escaping from a snake on the floor. "I don't want to fight!" he shouted. "I don't want to fight!"

The cowboy stretched his long legs indolently and deliberately. His hands were in his pockets. He spat into the sawdust-box. "Well, who the hell thought you did?" he inquired.

The Swede backed rapidly toward a corner of the room. His hands were out protectingly in front of his chest, but he was making an obvious struggle to control his fright. "Gentlemen," he quavered, "I suppose I am going to be killed before I can leave this house!" In his eyes was the dying-swan look. Through the windows could be seen the snow turning blue in the shadow of dusk. The wind tore at the house, and some loose thing beat regularly against the clapboards like a spirit tapping.

A door opened, and Scully himself entered. He paused in surprise as he noted the tragic attitude of the Swede. Then he said, "What's the matter here?"

The Swede answered him swiftly and eagerly: "These men are going to kill me."

"Kill you!" ejaculated Scully. "Kill you! What are you talkin'?"

The Swede made the gesture of a martyr.

Scully wheeled sternly upon his son. "What is this, Johnnie?"

The lad had grown sullen. "Damned if I know," he answered. "I can't make no sense to it." He began to shuffle the cards, fluttering them together with an angry snap. "He says a good many men have been killed in this room, or something like that. And he says he's goin' to be killed here too. I don't know what ails him. He's crazy, I shouldn't wonder."

Scully then looked for explanation to the cowboy, but the cowboy simply shrugged his shoulders.

"Kill you?" said Scully again to the Swede. "Kill you? Man, you're off your nut."

"Oh, I know," burst out the Swede. "I know what will happen. Yes, I'm crazy — yes. Yes, of course, I'm crazy — yes. But I know one thing —" There was a sort of sweat of misery and terror upon his face. "I know I won't get out of here alive."

The cowboy drew a deep breath as if his mind was passing into the last stages of dissolution. "Well, I'm doggoned," he whispered to himself.

Scully wheeled suddenly and faced his son. "You've been troublin' this man!"

Johnnie's voice was loud with its burden of grievance. "Why, good Gawd, I ain't done nothin' to 'im."

The Swede broke in. "Gentlemen, do not disturb yourselves. I will leave this house. I will go away, because" — he accused them dramatically with his glance — "because I do not want to be killed."

Scully was furious with his son. "Will you tell me what is the matter, you young divil? What's the matter, anyhow? Speak out!"

"Blame it!" cried Johnnie in despair, "don't I tell you I don't know? He — he says we want to kill him, and that's all I know. I can't tell what ails him."

The Swede continued to repeat: "Never mind, Mr. Scully; never mind. I will leave this house. I will go away, because I do not wish to be killed. Yes, of course, I am crazy — yes. But I know one thing! I will go away. I will leave this house. Never mind, Mr. Scully; never mind. I will go away."

"You will not go 'way," said Scully. "You will not go 'way until I hear the reason of this business. If anybody has troubled you I will take care of him. This is my house. You are under my roof, and I will not allow any peaceable man to be troubled here." He cast a terrible eye upon Johnnie, the cowboy, and the Easterner.

"Never mind, Mr. Scully; never mind. I will go away. I do not wish to be killed." The Swede moved toward the door which opened upon the stairs. It was evidently his intention to go at once for his baggage.

"No, no," shouted Scully peremptorily; but the white-faced man slid by him and disappeared. "Now," said Scully severely, "what does this mane?"

Johnnie and the cowboy cried together: "Why, we didn't do nothin' to 'im!"

Scully's eyes were cold. "No," he said, "you didn't?"

Johnnie swore a deep oath. "Why, this is the wildest loon I ever see. We didn't do nothin' at all. We were jest sittin' here playin' cards, and he — "

The father suddenly spoke to the Easterner. "Mr. Blanc," he asked, "what has these boys been doin'?"

The Easterner reflected again. "I didn't see anything wrong at all," he said at last, slowly.

Scully began to howl. "But what does it mane?" He stared ferociously at his son. "I have a mind to lather you for this, me boy."

Johnnie was frantic. "Well, what have I done?" he bawled at his father.

III

"I think you are tongue-tied," said Scully finally to his son, the cowboy, and the Easterner; and at the end of this scornful sentence he left the room.

Upstairs the Swede was swiftly fastening the straps of his great valise. Once his back happened to be half turned toward the door, and, hearing a noise there, he wheeled and sprang up, uttering a loud cry. Scully's wrinkled visage showed grimly in the light of the small lamp he carried. This yellow effulgence, streaming upward, coloured only his prominent features, and left his eyes, for instance, in mysterious shadow. He resembled a murderer.

"Man! man!" he exclaimed, "have you gone daffy?"

"Oh, no! Oh, no!" rejoined the other. "There are people in this world who know pretty nearly as much as you do — understand?"

For a moment they stood gazing at each other. Upon the Swede's deathly pale cheeks were two spots brightly crimson and sharply edged, as if they had been carefully painted. Scully placed the light on the table and sat himself on the edge of the bed. He spoke ruminatively. "By cracky, I never heard of such a thing in my life. It's a complete muddle. I can't, for the soul of me, think how you ever got this idea into your head." Presently he lifted his eyes and asked: "And did you sure think they were going to kill you?"

The Swede scanned the old man as if he wished to see into his mind. "I did," he said at last. He obviously suspected that this answer might precipitate an outbreak. As he pulled on a strap his whole arm shook, the elbow wavering like a bit of paper.

Scully banged his hand impressively on the footboard of the bed. "Why, man, we're goin' to have a line of ilictric street-cars in this town next spring."

" 'A line of electric street-cars,' " repeated the Swede, stupidly.

"And," said Scully, "there's a new railroad goin' to be built down from Broken Arm to here. Not to mention the four churches and the smashin' big brick schoolhouse. Then there's the big factory, too. Why, in two years Romper'll be a met-tro-*pol*-is."

Having finished the preparation of his baggage, the Swede straightened himself. "Mr. Scully," he said, with sudden hardihood, "how much do I owe you?"

"You don't owe me anythin'," said the old man, angrily.

"Yes, I do," retorted the Swede. He took seventy-five cents from his pocket and tendered it to Scully; but the latter snapped his fingers in disdainful refusal. However, it happened that they both stood gazing in a strange fashion at three silver pieces on the Swede's open palm.

"I'll not take your money," said Scully at last. "Not after what's been goin' on here." Then a plan seemed to strike him. "Here," he cried, picking up his lamp and moving toward the door. "Here! Come with me a minute."

"No," said the Swede, in overwhelming alarm.

"Yes," urged the old man. "Come on! I want you to come and see a picter — just across the hall — in my room."

The Swede must have concluded that his hour was come. His jaw dropped and his teeth showed like a dead man's. He ultimately followed Scully across the corridor, but he had the step of one hung in chains.

Scully flashed the light high on the wall of his own chamber. There was revealed a ridiculous photograph of a little girl. She was leaning against a balustrade of gorgeous decoration, and the formidable bang to her hair was prominent. The figure was as graceful as an upright sled-stake, and, withal, it was of the hue of lead. "There," said Scully, tenderly, "that's the picter of my little girl that died. Her name was Carrie. She had the purtiest hair you ever saw! I was that fond of her, she — "

Turning then, he saw that the Swede was not contemplating the picture at all, but, instead, was keeping keen watch on the gloom in the rear.

"Look, man!" cried Scully, heartily. "That's the picter of my little gal that died. Her name was Carrie. And then here's the picter of my oldest boy, Michael. He's a lawyer in Lincoln, an' doin' well. I gave that boy a grand eddication, and I'm glad for it now. He's a fine boy. Look at 'im now. Ain't he bold as blazes, him there in Lincoln, an honoured an' respicted gintleman! An honoured and respicted gintleman," concluded Scully with a flourish. And, so saying, he smote the Swede jovially on the back.

The Swede faintly smiled.

"Now," said the old man, "there's only one more thing." He dropped suddenly to the floor and thrust his head beneath the bed. The Swede could hear his muffled voice. "I'd keep it under me piller if it wasn't for that boy Johnnie. Then there's the old woman — Where is it now? I never put it twice in the same place. Ah, now come out with you!"

Presently he backed clumsily from under the bed, dragging

with him an old coat rolled into a bundle. "I've fetched him," he muttered. Kneeling on the floor, he unrolled the coat and extracted from its heart a large yellow-brown whisky-bottle.

His first manœuvre was to hold the bottle up to the light. Reassured, apparently, that nobody had been tampering with it, he thrust it with a generous movement toward the Swede.

The weak-kneed Swede was about to eagerly clutch this element of strength, but he suddenly jerked his hand away and cast a look of horror upon Scully.

"Drink," said the old man affectionately. He had risen to his feet, and now stood facing the Swede.

There was a silence. Then again Scully said: "Drink!"

The Swede laughed wildly. He grabbed the bottle, put it to his mouth; and as his lips curled absurdly around the opening and his throat worked, he kept his glance, burning with hatred, upon the old man's face.

IV

After the departure of Scully the three men, with the cardboard still upon their knees, preserved for a long time an astounded silence. Then Johnnie said: "That's the doddangedest Swede I ever see."

"He ain't no Swede," said the cowboy, scornfully.

"Well, what is he then?" cried Johnnie. "What is he then?"

"It's my opinion," replied the cowboy deliberately, "he's some kind of a Dutchman." It was a venerable custom of the country to entitle as Swedes all light-haired men who spoke with a heavy tongue. In consequence the idea of the cowboy was not without its daring. "Yes, sir," he repeated. "It's my opinion this feller is some kind of a Dutchman."

"Well, he says he's a Swede, anyhow," muttered Johnnie, sulkily. He turned to the Easterner: "What do you think, Mr. Blanc?"

"Oh, I don't know," replied the Easterner.

"Well, what do you think makes him act that way?" asked the cowboy.

"Why, he's frightened." The Easterner knocked his pipe against a rim of the stove. "He's clear frightened out of his boots."

"What at?" cried Johnnie and the cowboy together.

The Easterner reflected over his answer.

"What at?" cried the others again.

"Oh, I don't know, but it seems to me this man has been reading dime novels, and he thinks he's right out in the middle of it — the shootin' and stabbin' and all."

"But," said the cowboy, deeply scandalized, "this ain't Wyoming, ner none of them places. This is Nebrasker."

"Yes," added Johnnie, "an' why don't he wait till he gits *out West?*"

The travelled Easterner laughed. "It isn't different there even — not in these days. But he thinks he's right in the middle of hell."

Johnnie and the cowboy mused long.

"It's awful funny," remarked Johnnie at last.

"Yes," said the cowboy, "This is a queer game. I hope we don't git snowed in, because then we'd have to stand this here man bein' around with us all the time. That wouldn't be no good."

"I wish Pop would throw him out," said Johnnie.

Presently they heard a loud stamping on the stairs, accompanied by ringing jokes in the voice of old Scully, and laughter, evidently from the Swede. The men around the stove stared vacantly at each other. "Gosh!" said the cowboy. The door flew open, and old Scully, flushed and anecdotal, came into the room. He was jabbering at the Swede, who followed him, laughing bravely. It was the entry of two roisterers from a banquet hall.

"Come now," said Scully sharply to the three seated men, "move up and give us a chance at the stove." The cowboy and the Easterner obediently sidled their chairs to make room for the new-comers. Johnnie, however, simply arranged himself in a more indolent attitude, and then remained motionless.

"Come! Git over, there," said Scully.

"Plenty of room on the other side of the stove," said Johnnie.

"Do you think we want to sit in the draught?" roared the father.

But the Swede here interposed with a grandeur of confidence. "No, no. Let the boy sit where he likes." he cried in a bullying voice to the father.

"All right! All right!" said Scully, deferentially. The cowboy and the Easterner exchanged glances of wonder.

The five chairs were formed in a crescent about one side of the stove. The Swede began to talk; he talked arrogantly, profanely, angrily. Johnnie, the cowboy, and the Easterner maintained a morose silence, while old Scully appeared to be receptive and eager, breaking in constantly with sympathetic ejaculations.

Finally the Swede announced that he was thirsty. He moved in his chair, and said that he would go for a drink of water.

"I'll git it for you," cried Scully at once.

"No," said the Swede, contemptuously. "I'll get it for myself." He arose and stalked with the air of an owner off into the executive parts of the hotel.

As soon as the Swede was out of hearing Scully sprang to his feet and whispered intensely to the others: "Upstairs he thought I was tryin' to poison 'im."

"Say," said Johnnie, "this makes me sick. Why don't you throw 'im out in the snow?"

"Why, he's all right now," declared Scully. "It was only that he was from the East, and he thought this was a tough place. That's all. He's all right now."

The cowboy looked with admiration upon the Easterner. "You were straight," he said. "You were on to that there Dutchman."

"Well," said Johnnie to his father, "he may be all right now, but I don't see it. Other time he was scared, but now he's too fresh."

Scully's speech was always a combination of Irish brogue and idiom, Western twang and idiom, and scraps of curiously formal diction taken from the story-books and newspapers. He now hurled a strange mass of language at the head of his son. "What do I keep? What do I keep? What do I keep?" he demanded, in a voice of thunder. He slapped his knee impressively, to indicate that he himself was going to make reply, and that all should heed. "I keep a hotel," he shouted. "A hotel, do you mind? A guest under my roof has sacred privileges. He is to be intimidated by none. Not one word shall he hear that would prijudice him in favour of goin' away. I'll not have it. There's no place in this here town where they can say they iver took in a guest of mine because he was afraid to stay here." He wheeled suddenly upon the cowboy and the Easterner. "Am I right?"

"Yes, Mr. Scully," said the cowboy, "I think you're right."

"Yes, Mr. Scully," said the Easterner, "I think you're right."

V

At six-o'clock supper, the Swede fizzed like a fire-wheel. He sometimes seemed on the point of bursting into riotous song, and in all his madness he was encouraged by old Scully. The Easterner was encased in reserve; the cowboy sat in wide-mouthed amazement, forgetting to eat, while Johnnie wrathily demolished great plates of food. The daughters of the house, when they were obliged to replenish the biscuits, approached as warily as Indians, and, having succeeded in their purpose, fled with ill-concealed trepidation. The Swede domineered the whole feast, and he gave it the appearance of a cruel bacchanal. He seemed to have grown suddenly taller; he gazed, brutally disdainful, into every face. His voice rang through the room. Once when he jabbed out harpoon-fashion with his fork to pinion a biscuit, the weapon nearly impaled the hand of the Easterner, which had been stretched quietly out for the same biscuit.

After supper, as the men filed toward the other room, the Swede smote Scully ruthlessly on the shoulder. "Well, old boy, that was a good, square meal." Johnnie looked hopefully at his father; he knew that shoulder was tender from an old fall; and, indeed, it appeared for a moment as if Scully was going to flame out over the matter, but in the end he smiled a sickly smile and remained silent. The others understood from his manner that he was admitting his responsibility for the Swede's new view-point.

Johnnie, however, addressed his parent in an aside. "Why don't you license somebody to kick you downstairs?" Scully scowled darkly by way of reply.

When they were gathered about the stove, the Swede insisted on another game of High-Five. Scully gently deprecated the plan at first, but the Swede turned a wolfish glare upon him. The old man subsided, and the Swede canvassed the others. In his tone there was always a great threat. The cowboy and the Easterner both remarked indifferently that they would play. Scully said that he would presently have to go to meet the 6.58 train, and so the Swede turned menacingly upon Johnnie. For a moment their glances crossed like blades, and then Johnnie smiled and said, "Yes, I'll play."

They formed a square, with the little board on their knee. The Easterner and the Swede were again partners. As the play went on, it was noticeable that the cowboy was not board-whacking as usual. Meanwhile, Scully, near the lamp, had put on his spectacles and, with an appearance curiously like an old priest, was reading a newspaper. In time he went out to meet the 6.58 train, and, despite his precautions, a gust of polar wind whirled into the room as he opened the door. Besides scattering the cards, it chilled the players to the marrow. The Swede cursed frightfully. When Scully returned, his entrance disturbed a cosy and friendly scene. The Swede again cursed. But presently they were once more intent, their heads bent forward and their hands moving swiftly. The Swede had adopted the fashion of board-whacking.

Scully took up his paper and for a long time remained immersed in matters which were extraordinarily remote from him. The lamp burned badly, and once he stopped to adjust the wick. The newspaper, as he turned from page to page, rustled with a slow and comfortable sound. Then suddenly he heard three terrible words: "You are cheatin'!"

Such scenes often prove that there can be little of dramatic import in environment. Any room can present a tragic front; any room can be comic. This little den was now hideous as a torture-chamber. The new faces of the men themselves had changed it upon the instant. The Swede held a huge fist in front of Johnnie's face, while the latter looked steadily over it into the blazing orbs of his accuser. The Easterner had grown pallid; the cowboy's jaw had dropped in that expression of bovine amazement which was one of his important mannerisms. After the three words, the first sound in the room was made by Scully's paper as it floated forgotten to his feet. His spectacles had also fallen from his nose, but by a clutch he had saved them in air. His hand, grasping the spectacles, now remained poised awkwardly and near his shoulder. He stared at the card-players.

Probably the silence was while a second elapsed. Then, if the floor had been suddenly twitched out from under the men they could not have moved quicker. The five had projected themselves headlong toward a common point. It happened that Johnnie, in rising to hurl himself upon the Swede, had stumbled slightly because of his curiously instinctive care for the cards and the board. The loss of the moment allowed time for the arrival of

Scully, and also allowed the cowboy time to give the Swede a
great push which sent him staggering back. The men found
tongue together, and hoarse shouts of rage, appeal, or fear burst
from every throat. The cowboy pushed and jostled feverishly at
the Swede, and the Easterner and Scully clung wildly to Johnnie;
but through the smoky air, above the swaying bodies of the peace-
compellers, the eyes of the two warriors ever sought each other
in glances of challenge that were at once hot and steely.

Of course the board had been overturned, and now the whole
company of cards was scattered over the floor, where the boots of
the men trampled the fat and painted kings and queens as they
gazed with their silly eyes at the war that was waging above them.

Scully's voice was dominating the yells. "Stop now! Stop, I
say! Stop, now — "

Johnnie, as he struggled to burst through the rank formed by
Scully and the Easterner, was crying, "Well, he says I cheated!
He says I cheated! I won't allow no man to say I cheated! If he
says I cheated, he's a —— ——!"

The cowboy was telling the Swede, "Quit, now! Quit, d'ye
hear — "

The screams of the Swede never ceased: "He did cheat! I saw
him! I saw him — "

As for the Easterner, he was importuning in a voice that was
not heeded: "Wait a moment, can't you? Oh, wait a moment.
What's the good of a fight over a game of cards? Wait a moment — "

In this tumult no complete sentences were clear. "Cheat" —
"Quit" — "He says" — these fragments pierced the uproar and
rang out sharply. It was remarkable that, whereas Scully undoubtedly made the most noise, he was the least heard of any
of the riotous band.

Then suddenly there was a great cessation. It was as if each
man had paused for breath; and although the room was still
lighted with the anger of men, it could be seen that there was no
danger of immediate conflict, and at once Johnnie, shouldering
his way forward, almost succeeded in confronting the Swede.
"What did you say I cheated for? What did you say I cheated for?
I don't cheat, and I won't let no man say I do!"

The Swede said, "I saw you! I saw you!"

"Well," cried Johnnie, "I'll fight any man what says I cheat!"

"No, you won't," said the cowboy. "Not here."

"Ah, be still, can't you?" said Scully, coming between them. The quiet was sufficient to allow the Easterner's voice to be heard. He was repeating, "Oh, wait a moment, can't you? What's the good of a fight over a game of cards? Wait a moment!"

Johnnie, his red face appearing above his father's shoulder, hailed the Swede again. "Did you say I cheated?"

The Swede showed his teeth. "Yes."

"Then," said Johnnie, "we must fight."

"Yes, fight," roared the Swede. He was like a demoniac. "Yes, fight! I'll show you what kind of a man I am! I'll show you who you want to fight! Maybe you think I can't fight! Maybe you think I can't! I'll show you, you skin, you card-sharp! Yes, you cheated! You cheated! You cheated!"

"Well, let's go at it, then, mister," said Johnnie, coolly.

The cowboy's brow was beaded with sweat from his efforts in intercepting all sorts of raids. He turned in despair to Scully. "What are you goin' to do now?"

A change had come over the Celtic visage of the old man. He now seemed all eagerness; his eyes glowed.

"We'll let them fight," he answered, stalwartly. "I can't put up with it any longer. I've stood this damned Swede till I'm sick. We'll let them fight."

VI

The men prepared to go out of doors. The Easterner was so nervous that he had great difficulty in getting his arms into the sleeves of his new leather coat. As the cowboy drew his fur cap down over his ears his hands trembled. In fact, Johnnie and old Scully were the only ones who displayed no agitation. These preliminaries were conducted without words.

Scully threw open the door. "Well, come on," he said. Instantly a terrific wind caused the flame of the lamp to struggle at its wick, while a puff of black smoke sprang from the chimney-top. The stove was in mid-current of the blast, and its voice swelled to equal the roar of the storm. Some of the scarred and bedabbled cards were caught up from the floor and dashed helplessly against the farther wall. The men lowered their heads and plunged into the tempest as into a sea.

No snow was falling, but great whirls and clouds of flakes, swept up from the ground by the frantic winds, were streaming southward with the speed of bullets. The covered land was blue with the sheen of an unearthly satin, and there was no other hue save where, at the low, black railway station — which seemed incredibly distant — one light gleamed like a tiny jewel. As the men floundered into a thigh-deep drift, it was known that the Swede was bawling out something. Scully went to him, put a hand on his shoulder, and projected an ear. "What's that you say?" he shouted.

"I say," bawled the Swede again, "I won't stand much show against this gang. I know you'll all pitch on me."

Scully smote him reproachfully on the arm. "Tut, man!" he yelled. The wind tore the words from Scully's lips and scattered them far alee.

"You are all a gang of —" boomed the Swede, but the storm also seized the remainder of this sentence.

Immediately turning their backs upon the wind, the men had swung around a corner to the sheltered side of the hotel. It was the function of the little house to preserve here, amid this great devastation of snow, an irregular V-shape of heavily encrusted grass, which crackled beneath the feet. One could imagine the great drifts piled against the windward side. When the party reached the comparative peace of this spot it was found that the Swede was still bellowing.

"Oh, I know what kind of a thing this is! I know you'll all pitch on me. I can't lick you all!"

Scully turned upon him panther-fashion. "You'll not have to whip all of us. You'll have to whip my son Johnnie. An' the man what troubles you durin' that time will have me to dale with."

The arrangements were swiftly made. The two men faced each other, obedient to the harsh commands of Scully, whose face, in the subtly luminous gloom, could be seen set in the austere impersonal lines that are pictured on the countenances of the Roman veterans. The Easterner's teeth were chattering, and he was hopping up and down like a mechanical toy. The cowboy stood rock-like.

The contestants had not stripped off any clothing. Each was in his ordinary attire. Their fists were up, and they eyed each other in a calm that had the elements of leonine cruelty in it.

During this pause, the Easterner's mind, like a film, took last-ing impressions of three men — the iron-nerved master of the ceremony; the Swede, pale, motionless, terrible; and Johnnie, serene yet ferocious, brutish yet heroic. The entire prelude had in it a tragedy greater than the tragedy of action, and this aspect was accentuated by the long, mellow cry of the blizzard, as it sped the tumbling and wailing flakes into the black abyss of the south.

"Now!" said Scully.

The two combatants leaped forward and crashed together like bullocks. There was heard the cushioned sound of blows, and of a curse squeezing out from between the tight teeth of one.

As for the spectators, the Easterner's pent-up breath exploded from him with a pop of relief, absolute relief from the tension of the preliminaries. The cowboy bounded into the air with a yowl. Scully was immovable as from supreme amazement and fear at the fury of the fight which he himself had permitted and arranged.

For a time the encounter in the darkness was such a perplexity of flying arms that it presented no more detail than would a swiftly revolving wheel. Occasionally a face, as if illumined by a flash of light, would shine out, ghastly and marked with pink spots. A moment later, the men might have been known as shadows, if it were not for the involuntary utterance of oaths that came from them in whispers.

Suddenly a holocaust of warlike desire caught the cowboy, and he bolted forward with the speed of a broncho. "Go it, Johnnie! go it! Kill him! Kill him!"

Scully confronted him. "Kape back," he said; and by his glance the cowboy could tell that this man was Johnnie's father.

To the Easterner there was a monotony of unchangeable fight-ing that was an abomination. This confused mingling was eternal to his sense, which was concentrated in a longing for the end, the priceless end. Once the fighters lurched near him, and as he scrambled hastily backward he heard them breathe like men on the rack.

"Kill him, Johnnie! Kill him! Kill him! Kill him!" The cow-boy's face was contorted like one of those agony masks in mu-seums.

"Keep still," said Scully icily.

Then there was a sudden loud grunt, incomplete, cut short, and Johnnie's body swung away from the Swede and fell with sickening heaviness to the grass. The cowboy was barely in time to prevent the mad Swede from flinging himself upon his prone adversary. "No, you don't," said the cowboy, interposing an arm. "Wait a second."

Scully was at his son's side. "Johnnie! Johnnie, me boy!" His voice had a quality of melancholy tenderness. "Johnnie! Can you go on with it?" He looked anxiously down into the bloody, pulpy face of his son.

There was a moment of silence, and then Johnnie answered in his ordinary voice, "Yes, I — it — yes."

Assisted by his father he struggled to his feet. "Wait a bit now till you git your wind," said the old man.

A few paces away the cowboy was lecturing the Swede. "No, you don't! Wait a second!"

The Easterner was plucking at Scully's sleeve. "Oh, this is enough," he pleaded. "This is enough! Let it go as it stands. This is enough!"

"Bill," said Scully, "git out of the road." The cowboy stepped aside. "Now." The combatants were actuated by a new caution as they advanced toward collision. They glared at each other, and then the Swede aimed a lightning blow that carried with it his entire weight. Johnnie was evidently half stupid from weakness, but he miraculously dodged, and his fist sent the over-balanced Swede sprawling.

The cowboy, Scully, and the Easterner burst into a cheer that was like a chorus of triumphant soldiery, but before its conclusion the Swede had scuffled agilely to his feet and come in berserk abandon at his foe. There was another perplexity of flying arms, and Johnnie's body again swung away and fell, even as a bundle might fall from a roof. The Swede instantly staggered to a little wind-waved tree and leaned upon it, breathing like an engine, while his savage and flame-lit eyes roamed from face to face as the men bent over Johnnie. There was a splendour of isolation in his situation at this time which the Easterner felt once when, lifting his eyes from the man on the ground, he beheld that mysterious and lonely figure, waiting.

"Are you any good yet, Johnnie?" asked Scully in a broken voice.

The son gasped and opened his eyes languidly. After a moment he answered, "No — I ain't — any good — any — more." Then, from shame and bodily ill, he began to weep, the tears furrowing down through the blood-stains on his face. "He was too — too — too heavy for me."

Scully straightened and addressed the waiting figure. "Stranger," he said, evenly, "it's all up with our side." Then his voice changed into that vibrant huskiness which is commonly the tone of the most simple and deadly announcements. "Johnnie is whipped."

Without replying, the victor moved off on the route to the front door of the hotel.

The cowboy was formulating new and unspellable blasphemies. The Easterner was startled to find that they were out in a wind that seemed to come direct from the shadowed arctic floes. He heard again the wail of the snow as it was flung to its grave in the south. He knew now that all this time the cold had been sinking into him deeper and deeper, and he wondered that he had not perished. He felt indifferent to the condition of the vanquished man.

"Johnnie, can you walk?" asked Scully.

"Did I hurt — hurt him any?" asked the son.

"Can you walk, boy? Can you walk?"

Johnnie's voice was suddenly strong. There was a robust impatience in it. "I asked you whether I hurt him any!"

"Yes, yes, Johnnie," answered the cowboy, consolingly; "he's hurt a good deal."

They raised him from the ground, and as soon as he was on his feet he went tottering off, rebuffing all attempts at assistance. When the party rounded the corner they were fairly blinded by the pelting of the snow. It burned their faces like fire. The cowboy carried Johnnie through the drift to the door. As they entered, some cards again rose from the floor and beat against the wall.

The Easterner rushed to the stove. He was so profoundly chilled that he almost dared to embrace the glowing iron. The Swede was not in the room. Johnnie sank into a chair and, folding his arms on his knees, buried his face in them. Scully, warming one foot and then the other at a rim of the stove, muttered to himself with Celtic mournfulness. The cowboy had removed his fur cap, and with a dazed and rueful air he was running one hand through his tousled locks. From overhead they could hear the creaking of boards, as the Swede tramped here and there in his room.

The sad quiet was broken by the sudden flinging open of a door that led toward the kitchen. It was instantly followed by an inrush of women. They precipitated themselves upon Johnnie amid a chorus of lamentation. Before they carried their prey off to the kitchen, there to be bathed and harangued with that mixture of sympathy and abuse which is a feat of their sex, the mother straightened herself and fixed old Scully with an eye of stern reproach. "Shame be upon you, Patrick Scully!" she cried. "Your own son, too. Shame be upon you!"

"There, now! Be quiet, now!" said the old man, weakly.

"Shame be upon you, Patrick Scully!" The girls, rallying to this slogan, sniffed disdainfully in the direction of those trembling accomplices, the cowboy and the Easterner. Presently they bore Johnnie away, and left the three men to dismal reflection.

VII

"I'd like to fight this here Dutchman myself," said the cowboy, breaking a long silence.

Scully wagged his head sadly. "No, that wouldn't do. It wouldn't be right. It wouldn't be right."

"Well, why wouldn't it?" argued the cowboy. "I don't see no harm in it."

"No," answered Scully, with mournful heroism. "It wouldn't be right. It was Johnnie's fight, and now we mustn't whip the man just because he whipped Johnnie."

"Yes, that's true enough," said the cowboy; "but — he better not get fresh with me, because I couldn't stand no more of it."

"You'll not say a word to him," commanded Scully, and even then they heard the tread of the Swede on the stairs. His entrance was made theatric. He swept the door back with a bang and swaggered to the middle of the room. No one looked at him. "Well," he cried, insolently, at Scully, "I s'pose you'll tell me now how much I owe you?"

The old man remained stolid. "You don't owe me nothin'."

"Huh!" said the Swede, "huh! Don't owe 'im nothin'."

The cowboy addressed the Swede. "Stranger, I don't see how you come to be so gay around here."

Old Scully was instantly alert. "Stop!" he shouted, holding his hand forth, fingers upward. "Bill, you shut up!"

The cowboy spat carelessly into the sawdust-box. "I didn't say a word, did I?" he asked.

"Mr. Scully," called the Swede, "how much do I owe you?" It was seen that he was attired for departure, and that he had his valise in his hand.

"You don't owe me nothin'," repeated Scully in the same imperturbable way.

"Huh!" said the Swede. "I guess you're right. I guess if it was any way at all, you'd owe me somethin'. Thats' what I guess." He turned to the cowboy. " 'Kill him! Kill him! Kill him!' " he mimicked, and then guffawed victoriously. " 'Kill him!' " He was convulsed with ironical humour.

But he might have been jeering the dead. The three men were immovable and silent, staring with glassy eyes at the stove.

The Swede opened the door and passed into the storm, giving one derisive glance backward at the still group.

As soon as the door was closed, Scully and the cowboy leaped to their feet and began to curse. They trampled to and fro, waving their arms and smashing into the air with their fists. "Oh, but that was a hard minute!" wailed Scully. "That was a hard minute! Him there leerin' and scoffin'! One bang at his nose was worth forty dollars to me that minute! How did you stand it, Bill?"

"How did I stand it?" cried the cowboy in a quivering voice. "How did I stand it? Oh!"

The old man burst into sudden brogue. "I'd loike to take that Swade," he wailed, "and hould 'im down on a shtone flure and bate 'im to a jelly wid a shtick!"

The cowboy groaned in sympathy. "I'd like to git him by the neck and ha-ammer him" — he brought his hand down on a chair with a noise like a pistol-shot — "hammer that there Dutchman until he couldn't tell himself from a dead coyote!"

"I'd bate 'im until he — "

"I'd show *him* some things — "

And then together they raised a yearning, fanatic cry —
"Oh-o-oh! if we only could — "

"Yes!"

"Yes!"

"And then I'd — "

"O-o-oh!"

VIII

The Swede, tightly gripping his valise, tacked across the face of the storm as if he carried sails. He was following a line of little naked, gasping trees which, he knew, must mark the way of the road. His face, fresh from the pounding of Johnnie's fists, felt more pleasure than pain in the wind and the driving snow. A number of square shapes loomed upon him finally, and he knew them as the houses of the main body of the town. He found a street and made travel along it, leaning heavily upon the wind whenever, at a corner, a terrific blast caught him.

He might have been in a deserted village. We picture the world as thick with conquering and elate humanity, but here, with the bugles of the tempest pealing, it was hard to imagine a peopled earth. One viewed the existence of man then as a marvel, and conceded a glamour of wonder to these lice which were caused to cling to a whirling, fire-smitten, ice-locked, disease-stricken, space-lost bulb. The conceit of man was explained by this storm to be the very engine of life. One was a coxcomb not to die in it. However, the Swede found a saloon.

In front of it an indomitable red light was burning, and the snowflakes were made blood-colour as they flew through the circumscribed territory of the lamp's shining. The Swede pushed open the door of the saloon and entered. A sanded expanse was before him, and at the end of it four men sat about a table drinking. Down one side of the room extended a radiant bar, and its guardian was leaning upon his elbows listening to the talk of the men at the table. The Swede dropped his valise upon the floor and, smiling fraternally upon the barkeeper, said, "Gimme some whisky, will you?" The man placed a bottle, a whisky-glass, and a glass of ice-thick water upon the bar. The Swede poured himself an abnormal portion of whisky and drank it in three gulps. "Pretty bad night," remarked the bartender, indifferently. He was making the pretension of blindness which is usually a distinction of his class; but it could have been seen that he was furtively studying the half-erased blood-stains on the face of the Swede. "Bad night," he said again.

"Oh, it's good enough for me," replied the Swede, hardily, as he poured himself some more whisky. The barkeeper took his coin and manœuvred it through its reception by the highly nickelled cash-machine. A bell rang; a card labelled "20 cts." had appeared.

"No," continued the Swede, "this isn't too bad weather. It's good enough for me."

"So?" murmured the barkeeper, languidly.

The copious drams made the Swede's eyes swim, and he breathed a trifle heavier. "Yes, I like this weather. I like it. It suits me." It was apparently his design to impart a deep significance to these words.

"So?" murmured the bartender again. He turned to gaze dreamily at the scroll-like birds and bird-like scrolls which had been drawn with soap upon the mirrors in back of the bar.

"Well, I guess I'll take another drink," said the Swede, presently. "Have something?"

"No, thanks; I'm not drinkin'," answered the bartender. Afterward he asked, "How did you hurt your face?"

The Swede immediately began to boast loudly.

"Why, in a fight. I thumped the soul out of a man down here at Scully's hotel."

The interest of the four men at the table was at last aroused.

"Who was it?" said one.

"Johnnie Scully," blustered the Swede. "Son of the man what runs it. He will be pretty near dead for some weeks, I can tell you. I made a nice thing of him, I did. He couldn't get up. They carried him in the house. Have a drink?"

Instantly the men in some subtle way encased themselves in reserve. "No, thanks," said one. The group was of curious formation. Two were prominent local business men; one was the district attorney; and one was a professional gambler of the kind known as "square." But a scrutiny of the group would not have enabled an observer to pick the gambler from the men of more reputable pursuits. He was, in fact, a man so delicate in manner, when among people of fair class, and so judicious in his choice of victims, that in the strictly masculine part of the town's life he had come to be explicitly trusted and admired. People called him a thoroughbred. The fear and contempt with which his craft was regarded were undoubtedly the reason why his quiet dignity shone conspicuous above the quiet dignity of men who might be merely hatters, billiard-markers, or grocery clerks. Beyond an occasional unwary traveller who came by rail, this gambler was supposed to prey solely upon reckless and senile farmers, who, when flush with good crops, drove into town in all the pride and confidence of an absolutely invulnerable stupidity. Hearing at times in circuitous fashion of the despoilment of such a farmer, the important men of Romper invariably laughed in contempt of the victim, and if they thought of the wolf at all, it was with a kind of pride at the knowledge that he would never dare think of attacking their wisdom and courage. Besides, it was popular that this gambler had a real wife and two real children in a neat cottage in a suburb, where he led an exemplary home life; and when any one even suggested a discrepancy in his character, the crowd immediately vociferated descriptions of this virtuous family circle. Then men who led exemplary home lives, and men who did not lead exemplary home lives, all subsided in a bunch, remarking that there was nothing more to be said.

However, when a restriction was placed upon him — as, for instance, when a strong clique of members of the new Pollywog Club refused to permit him, even as a spectator, to appear in the rooms of the organization — the candour and gentleness with which he accepted the judgment disarmed many of his foes and made his friends more desperately partisan. He invariably distinguished between himself and a respectable Romper man so quickly and frankly that his manner actually appeared to be a continual broadcast compliment.

And one must not forget to declare the fundamental fact of his entire position in Romper. It is irrefutable that in all affairs outside his business, in all matters that occur eternally and commonly between man and man, this thieving card-player was so generous, so just, so moral, that, in a contest, he could have put to flight the consciences of nine tenths of the citizens of Romper.

And so it happened that he was seated in this saloon with the two prominent local merchants and the district attorney.

The Swede continued to drink raw whisky, meanwhile babbling at the barkeeper and trying to induce him to indulge in pota-

tions. "Come on. Have a drink. Come on. What — no? Well,
have a little one, then. By gawd, I've whipped a man to-night,
and I want to celebrate. I whipped him good, too. Gentlemen,"
the Swede cried to the men at the table, "have a drink?"

"Ssh!" said the barkeeper.

The group at the table, although furtively attentive, had been
pretending to be deep in talk, but now a man lifted his eyes
toward the Swede and said, shortly, "Thanks. We don't want
any more."

At this reply the Swede ruffled out his chest like a rooster.
"Well," he exploded, "it seems I can't get anybody to drink with
me in this town. Seems so, don't it? Well!"

"Ssh!" said the barkeeper.

"Say," snarled the Swede, "don't you try to shut me up. I
won't have it. I'm a gentleman, and I want people to drink with
me. And I want 'em to drink with me now. *Now* — do you understand?" He rapped the bar with his knuckles.

Years of experience had calloused the bartender. He merely
grew sulky. "I hear you," he answered.

"Well," cried the Swede, "listen hard then. See those men over
there? Well, they're going to drink with me, and don't you forget
it. Now you watch."

"Hi!" yelled the barkeeper, "this won't do!"

"Why won't it?" demanded the Swede. He stalked over to the
table, and by chance laid his hand upon the shoulder of the
gambler. "How about this?" he asked wrathfully. "I asked you
to drink with me."

The gambler simply twisted his head and spoke over his shoulder. "My friend, I don't know you."

"Oh, hell!" answered the Swede, "come and have a drink."

"Now, my boy," advised the gambler, kindly, "take your hand
off my shoulder and go 'way and mind your own business." He
was a little, slim man, and it seemed strange to hear him use this
tone of heroic patronage to the burly Swede. The other men at
the table said nothing.

"What! You won't drink with me, you little dude? I'll make
you, then! I'll make you!" The Swede had grasped the gambler
frenziedly at the throat, and was dragging him from his chair. The
other men sprang up. The barkeeper dashed around the corner

of his bar. There was a great tumult, and then was seen a long blade in the hand of the gambler. It shot forward, and a human body, this citadel of virtue, wisdom, power, was pierced as easily as if it had been a melon. The Swede fell with a cry of supreme astonishment.

The prominent merchants and the district attorney must have at once tumbled out of the place backward. The bartender found himself hanging limply to the arm of a chair and gazing into the eyes of a murderer.

"Henry," said the latter, as he wiped his knife on one of the towels that hung beneath the bar rail, "you tell 'em where to find me. I'll be home, waiting for 'em." Then he vanished. A moment afterward the barkeeper was in the street dinning through the storm for help and, moreover, companionship.

The corpse of the Swede, alone in the saloon, had its eyes fixed upon a dreadful legend that dwelt atop of the cash-machine: "This registers the amount of your purchase."

IX

Months later, the cowboy was frying pork over the stove of a little ranch near the Dakota line, when there was a quick thud of hoofs outside, and presently the Easterner entered with the letters and the papers.

"Well," said the Easterner at once, "the chap that killed the Swede has got three years. Wasn't much, was it?"

"He has? Three years?" The cowboy poised his pan of pork, while he ruminated upon the news. "Three years. That ain't much."

"No. It was a light sentence," replied the Easterner as he unbuckled his spurs. "Seems there was a good deal of sympathy for him in Romper."

"If the bartender had been any good," observed the cowboy, thoughtfully, "he would have gone in and cracked that there Dutchman on the head with a bottle in the beginnin' of it and stopped all this here murderin'."

"Yes, a thousand things might have happened," said the Easterner, tartly.

The cowboy returned his pan of pork to the fire, but his philosophy continued. "It's funny, ain't it? If he hadn't said Johnnie was cheatin' he'd be alive this minute. He was an awful fool. Game played for fun, too. Not for money. I believe he was crazy."

"I feel sorry for that gambler," said the Easterner.

"Oh, so do I," said the cowboy. "He don't deserve none of it for killin' who he did."

"The Swede might not have been killed if everything had been square."

"Might not have been killed?" exclaimed the cowboy. "Everythin' square? Why, when he said that Johnnie was cheatin' and acted like such a jackass? And then in the saloon he fairly walked up to git hurt?" With these arguments the cowboy browbeat the Easterner and reduced him to rage.

"You're a fool!" cried the Easterner, viciously. "You're a bigger jackass than the Swede by a million majority. Now let me tell you one thing. Let me tell you something. Listen! Johnnie *was* cheating!"

" 'Johnnie,' " said the cowboy, blankly. There was a minute of silence, and then he said, robustly, "Why, no. The game was only for fun."

"Fun or not," said the Easterner, "Johnnie was cheating. I saw him. I know it. I saw him. And I refused to stand up and be a man. I let the Swede fight it out alone. And you — you were simply puffing around the place and wanting to fight. And then old Scully himself! We are all in it! This poor gambler isn't even a noun. He is kind of an adverb. Every sin is the result of a collaboration. We, five of us, have collaborated in the murder of this Swede. Usually there are from a dozen to forty women really involved in every murder, but in this case it seems to be only five men — you, I, Johnnie, old Scully; and that fool of an unfortunate gambler came merely as a culmination, the apex of a human movement, and gets all the punishment."

The cowboy, injured and rebellious, cried out blindly into this fog of mysterious theory: "Well, I didn't do anythin', did I?"

HUGO VON HOFMANNSTHAL (1874–1929) Hofmannsthal was born in Vienna, studied law at the University of Vienna, and, after military service, obtained a Ph.D. in romance philology. When he was twenty-seven he married and lived in a village near Vienna. His travels included Europe, England, Greece, Morocco, and Sicily; he also helped institute the Salzburg Festival.

Hofmannsthal's literary career is rather peculiarly divided. From 1890–1899 he wrote lyrical poems and short verse plays and was acclaimed for both. In 1899 he renounced the lyric form and began composing dramas which he continued writing until his death. His essays were "his constant medium of self-contemplation and self-interpretation, his philosophical diary in the course of existence."

Beginning in 1908 he wrote librettos for Richard Strauss: *Elektra* (1909), *Der Rosenkavalier* (1911), *Ariadne auf Naxos* (1912), *The Woman Without a Shadow* (1919), *The Egyptian Helen* (1928), and *Arabella* which was first performed in 1933 after his death.

Herman Broch writes of Hofmannsthal: "On leafing through Hofmannsthal's poems, on opening at random his diary-like letters, one sees on every page evidence of his visual memory" (as in "Twilight and Nocturnal Storm"). And one "is continually surprised by the manifold diversity [of] images." Within Hofmannsthal's landscapes, "man is nought but a prop, nought but — in the truest sense of the word — an optical figure, a non-living being whose shadow-existence follows some abstract moralizing, some idealistically romanticized conventions and knows no genuine human desire."

TWILIGHT AND NOCTURNAL STORM

Hugo von Hofmannsthal

The sparrow-hawk which the boys had nailed to the barn door twisted itself dreadfully towards the breaking night. Euseb, the eldest of those who had done it, stood in the dusk and stared at the bird, from whose shining eyes fury shot forth while it jerked itself to death on the iron nails that pierced its wings. Then its mate dived down from the darkening air; with a shrill cry she flew as though bereft of her senses in giddy little circles, then hung rigid in the air with outspread wings and glimmering eyes, flung herself upwards, backwards, towards the mountain wall, vanishing, then reappearing in wild flights of frenzy. It seemed as though her screams were intended to attract the night-black storm that lay there, its own body afire with suppressed lightning, and with magic circles pull it down on the village. The boy Euseb could hardly stand on his legs; terror gripped him by the neck so that he dared not move his eyeballs. But when, under a silent flash of lightning, the whole barn blazed out in an ashen light, and when to his right a bearded goat-owl, disturbed by a gust of wind, shot out of a hole in the wall to spear a beetle and to his left a bat tumbled down, then horror seized him and drove him with chattering teeth down into the village. And now right in front of him a fresh flash revealed the cemetery wall with all its crevices wherein wood-lice lived; under the sudden glare the crosses seemed to stretch, and on the one fresh child's grave a bush, its blossoms of bleeding hearts hanging by threads, began to shake. But as the lightning flickered out and darkness settled down with the weight of a blanket, a gleam of light fell slantingly from the rear window of a small house on to the cemetery wall. In this chamber slept the butcher's daughter, the most beautiful girl in the village; and it was common knowledge that here one evening, while she was undressing and until she blew out the light, one of the older boys had been able to see the shadows of her breasts upon the curtains.

So Euseb pressed himself under a projecting roof where shingles lay piled up high; and his heart beat differently from hitherto. Facing him, its head dangling, hung the calf he had seen being led past in the afternoon; warm breath still seemed to be coming from its soft mouth. To the boy Euseb the time he spent lying here in wait passed like nothing; the quarter-hours striking almost over his head and booming on the fearful air he failed to hear. Nor did he heed the lightning that laid bare in dazzling brightness the bells in their belfry; he was absorbed only with the calf, absorbed only with the girl who there in the house would soon be preparing for bed in her chamber. Now she was busying herself in the parlour, wherein sat two or three men, for the butcher was pouring out some year-old wine.

Presently two dark figures approached the house; they were menservants of townsfolk who owned country estates round about the village and on the slopes of the mountains; one was in livery and knee-breeches, the other clad as a gamekeeper. While the first remained behind, the other strode ahead and entered the parlour. Whereupon, from a dark spot close to a gushing well, a wench stepped forth in the direction of the man who had remained behind, raised her hands towards him, and tried to take his arm. The lower half of her figure was shapelessly broad and Euseb knew immediately that she was the maidservant to the keeper of the "Crown," a young stranger to the place at whom he and the other boys would steal glances when, with heavy body, she knelt down beside the dammed-up mill-stream to rinse the washing, for all were aware that she was with child. Now the servant shook the pleading woman with such force that she had to support herself with one hand on the edge of the well, while with the other she convulsively grasped her belly, and the sound of her sobbing drowned out the gushing of the water. Soon there appeared on the threshold the other servant with the butcher's beautiful daughter, and the one in livery lent to his speech, while half turning towards the maid standing in the dark, a loud and strangely superior tone. "That was last year," he shouted back. "Now we are in another year. Amen." And when, with a "Joseph, Joseph!" from a mouth stretched wide in fear, she tried once more to come near him, he reproached her with knife-sharp words that actually had the power to strike her dumb — to the effect that a person in her condition should be ashamed of loitering in the streets and outside inns, that he regretted the time he had wasted with her during the bygone year and even now would regret every additional minute, since he had better things to do than hang about here with her.

These knife-sharp words penetrated the boy Euseb in his hiding-place with a kind of cruel delight; the skill wherewith the servant had uttered his words and then, whistling three bars and without turning round, disappeared into the inn, gave him much the same sensation he frequently felt when the dresses of women and girls from the town brushed against him: they cast off a subtle, benumbing fragrance which, as he inhaled it, filled him with a divided feeling of sinking down, gently surrendering, while at the same time something within him violently revolted. The twofold sensation now seized him again; it seemed as if, like a door in the dark, the secret splendour of the life of the townsfolk and their servants opened up to him and he was driven to prowl after the maid who stumbled away before him, moaning to herself, hand in mouth, face distorted, to continue following her unobserved and to play a cruel game with the unsuspecting girl. As she walked in heavy despair down the middle of the road, he slipped sideways between the hedges hunched in the storm, under the trees shaken by the storm, past barns that groaned in their beams. Though the nocturnal storm flung dust and chaff into his wide-stretched eyes, he paid no heed; he had lost consciousness of his body, for minutes on end he felt no bigger than the weasels, the toads, or any of the other things that lay in wait and rustled on the trembling earth; an instant later he was of gigantic stature, he stretched up between the trees and it was he who seized their crests and bent them, groaning, down; he was the Terrible who lies in wait in the dark and leaps forth at the cross-roads, yet in him was the timidity of a frightened deer, and all the dread that emanated from him he felt rippling down his spine. She who stumbled along before him had become his prey; he was a gentleman from town and had several of her kind; the new ones he had locked into his house and this one he was now driving to join them; he was the butcher who sneaked up on a runaway animal to lead it to its death, but the animal was an animal bewitched; it was this woman here before him.

He ducked when the wind ceased and sprang forth again when it roared; between the breath of the wind and his wild secret chase lay an intimate harmony; the wind was his ally and the brilliant lightning illuminated the road with its cart-tracks, cast its light on the chalk walls of the houses and between the hedges, shone into the forest and revealed the roots of the trees — all that he might keep his victim in sight should she try to slip away from him in the dark.

(Translated by James and Tanya Stern)

THOMAS MANN (1875–1955) Born in the Hanseatic city of Lübeck, Germany, Mann was the son of a prosperous grain merchant and senator and was next to the oldest of five children. His beautiful German-Brazilian mother loved music and music plays an important thematic role in Mann's works. Mann hated his early rigorous Prussian education and dreaded returning to school after his summers on the Baltic.

At nineteen, he joined his family in Munich and worked briefly in a fire insurance office where he wrote *Gefallen* (1894). Mann studied the humanities at the University of Munich; here he first read Schopenhauer and Nietzsche, both of whom had a profound effect on him. *Little Herr Friedemann,* a collection of short stories, was published in 1898, and, after the successful publication of *Buddenbrooks* in 1901, Mann devoted himself entirely to writing. In 1905 Mann married a girl of German-Jewish parentage; they had six children — two of whom became important literary persons and one became an historian.

Death and sickness (central images in Mann's work) hung ominously over Mann's life. One sister committed suicide in 1910, and his mother died after a long illness in 1922. "I assume that I shall die in 1945 when I have reached the age of my mother." Five years later his other sister committed suicide. "It seems that the nourishing love has given more resistance to life to us, the sons, than to the girls." His wife suffered from a lung infection and was in sanatoriums repeatedly.

In 1924 *The Magic Mountain* was published, and five years later Mann was awarded the Nobel Prize for literature. A few days after Hitler gained the chancellorship in Germany, Mann gave a lecture entitled "Suffering and Greatness of Richard Wagner." He left the following day for Switzerland and never again lived in Germany. For a while, fearful of losing his German readers, Mann had little public comment about the Nazi regime. In 1936, however, he wrote an open letter to a Nazi newspaper which resulted in his books being banned. His manifesto against Hitler, *Achtung, Europa!,* appeared in 1938.

From 1938–1952 Mann lived in the United States and wrote *Dr. Faustus* (1947) and *The Holy Sinner* (1951). In 1944 he became a naturalized citizen. The last three years of his life Mann lived in

Switzerland where he wrote *The Confessions of Felix Krull, Confidence Man*. "The Fight Between Jappe and Do Escobar" is an early treatment of the theme of antagonistic nationalism — a theme Mann came to explore fully in both its psychological and political aspects and in the ways adult hostilities infect the attitudes of children.

THE FIGHT BETWEEN JAPPE
AND DO ESCOBAR

Thomas Mann

I was very much taken aback when Johnny Bishop told me that Jappe and Do Escobar were going to fight each other and that we must go and watch them do it.

It was in the summer holidays at Travemünde, on a sultry day with a slight land breeze and a flat sea ever so far away across the sands. We had been some three-quarters of an hour in the water and were lying on the hard sand under the props of the bathing-cabins — we two and Jürgen Brattström the shipowner's son. Johnny and Brattström were lying on their backs entirely naked; I felt more comfortable with my towel wrapped round my hips. Brattström asked me why I did it and I could not think of any sensible answer; so Johnny said with his winning smile that I was probably too big now to lie naked. I really was larger and more developed than Johnny and Brattström; also a little older, about thirteen; so I accepted Johnny's explanation in silence, although with a certain feeling of mortification. For in Johnny Bishop's presence you actually felt rather out of it if you were any less small, fine, and physically childlike than he, who was all these things in such a very high degree. He knew how to look up at you with his pretty, friendly blue eyes, which had a certain mocking smile in them too, with an expression that said: "What a great, gawky thing you are, to be sure!" The ideal of manliness and long trousers had no validity in his presence — and that at a time, not long after the war, when strength, courage, and every hardy virtue stood very high among us youth and all sorts of conduct were banned as effeminate. But Johnny, as a foreigner — or half-foreigner — was exempt from this atmosphere. He was a little like a woman who preserves her youth and looks down on other women who are less successful at the feat. Besides he was far and away the best-dressed boy in town, distinctly aristocratic and elegant in his real English sailor suit with the linen collar, sailor's knot, laces, a silver whistle in his pocket, and an anchor on the sleeves that narrowed round his wrists. Anyone else would have been laughed at for that sort of thing — it would have been jeered at as "girls' clothes." But he wore them with such a disarming and confident air that he never suffered in the least.

He looked rather like a thin little cupid as he lay there, with his pretty, soft blond curls and his arms up over the narrow English head that rested on the sand. His father had been a German business man who had been naturalized in England and died some years since. His mother was English by blood, a long-featured lady with quiet, gentle ways, who had settled in our town with her two children, Johnny and a mischievous little girl just as pretty as he. She still wore black for her husband, and she was probably honouring his last wishes when she brought the children to grow up in Germany. Obviously they were in easy circumstances. She owned a spacious house outside the city and a villa at the sea and from time to time she travelled with Johnny and Sissie to more distant resorts. She did not move in society, although it would have been open to her. Whether on account of her mourning or perhaps because the horizon of our best families was too narrow for her, she herself led a retired life, but she managed that her children should have social intercourse. She invited other children to play with them and sent them to dancing and deportment lessons, thus quietly arranging that Johnny and Sissie should associate exclusively with the children of well-to-do families — of course not in pursuance of any well-defined principle, but just as a matter of course. Mrs. Bishop contributed, remotely, to my own education: it was from her I learned that to be well thought of by others no more is needed than to think well of yourself. Though deprived of its male head the little family showed none of the marks of neglect or disruption which often in such cases make people fight shy. Without further family connection, without title, tradition, influence, or public office, and living a life apart, Mrs. Bishop by no means lacked social security or pretensions. She was definitely accepted at her own valuation and the friendship of her children was much sought after by their young contemporaries.

As for Jürgen Brattström, I may say in passing that his father had made his own money, achieved public office, and built for himself and his family the red sandstone house on the Burgfeld, next to Mrs. Bishop's. And that lady had quietly accepted his son as Johnny's playmate and let the two go to school together. Jürgen was a decent, phlegmatic, short-legged lad without any prominent characteristics. He had begun to do a little private business in licorice sticks.

As I said, I was extremely shocked when Johnny told me about the impending meeting between Jappe and Do Escobar which was to take place at twelve o'clock that day on the Leuchtenfeld. It was dead earnest — might have a serious outcome, for Jappe and Do Escobar were both stout and reckless fellows and had strong feelings about knightly honour. The issue might well be frightful. In my memory they still seem as tall and manly as they did then, though they could not have been more than fifteen at the time. Jappe came from the middle class of the city; he was not much looked after at home, he was already almost his own master, a combination of loafer and man-about-town. Do Escobar was an exotic and bohemian foreigner, who did not even come regularly to school but only attended lectures now and then — an irregular but paradisial existence! He lived *en pension* with some middle-class people and rejoiced in complete independence. Both were people who went late to bed, visited publichouses, strolled of evenings in the Broad Street, followed girls about, performed crazy "stunts" — in short, were regular blades. Although they did not live in the Kurhotel at Travemünde — where they would scarcely have been acceptable — but somewhere in the village, they frequented the Kurhaus and garden and were at home there as cosmopolitans. In the evening, especially on a Sunday, when I had long since been in my bed in one of the chalets and gone off to sleep to the pleasant sound of the Kurhaus band, they, and other members of the young generation — as I was aware — still sauntered up and down in the stream of tourists and guests, loitered in front of the long awning of the café, and sought and found grown-up entertainment. And here they had come to blows, goodness knows how and why. It is possible that they had only brushed against each other in passing and in the sensitiveness of their knightly honour had made a fighting matter of the encounter. Johnny, who of course had been long since in bed too and was instructed only by hearsay in what happened, expressed himself in his pleasant, slightly husky childish voice, that the quarrel was probably about some "gal" — an easy assumption, considering Jappe's and Do Escobar's precocity and boldness. In short, they had made no scene among the guests, but in few and biting words agreed upon hour and place and witnesses for the satisfaction of their honour. The next day, at twelve, rendezvous at such and such a spot on the Leuchtenfeld. Good evening. — Ballet-master Knaak from Hamburg, master of ceremonies and leader of the Kurhaus cotillions, had been on the scene and promised his presence at the appointed hour and place.

Johnny rejoiced wholeheartedly in the fray — I think that neither he nor Brattström would have shared my apprehensions. Johnny repeatedly assured me, forming the *r* far forward on his palate, with his pretty enunciation, that they were both "in dead eahnest" and certainly meant business. Complacently and with a rather ironic objectivity he weighed the chances of victory for each. They were both frightfully strong, he grinned; both of them great fighters — it would be fun to have it settled which of them was the greater. Jappe, Johnny thought, had a broad chest and capital arm and leg muscles, he could tell that from seeing him swimming. But Do Escobar was uncommonly wiry and savage — hard to tell beforehand who would get the upper hand. It was strange to hear Johnny discourse so sovereignly upon Jappe's and Do Escobar's qualifications, looking at his childish arms, which could never have given or warded off a blow. As for me, I was indeed far from absenting myself from the spectacle. That would have been absurd and moreover the proceedings had a great fascination for me. Of course I must go, I must see it all, now that I knew about it. I felt a certain sense of duty, along with other and conflicting emotions: a great shyness and shame, all unwarlike as I was, and not at all minded to trust myself upon the scene of manly exploits. I had a nervous dread of the shock which the sight of a duel *à outrance*, a fight for life and death, as it were, would give me. I was cowardly enough to ask myself whether, once on the field, I might not be caught up in the struggle and have to expose my own person to a proof of valour which I knew in my inmost heart I was far from being able or willing to give. On the other hand I kept putting myself in Jappe's and Do Escobar's place and feeling consuming sensations which I assumed to be what they were feeling. I visualized the scene of the insult and the challenge, summoned my sense of good form and with Jappe and Do Escobar resisted the impulse to fall to there and then. I experienced the agony of an overwrought passion for justice, the flaring, shattering hatred, the attacks of raving impatience for revenge, in which they must have passed the night. Arrived at the last ditch, lost to all sense of fear, I fought myself blind and bloody with an adversary just as inhuman, drove my fist into his hated jaw with all the strength of my being, so that all his teeth were broken, received in exchange a brutal kick in the stomach and went under in a sea of blood. After which I woke in my bed with ice-bags, quieted nerves, and a chorus of mild reproaches from my family. In short, when it was half past twelve and we got up to dress I was half worn out with my apprehensions. In the cabin and afterwards when we were dressed and went outdoors, my heart throbbed exactly as though it was I myself who was to fight with Jappe or Do Escobar, in public and with all the rigours of the game.

I still remember how we took the narrow wooden bridge which ran diagonally up from the beach to the cabins. Of course we jumped, in order to make it sway as much as possible, so that we bounced as though on a spring-board. But once below we did not follow the board walk which led along the beach past the tents and the basket chairs; but held inland in the general direction of the Kurhaus but rather more leftwards. The sun brooded over the dunes and sucked a dry, hot odour from the sparse and withered vegetation, the reeds and thistles that stuck into our legs. There was no sound but the ceaseless humming of the blue-bottle flies which hung apparently motionless in the heavy warmth, suddenly to shift to another spot and begin afresh their sharp, monotonous whine. The cooling effect of the bath was long since spent. Brattström and I kept lifting our hats, he his Swedish sailor cap with the oilcloth visor, I my round Heligoland woollen bonnet — the so-called tam-o'-shanter — to wipe our brows. Johnny suffered little from heat, thanks to his slightness and also because his clothing was more elegantly adapted than ours to the summer day. In his light and comfortable sailor suit of striped washing material which left bare his throat and legs, the blue, short-ribboned cap with English lettering on his pretty little head, the long slender feet in fine, almost heelless white leather shoes, he walked with mounting strides and somewhat bent knees between Brattström and me and sang with his charming accent "Little Fisher Maiden" — a ditty which was then the rage. He sang it with some vulgar variation in the words, such as boys like to invent. Curiously enough, in all his childishness he knew a good deal about various matters and was not at all too prudish to take them in his mouth. But always he would make a sanctimonious little face and say: "Fie! Who would sing such dirty songs?" — as though Brattström and I had been the ones to make indecent advances to the little fisher maiden.

I did not feel at all like singing, we were too near the fatal spot. The prickly grass of the dunes had changed to the sand and sea moss of a barren meadow; this was the Leuchtenfeld, so called after the yellow lighthouse towering up in the far distance. We soon found ourselves at our goal.

It was a warm, peaceful spot, where almost nobody ever came: protected from view by scrubby willow trees. On the free space among the bushes a crowd of youths lay or sat in a circle. They were almost all older than we and from various strata of society. We seemed to be the last spectators to arrive. Everybody was waiting for Knaak the dancing-master, who was needed in the capacity of neutral and umpire. Both Jappe and Do Escobar were there — I saw them at once. They were sitting far apart in the circle and pretending not to see each other. We greeted a few acquaintances with silent nods and squatted in our turn on the sun-warmed ground.

Some of the group were smoking. Both Jappe and Do Escobar held cigarettes in the corners of their mouths. Each kept one eye shut against the smoke and I instantly felt and knew that they were aware how grand it was to sit there and smoke before entering the ring. They were both dressed in grown-up clothes, but Do Escobar's were more gentlemanly than Jappe's. He wore yellow shoes with pointed toes, a light-grey summer suit, a rose-coloured shirt with cuffs, a coloured silk cravat, and a round, narrow-brimmed straw hat sitting far back on his head, so that his mop of shiny black hair showed on one side beneath it, in a big hummock. He kept raising his right hand to shake back the silver bangle he wore under his cuff. Jappe's appearance was distinctly less pretentious. His legs were encased in tight trousers of a lighter colour than his coat and waistcoat and fastened with straps under his waxed black boots. A checked cap covered his

curly blond hair; in contrast to Do Escobar's jaunty headgear he
wore it pulled down over his forehead. He sat with his arms
clasped round one knee; you could see that he had on loose cuffs
over his shirt-sleeves, also that his finger-nails were either cut too
short or else that he indulged in the vice of biting them. Despite
the smoking and the assumed nonchalance, the whole circle was
serious and silent, restraint was in the air. The only one to make
head against it was Do Escobar, who talked without stopping to
his neighbours, in a loud, strained voice, rolling his *r*'s and blowing smoke out of his nose.

I was rather put off by his volubility; it inclined me, despite
the bitten finger-nails, to side with Jappe, who at most addressed
a word or two over his shoulder to his neighbour and for the
rest gazed in apparent composure at the smoke of his cigarette.

Then came Herr Knaak — I can still see him, in his blue striped
flannel morning suit, coming with winged tread from the direction of the Kurhaus and lifting his hat as he paused outside the
circle. That he wanted to come I do not believe; I am convinced
rather that he had made a virtue of necessity when he honoured
the fight with his presence. And the necessity, the compulsion,
was due to his equivocal position in the eyes of martially- and
masculinely-minded youth. Dark-skinned and comely, plump,
particularly in the region of the hips, he gave us dancing and deportment lessons in the wintertime — private, family lessons as
well as public classes in the Casino; and in the summer he acted
as bathing-master and social manager at Travemünde. He rocked
on his hips and weaved in his walk, turning out his toes very
much and setting them first on the ground as he stepped. His
eyes had a vain expression, his speech was pleasant but affected,
and his way of entering a room as though it were a stage, his
extraordinary and fastidious mannerisms charmed all the female
sex, while the masculine world, and especially critical youth,
viewed him with suspicion. I have often pondered over the position of François Knaak in life and always I have found it strange
and fantastic. He was of humble origins, his parents were poor,
and his taste for the social graces left him as it were hanging in
the air — not a member of society, yet paid by it as a guardian
and instructor of its conventions. Jappe and Do Escobar were
his pupils too; not in private lessons, like Johnny, Brattström,
and me, but in the public classes in the Casino. It was in these

that Herr Knaak's character and position were most sharply criticized. We of the private classes were less austere. A fellow who taught you the proper deportment towards little girls, who was thrillingly reported to wear a corset, who picked up the edge of his frock-coat with his fingertips, curtsied, cut capers, leaped suddenly into the air, where he twirled his toes before he came down again — what sort of chap was he, after all? These were the suspicions harboured by militant youth on the score of Herr Knaak's character and mode of life, and his exaggerated airs did nothing to allay them. Of course, he was a grown-up man (he was even, comically enough, said to have a wife and children in Hamburg); and his advantage in years and the fact that he was never seen except officially and in the dance-hall, prevented him from being convicted and unmasked. Could he do gymnastics? Had he ever been able to? Had he courage? Had he parts? In short, could one accept him as an equal? He was never in a position to display the soldier characteristics which might have balanced his salon arts and made him a decent chap. So there were youths who made no bones of calling him straight out a coward and a jackanapes. All this he knew and therefore he was here today to manifest his interest in a good stand-up fight and to put himself on terms with the young, though in his official position he should not have countenanced such goings-on. I am convinced, however, that he was not comfortable — he knew he was treading on thin ice. Some of the audience looked coldly at him and he himself gazed uneasily round to see if anybody was coming.

He politely excused his late arrival, saying that he had been kept by a consultation with the management of the Kurhaus about the next Sunday's ball. "Are the combatants present?" he next inquired in official tones. "Then we can begin." Leaning on his stick with his feet crossed he gnawed his soft brown moustache with his under lip and made owl eyes to look like a connoisseur.

Jappe and Do Escobar stood up, threw away their cigarettes, and began to prepare for the fray. Do Escobar did it in a hurry, with impressive speed. He threw hat, coat, and waistcoat on the ground, unfastened tie, collar, and braces and added them to the pile. He even drew his rose-coloured shirt out of his trousers, pulled his arms briskly out of the sleeves, and stood up in a red and white striped undershirt which exposed the larger part of his yellow arms, already covered with a thick black fell. "At your service, sir," he said, with a rolling *r*, stepping into the middle of the ring, expanding his chest and throwing back his shoulders. He still wore the silver bangle.

Jappe was not ready yet. He turned his head, elevated his brows, and looked at Do Escobar's feet a moment with narrowed eyes — as much as to say: "Wait a bit — I'll get there too, even if I don't swagger so much." He was broader in the shoulder; but as he took his place beside Do Escobar he seemed nowhere near so fit or athletic. His legs in the tight strapped boots inclined to be knock-kneed and his fit-out was not impressive — grey braces over a yellowed white shirt with loose buttoned sleeves. By contrast Do Escobar's striped tricot and the black hair on his arms looked uncommonly grim and businesslike. Both were pale but it showed more in Jappe as he was otherwise blond and red-cheeked, with jolly, not-too-refined features including a rather turned-up nose with a saddle of freckles. Do Escobar's nose was short, straight, and drooping and there was a downy black growth on his full upper lip.

They stood with hanging arms almost breast to breast, and looked at one another darkly and haughtily in the region of the stomach. They obviously did not know how to begin — and how well I could understand that! A night and half a day had intervened since the unpleasantness. They had wanted to fly at each other's throats and had only been held in check by the rules of the game. But they had had time to cool off. To do to order, as it were, before an audience, by appointment, in cold blood, what they had wanted to do yesterday when the fit was on them — it was not the same thing at all. After all, they were not gladiators. They were civilized young men. And in possession of one's senses one has a certain reluctance to smash a sound human body with one's fists. So I thought, and so, very likely, it was.

But something had to be done, that honour might be satisfied, so each began to work the other up by hitting him contemptuously with the finger-tips on the breast, as though that would be enough to finish him off. And, indeed, Jappe's face began to be distorted with anger — but just at that moment Do Escobar broke off the skirmish.

"Pardon," said he, taking two steps backwards and turning aside. He had to tighten the buckle at the back of his trousers, for he was narrow-hipped and in the absence of braces they had begun to slip. He took his position again almost at once, throwing out his chest and saying something in guttural and rattling Spanish, probably to the effect that he was again at Jappe's service. It was clear that he was inordinately vain.

The skirmishing with shoulders and buffeting with palms began again. Then unexpectedly there ensued a blind and raging hand-to-hand scuffle with the fists, which lasted three seconds and broke off without notice.

"Now they are warming up," said Johnny, sitting next to me with a dry grass in his mouth. "I'll wager Jappe beats him. Look how he keeps squinting over at us — Jappe keeps his mind on his job. Will you bet he won't give him a good hiding?"

They had now recoiled and stood, fists on hips, their chests heaving. Both had doubtless taken some punishment, for they both looked angry, sticking out their lips furiously as much as to say: "What do you mean by hurting me like that?" Jappe was red-eyed and Do Escobar showed his white teeth as they fell to again.

They were hitting out now with all their strength on shoulders, forearms, and breasts by turns and in quick succession. "That's nothing," Johnny said, with his charming accent. "They won't get anywhere that way, either of them. They must go at it under the chin, with an uppercut to the jaw. That does it." But meanwhile Do Escobar had caught both Jappe's arms with his left arm, pressed them as in a vise against his chest, and with his right when on pummelling Jappe's flanks.

There was great excitement. "No clinching!" several voices cried out, and people jumped up. Herr Knaak hastened between the combatants, in horror. "You are holding him fast, my dear friend. That is against all the rules." He separated them and again instructed Do Escobar in the regulations. Then he withdrew once more outside the ring.

Jappe was obviously in a fury. He was quite white, rubbing his side and looking at Do Escobar with a slow nod that boded no good. When the next round began, his face looked so grim that everybody expected him to deliver a decisive blow.

And actually as soon as contact had been renewed Jappe carried out a coup — he practised a feint which he had probably planned beforehand. A thrust with his left caused Do Escobar to protect his head; but as he did so Jappe's right hit him so hard in the stomach that he crumpled forwards and his face took on the colour of yellow wax.

"That went home," said Johnny. "That's where it hurts. Maybe now he will pull himself together and take things seriously, so as to pay it back." But the blow to the stomach had been too telling, Do Escobar's nerve was visibly shaken. It was clear he could not even clench his fists properly, and his eyes took on a glazed look. However, finding his muscles thus affected, his vanity counselled him to play the agile southron, dancing round the German bear and rendering him desperate by his own dexterity. He took tiny steps and made all sorts of useless passes, moving round Jappe in little circles and trying to assume an arrogant smile — which in his reduced condition struck me as really heroic. But it did not upset Jappe at all — he simply turned round on his heel and got in many a good blow with his right while with his left he warded off Do Escobar's feeble attack. But what sealed Do Escobar's fate was that his trousers kept slipping. His tricot shirt even came outside and rucked up, showing a little strip of his bare yellow skin — some of the audience sniggered. But why had he taken off his braces? He would have done better to leave æsthetic considerations on one side. For now his trousers bothered him, they had bothered him during the whole fight. He kept wanting to pull them up and stuff in his shirt, for however much he was punished he could bear it better than the thought that he might be cutting a ridiculous figure. In the end he was fighting with one hand while the other tried to put himself to rights; and thus Jappe was able to land such a blow on his nose that to this day I do not understand why it was not broken.

But the blood poured out, and Do Escobar turned and went apart from Jappe, trying with his right hand to stop the bleeding and with his left making an eloquent gesture behind him as he went. Jappe stood there with his knock-kneed legs spread out and waited for Do Escobar to come back. But Do Escobar was finished with the business. If I interpret him aright he was the more civilized of the two and felt that it was high time to call a halt. Jappe would beyond doubt have fought on with his nose bleeding; but almost as certainly Do Escobar would equally have refused to go on, and he did so with even more conviction in that it was himself that bled. They had made the claret run out of his nose — in his view things should never have been allowed to go so far, devil take it! The blood ran between his fingers onto his clothes, it soiled his light trousers and dripped on his yellow shoes. It was beastly and nothing but beastly — and under such circumstances he declined to take part in more fighting. It would be inhuman.

And his attitude was accepted by the majority of the spectators. Herr Knaak came into the ring and declared that the fight was over. Both sides had behaved with distinction. You could see how relieved he felt that the affair had gone off so smoothly.

"But neither of them was brought to a fall," said Johnny, surprised and disappointed. However, even Jappe was quite satisfied to consider the affair as settled. Drawing a long breath he went to fetch his clothes. Everybody generally accepted Herr Knaak's delicate fiction that the issue was a draw. Jappe was congratulated, but only surreptitiously; on the other hand some people lent Do Escobar their handkerchiefs, as his own was soon drenched. And now the cry was for more. Let two other fellows fight. That was the sense of the meeting; Jappe's and Do Escobar's business had taken so little time, hardly ten minutes; since they were all there and it was still quite early something more ought to come. Another pair must enter the arena — whoever wanted to show that he deserved being called a lad of parts.

Nobody offered. But why at this summons did my heart begin to beat like a little drum? What I had feared had come to pass: the challenge had become general. Why did I feel as though I had all the time been awaiting this very moment with shivers of delicious anticipation and now when it had come why was I plunged into a whirl of conflicting emotions? I looked at Johnny. Perfectly calm and detached he sat beside me, turned his straw about in his mouth and looked about the ring with a frankly curious air, to see whether a couple of stout chaps would not be found to let their noses be broken for his amusement. Why was it that I had to feel personally challenged to conquer my nervous timidity, to make an unnatural effort and draw all eyes upon myself by heroically stepping into the ring? In an access of self-consciousness mingled with vanity I was about to raise my hand and offer myself for combat when somewhere in the circle the shout arose:

"Herr Knaak ought to fight!"

All eyes fastened themselves upon Herr Knaak. I have said that he was walking upon slippery ice in exposing himself to the danger of such a test of his kidney. But he simply answered:

"No, thanks, very much — I had enough beatings when I was young."

He was safe. He had slipped like an eel out of the trap. How astute of him, to bring in his superiority in years, to imply that at our age he would not have avoided an honourable fight — and that without boasting at all, even making his words carry irresistible conviction by admitting with a disarming laugh at himself that he too had taken beatings in his time. They let him alone. They perceived that it was hard, if not impossible, to bring him to book.

"Then somebody must wrestle!" was the next cry. This suggestion was not taken up either; but in the midst of the discussion over it (and I shall never forget the painful impression it made) Do Escobar said in his hoarse Spanish voice from behind his gory handkerchief: "Wrestling is for cowards. Only Germans wrestle." It was an unheard-of piece of tactlessness, coming from him, and got its reward at once in the capital retort made by Herr Knaak: "Possibly," said he. "But it looks as though the Germans know how to give pretty good beatings sometimes too!" He was rewarded by shouts of approving laughter; his whole position was improved, and Do Escobar definitely put down for the day.

But it was the general opinion that wrestling was a good deal of a bore, and so various athletic feats were resorted to instead: leap-frog, standing on one's head, handsprings and so on, to fill in the time.

"Come on, let's go," said Johnny to Brattström and me, and got up. That was Johnny Bishop for you. He had come to see something real, with the possibility of a bloody issue. But the thing had petered out and so he left.

He gave me my first impression of the peculiar superiority of the English character, which later on I came so greatly to admire.

(Translated by H. T. Lowe-Porter)

JAMES JOYCE (1882–1941) Born in Dublin, Ireland, Joyce was the son of a government rate collector and the eldest of ten children. He studied at Jesuit schools and University College in Dublin.

Joyce's family enjoyed singing together. Twice during his twenties Joyce decided, without success, to become a professional singer to earn money. The theme of music, as well as the technique of the recurrent motif, are prominent in Joyce's writing from *Chamber Music* (an early collection of poems) to *Finnegan's Wake*. "The Dead" is particularly rich in musical allusions.

In October 1891, the death of Charles Stuart Parnell, the leader for Irish independence, captured Joyce's boyhood imagination as it captured that of the great Irish poet, W. B. Yeats, seventeen years older than Joyce. That year — Joyce was nine — he wrote a poem about the conspiracy against Parnell and his death. In *Portrait of the Artist As a Young Man* (1916), young Stephen Daedalus identifies with Parnell.

When he was twenty-two, Joyce left Ireland for the continent. Although he returned to Ireland several times, in 1912 he left forever. His was a self-imposed exile from both country and church since he strongly objected to the Irish nationalist movement. In terms of political reality, Ireland became "the sow that eats her farrow." Emotionally and artistically, however, Joyce never left Ireland, and the Dublin of his youth is the home of his characters. Richard Ellman says in his definitive biography that Joyce had to leave Ireland to become a Dubliner and that "The Dead" is Joyce's "first song of exile."

The Dubliners, published in 1914 in London, is a collection of stories about quotidian events of Dublin life. In these stories Joyce already employed the techniques of epiphany and parody which he continued to develop throughout his career. *Ulysses* was published in 1922 and *Finnegan's Wake,* in 1939. *Ulysses* was banned by the censors in Ireland and in the United States as well until 1933.

Joyce's life on the continent was a struggle against poverty and blindness. He worked briefly as a bank clerk in Rome and lived in London, Paris, and Zurich, fighting to have his works published and seeking patronage. He fled to Zurich to escape the Nazi invasion of France and died there in 1941.

EVELINE

James Joyce

She sat at the window watching the evening invade the avenue. Her head was leaned against the window curtains and in her nostrils was the odour of dusty cretonne. She was tired.

Few people passed. The man out of the last house passed on his way home; she heard his footsteps clacking along the concrete pavement and afterwards crunching on the cinder path before the new red houses. One time there used to be a field there in which they used to play every evening with other people's children. Then a man from Belfast bought the field and built houses in it — not like their little brown houses but bright brick houses with shining roofs. The children of the avenue used to play together in that field — the Devines, the Waters, the Dunns, little Keogh the cripple, she and her brothers and sisters. Ernest, however, never played: he was too grown up. Her father used often to hunt them in out of the field with his blackthorn stick; but usually little Keogh used to keep *nix* and call out when he saw her father coming. Still they seemed to have been rather happy then. Her father was not so bad then; and besides, her mother was alive. That was a long time ago; she and her brothers and sisters were all grown up; her mother was dead. Tizzie Dunn was dead, too, and the Waters had gone back to England. Everything changes. Now she was going to go away like the others, to leave her home.

Home! She looked round the room, reviewing all its familiar objects which she had dusted once a week for so many years, wondering where on earth all the dust came from. Perhaps she would never see again those familiar objects from which she had never dreamed of being divided. And yet during all those years she had never found out the name of the priest whose yellowing photograph hung on the wall above the broken harmonium beside the coloured print of the promises made to Blessed Margaret Mary Alacoque. He had been a school friend of her father. Whenever he showed the photograph to a visitor her father used to pass it with a casual word:

"He is in Melbourne now."

She had consented to go away, to leave her home. Was that wise? She tried to weigh each side of the question. In her home anyway she had shelter and food; she had those whom she had known all her life about her. Of course she had to work hard, both in the house and at business. What would they say of her in the Stores when they found out that she had run away with a fellow? Say she was a fool, perhaps; and her place would be filled up by advertisement. Miss Gavan would be glad. She had always had an edge on her, especially whenever there were people listening.

"Miss Hill, don't you see these ladies are waiting?"

"Look lively, Miss Hill, please."

She would not cry many tears at leaving the Stores.

But in her new home, in a distant unknown country, it would not be like that. Then she would be married — she, Eveline. People would treat her with respect then. She would not be treated as her mother had been. Even now, though she was over nineteen, she sometimes felt herself in danger of her father's violence. She knew it was that that had given her the palpitations. When they were growing up he had never gone for her, like he used to go for Harry and Ernest, because she was a girl; but latterly he had begun to threaten her and say what he would do to her only for her dead mother's sake. And now she had nobody to protect her. Ernest was dead and Harry, who was in the church decorating business, was nearly always down somewhere in the country. Besides, the invariable squabble for money on Saturday nights had begun to weary her unspeakably. She always gave her entire wages — seven shillings — and Harry always sent up what he could but the trouble was to get any money from her father. He said she used to squander the money, that she had no head, that he wasn't going to give her his hard-earned money to throw about the streets, and much more, for he was usually fairly bad on Saturday night. In the end he would give her the money and ask her had she any intention of buying Sunday's dinner. Then she had to rush out as quickly as she

could and do her marketing, holding her black leather purse
tightly in her hand as she elbowed her way through the crowds
and returning home late under her load of provisions. She had
hard work to keep the house together and to see that the two
young children who had been left to her charge went to school
regularly and got their meals regularly. It was hard work — a
hard life — but now that she was about to leave it she did not
find it a wholly undesirable life.

She was about to explore another life with Frank. Frank was
very kind, manly, open-hearted. She was to go away with him
by the night-boat to be his wife and to live with him in Buenos
Ayres where he had a home waiting for her. How well she
remembered the first time she had seen him; he was lodging in a
house on the main road where she used to visit. It seemed a few
weeks ago. He was standing at the gate, his peaked cap pushed
back on his head and his hair tumbled forward over a face of
bronze. Then they had come to know each other. He used to
meet her outside the Stores every evening and see her home. He
took her to see *The Bohemian Girl* and she felt elated as she sat
in an unaccustomed part of the theatre with him. He was awfully
fond of music and sang a little. People knew that they were
courting and, when he sang about the lass that loves a sailor, she
always felt pleasantly confused. He used to call her Poppens out
of fun. First of all it had been an excitement for her to have a
fellow and then she had begun to like him. He had tales of distant countries. He had started as a deck boy at a pound a month
on a ship of the Allan Line going out to Canada. He told her
the names of the ships he had been on and the names of the
different services. He had sailed through the Straits of Magellan
and he told her stories of the terrible Patagonians. He had fallen
on his feet in Buenos Ayres, he said, and had come over to the
old country just for a holiday. Of course, her father had found
out the affair and had forbidden her to have anything to say to
him.

"I know these sailor chaps," he said.

One day he had quarrelled with Frank and after that she had
to meet her lover secretly.

The evening deepened in the avenue. The white of two letters
in her lap grew indistinct. One was to Harry; the other was to
her father. Ernest had been her favourite but she liked Harry

too. Her father was becoming old lately, she noticed; he would miss her. Sometimes he could be very nice. Not long before, when she had been laid up for a day, he had read her out a ghost story and made toast for her at the fire. Another day, when their mother was alive, they had all gone for a picnic to the Hill of Howth. She remembered her father putting on her mother's bonnet to make the children laugh.

Her time was running out but she continued to sit by the window, leaning her head against the window curtain, inhaling the odour of dusty cretonne. Down far in the avenue she could hear a street organ playing. She knew the air. Strange that it should come that very night to remind her of the promise to her mother, her promise to keep the home together as long as she could. She remembered the last night of her mother's illness; she was again in the close dark room at the other side of the hall and outside she heard a melancholy air of Italy. The organ-player had been ordered to go away and given sixpence. She remembered her father strutting back into the sickroom saying:

"Damned Italians! coming over here!"

As she mused the pitiful vision of her mother's life laid its spell on the very quick of her being — that life of commonplace sacrifices closing in final craziness. She trembled as she heard again her mother's voice saying constantly with foolish insistence:

"Derevaun Seraun! Derevaun Seraun!"

She stood up in a sudden impulse of terror. Escape! She must escape! Frank would save her. He would give her life, perhaps love, too. But she wanted to live. Why should she be unhappy? She had a right to happiness. Frank would take her in his arms, fold her in his arms. He would save her.

She stood among the swaying crowd in the station at the North Wall. He held her hand and she knew that he was speaking to her, saying something about the passage over and over again. The station was full of soldiers with brown baggages. Through the wide doors of the sheds she caught a glimpse of the black mass of the boat, lying in beside the quay wall, with illumined portholes. She answered nothing. She felt her cheek pale and cold and, out of a maze of distress, she prayed to God to direct her, to show her what was her duty. The boat blew a long mournful whistle into the mist. If she went, tomorrow she would be on the sea with Frank, steaming towards Buenos Ayres. Their passage had been booked. Could she still draw back after all he had done for her? Her distress awoke a nausea in her body and she kept moving her lips in silent fervent prayer.

A bell clanged upon her heart. She felt him seize her hand:

"Come!"

All the seas of the world tumbled about her heart. He was drawing her into them: he would drown her. She gripped with both hands at the iron railing.

"Come!"

No! No! No! It was impossible. Her hands clutched the iron in frenzy. Amid the seas she sent a cry of anguish.

"Eveline! Evvy!"

He rushed beyond the barrier and called to her to follow. He was shouted at to go on but he still called to her. She set her white face to him, passive, like a helpless animal. Her eyes gave him no sign of love or farewell or recognition.

THE DEAD

James Joyce

Lily, the caretaker's daughter, was literally run off her feet. Hardly had she brought one gentleman into the little pantry behind the office on the ground floor and helped him off with his overcoat than the wheezy hall-door bell clanged again and she had to scamper along the bare hallway to let in another guest. It was well for her she had not to attend to the ladies also. But Miss Kate and Miss Julia had thought of that and had converted the bathroom upstairs into a ladies' dressing-room. Miss Kate and Miss Julia were there, gossiping and laughing and fussing, walking after each other to the head of the stairs, peering down over the banisters and calling down to Lily to ask her who had come.

It was always a great affair, the Misses Morkan's annual dance. Everybody who knew them came to it, members of the family, old friends of the family, the members of Julia's choir, any of Kate's pupils that were grown up enough, and even some of Mary Jane's pupils too. Never once had it fallen flat. For years and years it had gone off in splendid style, as long as anyone could remember; ever since Kate and Julia, after the death of their brother Pat, had left the house in Stoney Batter and taken Mary Jane, their only niece, to live with them in the dark, gaunt house on Usher's Island, the upper part of which they had rented from Mr. Fulham, the corn-factor on the ground floor. That was a good thirty years ago if it was a day. Mary Jane, who was then a little girl in short clothes, was now the main prop of the household, for she had the organ in Haddington Road. She had been through the Academy and gave a pupils' concert every year in the upper room of the Antient Concert Rooms. Many of her pupils belonged to the better-class families on the Kingstown and Dalkey line. Old as they were, her aunts also did their share. Julia, though she was quite grey, was still the leading soprano in Adam and Eve's, and Kate, being too feeble to go about much, gave music lessons to beginners on the old square piano in the back room. Lily, the caretaker's daughter, did housemaid's work. for them. Though their life was modest, they believed in eating well; the best of everything: diamond-bone sirloins, three-shilling tea and the best bottled stout. But Lily seldom made a mistake in the orders, so that she got on well with her three mistresses. They were fussy, that was all. But the only thing they would not stand was back answers.

Of course, they had good reason to be fussy on such a night. And then it was long after ten o'clock and yet there was no sign of Gabriel and his wife. Besides they were dreadfully afraid that Freddy Malins might turn up screwed. They would not wish for worlds that any of Mary Jane's pupils should see him under the influence; and when he was like that it was sometimes very hard to manage him. Freddy Malins always came late, but they wondered what could be keeping Gabriel: and that was what brought them every two minutes to the banisters to ask Lily had Gabriel or Freddy come.

"O, Mr. Conroy," said Lily to Gabriel when she opened the door for him, "Miss Kate and Miss Julia thought you were never coming. Good-night, Mrs. Conroy."

"I'll engage they did," said Gabriel, "but they forget that my wife here takes three mortal hours to dress herself."

He stood on the mat, scraping the snow from his goloshes, while Lily led his wife to the foot of the stairs and called out:

"Miss Kate, here's Mrs. Conroy."

Kate and Julia came toddling down the dark stairs at once. Both of them kissed Gabriel's wife, said she must be perished alive, and asked was Gabriel with her.

"Here I am as right as the mail, Aunt Kate! Go on up. I'll follow," called out Gabriel from the dark.

He continued scraping his feet vigorously while the three women went upstairs, laughing, to the ladies' dressing-room. A light fringe of snow lay like a cape on the shoulders of his overcoat and like toecaps on the toes of his goloshes; and, as the buttons of his overcoat slipped with a squeaking noise through the snow-stiffened frieze, a cold, fragrant air from out-of-doors escaped from crevices and folds.

"Is it snowing again, Mr. Conroy?" asked Lily.

She had preceded him into the pantry to help him off with his overcoat. Gabriel smiled at the three syllables she had given his surname and glanced at her. She was a slim, growing girl, pale in complexion and with hay-coloured hair. The gas in the pantry made her look still paler. Gabriel had known her when she was a child and used to sit on the lowest step nursing a rag doll.

"Yes, Lily," he answered, "and I think we're in for a night of it."

He looked up at the pantry ceiling, which was shaking with the stamping and shuffling of feet on the floor above, listened for a moment to the piano and then glanced at the girl, who was folding his overcoat carefully at the end of a shelf.

"Tell me, Lily," he said in a friendly tone, "do you still go to school?"

"O no, sir," she answered. "I'm done schooling this year and more."

"O, then," said Gabriel gaily, "I suppose we'll be going to your wedding one of these fine days with your young man, eh?"

The girl glanced back at him over her shoulder and said with great bitterness:

"The men that is now is only all palaver and what they can get out of you."

Gabriel coloured, as if he felt he had made a mistake and, without looking at her, kicked off his goloshes and flicked actively with his muffler at his patent-leather shoes.

He was a stout, tallish young man. The high colour of his cheeks pushed upwards even to his forehead, where it scattered itself in a few formless patches of pale red; and on his hairless face there scintillated restlessly the polished lenses and the bright gilt rims of the glasses which screened his delicate and restless eyes. His glossy black hair was parted in the middle and brushed in a long curve behind his ears where it curled slightly beneath the groove left by his hat.

When he had flicked lustre into his shoes he stood up and pulled his waistcoat down more tightly on his plump body. Then he took a coin rapidly from his pocket.

"O Lily," he said, thrusting it into her hands, "it's Christmastime, isn't it? Just . . . here's a little. . . ."

He walked rapidly towards the door.

"O no, sir!" cried the girl, following him. "Really, sir, I wouldn't take it."

"Christmas-time! Christmas-time!" said Gabriel, almost trotting to the stairs and waving his hand to her in deprecation.

The girl, seeing that he had gained the stairs, called out after him:

"Well, thank you, sir."

He waited outside the drawing-room door until the waltz should finish, listening to the skirts that swept against it and to the shuffling of feet. He was still discomposed by the girl's bitter and sudden retort. It had cast a gloom over him which he tried to dispel by arranging his cuffs and the bows of his tie. He then took from his waistcoat pocket a little paper and glanced at the headings he had made for his speech. He was undecided about the lines from Robert Browning, for he feared they would be above the heads of his hearers. Some quotation that they would recognise from Shakespeare or from the Melodies would be better. The indelicate clacking of the men's heels and the shuffling of their soles reminded him that their grade of culture differed from his. He would only make himself ridiculous by quoting poetry to them which they could not understand. They would think that he was airing his superior education. He would fail with them just as he had failed with the girl in the pantry. He had taken up a wrong tone. His whole speech was a mistake from first to last, an utter failure.

Just then his aunts and his wife came out of the ladies' dressing-room. His aunts were two small, plainly dressed old women. Aunt Julia was an inch or so the taller. Her hair, drawn low over the tops of her ears, was grey; and grey also, with darker shadows, was her large flaccid face. Though she was stout in build and stood erect, her slow eyes and parted lips gave her the appearance of a woman who did not know where she was or where she was going. Aunt Kate was more vivacious. Her face, healthier than her sister's, was all puckers and creases, like a shrivelled red apple, and her hair, braided in the same old-fashioned way, had not lost its ripe nut colour.

They both kissed Gabriel frankly. He was their favourite nephew, the son of their dead elder sister, Ellen, who had married T. J. Conroy of the Port and Docks.

"Gretta tells me you're not going to take a cab back to Monkstown tonight, Gabriel," said Aunt Kate.

"No," said Gabriel, turning to his wife, "we had quite enough of that last year, hadn't we? Don't you remember, Aunt Kate, what a cold Gretta got out of it? Cab windows rattling all the way, and the east wind blowing in after we passed Merrion. Very jolly it was. Gretta caught a dreadful cold."

Aunt Kate frowned severely and nodded her head at every word.

"Quite right, Gabriel, quite right," she said. "You can't be too careful."

"But as for Gretta there," said Gabriel, "she'd walk home in the snow if she were let."

Mrs. Conroy laughed.

"Don't mind him, Aunt Kate," she said. "He's really an awful bother, what with green shades for Tom's eyes at night and making him do the dumb-bells, and forcing Eva to eat the stirabout. The poor child! And she simply hates the sight of it! . . . O, but you'll never guess what he makes me wear now!"

She broke out into a peal of laughter and glanced at her husband, whose admiring and happy eyes had been wandering from her dress to her face and hair. The two aunts laughed heartily, too, for Gabriel's solicitude was a standing joke with them.

"Goloshes!" said Mrs. Conroy. "That's the latest. Whenever it's wet underfoot I must put on my goloshes. Tonight even, he wanted me to put them on, but I wouldn't. The next thing he'll buy me will be a diving suit."

Gabriel laughed nervously and patted his tie reassuringly, while Aunt Kate nearly doubled herself, so heartily did she enjoy the joke. The smile soon faded from Aunt Julia's face and her mirthless eyes were directed towards her nephew's face. After a pause she asked:

"And what are goloshes, Gabriel?"

"Goloshes, Julia!" exclaimed her sister. "Goodness me, don't you know what goloshes are? You wear them over your . . . over your boots, Gretta, isn't it?"

"Yes," said Mrs. Conroy. "Guttapercha things. We both have a pair now. Gabriel says everyone wears them on the Continent."

"O, on the Continent," murmured Aunt Julia, nodding her head slowly.

Gabriel knitted his brows and said, as if he were slightly angered:

"It's nothing very wonderful, but Gretta thinks it very funny because she says the word reminds her of Christy Minstrels."

"But tell me, Gabriel," said Aunt Kate, with brisk tact. "Of course, you've seen about the room. Gretta was saying . . ."

"O, the room is all right," replied Gabriel. "I've taken one in the Gresham."

"To be sure," said Aunt Kate, "by far the best thing to do. And the children, Gretta, you're not anxious about them?"

"O, for one night," said Mrs. Conroy. "Besides, Bessie will look after them."

"To be sure," said Aunt Kate again. "What a comfort it is to have a girl like that, one you can depend on! There's that Lily, I'm sure I don't know what has come over her lately. She's not the girl she was at all."

Gabriel was about to ask her aunt some questions on this point, but she broke off suddenly to gaze after her sister, who had wandered down the stairs and was craning her neck over the banisters.

"Now, I ask you," she said almost testily, "where is Julia going? Julia! Julia! Where are you going?"

Julia, who had gone half way down one flight, came back and announced blandly:

"Here's Freddy."

At the same moment a clapping of hands and a final flourish of the pianist told that the waltz had ended. The drawing-room door was opened from within and some couples came out. Aunt Kate drew Gabriel aside hurriedly and whispered into his ear:

"Slip down, Gabriel, like a good fellow and see if he's all right, and don't let him up if he's screwed. I'm sure he's screwed. I'm sure he is."

Gabriel went to the stairs and listened over the banisters. He could hear two persons talking in the pantry. Then he recognised Freddy Malins' laugh. He went down the stairs noisily.

"It's such a relief," said Aunt Kate to Mrs. Conroy, "that Gabriel is here, I always feel easier in my mind when he's here. . . . Julia, there's Miss Daly and Miss Power will take some refreshment. Thanks for your beautiful waltz, Miss Daly. It made lovely time."

A tall wizen-faced man, with a stiff grizzled moustache and swarthy skin, who was passing out with his partner, said:

"And may we have some refreshment, too, Miss Morkan?"

"Julia," said Aunt Kate summarily, "and here's Mr. Browne and Miss Furlong. Take them in, Julia, with Miss Daly and Miss Power."

"I'm the man for the ladies," said Mr. Browne, pursing his lips until his moustache bristled and smiling in all his wrinkles. "You know, Miss Morkan, the reason they are so fond of me is — "

He did not finish his sentence, but, seeing that Aunt Kate was out of earshot, at once led the three young ladies into the back room. The middle of the room was occupied by two square tables placed end to end, and on these Aunt Julia and the caretaker were straightening and smoothing a large cloth. On the sideboard were arrayed dishes and plates, and glasses and bundles of knives and forks and spoons. The top of the closed square piano served also as a sideboard for viands and sweets. At a smaller sideboard in one corner two young men were standing, drinking hop-bitters.

Mr. Browne led his charges thither and invited them all, in jest, to some ladies' punch, hot, strong and sweet. As they said they never took anything strong, he opened three bottles of lemonade for them. Then he asked one of the young men to move aside, and, taking hold of the decanter, filled out for himself a goodly measure of whisky. The young men eyed him respectfully while he took a trial sip.

"God help me," he said, smiling, "it's the doctor's orders."

His wizened face broke into a broader smile, and the three young ladies laughed in musical echo to his pleasantry, swaying their bodies to and fro, with nervous jerks of their shoulders. The boldest said:

"O, now, Mr. Browne, I'm sure the doctor never ordered anything of the kind."

Mr. Browne took another sip of his whisky and said, with sidling mimicry:

"Well, you see, I'm like the famous Mrs. Cassidy, who is reported to have said: 'Now, Mary Grimes, if I don't take it, make me take it, for I feel I want it.'"

His hot face had leaned forward a little too confidentially and he had assumed a very low Dublin accent so that the young ladies, with one instinct, received his speech in silence. Miss Furlong, who was one of Mary Jane's pupils, asked Miss Daly what was the name of the pretty waltz she had played; and Mr. Browne, seeing that he was ignored, turned promptly to the two young men who were more appreciative.

A red-faced young woman, dressed in pansy, came into the room, excitedly clapping her hands and crying:

"Quadrilles! Quadrilles!"

Close on her heels came Aunt Kate, crying:

"Two gentlemen and three ladies, Mary Jane!"

"O, here's Mr. Bergin and Mr. Kerrigan," said Mary Jane. "Mr. Kerrigan, will you take Miss Power? Miss Furlong, may I get you a partner, Mr. Bergin. O, that'll just do now."

"Three ladies, Mary Jane," said Aunt Kate.

The two young gentlemen asked the ladies if they might have the pleasure, and Mary Jane turned to Miss Daly.

"O, Miss Daly, you're really awfully good, after playing for the last two dances, but really we're so short of ladies tonight."

"I don't mind in the least, Miss Morkan."

"But I've a nice partner for you, Mr. Bartell D'Arcy, the tenor. I'll get him to sing later on. All Dublin is raving about him."

"Lovely voice, lovely voice!" said Aunt Kate.

As the piano had twice begun the prelude to the first figure Mary Jane led her recruits quickly from the room. They had hardly gone when Aunt Julia wandered slowly into the room, looking behind her at something.

"What is the matter, Julia?" asked Aunt Kate anxiously. "Who is it?"

Julia, who was carrying in a column of table-napkins, turned to her sister and said, simply, as if the question had surprised her:

"It's only Freddy, Kate, and Gabriel with him."

In fact right behind her Gabriel could be seen piloting Freddy Malins across the landing. The latter, a young man of about forty, was of Gabriel's size and build, with very round shoulders. His face was fleshy and pallid, touched with colour only at the thick hanging lobes of his ears and at the wide wings of his nose. He had coarse features, a blunt nose, a convex and receding brow, tumid and protruded lips. His heavy-lidded eyes and the disorder of his scanty hair made him look sleepy. He was laughing heartily in a high key at a story which he had been telling Gabriel on the stairs and at the same time rubbing the knuckles of his left fist backwards and forwards into his left eye.

"Good-evening, Freddy," said Aunt Julia.

Freddy Malins bade the Misses Morkan good-evening in what seemed an offhand fashion by reason of the habitual catch in his voice and then, seeing that Mr. Browne was grinning at him from the sideboard, crossed the room on rather shaky legs and began to repeat in an undertone the story he had just told to Gabriel.

"He's not so bad, is he?" said Aunt Kate to Gabriel.

Gabriel's brows were dark but he raised them quickly and answered: "O, no, hardly noticeable."

"Now, isn't he a terrible fellow!" she said. "And his poor mother made him take the pledge on New Year's Eve. But come on, Gabriel, into the drawing-room."

Before leaving the room with Gabriel she signalled to Mr. Browne by frowning and shaking her forefinger in warning to and fro. Mr. Browne nodded in answer and, when she had gone, said to Freddy Malins:

"Now, then, Teddy, I'm going to fill you out a good glass of lemonade just to buck you up."

Freddy Malins, who was nearing the climax of his story, waved the offer aside impatiently but Mr. Browne, having first called Freddy Malins' attention to a disarray in his dress, filled out and handed him a full glass of lemonade. Freddy Malin's left hand accepted the glass mechanically, his right hand being engaged in the mechanical readjustment of his dress. Mr. Browne, whose face was once more wrinkling with mirth, poured out for himself a glass of whisky while Freddy Malins exploded, before he had well reached the climax of his story, in a kink of high-pitched bronchitic laughter and, setting down his untasted and overflowing glass, began to rub the knuckles of his left fist backwards and forwards into his left eye, repeating words of his last phrase as well as his fit of laughter would allow him.

Gabriel could not listen while Mary Jane was playing her Academy piece, full of runs and difficult passages, to the hushed drawing-room. He liked music but the piece she was playing had no melody for him and he doubted whether it had any melody for the other listeners, though they had begged Mary Jane to play something. Four young men, who had come from the refreshment-room to stand in the doorway at the sound of the piano, had gone away quietly in couples after a few minutes. The only persons who seemed to follow the music were Mary Jane herself, her hands racing along the key-board or lifted from it at the pauses like those of a priestess in momentary imprecation, and Aunt Kate standing at her elbow to turn the page.

Gabriel's eyes, irritated by the floor, which glittered with bees-wax under the heavy chandelier, wandered to the wall above the piano. A picture of the balcony scene in *Romeo and Juliet* hung there and beside it was a picture of the two murdered princes in the Tower which Aunt Julia had worked in red, blue and brown wools when she was a girl. Probably in the school they had gone to as girls that kind of work had been taught for one year. His mother had worked for him as a birthday present a waistcoat of purple tabinet, with little foxes' heads upon it, lined with brown satin and having round mulberry buttons. It was strange that his mother had had no musical talent though Aunt Kate used to call her the brains carrier of the Morkan family. Both she and Julia had always seemed a little proud of their serious and matronly sister. Her photograph stood before the pierglass. She held an open book on her knees and was pointing out something in it to Constantine who, dressed in a man-o'-war suit, lay at her feet. It was she who had chosen the names of her sons for she was very sensible of the dignity of family life. Thanks to her, Constantine was now senior curate in Balbriggan and, thanks to her, Gabriel himself had taken his degree in the Royal University. A shadow passed over his face as he remembered her sullen opposition to his marriage. Some slighting phrases she had used still rankled in his memory; she had once spoken of Gretta as being country cute and that was not true of Gretta at all. It was Gretta who had nursed her during all her last long illness in their house at Monkstown.

He knew that Mary Jane must be near the end of her piece for she was playing again the opening melody with runs of scales after every bar and while he waited for the end the resentment died down in his heart. The piece ended with a trill of octaves in the treble and a final deep octave in the bass. Great applause greeted Mary Jane as, blushing and rolling up her music nervously, she escaped from the room. The most vigorous clapping came from the four young men in the doorway who had gone away to the refreshment-room at the beginning of the piece but had come back when the piano had stopped.

Lancers were arranged. Gabriel found himself partnered with Miss Ivors. She was a frank-mannered talkative young lady, with a freckled face and prominent brown eyes. She did not wear a low-cut bodice and the large brooch which was fixed in the front of her collar bore on it an Irish device and motto.

When they had taken their places she said abruptly:

"I have a crow to pluck with you."

"With me?" said Gabriel.

She nodded her head gravely.

"What is it?" asked Gabriel, smiling at her solemn manner.

"Who is G. C.?" answered Miss Ivors, turning her eyes upon him.

Gabriel coloured and was about to knit his brows, as if he did not understand, when she said bluntly:

"O, innocent Amy! I have found out that you write for *The Daily Express*. Now, aren't you ashamed of yourself?"

"Why should I be ashamed of myself?" asked Gabriel, blinking his eyes and trying to smile.

"Well, I'm ashamed of you," said Miss Ivors frankly. "To say you'd write for a paper like that. I didn't think you were a West Briton."

A look of perplexity appeared on Gabriel's face. It was true that he wrote a literary column every Wednesday in *The Daily Express,* for which he was paid fifteen shillings. But that did not make him a West Briton surely. The books he received for review were almost more welcome than the paltry cheque. He loved to feel the covers and turn over the pages of newly printed books. Nearly every day when his teaching in the college was ended he used to wander down the quays to the second-hand booksellers, to Hickey's on Bachelor's Walk, to Web's or Massey's on Aston's Quay, or to O'Clohissey's in the bystreet. He did not know how to meet her charge. He wanted to say that literature was above politics. But they were friends of many years' standing and their careers had been parallel, first at the University and then as teachers: he could not risk a grandiose phrase with her. He continued blinking his eyes and trying to smile and murmured lamely that he saw nothing political in writing reviews of books.

When their turn to cross had come he was still perplexed and inattentive. Miss Ivors promptly took his hand in a warm grasp and said in a soft friendly tone:

"Of course, I was only joking. Come, we cross now."

When they were together again she spoke of the University question and Gabriel felt more at ease. A friend of hers had shown her his review of Browning's poems. That was how she had found out the secret: but she liked the review immensely. Then she said suddenly:

"O, Mr. Conroy, will you come for an excursion to the Aran Isles this summer? We're going to stay there a whole month. It will be splendid out in the Atlantic. You ought to come. Mr. Clancy is coming, and Mr. Kilkelly and Kathleen Kearney. It would be splendid for Gretta too if she'd come. She's from Connacht, isn't she?"

"Her people are," said Gabriel shortly.

"But you will come, won't you?" said Miss Ivors, laying her warm hand eagerly on his arm.

"The fact is," said Gabriel, "I have just arranged to go — "

"Go where?" asked Miss Ivors.

"Well, you know, every year I go for a cycling tour with some fellows and so — "

"But where?" asked Miss Ivors.

"Well, we usually go to France or Belgium or perhaps Germany," said Gabriel awkwardly.

"And why do you go to France and Belgium," said Miss Ivors, "instead of visiting your own land?"

"Well," said Gabriel, "it's partly to keep in touch with the languages and partly for a change."

"And haven't you your own language to keep in touch with — Irish?" asked Miss Ivors.

"Well," said Gabriel, "if it comes to that, you know, Irish is not my language."

Their neighbours had turned to listen to the cross-examination. Gabriel glanced right and left nervously and tried to keep his good humour under the ordeal which was making a blush invade his forehead.

"And haven't you your own land to visit," continued Miss Ivors, "that you know nothing of, your own people, and your own country?"

"Oh, to tell you the truth," retorted Gabriel suddenly, "I'm sick of my own country, sick of it!"

"Why?" asked Miss Ivors.

Gabriel did not answer for his retort had heated him.

"Why?" repeated Miss Ivors.

They had to go visiting together and, as he had not answered her, Miss Ivors said warmly:

"Of course, you've no answer."

Gabriel tried to cover his agitation by taking part in the dance with great energy. He avoided her eyes for he had seen a sour expression on her face. But when they met in the long chain he was surprised to feel his hand firmly pressed. She looked at him from under her brows for a moment quizzically until he smiled. Then, just as the chain was about to start again, she stood on tip-toe and whispered into his ear:

"West Briton!"

When the lancers were over Gabriel went away to a remote corner of the room where Freddy Malins' mother was sitting. She was a stout feeble old woman with white hair. Her voice had a catch in it like her son's and she stuttered slightly. She had been told that Freddy had come and that he was nearly all right. Gabriel asked her whether she had had a good crossing. She lived with her married daughter in Glasgow and came to Dublin on a visit once a year. She answered placidly that she had had a beautiful crossing and that the captain had been most attentive to her. She spoke also of the beautiful house her daughter kept in Glasgow, and of all the friends they had there. While her tongue rambled on Gabriel tried to banish from his mind all memory of the unpleasant incident with Miss Ivors. Of course the girl or woman, or whatever she was, was an enthusiast but there was a time for all things. Perhaps he ought not to have answered her like that. But she had no right to call him a West Briton before people, even in joke. She had tried to make him ridiculous before people, heckling him and staring at him with her rabbit's eyes.

He saw his wife making her way towards him through the waltzing couples. When she reached him she said into his ear:

"Gabriel, Aunt Kate wants to know won't you carve the goose as usual. Miss Daly will carve the ham and I'll do the pudding."

"All right," said Gabriel.

"She's sending in the younger ones first as soon as this waltz is over so that we'll have the table to ourselves."

"Were you dancing?" asked Gabriel.

"Of course I was. Didn't you see me? What row had you with Molly Ivors?"

"No row. Why? Did she say so?"

"Something like that. I'm trying to get that Mr. D'Arcy to sing. He's full of conceit, I think."

"There was no row," said Gabriel moodily, "only she wanted me to go for a trip to the west of Ireland and I said I wouldn't."

His wife clasped her hand excitedly and gave a little jump.

"O, do go, Gabriel," she cried. "I'd love to see Galway again."

"You can go if you like," said Gabriel coldly.

She looked at him for a moment, then turned to Mrs. Malins and said:

"There's a nice husband for you, Mrs. Malins."

While she was threading her way back across the room Mrs. Malins, without adverting to the interruption, went on to tell Gabriel what beautiful places there were in Scotland and beautiful scenery. Her son-in-law brought them every year to the lakes and they used to go fishing. Her son-in-law was a splendid fisher. One day he caught a beautiful big fish and the man in the hotel cooked it for their dinner.

Gabriel hardly heard what she said. Now that supper was coming near he began to think again about his speech and about the quotation. When he saw Freddy Malins coming across the room to visit his mother Gabriel left the chair free for him and retired into the embrasure of the window. The room had already cleared and from the back room came the clatter of plates and knives. Those who still remained in the drawing-room seemed tired of dancing and were conversing quietly in little groups. Gabriel's warm trembling fingers tapped the cold pane of the window. How cool it must be outside! How pleasant it would be to walk out alone, first along by the river and then through the park! The snow would be lying on the branches of the trees and forming a bright cap on the top of the Wellington Monument. How much more pleasant it would be there than at the supper-table!

He ran over the headings of his speech: Irish hospitality, sad memories, the Three Graces, Paris, the quotation from Browning. He repeated to himself a phrase he had written in his review:

"One feels that one is listening to a thought-tormented music." Miss Ivors had praised the review. Was she sincere? Had she really any life of her own behind all her propagandism? There had never been any ill-feeling between them until that night. It unnerved him to think that she would be at the supper-table, looking up at him while he spoke with her critical quizzing eyes. Perhaps she would not be sorry to see him fail in his speech. An idea came into his mind and gave him courage. He would say, alluding to Aunt Kate and Julia: "Ladies and Gentlemen, the generation which is now on the wane among us may have had its faults but for my part I think it had certain qualities of hospitality, of humour, of humanity, which the new and very serious and hypereducated generation that is growing up around us seems to me to lack." Very good: that was one for Miss Ivors. What did he care that his aunts were only two ignorant old women?

A murmur in the room attracted his attention. Mr. Browne was advancing from the door, gallantly escorting Aunt Julia, who leaned upon his arm, smiling and hanging her head. An irregular musketry of applause escorted her also as far as the piano and then, as Mary Jane seated herself on the stool, and Aunt Julia, no longer smiling, half turned so as to pitch her voice fairly into the room, gradually ceased. Gabriel recognised the prelude. It was that of an old song of Aunt Julia's — *Arrayed for the Bridal.* Her voice, strong and clear in tone, attacked with great spirit the runs which embellish the air and though she sang very rapidly she did not miss even the smallest of the grace notes. To follow the voice, without looking at the singer's face, was to feel and share the excitement of swift and secure flight. Gabriel applauded loudly with all the others at the close of the song and loud applause was borne in from the invisible supper-table. It sounded so genuine that a little colour struggled into Aunt Julia's face as she bent to replace in the music-stand the old leather-bound songbook that had her initials on the cover. Freddy Malins, who had listened with his head perched sideways to hear her better, was still applauding when everyone else had ceased and talking animatedly to his mother who nodded her head gravely and slowly in acquiescence. At last, when he could clap no more, he stood up suddenly and hurried across the room to Aunt Julia whose hand he seized and held in both his hands, shaking it when words failed him or the catch in his voice proved too much for him.

"I was just telling my mother," he said, "I never heard you sing so well, never. No, I never heard your voice so good as it is to-night. Now! Would you believe that now? That's the truth. Upon my word and honour that's the truth. I never heard your voice sound so fresh and so . . . so clear and fresh, never."

Aunt Julia smiled broadly and murmured something about compliments as she released her hand from his grasp. Mr. Browne extended his open hand towards her and said to those who were near him in the manner of a showman introducing a prodigy to an audience:

"Miss Julia Morkan, my latest discovery!"

He was laughing very heartily at this himself when Freddy Malins turned to him and said:

"Well, Browne, if you're serious you might make a worse discovery. All I can say is I never heard her sing half so well as long as I am coming here. And that's the honest truth."

"Neither did I," said Mr. Browne. "I think her voice has greatly improved."

Aunt Julia shrugged her shoulders and said with meek pride:

"Thirty years ago I hadn't a bad voice as voices go."

"I often told Julia," said Aunt Kate emphatically, "that she was simply thrown away in that choir. But she never would be said by me."

She turned as if to appeal to the good sense of the others against a refractory child while Aunt Julia gazed in front of her, a vague smile of reminiscence playing on her face.

"No," continued Aunt Kate, "she wouldn't be said or led by anyone, slaving there in that choir night and day, night and day. Six o'clock on Christmas morning! And all for what?"

"Well, isn't it for the honour of God, Aunt Kate?" asked Mary Jane, twisting round on the piano-stool and smiling.

Aunt Kate turned fiercely on her niece and said:

"I know all about the honour of God, Mary Jane, but I think it's not at all honourable for the pope to turn out the women out of the choirs that have slaved there all their lives and put little whippersnappers of boys over their heads. I suppose it is for the good of the Church if the pope does it. But it's not just, Mary Jane, and it's not right."

She had worked herself into a passion and would have continued in defence of her sister for it was a sore subject with her but Mary Jane, seeing that all the dancers had come back, intervened pacifically:

"Now, Aunt Kate, you're giving scandal to Mr. Browne who is of the other persuasion."

Aunt Kate turned to Mr. Browne, who was grinning at this allusion to his religion, and said hastily:

"O, I don't question the pope's being right. I'm only a stupid old woman and I wouldn't presume to do such a thing. But there's such a thing as common everyday politeness and gratitude. And if I were in Julia's place I'd tell that Father Healey straight up to his face . . ."

"And besides, Aunt Kate," said Mary Jane, "we really are all hungry and when we are hungry we are all very quarrelsome."

"And when we are thirsty we are also quarrelsome," added Mr. Browne.

"So that we had better go to supper," said Mary Jane, "and finish the discussion afterwards."

On the landing outside the drawing-room Gabriel found his wife and Mary Jane trying to persuade Miss Ivors to stay for supper. But Miss Ivors, who had put on her hat and was buttoning her cloak, would not stay. She did not feel in the least hungry and she had already overstayed her time.

"But only for ten minutes, Molly," said Mrs. Conroy. "That won't delay you."

"To take a pick itself," said Mary Jane, "after all your dancing."

"I really couldn't," said Miss Ivors.

"I am afraid you didn't enjoy yourself at all," said Mary Jane hopelessly.

"Ever so much, I assure you," said Miss Ivors, "but you really must let me run off now."

"But how can you get home?" asked Mrs. Conroy.

"O, it's only two steps up the quay."

Gabriel hesitated a moment and said:

"If you will allow me, Miss Ivors, I'll see you home if you are really obliged to go."

But Miss Ivors broke away from them.

"I won't hear of it," she cried. "For goodness' sake go in to your suppers and don't mind me. I'm quite well able to take care of myself."

"Well, you're the comical girl, Molly," said Mrs. Conroy frankly.

"*Beannacht libh*," cried Miss Ivors, with a laugh, as she ran down the staircase.

Mary Jane gazed after her, a moody puzzled expression on her face, while Mrs. Conroy leaned over the banisters to listen for the hall-door. Gabriel asked himself was he the cause of her abrupt departure. But she did not seem to be in ill humour: she had gone away laughing. He stared blankly down the staircase.

At the moment Aunt Kate came toddling out of the supper-room, almost wringing her hands in despair.

"Where is Gabriel?" she cried. "Where on earth is Gabriel? There's everyone waiting in there, stage to let, and nobody to carve the goose!"

"Here I am, Aunt Kate!" cried Gabriel, with sudden animation, "ready to carve a flock of geese, if necessary."

A fat brown goose lay at one end of the table and at the other end, on a bed of creased paper strewn with sprigs of parsley, lay a great ham, stripped of its outer skin and peppered over with crust crumbs, a neat paper frill round its shin and beside this was a round of spiced beef. Between these rival ends ran parallel lines of side-dishes: two little minsters of jelly, red and yellow; a shallow dish full of blocks of blancmange and red jam, a large green leaf-shaped dish with a· stalk-shaped handle, on which lay bunches of purple raisins and peeled almonds, a companion dish on which lay a solid rectangle of Smyrna figs, a dish of custard topped with grated nutmeg, a small bowl full of chocolates and sweets wrapped in gold and silver papers and a glass vase in which stood some tall celery stalks. In the centre of the table there stood, as sentries to a fruit-stand which upheld a pyramid of oranges and American apples, two squat old-fashioned decanters of cut glass, one containing port and the other dark sherry. On the closed square piano a pudding in a huge yellow dish lay in waiting and behind it were three squads of bottles of stout and ale and minerals, drawn up according to the colours of their uniforms, the first two black, with brown and red labels, the third and smallest squad white, with transverse green sashes.

Gabriel took his seat boldly at the head of the table and, having looked to the edge of the carver, plunged his fork firmly into the goose. He felt quite at ease now for he was an expert carver and liked nothing better than to find himself at the head of a well-laden table.

"Miss Furlong, what shall I send you?" he asked. "A wing or a slice of the breast?"

"Just a small slice of the breast."

"Miss Higgins, what for you?"

"O, anything at all, Mr. Conroy."

While Gabriel and Miss Daly exchanged plates of goose and plates of ham and spiced beef Lily went from guest to guest with a dish of hot floury potatoes wrapped in a white napkin. This was Mary Jane's idea and she had also suggested apple sauce for the goose but Aunt Kate had said that plain roast goose without any apple sauce had always been good enough for her and she hoped she might never eat worse. Mary Jane waited on her pupils and saw that they got the best slices and Aunt Kate and Aunt Julia opened and carried across from the piano bottles of stout and ale for the gentlemen and bottles of minerals for the ladies. There was a great deal of confusion and laughter and noise, the noise of orders and counter-orders, of knives and forks, of corks and glass-stoppers. Gabriel began to carve second helpings as soon as he had finished the first round without serving himself. Everyone protested loudly so that he compromised by taking a long draught of stout for he had found the carving hot work. Mary Jane settled down quietly to her supper but Aunt Kate and Aunt Julia were still toddling round the table, walking on each other's heels, getting in each other's way and giving each other unheeded orders. Mr. Browne begged of them to sit down and eat their suppers and so did Gabriel but they said there was time enough, so that, at last, Freddy Malins stood up and, capturing Aunt Kate, plumped her down on her chair amid general laughter.

When everyone had been well served Gabriel said, smiling:

"Now, if anyone wants a little more of what vulgar people call stuffing let him or her speak."

A chorus of voices invited him to begin his own supper and Lily came forward with three potatoes which she had reserved for him.

"Very well," said Gabriel amiably, as he took another prepara-
tory draught, "kindly forget my existence, ladies and gentlemen,
for a few minutes."

He set to his supper and took no part in the conversation with
which the table covered Lily's removal of the plates. The subject
of talk was the opera company which was then at the Theatre
Royal. Mr. Bartell D'Arcy, the tenor, a dark-complexioned young
man with a smart moustache, praised very highly the leading
contralto of the company but Miss Furlong thought she had a
rather vulgar style of production. Freddy Malins said there was a
Negro chieftain singing in the second part of the Gaiety panto-
mime who had one of the finest tenor voices he had ever heard.

"Have you heard him?" he asked Mr. Bartell D'Arcy across the
table.

"No," answered Mr. Bartell D'Arcy carelessly.

"Because," Freddy Malins explained, "now I'd be curious to
hear your opinion of him. I think he has a grand voice."

"It takes Teddy to find out the really good things," said Mr.
Browne familiarly to the table.

"And why couldn't he have a voice too?" asked Freddy Malins
sharply. "Is it because he's only a black?"

Nobody answered this question and Mary Jane led the table
back to the legitimate opera. One of her pupils had given her a
pass for *Mignon*. Of course it was very fine, she said, but it made
her think of poor Georgina Burns. Mr. Browne could go back
farther still, to the old Italian companies that used to come to
Dublin — Tietjens, Ilma de Murzka, Campanini, the great Tre-
belli, Giuglini, Ravelli, Aramburo. Those were the days, he said,
when there was something like singing to be heard in Dublin.
He told too of how the top gallery of the old Royal used to be
packed night after night, of how one night an Italian tenor had
sung five encores to *Let me like a Soldier fall,* introducing a high
C every time, and of how the gallery boys would sometimes in
their enthusiasm unyoke the horses from the carriage of some
great *prima donna* and pull her themselves through the streets
to her hotel. Why did they never play the grand old operas now,
he asked, *Dinorah, Lucrezia Borgia?* Because they could not get
the voices to sing them: that was why.

"Oh, well," said Mr. Bartell D'Arcy, "I presume there are as
good singers today as there were then."

"Where are they?" asked Mr. Browne defiantly.

"In London, Paris, Milan," said Mr. Bartell D'Arcy warmly. "I suppose Caruso, for example, is quite as good, if not better than any of the men you have mentioned."

"Maybe so," said Mr. Browne. "But I may tell you I doubt it strongly."

"O, I'd give anything to hear Caruso sing," said Mary Jane.

"For me," said Aunt Kate, who had been picking a bone, "there was only one tenor. To please me, I mean. But I suppose none of you ever heard of him."

"Who was he, Miss Morkan?" asked Mr. Bartell D'Arcy politely.

"His name," said Aunt Kate, "was Parkinson. I heard him when he was in his prime and I think he had then the purest tenor voice that was ever put into a man's throat."

"Strange," said Mr. Bartell D'Arcy. "I never even heard of him."

"Yes, yes, Miss Morkan is right," said Mr. Browne. "I remember hearing of old Parkinson but he's too far back for me."

"A beautiful, pure, sweet, mellow English tenor," said Aunt Kate with enthusiasm.

Gabriel having finished, the huge pudding was transferred to the table. The clatter of forks and spoons began again. Gabriel's wife served out spoonfuls of the pudding and passed the plates down the table. Midway down they were held up by Mary Jane, who replenished them with raspberry or orange jelly or with blancmange and jam. The pudding was of Aunt Julia's making and she received praises for it from all quarters. She herself said that it was not quite brown enough.

"Well, I hope, Miss Morkan," said Mr. Browne, "that I'm brown enough for you because, you know, I'm all brown."

All the gentlemen, except Gabriel, ate some of the pudding out of compliment to Aunt Julia. As Gabriel never ate sweets the celery had been left for him. Freddy Malins also took a stalk of celery and ate it with his pudding. He had been told that celery was a capital thing for the blood and he was just then under doctor's care. Mrs. Malins, who had been silent all through the supper, said that her son was going down to Mount Melleray in a week or so. The table then spoke of Mount Melleray, how bracing the air was down there, how hospitable the monks were and how they never asked for a penny-piece from their guests.

"And do you mean to say," asked Mr. Browne incredulously, "that a chap can go down there and put up there as if it were a hotel and live on the fat of the land and then come away without paying anything?"

"O, most people give some donation to the monastery when they leave," said Mary Jane.

"I wish we had an institution like that in our Church," said Mr. Browne candidly.

He was astonished to hear that the monks never spoke, got up at two in the morning and slept in their coffins. He asked what they did it for.

"That's the rule of the order," said Aunt Kate firmly.

"Yes, but why?" asked Mr. Browne.

Aunt Kate repeated that it was the rule, that was all. Mr. Browne still seemed not to understand. Freddy Malins explained to him, as best he could, that the monks were trying to make up for the sins committed by all the sinners in the outside world. The explanation was not very clear for Mr. Browne grinned and said:

"I like that idea very much but wouldn't a comfortable spring bed do them as well as a coffin?"

"The coffin," said Mary Jane, "is to remind them of their last end."

As the subject had grown lugubrious it was buried in a silence of the table during which Mrs. Malins could be heard saying to her neighbour in an indistinct undertone:

"They are very good men, the monks, very pious men."

The raisins and almonds and figs and apples and oranges and chocolates and sweets were now passed about the table and Aunt Julia invited all the guests to have either port or sherry. At first Mr. Bartell D'Arcy refused to take either but one of his neighbours nudged him and whispered something to him upon which he allowed his glass to be filled. Gradually as the last glasses were being filled the conversation ceased. A pause followed, broken only by the noise of the wine and by unsettlings of chairs. The Misses Morkan, all three, looked down at the tablecloth. Someone coughed once or twice and then a few gentlemen patted the table gently as a signal for silence. The silence came and Gabriel pushed back his chair and stood up.

The patting at once grew louder in encouragement and then ceased altogether. Gabriel leaned his ten trembling fingers on the tablecloth and smiled nervously at the company. Meeting a row of upturned faces he raised his eyes to the chandelier. The piano was playing a waltz tune and he could hear the skirts sweeping against the drawing-room door. People, perhaps, were standing in the snow on the quay outside, gazing up at the lighted windows and listening to the waltz music. The air was pure there. In the distance lay the park where the trees were weighted with snow. The Wellington Monument wore a gleaming cap of snow that flashed westward over the white field of Fifteen Acres.

He began:

"Ladies and Gentlemen,

"It has fallen to my lot this evening, as in years past, to perform a very pleasing task but a task for which I am afraid my poor powers as a speaker are all too inadequate."

"No, no!" said Mr. Browne.

"But, however that may be, I can only ask you tonight to take the will for the deed and to lend me your attention for a few moments while I endeavour to express to you in words what my feelings are on this occasion.

"Ladies and Gentlemen, it is not the first time that we have gathered together under this hospitable roof, around this hospitable board. It is not the first time that we have been the recipients — or perhaps, I had better say, the victims — of the hospitality of certain good ladies."

He made a circle in the air with his arm and paused. Everyone laughed or smiled at Aunt Kate and Aunt Julia and Mary Jane who all turned crimson with pleasure. Gabriel went on more boldly:

"I feel more strongly with every recurring year that our country has no tradition which does it so much honour and which it should guard so jealously as that of its hospitality. It is a tradition that is unique as far as my experience goes (and I have visited not a few places abroad) among the modern nations. Some would say, perhaps, that with us it is rather a failing than anything to be boasted of. But granted even that, it is, to my mind, a princely failing, and one that I trust will long be cultivated among us. Of one thing, at least, I am sure. As long as this one roof shelters the good ladies aforesaid — and I wish from

my heart it may do so for many and many a long year to come
— the tradition of genuine warm-hearted courteous Irish hospitality, which our forefathers have handed down to us and which
we in turn must hand down to our descendants, is still alive
among us."

A hearty murmur of assent ran round the table. It shot through
Gabriel's mind that Miss Ivors was not there and that she had
gone away discourteously: and he said with confidence in himself:

"Ladies and Gentlemen,

"A new generation is growing up in our midst, a generation
actuated by new ideas and new principles. It is serious and en-
thusiastic for these new ideas and its enthusiasm, even when it is
misdirected, is, I believe, in the main sincere. But we are living
in a sceptical and, if I may use the phrase, a thought-tormented
age: and sometimes I fear that this new generation, educated or
hypereducated as it is, will lack those qualities of humanity, of
hospitality, of kindly humour which belonged to an older day.
Listening tonight to the names of all those great singers of the
past it seemed to me, I must confess, that we were living in a less
spacious age. Those days might, without exaggeration, be called
spacious days: and if they are gone beyond recall let us hope,
at least, that in gatherings such as this we shall still speak of them
with pride and affection, still cherish in our hearts the memory
of those dead and gone great ones whose fame the world will
not willingly let die."

"Hear, hear!" said Mr. Browne loudly.

"But yet," continued Gabriel, his voice falling into a softer in-
flection, "there are always in gatherings such as this sadder
thoughts that will recur to our minds: thoughts of the past, of
youth, of changes, of absent faces that we miss here tonight. Our
path through life is strewn with many such sad memories: and
were we to brood upon them always we could not find the heart
to go on bravely with our work among the living. We have all of
us living duties and living affections which claim, and rightly
claim, our strenuous endeavours.

"Therefore, I will not linger on the past. I will not let any
gloomy moralising intrude upon us here tonight. Here we are
gathered together for a brief moment from the bustle and rush
of our everyday routine. We are met here as friends, in the spirit

of good-fellowship, as colleagues, also to a certain extent, in the true spirit of *camaraderie,* and as the guests of — what shall I call them? — the Three Graces of the Dublin musical world."

The table burst into applause and laughter at this allusion. Aunt Julia vainly asked each of her neighbours in turn to tell her what Gabriel had said.

"He says we are the Three Graces, Aunt Julia," said Mary Jane.

Aunt Julia did not understand but she looked up, smiling, at Gabriel, who continued in the same vein:

"Ladies and Gentlemen,

"I will not attempt to play tonight the part that Paris played on another occasion. I will not attempt to choose between them. The task would be an invidious one and one beyond my poor powers. For when I view them in turn, whether it be our chief hostess herself, whose good heart, whose too good heart, has become a byword with all who know her, or her sister, who seems to be gifted with perennial youth and whose singing must have been a surprise and a revelation to us all tonight, or, last but not least, when I consider our youngest hostess, talented, cheerful, hard-working and the best of nieces, I confess, Ladies and Gentlemen, that I do not know to which of them I should award the prize."

Gabriel glanced down at his aunts and, seeing the large smile on Aunt Julia's face and the tears which had risen to Aunt Kate's eyes, hastened to his close. He raised his glass of port gallantly, while every member of the company fingered a glass expectantly, and said loudly:

"Let us toast them all three together. Let us drink to their health, wealth, long life, happiness and prosperity and may they long continue to hold the proud and self-won position which they hold in their profession and the position of honour and affection which they hold in our hearts."

All the guests stood up, glass in hand, and turning towards the three seated ladies, sang in unison, with Mr. Browne as leader:

> *For they are jolly gay fellows,*
> *For they are jolly gay fellows,*
> *For they are jolly gay fellows,*
> *Which nobody can deny.*

Aunt Kate was making frank use of her handkerchief and even Aunt Julia seemed moved. Freddy Malins beat time with his pudding-fork and the singers turned towards one another, as if in melodious conference, while they sang with emphasis:

> *Unless he tells a lie,*
> *Unless he tells a lie,*

Then, turning once more towards their hostesses, they sang:

> *For they are jolly gay fellows,*
> *For they are jolly gay fellows,*
> *For they are jolly gay fellows,*
> *Which nobody can deny.*

The acclamation which followed was taken up beyond the door of the supper-room by many of the other guests and renewed time after time. Freddy Malins acting as officer with his fork on high.

The piercing morning air came into the hall where they were standing so that Aunt Kate said:

"Close the door, somebody. Mrs. Malins will get her death of cold."

"Browne is out there, Aunt Kate," said Mary Jane.

"Browne is everywhere," said Aunt Kate, lowering her voice.

Mary Jane laughed at her tone.

"Really," she said archly, "he is very attentive."

"He has been laid on here like the gas," said Aunt Kate in the same tone, "all during the Christmas."

She laughed herself this time good-humouredly and then added quickly:

"But tell him to come in, Mary Jane, and close the door. I hope to goodness he didn't hear me."

At that moment the hall-door was opened and Mr. Browne came in from the doorstep, laughing as if his heart would break. He was dressed in a long green overcoat with mock astrakhan cuffs and collar and wore on his head an oval fur cap. He pointed down the snow-covered quay from where the sound of shrill prolonged whistling was borne in.

"Teddy will have all the cabs in Dublin out," he said.

Gabriel advanced from the little pantry behind the office, struggling into his overcoat and, looking round the hall, said:

"Gretta not down yet?"

"She's getting on her things, Gabriel," said Aunt Kate.

"Who's playing up there?" asked Gabriel.

"Nobody. They're all gone."

"O no, Aunt Kate," said Mary Jane. "Bartell D'Arcy and Miss O'Callaghan aren't gone yet."

"Someone is fooling at the piano anyhow," said Gabriel.

Mary Jane glanced at Gabriel and Mr. Browne and said with a shiver:

"It makes me feel cold to look at you two gentlemen muffled up like that. I wouldn't like to face your journey home at this hour."

"I'd like nothing better this minute," said Mr. Browne stoutly, "than a rattling fine walk in the country or a fast drive with a good spanking goer between the shafts."

"We used to have a very good horse and trap at home," said Aunt Julia sadly.

"The never-to-be-forgotten Johnny," said Mary Jane, laughing.

Aunt Kate and Gabriel laughed too.

"Why, what was wonderful about Johnny?" asked Mr. Browne.

"The late lamented Patrick Morkan, our grandfather, that is," explained Gabriel, "commonly known in his later years as the old gentleman, was a glue-boiler."

"Oh, now, Gabriel," said Aunt Kate, laughing, "he had a starch mill."

"Well, glue or starch," said Gabriel, "the old gentleman had a horse by the name of Johnny. And Johnny used to work in the old gentleman's mill, walking round and round in order to drive the mill. That was all very well; but now comes the tragic part about Johnny. One fine day the old gentleman thought he'd like to drive out with the quality to a military review in the park."

"The Lord have mercy on his soul," said Aunt Kate compassionately.

"Amen," said Gabriel. "So the old gentleman, as I said, harnessed Johnny and put on his very best tall hat and his very best stock collar and drove out in grand style from his ancestral mansion somewhere near Back Lane, I think."

Everyone laughed, even Mrs. Malins, at Gabriel's manner and Aunt Kate said:

"O, now, Gabriel, he didn't live in Back Lane, really. Only the mill was there."

"Out from the mansion of his forefathers," continued Gabriel, "he drove with Johnny. And everything went on beautifully until Johnny came in sight of King Billy's statue: and whether he fell in love with the horse King Billy sits on or whether he thought he was back again in the mill, anyhow he began to walk round the statue."

Gabriel paced in a circle round the hall in his goloshes amid the laughter of the others.

"Round and round he went," said Gabriel, "and the old gentleman, who was a very pompous old gentleman, was highly indignant. 'Go on, sir! What do you mean, sir? Johnny! Johnny! Most extraordinary conduct! Can't understand the horse!' "

The peal of laughter which followed Gabriel's imitation of the incident was interrupted by a resounding knock at the hall door. Mary Jane ran to open it and let in Freddy Malins. Freddy Malins, with his hat well back on his head and his shoulders humped with cold, was puffing and steaming after his exertions.

"I could only get one cab," he said.

"O, we'll find another along the quay," said Gabriel.

"Yes," said Aunt Kate. "Better not keep Mrs. Malins standing in the draught."

Mrs. Malins was helped down the front steps by her son and Mr. Browne and, after many manœuvres, hoisted into the cab. Freddy Malins clambered in after her and spent a long time settling her on the seat, Mr. Browne helping him with advice. At last she was settled comfortably and Freddy Malins invited Mr. Browne into the cab. There was a good deal of confused talk, and then Mr. Browne got into the cab. The cabman settled his rug over his knees, and bent down for the address. The confusion grew greater and the cabman was directed differently by Freddy Malins and Mr. Browne, each of whom had his head out through a window of the cab. The difficulty was to know where to drop Mr. Browne along the route, and Aunt Kate, Aunt Julia and Mary Jane helped the discussion from the doorstep with cross-directions and contradictions and abundance of laughter. As for Freddy Malins he was speechless with laughter. He popped his head in and out of the window every moment to the great danger of his hat, and told his mother how the discussion was progressing, till at last Mr. Browne shouted to the bewildered cabman above the din of everybody's laughter:

"Do you know Trinity College?"

"Yes, sir," said the cabman.

"Well, drive bang up against Trinity College gates," said Mr. Browne, "and then we'll tell you where to go. You understand now?"

"Yes, sir," said the cabman.

"Make like a bird for Trinity College."

"Right, sir," said the cabman.

The horse was whipped up and the cab rattled off along the quay amid a chorus of laughter and adieus.

Gabriel had not gone to the door with the others. He was in a dark part of the hall gazing up the staircase. A woman was standing near the top of the first flight, in the shadow also. He could not see her face but he could see the terra-cotta and salmon-pink panels of her skirt which the shadow made appear black and white. It was his wife. She was leaning on the banisters, listening to something. Gabriel was surprised at her stillness and strained his ear to listen also. But he could hear little save the noise of laughter and dispute on the front steps, a few chords struck on the piano and a few notes of a man's voice singing.

He stood still in the gloom of the hall, trying to catch the air that the voice was singing and gazing up at his wife. There was grace and mystery in her attitude as if she were a symbol of something. He asked himself what is a woman standing on the stairs in the shadow, listening to distant music, a symbol of. If he were a painter he would paint her in that attitude. Her blue felt hat would show off the bronze of her hair against the darkness and the dark panels of her skirt would show off the light ones. *Distant Music* he would call the picture if he were a painter.

The hall-door was closed; and Aunt Kate, Aunt Julia and Mary Jane came down the hall, still laughing.

"Well, isn't Freddy terrible?" said Mary Jane. "He's really terrible."

Gabriel said nothing but pointed up the stairs towards where his wife was standing. Now that the hall-door was closed the voice and the piano could be heard more clearly. Gabriel held up his hand for them to be silent. The song seemed to be in the old Irish tonality and the singer seemed uncertain both of his

words and of his voice. The voice, made plaintive by distance and
by the singer's hoarseness, faintly illuminated the cadence of the
air with words expressing grief:

> *O, the rain falls on my heavy locks*
> *And the dew wets my skin,*
> *My babe lies cold ...*

"O," exclaimed Mary Jane. "It's Bartell D'Arcy singing and he
wouldn't sing all the night. O, I'll get him to sing a song before
he goes."

"O, do, Mary Jane," said Aunt Kate.

Mary Jane brushed past the others and ran to the staircase, but
before she reached it the singing stopped and the piano was
closed abruptly.

"O, what a pity!" she cried. "Is he coming down, Gretta?"

Gabriel heard his wife answer yes and saw her come down towards them. A few steps behind her were Mr. Bartell D'Arcy and
Miss O'Callaghan.

"O, Mr. D'Arcy," cried Mary Jane, "it's downright mean of you
to break off like that when we were all in raptures listening to
you."

"I have been at him all the evening," said Miss O'Callaghan,
"and Mrs. Conroy, too, and he told us he had a dreadful cold
and couldn't sing."

"O, Mr. D'Arcy," said Aunt Kate, "now that was a great fib to
tell."

"Can't you see that I'm as hoarse as a crow?" said Mr. D'Arcy
roughly.

He went into the pantry hastily and put on his overcoat. The
others, taken aback by his rude speech, could find nothing to
say. Aunt Kate wrinkled her brows and made signs to the others
to drop the subject. Mr. D'Arcy stood swathing his neck carefully
and frowning.

"It's the weather," said Aunt Julia, after a pause.

"Yes, everybody has colds," said Aunt Kate readily, "everybody."

"They say," said Mary Jane, "we haven't had snow like it for
thirty years; and I read this morning in the newspapers that the
snow is general all over Ireland."

"I love the look of snow," said Aunt Julia sadly.

"So do I," said Miss O'Callaghan. "I think Christmas is never really Christmas unless we have the snow on the ground."

"But poor Mr. D'Arcy doesn't like the snow," said Aunt Kate, smiling.

Mr. D'Arcy came from the pantry, fully swathed and buttoned, and in a repentant tone told them the history of his cold. Everyone gave him advice and said it was a great pity and urged him to be very careful of his throat in the night air. Gabriel watched his wife, who did not join in the conversation. She was standing right under the dusty fanlight and the flame of the gas lit up the rich bronze of her hair, which he had seen her drying at the fire a few days before. She was in the same attitude and seemed unaware of the talk about her. At last she turned towards them and Gabriel saw that there was colour on her cheeks and that her eyes were shining. A sudden tide of joy went leaping out of his heart.

"Mr. D'Arcy," she said, "what is the name of that song you were singing?"

"It's called *The Lass of Aughrim*," said Mr. D'Arcy, "but I couldn't remember it properly. Why? Do you know it?"

"*The Lass of Aughrim*," she repeated. "I couldn't think of the name."

"It's a very nice air," said Mary Jane. "I'm sorry you were not in voice tonight."

"Now, Mary Jane," said Aunt Kate, "don't annoy Mr. D'Arcy. I won't have him annoyed."

Seeing that all were ready to start she shepherded them to the door, where good-night was said:

"Well, good-night, Aunt Kate, and thanks for the pleasant evening."

"Good-night, Gabriel. Good-night, Gretta!"

"Good-night, Aunt Kate, and thanks ever so much. Goodnight, Aunt Julia."

"O, good-night, Gretta, I didn't see you."

"Good-night, Mr. D'Arcy. Good-night, Miss O'Callaghan."

"Good-night, Miss Morkan."

"Good-night, again."

"Good-night, all. Safe home."

"Good-night. Good night."

The morning was still dark. A dull, yellow light brooded over the houses and the river; and the sky seemed to be descending. It was slushy underfoot; and only streaks and patches of snow lay on the roofs, on the parapets of the quay and on the area railings. The lamps were still burning redly in the murky air and, across the river, the palace of the Four Courts stood out menacingly against the heavy sky.

She was walking on before him with Mr. Bartell D'Arcy, her shoes in a brown parcel tucked under one arm and her hands holding her skirt up from the slush. She had no longer any grace of attitude, but Gabriel's eyes were still bright with happiness. The blood went bounding along his veins; and the thoughts went rioting through his brain, proud, joyful, tender, valorous.

She was walking on before him so lightly and so erect that he longed to run after her noiselessly, catch her by the shoulder and say something foolish and affectionate into her ear. She seemed to him so frail that he longed to defend her against something and then to be alone with her. Moments of their secret life together burst like stars upon his memory. A heliotrope envelope was lying beside his breakfast-cup and he was caressing it with his hand. Birds were twittering in the ivy and the sunny web of the curtain was shimmering along the floor: he could not eat for happiness. They were standing on the crowded platform and he was placing a ticket inside the warm palm of her glove. He was standing with her in the cold, looking in through a grated window at a man making bottles in a roaring furnace. It was very cold. Her face, fragrant in the cold air, was quite close to his; and suddenly he called out to the man at the furnace:

"Is the fire hot, sir?"

But the man could not hear with the noise of the furnace. It was just as well. He might have answered rudely.

A wave of yet more tender joy escaped from his heart and went coursing in warm flood along his arteries. Like the tender fire of stars moments of their life together, that no one knew of or would ever know of, broke upon and illuminated his memory. He longed to recall to her those moments, to make her forget the years of their dull existence together and remember only their moments of ecstasy. For the years, he felt, had not quenched his soul or hers. Their children, his writing, her household cares had not quenched all their souls' tender fire. In one letter that he had written to her then he had said: "Why is it that words like these seem to me so dull and cold? Is it because there is no word tender enough to be your name?"

Like distant music these words that he had written years before were borne towards him from the past. He longed to be alone with her. When the others had gone away, when he and she were in the room in the hotel, then they would be alone together. He would call her softly:

"Gretta!"

Perhaps she would not hear at once: she would be undressing. Then something in his voice would strike her. She would turn and look at him. . . .

At the corner of Winetavern Street they met a cab. He was glad of its rattling noise as it saved him from conversation. She was looking out of the window and seemed tired. The others spoke only a few words, pointing out some building or street. The horse galloped along wearily under the murky morning sky, dragging his old rattling box after his heels, and Gabriel was again in a cab with her, galloping to catch the boat, galloping to their honeymoon.

As the cab drove across O'Connell Bridge Miss O'Callaghan said:

"They say you never cross O'Connell Bridge without seeing a white horse."

"I see a white man this time," said Gabriel.

"Where?" asked Mr. Bartell D'Arcy.

Gabriel pointed to the statue, on which lay patches of snow. Then he nodded familiarly to it and waved his hand.

"Good-night, Dan," he said gaily.

When the cab drew up before the hotel, Gabriel jumped out and, in spite of Mr. Bartell D'Arcy's protest, paid the driver. He gave the man a shilling over his fare. The man saluted and said:

"A prosperous New Year to you, sir."

"The same to you," said Gabriel cordially.

She leaned for a moment on his arm in getting out of the cab and while standing at the curbstone, bidding the others good-night. She leaned lightly on his arm, as lightly as when she had danced with him a few hours before. He had felt proud and happy then, happy that she was his, proud of her grace and wifely carriage. But now, after the kindling again of so many memories, the first touch of her body, musical and strange and perfumed, sent through him a keen pang of lust. Under cover of her silence he pressed her arm closely to his side; and, as they stood at the hotel door, he felt that they had escaped from their lives and duties, escaped from home and friends and run away together with wild and radiant hearts to a new adventure.

An old man was dozing in a great hooded chair in the hall. He lit a candle in the office and went before them to the stairs. They followed him in silence, their feet falling in soft thuds on the thickly carpeted stairs. She mounted the stairs behind the porter, her head bowed in the ascent, her frail shoulders curved as with a burden, her skirt girt tightly about her. He could have flung his arms about her hips and held her still, for his arms were trembling with desire to seize her and only the stress of his nails against the palms of his hands held the wild impulse of his body in check. The porter halted on the stairs to settle his guttering candle. They halted, too, on the steps below him. In the silence Gabriel could hear the falling of the molten wax into the tray and the thumping of his own heart against his ribs.

The porter led them along a corridor and opened a door. Then he set his unstable candle down on a toilet-table and asked at what hour they were to be called in the morning.

"Eight," said Gabriel.

The porter pointed to the tap of the electric-bulb and began a muttered apology, but Gabriel cut him short.

"We don't want any light. We have light enough from the street. And I say," he added, pointing to the candle, "you might remove that handsome article, like a good man."

The porter took up his candle again, but slowly, for he was surprised by such a novel idea. Then he mumbled good-night and went out. Gabriel shot the lock to.

A ghastly light from the street lamp lay in a long shaft from one window to the door. Gabriel threw his overcoat and hat on a couch and crossed the room towards the window. He looked down into the street in order that his emotion might calm a little. Then he turned and leaned against a chest of drawers with his back to the light. She had taken off her hat and cloak and was standing before a large swinging mirror, unhooking her waist. Gabriel paused for a few moments, watching her, and then said:

"Gretta!"

She turned away from the mirror slowly and walked along the shaft of light towards him. Her face looked so serious and weary that the words would not pass Gabriel's lips. No, it was not the moment yet.

"You looked tired," he said.

"I am a little," she answered.

"You don't feel ill or weak?"

"No, tired: that's all."

She went on to the window and stood there, looking out. Gabriel waited again and then, fearing that diffidence was about to conquer him, he said abruptly:

"By the way, Gretta!"

"What is it?"

"You know that poor fellow Malins?" he said quickly.

"Yes. What about him?"

"Well, poor fellow, he's a decent sort of chap, after all," continued Gabriel in a false voice. "He gave me back that sovereign I lent him, and I didn't expect it, really. It's a pity he wouldn't keep away from that Browne, because he's not a bad fellow, really."

He was trembling now with annoyance. Why did she seem so abstracted? He did not know how he could begin. Was she annoyed, too, about something? If she would only turn to him or come to him of her own accord! To take her as she was would be brutal. No, he must see some ardour in her eyes first. He longed to be master of her strange mood.

"When did you lend him the pound?" she asked, after a pause.

Gabriel strove to restrain himself from breaking out into brutal language about the sottish Malins and his pound. He longed to cry to her from his soul, to crush her body against his, to overmaster her. But he said:

"O, at Christmas, when he opened that little Christmas-card shop in Henry Street."

He was in such a fever of rage and desire that he did not hear her come from the window. She stood before him for an instant, looking at him strangely. Then, suddenly raising herself on tiptoe and resting her hands lightly on his shoulders, she kissed him.

"You are a very generous person, Gabriel," she said.

Gabriel, trembling with delight at her sudden kiss and at the quaintness of her phrase, put his hands on her hair and began smoothing it back, scarcely touching it with his fingers. The washing had made it fine and brilliant. His heart was brimming over with happiness. Just when he was wishing for it she had come to him of her own accord. Perhaps her thoughts had been running with his. Perhaps she had felt the impetuous desire that was in him, and then the yielding mood had come upon her. Now that she had fallen to him so easily, he wondered why he had been so diffident.

He stood, holding her head between his hands. Then, slipping one arm swiftly about her body and drawing her towards him, he said softly:

"Gretta, dear, what are you thinking about?"

She did not answer nor yield wholly to his arm. He said again, softly:

"Tell me what it is, Gretta. I think I know what is the matter. Do I know?"

She did not answer at once. Then she said in an outburst of tears:

"O, I am thinking about that song, *The Lass of Aughrim.*"

She broke loose from him and ran to the bed and, throwing her arms across the bed-rail, hid her face. Gabriel stood stock-still for a moment in astonishment and then followed her. As he passed in the way of the cheval-glass he caught sight of himself in full length, his broad, well-filled shirt-front, the face whose expression always puzzled him when he saw it in a mirror, and his glimmering gilt-rimmed eyeglasses. He halted a few paces from her and said:

"What about the song? Why does that make you cry?"

She raised her head from her arms and dried her eyes with the back of her hand like a child. A kinder note than he had intended went into his voice.

"Why, Gretta?" he asked.

"I am thinking about a person long ago who used to sing that song."

"And who was the person long ago?" asked Gabriel, smiling.

"It was a person I used to know in Galway when I was living with my grandmother," she said.

The smile passed away from Gabriel's face. A dull anger began to gather again at the back of his mind and the dull fires of his lust began to glow angrily in his veins.

"Someone you were in love with?" he asked ironically.

"It was a young boy I used to know," she answered, "named Michael Furey. He used to sing that song *The Lass of Aughrim.* He was very delicate."

Gabriel was silent. He did not wish her to think that he was interested in this delicate boy.

"I can see him so plainly," she said, after a moment. "Such eyes as he had: big, dark eyes! And such an expression in them — an expression!"

"O, then, you are in love with him?" said Gabriel.

"I used to go out walking with him," she said, "when I was in Galway."

A thought flew across Gabriel's mind.

"Perhaps that was why you wanted to go to Galway with that Ivors girl?" he said coldly.

She looked at him and asked in surprise:

"What for?"

Her eyes made Gabriel feel awkward. He shrugged his shoulders and said:

"How do I know? To see him, perhaps."

She looked away from him along the shaft of light towards the window in silence.

"He is dead," she said at length. "He died when he was only seventeen. Isn't it a terrible thing to die so young as that?"

"What was he?" asked Gabriel, still ironically.

"He was in the gasworks," she said.

Gabriel felt humiliated by the failure of his irony and by the evocation of this figure from the dead, a boy in the gasworks. While he had been full of memories of their secret life together, full of tenderness and joy and desire, she had been comparing him in her mind with another. A shameful consciousness of his own person assailed him. He saw himself as a ludicrous figure, acting as a penny-boy for his aunts, a nervous, well-meaning sentimentalist, orating to vulgarians and idealising his own clownish lusts, the pitiable fatuous fellow he had caught a glimpse of in the mirror. Instinctively he turned his back more to the light lest she might see the shame that burned upon his forehead.

He tried to keep up his tone of cold interrogation, but his voice when he spoke was humble and indifferent.

"I suppose you were in love with this Michael Furey, Gretta," he said.

"I was great with him at that time," she said.

Her voice was veiled and sad. Gabriel, feeling now how vain it would be to try to lead her whither he had purposed, caressed one of her hands and said, also sadly:

"And what did he die of so young, Gretta? Consumption, was it?"

"I think he died for me," she answered.

A vague terror seized Gabriel at this answer, as if, at that hour when he had hoped to triumph, some impalpable and vindictive being was coming against him, gathering forces against him in its vague world. But he shook himself free of it with an effort of reason and continued to caress her hand. He did not question her again, for he felt that she would tell him of herself. Her hand was warm and moist: it did not respond to his touch, but he continued to caress it just as he had caressed her first letter to him that spring morning.

"It was in the winter," she said, "about the beginning of the winter when I was going to leave my grandmother's and come up here to the convent. And he was ill at the time in his lodgings in Galway and wouldn't be let out, and his people in Oughterard were written to. He was in decline, they said, or something like that. I never knew rightly."

She paused for a moment and sighed.

"Poor fellow," she said. "He was very fond of me and he was such a gentle boy. We used to go out together, walking, you know, Gabriel, like the way they do in the country. He was going to study singing only for his health. He had a very good voice, poor Michael Furey."

"Well; and then?" asked Gabriel.

"And then when it came to the time for me to leave Galway and come up to the convent he was much worse and I wouldn't be let see him so I wrote a letter saying I was going up to Dublin and would be back in the summer, and hoping he would be better then."

She paused for a moment to get her voice under control, and then went on:

"Then the night before I left, I was in my grandmother's house in Nuns' Island, packing up, and I heard gravel thrown up against the window. The window was so wet I couldn't see, so I ran downstairs as I was and slipped out the back into the garden and there was the poor fellow at the end of the garden, shivering."

"And did you not tell him to go back?" asked Gabriel.

"I implored of him to go home at once and I told him he would get his death in the rain. But he said he did not want to live. I can see his eyes as well as well! He was standing at the end of the wall where there was a tree."

"And did he go home?" asked Gabriel.

"Yes, he went home. And when I was only a week in the convent he died and he was buried in Oughterard, where his people came from. O, the day I heard that, that he was dead!"

She stopped, choking with sobs, and, overcome by emotion, flung herself face downward on the bed, sobbing in the quilt. Gabriel held her hand for a moment longer, irresolutely, and then, shy of intruding on her grief, let it fall gently and walked quietly to the window.

She was fast asleep.

Gabriel, leaning on his elbow, looked for a few moments unresentfully on her tangled hair and half-open mouth, listening to her deep-drawn breath. So she had had that romance in her life: a man had died for her sake. It hardly pained him now to think how poor a part he, her husband, had played in her life. He watched her while she slept, as though he and she had never lived together as man and wife. His curious eyes rested long upon her face and on her hair; and, as he thought of what she must have been then, in that time of her first girlish beauty, a strange, friendly pity for her entered his soul. He did not like to say even to himself that her face was no longer beautiful, but he knew that it was no longer the face for which Michael Furey had braved death.

Perhaps she had not told him all the story. His eyes moved to the chair over which she had thrown some of her clothes. A petticoat string dangled to the floor. One boot stood upright, its limp upper fallen down: the fellow of it lay upon its side. He wondered at his riot of emotions of an hour before. From what had it proceeded? From his aunt's supper, from his own foolish speech, from the wine and dancing, the merry-making when saying good-night in the hall, the pleasure of the walk along the river in the snow. Poor Aunt Julia! She, too, would soon be a shade with the shade of Patrick Morkan and his horse. He had caught that haggard look upon her face for a moment when she was singing *Arrayed for the Bridal.* Soon, perhaps, he would be sitting in that same drawing-room, dressed in black, his silk hat on his knees. The blinds would be drawn down and Aunt Kate would be sitting beside him, crying and blowing her nose and telling him how Julia had died. He would cast about in his mind for some words that might console her, and would find only lame and useless ones. Yes, yes: that would happen very soon.

The air of the room chilled his shoulders. He stretched himself cautiously along under the sheets and lay down beside his wife. One by one, they were all becoming shades. Better pass boldly into that other world, in the full glory of some passion, than fade and wither dismally with age. He thought of how she who lay beside him had locked in her heart for so many years that image of her lover's eyes when he had told her that he did not wish to live.

Generous tears filled Gabriel's eyes. He had never felt like that himself towards any woman, but he knew that such a feeling must be love. The tears gathered more thickly in his eyes and in the partial darkness he imagined he saw the form of a young man standing under a dripping tree. Other forms were near. His soul had approached that region where dwell the vast hosts of the dead. He was conscious of, but could not apprehend, their wayward and flickering existence. His own identity was fading out into a grey impalpable world: the solid world itself, which these dead had one time reared and lived in, was dissolving and dwindling.

A few light taps upon the pane made him turn to the window. It had begun to snow again. He watched sleepily the flakes, silver and dark, falling obliquely against the lamplight. The time had come for him to set out on his journey westward. Yes, the newspapers were right: snow was general all over Ireland. It was falling on every part of the dark central plain, on the treeless hills, falling softly upon the Bog of Allen and, farther westward, softly falling into the dark mutinous Shannon waves. It was falling, too, upon every part of the lonely churchyard on the hill where Michael Furey lay buried. It lay thickly drifted on the crooked crosses and headstones, on the spears of the little gate, on the barren thorns. His soul swooned slowly as he heard the snow falling faintly through the universe and faintly falling, like the descent of their last end, upon all the living and the dead.

FRANZ KAFKA (1883–1924) Kafka was born in Prague, Czechoslovakia of middle-class German-Jewish parents. He studied law and was employed by the Workmen's Compensation bureau of the Austrian government where he assisted injured workers in making their insurance claims. His primary concern, nevertheless, was his writing.

Kafka's ambivalent response to his father is crucial to an understanding of his works. As a boy, he stuttered whenever his father was near. "For me, you began to have that mysterious quality which all tyrants have, whose privilege is based on their personality, not on reason." In his later works the "primal" father was transformed into authoritarian concepts as the Law, the Court, and the officials at the Castle.

Kafka was a man of enormous anxieties, guilts, and self-doubts. He was so intrigued with Balzac's walking stick on which was engraved: "I overcome all obstacles" that he had one engraved for himself which read: "All obstacles overcome me." In 1912 he twice broke his engagement to the girl he loved on the basis of his own inadequacies. Ironically, 1912 was the year he wrote "The Judgment" in one night, the year he began *Amerika* and completed *The Metamorphosis*. He did marry in 1923 but died of tuberculosis in 1924.

The Metamorphosis was published while he was alive although most of his works were published posthumously by Max Brod, a friend whom Kafka had instructed to destroy all his manuscripts upon his death. *The Trial* was published in 1925, *The Castle* in 1926, and *Amerika* in 1927. The surrealistic images and effects of his stories and novels unfold in a realistic and recognizable context. The narrator speaks of bizarre happenings, as in "The Judgment," in a tone that reveals no surprise at the feasibility of such occurrences. Kafka does not differentiate ordinary reality from the fantastic or the nightmare vision.

THE BUCKET-RIDER

Franz Kafka

Coal all spent; the bucket empty; the shovel useless; the stove breathing out cold; the room freezing; the leaves outside the window rigid, covered with rime; the sky a silver shield against anyone who looks for help from it. I must have coal; I cannot freeze to death; behind me is the pitiless stove, before me the pitiless sky, so I must ride out between them and on my journey seek aid from the coal-dealer. But he has already grown deaf to ordinary appeals; I must prove irrefutably to him that I have not a single grain of coal left, and that he means to me the very sun in the firmament. I must approach like a beggar who, with the death-rattle already in his throat, insists on dying on the doorstep, and to whom the grand people's cook accordingly decides to give the dregs of the coffee-pot; just so must the coal-dealer, filled with rage, but acknowledging the command, "Thou shalt not kill," fling a shovelful of coal into my bucket.

My mode of arrival must decide the matter; so I ride off on the bucket. Seated on the bucket, my hands on the handle, the simplest kind of bridle, I propel myself with difficulty down the stairs; but once down below my bucket ascends, superbly, superbly; camels humbly squatting on the ground do not rise with more dignity, shaking themselves under the sticks of their drivers. Through the hard frozen streets we go at a regular canter; often I am upraised as high as the first story of a house; never do I sink as low as the house doors. And at last I float at an extraordinary height above the vaulted cellar of the dealer, whom I see far below crouching over his table, where he is writing; he has opened the door to let out the excessive heat.

"Coal-dealer!" I cry in a voice burned hollow by the frost and muffled in the cloud made by my breath, "please, coal-dealer, give me a little coal. My bucket is so light that I can ride on it. Be kind. When I can I'll pay you."

The dealer puts his hand to his ear. "Do I hear rightly?" He throws the question over his shoulder to his wife. "Do I hear rightly? A customer."

"I hear nothing," says his wife, breathing in and out peacefully while she knits on, her back pleasantly warmed by the heat.

"Oh, yes, you must hear," I cry. "It's me; an old customer; faithful and true; only without means at the moment."

"Wife," says the dealer, "it's some one, it must be; my ears can't have deceived me so much as that; it must be an old, a very old customer, that can move me so deeply."

"What ails you, man?" says his wife, ceasing from her work for a moment and pressing her knitting to her bosom. "It's nobody, the street is empty, all our customers are provided for; we could close down the shop for several days and take a rest."

"But I'm sitting up here on the bucket," I cry, and unfeeling frozen tears dim my eyes, "please look up here, just once; you'll see me directly; I beg you, just a shovelful; and if you give me more it'll make me so happy that I won't know what to do. All the other customers are provided for. Oh, if I could only hear the coal clattering into the bucket!"

"I'm coming," says the coal-dealer, and on his short legs he makes to climb the steps of the cellar, but his wife is already beside him, holds him back by the arm and says: "You stay here; seeing you persist in your fancies I'll go myself. Think of the bad fit of coughing you had during the night. But for a piece of business, even if it's one you've only fancied in your head, you're prepared to forget your wife and child and sacrifice your lungs. I'll go."

"Then be sure to tell him all the kinds of coal we have in stock; I'll shout out the prices after you."

"Right," says his wife, climbing up to the street. Naturally she sees me at once. "Frau Coal-dealer," I cry, "my humblest greetings; just one shovelful of coal; here in my bucket; I'll carry it home myself. One shovelful of the worst you have. I'll pay you in full for it, of course, but not just now, not just now." What a knell-like sound the words "not just now" have, and how bewilderingly they mingle with the evening chimes that fall from the church steeple nearby!

"Well, what does he want?" shouts the dealer. "Nothing," his wife shouts back, "there's nothing here; I see nothing, I hear nothing; only six striking, and now we must shut up the shop. The cold is terrible; tomorrow we'll likely have lots to do again."

She sees nothing and hears nothing; but all the same she loosens her apron-strings and waves her apron to waft me away. She succeeds, unluckily. My bucket has all the virtues of a good steed except powers of resistance, which it has not; it is too light; a woman's apron can make it fly through the air.

"You bad woman!" I shout back, while she, turning into the shop, half-contemptuous, half-reassured, flourishes her fist in the air. "You bad woman! I begged you for a shovelful of the worst coal and you would not give me it." And with that I ascend into the regions of the ice mountains and am lost forever.

(Translated by Willa and Edwin Muir)

THE JUDGMENT

Franz Kafka

It was a Sunday morning in the very height of spring. Georg Bendemann, a young merchant, was sitting in his own room on the first floor of one of a long row of small, ramshackle houses stretching beside the river which were scarcely distinguishable from each other except in height and coloring. He had just finished a letter to an old friend of his who was now living abroad, had put it into its envelope in a slow and dreamy fashion, and with his elbows propped on the writing table was gazing out of the window at the river, the bridge and the hills on the farther bank with their tender green.

He was thinking about his friend, who had actually run away to Russia some years before, being dissatisfied with his prospects at home. Now he was carrying on a business in St. Petersburg, which had flourished to begin with but had long been going downhill, as he always complained on his increasingly rare visits. So he was wearing himself out to no purpose in a foreign country, the unfamiliar full beard he wore did not quite conceal the face Georg had known so well since childhood, and his skin was growing so yellow as to indicate some latent disease. By his own account he had no regular connection with the colony of his fellow countrymen out there and almost no social intercourse with Russian families, so that he was resigning himself to becoming a permanent bachelor.

What could one write to such a man, who had obviously run off the rails, a man one could be sorry for but could not help. Should one advise him to come home, to transplant himself and take up his old friendships again — there was nothing to hinder him — and in general to rely on the help of his friends? But that was as good as telling him, and the more kindly the more offensively, that all his efforts hitherto had miscarried, that he should finally give up, come back home, and be gaped at by everyone as a returned prodigal, that only his friends knew what was what and that he himself was just a big child who should do what his successful and home-keeping friends prescribed. And was it certain, besides, that all the pain one would have to inflict on him would achieve its object? Perhaps it would not even be possible to get him to come home at all — he said himself that he was now out of touch with commerce in his native country — and then he would still be left an alien in a foreign land embittered by his friends' advice and more than ever estranged from them. But if he did follow their advice and then didn't fit in at home — not out of malice, of course, but through force of circumstances — couldn't get on with his friends or without them, felt humiliated, couldn't be said to have either friends or a country of his own any longer, wouldn't it have been better for him to stay abroad just as he was? Taking all this into account, how could one be sure that he would make a success of his life at home?

For such reasons, supposing one wanted to keep up correspondence with him, one could not send him any real news such as could frankly be told to the most distant acquaintance. It was more than three years since his last visit, and for this he offered the lame excuse that the political situation in Russia was too uncertain, which apparently would not permit even the briefest absence of a small business man while it allowed hundreds of thousands of Russians to travel peacefully abroad. But during these three years Georg's own position in life had changed a lot. Two years ago his mother had died, since when he and his father had shared the household together, and his friend had of course been informed of that and had expressed his sympathy in a letter phrased so dryly that the grief caused by such an event, one had to conclude, could not be realized in a distant country. Since that time, however, Georg had applied himself with greater determination to the business as well as to everything else.

Perhaps during his mother's lifetime his father's insistence on having everything his own way in the business had hindered him from developing any real activity of his own, perhaps since her death his father had become less aggressive, although he was still active in the business, perhaps it was mostly due to an accidental run of good fortune — which was very probable indeed — but at any rate during those two years the business had developed in a most unexpected way, the staff had had to be doubled, the turnover was five times as great, no doubt about it, farther progress lay just ahead.

But Georg's friend had no inkling of this improvement. In earlier years, perhaps for the last time in that letter of condolence, he had tried to persuade Georg to emigrate to Russia and had enlarged upon the prospects of success for precisely Georg's branch of trade. The figures quoted were microscopic by comparison with the range of Georg's present operations. Yet he shrank from letting his friend know about his business success, and if he were to do it now retrospectively that certainly would look peculiar.

So Georg confined himself to giving his friend unimportant items of gossip such as rise at random in the memory when one is idly thinking things over on a quiet Sunday. All he desired was to leave undisturbed the idea of the home town which his friend must have built up to his own content during the long interval. And so it happened to Georg that three times in three fairly widely separated letters he had told his friend about the engagement of an unimportant man to an equally unimportant girl, until indeed, quite contrary to his intentions, his friend began to show some interest in this notable event.

Yet Georg preferred to write about things like these rather than to confess that he himself had got engaged a month ago to a Fräulein Frieda Brandenfeld, a girl from a well-to-do family. He often discussed this friend of his with his fiancée and the peculiar relationship that had developed between them in their correspondence. "So he won't be coming to our wedding," said she, "and yet I have a right to get to know all your friends." "I don't want to trouble him," answered Georg, "don't misunderstand me, he would probably come, at least I think so, but he would feel that his hand had been forced and he would be hurt, perhaps he would envy me and certainly he'd be discontented and without being able to do anything about his discontent he'd have to go away again alone. Alone — do you know what that means?" "Yes, but may he not hear about our wedding in some other fashion?" "I can't prevent that, of course, but it's unlikely, considering the way he lives." "Since your friends are like that, Georg, you shouldn't ever have got engaged at all." "Well, we're both to blame for that; but I wouldn't have it any other way now." And when, breathing quickly under his kisses, she still brought out: "All the same, I do feel upset," he thought it could not really involve him in trouble were he to send the news to his friend. "That's the kind of man I am and he'll just have to take me as I am," he said to himself, "I can't cut myself to another pattern that might make a more suitable friend for him."

And in fact he did inform his friend, in the long letter he had been writing that Sunday morning, about his engagement, with these words: "I have saved my best news to the end. I have got engaged to a Fräulein Frieda Brandenfeld, a girl from a well-to-do family, who only came to live here a long time after you went away, so that you're hardly likely to know her. There will be time to tell you more about her later, for today let me just say that I am very happy and as between you and me the only difference in our relationship is that instead of a quite ordinary kind of friend you will now have in me a happy friend. Besides that, you will acquire in my fiancée, who sends her warm greetings and will soon write you herself, a genuine friend of the opposite sex, which is not without importance to a bachelor. I know that there are many reasons why you can't come to see us, but would not my wedding be precisely the right occasion for giving all obstacles the go-by? Still, however that may be, do just as seems good to you without regarding any interests but your own."

With this letter in his hand Georg had been sitting a long time at the writing table, his face turned towards the window. He had barely acknowleged, with an absent smile, a greeting waved to him from the street by a passing acquaintance.

At last he put the letter in his pocket and went out of his room across a small lobby into his father's room, which he had not entered for months. There was in fact no need for him to enter it, since he saw his father daily at business and they took their midday meal together at an eating house; in the evening, it was true, each did as he pleased, yet even then, unless Georg — as mostly happened — went out with friends or, more recently, visited his fiancée, they always sat for a while, each with his newspaper, in their common sitting room.

It surprised Georg how dark his father's room was even on this sunny morning. So it was overshadowed as much as that by the high wall on the other side of the narrow courtyard. His father was sitting by the window in a corner hung with various mementoes of Georg's dead mother, reading a newspaper which he held to one side before his eyes in an attempt to overcome a defect of vision. On the table stood the remains of his breakfast, not much of which seemed to have been eaten.

"Ah, Georg," said his father, rising at once to meet him. His heavy dressing gown swung open as he walked and the skirts of it fluttered round him. — "My father is still a giant of a man," said Georg to himself.

"It's unbearably dark here," he said aloud.

"Yes, it's dark enough," answered his father.

"And you've shut the window, too?"

"I prefer it like that."

"Well, it's quite warm outside," said Georg, as if continuing his previous remark, and sat down.

His father cleared away the breakfast dishes and set them on a chest.

"I really only wanted to tell you," went on Georg, who had been vacantly following the old man's movements, "that I am now sending the news of my engagement to St. Petersburg." He drew the letter a little way from his pocket and let it drop back again.

"To St. Petersburg?" asked his father.

"To my friend there," said Georg, trying to meet his father's eye. — In business hours he's quite different, he was thinking, how solidly he sits here with his arms crossed.

"Oh yes. To your friend," said his father, with peculiar emphasis.

"Well, you know, Father, that I wanted not to tell him about my engagement at first. Out of consideration for him, that was the only reason. You know yourself he's a difficult man. I said to myself that someone else might tell him about my engagement, although he's such a solitary creature that that was hardly likely — I couldn't prevent that — but I wasn't ever going to tell him myself."

"And now you've changed your mind?" asked his father, laying his enormous newspaper on the window sill and on top of it his spectacles, which he covered with one hand.

"Yes, I've been thinking it over. If he's a good friend of mine,

I said to myself, my being happily engaged should make him happy too. And so I wouldn't put off telling him any longer. But before I posted the letter I wanted to let you know."

"Georg," said his father, lengthening his toothless mouth, "listen to me! You've come to me about this business, to talk it over with me. No doubt that does you honor. But it's nothing, it's worse than nothing, if you don't tell me the whole truth. I don't want to stir up matters that shouldn't be mentioned here. Since the death of our dear mother certain things have been done that aren't right. Maybe the time will come for mentioning them, and maybe sooner than we think. There's many a thing in the business I'm not aware of, maybe it's not done behind my back — I'm not going to say that it's done behind my back — I'm not equal to things any longer, my memory's failing, I haven't an eye for so many things any longer. That's the course of nature in the first place, and in the second place the death of our dear mother hit me harder than it did you. — But since we're talking about it, about this letter, I beg you, Georg, don't deceive me. It's a trivial affair, it's hardly worth mentioning, so don't deceive me. Do you really have this friend in St. Petersburg?"

Georg rose in embarrassment. "Never mind my friends. A thousand friends wouldn't make up to me for my father. Do you know what I think? You're not taking enough care of yourself. But old age must be taken care of. I can't do without you in the business, you know that very well, but if the business is going to undermine your health, I'm ready to close it down tomorrow forever. And that won't do. We'll have to make a change in your way of living. But a radical change. You sit here in the dark, and in the sitting room you would have plenty of light. You just take a bite of breakfast instead of properly keeping up your strength. You sit by a closed window, and the air would be so good for you. No, Father! I'll get the doctor to come, and we'll follow his orders. We'll change your room, you can move into the front room and I'll move in here. You won't notice the change, all your things will be moved with you. But there's time for all that later, I'll put you to bed now for a little, I'm sure you need to rest. Come, I'll help you to take off your things, you'll see I can do it. Or if you would rather go into the front room at once, you can lie down in my bed for the present. That would be the most sensible thing."

Georg stood close beside his father, who had let his head with its unkempt white hair sink on his chest.

"Georg," said his father in a low voice, without moving.

Georg knelt down at once beside his father, in the old man's weary face he saw the pupils, over-large, fixedly looking at him from the corners of the eyes.

"You have no friend in St. Petersburg. You've always been a leg-puller and you haven't even shrunk from pulling my leg. How could you have a friend out there! I can't believe it."

"Just think back a bit, Father," said Georg, lifting his father from the chair and slipping off his dressing gown as he stood feebly enough, "it'll soon be three years since my friend came to see us last. I remember that you used not to like him very much. At least twice I kept you from seeing him, although he was actually sitting with me in my room. I could quite well understand your dislike of him, my friend has his peculiarities. But then, later, you got on with him very well. I was proud because you listened to him and nodded and asked him questions. If you think back you're bound to remember. He used to tell us the most incredible stories of the Russian Revolution. For instance, when he was on a business trip to Kiev and ran into a riot, and saw a priest on a balcony who cut a broad cross in blood on the palm of his hand and held the hand up and appealed to the mob. You've told that story yourself once or twice since."

Meanwhile Georg had succeeded in lowering his father down again and carefully taking off the woollen drawers he wore over his linen underpants and his socks. The not particularly clean appearance of this underwear made him reproach himself for having been neglectful. It should have certainly been his duty to see that his father had clean changes of underwear. He had not yet explicitly discussed with his bride-to-be what arrangements should be made for his father in the future, for they had both of them silently taken it for granted that the old man would go on living alone in the old house. But now he made a quick, firm decision to take him into his own future establishment. It almost looked, on closer inspection, as if the care he meant to lavish there on his father might come too late.

He carried his father to bed in his arms. It gave him a dreadful feeling to notice that while he took the few steps towards the bed the old man on his breast was playing with his watch chain. He could not lay him down on the bed for a moment, so firmly did he hang on to the watch chain.

But as soon as he was laid in bed, all seemed well. He covered himself up and even drew the blankets farther than usual over his shoulders. He looked up at George with a not unfriendly eye.

"You begin to remember my friend, don't you?" asked Georg, giving him an encouraging nod.

"Am I well covered up now?" asked his father, as if he were not able to see whether his feet were properly tucked in or not.

"So you find it snug in bed already," said Georg, and tucked the blankets more closely round him.

"Am I well covered up?" asked the father once more, seeming to be strangely intent upon the answer.

"Don't worry, you're well covered up."

"No!" cried his father, cutting short the answer, threw the blankets off with a strength that sent them all flying in a moment and sprang erect in bed. Only one hand lightly touched the ceiling to steady him.

"You wanted to cover me up, I know, my young sprig, but I'm far from being covered up yet. And even if this is the last strength I have, it's enough for you, too much for you. Of course I know your friend. He would have been a son after my own heart. That's why you've been playing him false all these years. Why else? Do you think I haven't been sorry for him? And that's why you had to lock yourself up in your office — the Chief is busy, mustn't be disturbed — just so that you could write your lying little letters to Russia. But thank goodness a father doesn't need to be taught how to see through his son. And now that you thought you'd got him down, so far down that you could set your bottom on him and sit on him and he wouldn't move, then my fine son makes up his mind to get married!"

Georg stared at the bogey conjured up by his father. His friend in St. Petersburg, whom his father suddenly knew too well, touched his imagination as never before. Lost in the vastness of Russia he saw him. At the door of an empty, plundered warehouse he saw him. Among the wreckage of his showcases, the slashed remnants of his wares, the falling gas brackets, he was just standing up. Why did he have to go so far away!

"But attend to me!" cried his father, and Georg, almost distracted, ran towards the bed to take everything in, yet came to a stop halfway.

"Because she lifted up her skirts," his father began to flute, "because she lifted her skirts like this, the nasty creature," and mimicking her he lifted his shirt so high that one could see the scar on his thigh from his war wound, "because she lifted her skirts like this and this you made up to her, and in order to make free with her undisturbed you have disgraced your mother's memory, betrayed your friend and stuck your father into bed so that he can't move. But he can move, or can't he?"

And he stood up quite unsupported and kicked his legs out. His insight made him radiant.

Georg shrank into a corner, as far away from his father as possible. A long time ago he had firmly made up his mind to watch closely every least movement so that he should not be surprised by any indirect attack, a pounce from behind or above. At this moment he recalled this long-forgotten resolve and forgot it again, like a man drawing a short thread through the eye of a needle.

"But your friend hasn't been betrayed after all!" cried his father, emphasizing the point with stabs of his forefinger. "I've been representing him here on the spot."

"You comedian!" Georg could not resist the retort, realized at once the harm done and, his eyes starting in his head, bit his tongue back, only too late, till the pain made his knees give.

"Yes, of course I've been playing a comedy! A comedy! That's a good expression! What other comfort was left to a poor old widower? Tell me — and while you're answering me be you still my living son — what else was left to me, in my back room, plagued by a disloyal staff, old to the marrow of my bones? And my son strutting through the world, finishing off deals that I had prepared for him, bursting with triumphant glee and stalking away from his father with the closed face of a respectable business man! Do you think I didn't love you, I, from whom you are sprung?"

Now he'll lean forward, thought Georg, what if he topples and smashes himself! These words went hissing through his mind.

His father leaned forward but did not topple. Since Georg did not come any nearer, as he had expected, he straightened himself again.

"Stay where you are, I don't need you! You think you have strength enough to come over here and that you're only hanging back of your own accord. Don't be too sure! I am still much the stronger of us two. All by myself I might have had to give way, but your mother has given me so much of her strength that I've established a fine connection with your friend and I have your customers here in my pocket!"

"He has pockets even in his shirt!" said Georg to himself, and believed that with this remark he could make him an impossible figure for all the world. Only for a moment did he think so, since he kept on forgetting everything.

"Just take your bride on your arm and try getting in my way! I'll sweep her from your very side, you don't know how!"

Georg made a grimace of disbelief. His father only nodded, confirming the truth of his words, towards Georg's corner.

"How you amused me today, coming to ask me if you should tell your friend about your engagement. He knows it already, you stupid boy, he knows it all! I've been writing to him, for you forgot to take my writing things away from me. That's why he hasn't been here for years, he knows everything a hundred times better than you do yourself, in his left hand he crumples your letters unopened while in his right hand he holds up my letters to read through!"

In his enthusiasm he waved his arm over his head. "He knows everything a thousand times better!" he cried.

"Ten thousand times!" said Georg, to make fun of his father, but in his very mouth the words turned into deadly earnest.

"For years I've been waiting for you to come with some such question! Do you think I concern myself with anything else? Do you think I read my newspapers? Look!" and he threw Georg a newspaper sheet which he had somehow taken to bed with him. An old newspaper, with a name entirely unknown to Georg.

"How long a time you've taken to grow up! Your mother had to die, she couldn't see the happy day, your friend is going to pieces in Russia, even three years ago he was yellow enough to be thrown away, and as for me, you see what condition I'm in. You have eyes in your head for that!"

"So you've been lying in wait for me!" cried Georg.

His father said pityingly, in an offhand manner: "I suppose you wanted to say that sooner. But now it doesn't matter." And in a louder voice: "So now you know what else there was in the world besides yourself, till now you've known only about yourself! An innocent child, yes, that you were, truly, but still more truly have you been a devilish human being! — And therefore take note: I sentence you now to death by drowning!"

Georg felt himself urged from the room, the crash with which his father fell on the bed behind him was still in his ears as he fled. On the staircase, which he rushed down as if its steps were an inclined plane, he ran into his charwoman on her way up to do the morning cleaning of the room. "Jesus!" she cried, and covered her face with her apron, but he was already gone. Out of the front door he rushed, across the roadway, driven towards the water. Already he was grasping at the railings as a starving man clutches food. He swung himself over, like the distinguished gymnast he had once been in his youth, to his parents' pride. With weakening grip he was still holding on when he spied between the railings a motor-bus coming which would easily cover the noise of his fall, called in a low voice: "Dear parents, I have always loved you, all the same," and let himself drop.

At this moment an unending stream of traffic was just going over the bridge.

                    (*Translated by Willa and Edwin Muir*)

D. H. LAWRENCE (1885–1930) Lawrence was born in the English Midland's community of Eastwood, Nottinghamshire. He was the son of a miner and a former schoolteacher. The coal-mining community and its environs provided the setting for some of his writing, notably *Sons and Lovers*. His barely literate, jovial father and dominating, reproving mother provided a major theme in his works — that of the problems of the relationship between a man and a woman in love, in marriage, and as son and mother.

Lawrence was a frail child, having suffered from early pneumonia. He attended Nottingham high school, studied briefly at Nottingham University, and taught biology until 1911 when *The White Peacock* was published. His attachment to his mother was reinforced by her death when he was twenty-five, and he did not commit himself to another woman until he eloped with Frieda von Richthofen, herself a mother of three children. They probed the world — Italy, Mexico, Ceylon, Australia, New Mexico — seeking mystical communion with the rituals of primitive man. Lawrence believed that civilization had severed the natural bond between man's body and his soul and had destroyed the balance between body and mind.

Among his most important novels are *Sons and Lovers* (1913), *Women in Love* (1920), *Lady Chatterly's Lover* (1928). *The Rainbow* (1915) incited the censors, and from then on Lawrence, like Joyce, was plagued by the censorship of his novels. "The Blue Moccasins" is one of the last of Lawrence's many short stories. Lawrence died of tuberculosis in France. On his tombstone is a phoenix which was carved by a peasant.

THE BLUE MOCCASINS

D. H. Lawrence

The fashion in women changes nowadays even faster than women's fashions. At twenty, Lina M'Leod was almost painfully modern. At sixty, almost obsolete!

She started off in life to be really independent. In that remote day, forty years ago, when a woman said she was going to be independent, it meant she was having no nonsense with men. She was kicking over the masculine traces, and living her own life, manless.

To-day, when a girl says she is going to be independent, it means she is going to devote her attentions almost exclusively to men; though not necessarily to "a man."

Miss M'Leod had an income from her mother. Therefore, at the age of twenty, she turned her back on that image of tyranny, her father, and went to Paris to study art. Art having been studied, she turned her attention to the globe of earth. Being terribly independent, she soon made Africa look small: she dallied energetically with vast hinterlands of China: and she knew the Rocky Mountains and the deserts of Arizona as if she had been married to them. All this, to escape mere man.

It was in New Mexico she purchased the blue moccasins, blue bead moccasins, from an Indian who was her guide and her subordinate. In her independence she made use of men, of course, but merely as servants, subordinates.

When the war broke out she came home. She was then forty-five, and already going grey. Her brother, two years older than herself, but a bachelor, went off to the war; she stayed at home in the small family mansion in the country, and did what she could. She was small and erect and brief in her speech, her face was like pale ivory, her skin like a very delicate parchment, and her eyes were very blue. There was no nonsense about her, though she did paint pictures. She never even touched her delicate parchment face with pigment. She was good enough as she was, honest-to-God, and the country town had a tremendous respect for her.

In her various activities she came pretty often into contact with Percy Barlow, the clerk at the bank. He was only twenty-two when she first set eyes on him in 1914, and she immediately liked him. He was a stranger in the town, his father being a poor country vicar in Yorkshire. But he was of the confiding sort. He soon confided in Miss M'Leod, for whom he had a towering respect, how he disliked his stepmother, how he feared his father, was but as wax in the hands of that downright woman, and how, in consequence, he was homeless. Wrath shone in his pleasant features, but somehow it was an amusing wrath; at least to Miss M'Leod.

He was distinctly a good-looking boy, with stiff dark hair and odd, twinkling grey eyes under thick dark brows, and a rather full mouth and a queer, deep voice that had a caressing touch of hoarseness. It was his voice that somehow got behind Miss M'Leod's reserve. Not that he had the faintest intention of so doing. He looked up to her immensely: "She's miles above me."

When she watched him playing tennis, letting himself go a bit too much, hitting too hard, running too fast, being too nice to his partner, her heart yearned over him. The orphan in him! Why should he go and be shot? She kept him at home as long as possible, working with her at all kinds of war-work. He was so absolutely willing to do everything she wanted: devoted to her.

But at last the time came when he must go. He was now twenty-four and she forty-seven. He came to say good-bye, in his awkward fashion. She suddenly turned away, leaned her forehead against the wall, and burst into bitter tears. He was frightened out of his wits. Before he knew what was happening he had his arm in front of his face and was sobbing too.

She came to comfort him. "Don't cry, dear, don't! It will all be all right."

At last he wiped his face on his sleeve and looked at her sheepishly. "It was you crying as did me in," he said. Her blue eyes were brilliant with tears. She suddenly kissed him.

"You are such a dear!" she said wistfully. Then she added, flushing suddenly vivid pink under her transparent parchment skin: "It wouldn't be right for you to marry an old thing like me, would it?"

He looked at her dumbfounded.

"No, I'm too old," she added hastily.

"Don't talk about old! You're not old!" he said hotly.

"At least I'm too old for *that*," she said sadly.

"Not as far as I'm concerned," he said. "You're younger than me, in most ways, I'm hanged if you're not!"

"Are you hanged if I'm not?" she teased wistfully.

"I am," he said. "And if I thought you wanted me, I'd be jolly proud if you married me. I would, I assure you."

"Would you?" she said, still teasing him.

Nevertheless, the next time he was home on leave she married him, very quietly, but very definitely. He was a young lieutenant. They stayed in her family home, Twybit Hall, for the honeymoon. It was her house now, her brother being dead. And they had a strangely happy month. She had made a strange discovery: a man.

He went off to Gallipoli, and became a captain. He came home in 1919, still green with malaria, but otherwise sound. She was in her fiftieth year. And she was almost white-haired; long, thick, white hair, done perfectly, and perfectly creamy, colourless face, with very blue eyes.

He had been true to her, not being very forward with women. But he was a bit startled by her white hair. However, he shut his eyes to it, and loved her. And she, though frightened and somewhat bewildered, was happy. But she was bewildered. It always seemed awkward to her, that he should come wandering into her room in his pyjamas when she was half dressed, and brushing her hair. And he would sit there silent, watching her brush the long swinging river of silver, of her white hair, the bare, ivory-white, slender arm working with a strange mechanical motion, sharp and forcible, brushing down the long silvery stream of hair. He would sit as if mesmerised, just gazing. And she would at last glance round sharply, and he would rise, saying some little casual thing to her and smiling to her oddly with his eyes. Then he would go out, his thin cotton pyjamas hitching up over his hips, for he was a rather big-built fellow. And she would feel dazed, as if she did not quite know her own self any more. And the queer, ducking motion of his silently going out of her door impressed her ominously, his curious cat head, his big hips and limbs.

They were alone in the house, save for the servants. He had no work. They lived modestly, for a good deal of her money had been lost during the war. But she still painted pictures. Marriage had only stimulated her to this. She painted canvases of flowers, beautiful flowers that thrilled her soul. And he would sit, pipe in fist, silent, and watch her. He had nothing to do. He just sat and watched her small, neat figure and her concentrated movements as she painted. Then he knocked out his pipe and filled it again.

She said that at last she was perfectly happy. And he said that he was perfectly happy. They were always together. He hardly went out, save riding in the lanes. And practically nobody came to the house.

But still, they were very silent with one another. The old chatter had died out. And he did not read much. He just sat still, and smoked, and was silent. It got on her nerves sometimes, and she would think as she had thought in the past, that the highest bliss a human being can experience is perhaps the bliss of being quite alone, quite, quite alone.

His bank firm offered to make him manager of the local branch, and, at her advice, he accepted. Now he went out of the house every morning and came home every evening, which was much more agreeable. The rector begged him to sing again in the church choir: and again she advised him to accept. These were the old grooves in which his bachelor life had run. He felt more like himself.

He was popular: a nice, harmless fellow, everyone said of him. Some of the men secretly pitied him. They made rather much of him, took him home to luncheon, and let him loose with their daughters. He was popular among the daughters too: naturally, for if a girl expressed a wish, he would instinctively say: "What! Would you like it? I'll get it for you." And if he were not in a position to satisfy the desire, he would say: "I only wish I could do it for you. I'd do it like a shot." All of which he meant.

At the same time, though he got on so well with the maidens of the town, there was no coming forward about him. He was, in some way, not wakened up. Good-looking, and big, and serviceable, he was inwardly remote, without self-confidence, almost without a self at all.

The rector's daughter took upon herself to wake him up. She

was exactly as old as he was, a smallish, rather sharp-faced young woman who had lost her husband in the war, and it had been a grief to her. But she took the stoic attitude of the young: You've got to live, so you may as well do it! She was a kindly soul, in spite of her sharpness. And she had a very perky little red-brown Pomeranian dog that she had bought in Florence in the street, but which had turned out a handsome little fellow. Miss M'Leod looked down a bit on Alice Howells and her pom, so Mrs. Howells felt no special love for Miss M'Leod — "Mrs. Barlow, that is!" she would add sharply. "For it's quite impossible to think of her as anything but Miss M'Leod!"

Percy was really more at ease at the rectory, where the pom yapped and Mrs. Howells changed her dress three or four times a day, and looked it, than in the semi-cloisteral atmosphere of Twybit Hall, where Miss M'Leod wore tweeds and a natural knitted jumper, her skirts rather long, her hair done up pure silver, and painted her wonderful flower pictures in the deepening silence of the daytime. At evening she would go up to change, after he came home. And though it thrilled her to have a man coming into her room as he dressed, snapping his collar-stud, to tell her something trivial as she stood bare-armed in her silk slip, rapidly coiling up the rope of silver hair behind her head, still, it worried her. When he was there, he couldn't keep away from her. And he would watch her, watch her, watch her as if she was the ultimate revelation. Sometimes it made her irritable. She was so absolutely used to her own privacy. What was he looking at? She never watched *him*. Rather she looked the other way. His watching tried her nerves. She was turned fifty. And his great silent body loomed almost dreadful.

He was quite happy playing tennis or croquet with Alice Howells and the rest. Alice was choir-mistress, a bossy little person outwardly, inwardly rather forlorn and affectionate, and not very sure that life hadn't let her down for good. She was now over thirty — and had no one but the pom and her father and the parish — nothing in her really intimate life. But she was very cheerful, busy, even gay, with her choir and school work, her dancing, and flirting, and dressmaking.

She was intrigued by Percy Barlow. "How *can* a man be so nice to *everybody?*" she asked him, a little exasperated. "Well, why not?" he replied, with the odd smile of his eyes. "It's not why he shouldn't, but how he manages to do it! How can you have so much good-nature? I *have* to be catty to some people, but you're nice to *everybody*."

"Oh, am I!" he said ominously.

He was like a man in a dream, or in a cloud. He was quite a good bank-manager, in fact very intelligent. Even in appearance, his great charm was his beautifully-shaped head. He had plenty of brains, really. But in his will, in his body, he was asleep. And sometimes this lethargy, or coma, made him look haggard. And sometimes it made his body seem inert and despicable, meaningless.

Alice Howells longed to ask him about his wife. "*Do* you love her? *Can* you really care for her?" But she daren't. She daren't ask him one word about his wife. Another thing she couldn't do, she couldn't persuade him to dance. Never, not once. But in everything else he was pliable as wax.

Mrs. Barlow — Miss M'Leod — stayed out at Twybit all the time. She did not even come in to church on Sunday. She had shaken off church, among other things. And she watched Percy depart, and felt just a little humiliated. He was going to sing in the choir! Yes, marriage was also a humiliation to her. She had distinctly married beneath her.

The years had gone by: she was now fifty-seven, Percy was thirty-four. He was still, in many ways, a boy. But in his curious silence, he was ageless. She managed him with perfect ease. If she expressed a wish, he acquiesced at once. So now it was agreed he should not come to her room any more. And he never did. But sometimes she went to him in his room, and was winsome in a pathetic, heart-breaking way.

She twisted him round her little finger, as the saying goes. And yet secretly she was afraid of him. In the early years he had displayed a clumsy but violent sort of passion, from which she had shrunk away. She felt it had nothing to do with her. It was just his indiscriminating desire for Woman, and for his own satisfaction. Whereas she was not just unidentified Woman, to give him his general satisfaction. So she had recoiled, and withdrawn herself. She had put him off. She had regained the absolute privacy of her room.

He was perfectly sweet about it. Yet she was uneasy with him now. She was afraid of him; or rather, not of him, but of a mys-

terious something in him. She was not a bit afraid of *him,* oh no!
And when she went to him now, to be nice to him, in her
pathetic winsomeness of an unused woman of fifty-seven, she
found him sweet-natured as ever, but really indifferent. He saw
her pathos and her winsomeness. In some way, the mystery of
her, her thick white hair, her vivid blue eyes, her ladylike refinement still fascinated him. But his bodily desire for her had gone,
utterly gone. And secretly, she was rather glad. But as he looked
at her, looked at her, as he lay there so silent, she was afraid, as
if some finger were pointed at her. Yet she knew, the moment she
spoke to him, he would twist his eyes to that good-natured and
"kindly" smile of his.

It was in the late, dark months of this year that she missed the
blue moccasins. She had hung them on a nail in his room. Not
that he ever wore them: they were too small. Nor did she: they
were too big. Moccasins are male footwear, among the Indians,
not female. But they were of a lovely turquoise-blue colour, made
all of little turquoise beads, with little forked flames of dead-
white and dark-green. When, at the beginning of their marriage,
he had exclaimed over them, she had said: "Yes! Aren't they a
lovely colour! So blue!" And he had replied: "Not as blue as your
eyes, even then."

So, naturally, she had hung them up on the wall in his room,
and there they had stayed. Till, one November day, when there
were no flowers, and she was pining to paint a still-life with
something blue in it — oh, so blue, like delphiniums! — she had
gone to his room for the moccasins. And they were not there.
And though she hunted, she could not find them. Nor did the
maids know anything of them.

So she asked him: "Percy, do you know where those blue moccasins are, which hung in your room?" There was a moment's
dead silence. Then he looked at her with his good-naturedly
twinkling eyes, and said: "No, *I* know nothing of them." There
was another dead pause. She did not believe him. But being a
perfect lady, she only said, as she turned away: "Well then, how
curious it is!" And there was another dead pause. Out of which
he asked her what she wanted them for, and she told him.
Whereon the matter lapsed.

It was November, and Percy was out in the evening fairly

often now. He was rehearsing for a "play" which was to be given in the church schoolroom at Christmas. He had asked her about it. "Do you think it's a bit *infra dig,* if I play one of the characters?" She had looked at him mildly, disguising her real feeling. "If you don't feel *personally* humiliated," she said, "then there's nothing else to consider." And he had answered: "Oh, it doesn't upset *me* at all." So she mildly said: "Then do it, by all means." Adding at the back of her mind: If it amuses you, child! — but she thought, a change had indeed come over the world, when the master of Twybit Hall, or even, for that matter, the manager of the dignified Stubbs' Bank, should perform in public on a schoolroom stage in amateur theatricals. And she kept calmly aloof, preferring not to know any details. She had a world of her own.

When he had said to Alice Howells: "You don't think other folk'll mind — clients of the bank and so forth — think it beneath my dignity?" she had cried, looking up into his twinkling eyes: "Oh, you don't have to keep *your* dignity on ice, Percy — any more than I do mine."

The play was to be performed for the first time on Christmas Eve: and after the play, there was the midnight service in church. Percy therefore told his wife not to expect him home till the small hours, at least. So he drove himself off in the car.

As night fell, and rain, Miss M'Leod felt a little forlorn. She was left out of everything. Life was slipping past her. It was Christmas Eve, and she was more alone than she had ever been. Percy only seemed to intensify her aloneness, leaving her in this fashion.

She decided not to be left out. She would go to the play too. It was past six o'clock, and she had worked herself into a highly nervous state. Outside was darkness and rain: inside was silence, forlornness. She went to the telephone and rang up the garage in Shewbury. It was with great difficulty she got them to promise to send a car for her: Mr. Slater would have to fetch her himself in the two-seater runabout: everything else was out.

She dressed nervously, in a dark-green dress with a few modest jewels. Looking at herself in the mirror, she still thought herself slim, young looking and distinguished. She did not see how old-fashioned she was, with her uncompromising erectness, her glistening knob of silver hair sticking out behind, and her long dress.

It was a three-mile drive in the rain, to the small country town. She sat next to old Slater, who was used to driving horses and was nervous and clumsy with a car, without saying a word. He thankfully deposited her at the gate of St. Barnabas' School.

It was almost half-past seven. The schoolroom was packed and buzzing with excitement. "I'm afraid we haven't a seat left, Mrs. Barlow!" said Jackson, one of the church sidesmen, who was standing guard in the school porch, where people were still fighting to get in. He faced her in consternation. She faced him in consternation. "Well, I shall have to stay somewhere, till Mr. Barlow can drive me home," she said. "Couldn't you put me a chair somewhere?"

Worried and flustered, he went worrying and flustering the other people in charge. The schoolroom was simply packed solid. But Mr. Simmons, the leading grocer, gave up his chair in the front row to Mrs. Barlow, whilst he sat in a chair right under the stage, where he couldn't see a thing. But he could see Mrs. Barlow seated between his wife and daughter, speaking a word or two to them occasionally, and that was enough.

The lights went down: *The Shoes of Shagput* was about to begin. The amateur curtains were drawn back, disclosing the little amateur stage with a white amateur back-cloth daubed to represent a Moorish courtyard. In stalked Percy, dressed as a Moor, his face darkened. He looked quite handsome, his pale grey eyes queer and startling in his dark face. But he was afraid of the audience — he spoke away from them, stalking around clumsily. After a certain amount of would-be funny dialogue, in tripped the heroine, Alice Howells, of course. She was an Eastern houri, in white gauze Turkish trousers, silver veil, and — the blue moccasins. The whole stage was white, save for her blue moccasins, Percy's dark-green sash, and a negro boy's red fez.

When Mrs. Barlow saw the blue moccasins, a little bomb of rage exploded in her. This, of all places! The blue moccasins that she had bought in the western deserts! The blue moccasins that were not so blue as her own eyes! *Her* blue moccasins! On the feet of that creature, Mrs. Howells.

Alice Howells was not afraid of the audience. She looked full at them, lifting her silver veil. And of course she saw Mrs. Barlow, sitting there like the Ancient of Days in judgment, in the front row. And a bomb of rage exploded in *her* breast too.

In the play, Alice was the wife of the grey-bearded old Caliph, but she captured the love of the young Ali, otherwise Percy, and the whole business was the attempt of these two to evade Caliph and negro-eunuchs and ancient crones, and get into each other's arms. The blue shoes were very important: for while the sweet Leila wore them, the gallant Ali was to know there was danger. But when she took them off, he might approach her.

It was all quite childish, and everybody loved it, and Miss M'Leod might have been quite complacent about it all, had not Alice Howells got her monkey up, so to speak. Alice with a lot of make-up, looked boldly handsome. And suddenly bold she was, bold as the devil. All these years the poor young widow had been "good," slaving in the parish, and only even flirting just to cheer things up, never going very far and knowing she could never get anything out of it, but determined never to mope.

Now the sight of Miss M'Leod sitting there so erect, so coolly "higher plane," and calmly superior, suddenly let loose a devil in Alice Howells. All her limbs went suave and molten, as her young sex, long pent up, flooded even to her finger-tips. Her voice was strange, even to herself, with its long, plaintive notes. She felt all her movements soft and fluid, she felt herself like living liquid. And it was lovely. Underneath it all was the sting of malice against Miss M'Leod, sitting there so erect, with her great knob of white hair.

Alice's business, as the lovely Leila, was to be seductive to the rather heavy Percy. And seductive she was. In two minutes, she had him spellbound. He saw nothing of the audience. A faint, fascinated grin came on to his face, as he acted up to the young woman in the Turkish trousers. His rather full, hoarse voice changed and became clear, with a new, naked clang in it. When the two sang together, in the simple banal duets of the play, it was with a most fascinating intimacy. And when, at the end of Act One, the lovely Leila kicked off the blue moccasins, saying: "Away, shoes of bondage, shoes of sorrow!" and danced a little dance all alone, barefoot, in her Turkish trousers, in front of her fascinated hero, his smile was so spellbound that everybody else was spellbound too.

Miss M'Leod's indignation knew no bounds. When the blue moccasins were kicked across the stage by the brazen Alice, with the words: "Away, shoes of bondage, shoes of sorrow!" the elder woman grew pink with fury, and it was all she could do not to rise and snatch the moccasins from the stage, and bear them away. She sat in speechless indignation during the brief curtain between Act One and Act Two. Her moccasins! Her blue moccasins! Of the sacred blue colour, the turquoise of heaven.

But there they were, in Act Two, on the feet of the bold Alice. It was becoming too much. And the love-scenes between Percy and the young woman were becoming nakedly shameful. Alice grew worse and worse. She was worked up now, caught in her own spell, and unconscious of everything save of him, and the sting of that other woman, who presumed to own him. Own him? Ha-ha! For he was fascinated. The queer smile on his face, the concentrated gleam of his eyes, the queer way he leaned forward from his loins towards her, the new, reckless, throaty twang in his voice — the audience had before their eyes a man spellbound and lost in passion.

Miss M'Leod sat in shame and torment, as if her chair was red-hot. She too was fast losing her normal consciousness, in the spell of rage. She was outraged. The second Act was working to its climax. The climax came. The lovely Leila kicked off the blue shoes: "Away, shoes of bondage, away!" and flew barefoot to the enraptured Ali, flinging herself into his arms. And if ever a man was gone in sheer desire, it was Percy, as he pressed the woman's lithe form against his body, and seemed unconsciously to envelop her, unaware of everything else. While she, blissful in his spell, but still aware of the audience and of the superior Miss M'Leod, let herself be wrapped closer and closer.

Miss M'Leod rose to her feet and looked towards the door. But the way out was packed with people standing holding their breath as the two on the stage remained wrapped in each other's arms, and the three fiddles and the flute softly woke up. Miss M'Leod could not bear it. She was on her feet, and beside herself. She could not get out. She could not sit down again.

"Percy!" she said, in a low clear voice. "Will you hand me my moccasins?"

He lifted his face like a man startled in a dream, lifted his face from the shoulder of his Leila. His gold-grey eyes were like softly-startled flames. He looked in sheer horrified wonder at the little white-haired woman standing below.

"Eh!" he said, purely dazed.

"Will you please hand me my moccasins!" — and she pointed to where they lay on the stage.

Alice had stepped away from him, and was gazing at the risen viper of the little elderly woman on the tip of the audience. Then she watched him move across the stage, bending forward from the loins in his queer mesmerized way, pick up the blue moccasins, and stoop down to hand them over the edge of the stage to his wife, who reached up for them.

"Thank you!" Miss M'Leod, seating herself, with the blue moccasins in her lap.

Alice recovered her composure, gave a sign to the little orchestra, and began to sing at once, strong and assured, to sing her part in the duet that closed the Act. She knew she could command public opinion in her favour.

He too recovered at once, the little smile came back on his face, he calmly forgot his wife again as he sang his share in the duet. It was finished. The curtains were pulled to. There was immense cheering. The curtains opened, and Alice and Percy bowed to the audience, smiling both of them their peculiar secret smile, while Miss M'Leod sat with the blue moccasins in her lap.

The curtains were closed, it was the long interval. After a few moments of hesitation, Mrs. Barlow rose with dignity, gathered her wrap over her arm, and with the blue moccasins in her hand, moved towards the door. Way was respectfully made for her.

"I should like to speak to Mr. Barlow," she said to Jackson, who had anxiously ushered her in, and now would anxiously usher her out.

"Yes, Mrs. Barlow."

He led her round to the smaller class-room at the back, that acted as dressing-room. The amateur actors were drinking lemonade, and chattering freely. Mrs. Howells came forward, and Jackson whispered the news to her. She turned to Percy.

"Percy, Mrs. Barlow wants to speak to you. Shall I come with you?"

"Speak to me? Aye, come on with me."

The two followed the anxious Jackson into the other half-lighted class-room, where Mrs. Barlow stood in her wrap, holding the moccasins. She was very pale, and she watched the two butter-muslin Turkish figures enter, as if they could not possibly be real. She ignored Mrs. Howells entirely.

"Percy," she said, "I want you to drive me home."

"Drive you home!" he echoed.

"Yes, please!"

"Why — when?" he said, with vague bluntness.

"Now — if you don't mind ——"

"What — in this get-up?" He looked at himself.

"I could wait while you changed."

There was a pause. He turned and looked at Alice Howells, and Alice Howells looked at him. The two women saw each other out of the corners of their eyes: but it was beneath notice. He turned to his wife, his black face ludicrously blank, his eyebrows cocked.

"Well, you see," he said, "it's rather awkward. I can hardly hold up the third Act while I've taken you home and got back here again, can I?"

"So you intend to play in the third Act?" she asked with cold ferocity.

"Why, I must, mustn't I?" he said blankly.

"Do you *wish* to?" she said, in all her intensity.

"I do, naturally. I want to finish the thing up properly," he replied, in the utter innocence of his head; about his heart he knew nothing.

She turned sharply away.

"Very well!" she said. And she called to Jackson, who was standing dejectedly by the door: "Mr. Jackson, will you please find some car or conveyance to take me home?"

"Aye! I say, Mr. Jackson," called Percy in his strong, democratic voice, going forward to the man. "Ask Tom Lomas if he'll do me a good turn and get my car out of the rectory garage, to drive Mrs. Barlow home. Aye, ask Tom Lomas! And if not him, ask Mr. Pilkington — Leonard. The key's there. You don't mind do you? I'm ever so much obliged ——"

The three were left awkwardly alone again.

"I expect you've had enough with two acts," said Percy soothingly to his wife. "These things aren't up to your mark. I know it. They're only child's play. But, you see, they please the people. We've got a packed house, haven't we?"

His wife had nothing to answer. He looked so ludicrous, with his dark-brown face and butter-muslin bloomers. And his mind was so ludicrously innocent. His body, however, was not so ridiculously innocent as his mind, as she knew when he turned to the other woman.

"You and I, we're more on the nonsense level, aren't we?" he said, with the new, throaty clang of naked intimacy in his voice. His wife shivered.

"Absolutely on the nonsense level," said Alice, with easy assurance.

She looked into his eyes, then she looked at the blue moccasins in the hand of the other woman. He gave a little start, as if realising something for himself.

At that moment Tom Lomas looked in, saying heartily: "Right you are, Percy! I'll have my car here in half a tick. I'm more handy with it than yours."

"Thanks, old man! You're a Christian."

"Try to be — especially when you turn Turk! Well ——" He disappeared.

"I say, Lina," said Percy in his most amiable democratic way, "would you mind leaving the moccasins for the next act? We s'll be in a bit of a hole without them."

Miss M'Leod faced him and stared at him with the full blast of her forget-me-not blue eyes, from her white face.

"Will you pardon me if I don't?" she said.

"What!" he exclaimed. "Why? Why not? It's nothing but play, to amuse the people. I can't see how it can hurt the *moccasins*. I understand you don't quite like seeing me make a fool of myself. But, anyhow, I'm a bit of a born fool. What?" — and his blackened face laughed with a Turkish laugh. "Oh, yes, you have to realise I rather enjoy playing the fool," he resumed. "And, after all, it doesn't really hurt *you*, now does it? Shan't you leave us those moccasins for the last act?"

She looked at him, then at the moccasins in her hand. No, it was useless to yield to so ludicrous a person. The vulgarity of his wheedling, the commonness of the whole performance! It was useless to yield even the moccasins. It would be treachery to herself.

"I'm sorry," she said. "But I'd so much rather they weren't used for this kind of thing. I never intended them to be." She stood with her face averted from the ridiculous couple.

He changed as if she had slapped his face. He sat down on top of the low pupils' desk and gazed with glazed interest round the class-room. Alice sat beside him, in her white gauze and her bedizened face. They were like two rebuked sparrows on one twig, he with his great, easy, intimate limbs, she so light and alert. And as he sat he sank into an unconscious physical sympathy with her. Miss M'Leod walked towards the door.

"You'll have to think of something as'll do instead," he muttered to Alice in a low voice, meaning the blue moccasins. And leaning down, he drew off one of the grey shoes she had on, caressing her foot with the slip of his hand over its slim, bare shape. She hastily put the bare foot behind her other, shod foot.

Tom Lomas poked in his head, his overcoat collar turned up to his ears.

"Car's here," he said.

"Right-o! Tom! I'll chalk it up to thee, lad!" said Percy with heavy breeziness. Then, making a great effort with himself, he rose heavily and went across to the door, to his wife, saying to her, in the same stiff voice of false heartiness:

"You'll be as right as rain with Tom. You won't mind if I don't come out? No! I'd better not show myself to the audience. Well — I'm glad you came, if only for a while. Good-bye then! I'll be home after the service — but I shan't disturb you. Good-bye! Don't get wet now ——" And his voice, falsely cheerful, stiff with anger, ended in a clang of indignation.

Alice Howells sat on the infants' bench in silence. She was ignored. And she was unhappy, uneasy, because of the scene.

Percy closed the door after his wife. Then he turned with a looming slowness to Alice, and said in a hoarse whisper: "Think o' that, now!"

She looked up at him anxiously. His face, in its dark pigment, was transfigured with indignant anger. His yellow-grey eyes blazed, and a great rush of anger seemed to be surging up volcanic in him. For a second his eyes rested on her upturned, troubled, dark-blue eyes, then glanced away, as if he didn't want to look at her in his anger. Even so, she felt a touch of tenderness in his glance.

"And that's all she's ever cared about — her own things and her own way," he said, in the same hoarse whisper, hoarse with suddenly-released rage. Alice Howells hung her head in silence.

"Not another damned thing, but what's her own, her own —
and her own holy way — damned holy-holy-holy, all to herself."
His voice shook with hoarse, whispering rage, burst out at last.

Alice Howells looked up at him in distress.

"Oh, don't say it!" she said. "I'm sure she's fond of you."

"*Fond* of me! Fond of *me!*" he blazed, with a grin of trans-
cendent irony. "It makes her sick to look at me. I am a hairy
brute, I own it. Why, she's never once touched me to be fond
of me — never once — though she pretends sometimes. But a
man knows ———" and he made a grimace of contempt. "He
knows when a woman's just stroking him, good doggie! — and
when she's really a bit woman-fond of him. That woman's never
been real fond of anybody or anything, all her life — she couldn't,
for all her show of kindness. She's limited to herself, that woman
is; and I've looked up to her as if she was God. More fool me!
If God's not good-natured and good-hearted, then what is
He ——— ?"

Alice sat with her head dropped, realising once more that men
aren't really fooled. She was upset, shaken by his rage, and frightened, as if she too were guilty. He had sat down blankly beside
her. She glanced up at him.

"Never mind!" she said soothingly. "You'll like her again tomorrow."

He looked down at her with a grin, a grey sort of grin. "Are
you going to stroke me 'good doggie!' as well?" he said.

"Why?" she asked, blank.

But he did not answer. Then after a while he resumed:
"Wouldn't even leave the moccasins! And she's hung them up in
my room, left them there for years — any man'd consider they
were his. And I did want this show to-night to be a success! What
are you going to do about it?"

"I've sent over for a pair of pale-blue satin bed-slippers of
mine — they'll do just as well," she replied.

"Aye! For all that, it's done me in."

"You'll get over it."

"Happen so! She's curdled my inside, for all that. I don't know
how I'm going to be civil to her."

"Perhaps you'd better stay at the rectory to-night," she said
softly.

He looked into her eyes. And in that look, he transferred his allegiance.

"*You* don't want to be drawn in, do you?" he asked, with troubled tenderness.

But she only gazed with wide, darkened eyes into his eyes, so she was like an open, dark doorway to him. His heart beat thick, and the faint, breathless smile of passion came into his eyes again.

"You'll have to go on, Mrs. Howells. We can't keep them waiting any longer."

It was Jim Stokes, who was directing the show. They heard the clapping and stamping of the impatient audience.

"Goodness!" cried Alice Howells, darting to the door.

ISAAC BABEL (1894–1939 or 1940)   Babel, the son of a Jewish shopkeeper, was born into the ghetto Moldavanka in Odessa, Russia. He had a typical Orthodox Jewish education which he found unreal and stifling. Although anti-semitism was strong in Russia at this time, the Jews in cosmopolitan Odessa did well — many were rich, and Jewish intellectual life flourished. The Jewish gangs of Babel's ghetto appear in many of his comic stories.

According to Lionel Trilling's introduction to the *Collected Stories of Isaac Babel,* the crucial event in Babel's life occurred at the age of nine when he saw his father kneeling in suppliance before a "Cossack captain on a horse, who said 'At your service,' and touched his fur cap with his yellow-gloved hand and politely paid no heed to the mob looting the Babel store." The initiation rites which pervade Babel's stories suggest the humiliation or terror that precedes the quest for strength, endurance, mastery, or some form of manly proof.

As a boy, Babel wrote stories in French and admired the works of Flaubert and Maupassant. He was a physically awkward child and at twenty-one left Odessa to be an intellectual — "a man, with spectacles on his nose and autumn in his heart." He lived illegally in St. Petersburg where Gorky published two of his stories. Gorky came to believe that these early stories were literary accidents of fate and advised Babel to leave the intellectual life and "go among the people." Babel then enlisted with the Tsar's army and served in other military expeditions. At twenty-six he was made supply officer to a Cossack regiment in Poland — a rare position for a Jew — and his collection of stories entitled *Red Cavalry* came from this experience.

Babel made a speech before the Writer's Congress in Russia in 1934 during a time of apparent leniency in which he said that he was "the master of the genre of silence." In 1937 he was arrested and put in a concentration camp where he died.

DI GRASSO
A Tale of Odessa

Isaac Babel

I was fourteen, and of the undauntable fellowship of dealers in theater tickets. My boss was a tricky customer with a permanently screwed-up eye and enormous silky handle bars; Nick Schwarz was his name. I came under his sway in that unhappy year when the Italian Opera flopped in Odessa. Taking a lead from the critics on the local paper, our impresario decided not to import Anselmi and Tito Ruffo as guest artistes but to make do with a good stock company. For this he was sorely punished; he went bankrupt, and we with him. We were promised Chaliapin to straighten out our affairs, but Chaliapin wanted three thousand a performance; so instead we had the Sicilian tragedian Di Grasso with his troupe. They arrived at the hotel in peasant carts crammed with children, cats, cages in which Italian birds hopped and skipped. Casting an eye over this gypsy crew, Nick Schwarz opined:

"Children, this stuff won't sell."

When he had settled in, the tragedian made his way to the market with a bag. In the evening he arrived at the theater with another bag. Hardly fifty people had turned up. We tried selling tickets at half-price, but there were no takers.

That evening they staged a Sicilian folk drama, a tale as commonplace as the change from night to day and vice versa. The daughter of a rich peasant pledges her troth to a shepherd. She is faithful to him till one day there drives out from the city a young slicker in a velvet waistcoat. Passing the time of day with the new arrival, the maiden giggled in all the wrong places and fell silent when she shouldn't have. As he listened to them, the shepherd twisted his head this way and that like a startled bird. During the whole of the first act he kept flattening himself against walls, dashing off somewhere, his pants flapping, and on his return gazing wildly about.

"This stuff stinks," said Nick Schwarz in the intermission. "Only place it might go down is some dump like Kremenchug."

The intermission was designed to give the maiden time to grow ripe for betrayal. In the second act we just couldn't recognize her: she behaved insufferably, her thoughts were clearly elsewhere, and she lost no time in handing the shepherd back his ring. Thereupon he led her over to a poverty-stricken but brightly painted image of the Holy Virgin, and said in his Sicilian patois:

"Signora," said he in a low voice, turning away, "the Holy Virgin desires you to give me a hearing. To Giovanni, the fellow from the city, the Holy Virgin will grant as many women as he can cope with; but I need none save you. The Virgin Mary, our stainless intercessor, will tell you exactly the same thing if you ask Her."

The maiden stood with her back to the painted wooden image. As she listened she kept impatiently tapping her foot.

In the third act Giovanni, the city slicker, met his fate. He was having a shave at the village barber's, his powerful male legs thrust out all over the front of the stage. Beneath the Sicilian sun the pleats in his waistcoat gleamed. The scene represented a village fair. In a far corner stood the shepherd; silent he stood there amid the carefree crowd. First he hung his head; then he raised it, and beneath the weight of his attentive and burning gaze Giovanni started stirring and fidgeting in his barber chair, till pushing the barber aside he leaped to his feet. In a voice shaking with passion he demanded that the policeman should remove from the village square all persons of a gloomy and suspicious aspect. The shepherd — the part was played by Di Grasso himself — stood there lost in thought; then he gave a smile, soared into the air, sailed across the stage, plunged down on Giovanni's shoulders, and having bitten through the latter's throat, began, growling and squinting, to suck blood from the wound. Giovanni collapsed, and the curtain, falling noiselessly and full of menace, hid from us killed and killer. Waiting for no more, we dashed to the box office in Theater Lane, which was to open next day, Nick Schwarz beating the rest by a short neck. Came the dawn, and with it the *Odessa News* informed the few people who had been at the theater that they had seen the most remarkable actor of the century.

On this visit Di Grasso played *King Lear, Othello, Civil Death,* Turgenev's *The Parasite,* confirming with every word and every gesture that there is more justice in outbursts of noble passion than in all the joyless rules that run the world.

Tickets for these shows were snapped up at five times face value. Scouting round for ticket-traders, would-be purchasers found them at the inn, yelling their heads off, purple, vomiting a harmless sacrilege.

A pink and dusty sultriness was injected into Theater Lane. Shopkeepers in felt slippers bore green bottles of wine and barrels of olives out onto the pavement. In tubs outside the shops macaroni seethed in foaming water, and the steam from it melted in the distant skies. Old women in men's boots dealt in seashells and souvenirs, pursuing hesitant purchasers with loud cries. Moneyed Jews with beards parted down the middle and combed to either side would drive up to the Northern Hotel and tap discreetly on the doors of fat women with raven hair and little mustaches, Di Grasso's actresses. All were happy in Theater Lane; all, that is, save for one person. I was that person. In those days catastrophe was approaching me: at any moment my father might miss the watch I had taken without his permission and pawned to Nick Schwarz. Having had the gold turnip long enough to get used to it, and being a man who replaced tea as his morning drink by Bessarabian wine, Nick Schwarz, even with his money back, could still not bring himself to return the watch to me. Such was his character. And my father's character differed in no wise from his. Hemmed in by these two characters, I sorrowfully watched other people enjoying themselves. Nothing remained for me but to run away to Constantinople. I had made all the arrangements with the second engineer of the S.S. *Duke of Kent,* but before embarking on the deep I decided to say goodbye to Di Grasso. For the last time he was playing the shepherd who is swung aloft by an incomprehensible power. In the audience were all the Italian colony, with the bald but shapely consul at their head. There were fidgety Greeks and bearded externs with their gaze fastened fanatically upon some point invisible to all other mortals; there was the long-armed Utochkin. Nick Schwarz had even brought his missis, in a violet shawl with a fringe; a woman with all the makings of a grenadier she was, stretching right out to the steppes, and with a sleepy little crumpled face at the far end. When the curtain fell this face was drenched in tears.

"Now you see what love means," she said to Nick as they were leaving the theater.

Stomping ponderously, Madam Schwarz moved along Langeron Street; tears rolled from her fishlike eyes, and the shawl with the fringe shuddered on her obese shoulders. Dragging her mannish soles, rocking her head, she reckoned up, in a voice that made the street re-echo, the women who got on well with their husbands.

" 'Ducky' they're called by their husbands; 'sweetypie' they're called . . ."

The cowed Nick walked along by his wife, quietly blowing on his silky mustaches. From force of habit I followed on behind, sobbing. During a momentary pause Madam Schwarz heard my sobs and turned around.

"See here," she said to her husband, her fisheyes agoggle, "may I not die a beautiful death if you don't give the boy his watch back!"

Nick froze, mouth agape; then came to and, giving me a vicious pinch, thrust the watch at me sideways.

"What can I expect of him," the coarse and tear-muffled voice of Madam Schwarz wailed disconsolately as it moved off into the distance, "what can I expect but beastliness today and beastliness tomorrow? I ask you, how long is a woman supposed to put up with it?"

They reached the corner and turned into Pushkin Street. I stood there clutching the watch, alone; and suddenly, with a distinctness such as I had never before experienced, I saw the columns of the Municipal Building soaring up into the heights, the gas-lit foliage of the boulevard, Pushkin's bronze head touched by the dim gleam of the moon; saw for the first time the things surrounding me as they really were: frozen in silence and ineffably beautiful.

(Translated by Walter Morison)

WILLIAM FAULKNER (1897–1962) Faulkner, the oldest of four brothers, was born in New Albany, Mississippi. The family moved to Oxford when Faulkner's father became treasurer of the University of Mississippi. Faulkner's education was sparse — he left Oxford high school and the University of Mississippi without degrees. After Faulkner had returned from the British Royal Air Force in World War I (before entering the University of Mississippi), he began writing poems and stories. His knowledge of literature came from his voracious reading of Keats, Balzac, Flaubert, Swinburne, Housman, Mallarmé, Wilde, Joyce, Eliot, and Sherwood Anderson. Faulkner mainly worked alone and cared little about a public response: "I think I have written a lot and sent it off to print before I actually realized strangers might read it."

Faulkner's brief journeys — including a stay with Sherwood Anderson, a bookstore job in New York, and a walking trip through Europe — ended back at home in Oxford, Mississippi where he created the saga of Yoknapatawpha County, a comprehensive legend of the Deep South. The fictitious Yoknapatawpha County — "sole owner and proprietor William Faulkner" — is peopled with the old cotton aristocracy, the new planters, storekeepers, mechanics, tenant farmers, carpetbaggers, slaves, sewing machine agents, sharecroppers, woodsmen, housewives, townsmen — black and white, good and bad. Faulkner's characters exist in a "dream state in which you run without moving from a terror in which you cannot believe, toward a safety in which you have no faith." Faulkner dramatizes a fate which his characters cannot change nor understand; he portrays the blind journey on which they are driven. This is the doom Faulkner saw in the South's defeat, corruption, and decline.

In 1950 Faulkner was awarded the Nobel Prize. Among his novels are *The Sound and the Fury* (1929), *As I Lay Dying* (1930), *Light in August* (1932), *Absalom, Absalom!* (1936), *The Hamlet* (1940), *Go Down, Moses* (1942), *Requiem for a Nun* (1951), and *A Fable* (1954). Forty-two of his short stories are included in his *Collected Stories*.

SHINGLES FOR THE LORD

William Faulkner

Pap got up a good hour before daylight and caught the mule and rid down to Killegrew's to borrow the froe and maul. He ought to been back with it in forty minutes. But the sun had rose and I had done milked and fed and was eating my breakfast when he got back, with the mule not only in a lather but right on the edge of the thumps too.

"Fox hunting," he said. "Fox hunting. A seventy-year-old man, with both feet and one knee, too, already in the grave, squatting all night on a hill and calling himself listening to a fox race that he couldn't even hear unless they had come right up onto the same log he was setting on and bayed into his ear trumpet. Give me my breakfast," he told maw. "Whitfield is standing there right this minute, straddle of that board tree with his watch in his hand."

And he was. We rid on past the church, and there was not only Solon Quick's school-bus truck but Reverend Whitfield's old mare too. We tied the mule to a sapling and hung our dinner bucket on a limb, and with pap toting Killegrew's froe and maul and the wedges and me toting our ax, we went on to the board tree where Solon and Homer Bookwright, with their froes and mauls and axes and wedges, was setting on two upended cuts, and Whitfield was standing jest like pap said, in his boiled shirt and his black hat and pants and necktie, holding his watch in his hand. It was gold and in the morning sunlight it looked big as a full-growed squash.

"You're late," he said.

So pap told again about how Old Man Killegrew had been off fox hunting all night, and nobody at home to lend him the froe but Mrs. Killegrew and the cook. And naturally, the cook wasn't going to lend none of Killegrew's tools out, and Mrs. Killegrew was worser deaf than even Killegrew. If you was to run in and tell her the house was afire, she would jest keep on rocking and say she thought so, too, unless she began to holler back to the cook to turn the dogs loose before you could even open your mouth.

"You could have gone yesterday and borrowed the froe," Whitfield said. "You have known for a month now that you had promised this one day out of a whole summer toward putting a roof on the house of God."

"We ain't but two hours late," pap said. "I reckon the Lord will forgive it. He ain't interested in time, nohow. He's interested in salvation."

Whitfield never even waited for pap to finish. It looked to me like he even got taller, thundering down at pap like a cloudburst. "He ain't interested in neither! Why should He be, when He owns them both? And why He should turn around for the poor, mizzling souls of men that can't even borrow tools in time to replace the shingles on His church, I don't know either. Maybe it's just because He made them. Maybe He just said to Himself: 'I made them; I don't know why. But since I did, I Godfrey, I'll roll My sleeves up and drag them into glory whether they will or no!'"

But that wasn't here nor there either now, and I reckon he knowed it, jest like he knowed there wasn't going to be nothing atall here as long as he stayed. So he put the watch back into his pocket and motioned Solon and Homer up, and we all taken off our hats except him while he stood there with his face raised into the sun and his eyes shut and his eyebrows looking like a big iron-gray caterpillar lying along the edge of a cliff. "Lord," he said, "make them good straight shingles to lay smooth, and let them split out easy; they're for You," and opened his eyes and looked at us again, mostly at pap, and went and untied his mare and clumb up slow and stiff, like old men do, and rid away.

Pap put down the froe and maul and laid the three wedges in a neat row on the ground and taken up the ax.

"Well, men," he said, "let's get started. We're already late."

"Me and Homer ain't," Solon said. "We was here." This time him and Homer didn't set on the cuts. They squatted on their heels. Then I seen that Homer was whittling on a stick. I hadn't noticed it before.

"I make it two hours and a little over," Solon said. "More or less."

Pap was still about half stooped over, holding the ax. "It's nigher one," he said. "But call it two for the sake of the argument. What about it?"

"What argument?" Homer said.

"All right," pap said. "Two hours then. What about it?"

"Which is three man-hour units a hour, multiplied by two hours," Solon said. "Or a total of six work units." When the WPA first come to Yoknapatawpha County and started to giving out jobs and grub and mattresses, Solon went in to Jefferson to get on it. He would drive his school-bus truck the twenty-two miles in to town every morning and come back that night. He done that for almost a week before he found out he would not only have to sign his farm off into somebody else's name, he couldn't even own and run the school bus that he had built himself. So he come back that night and never went back no more, and since then hadn't nobody better mention WPA to him unless they aimed to fight, too, though every now and then he would turn up with something all figured down into work units like he done now. "Six units short."

"Four of which you and Homer could have already worked out while you was setting here waiting on me," pap said.

"Except that we didn't," Solon said. "We promised Whitfield two units of twelve three-unit hours toward getting some new shingles on the church roof. We been here ever since sunup, waiting for the third unit to show up, so we could start. You don't seem to kept up with these modren ideas about work that's been flooding and uplifting the country in the last few years."

"What modren ideas?" pap said. "I didn't know there was but one idea about work — until it is done, it ain't done, and when it is done, it is."

Homer made another long, steady whittle on the stick. His knife was sharp as a razor.

Solon taken out his snuffbox and filled the top and tilted the snuff into his lip and offered the box to Homer, and Homer shaken his head, and Solon put the top back on the box and put the box back into his pocket.

"So," pap said, "jest because I had to wait two hours for a old seventy-year man to get back from fox hunting that never had no more business setting out in the woods all night than he would ·'a' had setting all night in a highway juke joint, we all three have got to come back here tomorrow to finish them two hours that you and Homer — "

"I ain't," Solon said. "I don't know about Homer. I promised Whitfield one day. I was here at sunup to start it. When the sun goes down, I will consider I have done finished it."

"I see," pap said. "I see. It's me that's got to come back. By myself. I got to break into a full morning to make up them two hours that you and Homer spent resting. I got to spend two hours of the next day making up for the two hours of the day before that you and Homer never even worked."

"It's going to more than jest break into a morning," Solon said. "It's going to wreck it. There's six units left over. Six one-man-hour units. Maybe you can work twice as fast as me and Homer put together and finish them in four hours, but I don't believe you can work three times as fast and finish in two."

Pap was standing up now. He was breathing hard. We could hear him. "So," he said. "So." He swung the ax and druv the blade into one of the cuts and snatched it up onto its flat end, ready to split. "So I'm to be penalized a half day of my own time, from my own work that's waiting for me at home right this minute, to do six hours more work than the work you fellers lacked two hours of even doing atall, purely and simply because I am jest a average hard-working farmer trying to do the best he can, instead of a durn froe-owning millionaire named Quick or Bookwright."

They went to work then, splitting the cuts into bolts and riving the bolts into shingles for Tull and Snopes and the others that had promised for tomorrow to start nailing onto the church roof when they finished pulling the old shingles off. They set flat on the ground in a kind of circle, with their legs spraddled out on either side of the propped-up bolt, Solon and Homer working light and easy and steady as two clocks ticking, but pap making every lick of hisn like he was killing a moccasin. If he had jest swung the maul half as fast as he swung it hard, he would have rove as many shingles as Solon and Homer together, swinging the maul up over his head and holding it there for what looked like a whole minute sometimes and then swinging it down onto the blade of the froe, and not only a shingle flying off every lick but the froe going on into the ground clean up to the helve eye, and pap setting there wrenching at it slow and steady and hard, like he jest wished it would try to hang on a root or a rock and stay there.

"Here, here," Solon said. "If you don't watch out you won't have nothing to do neither during the six extra units tomorrow morning but rest."

Pap never even looked up. "Get out of the way," he said. And Solon done it. If he hadn't moved the water bucket, pap would have split it, too, right on top of the bolt, and this time the whole shingle went whirling past Solon's shin jest like a scythe blade.

"What you ought to do is to hire somebody to work out them extra overtime units," Solon said.

"With what?" pap said. "I ain't had no WPA experience in dickering over labor. Get out of the way."

But Solon had already moved this time. Pap would have had to change his whole position or else made this one curve. So this one missed Solon, too, and pap set there wrenching the froe, slow and hard and steady, back out of the ground.

"Maybe there's something else besides cash you might be able to trade with," Solon said. "You might use that dog."

That was when pap actually stopped. I didn't know it myself then either, but I found it out a good long time before Solon did. Pap set there with the maul up over his head and the blade of the froe set against the block for the next lick, looking up at Solon. "The dog?" he said.

It was a kind of mixed hound, with a little bird dog and some collie and maybe a considerable of almost anything else, but it would ease through the woods without no more noise than a hant and pick up a squirrel's trail on the ground and bark jest once, unless it knowed you was where you could see it, and then tip-toe that trail out jest like a man and never make another sound until it treed, and only then when it knowed you hadn't kept in sight of it. It belonged to pap and Vernon Tull together. Will Varner give it to Tull as a puppy, and pap raised it for a half interest; me and him trained it and it slept in my bed with me until it got so big maw finally run it out of the house, and for the last six months Solon had been trying to buy it. Him and Tull had agreed on two dollars for Tull's half of it, but Solon and pap was still six dollars apart on ourn, because pap said it was worth ten dollars of anybody's money and if Tull wasn't going to collect his full half of that, he was going to collect it for him.

"So that's it," pap said. "Them things wasn't work units atall. They was dog units."

"Jest a suggestion," Solon said. "Jest a friendly offer to keep them runaway shingles from breaking up your private business for six hours tomorrow morning. You sell me your half of that trick overgrown fyce and I'll finish these shingles for you."

"Naturally including them six extra units of one dollars," pap said.

"No, no," Solon said. "I'll pay you the same two dollars for your half of that dog that me and Tull agreed on for his half of it. You meet me here tomorrow morning with the dog and you can go on back home or wherever them urgent private affairs are located, and forget about that church roof."

For about ten seconds more, pap set there with the maul up over his head, looking at Solon. Then for about three seconds he wasn't looking at Solon or at nothing else. Then he was looking at Solon again. It was jest exactly like after about two and nine-tenths seconds he found out he wasn't looking at Solon, so he looked back at him as quick as he could. "Hah," he said. Then he began to laugh. It was laughing all right, because his mouth was open and that's what it sounded like. But it never went no further back than his teeth and it never come nowhere near reaching as high up as his eyes. And he never said "Look out" this time neither. He jest shifted fast on his hips and swung the maul down, the froe done already druv through the bolt and into the ground while the shingle was still whirling off to slap Solon across the shin.

Then they went back at it again. Up to this time I could tell pap's licks from Solon's and Homer's, even with my back turned, not because they was louder or steadier, because Solon and Homer worked steady, too, and the froe never made no especial noise jest going into the ground, but because they was so infrequent; you would hear five or six of Solon's and Homer's little polite chipping licks before you would hear pap's froe go "chug!" and know that another shingle had went whirling off somewhere. But from now on pap's sounded jest as light and quick and polite as Solon's or Homer's either, and, if anything, even a little faster, with the shingles piling up steadier than I could stack them, almost; until now there was going to be more than a plenty of them for Tull and the others to shingle with tomorrow, right on up to noon, when we heard Armstid's farm bell, and Solon laid his froe and maul down and looked at his watch too. And I wasn't so far away neither, but by the time I caught up with pap he had untied the mule from the sapling and was already on it. And maybe Solon and Homer thought they had pap, and maybe for a minute I did, too, but I jest wish they could have seen his face then. He reached our dinner bucket down from the limb and handed it to me.

"Go on and eat," he said. "Don't wait for me. Him and his work units. If he wants to know where I went, tell him I forgot something and went home to get it. Tell him I had to go back home to get two spoons for us to eat our dinner with. No, don't tell him that. If he hears I went somewhere to get something I needed to use, even if it's jest a tool to eat with, he will refuse to believe I jest went home, for the reason that I don't own anything there that even I would borrow." He hauled the mule around and heeled him in the flank. Then he pulled up again. "And when I come back, no matter what I say, don't pay no attention to it. No matter what happens, don't you say nothing. Don't open your mouth a-tall, you hear?"

Then he went on, and I went back to where Solon and Homer was setting on the running board of Solon's school-bus truck, eating, and sho enough Solon said jest exactly what pap said he was going to.

"I admire his optimism, but he's mistaken. If it's something he needs that he can't use his natural hands and feet for, he's going somewhere else than jest his own house."

We had jest went back to the shingles when pap rid up and got down and tied the mule back to the sapling and come and taken up the ax and snicked the blade into the next cut.

"Well, men," he said, "I been thinking about it. I still don't think it's right, but I still ain't thought of anything to do about it. But somebody's got to make up for them two hours nobody worked this morning, and since you fellers are two to one against me, it looks like it's going to be me that makes them up. But I got work waiting at home for me tomorrow. I got corn that's crying out loud for me right now. Or maybe that's jest a lie too.

Maybe the whole thing is, I don't mind admitting here in private that I been outfigured, but I be dog if I'm going to set here by myself tomorrow morning admitting it in public. Anyway, I ain't. So I'm going to trade with you, Solon. You can have the dog."

Solon looked at pap. "I don't know as I want to trade now," he said.

"I see," pap said. The ax was still stuck in the cut. He began to pump it up and down to back it out.

"Wait," Solon said. "Put that durn ax down." But pap held the ax raised for the lick, looking at Solon and waiting. "You're swapping me half a dog for a half a day's work," Solon said.

"Your half of the dog for that half a day's work you still owe on these shingles."

"And the two dollars," pap said. "That you and Tull agreed on. I sell you half the dog for two dollars, and you come back here tomorrow and finish the shingles. You give me the two dollars now, and I'll meet you here in the morning with the dog, and you can show me the receipt from Tull for his half then."

"Me and Tull have already agreed," Solon said.

"All right," pap said. "Then you can pay Tull his two dollars and bring his receipt with you without no trouble."

"Tull will be at the church tomorrow morning, pulling off them old shingles," Solon said.

"All right," pap said. "Then it won't be no trouble at all for you to get a receipt from him. You can stop at the church when you pass. Tull ain't named Grier. He won't need to be off somewhere borrowing a crowbar."

So Solon taken out his purse and paid pap the two dollars and they went back to work. And now it looked like they really was trying to finish that afternoon, not jest Solon, but even Homer, that didn't seem to be concerned in it nohow, and pap, that had already swapped a half a dog to get rid of whatever work Solon claimed would be left over. I quit trying to stay up with them; I jest stacked shingles.

Then Solon laid his froe and maul down. "Well, men," he said, "I don't know what you fellers think, but I consider this a day."

"All right," pap said. "You are the one to decide when to quit, since whatever elbow units you consider are going to be shy tomorrow will be yourn."

"That's a fact," Solon said, "And since I am giving a day and a half to the church instead of jest a day, like I started out doing, I reckon I better get on home and tend to a little of my own work." He picked up his froe and maul and ax, and went to his truck and stood waiting for Homer to come and get in.

"I'll be here in the morning with the dog," pap said.

"Sholy," Solon said. It sounded like he had forgot about the dog, or that it wasn't no longer any importance. But he stood there again and looked hard and quiet at pap for about a second. "And a bill of sale from Tull for his half of it. As you say, it won't be no trouble a-tall to get that from him." Him and Homer got into the truck and he started the engine. You couldn't say jest what it was. It was almost like Solon was hurrying himself, so pap wouldn't have to make any excuse or pretense toward doing or not doing anything. "I have always understood the fact that lightning don't have to hit twice is one of the reasons why they named it lightning. So getting lightning-struck is a mistake that might happen to any man. The mistake I seem to made is, I never realized in time that what I was looking at was a cloud. I'll see you in the morning."

"With the dog," pap said.

"Certainly," Solon said, again like it had slipped his mind completely. "With the dog."

Then him and Homer drove off. Then pap got up.

"What?" I said. "What? You swapped him your half of Tull's dog for that half a day's work tomorrow. Now what?"

"Yes," pap said. "Only before that I had already swapped Tull a half a day's work pulling off them old shingles tomorrow, for Tull's half of that dog. Only we ain't going to wait until tomorrow. We're going to pull them shingles off tonight, and without no more racket about it than is necessary. I don't aim to have nothing on my mind tomorrow but watching Mr. Solon Work-Unit Quick trying to get a bill of sale for two dollars or ten dollars either on the other half of that dog. And we'll do it tonight. I don't want him jest to find out at sunup tomorrow that he is too late. I want him to find out then that even when he laid down to sleep he was already too late."

So we went back home and I fed and milked while pap went down to Killegrew's to carry the froe and maul back and to borrow a crowbar. But of all places in the world and doing what under the sun with it. Old Man Killegrew had went and lost his crowbar out of a boat into forty feet of water. And pap said how he come within a inch of going to Solon's and borrowing his crowbar out of pure poetic justice, only Solon might have smelled the rat jest from the idea of the crowbar. So pap went to Armstid's and borrowed hisn and come back and we et supper and cleaned and filled the lantern while maw still tried to find out what we was up to that couldn't wait till morning.

We left her still talking, even as far as the front gate, and come on back to the church, walking this time, with the rope and crowbar and a hammer for me, and the lantern still dark. Whitfield and Snopes was unloading a ladder from Snopes' wagon when we passed the church on the way home before dark, so all we had to do was to set the ladder up against the church. Then pap clumb up onto the roof with the lantern and pulled off shingles until he could hang the lantern inside behind the decking, where it could shine out through the cracks in the planks, but you couldn't see it unless you was passing in the road, and by that time anybody would 'a' already heard us. Then I clumb up with the rope, and pap reached it through the decking and around a rafter and back and tied the ends around our waists, and we started. And we went at it. We had them old shingles jest raining down, me using the claw hammer and pap using the crowbar, working the bar under a whole patch of shingles at one time and then laying back on the bar like in one more lick or if the crowbar ever happened for one second to get a solid holt, he would tilt up that whole roof at one time like a hinged box lid.

That's exactly what he finally done. He laid back on the bar and this time it got a holt. It wasn't jest a patch of shingles, it was a whole section of decking, so that when he lunged back he snatched that whole section of roof from around the lantern like you would shuck a corn nubbin. The lantern was hanging on a nail. He never even moved the nail, he just pulled the board off of it, so that it looked like for a whole minute I watched the lantern, and the crowbar, too, setting there in the empty air in a little mess of floating shingles, with the empty nail still sticking through the bail of the lantern, before the whole thing started down into the church. It hit the floor and bounced once. Then it hit the floor again, and this time the whole church jest blowed up into a pit of yellow jumping fire, with me and pap hanging over the edge of it on two ropes.

I don't know what become of the rope nor how we got out of it. I don't remember climbing down. Jest pap yelling behind me and pushing me about halfway down the ladder and then throwing me the rest of the way by a handful of my overhalls, and then we was both on the ground, running for the water barrel. It set under the gutter spout at the side, and Armstid was there then; he had happened to go out to his lot about a hour back and seen the lantern on the church roof, and it stayed on his mind until finally he come up to see what was going on, and got there jest in time to stand yelling back and forth with pap across the water barrel. And I believe we still would have put it out. Pap turned and squatted against the barrel and got a holt of it over his shoulder and stood up with that barrel that was almost full and run around the corner and up the steps of the church and hooked his toe on the top step and come down with the barrel busting on top of him and knocking him cold out as a wedge.

So we had to drag him back first, and maw was there then, and Mrs. Armstid about the same time, and me and Armstid run with the two fire buckets to the spring, and when we got back there was a plenty there, Whitfield, too, with more buckets, and we done what we could, but the spring was two hundred yards away and ten buckets emptied it and it taken five minutes to fill again, and so finally we all jest stood around where pap had come to again with a big cut on his head and watched it go. It was a old church, long dried out, and full of old colored-picture charts that Whitfield had accumulated for more than fifty years, that the lantern had lit right in the middle of when it finally exploded. There was a special nail where he would keep a old long nightshirt he would wear to baptize in. I would use to watch it all the time during church and Sunday school, and me and the other boys would go past the church sometimes jest to peep in at it, because to a boy of ten it wasn't jest a cloth garment or even a iron armor; it was the old strong Archangel Michael his self, that had fit and strove and conquered sin for so long that it finally had the same contempt for the human beings that returned always to sin as hogs and dogs done that the old strong archangel his self must have had.

For a long time it never burned, even after everything else inside had. We could watch it, hanging there among the fire, not like it had knowed in its time too much water to burn easy, but like it had strove and fit with the devil and all the hosts of hell too long to burn in jest a fire that Res Grier started, trying to beat Solon Quick out of half a dog. But at last it went, too, not in a hurry still, but jest all at once, kind of roaring right on up and out against the stars and the far dark spaces. And then there wasn't nothing but jest pap, drenched and groggy-looking, on the ground, with the rest of us around him, and Whitfield like always in his boiled shirt and his black hat and pants, standing there with his hat on, too, like he had strove too long to save what hadn't ought to been created in the first place, from the damnation it didn't even want to escape, to bother to need to take his hat off in any presence. He looked around at us from under it; we was all there now, all that belonged to that church and used it to be born and marry and die from — us and the Armstids and Tulls, and Bookwright and Quick and Snopes.

"I was wrong," Whitfield said. "I told you we would meet here tomorrow to roof a church. We'll meet here in the morning to raise one."

"Of course we got to have a church," pap said. "We're going to have one. And we're going to have it soon. But there's some of us done already give a day or so this week, at the cost of our own work. Which is right and just, and we're going to give more, and glad to. But I don't believe that the Lord — "

Whitfield let him finish. He never moved. He jest stood there until pap finally run down of his own accord and hushed and set there on the ground mostly not looking at maw, before Whitfield opened his mouth.

"Not you," Whitfield said. "Arsonist."

"Arsonist?" pap said.

"Yes," Whitfield said. "If there is any pursuit in which you can engage without carrying flood and fire and destruction and death behind you, do it. But not one hand shall you lay to this new house until you have proved to us that you are to be trusted again with the powers and capacities of a man." He looked about at us again. "Tull and Snopes and Armstid have already promised for tomorrow. I understand that Quick had another half day he intended — "

"I can give another day," Solon said.

"I can give the rest of the week," Homer said.

"I ain't rushed neither," Snopes said.

"That will be enough to start with, then," Whitfield said. "It's late now. Let us all go home."

He went first. He didn't look back once, at the church or at us. He went to the old mare and clumb up slow and stiff and powerful, and was gone, and we went too, scattering. But I looked back at it. It was jest a shell now, with a red and fading core, and I had hated it at times and feared it at others, and I should have been glad. But there was something that even that fire hadn't even touched. Maybe that's all it was — jest indestructibility — that old man that could plan to build it back while its walls was still fire-fierce and then calmly turn his back and go away because he knowed that the men that never had nothing to give toward the new one but their work would be there at sunup tomorrow, and the day after that, and the day after that, too, as long as it was needed, to give that work to build it back again. So it hadn't gone a-tall; it didn't no more care for that little fire and flood than Whitfield's old baptizing gown had done. Then we was home. Maw had left so fast the lamp was still lit, and we could see pap now, still leaving a puddle where he stood, with a cut across the back of his head where the barrel had busted and the blood-streaked water soaking him to the waist.

"Get them wet clothes off," maw said.

"I don't know as I will or not," pap said. "I been publicly notified that I ain't fitten to associate with white folks, so I publicly notify them same white folks and Methodists, too, not to try to associate with me, or the devil can have the hindmost."

But maw hadn't even listened. When she come back with a pan of water and a towel and the liniment bottle, pap was already in his nightshirt.

"I don't want none of that neither," he said. "If my head wasn't worth busting, it ain't worth patching." But she never paid no mind to that neither. She washed his head off and dried it and put the bandage on and went out again, and pap went and got into bed.

"Hand me my snuff; then you get out of here and stay out too," he said.

But before I could do that maw come back. She had a glass of hot toddy, and she went to the bed and stood there with it, and pap turned his head and looked at it.

"What's that?" he said.

But maw never answered, and then he set up in bed and drawed a long, shuddering breath — we could hear it — and after a minute he put out his hand for the toddy and set there holding it and drawing his breath, and then he taken a sip of it.

"I Godfrey, if him and all of them put together think they can keep me from working on my own church like ary other man, he better be a good man to try it." He taken another sip of the toddy. Then he taken a long one. "Arsonist," he said. "Work units. Dog units. And now arsonist. I Godfrey, what a day!"

ERNEST HEMINGWAY (1899–1961) Hemingway, the son of a doctor, was born and grew up in the fashionable Chicago suburb of Oak Park. He spent his summers in the northern woods of Michigan where his family owned a cabin. Traveling around the woods with his father, Hemingway became aware of the brutality and violence in woodsmen and nature that was later paralleled by the horrors of war. After graduation from high school, he worked for a few months as a reporter on the Kansas City *Star*. In 1918 he served with the Red Cross ambulance corps on the Italian front; his service was cut short, however, when he was severely wounded by the explosion of a mortar shell. He came back to America for a brief period and then returned to Europe, settling in Paris where, for a while, he was foreign correspondent for Hearst's Syndicated News Service.

His early experiences in the Michigan woods, his wound, and his companions among the disillusioned expatriates of post-war Paris — these biographical facts form the central pattern in all of Hemingway's fiction which is, as the critic Philip Young has pointed out, "violence, psychological wounding, escape, and death." Alfred Kazin describes the Hemingway hero in the following terms: "And always below that level of native memories, interspersed with passing sketches of gangsters and bullfights, lay the war. The glazed face of the Hemingway hero, which through its various phases was to become, like Al Capone's, the face of a decade and to appear on a succession of soldiers, bullfighters, explorers, gangsters, and unhappy revolutionaries, emerged slowly in *In Our Time*"(a collection of stories on his youth published in 1924).

Hemingway achieved his first great fame in 1926 with the publication of *The Sun Also Rises* and his fame was confirmed in 1929 with *A Farewell to Arms*. His fascination with bullfighting is reflected in *Death in the Afternoon* (1932). Other works include "The Snows of Kilimanjaro" (1936), *For Whom the Bell Tolls* (1940), and *The Old Man and the Sea* (1952). In 1954 he was awarded the Nobel Prize for Literature.

THE SNOWS OF KILIMANJARO

Ernest Hemingway

Kilimanjaro is a snow covered mountain 19,710 feet high, and is said to be the highest mountain in Africa. Its western summit is called the Masai "Ngàje Ngài," the House of God. Close to the western summit there is the dried and frozen carcass of a leopard. No one has explained what the leopard was seeking at that altitude.

"The marvellous thing is that it's painless," he said. "That's how you know when it starts."

"Is it really?"

"Absolutely. I'm awfully sorry about the odor though. That must bother you."

"Don't! Please don't."

"Look at them," he said. "Now is it sight or is it scent that brings them like that?"

The cot the man lay on was in the wide shade of a mimosa tree and as he looked out past the shade onto the glare of the plain there were three of the big birds squatted obscenely, while in the sky a dozen more sailed, making quick-moving shadows as they passed.

"They've been there since the day the truck broke down," he said. "Today's the first time any have lit on the ground. I watched the way they sailed very carefully at first in case I ever wanted to use them in a story. That's funny now."

"I wish you wouldn't," she said.

"I'm only talking," he said. "It's much easier if I talk. But I don't want to bother you."

"You know it doesn't bother me," she said. "It's that I've gotten so very nervous not being able to do anything. I think we might make it as easy as we can until the plane comes."

"Or until the plane doesn't come."

"Please tell me what I can do. There must be something I can do."

"You can take the leg off and that might stop it, though I doubt it. Or you can shoot me. You're a good shot now. I taught you to shoot didn't I?"

"Please don't talk that way. Couldn't I read to you?"

"Read what?"

"Anything in the book bag that we haven't read."

"I can't listen to it," he said. "Talking is the easiest. We quarrel and that makes the time pass."

"I don't quarrel. I never want to quarrel. Let's not quarrel any more. No matter how nervous we get. Maybe they will be back with another truck today. Maybe the plane will come."

"I don't want to move," the man said. "There is no sense in moving now except to make it easier for you."

"That's cowardly."

"Can't you let a man die as comfortably as he can without calling him names? What's the use of slanging me?"

"You're not going to die."

"Don't be silly. I'm dying now. Ask those bastards." He looked over to where the huge, filthy birds sat, their naked heads sunk in the hunched feathers. A fourth planed down, to run quick-legged and then waddle slowly toward the others.

"They are around every camp. You never notice them. You can't die if you don't give up."

"Where did you read that? You're such a bloody fool."

"You might think about some one else."

"For Christ's sake," he said, "That's been my trade."

He lay then and was quiet for a while and looked across the heat shimmer of the plain to the edge of the bush. There were a few Tommies that showed minute and white against the yellow and, far off, he saw a herd of zebra, white against the green of the bush. This was a pleasant camp under big trees against a hill, with good water, and close by, a nearly dry water hole where sand grouse flighted in the mornings.

"Wouldn't you like me to read?" she asked. She was sitting on a canvas chair beside his cot. "There's a breeze coming up."

"No thanks."

"Maybe the truck will come."

"I don't give a damn about the truck."

"I do."

"You give a damn about so many things that I don't."

"Not so many, Harry."

"What about a drink?"

"It's supposed to be bad for you. It said in Black's to avoid all alcohol. You shouldn't drink."

"Molo!" he shouted.

"Yes Bwana."

"Bring whiskey-soda."

"Yes Bwana."

"You shouldn't," she said. "That's what I mean by giving up. It says it's bad for you. I know it's bad for you."

"No," he said. "It's good for me."

So now it was all over, he thought. So now he would never have a chance to finish it. So this was the way it ended in a bickering over a drink. Since the gangrene started in his right leg he had no pain and with the pain the horror had gone and all he felt now was a great tiredness and anger that this was the end of it. For this, that now was coming, he had very little curiosity. For years it had obsessed him; but now it meant nothing in itself. It was strange how easy being tired enough made it.

Now he would never write the things that he had saved to write until he knew enough to write them well. Well, he would not have to fail at trying to write them either. Maybe you could never write them, and that was why you put them off and delayed the starting. Well he would never know, now.

"I wish we'd never come," the woman said. She was looking at him holding the glass and biting her lip. "You never would have gotten anything like this in Paris. You always said you loved Paris. We could have stayed in Paris or gone anywhere. I'd have gone anywhere. I said I'd go anywhere you wanted. If you wanted to shoot we could have gone shooting in Hungary and been comfortable."

"Your bloody money," he said.

"That's not fair," she said. "It was always yours as much as mine. I left everything and I went wherever you wanted to go and I've done what you wanted to do. But I wish we'd never come here."

"You said you loved it."

"I did when you were all right. But now I hate it. I don't see why that had to happen to your leg. What have we done to have that happen to us?"

"I suppose what I did was to forget to put iodine on it when I first scratched it. Then I didn't pay any attention to it because I never infect. Then, later, when it got bad, it was probably using that weak carbolic solution when the other antiseptics ran out that paralyzed the minute blood vessels and started the gangrene." He looked at her, "What else?"

"I don't mean that."

"If we would have hired a good mechanic instead of a half baked kikuyu driver, he would have checked the oil and never burned out that bearing in the truck."

"I don't mean that."

"If you hadn't left your own people, your goddamned Old Westbury, Saratoga, Palm Beach people to take me on ———"

"Why, I loved you. That's not fair. I love you now. I'll always love you. Don't you love me?"

"No," said the man. "I don't think so. I never have."

"Harry, what are you saying? You're out of your head."

"No. I haven't any head to go out of."

"Don't drink that," she said. "Darling, please don't drink that. We have to do everything we can."

"You do it," he said. "I'm tired."

Now in his mind he saw a railway station at Karagatch and he was standing with his pack and that was the headlight of the Simplon-Orient cutting the dark now and he was leaving Thrace then after the retreat. That was one of the things he had saved to write with, in the morning at breakfast, looking out the window and seeing snow on the mountains in Bulgaria and Nansen's Secretary asking the old man if it were snow and the old man looking at it and saying, No, that's not snow. It's too early for snow. And the Secretary repeating to the other girls, No, you see. It's not snow and them all saying, It's not snow we were mistaken. But it was the snow all right and he sent them on into it when he evolved exchange of populations. And it was snow they tramped along in until they died that winter.

It was snow too that fell all Christmas week that year up in the Gauertal, that year they lived in the woodcutter's house with

*the big square porcelain stove that filled half the room, and they
slept on mattresses filled with beech leaves, the time the deserter
came with his feet bloody in the snow. He said the police were
right behind him and they gave him woolen socks and held the
gendarmes talking until the tracks had drifted over.*

*In Schrunz, on Christmas day, the snow was so bright it hurt
your eyes when you looked out from the weinstube and saw every
one coming home from church. That was where they walked up
the sleigh-smoothed urine-yellowed road along the river with
the steep pine hills, skis heavy on the shoulder, and where they
ran that great run down the glacier above the Madlener-haus,
the snow as smooth to see as cake frosting and as light as powder
and he remembered the noiseless rush the speed made as you
dropped down like a bird.*

*They were snow-bound a week in the Madlener-haus that time
in the blizzard playing cards in the smoke by the lantern light
and the stakes were higher all the time as Herr Lent lost more.
Finally he lost it all. Everything, the skischule money and all the
season's profit and then his capital. He could see him with his
long nose, picking up the cards and then opening, "Sans Voir."
There was always gambling then. When there was no snow you
gambled and when there was too much you gambled. He thought
of all the time in his life he had spent gambling.*

*But he had never written a line of that, nor of that cold, bright
Christmas day with the mountains showing across the plain that
Gardner had flown across the lines to bomb the Austrian officers'
leave train, machine-gunning them as they scattered and ran. He
remembered Gardner afterwards coming into the mess and starting to tell about it. And how quiet it got and then somebody
saying, "You bloody murderous bastard."*

*Those were the same Austrians they killed then that he skied
with later. No not the same. Hans, that he skied with all that
year, had been in the Kaiser-Jägers and when they went hunting
hares together up the little valley above the saw-mill they had
talked of the fighting on Pasubio and of the attack on Pertica
and Asalone and he had never written a word of that. Nor of
Monte Corno, nor the Siete Commum nor of Arsiedo.*

*How many winters had he lived in the Voralberg and the Arl-
berg? It was four and then he remembered the man who had the
fox to sell when they had walked into Bludenz, that time to buy*

*presents, and the cherry-pit taste of good kirsch, the fast-slipping
rush of running powder-snow on crust, singing "Hi! Ho! said
Rolly!" as you ran down the last stretch to the steep drop, taking
it straight, then running the orchard in three turns and out
across the ditch and onto the icy road behind the inn. Knocking
your bindings loose, kicking the skis free and leaning them up
against the wooden wall of the inn, the lamplight coming from
the window, where inside, in the smoky, new-wine smelling
warmth, they were playing the accordion.*

"Where did we stay in Paris?" he asked the woman who was
sitting by him in a canvas chair, now, in Africa.

"At the Crillon. You know that."

"Why do I know that?"

"That's where we always stayed."

"No. Not always."

"There and at the Pavillion Henri-Quatre in St. Germain. You
said you loved it there."

"Love is a dunghill," said Harry. "And I'm the cock that gets
on it to crow."

"If you have to go away," she said, "is it absolutely necessary
to kill off everything you leave behind? I mean do you have to
take away everything? Do you have to kill your horse, and your
wife and burn your saddle and your armour?"

"Yes," he said. "Your damned money was my armour. My Swift
and my Armour."

"Don't."

"All right. I'll stop that. I don't want to hurt you."

"It's a little bit late now."

"All right then. I'll go on hurting you. It's more amusing. The
only thing I ever really liked to do with you I can't do now."

"No, that's not true. You liked to do many things and everything you wanted to do I did."

"Oh, for Christ sake stop bragging, will you?"

He looked at her and saw her crying.

"Listen," he said. "Do you think that it is fun to do this? I
don't know why I'm doing it. It's trying to kill to keep yourself
alive, I imagine. I was all right when we started talking. I didn't
mean to start this, and now I'm crazy as a coot and being as
cruel to you as I can be. Don't pay any attention, darling, to

what I say. I love you, really. You know I love you. I've never
loved any one else the way I love you."

He slipped into the familiar lie he made his bread and butter
by.

"You're sweet to me."

"You bitch," he said. "You rich bitch. That's poetry. I'm full
of poetry now. Rot and poetry. Rotten poetry."

"Stop it. Harry, why do you have to turn into a devil now?"

"I don't like to leave anything," the man said. "I don't like to
leave things behind."

                                *   *   *

It was evening now and he had been asleep. The sun was gone
behind the hill and there was a shadow all across the plain and
the small animals were feeding close to camp; quick dropping
heads and switching tails, he watched them keeping well out
away from the bush now. The birds no longer waited on the
ground. They were all perched heavily in a tree. There were
many more of them. His personal boy was sitting by the bed.

"Memsahib's gone to shoot," the boy said. "Does Bwana want?"

"Nothing."

She had gone to kill a piece of meat and, knowing how he liked
to watch the game, she had gone well away so she would not
disturb this little pocket of the plain that he could see. She was
always thoughtful, he thought. On anything she knew about, or
had read, or that she had ever heard.

It was not her fault that when he went to her he was already
over. How could a woman know that you meant nothing that
you said; that you spoke only from habit and to be comfortable?
After he no longer meant what he said, his lies were more successful with women than when he had told them the truth.

It was not so much that he lied as that there was no truth to
tell. He had had his life and it was over and then he went on
living it again with different people and more money, with the
best of the same places, and some new ones.

You kept from thinking and it was all marvellous. You were
equipped with good insides so that you did not go to pieces that
way, the way most of them had, and you made an attitude that
you cared nothing for the work you used to do, now that you
could no longer do it. But, in yourself, you said that you would
write about these people; about the very rich; that you were

really not of them but a spy in their country; that you would leave it and write of it and for once it would be written by some one who knew what he was writing of. But he would never do it, because each day of not writing, of comfort, of being that which he despised, dulled his ability and softened his will to work so that, finally, he did no work at all. The people he knew now were all much more comfortable when he did not work. Africa was where he had been happiest in the good time of his life, so he had come out here to start again. They had made this safari with the minimum of comfort. There was no hardship; but there was no luxury and he had thought that he could get back into training that way. That in some way he could work the fat off his soul the way a fighter went into the mountains to work and train in order to burn it out of his body.

She had liked it. She said she loved it. She loved anything that was exciting, that involved a change of scene, where there were new people and where things were pleasant. And he had felt the illusion of returning strength of will to work. Now if this was how it ended, and he knew it was, he must not turn like some snake biting itself because its back was broken. It wasn't this woman's fault. If it had not been she it would have been another. If he lived by a lie he should try to die by it. He heard a shot beyond the hill.

She shot very well this good, this rich bitch, this kindly caretaker and destroyer of his talent. Nonsense. He had destroyed his talent himself. Why should he blame this woman because she kept him well? He had destroyed his talent by not using it, by betrayals of himself and what he believed in, by drinking so much that he blunted the edge of his perceptions, by laziness, by sloth, and by snobbery, by pride and by prejudice, by hook and by crook. What was this? A catalogue of old books? What was his talent anyway? It was a talent all right but instead of using it, he had traded on it. It was never what he had done, but always what he could do. And he had chosen to make his living with something else instead of a pen or a pencil. It was strange, too, wasn't it, that when he fell in love with another woman, that woman should always have more money than the last one? But when he no longer was in love, when he was only lying, as to this woman, now, who had the most money of all, who had all the money there was, who had had a husband and children, who had

taken lovers and been dissatisfied with them, and who loved him
dearly as a writer, as a man, as a companion and as a proud possession; it was strange that when he did not love her at all and
was lying, that he should be able to give her more for her money
than when he had really loved.

We must all be cut out for what we do, he thought. However
you make your living is where your talent lies. He had sold
vitality, in one form or another, all his life and when your affections are not too involved you give much better value for the
money. He had found that out but he would never write that,
now, either. No, he would not write that, although it was well
worth writing.

Now she came in sight, walking across the open toward the
camp. She was wearing jodphurs and carrying her rifle. The two
boys had a Tommie slung and they were coming along behind
her. She was still a good-looking woman, he thought, and she had
a pleasant body. She had a great talent and appreciation for the
bed, she was not pretty, but he liked her face, she read enor-
mously, liked to ride and shoot and, certainly, she drank too
much. Her husband had died when she was still a comparatively
young woman and for a while she had devoted herself to her
two just-grown children, who did not need her and were embarrassed at having her about, to her stable of horses, to books,
and to bottles. She liked to read in the evening before dinner
and she drank Scotch and soda while she read. By dinner she was
fairly drunk and after a bottle of wine at dinner she was usually
drunk enough to sleep.

That was before the lovers. After she had the lovers she did
not drink so much because she did not have to be drunk to sleep.
But the lovers bored her. She had been married to a man who
had never bored her and these people bored her very much.

Then one of her two children was killed in a plane crash and
after that was over she did not want the lovers, and drink being
no anæsthetic she had to make another life. Suddenly, she had
been acutely frightened of being alone. But she wanted some
one that she respected with her.

It had begun very simply. She liked what he wrote and she had
always envied the life he led. She thought he did exactly what he
wanted to. The steps by which she had acquired him and the way
in which she had finally fallen in love with him were all part of

a regular progression in which she had built herself a new life and he had traded away what remained of his old life.

He had traded it for security, for comfort too, there was no denying that, and for what else? He did not know. She would have bought him anything he wanted. He knew that. She was a damned nice woman too. He would as soon be in bed with her as any one; rather with her, because she was richer, because she was very pleasant and appreciative and because she never made scenes. And now this life that she had built again was coming to a term because he had not used iodine two weeks ago when a thorn had scratched his knee as they moved forward trying to photograph a herd of waterbuck standing, their heads up, peering while their nostrils searched the air, their ears spread wide to hear the first noise that would send them rushing into the bush. They had bolted, too, before he got the picture.

Here she came now.

He turned his head on the cot to look toward her. "Hello," he said.

"I shot a Tommy ram," she told him. "He'll make you good broth and I'll have them mash some potatoes with the Klim. How do you feel?"

"Much better."

"Isn't that lovely? You know I thought perhaps you would. You were sleeping when I left."

"I had a good sleep. Did you walk far?"

"No. Just around behind the hill. I made quite a good shot on the Tommy."

"You shoot marvellously, you know."

"I love it. I've loved Africa. Really. If *you're* all right it's the most fun that I've ever had. You don't know the fun it's been to shoot with you. I've loved the country."

"I love it too."

"Darling, you don't know how marvellous it is to see you feeling better. I couldn't stand it when you felt that way. You won't talk to me like that again, will you? Promise me?"

"No," he said. "I don't remember what I said."

"You don't have to destroy me. Do you? I'm only a middle-aged woman who loves you and wants to do what you want to do. I've been destroyed two or three times already. You wouldn't want to destroy me again, would you?"

"I'd like to destroy you a few times in bed," he said.

"Yes. That's the good destruction. That's the way we're made to be destroyed. The plane will be here tomorrow."

"How do you know?"

"I'm sure. It's bound to come. The boys have the wood all ready and the grass to make the smudge. I went down and looked at it again today. There's plenty of room to land and we have the smudges ready at both ends."

"What makes you think it will come tomorrow?"

"I'm sure it will. It's overdue now. Then, in town, they will fix up your leg and then we will have some good destruction. Not that dreadful talking kind."

"Should we have a drink? The sun is down."

"Do you think you should?"

"I'm having one."

"We'll have one together. *Molo, letti dui whiskey-soda!*" she called.

"You'd better put on your mosquito boots," he told her.

"I'll wait till I bathe . . ."

While it grew dark they drank and just before it was dark and there was no longer enough light to shoot, a hyena crossed the open on his way around the hill.

"That bastard crosses there every night," the man said. "Every night for two weeks."

"He's the one makes the noise at night. I don't mind it. They're a filthy animal though."

Drinking together, with no pain now except the discomfort of lying in the one position, the boys lighting a fire, its shadow jumping on the tents, he could feel the return of acquiescence in this life of pleasant surrender. She *was* very good to him. He had been cruel and unjust in the afternoon. She was a fine woman, marvellous really. And just then it occurred to him that he was going to die.

It came with a rush; not as a rush of water nor of wind; but of a sudden evil-smelling emptiness and the odd thing was that the hyena slipped lightly along the edge of it.

"What is it, Harry?" she asked him.

"Nothing," he said. "You had better move over to the other side. To windward."

"Did Molo change the dressing?"

"Yes. I'm just using the boric now."

"How do you feel?"

"A little wobbly."

"I'm going in to bathe," she said. "I'll be right out. I'll eat with you and then we'll put the cot in."

So, he said to himself, we did well to stop the quarrelling. He had never quarrelled much with this woman, while with the women that he loved he had quarrelled so much they had finally, always, with the corrosion of the quarrelling, killed what they had together. He had loved too much, demanded too much, and he wore it all out.

He thought about, alone in Constantinople that time, having quarrelled in Paris before he had gone out. He had whored the whole time and then, when that was over, and he had failed to kill his loneliness, but only made it worse, he had written her, the first one, the one who left him, a letter telling her how he had never been able to kill it. . . . How when he thought he saw her outside the Regence one time it made him go all faint and sick inside, and that he would follow a woman who looked like her in some way, along the Boulevard, afraid to see it was not she, afraid to lose the feeling it gave him. How every one he had slept with had only made him miss her more. How what she had done could never matter since he knew he could not cure himself of loving her. He wrote this letter at the Club, cold sober, and mailed it to New York asking her to write him at the office in Paris. That seemed safe. And that night missing her so much it made him feel hollow sick inside, he wandered up past Taxim's, picked a girl up and took her out to supper. He had gone to a place to dance with her afterward, she danced badly, and left her for a hot Armenian slut, that swung her belly against him so it almost scalded. He took her away from a British gunner subaltern after a row. The gunner asked him outside and they fought in the street on the cobbles in the dark. He'd hit him twice, hard, on the side of the jaw and when he didn't go down he knew he was in for a fight. The gunner hit him in the body, then beside his eye. He swung with his left again and landed and the gunner fell on him and grabbed his coat and tore the sleeve off and he clubbed him twice behind the ear and then smashed him with his right as he pushed him away. When the gunner went down his head hit first and he ran with the girl because they heard the M.P.'s coming. They got into a taxi and drove out to Rimmily Hissa along the Bosphorus, and around, and back in the cool night and went to bed and she felt as over-ripe as she looked but smooth, rose-petal, syrupy, smooth-bellied, big-breasted and needed no pillow under her buttocks, and he left her before she was awake looking blousy enough in the first daylight and turned up at the Pera Palace with a black eye, carrying his coat because one sleeve was missing.

That same night he left for Anatolia and he remembered, later on that trip, riding all day through fields of the poppies that they raised for opium and how strange it made you feel, finally, and all the distances seemed wrong, to where they had made the attack with the newly arrived Constantine officers, that did not know a god-damned thing, and the artillery had fired into the troops and the British observer had cried like a child.

That was the day he'd first seen dead men wearing white ballet skirts and upturned shoes with pompons on them. The Turks had come steadily and lumpily and he had seen the skirted men running and the officers shooting into them and running then themselves and he and the British observer had run too until his lungs ached and his mouth was full of the taste of pennies and they stopped behind some rocks and there were the Turks coming as lumpily as ever. Later he had seen the things that he could never think of and later still he had seen much worse. So when he got back to Paris that time he could not talk about it or stand to have it mentioned. And there in the café as he passed was that American poet with a pile of saucers in front of him and a stupid look on his potato face talking about the Dada movement with a Roumanian who said his name was Tristan Tzara, who always wore a monocle and had a headache, and, back at the apartment with his wife that now he loved again, the quarrel all over, the madness all over, glad to be home, the office sent his mail up to the flat. So then the letter in answer to the one he'd written came in on a platter one morning and when he saw the handwriting he went cold all over and tried to slip the letter underneath another. But his wife said, "Who is that letter from, dear?" and that was the end of the beginning of that.

He remembered the good times with them all, and the quarrels. They always picked the finest places to have the quarrels.

And why had they always quarrelled when he was feeling best? He had never written any of that because, at first, he never wanted to hurt any one and then it seemed as though there was enough to write without it. But he had always thought that he would write it finally. There was so much to write. He had seen the world change; not just the events; although he had seen many of them and had watched the people, but he had seen the subtler change and he could remember how the people were at different times. He had been in it and he had watched it and it was his duty to write of it; but now he never would.

"How do you feel?" she said. She had come out from the tent now after her bath.

"All right."

"Could you eat now?" He saw Molo behind her with the folding table and the other boy with the dishes.

"I want to write," he said.

"You ought to take some broth to keep your strength up."

"I'm going to die tonight," he said. "I don't need my strength up."

"Don't be melodramatic, Harry, please," she said.

"Why don't you use your nose? I'm rotted half way up my thigh now. What the hell should I fool with broth for? Molo bring whiskey-soda."

"Please take the broth," she said gently.

"All right."

The broth was too hot. He had to hold it in the cup until it cooled enough to take it and then he just got it down without gagging.

"You're a fine woman," he said. "Don't pay any attention to me."

She looked at him with her well-known, well-loved face from *Spur* and *Town and Country,* only a little the worse for drink, only a little the worse for bed, but *Town and Country* never showed those good breasts and those useful thighs and those lightly small-of-back-caressing hands, and as he looked and saw her well known pleasant smile, he felt death come again. This time there was no rush. It was a puff, as of a wind that makes a candle flicker and the flame go tall.

"They can bring my net out later and hang it from the tree

and build the fire up. I'm not going in the tent tonight. It's not worth moving. It's a clear night. There won't be any rain."

So this was how you died, in whispers that you did not hear. Well, there would be no more quarrelling. He could promise that. The one experience that he had never had he was not going to spoil now. He probably would. You spoiled everything. But perhaps he wouldn't.

"You can't take dictation, can you?"

"I never learned," she told him.

"That's all right."

There wasn't time, of course, although it seemed as though it telescoped so that you might put it all into one paragraph if you could get it right.

There was a log house, chinked white with mortar, on a hill above the lake. There was a bell on a pole by the door to call the people in to meals. Behind the house were fields and behind the fields was the timber. A line of lombardy poplars ran from the house to the dock. Other poplars ran along the point. A road went up to the hills along the edge of the timber and along that road he picked blackberries. Then that log house was burned down and all the guns that had been on deer foot racks above the open fire place were burned and afterwards their barrels, with the lead melted in the magazines, and the stocks burned away, lay out on the heap of ashes that were used to make lye for the big iron soap kettles, and you asked Grandfather if you could have them to play with, and he said, no. You see they were his guns still and he never bought any others. Nor did he hunt any more. The house was rebuilt in the same place out of lumber now and painted white and from its porch you saw the poplars and the lake beyond; but there were never any more guns. The barrels of the guns that had hung on the deer feet on the wall of the log house lay out there on the heap of ashes and no one ever touched them.

In the Black Forest, after the war, we rented a trout stream and there were two ways to walk to it. One was down the valley from Triberg and around the valley road in the shade of the trees that bordered the white road, and then up a side road that went up through the hills past many small farms, with the big

Schwarzwald houses, until that road crossed the stream. That was where our fishing began.

The other way was to climb steeply up to the edge of the woods and then go across the top of the hills through the pine woods, and then out to the edge of a meadow and down across this meadow to the bridge. There were birches along the stream and it was not big, but narrow, clear and fast, with pools where it had cut under the roots of the birches. At the Hotel in Triberg the proprietor had a fine season. It was very pleasant and we were all great friends. The next year came the inflation and the money he had made the year before was not enough to buy supplies to open the hotel and he hanged himself.

You could dictate that, but you could not dictate the Place Contrescarpe where the flower sellers dyed their flowers in the street and the dye ran over the paving where the autobus started and the old men and the women, always drunk on wine and bad marc; and the children with their noses running in the cold; the smell of dirty sweat and poverty and drunkenness at the Café des Amateurs and the whores at the Bal Musette they lived above. The Concierge who entertained the trooper of the Garde Republicaine in her loge, his horse-hair-plumed helmet on a chair. The locataire across the hall whose husband was a bicycle racer and her joy that morning at the Cremerie when she had opened L'Auto and seen where he placed third in Paris-Tours, his first big race. She had blushed and laughed and then gone upstairs crying with the yellow sporting paper in her hand. The husband of the woman who ran the Bal Musette drove a taxi and when he, Harry, had to take an early plane the husband knocked upon the door to wake him and they drank a glass of white wine at the zinc of the bar before they started. He knew his neighbors in that quarter then because they all were poor.

Around that Place there were two kinds; the drunkards and the sportifs. The drunkards killed their poverty that way; the sportifs took it out in exercise. They were the descendants of the Communards and it was no struggle for them to know their politics. They knew who had shot their fathers, their relatives, their brothers, and their friends when the Versailles troops came in and took the town after the Commune and executed any one they could catch with calloused hands, or who wore a cap, or carried any other sign he was a working man. And in that poverty, and in that quarter across the street from a Boucherie Chevaline and a wine co-operative he had written the start of all he was to do. There never was another part of Paris that he loved like that, the sprawling trees, the old white plastered houses painted brown below, the long green of the autobus in that round square, the purple flower dye upon the paving, the sudden drop down the hill of the rue Cardinal Lemoine to the River, and the other way the narrow crowded world of the rue Mouffetard. The street that ran up toward the Pantheon and the other that he always took with the bicycle, the only asphalted street in all that quarter, smooth under the tires, with the high narrow houses and the cheap tall hotel where Paul Verlaine had died. There were only two rooms in the apartments where they lived and he had a room on the top floor of that hotel that cost him sixty francs a month where he did his writing, and from it he could see the roofs and chimney pots and all the hills of Paris.

From the apartment you could only see the wood and coal man's place. He sold wine too, bad wine. The golden horse's head outside the Boucherie Chevaline where the carcasses hung yellow gold and red in the open window, and the green painted co-operative where they bought their wine; good wine and cheap. The rest was plaster walls and the windows of the neighbors. The neighbors who, at night, when some one lay drunk in the street, moaning and groaning in that typical French ivresse *that you were propaganded to believe did not exist, would open their windows and then the murmur of talk.*

"Where is the policeman? When you don't want him the bugger is always there. He's sleeping with some concierge. Get the Agent." Till some one threw a bucket of water from a window and the moaning stopped. "What's that? Water. Ah, that's intelligent." And the windows shutting. Marie, his femme de menage, protesting against the eight-hour day saying, "If a husband works until six he gets only a little drunk on the way home and does not waste too much. If he works only until five he is drunk every night and one has no money. It is the wife of the working man who suffers from this shortening of hours."

"Wouldn't you like some more broth?" the woman asked him now.

"No, thank you very much. It is awfully good."

"Try just a little."

"I would like a whiskey-soda."

"It's not good for you."

"No. It's bad for me. Cole Porter wrote the words and the music. This knowledge that you're going mad for me."

"You know I like you to drink."

"Oh yes. Only it's bad for me."

When she goes, he thought. I'll have all I want. Not all I want but all there is. Ayee he was tired. Too tired. He was going to sleep a little while. He lay still and death was not there. It must have gone around another street. It went in pairs, on bicycles, and moved absolutely silently on the pavements.

No, he had never written about Paris. Not the Paris that he cared about. But what about the rest that he had never written?

What about the ranch and the silvered gray of the sage brush, the quick, clear water in the irrigation ditches, and the heavy green of the alfalfa. The trail went up into the hills and the cattle in the summer were shy as deer. The bawling and the steady noise and slow moving mass raising a dust as you brought them down in the fall. And behind the mountains, the clear sharpness of the peak in the evening light and, riding down along the trail in the moonlight, bright across the valley. Now he remembered coming down through the timber in the dark holding the horse's tail when you could not see and all the stories that he meant to write.

About the half-wit chore boy who was left at the ranch that time and told not to let any one get any hay, and that old bastard from the Forks who had beaten the boy when he had worked for him stopping to get some feed. The boy refusing and the old man saying he would beat him again. The boy got the rifle from the kitchen and shot him when he tried to come into the barn and when they came back to the ranch he'd been dead a week, frozen in the corral, and the dogs had eaten part of him. But what was left you packed on a sled wrapped in a blanket and roped on and you got the boy to help you haul it, and the two of you took it out over the road on skis, and sixty miles down to town to turn the boy over. He having no idea that he would be arrested. Thinking he had done his duty and that you were his friend and he would be rewarded. He'd helped to haul the old man in so everybody could know how bad the old man had been and how he'd tried to steal some feed that didn't belong to him, and when the sheriff put the handcuffs on the boy he couldn't believe it. Then he'd started to cry. That was one story he had saved to write. He knew at least twenty good stories from out there and he had never written one. Why?

"You tell them why," he said.

"Why what, dear?"

"Why nothing."

She didn't drink so much, now, since she had him. But if he lived he would never write about her, he knew that now. Nor about any of them. The rich were dull and they drank too much, or they played too much backgammon. They were dull and they were repetitious. He remembered poor Julian and his romantic awe of them and how he had started a story once that began, "The very rich are different from you and me." And how some one had said to Julian, Yes, they have more money. But that was not humorous to Julian. He thought they were a special glamourous race and when he found they weren't it wrecked him just as much as any other thing that wrecked him.

He had been contemptuous of those who wrecked. You did not have to like it because you understood it. He could beat anything, he thought, because no thing could hurt him if he did not care.

All right. Now he would not care for death. One thing he had always dreaded was the pain. He could stand pain as well as any man, until it went on too long, and wore him out, but here he had something that had hurt frightfully and just when he had felt it breaking him, the pain had stopped.

He remembered long ago when Williamson, the bombing officer, had been hit by a stick bomb some one in a German patrol had thrown as he was coming in through the wire that night and, screaming, had begged every one to kill him. He was a fat man, very brave, and a good officer, although addicted to fantastic shows. But that night he was caught in the wire, with a flare lighting him up and his bowels spilled out into the wire, so when they brought him in, alive, they had to cut him loose. Shoot me, Harry. For Christ sake shoot me. They had had an argument one time about our Lord never sending you anything you could not bear and some one's theory had been that meant that at a certain time the pain passed you out automatically. But he had always remembered Williamson, that night. Nothing passed out Williamson until he gave him all his morphine tablets that he had always saved to use himself and then they did not work right away.

Still this now, that he had, was very easy; and if it was no worse as it went on there was nothing to worry about. Except that he would rather be in better company.

He thought a little about the company that he would like to have.

No, he thought, when everything you do, you do too long, and do too late, you can't expect to find the people still there. The people all are gone. The party's over and you are with your hostess now.

I'm getting as bored with dying as with everything else, he thought.

"It's a bore," he said out loud.

"What is, my dear?"

"Anything you do too bloody long."

He looked at her face between him and the fire. She was leaning back in the chair and the firelight shone on her pleasantly lined face and he could see that she was sleepy. He heard the hyena make a noise just outside the range of the fire.

"I've been writing," he said. "But I got tired."

"Do you think you will be able to sleep?"

"Pretty sure. Why don't you turn in?"

"I like to sit here with you."

"Do you feel anything strange?" he asked her.

"No. Just a little sleepy."

"I do," he said.

He had just felt death come by again.

"You know the only thing I've never lost is curiosity," he said to her.

"You've never lost anything. You're the most complete man I've ever known."

"Christ," he said. "How little a woman knows. What is that? Your intuition?"

Because, just then, death had come and rested its head on the foot of the cot and he could smell its breath.

"Never believe any of that about a scythe and a skull," he told her. "It can be two bicycle policemen as easily, or be a bird. Or it can have a wide snout like a hyena."

It had moved up on him now, but it had no shape any more. It simply occupied space.

"Tell it to go away."

It did not go away but moved a little closer.

"You've got a hell of a breath," he told it. "You stinking bastard."

It moved up closer to him still and now he could not speak to it, and when it saw he could not speak it came a little closer, and now he tried to send it away without speaking, but it moved in on him so its weight was all upon his chest, and while it crouched there and he could not move, or speak, he heard the woman say, "Bwana is asleep now. Take the cot up very gently and carry it into the tent."

He could not speak to tell her to make it go away and it crouched now, heavier, so he could not breathe. And then, while they lifted the cot, suddenly it was all right and the weight went from his chest.

It was morning and had been morning for some time and he heard the plane. It showed very tiny and then made a wide circle and the boys ran out and lit the fires, using kerosene, and piled on grass so there were two big smudges at each end of the level place and the morning breeze blew them toward the camp and the plane circled twice more, low this time, and then glided down and levelled off and landed smoothly and, coming walking toward him, was old Compton in slacks, a tweed jacket and a brown felt hat.

"What's the matter, old cock?" Compton said.

"Bad leg," he told him. "Will you have some breakfast?"

"Thanks. I'll just have some tea. It's the Puss Moth you know. I won't be able to take the Memsahib. There's only room for one. Your lorry is on the way."

Helen had taken Compton aside and was speaking to him. Compton came back more cheery than ever.

"We'll get you right in," he said "I'll be back for the Mem. Now I'm afraid I'll have to stop at Arusha to refuel. We'd better get going."

"What about the tea?"

"I don't really care about it you know."

The boys had picked up the cot and carried it around the green tents and down along the rock and out onto the plain and along past the smudges that were burning brightly now, the grass all consumed, and the wind fanning the fire, to the little plane. It was difficult getting him in, but once in he lay back in the leather seat, and the leg was stuck straight out to one side of the seat where Compton sat. Compton started the motor and got in. He waved to Helen and to the boys and, as the clatter moved into the old familiar roar, they swung around with Compie watching for wart-hog holes and roared, bumping, along the stretch between the fires and with the last bump rose and he saw them all standing below, waving, and the camp beside the hill, flattening now, and the plain spreading, clumps of trees, and the bush flattening, while the game trails ran now smoothly to the dry waterholes, and there was a new water that he had never known of. The zebra, small rounded backs now, and the wildebeeste, big-headed dots seeming to climb as they moved in long fingers across the plain, now scattering as the shadow came toward them, they were tiny now, and the movement had no gallop, and the plain as far as you could see, gray-yellow now and ahead old Compie's tweed back and the brown felt hat. Then they were over the first hills and the wildebeeste were trailing up them, and then they were over mountains with sudden depths of green-rising forest and the solid bamboo slopes, and then the heavy forest again, sculptured into peaks and hollows until they crossed, and hills sloped down and then another plain, hot now, and purple brown, bumpy with heat and Compie looking back to see how he was riding. Then there were other mountains dark ahead.

And then instead of going on to Arusha they turned left, he evidently figured that they had the gas, and looking down he saw a pink sifting cloud, moving over the ground, and in the air, like the first snow in a blizzard, that comes from nowhere, and he knew the locusts were coming from the South. Then they began to climb and they were going to the East it seemed, and then it darkened and they were in a storm, the rain so thick it seemed like flying through a waterfall, and then they were out and Compie turned his head and grinned and pointed and there, ahead, all he could see, as wide as all the world, great, high, and unbelievably white in the sun, was the square top of Kilimanjaro. And then he knew that there was where he was going.

Just then the hyena stopped whimpering in the night and started to make a strange, human, almost crying sound. The woman heard it and stirred uneasily. She did not wake. In her dream she was at the house on Long Island and it was the night before her daughter's début. Somehow her father was there and he had been very rude. Then the noise the hyena made was so loud she woke and for a moment she did not know where she was and she was very afraid. Then she took the flashlight and shone it on the other cot that they had carried in after Harry had gone to sleep. She could see his bulk under the mosquito bar but somehow he had gotten his leg out and it hung down alongside the cot. The dressings had all come down and she could not look at it.

"Molo," she called, "Molo! Molo!"

Then she said, "Harry, Harry!" Then her voice rising, "Harry! Please, Oh Harry!"

There was no answer and she could not hear him breathing.

Outside the tent the hyena made the same strange noise that had awakened her. But she did not hear him for the beating of her heart.

VLADIMIR NABOKOV (b.1899)   Nabokov, the son of a wealthy jurist and statesman, was born in St. Petersburg, Russia. The life of his family, like that of other upper-class Russians, was entirely cosmopolitan. As a boy, Nabokov traveled extensively in Europe with his family and a retinue of servants. He learned to read English before he read Russian and received his Bachelor of Arts degree from Trinity College, Cambridge.

In 1919, with the coming of the Bolshevik Revolution, the family, suddenly impoverished, fled to Berlin. Nabokov's father, who had participated in the February-March Revolution of 1917, was assassinated in 1922 at a Berlin lecture. Nabokov supported himself by teaching English and tennis and by composing crossword puzzles for the Russian *emigré* daily newspaper. In 1937 he settled in Paris; in 1940 he came to the United States and became an American citizen. He now resides in Switzerland.

All of his novels written before 1940 — most of which have now been translated — were composed in Russian; his writing since then has been in English. Among his many novels, perhaps the best-known are *Lolita* (published in the United States in 1958), *Pale Fire* (1962), and *The Defense* (1966). "That in Aleppo Once . . ." was published first in 1943, and "Signs and Symbols," in 1948.

"THAT IN ALEPPO ONCE . . ."

Vladimir Nabokov

Dear V. — Among other things, this is to tell you that at last I am here, in the country whither so many sunsets have led. One of the first persons I saw was our good old Gleb Alexandrovich Gekko gloomily crossing Columbus Avenue in quest of the *petit café du coin* which none of us three will ever visit again. He seemed to think that somehow or other you were betraying our national literature, and he gave me your address with a deprecatory shake of his gray head, as if you did not deserve the treat of hearing from me.

I have a story for you. Which reminds me — I mean putting it like this reminds me — of the days when we wrote our first udder-warm bubbling verse, and all things, a rose, a puddle, a lighted window, cried out to us: "I'm a rhyme!" Yes, this is a most useful universe. We play, we die. *ig-rhyme, umi-rhyme*. And the sonorous souls of Russian verbs lend a meaning to the wild gesticulation of trees or to some discarded newspaper sliding and pausing, and shuffling again, with abortive flaps and apterous jerks along an endless wind-swept embankment. But just now I am not a poet. I come to you like that gushing lady in Chekhov who was dying to be described.

I married, let me see, about a month after you left France and a few weeks before the gentle Germans roared into Paris. Although I can produce documentary proofs of matrimony, I am positive now that my wife never existed. You may know her name from some other source, but that does not matter: it is the name of an illusion. Therefore, I am able to speak of her with as much detachment as I would of a character in a story (one of your stories, to be precise).

It was love at first touch rather than at first sight, for I had met her several times before without experiencing any special

420

emotions; but one night, as I was seeing her home, something quaint she had said made me stoop with a laugh and lightly kiss her on the hair — and of course we all know of that blinding blast which is caused by merely picking up a small doll from the floor of a carefully abandoned house: the soldier involved hears nothing; for him it is but an ecstatic soundless and boundless expansion of what had been during his life a pin point of light in the dark center of his being. And really, the reason we think of death in celestial terms is that the visible firmament, especially at night (above our blacked-out Paris with the gaunt arches of its Boulevard Exelmans and the ceaseless Alpine gurgle of desolate latrines), is the most adequate and ever-present symbol of that vast silent explosion.

But I cannot discern her. She remains as nebulous as my best poem — the one you made such gruesome fun of in the *Litera-turnïe Zapiski*. When I want to imagine her, I have to cling mentally to a tiny brown birthmark on her downy forearm, as one concentrates upon a punctuation mark in an illegible sentence. Perhaps, had she used a greater amount of make-up or used it more constantly, I might have visualized her face today, or at least the delicate transverse furrows of dry, hot rouged lips; but I fail, I fail — although I still feel their elusive touch now and then in the blindman's buff of my senses, in that sobbing sort of dream when she and I clumsily clutch at each other through a heartbreaking mist and I cannot see the color of her eyes for the blank luster of brimming tears drowning their irises.

She was much younger than I — not as much younger as was Nathalie of the lovely bare shoulders and long earrings in relation to swarthy Pushkin; but still there was a sufficient margin for that kind of retrospective romanticism which finds pleasure in imitating the destiny of a unique genius (down to the jealousy, down to the filth, down to the stab of seeing her almond-shaped eyes turn to her blond Cassio behind her peacock-feathered fan) even if one cannot imitate his verse. She liked mine though, and would scarcely have yawned as the other was wont to do every time her husband's poem happened to exceed the length of a sonnet. If she has remained a phantom to me, I may have been one to her: I suppose she had been solely attracted by the obscurity of my poetry; then tore a hole through its veil and saw a stranger's unlovable face.

As you know, I had been for some time planning to follow the example of your fortunate flight. She described to me an uncle of hers who lived, she said, in New York: he had taught riding at a Southern college and had wound up by marrying a wealthy American woman; they had a little daughter born deaf. She said she had lost their address long ago, but a few days later it miraculously turned up, and we wrote a dramatic letter to which we never received any reply. This did not much matter, as I had already obtained a sound affidavit from Professor Lomchenko of Chicago; but little else had been done in the way of getting the necessary papers, when the invasion began, whereas I foresaw that if we stayed on in Paris some helpful compatriot of mine would sooner or later point out to the interested party sundry passages in one of my books where I argued that, with all her many black sins, Germany was still bound to remain forever and ever the laughing stock of the world.

So we started upon our disastrous honeymoon. Crushed and jolted amid the apocalyptic exodus, waiting for unscheduled trains that were bound for unknown destinations, walking through the stale stage setting of abstract towns, living in a permanent twilight of physical exhaustion, we fled; and the farther we fled, the clearer it became that what was driving us on was something more than a booted and buckled fool with his assortment of variously propelled junk — something of which he was a mere symbol, something monstrous and impalpable, a timeless and faceless mass of immemorial horror that still keeps coming at me from behind even here, in the green vacuum of Central Park.

Oh, she bore it gamely enough — with a kind of dazed cheerfulness. Once, however, quite suddenly she started to sob in a sympathetic railway carriage. "The dog," she said, "the dog we left. I cannot forget the poor dog." The honesty of her grief shocked me, as we had never had any dog. "I know," she said, "But I tried to imagine we had actually bought that setter. And just think, he would be now whining behind a locked door." There had never been any talk of buying a setter.

I should also not like to forget a certain stretch of highroad and the sight of a family of refugees (two women, a child) whose old father, or grandfather, had died on the way. The sky was a chaos of black and flesh-colored clouds with an ugly sunburst beyond a hooded hill, and the dead man was lying on his back under a dusty plane tree. With a stick and their hands the women had tried to dig a roadside grave, but the soil was too hard; they had given it up and were sitting side by side, among the anemic poppies, a little apart from the corpse and its upturned beard. But the little boy was still scratching and scraping and tugging until he tumbled a flat stone and forgot the object of his solemn exertions as he crouched on his haunches, his thin, eloquent neck showing all its vertebrae to the headsman, and watched with surprise and delight thousands of minute brown ants seething, zigzagging, dispersing, heading for places of safety in the Gard, and the Aude, and the Drome, and the Var, and the Basses-Pyrénées — we two paused only in Pau.

Spain proved too difficult and we decided to move on to Nice. At a place called Faugères (a ten-minute stop) I squeezed out of the train to buy some food. When a couple of minutes later I came back, the train was gone, and the muddled old man responsible for the atrocious void that faced me (coal dust glittering in the heat between naked indifferent rails, and a lone piece of orange peel) brutally told me that, anyway, I had had no right to get out.

In a better world I could have had my wife located and told what to do (I had both tickets and most of the money); as it was, my nightmare struggle with the telephone proved futile, so I dismissed the whole series of diminutive voices barking at me from afar, sent two or three telegrams which are probably on their way only now, and late in the evening took the next local to Montpellier, farther than which her train would not stumble. Not finding her there, I had to choose between two alternatives: going on because she might have boarded the Marseilles train which I had just missed, or going back because she might have returned to Faugères. I forgot now what tangle of reasoning led me to Marseilles and Nice.

Beyond such routine action as forwarding false data to a few unlikely places, the police did nothing to help: one man bellowed at me for being a nuisance; another sidetracked the question by doubting the authenticity of my marriage certificate because it was stamped on what he contended to be the wrong side; a third, a fat *commissaire* with liquid brown eyes confessed that he wrote poetry in his spare time. I looked up various acquaintances among the numerous Russians domiciled or stranded in Nice. I heard those among them who chanced to have Jewish blood talk of their doomed kinsmen crammed into hell-bound trains; and my own plight, by contrast, acquired a commonplace air of irreality while I sat in some crowded café with the milky blue sea in front of me and a shell-hollow murmur behind telling and retelling the tale of massacre and misery, and the gray paradise beyond the ocean, and the ways and whims of harsh consuls.

A week after my arrival an indolent plain-clothes man called upon me and took me down a crooked and smelly street to a black-stained house with the word "hotel" almost erased by dirt and time; there, he said, my wife had been found. The girl he produced was an absolute stranger, of course; but my friend Holmes kept on trying for some time to make her and me confess we were married, while her taciturn and muscular bedfellow stood by and listened, his bare arms crossed on his striped chest.

When at length I got rid of those people and had wandered back to my neighborhood, I happened to pass by a compact queue waiting at the entrance of a food store; and there, at the very end, was my wife, straining on tiptoe to catch a glimpse of what exactly was being sold. I think the first thing she said to me was that she hoped it was oranges.

Her tale seemed a trifle hazy, but perfectly banal. She had returned to Faugères and gone straight to the Commissariat instead of making inquiries at the station, where I had left a message for her. A party of refugees suggested that she join them; she spent the night in a bicycle shop with no bicycles, on the floor, together with three elderly women who lay, she said, like three logs in a row. Next day she realized that she had not enough money to reach Nice. Eventually she borrowed some from one of the log-women. She got into the wrong train, however, and traveled to a town the name of which she could not remember. She had arrived at Nice two days ago and had found some friends at the Russian church. They had told her I was somewhere around, looking for her, and would surely turn up soon.

Some time later, as I sat on the edge of the only chair in my garret and held her by her slender young hips (she was combing her soft hair and tossing her head back with every stroke), her dim smile changed all at once into an odd quiver and she placed one hand on my shoulder, staring down at me as if I were a reflection in a pool, which she had noticed for the first time.

"I've been lying to you, dear," she said. *"Ya lgunia.* I stayed for several nights in Montpellier with a brute of a man I met on the train. I did not want it at all. He sold hair lotions."

The time, the place, the torture. Her fan, her gloves, her mask. I spent that night and many others getting it out of her bit by bit, but not getting it all. I was under the strange delusion that first I must find out every detail, reconstruct every minute, and only then decide whether I could bear it. But the limit of desired knowledge was unattainable, nor could I ever foretell the approximate point after which I might imagine myself satiated, because of course the denominator of every fraction of knowledge was potentially as infinite as the number of intervals between the fractions themselves.

Oh, the first time she had been too tired to mind, and the next had not minded because she was sure I had deserted her; and she apparently considered that such explanations ought to be a kind of consolation prize for me instead of the nonsense and agony they really were. It went on like that for eons, she breaking down every now and then, but soon rallying again, answering my unprintable questions in a breathless whisper or trying with a pitiful smile to wriggle into the semisecurity of irrelevant commentaries, and I crushing and crushing the mad molar till my jaw almost burst with pain, a flaming pain which seemed somehow preferable to the dull, humming ache of humble endurance.

And mark, in between the periods of this inquest, we were trying to get from reluctant authorities certain papers which in their turn would make it lawful to apply for a third kind which would serve as a steppingstone towards a permit enabling the holder to apply for yet other papers which might or might not give him the means of discovering how and why it had happened. For even if I could imagine the accursed recurrent scene, I failed to link up its sharp-angled grotesque shadows with the dim limbs of my wife as she shook and rattled and dissolved in my violent grasp.

So nothing remained but to torture each other, to wait for hours on end in the Prefecture, filling forms, conferring with friends who had already probed the innermost viscera of all visas, pleading with secretaries, and filling forms again, with the result that her lusty and versatile traveling salesman became blended in a ghastly mix-up with rat-whiskered snarling officials, rotting bundles of obsolete records, the reek of violet ink, bribes slipped under gangrenous blotting paper, fat flies tickling moist necks with their rapid cold padded feet, new-laid clumsy concave photographs of your six subhuman doubles, the tragic eyes and patient politeness of petitioners born in Slutzk, Starodub, or Bobruisk, the funnels and pulleys of the Holy Inquisition, the awful smile of the bald man with the glasses, who had been told that his passport could not be found.

I confess that one evening, after a particularly abominable day, I sank down on a stone bench weeping and cursing a mock world where millions of lives were being juggled by the clammy hands of consuls and *commissaires*. I noticed she was crying too, and then I told her that nothing would really have mattered the way it mattered now, had she not gone and done what she did.

"You will think me crazy," she said with a vehemence that, for a second, almost made a real person of her, "but I didn't — I swear that I didn't. Perhaps I live several lives at once. Perhaps I wanted to test you. Perhaps this bench is a dream and we are in Saratov or on some star."

It would be tedious to niggle the different stages through which I passed before accepting finally the first version of her delay. I did not talk to her and was a good deal alone. She would glimmer and fade, and reappear with some trifle she thought I would appreciate — a handful of cherries, three precious cigarettes or the like — treating me with the unruffled mute sweetness of a nurse that trips from and to a gruff convalescent. I ceased visiting most of our mutual friends because they had lost all interest in my passport affairs and seemed to have turned vaguely inimical. I composed several poems. I drank all the wine I could get. I clasped her one day to my groaning breast, and we went for a week to Caboule and lay on the round pink pebbles of the narrow beach. Strange to say, the happier our new relations seemed, the stronger I felt an undercurrent of poignant sadness, but I kept telling myself that this was an intrinsic feature of all true bliss.

In the meantime, something had shifted in the moving pattern of our fates and at last I emerged from a dark and hot office with a couple of plump *visas de sortie* cupped in my trembling hands. Into these the U.S.A. serum was duly injected, and I dashed to Marseilles and managed to get tickets for the very next boat. I returned and tramped up the stairs. I saw a rose in a glass on the table — the sugar pink of its obvious beauty, the parasitic air bubbles clinging to its stem. Her two spare dresses were gone, her comb was gone, her checkered coat was gone, and so was the mauve hairband with a mauve bow that had been her hat. There was no note pinned to the pillow, nothing at all in the room to enlighten me, for of course the rose was merely what French rhymsters call *une cheville*.

I went to the Veretennikovs, who could tell me nothing; to the Hellmans, who refused to say anything; and to the Elagins, who were not sure whether to tell me or not. Finally the old lady — and you know what Anna Vladimirovna is like at crucial moments — asked for her rubber-tipped cane, heavily but energetically dislodged her bulk from her favorite armchair, and took me into the garden. There she informed me that, being twice my age, she had the right to say I was a bully and a cad.

You must imagine the scene: the tiny graveled garden with its blue Arabian Nights jar and solitary cypress; the cracked terrace where the old lady's father had dozed with a rug on his knees when he retired from his Novgorod governorship to spend a few last evenings in Nice; the pale-green sky; a whiff of vanilla in the deepening dusk; the crickets emitting their metallic trill pitched at two octaves above middle C; and Anna Vladimirovna, the folds of her cheeks jerkily dangled as she flung at me a motherly but quite undeserved insult.

During several preceding weeks, my dear V., every time she had visited by herself the three or four families we both knew, my ghostly wife had filled the eager ears of all those kind people with an extraordinary story. To wit: that she had madly fallen in love with a young Frenchman who could give her a turreted home and a crested name; that she had implored me for a divorce and I had refused; that in fact I had said I would rather shoot her and myself than sail to New York alone; that she had said her father in a similar case had acted like a gentleman; that I had answered I did not give a hoot for her *cocu de père*.

There were loads of other preposterous details of the kind — but they all hung together in such a remarkable fashion that no wonder the old lady made me swear I would not seek to pursue the lovers with a cocked pistol. They had gone, she said, to a château in Lozère. I inquired whether she had ever set eyes upon the man. No, but she had been shown his picture. As I was about to leave, Anna Vladimirovna, who had slightly relaxed and had even given me her five fingers to kiss, suddenly flared up again, struck the gravel with her cane, and said in her deep strong voice: "But one thing I shall never forgive you — her dog, that poor beast which you hanged with your own hands before leaving Paris."

Whether the gentleman of leisure had changed into a traveling salesman, or whether the metamorphosis had been reversed, or whether again he was neither the one nor the other, but the nondescript Russian who had courted her before our marriage — all this was absolutely inessential. She had gone. That was the end. I should have been a fool had I begun the nightmare business of searching and waiting for her all over again.

On the fourth morning of a long and dismal sea voyage, I met on the deck a solemn but pleasant old doctor with whom I had played chess in Paris. He asked me whether my wife was very much incommoded by the rough seas. I answered that I had sailed alone; whereupon he looked taken aback and then said he had seen her a couple of days before going on board, namely in Marseilles, walking, rather aimlessly he thought, along the embankment. She said that I would presently join her with bag and tickets.

This is I gather, the point of the whole story — although if you write it, you had better not make him a doctor, as that kind of thing has been overdone. It was at that moment that I suddenly knew for certain that she had never existed at all. I shall tell you another thing. When I arrived I hastened to satisfy a certain morbid curiosity: I went to the address she had given me once; it proved to be an anonymous gap between two office buildings; I looked for her uncle's name in the directory; it was not there; I made some inquiries, and Gekko, who knows everything, informed me that the man and his horsey wife existed all right, but had moved to San Francisco after their deaf little girl had died.

Viewing the past graphically, I see our mangled romance engulfed in a deep valley of mist between the crags of two matter-of-fact mountains: life had been real before, life will be real from now on, I hope. Not tomorrow, though. Perhaps after tomorrow. You, happy mortal, with your lovely family (how is Ines? how are the twins?) and your diversified work (how are the lichens?), can hardly be expected to puzzle out my misfortune in terms of human communion, but you may clarify things for me through the prism of your art.

Yet the pity of it. Curse your art, I am hideously unhappy. She keeps on walking to and fro where the brown nets are spread to dry on the hot stone slabs and the dappled light of the water plays on the side of a moored fishing boat. Somewhere, somehow, I have made some fatal mistake. There are tiny pale bits of broken fish scales glistening here and there in the brown meshes. It may all end in *Aleppo* if I am not careful. Spare me, V.: you would load your dice with an unbearable implication if you took that for a title.

SIGNS AND SYMBOLS

Vladimir Nabokov

I

For the fourth time in as many years they were confronted with
the problem of what birthday present to bring a young man who
was incurably deranged in his mind. He had no desires. Man-
made objects were to him either hives of evil, vibrant with a
malignant activity that he alone could perceive, or gross comforts
for which no use could be found in his abstract world. After
eliminating a number of articles that might offend him or frighten
him (anything in the gadget line for instance was taboo), his
parents chose a dainty and innocent trifle: a basket with ten different fruit jellies in ten little jars.

At the time of his birth they had been married already for a
long time; a score of years had elapsed, and now they were quite
old. Her drab gray hair was done anyhow. She wore cheap black
dresses. Unlike other women of her age (such as Mrs. Sol, their
next-door neighbor, whose face was all pink and mauve with
paint and whose hat was a cluster of brookside flowers), she presented a naked white countenance to the fault-finding light of
spring days. Her husband, who in the old country had been a
fairly successful businessman, was now wholly dependent on his
brother Isaac, a real American of almost forty years standing.
They seldom saw him and had nicknamed him "the Prince."

That Friday everything went wrong. The underground train
lost its life current between two stations, and for a quarter of an
hour one could hear nothing but the dutiful beating of one's
heart and the rustling of newspapers. The bus they had to take
next kept them waiting for ages; and when it did come, it was
crammed with garrulous high-school children. It was raining hard
as they walked up the brown path leading to the sanitarium.
There they waited again; and instead of their boy shuffling into
the room as he usually did (his poor face blotched with acne, ill-

shaven, sullen, and confused), a nurse they knew, and did not care for, appeared at last and brightly explained that he had again attempted to take his life. He was all right, she said, but a visit might disturb him. The place was so miserably understaffed, and things got mislaid or mixed up so easily, that they decided not to leave their present in the office but to bring it to him next time they came.

She waited for her husband to open his umbrella and then took his arm. He kept clearing his throat in a special resonant way he had when he was upset. They reached the bus-stop shelter on the other side of the street and he closed his umbrella. A few feet away, under a swaying and dripping tree, a tiny half-dead unfledged bird was helplessly twitching in a puddle.

During the long ride to the subway station, she and her husband did not exchange a word; and every time she glanced at his old hands (swollen veins, brown-spotted skin), clasped and twitching upon the handle of his umbrella, she felt the mounting pressure of tears. As she looked around trying to hook her mind onto something, it gave her a kind of soft shock, a mixture of compassion and wonder, to notice that one of the passengers, a girl with dark hair and grubby red toenails, was weeping on the shoulder of an older woman. Whom did that woman resemble? She resembled Rebecca Borisovna, whose daughter had married one of the Soloveichiks — in Minsk, years ago.

The last time he had tried to do it, his method had been, in the doctor's words, a masterpiece of inventiveness; he would have succeeded, had not an envious fellow patient thought he was learning to fly — and stopped him. What he really wanted to do was to tear a hole in his world and escape.

The system of his delusions had been the subject of an elaborate paper in a scientific monthly, but long before that she and her husband had puzzled it out for themselves. "Referential mania," Herman Brink had called it. In these very rare cases the patient imagines that everything happening around him is a veiled reference to his personality and existence. He excludes real people from the conspiracy — because he considers himself to be so much more intelligent than other men. Phenomenal nature shadows him wherever he goes. Clouds in the staring sky transmit to one another, by means of slow signs, incredibly detailed information regarding him. His inmost thoughts are discussed at nightfall, in manual alphabet, by darkly gesticulating trees. Pebbles or stains or sun flecks form patterns representing in some awful way messages which he must intercept. Everything is a cipher and of everything he is the theme. Some of the spies are detached observers, such are glass surfaces and still pools; others, such as coats in store windows, are prejudiced witnesses, lynchers at heart; others again (running water, storms) are hysterical to the point of insanity, have a distorted opinion of him and grotesquely misinterpret his actions. He must be always on his guard and devote every minute and module of life to the decoding of the undulation of things. The very air he exhales is indexed and filed away. If only the interest he provokes were limited to his immediate surroundings — but alas it is not! With distance the torrents of wild scandal increase in volume and volubility. The silhouettes of his blood corpuscles, magnified a million times, flit over vast plains; and still farther, great mountains of unbearable solidity and height sum up in terms of granite and groaning firs the ultimate truth of his being.

II

When they emerged from the thunder and foul air of the subway, the last dregs of the day were mixed with the street lights. She wanted to buy some fish for supper, so she handed him the basket of jelly jars, telling him to go home. He walked up to the third landing and then remembered he had given her his keys earlier in the day.

In silence he sat down on the steps and in silence rose when some ten minutes later she came, heavily trudging upstairs, wanly smiling, shaking her head in deprecation of her silliness. They entered their two-room flat and he at once went to the mirror. Straining the corners of his mouth apart by means of his thumbs, with a horrible masklike grimace, he removed his new hopelessly uncomfortable dental plate and severed the long tusks of saliva connecting him to it. He read his Russian-language newspaper while she laid the table. Still reading, he ate the pale victuals that needed no teeth. She knew his moods and was also silent.

When he had gone to bed, she remained in the living room with her pack of soiled cards and her old albums. Across the narrow yard where the rain tinkled in the dark against some battered ash cans, windows were blandly alight and in one of them a black-trousered man with his bare elbows raised could be seen lying supine on an untidy bed. She pulled the blind down and examined the photographs. As a baby he looked more surprised than most babies. From a fold in the album, a German maid they had had in Leipzig and her fat-faced fiancé fell out. Minsk, the Revolution, Leipzig, Berlin, Leipzig, a slanting house front badly out of focus. Four years old, in a park: moodily, shyly, with puckered forehead, looking away from an eager squirrel as he would from any other stranger. Aunt Rosa, a fussy, angular, wild-eyed old lady, who had lived in a tremulous world of bad news, bankruptcies, train accidents, cancerous growths — until the Germans put her to death, together with all the people she had worried about. Age six — that was when he drew wonderful birds with human hands and feet, and suffered from insomnia like a grown-up man. His cousin, now a famous chess player. He again, aged about eight, already difficult to understand, afraid of the wallpaper in the passage, afraid of a certain picture in a book which merely showed an idyllic landscape with rocks on a hillside and an old cart wheel hanging from the branch of a leafless tree. Aged ten: the year they left Europe. The shame, the pity, the humiliating difficulties, the ugly, vicious, backward children he was with in that special school. And then came a time in his life, coinciding with a long convalescence after pneumonia, when those little phobias of his which his parents had stubbornly regarded as the eccentricities of a prodigiously gifted child hardened as it were into a dense tangle of logically interacting illusions, making him totally inaccessible to normal minds.

This, and much more, she accepted — for after all living did mean accepting the loss of one joy after another, not even joys in her case — mere possibilities of improvement. She thought of the endless waves of pain that for some reason or other she and her husband had to endure; of the invisible giants hurting her boy in some unimaginable fashion; of the incalculable amount of tenderness contained in the world; of the fate of this tenderness, which is either crushed, or wasted, or transformed into madness; of neglected children humming to themselves in unswept corners; of beautiful weeds that cannot hide from the farmer and helplessly have to watch the shadow of his simian stoop leave mangled flowers in its wake, as the monstrous darkness approaches.

III

It was past midnight when from the living room she heard her husband moan; and presently he staggered in, wearing over his nightgown the old overcoat with astrakhan collar which he much preferred to the nice blue bathrobe he had.

"I can't sleep," he cried.

"Why," she asked, "why can't you sleep? You were so tired."

"I can't sleep because I am dying," he said and lay down on the couch.

"Is it your stomach? Do you want me to call Dr. Solov?"

"No doctors, no doctors," he moaned, "To the devil with doctors! We must get him out of there quick. Otherwise we'll be responsible. Responsible!" he repeated and hurled himself into a sitting position, both feet on the floor, thumping his forehead with his clenched fist.

"All right," she said quietly, "we shall bring him home tomorrow morning."

Bending with difficulty, she retrieved some playing cards and a photograph or two that had slipped from the couch to the floor: knave of hearts, nine of spades, ace of spades, Elsa and her bestial beau.

He returned in high spirits, saying in a loud voice:

"I have it all figured out. We will give him the bedroom. Each of us will spend part of the night near him and the other part on this couch. By turns. We will have the doctor see him at least twice a week. It does not matter what the Prince says. He won't have to say much anyway because it will come out cheaper."

The telephone rang. It was an unusual hour for their telephone to ring. His left slipper had come off and he groped for it with his heel and toe as he stood in the middle of the room, and childishly, toothlessly, gaped at his wife. Having more English than he did, it was she who attended to calls.

"Can I speak to Charlie," said a girl's dull little voice.

"What number you want? No. That is not the right number."

The receiver was gently cradled. Her hand went to her old tired heart.

"It frightened me," she said.

He smiled a quick smile and immediately resumed his excited monologue. They would fetch him as soon as it was day. Knives would have to be kept in a locked drawer. Even at his worst he presented no danger to other people.

The telephone rang a second time. The same toneless anxious young voice asked for Charlie.

"You have the incorrect number. I will tell you what you are doing: you are turning the letter O instead of the zero."

They sat down to their unexpected festive midnight tea. The birthday present stood on the table. He sipped noisily; his face was flushed; every now and then he imparted a circular motion to his raised glass so as to make the sugar dissolve more thoroughly. The vein on the side of his bald head where there was a large birthmark stood out conspicuously and, although he had shaved that morning, a silvery bristle showed on his chin. While she poured him another glass of tea, he put on his spectacles and re-examined with pleasure the luminous yellow, green, red little jars. His clumsy moist lips spelled out their eloquent labels: apricot, grape, beech plum, quince. He had got to crab apple, when the telephone rang again.

ISAAC BASHEVIS SINGER (b.1904) Singer was born in Radzymin, Poland. His father and grandfather were rabbis, and his orthodox Jewish education culminated with his studies at the rabbinical seminary in Warsaw.

Although Singer began writing in Hebrew, he later wrote in Yiddish. *Satan In Goray* was published in 1935, the year he moved to the United States and joined the staff of the Jewish Daily Forward. His first short story collection was *Gimpel The Fool* which appeared in 1957. Like Kovrin in Chekhov's "The Black Monk," Gimpel is confronted with the problem of whether or not to reject his beliefs as mere illusions. But unlike Kovrin, Gimpel judges these beliefs according to the effect they have on his own inward life although they make him appear foolish and humiliate him in. public.

Singer's novels include *The Family Muskat* (1949), *The Magician of Lublin* (1960), and *The Slave* (1962). *The Spinoza of Market Street* (1958) and *Short Friday* (1961) are short story collections.

A folk quality, reminiscent of Chagall's paintings, is prevalent in his writings. The world of the supernatural is alive, and dybukks test and torment many of the characters of his Hasidic world which unfolds before the reader with the richness and narrative ease of a parable or fable.

GIMPEL THE FOOL

Isaac Bashevis Singer

I

I am Gimpel the fool. I don't think myself a fool. On the contrary. But that's what folks call me. They gave me the name while I was still in school. I had seven names in all: imbecile, donkey, flax-head, dope, glump, ninny, and fool. The last name stuck. What did my foolishness consist of? I was easy to take in. They said, "Gimpel, you know the rabbi's wife has been brought to childbed?" So I skipped school. Well, it turned out to be a lie. How was I supposed to know? She hadn't had a big belly. But I never looked at her belly. Was that really so foolish? The gang laughed and hee-hawed, stomped and danced and chanted a good-night prayer. And instead of the raisins they give when a woman's lying in, they stuffed my hand full of goat turds. I was no weakling. If I slapped someone he'd see all the way to Cracow. But I'm really not a slugger by nature. I think to myself: Let it pass. So they take advantage of me.

I was coming home from school and heard a dog barking. I'm not afraid of dogs, but of course I never want to start up with them. One of them may be mad, and if he bites there's not a Tartar in the world who can help you. So I made tracks. Then I looked around and saw the whole market place wild with laughter. It was no dog at all but Wolf-Leib the Thief. How was I supposed to know it was he? It sounded like a howling bitch.

When the pranksters and leg-pullers found that I was easy to fool, every one of them tried his luck with me. "Gimpel, the Czar is coming to Frampol; Gimpel, the moon fell down in Turbeen; Gimpel, little Hodel Furpiece found a treasure behind the bathhouse." And I like a golem believed everyone. In the first place, everything is possible, as it is written in the Wisdom of the Fathers, I've forgotten just how. Second, I had to believe when the whole town came down on me! If I ever dared to say, "Ah, you're kidding!" there was trouble. People got angry. "What do you mean! You want to call everyone a liar?" What was I to do? I believed them, and I hope at least that did them some good.

I was an orphan. My grandfather who brought me up was already bent toward the grave. So they turned me over to a baker, and what a time they gave me there! Every woman or girl who came to bake a batch of noodles had to fool me at least once. "Gimpel, there's a fair in heaven; Gimpel, the rabbi gave birth to a calf in the seventh month; Gimpel, a cow flew over the roof and laid brass eggs." A student from the yeshiva came once to buy a roll, and he said, "You, Gimpel, while you stand here scraping with your baker's shovel the Messiah has come. The dead have arisen." "What do you mean?" I said. "I heard no one blowing the ram's horn!" He said, "Are you deaf?" And all began to cry, "We heard it, we heard!" Then in came Rietze the Candle-dipper and called out in her hoarse voice, "Gimpel, your father and mother have stood up from the grave. They're looking for you."

To tell the truth, I knew very well that nothing of the sort had happened, but all the same, as folks were talking, I threw on my wool vest and went out. Maybe something had happened. What did I stand to lose by looking? Well, what a cat music went up! And then I took a vow to believe nothing more. But that was no go either. They confused me so that I didn't know the big end from the small.

I went to the rabbi to get some advice. He said, "It is written, better to be a fool all your days than for one hour to be evil. You are not a fool. They are the fools. For he who causes his neighbor to feel shame loses Paradise himself." Nevertheless the rabbi's daughter took me in. As I left the rabbinical court she said, "Have you kissed the wall yet?" I said, "No; what for?" She answered, "It's the law; you've got to do it after every visit." Well, there didn't seem to be any harm in it. And she burst out laughing. It was a fine trick. She put one over on me, all right.

I wanted to go off to another town, but then everyone got busy matchmaking, and they were after me so they nearly tore my coat tails off. They talked at me and talked until I got water on the ear. She was no chaste maiden, but they told me she was virgin pure. She had a limp, and they said it was deliberate, from coyness. She had a bastard, and they told me the child was her little brother. I cried, "You're wasting your time. I'll never marry that whore." But they said indignantly, "What a way to talk! Aren't you ashamed of yourself? We can take you to the rabbi and have you fined for giving her a bad name." I saw then that I wouldn't escape them so easily and I thought: They're set on making me their butt. But when you're married the husband's the master, and if that's all right with her it's agreeable to me too. Besides, you can't pass through life unscathed, nor expect to.

I went to her clay house, which was built on the sand, and the whole gang, hollering and chorusing, came after me. They acted like bear-baiters. When we came to the well they stopped all the same. They were afraid to start anything with Elka. Her mouth would open as if it were on a hinge, and she had a fierce tongue. I entered the house. Lines were strung from wall to wall and clothes were drying. Barefoot she stood by the tub, doing the wash. She was dressed in a worn hand-me-down gown of plush. She had her hair put up in braids and pinned across her head. It took my breath away, almost, the reek of it all.

Evidently she knew who I was. She took a look at me and said, "Look who's here! He's come, the drip. Grab a seat."

I told her all; I denied nothing. "Tell me the truth," I said, "are you really a virgin, and is that mischievous Yechiel actually your little brother? Don't be deceitful with me, for I'm an orphan."

"I'm an orphan myself," she answered, "and whoever tries to twist you up, may the end of his nose take a twist. But don't let them think they can take advantage of me. I want a dowry of fifty guilders, and let them take up a collection besides. Otherwise they can kiss my you-know-what." She was very plainspoken. I said, "It's the bride and not the groom who gives a dowry." Then she said, "Don't bargain with me. Either a flat 'yes' or a flat 'no' — Go back where you came from."

I thought: No bread will ever be baked from *this* dough. But ours is not a poor town. They consented to everything and proceeded with the wedding. It so happened that there was a dysentery epidemic at the time. The ceremony was held at the cemetery gates, near the little corpse-washing hut. The fellows got drunk. While the marriage contract was being drawn up I heard the most pious high rabbi ask, "Is the bride a widow or a divorced woman?" And the sexton's wife answered for her, "Both a widow and divorced." It was a black moment for me. But what was I to do, run away from under the marriage canopy?

There was singing and dancing. An old granny danced opposite me, hugging a braided white *chalah*. The master of revels made a "God 'a mercy" in memory of the bride's parents. The schoolboys threw burrs, as on Tishe b'Av fast day. There were a lot of gifts after the sermon: a noodle board, a kneading trough, a bucket, brooms, ladles, household articles galore. Then I took a look and saw two strapping young men carrying a crib. "What do we need this for?" I asked. So they said, "Don't rack your brains about it. It's all right, it'll come in handy." I realized I was going to be rooked. Take it another way though, what did I stand to lose? I reflected: I'll see what comes of it. A whole town can't go altogether crazy.

II

At night I came where my wife lay, but she wouldn't let me in. "Say, look here, is this what they married us for?" I said. And she said, "My monthly has come." "But yesterday they took you to the ritual bath, and that's afterward, isn't it supposed to be?" "Today isn't yesterday," said she, "and yesterday's not today. You can beat it if you don't like it." In short, I waited.

Not four months later she was in childbed. The townsfolk hid their laughter with their knuckles. But what could I do? She suffered intolerable pains and clawed at the walls. "Gimpel," she cried, "I'm going. Forgive me!" The house filled with women. They were boiling pans of water. The screams rose to the welkin.

The thing to do was to go to the House of Prayer to repeat Psalms, and that was what I did.

The townsfolk liked that, all right. I stood in a corner saying Psalms and prayers, and they shook their heads at me. "Pray, pray!" they told me. "Prayer never made any woman pregnant." One of the congregation put a straw to my mouth and said, "Hay for the cows." There was something to that too, by God!

She gave birth to a boy. Friday at the synagogue the sexton stood up before the Ark, pounded on the reading table, and announced, "The wealthy Reb Gimpel invites the congregation to a feast in honor of the birth of a son." The whole House of

Prayer rang with laughter. My face was flaming. But there was nothing I could do. After all, I *was* the one responsible for the circumcision honors and rituals.

Half the town came running. You couldn't wedge another soul in. Women brought peppered chick-peas, and there was a keg of beer from the tavern. I ate and drank as much as anyone, and they all congratulated me. Then there was a circumcision, and I named the boy after my father, may he rest in peace. When all were gone and I was left with my wife alone, she thrust her head through the bed-curtain and called me to her.

"Gimpel," said she, "why are you silent? Has your ship gone and sunk?"

"What shall I say?" I answered. "A fine thing you've done to me! If my mother had known of it she'd have died a second time."

She said, "Are you crazy, or what?"

"How can you make such a fool," I said, "of one who should be the lord and master?"

"What's the matter with you?" she said. "What have you taken it into your head to imagine?"

I saw that I must speak bluntly and openly. "Do you think this is the way to use an orphan?" I said. "You have borne a bastard."

She answered, "Drive this foolishness out of your head. The child is yours."

"How can he be mine?" I argued. "He was born seventeen weeks after the wedding."

She told me then that he was premature. I said, "Isn't he a little too premature?" She said, she had had a grandmother who carried just as short a time and she resembled this grandmother of hers as one drop of water does another. She swore to it with such oaths that you would have believed a peasant at the fair if he had used them. To tell the plain truth, I didn't believe her; but when I talked it over next day with the school-master he told me that the very same thing had happened to Adam and Eve. Two they went up to bed, and four they descended.

"There isn't a woman in the world who is not the grand-daughter of Eve," he said.

That was how it was; they argued me dumb. But then, who really knows how such things are?

I began to forget my sorrow. I loved the child madly, and he loved me too. As soon as he saw me he'd wave his little hands and want me to pick him up, and when he was colicky I was the only one who could pacify him. I bought him a little bone teething ring and a little gilded cap. He was forever catching the evil eye from someone, and then I had to run to get one of those abracadabras for him that would get him out of it. I worked like an ox. You know how expenses go up when there's an infant in the house. I don't want to lie about it; I didn't dislike Elka either, for that matter. She swore at me and cursed, and I couldn't get enough of her. What strength she had! One of her looks could rob you of the power of speech. And her orations! Pitch and sulphur, that's what they were full of, and yet somehow also full of charm. I adored her every word. She gave me bloody wounds though.

In the evening I brought her a white loaf as well as a dark one, and also poppyseed rolls I baked myself. I thieved because of her and swiped everything I could lay hands on: macaroons, raisins, almonds, cakes. I hope I may be forgiven for stealing from the Saturday pots the women left to warm in the baker's oven. I would take out scraps of meat, a chunk of pudding, a chicken leg or head, a piece of tripe, whatever I could nip quickly. She ate and became fat and handsome.

I had to sleep away from home all during the week, at the bakery. On Friday nights when I got home she always made an excuse of some sort. Either she had heartburn, or a stitch in the side, or hiccups, or headaches. You know what women's excuses are. I had a bitter time of it. It was rough. To add to it, this little brother of hers, the bastard, was growing bigger. He'd put lumps on me, and when I wanted to hit back she'd open her mouth and curse so powerfully I saw a green haze floating before my eyes. Ten times a day she threatened to divorce me. Another man in my place would have taken French leave and disappeared. But I'm the type that bears it and says nothing. What's one to do? Shoulders are from God, and burdens too.

One night there was a calamity in the bakery; the oven burst, and we almost had a fire. There was nothing to do but go home, so I went home. Let me, I thought, also taste the joy of sleeping in bed in mid-week. I didn't want to wake the sleeping mite and tiptoed into the house. Coming in, it seemed to me that I heard not the snoring of one but, as it were, a double snore, one a thin enough snore and the other like the snoring of a slaughtered ox. Oh, I didn't like that! I didn't like it at all. I went up to the bed, and things suddenly turned black. Next to Elka lay a man's form. Another in my place would have made an uproar, and enough noise to rouse the whole town, but the thought occurred to me that I might wake the child. A little thing like that — why frighten a little swallow, I thought. All right then, I went back to the bakery and stretched out on a sack of flour and till morning I never shut an eye. I shivered as if I had had malaria. "Enough of being a donkey," I said to myself. "Gimpel isn't going to be a sucker all his life. There's a limit even to the foolishness of a fool like Gimpel."

In the morning I went to the rabbi to get advice, and it made a great commotion in the town. They sent the beadle for Elka right away. She came, carrying the child. And what do you think she did? She denied it, denied everything, bone and stone! "He's out of his head," she said. "I know nothing of dreams or divinations." They yelled at her, warned her, hammered on the table, but she stuck to her guns: it was a false accusation, she said.

The butchers and the horse-traders took her part. One of the lads from the slaughterhouse came by and said to me, "We've got our eye on you, you're a marked man." Meanwhile the child started to bear down and soiled itself. In the rabbinical court there was an Ark of the Covenant, and they couldn't allow that, so they sent Elka away.

I said to the rabbi, "What shall I do?"

"You must divorce her at once," said he.

"And what if she refuses?" I asked.

He said, "You must serve the divorce. That's all you'll have to do."

I said, "Well, all right, Rabbi. Let me think about it."

"There's nothing to think about," said he. "You mustn't remain under the same roof with her."

"And if I want to see the child?" I asked.

"Let her go, the harlot," said he, "and her brood of bastards with her."

The verdict he gave was that I mustn't even cross her threshold — never again, as long as I should live.

During the day it didn't bother me so much. I thought: It was bound to happen, the abscess had to burst. But at night when I stretched out upon the sacks I felt it all very bitterly. A longing took me, for her and for the child. I wanted to be angry, but that's my misfortune exactly, I don't have it in me to be really angry. In the first place — this was how my thoughts went — there's bound to be a slip sometimes. You can't live without errors. Probably that lad who was with her led her on and gave her presents and what not, and women are often long on hair and short on sense, and so he got around her. And then since she denies it so, maybe I was only seeing things? Hallucinations do happen. You see a figure or a mannikin or something, but when you come up closer it's nothing, there's not a thing there. And if that's so, I'm doing her an injustice. And when I got so far in my thoughts I started to weep. I sobbed so that I wet the flour where I lay. In the morning I went to the rabbi and told him that I had made a mistake. The rabbi wrote on with his quill, and he said that if that were so he would have to reconsider the whole case. Until he had finished I wasn't to go near my wife, but I might send her bread and money by messenger.

III

Nine months passed before all the rabbis could come to an agreement. Letters went back and forth. I hadn't realized that there could be so much erudition about a matter like this.

Meanwhile Elka gave birth to still another child, a girl this time. On the Sabbath I went to the synagogue and invoked a blessing on her. They called me up to the Torah, and I named the child for my mother-in-law — may she rest in peace. The louts and loudmouths of the town who came into the bakery gave me a going over. All Frampol refreshed its spirits because of my trouble and grief. However, I resolved that I would always believe what I was told. What's the good of *not* believing? Today it's your wife you don't believe; tomorrow it's God Himself you won't take stock in.

By an apprentice who was her neighbor I sent her daily a corn or a wheat loaf, or a piece of pastry, rolls or bagels, or, when I got the chance, a slab of pudding, a slice of honeycake, or wedding strudel — whatever came my way. The apprentice was a goodhearted lad, and more than once he added something on his own. He had formerly annoyed me a lot, plucking my nose and digging me in the ribs, but when he started to be a visitor to my house he became kind and friendly. "Hey, you, Gimpel," he said to me, "you have a very decent little wife and two fine kids. You don't deserve them."

"But the things people say about her," I said.

"Well, they have long tongues," he said, "and nothing to do with them but babble. Ignore it as you ignore the cold of last winter."

One day the rabbi sent for me and said, "Are you certain, Gimpel, that you were wrong about your wife?"

I said, "I'm certain."

"Why, but look here! You yourself saw it."

"It must have been a shadow," I said.

"The shadow of what?"

"Just of one of the beams, I think."

"You can go home then. You owe thanks to the Yanover rabbi. He found an obscure reference in Maimonides that favored you."

I seized the rabbi's hand and kissed it.

I wanted to run home immediately. It's no small thing to be separated for so long a time from wife and child. Then I reflected: I'd better go back to work now, and go home in the evening. I said nothing to anyone, although as far as my heart was concerned it was like one of the Holy Days. The women teased and twitted me as they did every day, but my thought was: Go on, with your loose talk. The truth is out, like the oil upon the water. Maimonides says it's right, and therefore it is right!

At night, when I had covered the dough to let it rise, I took my share of bread and a little sack of flour and started homeward. The moon was full and the stars were glistening, something to terrify the soul. I hurried onward, and before me darted a long shadow. It was winter, and a fresh snow had fallen. I had a mind to sing, but it was growing late and I didn't want to wake the householders. Then I felt like whistling, but I remembered that you don't whistle at night because it brings the demons out. So I was silent and walked as fast as I could.

Dogs in the Christian yards barked at me when I passed, but I thought: Bark your teeth out! What are you but mere dogs? Whereas I am a man, the husband of a fine wife, the father of promising children.

As I approached the house my heart started to pound as though it were the heart of a criminal. I felt no fear, but my heart went thump! thump! Well, no drawing back. I quietly lifted the latch and went in. Elka was asleep. I looked at the infant's cradle. The shutter was closed, but the moon forced its way through the cracks. I saw the newborn child's face and loved it as soon as I saw it — immediately — each tiny bone.

Then I came nearer to the bed. And what did I see but the apprentice lying there beside Elka. The moon went out all at once. It was utterly black, and I trembled. My teeth chattered. The bread fell from my hands, and my wife waked and said, "Who is that, ah?"

I muttered, "It's me."

"Gimpel?" she asked. "How come you're here? I thought it was forbidden."

"The rabbi said," I answered and shook as with a fever.

"Listen to me, Gimpel," she said, "go out to the shed and see if the goat's all right. It seems she's been sick." I have forgotten to say that we had a goat. When I heard she was unwell I went into the yard. The nannygoat was a good little creature. I had a nearly human feeling for her.

With hesitant steps I went up to the shed and opened the door. The goat stood there on her four feet. I felt her everywhere, drew her by the horns, examined her udders, and found nothing wrong. She had probably eaten too much bark. "Good night, little goat," I said. "Keep well." And the little beast answered with a "Maa" as though to thank me for the good will.

I went back. The apprentice had vanished.

"Where," I asked, "is the lad?"

"What lad?" my wife answered.

"What do you mean?" I said. "The apprentice. You were sleeping with him."

"The things I have dreamed this night and the night before," she said, "may they come true and lay you low, body and soul! An evil spirit has taken root in you and dazzles your sight." She screamed out, "You hateful creature! You moon calf! You spook! You uncouth man! Get out, or I'll scream all Frampol out of bed!"

Before I could move, her brother sprang out from behind the oven and struck me a blow on the back of the head. I thought he had broken my neck. I felt that something about me was deeply wrong, and I said, "Don't make a scandal. All that's needed now is that people should accuse me of raising spooks and *dybbuks*." For that was what she had meant. "No one will touch bread of my baking."

In short, I somehow calmed her.

"Well," she said, "that's enough. Lie down, and be shattered by wheels."

Next morning I called the apprentice aside. "Listen here, brother!" I said. And so on and so forth. "What do you say?" He stared at me as though I had dropped from the roof or something.

"I swear," he said, "you'd better go to an herb doctor or some healer. I'm afraid you have a screw loose, but I'll hush it up for you." And that's how the thing stood.

To make a long story short, I lived twenty years with my wife. She bore me six children, four daughters and two sons. All kinds of things happened, but I neither saw nor heard. I believed, and that's all. The rabbi recently said to me, "Belief in itself is beneficial. It is written that a good man lives by his faith."

Suddenly my wife took sick. It began with a trifle, a little growth upon the breast. But she evidently was not destined to live long; she had no years. I spent a fortune on her. I have forgotten to say that by this time I had a bakery of my own and in Frampol was considered to be something of a rich man. Daily the healer came, and every witch doctor in the neighborhood was brought. They decided to use leeches, and after that to try cupping. They even called a doctor from Lublin, but it was too late. Before she died she called me to her bed and said, "Forgive me, Gimpel."

I said, "What is there to forgive? You have been a good and faithful wife."

"Woe, Gimpel!" she said. "It was ugly how I deceived you all these years. I want to go clean to my Maker, and so I have to tell you that the children are not yours."

If I had been clouted on the head with a piece of wood it couldn't have bewildered me more.

"Whose are they?" I asked.

"I don't know," she said. "There were a lot . . . but they're not yours." And as she spoke she tossed her head to the side, her eyes turned glassy, and it was all up with Elka. On her whitened lips there remained a smile.

I imagined that, dead as she was, she was saying, "I deceived Gimpel. That was the meaning of my brief life."

IV

One night, when the period of mourning was done, as I lay dreaming on the flour sacks, there came the Spirit of Evil himself and said to me, "Gimpel, why do you sleep?"

I said, "What should I be doing? Eating *kreplach?*"

"The whole world deceives you," he said, "and you ought to deceive the world in your turn."

"How can I deceive all the world?" I asked him.

He answered, "You might accumulate a bucket of urine every day and at night pour it into the dough. Let the sages of Frampol eat filth."

"What about the judgment in the world to come?" I said.

"There is no world to come," he said. "They've sold you a bill of goods and talked you into believing you carried a cat in your belly. What nonsense!"

"Well then," I said, "and is there a God?"

He answered, "There is no God either."

"What," I said, "*is* there, then?"

"A thick mire."

He stood before my eyes with a goatish beard and horn, long-toothed, and with a tail. Hearing such words, I wanted to snatch him by the tail, but I tumbled from the flour sacks and nearly broke a rib. Then it happened that I had to answer the call of nature, and, passing, I saw the risen dough, which seemed to say to me, "Do it!" In brief, I let myself be persuaded.

At dawn the apprentice came. We kneaded the bread, scattered caraway seeds on it, and set it to bake. Then the apprentice went away, and I was left sitting in the little trench by the oven, on a pile of rags. Well, Gimpel, I thought, you've revenged yourself on them for all the shame they've put on you. Outside the frost glittered, but it was warm beside the oven. The flames heated my face. I bent my head and fell into a doze.

I saw in a dream, at once, Elka in her shroud. She called to me, "What have you done, Gimpel?"

I said to her, "It's all your fault," and started to cry.

"You fool!" she said. "You fool! Because I was false is every-thing false too? I never deceived anyone but myself. I'm paying for it all, Gimpel. They spare you nothing here."

I looked at her face. It was black; I was startled and waked, and remained sitting dumb. I sensed that everything hung in the balance. A false step now and I'd lose Eternal Life. But God gave me His help. I seized the long shovel and took out the loaves, carried them into the yard, and started to dig a hole in the frozen earth.

My apprentice came back as I was doing it. "What are you doing boss?" he said, and grew pale as a corpse.

"I know what I'm doing," I said, and I buried it all before his very eyes.

Then I went home, took my hoard from its hiding place, and divided it among the children. "I saw your mother tonight," I said. "She's turning black, poor thing."

They were so astounded they couldn't speak a word.

"Be well," I said, "and forget that such a one as Gimpel ever existed." I put on my short coat, a pair of boots, took the bag that held my prayer shawl in one hand, my stock in the other, and kissed the *mezzuzah*. When people saw me in the street they were greatly surprised.

"Where are you going?" they said.

I answered, "Into the world." And so I departed from Frampol.

I wandered over the land, and good people did not neglect me. After many years I became old and white; I heard a great deal, many lies and falsehoods, but the longer I lived the more I under-stood that there were really no lies. Whatever doesn't really hap-pen is dreamed at night. It happens to one if it doesn't happen to another, tomorrow if not today, or a century hence if not next year. What difference can it make? Often I heard tales of which I said, "Now this is a thing that cannot happen." But before a year had elapsed I heard that it actually had come to pass some-where.

Going from place to place, eating at strange tables, it often happens that I spin yarns — improbable things that could never have happened — about devils, magicians, windmills, and the like. The children run after me, calling, "Grandfather, tell us a story." Sometimes they ask for particular stories, and I try to please them. A fat young boy once said to me, "Grandfather, it's the same story you told us before." The little rogue, he was right.

So it is with dreams too. It is many years since I left Frampol, but as soon as I shut my eyes I am there again. And whom do you think I see? Elka. She is standing by the washtub, as at our first encounter, but her face is shining and her eyes are as radiant as the eyes of a saint, and she speaks outlandish words to me, strange things. When I wake I have forgotten it all. But while the dream lasts I am comforted. She answers all my queries, and what comes out is that all is right. I weep and implore, "Let me be with you." And she consoles me and tells me to be patient. The time is nearer than it is far. Sometimes she strokes and kisses me and weeps upon my face. When I awaken I feel her lips and taste the salt of her tears.

No doubt the world is entirely an imaginary world, but it is only once removed from the true world. At the door of the hovel where I lie, there stands the plank on which the dead are taken away. The gravedigger Jew has his spade ready. The grave waits and the worms are hungry; the shrouds are prepared — I carry them in my beggar's sack. Another *shnorrer* is waiting to inherit my bed of straw. When the time comes I will go joyfully. Whatever may be there, it will be real, without complication, without ridicule, without deception. God be praised: there even Gimpel cannot be deceived.

(Translated by Saul Bellow)

JOHN CHEEVER (b. 1912) Cheever was born in Quincy, Massachusetts. Since 1930, when he wrote a fictional account of his expulsion from Thayer Academy in South Braintree, Massachusetts, he has published more than one hundred short stories, most of which have appeared in *The New Yorker.* Many of his stories employ as their subject ordinary, middle-class Americans whose lives are touched by a sense of romantic yearning. Cheever has received a number of awards and honors for his fiction; he received the O. Henry Award in 1956 for "The Country Husband."

Five collections of Cheever's stories have been published: *The Way Some People Live* (1943), *The Enormous Radio* (1953), *The Housebreaker of Shady Hill* (1958), *Some People, Places and Things That Will Not Appear in My Next Novel* (1961), and *The Brigadier and the Golf Widow* (1964). Cheever's novels are *The Wapshot Chronicle* (1957) and *The Wapshot Scandal* (1964).

THE COUNTRY HUSBAND

John Cheever

To begin at the beginning, the airplane from Minneapolis in which Francis Weed was travelling East ran into heavy weather. The sky had been a hazy blue, with the clouds below the plane lying so close together that nothing could be seen of the earth. Then mist began to form outside the windows, and they flew into a white cloud of such density that it reflected the exhaust fires. The color of the cloud darkened to gray, and the plane began to rock. Francis had been in heavy weather before, but he had never been shaken up so much. The man in the seat beside him pulled a flask out of his pocket and took a drink. Francis smiled at his neighbor, but the man looked away; he wasn't sharing his pain-killer with anyone. The plane had begun to drop and flounder wildly. A child was crying. The air in the cabin was overheated and stale, and Francis' left foot went to sleep. He read a little from a paper book that he had bought at the airport, but the violence of the storm divided his attention. The exhaust fires blazed and shed sparks in the dark, and, inside, the shaded lights, the stuffiness, and the window curtains gave the cabin an atmosphere of intense and misplaced domesticity. Then the lights flickered and went out. "You know what I've always wanted to do?" the man beside Francis said suddenly. "I've always wanted to buy a farm in New Hampshire and raise beef cattle." The stewardess announced that they were going to make an emergency landing. All but the child saw in their minds the spreading wings of the Angel of Death. The pilot could be heard singing faintly, "I've got sixpence, jolly, jolly sixpence. I've got sixpence to last me all my life . . ." There was no other sound.

The loud groaning of the hydraulic valves swallowed up the pilot's song, and there was a shrieking high in the air, like automobile brakes, and the plane hit flat on its belly in a cornfield and shook them so violently that an old man up forward howled, "Me kidneys! Me kidneys!" The stewardess flung open the door, and someone opened an emergency door at the back, letting in the sweet noise of their continuing mortality — the idle splash and smell of a heavy rain. Anxious for their lives, they filed out of the doors and scattered over the cornfield in all directions, praying that the thread would hold. It did. Nothing happened. When it was clear that the plane would not burn or explode, the crew and the stewardess gathered the passengers together and led them to the shelter of a barn. They were not far from Philadelphia, and in a little while a string of taxis took them into the city. "It's just like the Marne," someone said, but there was surprisingly little relaxation of that suspiciousness with which many Americans regard their fellow-travellers.

In Philadelphia, Francis Weed got a train to New York. At the end of that journey, he crossed the city and caught, just as it was about to pull out, the commuting train that he took five nights a week to his home in Shady Hill.

He sat with Trace Bearden. "You know, I was in that plane that just crashed outside Philadelphia," he said. "We came down in a field . . ." He had travelled faster than the newspapers or the rain, and the weather in New York was sunny and mild. It was a day in late September, as fragrant and shapely as an apple. Trace listened to the story, but how could he get excited? Francis had no powers that would let him re-create a brush with death — particularly in the atmosphere of a commuting train, journeying through a sunny countryside where already, in the slum gardens, there were signs of harvest. Trace picked up his newspaper, and Francis was left alone with his thoughts. He said good night to Trace on the platform at Shady Hill and drove in his second-hand Volkswagen up to the Blenhollow neighborhood, where he lived.

The Weeds' Dutch Colonial house was larger than it appeared to be from the driveway. The living room was spacious and divided like Gaul into three parts. Around an ell to the left as one entered from the vestibule was the long table, laid for six, with candles and a bowl of fruit in the center. The sounds and smells that came from the open kitchen door were appetizing, for Julia Weed was a good cook. The largest part of the living room centered around a fireplace. On the right were some bookshelves and a piano. The room was polished and tranquil, and from the windows that opened to the west there was some late-summer sunlight, brilliant and as clear as water. Nothing here was neglected; nothing had not been burnished. It was not the kind of household where, after prying open a stuck cigarette box, you would find an old shirt button and a tarnished nickel. The hearth was swept, the roses on the piano were reflected in the polish of the broad top, and there was an album of Schubert waltzes on the rack. Louisa Weed, a pretty girl of nine, was looking out the western windows. Her younger brother Henry was standing beside her. Her still younger brother, Toby, was studying the figures of some tonsured monks drinking beer on the polished brass of the wood box. Francis, taking off his hat and putting down his paper, was not consciously pleased with the scene; he was not that reflective. It was his element, his creation, and he returned to it with that sense of lightness and strength with which any creature returns to its home. "Hi, everybody," he said. "The plane from Minneapolis . . ."

Nine times out of ten, Francis would be greeted with affection, but tonight the children are absorbed in their own antagonisms. Francis had not finished his sentence about the plane crash before Henry plants a kick in Louisa's behind. Louisa swings around, saying *"Damn* you!" Francis makes the mistake of scolding Louisa for bad language before he punishes Henry. Now Louisa turns on her father and accuses him of favoritism. Henry is always right; she is persecuted and lonely; her lot is hopeless. Francis turns to his son, but the boy has justification for the kick — she hit him first; she hit him on the ear, which is dangerous. Louisa agrees with this passionately. She hit him on the ear, and she *meant* to hit him on the ear, because he messed up her china collection. Henry says that this is a lie. Little Toby turns away from the wood box to throw in some evidence for Louisa. Henry claps his hand over little Toby's mouth. Francis separates the two boys but accidentally pushes Toby into the wood box. Toby begins to cry. Louisa is already crying. Just then, Julia Weed comes into that part of the room where the table is laid. She is a pretty, intelligent woman, and the white in her hair is premature. She does not seem to notice the fracas. "Hello, darling," she says serenely to Francis. "Wash your hands, everyone. Dinner is ready." She strikes a match and lights the six candles in this vale of tears.

This simple announcement, like the war cries of the Scottish chieftains, only refreshes the ferocity of the combatants. Louisa gives Henry a blow on the shoulder. Henry, although he seldom cries, has pitched nine innings and is tired. He bursts into tears. Little Toby discovers a splinter in his hand and begins to howl. Francis says loudly that he has been in a plane crash and that he is tired. Julia appears again, from the kitchen, and, still ignoring the chaos, asks Francis to go upstairs and tell Helen that everything is ready. Francis is happy to go; it is like getting back to headquarters company. He is planning to tell his oldest daughter about the airplane crash, but Helen is lying on her bed reading a *True Romance* magazine, and the first thing Francis does is to take the magazine from her hand and remind Helen that he has forbidden her to buy it. She did not buy it, Helen replies. It was given to her by her best friend, Bessie Black. Everybody reads *True Romance*. Bessie Black's father reads *True Romance*. There isn't a girl in Helen's class who doesn't read *True Romance*. Francis expresses his detestation of the magazine and then tells her that dinner is ready — although from the sounds downstairs it doesn't seem so. Helen follows him down the stairs. Julia has seated herself in the candle-light and spread a napkin over her lap. Neither Louisa nor Henry has come to the table. Little Toby is still howling, lying face down on the floor. Francis speaks to him gently: "Daddy was in a plane crash this afternoon, Toby. Don't you want to hear about it?" Toby goes on crying. "If you don't come to the table now, Toby," Francis says, "I'll have to send you to bed without any supper." The little boy rises, gives him a cunning look, flies up the stairs to his bedroom, and slams the door. "Oh dear," Julia says, and starts to go after him. Francis says that she will spoil him. Julia says that Toby is ten pounds underweight and has to be encouraged to eat. Winter is coming, and he will spend the cold months in bed unless he has his dinner. Julia goes upstairs. Francis sits down at the table with Helen. Helen is suffering from the dismal feeling of having read too intently on a fine day, and she gives her father and the room a jaded look. She doesn't understand about the plane crash, because there wasn't a drop of rain in Shady Hill.

Julia returns with Toby, and they all sit down and are served.

"Do I have to look at that big, fat slob?" Henry says, of Louisa. Everybody but Toby enters into this skirmish, and it rages up and down the table for five minutes. Toward the end, Henry puts his napkin over his head and, trying to eat that way, spills spinach all over his shirt. Francis asks Julia if the children couldn't have their dinner earlier. Julia's guns are loaded for this. She can't cook two dinners and lay two tables. She paints with lightning strokes that panorama of drudgery in which her youth, her beauty, and her wit have been lost. Francis says that he must be understood; he was nearly killed in an airplane crash, and he doesn't like to come home every night to a battlefield. Now Julia is deeply committed. Her voice trembles. He doesn't come home every night to a battlefield. The accusation is stupid and mean. Everything was tranquil until he arrived. She stops speaking, puts down her knife and fork, and looks into her plate as if it is a gulf. She begins to cry. "Poor Mummy!" Toby says, and when Julia gets up from the table, drying her tears with a napkin, Toby goes to her side. "Poor Mummy," he says. "Poor Mummy!" And they climb the stairs together. The other children drift away from the battlefield, and Francis goes into the back garden for a cigarette and some air.

It was a pleasant garden, with walks and flower beds and places to sit. The sunset had nearly burned out, but there was still plenty of light. Put into a thoughtful mood by the crash and the battle, Francis listened to the evening sounds of Shady Hill. "Varmits! Rascals!" old Mr. Nixon shouted to the squirrels in his bird-feeding station. "Avaunt and quit my sight!" A door slammed. Someone was playing tennis on the Babcocks' court; someone was cutting grass. Then Donald Goslin, who lived at the corner, began to play the "Moonlight Sonata." He did this nearly every night. He threw the tempo out the window and played it *rubato* from beginning to end, like an outpouring of tearful petulance, lonesomeness, and self-pity — of everything it was Beethoven's greatness not to know. The music rang up and down the street beneath the trees like an appeal for love, for tenderness, aimed at some lonely housemaid — some fresh-faced, homesick girl from Galway, looking at old snapshots in her third-floor room. "Here, Jupiter, here Jupiter," Francis called to the

Mercers' retriever. Jupiter crashed through the tomato vines with the remains of a felt hat in his mouth.

Jupiter was an anomaly. His retrieving instincts and his high spirits were out of place in Shady Hill. He was as black as coal, with a long, alert, intelligent, rakehell face. His eyes gleamed with mischief, and he held his head high. It was the fierce, heavily collared dog's head that appears in heraldry, in tapestry, and that used to appear on umbrella handles and walking sticks. Jupiter went where he pleased, ransacking wastebaskets, clotheslines, garbage pails, and shoe bags. He broke up garden parties and tennis matches, and got mixed up in the processional at Christ's Church on Sunday, barking at the men in red dresses. He crashed through old Mr. Nixon's rose garden two or three times a day, cutting a wide swath through the Condesa de Sastagos, and as soon as Donald Goslin lighted his barbecue fire on Thursday nights, Jupiter would get the scent. Nothing the Goslins did could drive him away. Sticks and stones and rude commands only moved him to the edge of the terrace, where he remained, with his gallant and heraldic muzzle, waiting for Donald Goslin to turn his back and reach for the salt. Then he would spring onto the terrace, lift the steak lightly off the fire, and run away with the Goslins' dinner. Jupiter's days were numbered. The Wrightsons' German gardener or the Farquarsons' cook would soon poison him. Even old Mr. Nixon might put some arsenic in the garbage that Jupiter loved. "Here, Jupiter, Jupiter!" Francis called, but the dog pranced off, shaking the hat in his white teeth. Looking in at the windows of his house, Francis saw that Julia had come down and was blowing out the candles.

Julia and Francis Weed went out a great deal. Julia was well liked and gregarious, and her love of parties sprang from a most natural dread of chaos and loneliness. She went through her morning mail with real anxiety, looking for invitations, and she usually found some, but she was insatiable, and if she had gone out seven nights a week, it would not have cured her of a reflective look — the look of someone who hears distant music — for she would always suppose that there was a more brilliant party somewhere else. Francis limited her to two week-night parties, putting a flexible interpretation on Friday, and rode through the weekend like a dory in a gale. The day after the airplane crash, the Weeds were to have dinner with the Farquarsons.

Francis got home late from town, and Julia got the sitter while he dressed, and then hurried him out of the house. The party was small and pleasant, and Francis settled down to enjoy himself. A new maid passed the drinks. Her hair was dark, and her face was round and pale and seemed familiar to Francis. He had not developed his memory as a sentimental faculty. Wood smoke, lilac, and other such perfumes did not stir him, and his memory was something like his appendix — a vestigial repository. It was not his limitation at all to be unable to escape the past; it was perhaps his limitation that he had escaped it so successfully. He might have seen the maid at other parties, he might have seen her taking a walk on Sunday afternoons, but in either case he would not be searching his memory now. Her face was, in a wonderful way, a moon face — Norman or Irish — but it was not beautiful enough to account for his feeling that he had seen her before, in circumstances that he ought to be able to remember. He asked Nellie Farquarson who she was. Nellie said that the maid had come through an agency, and that her home was Trénon, in Normandy — a small place with a church and a restaurant that Nellie had once visited. While Nellie talked on about her travels abroad, Francis realized where he had seen the woman before. It had been at the end of the war. He had left a replacement depot with some other men and taken a three-day pass in Trénon. On their second day, they had walked out to a crossroads to see the public chastisement of a young woman who had lived with the German commandant during the Occupation.

It was a cool morning in the fall. The sky was overcast, and poured down onto the dirt crossroads a very discouraging light. They were on high land and could see how like one another the shapes of the clouds and the hills were as they stretched off toward the sea. The prisoner arrived sitting on a three-legged stool in a farm cart. She stood by the cart while the mayor read the accusation and the sentence. Her head was bent and her face was set in that empty half smile behind which the whipped soul is suspended. When the mayor was finished, she undid her hair and let it fall across her back. A little man with a gray mustache cut off her hair with shears and dropped it on the ground. Then, with a bowl of soapy water and a straight razor, he shaved her skull clean. A woman approached and began to undo the fastenings of her clothes, but the prisoner pushed her aside and undressed herself. When she pulled her chemise over her head and threw it on the ground, she was naked. The women jeered; the men were still. There was no change in the falseness or the plaintiveness of the prisoner's smile. The cold wind made her white skin rough and hardened the nipples of her breasts. The jeering ended gradually, put down by the recognition of their common humanity. One woman spat on her, but some inviolable grandeur in her nakedness lasted through the ordeal. When the crowd was quiet, she turned — she had begun to cry — and, with nothing on but a pair of worn black shoes and stockings, walked down the dirt road alone away from the village. The round white face had aged a little, but there was no question but that the maid who passed his cocktails and later served Francis his dinner was the woman who had been punished at the crossroads.

The war seemed now so distant and that world where the cost of partisanship had been death or torture so long ago. Francis had lost track of the men who had been with him in Vésey. He could not count on Julia's discretion. He could not tell anyone. And if he had told the story now, at the dinner table, it would have been a social as well as a human error. The people in the Farquarsons' living room seemed united in their tacit claim that there had been no past, no war — that there was no danger or trouble in the world. In the recorded history of human arrangements, this extraordinary meeting would have fallen into place, but the atmosphere of Shady Hill made the memory unseemly and impolite. The prisoner withdrew after passing the coffee, but the encounter left Francis feeling languid; it had opened his memory and his senses, and left them dilated. He and Julia drove home when the party ended, and Julia went into the house. Francis stayed in the car to take the sitter home.

Expecting to see Mrs. Henlein, the old lady who usually stayed with the children, he was surprised when a young girl opened the door and came out onto the lighted stoop. She stayed in the light to count her textbooks. She was frowning and beautiful. Now, the world is full of beautiful young girls, but Francis saw here the difference between beauty and perfection. All those endearing flaws, moles, birthmarks, and healed wounds were missing, and he experienced in his consciousness that moment when music breaks glass, and felt a pang of recognition as strange, deep, and wonderful as anything in his life. It hung from her frown, from an impalpable darkness in her face — a look that impressed him as a direct appeal for love. When she had counted her books, she came down the steps and opened the car door. In the light, he saw that her cheeks were wet. She got in and shut the door.

"You're new," Francis said.

"Yes, Mrs. Henlein is sick. I'm Anne Murchison."

"Did the children give you any trouble?"

"Oh, no, no." She turned and smiled at him unhappily in the dim dashboard light. Her light hair caught on the collar of her jacket, and she shook her head to set it loose.

"You've been crying."

"Yes."

"I hope it was nothing that happened in our house."

"No, no, it was nothing that happened in your house." Her voice was bleak. "It's no secret. Everybody in the village knows. Daddy's an alcoholic, and he just called me from some saloon and gave me a piece of his mind. He thinks I'm immoral. He called just before Mrs. Weed came back."

"I'm sorry."

"Oh, *Lord!*" She gasped and began to cry. She turned toward Francis, and he took her in his arms and let her cry on his shoulder. She shook in his embrace, and this movement accentuated his sense of the fineness of her flesh and bone. The layers of their clothing felt thin, and when her shuddering began to diminish, it was so much like a paroxysm of love that Francis lost his head and pulled her roughly against him. She drew away. "I live on Belleview Avenue," she said. "You go down Lansing Street to the railroad bridge."

"All right." He started the car.

"You turn left at that traffic light. . . . Now you turn right here and go straight on toward the tracks."

The road Francis took brought him out of his own neighborhood, across the tracks, and toward the river, to a street where the near-poor lived, in houses whose peaked gables and trimmings of wooden lace conveyed the purest feelings of pride and romance, although the houses themselves could not have offered much privacy or comfort, they were all so small. The street was dark, and, stirred by the grace and beauty of the troubled girl, he seemed, in turning into it, to have come into the deepest part of some submerged memory. In the distance, he saw a porch light burning. It was the only one, and she said that the house with the light was where she lived. When he stopped the car, he could see beyond the porch light into a dimly lighted hallway with an old-fashioned clothes tree. "Well, here we are," he said, conscious that a young man would have said something different.

She did not move her hands from the books, where they were folded, and she turned and faced him. There were tears of lust in his eyes. Determinedly — not sadly — he opened the door on his side and walked around to open hers. He took her free hand, letting his fingers in between hers, climbed at her side the two concrete steps, and went up a narrow walk through a front garden where dahlias, marigolds, and roses — things that had withstood the light frosts — still bloomed, and made a bittersweet smell in the night air. At the steps, she freed her hand and then turned and kissed him swiftly. Then she crossed the porch and shut the door. The porch light went out, then the light in the hall. A second later, a light went on upstairs at the side of the house, shining into a tree that was still covered with leaves. It took her only a few minutes to undress and get into bed, and then the house was dark.

Julia was asleep when Francis got home. He opened a second window and got into bed to shut his eyes on that night, but as soon as they were shut — as soon as he had dropped off to sleep — the girl entered his mind, moving with perfect freedom through its shut doors and filling chamber after chamber with her light, her perfume, and the music of her voice. He was crossing the Atlantic with her on the old Mauretania and, later, living with her in Paris. When he woke from this dream, he got up and smoked a cigarette at the open window. Getting back into bed, he cast around in his mind for something he desired to do that would injure no one, and he thought of skiing. Up through the dimness in his mind rose the image of a mountain deep in snow. It was late in the day. Wherever his eyes looked, he saw broad and heartening things. Over his shoulder, there was a snow-filled valley, rising into wooded hills where the trees dimmed the whiteness like a sparse coat of hair. The cold deadened all sound but the loud, iron clanking of the lift machinery.

The light on the trails was blue, and it was harder than it had been a minute or two earlier to pick the turns, harder to judge — now that the snow was all deep blue — the crust, the ice, the bare spots, and the deep piles of dry powder. Down the mountain he swung, matching his speed against the contours of a slope that had been formed in the first ice age, seeking with ardor some simplicity of feeling and circumstance. Night fell then, and he drank a Martini with some old friend in a dirty country bar.

In the morning, Francis' snow-covered mountain was gone, and he was left with his vivid memories of Paris and the Mauretania. He had been bitten gravely. He washed his body, shaved his jaws, drank his coffee, and missed the seven-thirty-one. The train pulled out just as he brought his car to the station, and the longing he felt for the coaches as they drew stubbornly away from him reminded him of the humors of love. He waited for the eight-two, on what was now an empty platform. It was a clear morning; the morning seemed thrown like a gleaming bridge of light over his mixed affairs. His spirits were feverish and high. The image of the girl seemed to put him into a relationship to the world that was mysterious and enthralling. Cars were beginning to fill up the parking lot, and he noticed that those that had driven down from the high land above Shady Hill were white with hoarfrost. This first clear sign of autumn thrilled him. An express train — a night train from Buffalo or Albany — came down the tracks between the platforms, and he saw that the roofs of the foremost cars were covered with a skin of ice. Struck by the miraculous physicalness of everything, he smiled at the passengers in the dining car, who could be seen eating eggs and wiping their mouths with napkins as they travelled. The sleeping-car compartments, with their soiled bed linen, trailed through the fresh morning like a string of rooming-house windows. Then he saw an extraordinary thing; at one of the bedroom windows sat an unclothed woman of exceptional beauty, combing her golden hair. She passed like an apparition through Shady Hill, combing and combing her hair, and Francis followed her with his eyes until she was out of sight. Then old Mrs. Wrightson joined him on the platform and began to talk.

"Well, I guess you must be surprised to see me here the third morning in a row," she said, "but because of my window curtains I'm becoming a regular commuter. The curtains I bought on

Monday I returned on Tuesday, and the curtains I bought on Tuesday, I'm returning today. On Monday, I got exactly what I wanted — it's a wool tapestry with roses and birds — but when I got them home, I found they were the wrong length. Well, I exchanged them yesterday, and when I got them home, I found they were still the wrong length. Now I'm praying to high Heaven that the decorator will have them in the right length, because you know my house, you *know* my living-room windows, and you can imagine what a problem they present. I don't know what to do with them."

"I know what to do with them," Francis said.

"What?"

"Paint them black on the inside, and shut up."

There was a gasp from Mrs. Wrightson, and Francis looked down at her to be sure that she knew he meant to be rude. She turned and walked away from him, so damaged in spirit that she limped. A wonderful feeling enveloped him, as if light were being shaken about him, and he thought again of Venus combing and combing her hair as she drifted through the Bronx. The realization of how many years had passed since he had enjoyed being deliberately impolite sobered him. Among his friends and neighbors, there were brilliant and gifted people — he saw that — but many of them, also, were bores and fools, and he had made the mistake of listening to them all with equal attention. He had confused a lack of discrimination with Christian love, and the confusion seemed general and destructive. He was grateful to the girl for this bracing sensation of independence. Birds were singing — cardinals and the last of the robins. The sky shone like enamel. Even the smell of ink from his morning paper honed his appetite for life, and the world that was spread out around him was plainly a paradise.

If Francis had believed in some hierarchy of love — in spirits armed with hunting bows, in the capriciousness of Venus and Eros — or even in magical potions, philtres, and stews, in scapulae and quarters of the moon, it might have explained his susceptibility and his feverish high spirits. The autumnal loves of middle age are well publicized, and he guessed that he was face to face with one of these, but there was not a trace of autumn in what he felt. He wanted to sport in the green woods, scratch where he itched, and drink from the same cup.

His secretary, Miss Rainey, was late that morning — she went
to a psychiatrist three mornings a week — and when she came in,
Francis wondered what advice a psychiatrist would have for him.
But the girl promised to bring back into his life something like
the sound of music. The realization that this music might lead
him straight to a trial for statutory rape at the county courthouse
collapsed his happiness. The photograph of his four children
laughing into the camera on the beach at Gay Head reproached
him. On the letterhead of his firm there was a drawing of the
Laocoön, and the figure of the priest and his sons in the coils
of the snake appeared to him to have the deepest meaning.

He had lunch with Pinky Trabert, who told him a couple of
dirty stories. At a conversational level, the mores of his friends
were robust and elastic, but he knew that the moral card house
would come down on them all — on Julia and the children as
well — if he got caught taking advantage of a baby-sitter. Looking back over the recent history of Shady Hill for some precedent,
he found there was none. There was no turpitude; there had not
been a divorce since he lived there; there had not even been a
breath of scandal. Things seemed arranged with more propriety
even than in the Kingdom of Heaven. After leaving Pinky, Francis went to a jeweller's and bought the girl a bracelet. How
happy this clandestine purchase made him, how stuffy and comical the jeweller's clerks seemed, how sweet the women who
passed at his back smelled! On Fifth Avenue, passing Atlas with
his shoulders bent under the weight of the world, Francis thought
of the strenuousness of containing his physicalness within the patterns he had chosen.

He did not know when he would see the girl next. He had the
bracelet in his inside pocket when he got home. Opening the
door of his house, he found her in the hall. Her back was to him,
and she turned when she heard the door close. Her smile was
open and loving. Her perfection stunned him like a fine day —
a day after a thunderstorm. He seized her and covered her lips
with his, and she struggled but she did not have to struggle for
long, because just then little Gertrude Flannery appeared from
somewhere and said, "Oh, Mr. Weed . . ."

Gertrude was a stray. She had been born with a taste for exploration, and she did not have it in her to center her life with

her affectionate parents. People who did not know the Flannerys concluded from Gertrude's behavior that she was the child of a bittterly divided family, where drunken quarrels were the rule. This was not true. The fact that little Gertrude's clothing was ragged and thin was her own triumph over her mother's struggle to dress her warmly and neatly. Garrulous, skinny, and unwashed, she drifted from house to house around the Blenhollow neighborhood, forming and breaking alliances based on an attachment to babies, animals, children her own age, adolescents, and sometimes adults. Opening your front door in the morning, you would find Gertrude sitting on your stoop. Going into the bathroom to shave, you would find Gertrude using the toilet. Looking into your son's crib, you would find it empty, and, looking further, you would find that Gertrude had pushed him in his baby carriage into the next village. She was helpful, pervasive, honest, hungry, and loyal. She never went home of her own choice. When the time to go arrived, she was indifferent to all its signs. "Go home, Gertrude," people could be heard saying in one house or another, night after night. "Go home, Gertrude." "It's time for you to go home now, Gertrude." "You had better go home and get your supper, Gertrude." "I told you to go home twenty minutes ago, Gertrude." "Your mother will be worrying about you, Gertrude." "Go home, Gertrude, go home."

There are times when the lines around the human eye seem like shelves of eroded stone and when the staring eye itself strikes us with such a wilderness of animal feeling that we are at a loss. The look Francis gave the little girl was ugly and queer, and it frightened her. He reached into his pocket — his hands were shaking — and took out a quarter. "Go home, Gertrude, go home, and don't tell anyone, Gertrude. Don't — " He choked and ran into the living room as Julia called down to him from upstairs to hurry and dress.

The thought that he would drive Anne Murchison home later that night ran like a golden thread through the events of the party that Francis and Julia went to, and he laughed uproariously at dull jokes, dried a tear when Mabel Mercer told him about the death of her kitten, and stretched, yawned, sighed, and grunted like any other man with a rendezvous at the back of his mind. The bracelet was in his pocket. As he sat talking, the smell of grass was in his nose, and he was wondering where he would park the car. Nobody lived in the old Parker mansion, and the driveway was used as a lovers' lane. Townsend Street was a dead end, and he could park there, beyond the last house. The old lane that used to connect Elm Street to the riverbanks was overgrown, but he had walked there with his children, and he could drive his car deep enough into the brushwoods to be concealed.

The Weeds were the last to leave the party, and their host and hostess spoke of their own married happiness while they all four stood in the hallway saying good night. "She's my girl," their host said, squeezing his wife. "She's my blue sky. After sixteen years, I still bite her shoulders. She makes me feel like Hannibal crossing the Alps."

The Weeds drove home in silence. Francis brought the car up the driveway and sat still, with the motor running. "You can put the car in the garage," Julia said as she got out. "I told the Murchison girl she could leave at eleven. Someone drove her home." She shut the door, and Francis sat in the dark. He would be spared nothing then, it seemed, that a fool was not spared: ravening lewdness, jealousy, this hurt to his feelings that put tears in his eyes, even scorn — for he could see clearly the image he now presented, his arms spread over the steering wheel and his head buried in them for love.

Francis had been a dedicated Boy Scout when he was young, and, remembering the precepts of his youth, he left his office early the next afternoon and played some round-robin squash, but, with his body toned up by exercise and a shower, he realized that he might better have stayed at his desk. It was a frosty night when he got home. The air smelled sharply of change. When he stepped into the house, he sensed an unusual stir. The children were in their best clothes, and when Julia came down, she was wearing a lavender dress and her diamond sunburst. She explained the stir: Mr. Hubber was coming at seven to take their photograph for the Christmas card. She had put out Francis' blue suit and a tie with some color in it, because the picture was going to be in color this year. Julia was lighthearted at the thought of being photographed for Christmas. It was the kind of ceremony she enjoyed.

Francis went upstairs to change his clothes. He was tired from the day's work and tired with longing, and sitting on the edge of the bed had the effect of deepening his weariness. He thought of Anne Murchison, and the physical need to express himself, instead of being restrained by the pink lamps on Julia's dressing table, engulfed him. He went to Julia's desk, took a piece of writing paper, and began to write on it. "Dear Anne, I love you, I love you, I love you . . ." No one would see the letter, and he used no restraint. He used phrases like "heavenly bliss," and "love nest." He salivated, sighed, and trembled. When Julia called him to come down, the abyss between his fantasy and the practical world opened so wide that he felt it affect the muscles of his heart.

Julia and the children were on the stoop, and the photographer and his assistant had set up a double battery of floodlights to show the family and the architectural beauty of the entrance to their house. People who had come home on a late train slowed their cars to see the Weeds being photographed for their Christmas card. A few waved and called to the family. It took half an hour of smiling and wetting their lips before Mr. Hubber was satisfied. The heat of the lights made an unfresh smell in the frosty air, and when they were turned off, they lingered on the retina of Francis' eyes.

Later that night, while Francis and Julia were drinking their coffee in the living room, the doorbell rang. Julia answered the door and let in Clayton Thomas. He had come to pay her for some theatre tickets that she had given his mother some time ago, and that Helen Thomas had scrupulously insisted on paying for, though Julia had asked her not to. Julia invited him in to have a cup of coffee. "I won't have any coffee," Clayton said, "but I will come in for a minute." He followed her into the living room, said good evening to Francis, and sat awkwardly in a chair.

Clayton's father had been killed in the war, and the young man's fatherlessness surrounded him like an element. This may have been conspicuous in Shady Hill because the Thomases were the only family that lacked a piece; all the other marriages were intact and productive. Clayton was in his second or third year of college, and he and his mother lived alone in a large house, which she hoped to sell. Clayton had once made some trouble.

Years ago, he had stolen some money and run away; he had got to California before they caught up with him. He was tall and homely, wore horn-rimmed glasses, and spoke in a deep voice.

"When do you go back to college, Clayton?" Francis asked.

"I'm not going back," Clayton said. "Mother doesn't have the money, and there's no sense in all this pretense. I'm going to get a job, and if we sell the house, we'll take an apartment in New York."

"Won't you miss Shady Hill?" Julia asked.

"No," Clayton said. "I don't like it."

"Why not?" Francis asked.

"Well, there's a lot here I don't approve of," Clayton said gravely. "Things like the club dances. Last Saturday night, I looked in toward the end and saw Mr. Granner trying to put Mrs. Minot into the trophy case. They were both drunk. I disapprove of so much drinking."

"It was Saturday night," Francis said.

"And all the dovecotes are phony," Clayton said. "And the way people clutter up their lives. I've thought about it a lot, and what seems to me to be really wrong with Shady Hill is that it doesn't have any future. So much energy is spent in perpetuating the place — in keeping out undesirables, and so forth — that the only idea of the future anyone has is just more and more commuting trains and more parties. I don't think that's healthy. I think people ought to be able to dream big dreams about the future. I think people ought to be able to dream great dreams."

"It's too bad you couldn't continue with college," Julia said.

"I wanted to go to divinity school," Clayton said.

"What's your church?" Francis asked.

"Unitarian, Theosophist, Transcendentalist, Humanist," Clayton said.

"Wasn't Emerson a transcendentalist?" Julia asked.

"I mean the English transcendentalists," Clayton said. "All the American transcendentalists were goops."

"What kind of a job do you expect to get?" Francis asked.

"Well, I'd like to work for a publisher," Clayton said, "but everyone tells me there's nothing doing. But it's the kind of thing I'm interested in. I'm writing a long verse play about good and evil. Uncle Charlie might get me into a bank, and that would be good for me. I need the discipline. I have a long way to go in forming my character. I have some terrible habits. I talk too much. I think I ought to take vows of silence. I ought to try not to speak for a week, and discipline myself. I've thought of making a retreat at one of the Episcopalian monasteries, but I don't like Trinitarianism."

"Do you have any girl friends?" Francis asked.

"I'm engaged to be married," Clayton said. "Of course, I'm not old enough or rich enough to have my engagement observed or respected or anything, but I bought a simulated emerald for Anne Murchison with the money I made cutting lawns this summer. We're going to be married as soon as she finishes school."

Francis recoiled at the mention of the girl's name. Then a dingy light seemed to emanate from his spirit, showing everything — Julia, the boy, the chairs — in their true colorlessness. It was like a bitter turn of the weather.

"We're going to have a large family," Clayton said. "Her father's a terrible rummy, and I've had my hard times, and we want to have lots of children. Oh, she's wonderful, Mr. and Mrs. Weed, and we have so much in common. We like all the same things. We sent out the same Christmas card last year without planning it, and we both have an allergy to tomatoes, and our eyebrows grow together in the middle. Well, good night."

Julia went to the door with him. When she returned, Francis said that Clayton was lazy, irresponsible, affected, and smelly. Julia said that Francis seemed to be getting intolerant; the Thomas boy was young and should be given a chance. Julia had noticed other cases where Francis had been short-tempered. "Mrs. Wrightson has asked everyone in Shady Hill to her anniversary party but us," she said.

"I'm sorry, Julia."

"Do you know why they didn't ask us?"

"Why?"

"Because you insulted Mrs. Wrightson."

"Then you know about it?"

"June Masterson told me. She was standing behind you."

Julia walked in front of the sofa with a small step that expressed, Francis knew, a feeling of anger.

"I did insult Mrs. Wrightson, Julia, and I meant to. I've never liked her parties, and I'm glad she's dropped us."

"What about Helen?"

"How does Helen come into this?"

"Mrs. Wrightson's the one who decides who goes to the assemblies."

"You mean she can keep Helen from going to the dances?"

"Yes."

"I hadn't thought of that."

"Oh, I knew you hadn't thought of it," Julia cried, thrusting hilt-deep into this chink of his armor. "And it makes me furious to see this kind of stupid thoughtlessness wreck everyone's happiness."

"I don't think I've wrecked anyone's happiness."

"Mrs. Wrightson runs Shady Hill and has run it for the last forty years. I don't know what makes you think that in a community like this you can indulge every impulse you have to be insulting, vulgar, and offensive."

"I have very good manners," Francis said, trying to give the evening a turn toward the light.

"Damn you, Francis Weed!" Julia cried, and the spit of her words struck him in the face. "I've worked hard for the social position we enjoy in this place, and I won't stand by and see you wreck it. You must have understood when you settled here that you couldn't expect to live like a bear in a cave."

"I've got to express my likes and dislikes."

"You can conceal your dislikes. You don't have to meet everything head-on, like a child. Unless you're anxious to be a social leper. It's no accident that we get asked out a great deal. It's no accident that Helen has so many friends. How would you like to spend your Saturday nights at the movies? How would you like to spend your Sundays raking up dead leaves? How would you like it if your daughter spent the assembly nights sitting at her window, listening to the music from the club? How would you like it — " He did something then that was, after all, not so unaccountable, since her words seemed to raise up between them a wall so deadening that he gagged: He struck her full in the face. She staggered and then, a moment later, seemed composed. She went up the stairs to their room. She didn't slam the door. When Francis followed, a few minutes later, he found her packing a suitcase.

"Julia, I'm very sorry."

"It doesn't matter," she said. She was crying.

"Where do you think you're going?"

"I don't know. I just looked at a timetable. There's an eleven-sixteen into New York. I'll take that."

"You can't go, Julia."

"I can't stay. I know that."

"I'm sorry about Mrs. Wrightson, Julia, and I'm — "

"It doesn't matter about Mrs. Wrightson. That isn't the trouble."

"What is the trouble?"

"You don't love me."

"I do love you, Julia."

"No, you don't."

"Julia, I do love you, and I would like to be as we were — sweet and bawdy and dark — but now there are so many people."

"You hate me."

"I don't hate you, Julia."

"You have no idea of how much you hate me. I think it's subconscious. You don't realize the cruel things you've done."

"What cruel things, Julia?"

"The cruel acts your subconscious drives you to in order to express your hatred of me."

"What, Julia?"

"I've never complained."

"Tell me."

"You don't know what you're doing."

"Tell me."

"Your clothes."

"What do you mean?"

"I mean the way you leave your dirty clothes around in order to express your subconscious hatred of me."

"I don't understand."

"I mean your dirty socks and your dirty pajamas and your dirty underwear and your dirty shirts!" She rose from kneeling by the suitcase and faced him, her eyes blazing and her voice ringing with emotion. "I'm talking about the fact that you've never learned to hang up anything. You just leave your clothes all over the floor where they drop, in order to humiliate me. You do it on purpose!" She fell on the bed, sobbing.

"Julia, darling!" he said, but when she felt his hand on her shoulder she got up.

"Leave me alone," she said. "I have to go." She brushed past him to the closet and came back with a dress. "I'm not taking any of the things you've given me," she said. "I'm leaving my pearls and the fur jacket."

"Oh, Julia!" Her figure, so helpless in its self-deceptions, bent over the suitcase made him nearly sick with pity. She did not understand how desolate her life would be without him. She didn't understand the hours that working women have to keep. She didn't understand that most of her friendships existed within the framework of their marriage, and that without this she would find herself alone. She didn't understand about travel, about hotels, about money. "Julia, I can't let you go! What you don't understand, Julia, is that you've come to be dependent on me."

She tossed her head back and covered her face with her hands. "Did you say that *I* was dependent on *you*?" she asked. "Is that what you said? And who is it that tells you what time to get up in the morning and when to go to bed at night? Who is it that prepares your meals and picks up your dirty closet and invites your friends to dinner? If it weren't for me, your neckties would be greasy and your clothing would be full of moth holes. You were alone when I met you, Francis Weed, and you'll be alone when I leave. When Mother asked you for a list to send out invitations to our wedding, how many names did you have to give her? Fourteen!"

"Cleveland wasn't my home, Julia."

"And how many of your friends came to the church? Two!"

"Cleveland wasn't my home, Julia."

"Since I'm not taking the fur jacket," she said quietly, "you'd better put it back into storage. There's an insurance policy on the pearls that comes due in January. The name of the laundry and the maid's telephone number — all those things are in my desk. I hope you won't drink too much, Francis. I hope that nothing bad will happen to you. If you do get into serious trouble, you can call me."

"Oh my darling, I can't let you go!" Francis said. "I can't let you go, Julia!" He took her in his arms.

"I guess I'd better stay and take care of you for a little while longer," she said.

Riding to work in the morning, Francis saw the girl walk down the aisle of the coach. He was surprised; he hadn't realized that the school she went to was in the city, but she was carrying books, she seemed to be going to school. His surprise delayed his reaction, but then he got up clumsily and stepped into the aisle. Several people had come between them, but he could see her ahead of him, waiting for someone to open the car door, and then, as the train swerved, putting out her hand to support herself as she crossed the platform into the next car. He followed her through that car and halfway through another before calling her name — "Anne! Anne!" — but she didn't turn. He followed her into still another car, and she sat down in an aisle seat. Coming up to her, all his feelings warm and bent in her direction, he put his hand on the back of her seat — even this touch warmed him — and, leaning down to speak to her, he saw that it was not Anne. It was an older woman wearing glasses. He went on deliberately into another car, his face red with embarrassment and the much deeper feeling of having his good sense challenged; for if he couldn't tell one person from another, what evidence was there that his life with Julia and the children had as much reality as his dreams of iniquity in Paris or the litter, the grass smell, and the cave-shaped trees in Lovers' Lane.

Late that afternoon, Julia called to remind Francis that they were going out for dinner. A few minutes later, Trace Bearden called. "Look, feller," Trace said. "I'm calling for Mrs. Thomas. You know? Clayton, that boy of hers, doesn't seem able to get a job, and I wondered if you could help. If you'd call Charlie Bell — I know he's indebted to you — and say a good word for the kid, I think Charlie would — "

"Trace, I hate to say this," Francis said, "but I don't feel that I can do anything for that boy. The kid's worthless. I know it's a harsh thing to say, but it's a fact. Any kindness done for him would backfire in everybody's face. He's just a worthless kid, Trace, and there's nothing to be done about it. Even if we got him a job, he wouldn't be able to keep it for a week. I know that to be a fact. It's an awful thing, Trace, and I know it is, but instead of recommending that kid, I'd feel obliged to warn people against him — people who knew his father and would naturally want to step in and do something. I'd feel obliged to warn them. He's a thief . . ."

The moment this conversation was finished, Miss Rainey came in and stood by his desk. "I'm not going to be able to work for you any more, Mr. Weed," she said. "I can stay until the seven-teenth if you need me, but I've been offered a whirlwind of a job, and I'd like to leave as soon as possible."

She went out, leaving him to face alone the wickedness of what he had done to the Thomas boy. His children in their photo-graph laughed and laughed, glazed with all the bright colors of summer, and he remembered that they had met a bagpiper on the beach that day and he had paid the piper a dollar to play them a battle song of the Black Watch. The girl would be at the house when he got home. He would spend another evening among his kind neighbors, picking and choosing dead-end streets, cart tracks, and the driveways of abandoned houses. There was nothing to mitigate his feeling — nothing that laughter or a game of soft-ball with the children would change — and, thinking back over the plane crash, the Farquarsons' new maid, and Anne Murchi-son's difficulties with her drunken father, he wondered how he could have avoided arriving at ·just where he was. He was in trouble. He had been lost once in his life, coming back from a trout stream in the north woods, and he had now the same bleak realization that no amount of cheerfulness or hopefulness or valor or perseverance could help him find, in the gathering dark, the path that he'd lost. He smelled the forest. The feeling of bleakness was intolerable, and he saw clearly that he had reached the point where he would have to make a choice.

He could go to a psychiatrist, like Miss Rainey; he could go to church and confess his lusts; he could go to a Danish massage parlor in the West Seventies that had been recommended by a salesman; he could rape the girl or trust that he would somehow be prevented from doing this; or he could get drunk. It was his life, his boat, and, like every other man, he was made to be the father of thousands, and what harm could there be in a tryst that would make them both feel more kindly toward the world? This was the wrong train of thought, and he came back to the first, the psychiatrist. He had the telephone number of Miss Rainey's doctor, and he called and asked for an immediate appointment. He was insistent with the doctor's secretary — it was his manner in business — and when she said that the doctor's schedule was full for the next few weeks, Francis demanded an appointment that day and was told to come at five.

The psychiatrist's office was in a building that was used mostly by doctors and dentists, and the hallways were filled with the candy smell of mouth-wash and memories of pain. Francis' character had been formed upon a series of private resolves — resolves about cleanliness, about going off the high diving board or repeating any other feat that challenged his courage, about punctuality, honesty, and virtue. To abdicate the prefect loneliness in which he had made his most vital decisions shattered his concept of character and left him now in a condition that felt like shock. He was stupefied. The scene for his *miserere mei Deus* was, like the waiting room of so many doctors' offices, a crude token gesture toward the sweets of domestic bliss: a place arranged with antiques, coffee tables, potted plants, and etchings of snow-covered bridges and geese in flight, although there were no children, no marriage bed, no stove, even, in this travesty of a house, where no one had ever spent the night and where the curtained windows looked straight onto a dark air shaft. Francis gave his name and address to a secretary and then saw, at the side of the room, a policeman moving toward him. "Hold it, hold it," the policeman said. "Don't move. Keep your hands where they are."

"I think it's all right, Officer," the secretary began. "I think it will be — "

"Let's make sure," the policeman said, and he began to slap Francis' clothes, looking for what — pistols, knives, an icepick? Finding nothing, he went off, and the secretary began a nervous apology: "When you called on the telephone, Mr. Weed, you seemed very excited, and one of the doctor's patients has been threatening his life, and we have to be careful. If you want to go in now?" Francis pushed open a door connected to an electrical chime, and in the doctor's lair sat down heavily, blew his nose into a handkerchief, searched in his pockets for cigarettes, for matches, for something, and said hoarsely, with tears in his eyes, "I'm in love, Dr. Herzog."

It is a week or ten days later in Shady Hill. The seven-fourteen has come and gone, and here and there dinner is finished and the dishes are in the dish-washing machine. The village hangs, morally and economically, from a thread; but it hangs by its thread in the evening light. Donald Goslin has begun to worry the "Moonlight Sonata" again. *Marcato ma sempre pianissimo!* He seems to be wringing out a wet bath towel, but the housemaid does not heed him. She is writing a letter to Arthur Godfrey. In the cellar of his house, Francis Weed is building a coffee table. Dr. Herzog recommended woodwork as a therapy, and Francis finds some true consolation in the simple arithmetic involved and in the holy smell of new wood. Francis is happy. Upstairs, little Toby is crying, because he is tired. He puts off his cowboy hat, gloves, and fringed jacket, unbuckles the belt studded with gold and rubies, the silver bullets and holsters, slips off his suspenders, his checked shirt, and Levis, and sits on the edge of his bed to pull off his high boots. Leaving this equipment in a heap, he goes to the closet and takes his space suit off a nail. It is a struggle for him to get into the long tights, but he succeeds. He loops the magic cape over his shoulders and, climbing onto the footboard of his bed, he spreads his arms and flies the short distance to the floor, landing with a thump that is audible to everyone in the house but himself.

"Go home, Gertrude, go home," Mrs. Masterson says. "I told you to go home an hour ago, Gertrude. It's way past your suppertime, and your mother will be worried. Go home!" A door on the Babcocks' terrace flies open, and out comes Mrs. Babcock without any clothes on, pursued by her naked husband. (Their children are away at boarding school, and their terrace is screened by a hedge.) Over the terrace they go and in at the kitchen door, as passionate and handsome a nymph and satyr as you will find on any wall in Venice. Cutting the last of the roses in her garden, Julia hears old Mr. Nixon shouting at the squirrels in his birdfeeding station. "Rapscallions! Varmits! Avaunt and quit my sight!" A miserable cat wanders into the garden, sunk in spiritual and physical discomfort. Tied to its head is a small straw hat — a doll's hat — and it is securely buttoned into a doll's dress, from the skirts of which protrudes its long, hairy tail. As it walks, it shakes its feet, as if it had fallen into water.

"Here, pussy, pussy, pussy!" Julia calls.

"Here, pussy, here, poor pussy!" But the cat gives her a skeptical look and stumbles away in its skirts. The last to come is Jupiter. He prances through the tomato vines, holding in his generous mouth the remains of an evening slipper. Then it is dark; it is a night where kings in golden suits ride elephants over the mountains.

DELMORE SCHWARTZ (1913–1966) Delmore Schwartz was born in Brooklyn of a middle-class Jewish family, and his early family life was the source of much of his writing. He studied at Columbia University, University of Wisconsin, Washington Square College, and Harvard University where he was a philosophy graduate student and an instructor. His first book was published when he was twenty-five. From 1943–1956 he was an editor of the Partisan Review.

Dwight Macdonald in his epitaph for Schwartz characterizes him as a great dialectical conversationalist: "An intellectual equivalent of the Borsch Circuit tummler, or stirrer-upper, his wide mouth grinning, his speedy, raucous New York voice running up and down the scale of sarcasm, invective, desperate rationality, grasping ridicule, his nervous hands clutching his head in despair at the obtuseness of his antagonist or flung wide in triumphant demonstration or stabbing the air with a minatory forefinger."

Summer Knowledge: New and Selected Poems 1938–1958 was published in 1959; *Successful Love and Other Stories* appeared in 1961. Besides his poems and stories, Schwartz wrote reviews of movies, television programs, and books, many of which appeared in *The New Republic*. He last taught at Syracuse University and died of a heart attack in 1966 outside the door of a lonely New York hotel room.

IN DREAMS BEGIN
RESPONSIBILITIES

Delmore Schwartz

I

I think it is the year 1909. I feel as if I were in a moving-picture theater, the long arm of light crossing the darkness and spinning, my eyes fixed upon the screen. It is a silent picture, as if an old Biograph one, in which the actors are dressed in ridiculously old-fashioned clothes, and one flash succeeds another with sudden jumps, and the actors, too, seem to jump about, walking too fast. The shots are full of rays and dots, as if it had been raining when the picture was photographed. The light is bad.

It is Sunday afternoon, June 12th, 1909, and my father is walking down the quiet streets of Brooklyn on his way to visit my mother. His clothes are newly pressed, and his tie is too tight in his high collar. He jingles the coins in his pocket, thinking of the witty things he will say. I feel as if I had by now relaxed entirely in the soft darkness of the theater; the organist peals out the obvious approximate emotions on which the audience rocks unknowingly. I am anonymous. I have forgotten myself: it is always so when one goes to a movie, it is, as they say, a drug.

My father walks from street to street of trees, lawns and houses, once in a while coming to an avenue on which a streetcar skates and yaws, progressing slowly. The motorman, who has a handle-bar mustache, helps a young lady wearing a hat like a feathered bowl onto the car. He leisurely makes change and rings his bell as the passengers mount the car. It is obviously Sunday, for everyone is wearing Sunday clothes and the streetcar's noises emphasize the quiet of the holiday. (Brooklyn is said to be the city of churches). The shops are closed and their shades drawn but for an occasional stationery store or drugstore with great green balls in the window.

My father has chosen to take this long walk because he likes to walk and think. He thinks about himself in the future and so arrives at the place he is to visit in a mild state of exaltation. He pays no attention to the houses he is passing, in which the Sunday dinner is being eaten, nor to the many trees which line each street, now coming to their full green and the time when they will enclose the whole street in leafy shadow. An occasional carriage passes, the horses' hooves falling like stones in the quiet afternoon, and once in a while an automobile, looking like an enormous upholstered sofa, puffs and passes.

My father thinks of my mother, of how lady-like she is, and of the pride which will be his when he introduces her to his family. They are not yet engaged and he is not yet sure that he loves my mother, so that, once in a while, he becomes panicky about the bond already established. But then he reassures himself by thinking of the big men he admires who are married: William Randolph Hearst and William Howard Taft, who has just become the President of the United States.

My father arrives at my mother's house. He has come too early and so is suddenly embarrassed. My aunt, my mother's younger sister, answers the loud bell with her napkin in her hand, for the family is still at dinner. As my father enters, my grandfather rises from the table and shakes hands with him. My mother has run upstairs to tidy herself. My grandmother asks my father if he has had dinner and tells him that my mother will be down soon. My grandfather opens the conversation by remarking about the mild June weather. My father sits uncomfortably near the table, holding his hat in his hand. My grandmother tells my aunt to take my father's hat. My uncle, twelve years old, runs into the house, his hair tousled. He shouts a greeting to my father, who has often given him nickles, and then runs upstairs, as my grandmother shouts after him. It is evident that the respect in which my father is held in this house is tempered by a good deal of mirth. He is impressive, but also very awkward.

II

Finally my mother comes downstairs and my father, being at the moment engaged in conversation with my grandfather, is made uneasy by her entrance, for he does not know whether to greet my mother or to continue the conversation. He gets up from his chair clumsily and says "Hello" gruffly. My grandfather

watches this, examining their congruence, such as it is, with a
critical eye, and meanwhile rubbing his bearded cheek roughly,
as he always does when he reasons. He is worried; he is afraid
that my father will not make a good husband for his oldest
daughter. At this point something happens to the film, just as my
father says something funny to my mother: I am awakened to
myself and my unhappiness just as my interest has become most
intense. The audience begins to clap impatiently. Then the
trouble is attended to, but the film has been returned to a portion just shown, and once more I see my grandfather rubbing his
bearded cheek, pondering my father's character. It is difficult to
get back into the picture once more and forget myself, but as my
mother giggles at my father's words, the darkness drowns me.

My father and mother depart from the house, my father shaking hands with my grandfather once more, out of some unknown
uneasiness. I stir uneasily also, slouched in the hard chair of the
theater. Where is the older uncle, my mother's older brother?
He is studying in his bedroom upstairs, studying for his final
examinations at the College of the City of New York, having
been dead of double pneumonia for the last twenty-one years.
My mother and father walk down the same quiet streets once
more. My mother is holding my father's arm and telling him of
the novel she has been reading and my father utters judgments
of the characters as the plot is made clear to him. This is a habit
which he very much enjoys, for he feels the utmost superiority
and confidence when he is approving or condemning the behavior of other people. At times he feels moved to utter a brief
"Ugh," whenever the story becomes what he would call sugary.
This tribute is the assertion of his manliness. My mother feels
satisfied by the interest she has awakened; and she is showing my
father how intelligent she is and how interesting.

They reach the avenue, and the streetcar leisurely arrives. They
are going to Coney Island this afternoon, although my mother
really considers such pleasures inferior. She has made up her
mind to indulge only in a walk on the boardwalk and a pleasant
dinner, avoiding the riotous amusements as being beneath the
dignity of so dignified a couple.

My father tells my mother how much money he has made in
the week just past, exaggerating an amount which need not have
been exaggerated. But my father has always felt that actualities

somehow fall short, no matter how fine they are. Suddenly I begin to weep. The determined old lady who sits next to me in the theater is annoyed and looks at me with an angry face, and being intimidated, I stop. I drag out my handkerchief and dry my face, licking the drop which has fallen near my lips. Meanwhile I have missed something, for here are my father and mother alighting from the streetcar at the last stop, Coney Island.

III

They walk toward the boardwalk and my mother commands my father to inhale the pungent air from the sea. They both breathe in deeply, both of them laughing as they do so. They have in common a great interest in health, although my father is strong and husky, and my mother is frail. They are both full of theories about what is good to eat and not good to eat, and sometimes have heated discussions about it, the whole matter ending in my father's announcement, made with a scornful bluster, that you have to die sooner or later anyway. On the boardwalk's flagpole, the American flag is pulsing in an intermittent wind from the sea.

My father and mother go to the rail of the boardwalk and look down on the beach where a good many bathers are casually walking about. A few are in the surf. A peanut whistle pierces the air with its pleasant and active whine, and my father goes to buy peanuts. My mother remains at the rail and stares at the ocean. The ocean seems merry to her; it pointedly sparkles and again and again the pony waves are released. She notices the children digging in the wet sand, and the bathing costumes of the girls who are her own age. My father returns with the peanuts. Overhead the sun's lightning strikes and strikes, but neither of them are at all aware of it. The boardwalk is full of people dressed in their Sunday clothes and casually strolling. The tide does not reach as far as the boardwalk, and the strollers would feel no danger if it did. My father and mother lean on the rail of the boardwalk and absently stare at the ocean. The ocean is becoming rough; the waves come in slowly, tugging strength from far back. The moment before they somersault, the moment when they arch their backs so beautifully, showing white veins in the green and black, that moment is intolerable. They finally crack, dashing fiercely upon the sand, actually driving, full force down-

ward, against it, bouncing upward and forward, and at last peter-
ing out into a small stream of bubbles which slides up the beach
and then is recalled. The sun overhead does not disturb my
father and my mother. They gaze idly at the ocean scarcely interested in its harshness. But I stare at the terrible sun which
breaks up sight, and the fatal merciless passionate ocean. I forget
my parents. I stare fascinated, and finally, shocked by their indifference, I burst out weeping once more. The old lady next to
me pats my shoulder and says: "There, there, young man, all of
this is only a movie, only a movie," but I look up once more at
the terrifying sun and the terrifying ocean, and being unable to
control my tears I get up and go to the men's room, stumbling
over the feet of the other people seated in my row.

IV

When I return, feeling as if I had just awakened in the morning sick for lack of sleep, several hours have apparently passed
and my parents are riding on the merry-go-round. My father is
on a black horse, my mother on a white one, and they seem to be
making an eternal circuit for the single purpose of snatching the
nickel rings which are attached to an arm of one of the posts. A
hand-organ is playing; it is inseparable from the ceaseless circling
of the merry-go-round.

For a moment it seems that they will never get off the carousel,
for it will never stop, and I feel as if I were looking down from
the fiftieth story of a building. But at length they do get off;
even the hand-organ has ceased for a moment. There is a sudden
and sweet stillness, as if the achievement of so much motion. My
mother has acquired only two rings, my father, however, ten of
them, although it was my mother who really wanted them.

They walk on along the boardwalk as the afternoon descends
by imperceptible degrees into the incredible violet of dusk.
Everything fades into a relaxed glow, even the ceaseless murmur-
ing from the beach. They look for a place to have dinner. My
father suggests the best restaurant on the boardwalk and my
mother demurs, according to her principles of economy and
housewifeliness.

However they do go to the best place, asking for a table near
the window so that they can look out upon the boardwalk and
the mobile ocean. My father feels omnipotent as he places a

quarter in the waiter's hand in asking for a table. The place is crowded and here too there is music, this time from a kind of string trio. My father orders with a fine confidence.

As their dinner goes on, my father tells of his plans for the future and my mother shows with expressive face how interested she is, and how impressed. My father becomes exultant, lifted up by the waltz that is being played and his own future begins to intoxicate him. My father tells my mother that he is going to expand his business, for there is a great deal of money to be made. He wants to settle down. After all, he is twenty-nine, he has lived by himself since his thirteenth year, he is making more and more money, and he is envious of his friends when he visits them in the security of their homes, surrounded, it seems, by the calm domestic pleasures, and by delightful children, and then as the waltz reaches the moment when the dancers all swing madly, then, then with awful daring, then he asks my mother to marry him, although awkwardly enough and puzzled as to how he had arrived at the question, and she, to make the whole business worse, begins to cry, and my father looks nervously about, not knowing at all what to do now, and my mother says: "It's all I've wanted from the first moment I saw you," sobbing, and he finds all of this very difficult, scarcely to his taste, scarcely as he thought it would be, on his long walks over Brooklyn Bridge in the revery of a fine cigar, and it was then, at that point, that I stood up in the theater and shouted: "Don't do it! It's not too late to change your minds, both of you. Nothing good will come of it, only remorse, hatred, scandal, and two children whose characters are monstrous." The whole audience turned to look at me, annoyed, the usher came hurrying down the aisle flashing his searchlight, and the old lady next to me tugged me down into my seat, saying: "Be quiet. You'll be put out, and you paid thirty-five cents to come in." And so I shut my eyes because I could not bear to see what was happening. I sat there quietly.

V

But after a while I begin to take brief glimpses and at length I watch again with thirsty interest, like a child who tries to maintain his sulk when he is offered a bribe of candy. My parents are now having their picture taken in a photographer's booth along the boardwalk. The place is shadowed in the mauve light which is apparently necessary. The camera is set to the side on its tripod and looks like a Martian man. The photographer is instructing my parents in how to pose. My father has his arm over my mother's shoulder, and both of them smile emphatically. The photographer brings my mother a bouquet of flowers to hold in her hand, but she holds it at the wrong angle. Then the photographer covers himself with the black cloth which drapes the camera and all that one sees of him is one protruding arm and his hand with which he holds tightly to the rubber ball which he squeezes when the picture is taken. But he is not satisfied with their appearance. He feels that somehow there is something wrong in their pose. Again and again he comes out from his hiding place with new directions. Each suggestion merely makes matters worse. My father is becoming impatient. They try a seated pose. The photographer explains that he has his pride, he wants to make beautiful pictures, he is not merely interested in all of this for the money. My father says: "Hurry up, will you? We haven't got all night." But the photographer only scurries about apologetically, issuing new directions. The photographer charms me, and I approve of him with all my heart, for I know exactly how he feels, and as he criticizes each revised pose according to some obscure idea of rightness, I become quite hopeful. But then my father says angrily: "Come on, you've had enough time, we're not going to wait any longer." And the photographer, sighing unhappily, goes back into the black covering, and holds out his hand, saying: "One, two, three, Now!" and the picture is taken, with my father's smile turned to a grimace and my mother's bright and false. It takes a few minutes for the picture to be developed and as my parents sit in the curious light they become depressed.

VI

They have passed a fortune-teller's booth and my mother wishes to go in, but my father does not. They begin to argue about it. My mother becomes stubborn, my father once more impatient. What my father would like to do now is walk off and leave my mother there, but he knows that that would never do. My mother refuses to budge. She is near tears, but she feels an uncontrollable desire to hear what the palm-reader will say. My father consents angrily and they both go into the booth which is, in a way, like the photographer's, since it is draped in black cloth and its light is colored and shadowed. The place is too warm, and my father keeps saying that this is all nonsense, pointing to the crystal ball on the table. The fortune-teller, a short, fat woman garbed in robes supposedly exotic, comes into the room and greets them, speaking with an accent, but suddenly my father feels that the whole thing is intolerable; he tugs at my mother's arm but my mother refuses to budge. And then, in terrible anger, my father lets go of my mother's arm and strides out, leaving my mother stunned. She makes a movement as if to go after him, but the fortune-teller holds her and begs her not to do so, and I in my seat in the darkness am shocked and horrified. I feel as if I were walking a tight-rope one hundred feet over a circus audience and suddenly the rope is showing signs of breaking, and I get up from my seat and begin to shout once more the first words I can think of to communicate my terrible fear, and once more the usher comes hurrying down the aisle flashing his searchlight, and the old lady pleads with me, and the shocked audience has turned to stare at me, and I keep shouting: "What are they doing? Don't they know what they are doing? Why doesn't my mother go after my father and beg him not to be angry? If she does not do that, what will she do? Doesn't my father know what he is doing?" But the usher has seized my arm, and is dragging me away, and as he does so, he says: "What are *you* doing? Don't you know you can't do things like this, you can't do whatever you want to do, even if other people aren't about? You will be sorry if you do not do what you should do. You can't carry on like this, it is not right, you will find that out soon enough, everything you do matters too much," and as he said that, dragging me through the lobby of the theatre, into the cold light, I woke up into the bleak winter morning of my twenty-first birthday, the window-sill shining with its lip of snow, and the morning already begun.

RALPH ELLISON (b.1914) Ellison was born in Oklahoma City and attended Tuskegee Institute where he studied music. In 1939 he began his career as a writer and since then has taught literature in a number of universities. Some of his essays on the subjects of writing, music, and race have been collected in *Shadow and Act* (1964).

Ellison's *Invisible Man* (1952) is considered by critics to be one of the most important American novels published since the end of World War II. Its hero is a Negro who attempts to discover his identity in terms of race, politics, culture, and history and is forced to realize that his identity exists outside of all of these terms; he is an invisible man. The story "King of the Bingo Game," published in 1944, in many ways foreshadows the novel. The technique is at once realistic and dreamlike; the Negro hero discovers identity neither with whites nor with Negroes; the universe in which the hero finds himself is intractably and ironically malevolent.

KING OF THE BINGO GAME

Ralph Ellison

The woman in front of him was eating roasted peanuts that smelled so good that he could barely contain his hunger. He could not even sleep and wished they'd hurry and begin the bingo game. There, on his right, two fellows were drinking wine out of a bottle wrapped in a paper bag, and he could hear soft gurgling in the dark. His stomach gave a low, gnawing growl. "If this was down South," he thought, "all I'd have to do is lean over and say, 'Lady, gimme a few of those peanuts, please ma'm,' and she'd pass me the bag and never think nothing of it." Or he could ask the fellows for a drink in the same way. Folks down South stuck together that way; they didn't even have to know you. But up here it was different. Ask somebody for something, and they'd think you were crazy. Well, I ain't crazy. I'm just broke, 'cause I got no birth certificate to get a job, and Laura 'bout to die 'cause we got no money for a doctor. But I ain't crazy. And yet a pinpoint of doubt was focused in his mind as he glanced toward the screen and saw the hero stealthily entering a dark room and sending the beam of a flashlight along a wall of bookcases. This is where he finds the trapdoor, he remembered. The man would pass abruptly through the wall and find the girl tied to a bed, her legs and arms spread wide, and her clothing torn to rags. He laughed softly to himself. He had seen the picture three times, and this was one of the best scenes.

On his right the fellow whispered wide-eyed to his companion, "Man, look a-yonder!"

"Damn!"

"Wouldn't I like to have her tied up like that . . ."

"Hey! That fool's letting her loose!"

"Aw, man, he loves her."

"Love or no love!"

The man moved impatiently beside him, and he tried to involve himself in the scene. But Laura was on his mind. Tiring quickly of watching the picture he looked back to where the white beam filtered from the projection room above the balcony. It started small and grew large, specks of dust dancing in its whiteness as it reached the screen. It was strange how the beam always landed right on the screen and didn't mess up and fall somewhere else. But they had it all fixed. Everything was fixed. Now suppose when they showed that girl with her dress torn the girl started taking off the rest of her clothes, and when the guy came in he didn't untie her but kept her there and went to taking off his own clothes? *That* would be something to see. If a picture got out of hand like that those guys up there would go nuts. Yeah, and there'd be so many folks in here you couldn't find a seat for nine months! A strange sensation played over his skin. He shuddered. Yesterday he'd seen a bedbug on a woman's neck as they walked out into the bright street. But exploring his thigh through a hole in his pocket he found only goose pimples and old scars.

The bottle gurgled again. He closed his eyes. Now a dreamy music was accompanying the film and train whistles were sounding in the distance, and he was a boy again walking along a railroad trestle down South, and seeing the train coming, and running back as fast as he could go, and hearing the whistle blowing, and getting off the trestle to solid ground just in time, with the earth trembling beneath his feet, and feeling relieved as he ran down the cinder-strewn embankment onto the highway, and looking back and seeing with terror that the train had left the track and was following him right down the middle of the street, and all the white people laughing as he ran screaming . . .

"Wake up there, buddy! What the hell do you mean hollering like that? Can't you see we trying to enjoy this here picture?"

He stared at the man with gratitude.

"I'm sorry, old man," he said. "I musta been dreaming."

"Well, here, have a drink. And don't be making no noise like that, damn!"

His hands trembled as he tilted his head. It was not wine, but whiskey. Cold rye whiskey. He took a deep swoller, decided it was better not to take another, and handed the bottle back to its owner.

"Thanks, old man," he said.

Now he felt the cold whiskey breaking a warm path straight through the middle of him, growing hotter and sharper as it moved. He had not eaten all day, and it made him light-headed. The smell of the peanuts stabbed him like a knife, and he got up and found a seat in the middle aisle. But no sooner did he sit than he saw a row of intense-faced young girls, and got up again, thinking, "You chicks musta been Lindy-hopping somewhere." He found a seat several rows ahead as the lights came on, and he saw the screen disappear behind a heavy red and gold curtain; then the curtain rising, and the man with the microphone and a uniformed attendant coming on the stage.

He felt for his bingo cards, smiling. The guy at the door wouldn't like it if he knew about his having *five* cards. Well, not everyone played the bingo game; and even with five cards he didn't have much of a chance. For Laura, though, he had to have faith. He studied the cards, each with its different numerals, punching the free center hole in each and spreading them neatly across his lap; and when the lights faded he sat slouched in his seat so that he could look from his cards to the bingo wheel with but a quick shifting of his eyes.

Ahead, at the end of the darkness, the man with the microphone was pressing a button attached to a long cord and spinning the bingo wheel and calling out the number each time the wheel came to rest. And each time the voice rang out his finger raced over the cards for the number. With five cards he had to move fast. He became nervous; there were too many cards, and the man went too fast with his grating voice. Perhaps he should just select one and throw the others away. But he was afraid. He became warm. Wonder how much Laura's doctor would cost? Damn that, watch the cards! And with despair he heard the man call three in a row which he missed on all five cards. This way he'd never win . . .

When he saw the row of holes punched across the third card, he sat paralyzed and heard the man call three more numbers before he stumbled forward, screaming,

"Bingo! Bingo!"

"Let that fool up there," someone called.

"Get up there, man!"

He stumbled down the aisle and up the steps to the stage into a light so sharp and bright that for a moment it blinded him, and he felt that he had moved into the spell of some strange, mysterious power. Yet it was as familiar as the sun, and he knew it was the perfectly familiar bingo.

The man with the microphone was saying something to the audience as he held out his card. A cold light flashed from the man's finger as the card left his hand. His knees trembled. The man stepped closer, checking the card against the numbers chalked on the board. Suppose he had made a mistake? The pomade on the man's hair made him feel faint, and he backed away. But the man was checking the card over the microphone now, and he had to stay. He stood tense, listening.

"Under the O, forty-four," the man chanted. "Under the I, seven. Under the G, three. Under the B, ninety-six. Under the N, thirteen!"

His breath came easier as the man smiled at the audience.

"Yessir, ladies and gentlemen, he's one of the chosen people!"

The audience rippled with laughter and applause.

"Step right up to the front of the stage."

He moved slowly forward, wishing that the light was not so bright.

"To win tonight's jackpot of $36.90 the wheel must stop between the double zero, understand?"

He nodded, knowing the ritual from the many days and nights he had watched the winners march across the stage to press the button that controlled the spinning wheel and receive the prizes. And now he followed the instructions as though he'd crossed the slippery stage a million prize-winning times.

The man was making some kind of a joke, and he nodded vacantly. So tense had he become that he felt a sudden desire to cry and shook it away. He felt vaguely that his whole life was determined by the bingo wheel; not only that which would happen now that he was at last before it, but all that had gone before, since his birth, and his mother's birth and the birth of his father. It had always been there, even though he had not been aware of it, handing out the unlucky cards and numbers of his days. The feeling persisted, and he started quickly away. I better get down from here before I make a fool of myself, he thought.

"Here, boy," the man called. "You haven't started yet."

Someone laughed as he went hesitantly back.

"Are you all reet?"

He grinned at the man's jive talk, but no words would come, and he knew it was not a convincing grin. For suddenly he knew that he stood on the slippery brink of some terrible embarrassment.

"Where are you from, boy?" the man asked.

"Down South."

"He's from down South, ladies and gentlemen," the man said. "Where from? Speak right into the mike."

"Rocky Mont," he said. "Rock' Mont, North Car'lina."

"So you decided to come down off that mountain to the U.S.," the man laughed. He felt that the man was making a fool of him, but then something cold was placed in his hand, and the lights were no longer behind him.

Standing before the wheel he felt alone, but that was somehow right, and he remembered his plan. He would give the wheel a short quick twirl. Just a touch of the button. He had watched it many times, and always it came close to double zero when it was short and quick. He steeled himself; the fear had left, and he felt a profound sense of promise, as though he were about to be repaid for all the things he'd suffered all his life. Trembling, he pressed the button. There was a whirl of lights, and in a second he realized with finality that though he wanted to, he could not stop. It was as though he held a high-powered line in his naked hand. His nerves tightened. As the wheel increased its speed it seemed to draw him more and more into its power, as though it held his fate; and with it came a deep need to submit, to whirl, to lose himself in its swirl of color. He could not stop it now, he knew. So let it be.

The button rested snuggly in his palm where the man had placed it. And now he became aware of the man beside him, advising him through the microphone, while behind the shadowy audience hummed with noisy voices. He shifted his feet. There was still that feeling of helplessness within him, making part of him desire to turn back, even now that the jackpot was right in his hand. He squeezed the button until his fist ached. Then, like the sudden shriek of a subway whistle, a doubt tore through his head. Suppose he did not spin the wheel long enough? What could he do, and how could he tell? And then he knew, even as he wondered, that as long as he pressed the button, he could control the jackpot. He and only he could determine whether or not it was to be his. Not even the man with the microphone could do anything about it now. He felt drunk. Then, as though he had come down from a high hill into a valley of people, he heard the audience yelling.

"Come down from there, you jerk!"

"Let somebody else have a chance . . ."

"Ole Jack thinks he done found the end of the rainbow . . ."

The last voice was not unfriendly, and he turned and smiled dreamily into the yelling mouths. Then he turned his back squarely on them.

"Don't take too long, boy," a voice said.

He nodded. They were yelling behind him. Those folks did not understand what had happened to him. They had been playing the bingo game day in and night out for years, trying to win rent money or hamburger change. But not one of those wise guys had discovered this wonderful thing. He watched the wheel whirling past the numbers and experienced a burst of exaltation: This is God! This is the really truly God! He said it aloud, "This is God!"

He said it with such absolute conviction that he feared he would fall fainting into the footlights. But the crowd yelled so loud that they could not hear. Those fools, he thought. I'm here trying to tell them the most wonderful secret in the world, and they're yelling like they gone crazy. A hand fell upon his shoulder.

"You'll have to make a choice now, boy. You've taken too long."

He brushed the hand violently away.

"Leave me alone, man. I know what I'm doing!"

The man looked surprised and held on to the microphone for support. And because he did not wish to hurt the man's feelings he smiled, realizing with a sudden pang that there was no way of explaining to the man just why he had to stand there pressing the button forever.

"Come here," he called tiredly.

The man approached, rolling the heavy microphone across the stage.

"Anybody can play this bingo game, right?" he said.

"Sure, but . . ."

He smiled, feeling inclined to be patient with this slick looking white man with his blue sport shirt and his sharp gabardine suit.

"That's what I thought," he said. "Anybody can win the jackpot as long as they get the lucky number, right?"

"That's the rule, but after all . . ."

"That's what I thought," he said. "And the big prize goes to the man who knows how to win it?"

The man nodded speechlessly.

"Well then, go on over there and watch me win like I want to. I ain't going to hurt nobody," he said "and I'll show you how to win. I mean to show the whole world how it's got to be done."

And because he understood, he smiled again to let the man know that he held nothing against him for being white and impatient. Then he refused to see the man any longer and stood pressing the button, the voices of the crowd reaching him like sounds in distant streets. Let them yell. All the Negroes down there were just ashamed because he was black like them. He smiled inwardly, knowing how it was. Most of the time he was ashamed of what Negroes did himself. Well, let them be ashamed for something this time. Like him. He was like a long thin black wire that was being stretched and wound upon the bingo wheel; wound until he wanted to scream; wound, but this time himself controlling the winding and the sadness and the shame, and because he did, Laura would be all right. Suddenly the lights flickered. He staggered backwards. Had something gone wrong? All this noise. Didn't they know that although he controlled the wheel, it also controlled him, and unless he pressed the button forever and forever and ever it would stop, leaving him high and dry, dry and high on this hard high slippery hill and Laura dead? There was only one chance; he had to do whatever the wheel demanded. And gripping the button in despair, he discovered with surprise that it imparted a nervous energy. His spine tingled. He felt a certain power.

Now he faced the raging crowd with defiance, its screams penetrating his eardrums like trumpets shrieking from a jukebox. The vague faces glowing in the bingo lights gave him a sense of himself that he had never known before. He was running the show, by God! They had to react to him, for he was their

luck. This is *me,* he thought. Let the bastards yell. Then someone was laughing inside him, and he realized that somehow he
had forgotten his own name. It was a sad, lost feeling to lose
your name, and a crazy thing to do. That name had been given
him by the white man who had owned his grandfather a long
lost time ago down South. But maybe those wise guys knew his
name.

"Who am I?" he screamed.

"Hurry up and bingo, you jerk!"

They didn't know either, he thought sadly. They didn't even
know their own names, they were all poor nameless bastards.
Well, he didn't need that old name; he was reborn. For as long
as he pressed the button he was The-man-who-pressed-the-button-
who-held-the-prize-who-was-the-King-of-Bingo. That was the way
it was, and he'd have to press the button even if nobody understood, even though Laura did not understand.

"Live!" he shouted.

The audience quieted like the dying of a huge fan.

"Live, Laura, baby. I got holt of it now, sugar. Live!"

He screamed it, tears streaming down his face. "I got nobody
but YOU!"

The screams tore from his very guts. He felt as though the rush
of blood to his head would burst out in baseball seams of small
red droplets, like a head beaten by police clubs. Bending over he
saw a trickle of blood splashing the toe of his shoe. With his free
hand he searched his head. It was his nose. God, suppose something has gone wrong? He felt that the whole audience had somehow entered him and was stamping its feet in his stomach, and
he was unable to throw them out. They wanted the prize, that
was it. They wanted the secret for themselves. But they'd never
get it; he would keep the bingo wheel whirling forever, and Laura
would be safe in the wheel. But would she? It had to be, because
if she were not safe the wheel would cease to turn; it could not go
on. He had to get away, *vomit* all, and his mind formed an image
of himself running with Laura in his arms down the tracks of the
subway just ahead of an A train, running desperately *vomit* with
people screaming for him to come out but knowing no way of
leaving the tracks because to stop would bring the train crushing
down upon him and to attempt to leave across the other tracks

would mean to run into a hot third rail as high as his waist which threw blue sparks that blinded his eyes until he could hardly see.

He heard singing and the audience was clapping its hands.

> *Shoot the liquor to him, Jim, boy!*
> *Clap-clap-clap*
> *Well a-calla the cop*
> *He's blowing his top!*
> *Shoot the liquor to him, Jim, boy!*

Bitter anger grew within him at the singing. They think I'm crazy. Well let 'em laugh. I'll do what I got to do.

He was standing in an attitude of intense listening when he saw that they were watching something on the stage behind him. He felt weak. But when he turned he saw no one. If only his thumb did not ache so. Now they were applauding. And for a moment he thought that the wheel had stopped. But that was impossible, his thumb still pressed the button. Then he saw them. Two men in uniform beckoned from the end of the stage. They were coming toward him, walking in step, slowly, like a tap-dance team returning for a third encore. But their shoulders shot forward, and he backed away, looking wildly about. There was nothing to fight them with. He had only the long black cord which led to a plug somewhere back stage, and he couldn't use that because it operated the bingo wheel. He backed slowly, fixing the men with his eyes as his lips stretched over his teeth in a tight, fixed grin; moved toward the end of the stage and realizing that he couldn't go much further, for suddenly the cord became taut and he couldn't afford to break the cord. But he had to do something. The audience was howling. Suddenly he stopped dead, seeing the men halt, their legs lifted as in an interrupted step of a slow-motion dance. There was nothing to do but run in the other direction and he dashed forward, slipping and sliding. The men fell back, surprised. He struck out violently going past.

"Grab him!"

He ran, but all too quickly the cord tightened, resistingly, and he turned and ran back again. This time he slipped them, and discovered by running in a circle before the wheel he could keep the cord from tightening. But this way he had to flail his arms to keep the men away. Why couldn't they leave a man alone? He ran, circling.

"Ring down the curtain," someone yelled. But they couldn't do that. If they did the wheel flashing from the projection room would be cut off. But they had him before he could tell them so, trying to pry open his fist, and he was wrestling and trying to bring his knees into the fight and holding on to the button, for it was his life. And now he was down, seeing a foot coming down, crushing his wrist cruelly, down, as he saw the wheel whirling serenely above.

"I can't give it up," he screamed. Then quietly, in a confidential tone, "Boys, I really can't give it up."

It landed hard against his head. And in the blank moment they had it away from him, completely now. He fought them trying to pull him up from the stage as he watched the wheel spin slowly to a stop. Without surprise he saw it rest at double-zero.

"You see," he pointed bitterly.

"Sure, boy, sure, it's O. K.," one of the men said smiling.

And seeing the man bow his head to someone he could not see, he felt very, very happy; he would receive what all the winners received.

But as he warmed in the justice of the man's tight smile he did not see the man's slow wink, nor see the bow-legged man behind him step clear of the swiftly descending curtain and set himself for a blow. He only felt the dull pain exploding in his skull, and he knew even as it slipped out of him that his luck had run out on the stage.

BERNARD MALAMUD (b.1914) Malamud was born in Brooklyn, New York and attended the City College of New York and Columbia University. He taught literature at Oregon State University and is now a member of the faculty of Bennington College.

Perhaps the distinguishing characteristic of Bernard Malamud's fiction has been a special combination of severe naturalism with mysticism. Most often, as is the case with "The Magic Barrel," Jewish life has provided him with his subject although Malamud has stressed repeatedly his intention to discover universal significances in the parochial lives of his Jewish characters. This is certainly true of his most recent novel *The Fixer*.

His stories have appeared in two collections: *The Magic Barrel* (1958) and *Idiots First* (1963). His novels are: *The Natural* (1952), *The Assistant* (1957), *A New Life* (1961), and *The Fixer* (1966).

THE MAGIC BARREL

Bernard Malamud

Not long ago there lived in uptown New York, in a small, almost
meager room, though crowded with books, Leon Finkle, a rabbinical student in the Yeshivah University. Finkle, after six
years of study, was to be ordained in June and had been advised
by an acquaintance that he might find it easier to win himself a
congregation if he were married. Since he had no present prospects of marriage, after two tormented days of turning it over in
his mind, he called in Pinye Salzman, a marriage broker, whose
two-line advertisement he had read in the *Forward*.

The matchmaker appeared one night out of the dark fourth-
floor hallway of the graystone rooming house, grasping a black,
strapped portfolio that had been worn thin with use. Salzman,
who had been long in the business, was of slight but dignified
build, wearing an old hat and an overcoat too short and tight for
him. He smelled frankly of fish, which he loved to eat, and although he was missing a few teeth, his presence was not displeas-
ing, because of an amiable manner curiously contrasted by
mournful eyes. His voice, his lips, his wisp of beard, his bony
fingers were animated, but give him a moment of repose, and his
mild blue eyes soon revealed a depth of sadness, a characteristic
that put Leo a little at ease although the situation, for him, was
inherently tense.

He at once informed Salzman why he had asked him to come,
explaining that his home was in Cleveland, and that but for his
parents, who had married comparatively late in life, he was alone
in the world. He had for six years devoted himself entirely to his
studies, as a result of which, quite understandably, he had found
himself without time for a social life and the company of young
women. Therefore he thought it the better part of trial and
error — of embarrassing fumbling — to call in an experienced

person to advise him in these matters. He remarked in passing that the function of the marriage broker was ancient and honorable, highly approved in the Jewish community, because it made practical the necessary without hindering joy. Moreover, his own parents had been brought together by a matchmaker. They had made, if not a financially profitable marriage — since neither had possessed any wordly goods to speak of — at least a successful one in the sense of their everlasting devotion to one another. Salzman listened in embarrassed surprise, sensing a sort of apology. Later, however, he experienced a glow of pride in his work, an emotion that had left him years ago, and he heartily approved of Finkle.

The two men went to their business. Leo had led Salzman to the only clear place in the room, a table near a window that overlooked the lamplit city. He seated himself at the matchmaker's side but facing him, attempting by an act of will to suppress the unpleasant tickle in his throat. Salzman eagerly unstrapped his portfolio and removed a loose rubber band from a thin packet of much-handled cards. As he flipped through them, a gesture and sound that physically hurt Leo, the student pretended not to see and gazed steadfastly out the window. Although it was still February, winter was on its last legs, signs of which he had for the first time in years begun to notice. He now observed the round white moon, moving high in the sky through a cloud-menagerie, and watched with half-open mouth as it penetrated a huge hen and dropped out of her like an egg laying itself. Salzman, though pretending through eyeglasses he had just slipped on, to be engaged in scanning the writing on the cards, stole occasional glances at the young man's distinguished face, noting with pleasure the long, severe scholar's nose, brown eyes heavy with learning, sensitive yet ascetic lips, and a certain almost hollow quality of the dark cheeks. He gazed around at shelves upon shelves of books and let out a soft but happy sigh.

When Leo's eyes fell upon the cards, he counted six spread out in Salzman's hand.

"So few?" he said in disappointment.

"You wouldn't believe me how much cards I got in my office," Salzman replied. "The drawers are already filled to the top, so I keep them now in a barrel, but is every girl good for a new rabbi?"

Leo blushed at this, regretting all he had revealed of himself in a curriculum vitae he had sent to Salzman. He had thought it best to acquaint him with his strict standards and specifications, but in having done so now felt he had told the marriage broker more than was absolutely necessary.

He hesitantly inquired, "Do you keep photographs of your clients on file?"

"First comes family, amount of dowry, also what kind promises," Salzman replied, unbuttoning his tight coat and settling himself in the chair. "After comes pictures, rabbi."

"Call me Mr. Finkle. I'm not a rabbi yet."

Salzman said he would, but instead called him doctor, which he changed to rabbi when Leo was not listening too attentively.

Salzman adjusted his horn-rimmed spectacles, gently cleared his throat and read in an eager voice the contents of the top card:

"Sophie P. Twenty-four years. Widow for one year. No children. Educated high school and two years college. Father promises eight thousand dollars. Has wonderful wholesale business. Also real estate. On mother's side comes teachers, also one actor. Well known on Second Avenue."

Leo gazed up in surprise. "Did you say a widow?"

"A widow don't mean spoiled, rabbi. She lived with her husband maybe four months. He was a sick boy, she made a mistake to marry him."

"Marrying a widow has never entered my mind."

"This is because you have no experience. A widow, specially if she is young and healthy like this girl, is a wonderful person to marry. She will be thankful to you the rest of her life. Believe me, if I was looking now for a bride, I would marry a widow."

Leo reflected, then shook his head.

Salzman hunched his shoulders in an almost imperceptible gesture of disappointment. He placed the card down on the wooden table and began to read another:

"Lily H. High-school teacher. Regular. Not a substitute. Has savings and new Dodge car. Lived in Paris one year. Father is successful dentist thirty-five years. Interested in professional man. Well Americanized family. Wonderful opportunity.

"I know her personally," said Salzman. "I wish you could see this girl. She is a doll. Also very intelligent. All day you could talk to her about books and theater and what not. She also knows current events."

"I don't believe you mentioned her age?"

"Her age?" Salzman said, raising his brows in surprise. "Her age is thirty-two years."

Leo said after a while, "I'm afraid that seems a little too old."

Salzman let out a laugh. "So how old are you, rabbi?"

"Twenty-seven."

"So what is the difference, tell me, between twenty-seven and thirty-two? My own wife is seven years older than me. So what did I suffer? — Nothing. If Rothschild's daughter wants to marry you, would you say on account of her age, no?"

"Yes," Leo said dryly.

Salzman shook off the no in the yes. "Five years don't mean a thing. I give you my word that when you will live with her for one week, you will forget her age. What does it mean five years — that she lived more and knows more than somebody who is younger? On this girl, God bless her, years are not wasted. Each one that it comes makes better the bargain."

"What subject does she teach in high school?"

"Languages. If you heard the way she reads French, you will think it is music. I am in the business twenty-five years, and I recommend her with my whole heart. Believe me, I know what I'm talking, rabbi."

"What's on the next card?" Leo said abruptly.

Salzman reluctantly turned up the third card:

"Ruth K. Nineteen years. Honor student. Father offers thirteen thousand dollars cash to the right bridegroom. He is a medical doctor. Stomach specialist with marvelous practice. Brother-in-law owns own garment business. Particular people."

Salzman looked up as if he had read his trump card.

"Did you say nineteen?" Leo asked with interest.

"On the dot."

"Is she attractive?" He blushed. "Pretty?"

Salzman kissed his fingertips. "A little doll. On this I give you my word. Let me call the father tonight and you will see what means pretty."

But Leo was troubled. "You're sure she's that young?"

"This I am positive. The father will show you the birth certificate."

"Are you positive there isn't something wrong with her?" Leo insisted.

"Who says there is wrong?"

"I don't understand why an American girl her age should go to a marriage broker."

A smile spread over Salzman's face.

"So for the same reason you went, she comes."

Leo flushed. "I am pressed for time."

Salzman, realizing he had been tactless, quickly explained. "The father came, not her. He wants she should have the best, so he looks around himself. When we will locate the right boy, he will introduce him and encourage. This makes a better marriage than if a young girl without experience takes for herself. I don't have to tell you this."

"But don't you think this young girl believes in love?" Leo spoke uneasily.

Salzman was about to guffaw, but caught himself and said soberly, "Love comes with the right person, not before."

Leo parted dry lips but did not speak. Noticing that Salzman had snatched a quick glance at the next card, he cleverly asked, "How is her health?"

"Perfect," Salzman said, breathing with difficulty. "Of course, she is a little lame on her right foot from an auto accident that it happened to her when she was twelve years, but nobody notices on account she is so brilliant and also beautiful."

Leo got up heavily and went to the window. He felt curiously bitter and upbraided himself for having called in the marriage broker. Finally, he shook his head.

"Why not?" Salzman persisted, the pitch of his voice rising.

"Because I hate stomach specialists."

"So what do you care what is his business? After you marry her, do you need him? Who says he must come every Friday night to your house?"

Ashamed of the way the talk was going, Leo dismissed Salzman, who went home with melancholy eyes.

Though he had felt only relief at the marriage broker's departure, Leo was in low spirits the next day. He explained it as arising from Salzman's failure to produce a suitable bride for him. He did not care for his type of clientele. But when Leo found himself hesitating over whether to seek out another matchmaker, one more polished than Pinye, he wondered if it could be — his protestations to the contrary, and although he honored his father and mother — that he did not, in essence, care for the matchmaking institution? This thought he quickly put out of his mind yet found himself still upset. All day he ran around in a fog — missed an important appointment, forgot to give out his laundry, walked out of a Broadway cafeteria without paying and had to run back with the ticket in his hand; had even not recognized his landlady in the street when she passed with a friend and courteously called out, "A good evening to you, Doctor Finkle." By nightfall, however, he had regained sufficient calm to sink his nose into a book and there found peace from his thoughts.

Almost at once there came a knock on the door. Before Leo could say enter, Salzman, commercial cupid, was standing in the room. His face was gray and meager, his expression hungry, and he looked as if he would expire on his feet. Yet the marriage broker managed, by some trick of the muscles, to display a broad smile.

"So good evening. I am invited?"

Leo nodded, disturbed to see him again, yet unwilling to ask him to leave.

Beaming still, Salzman laid his portfolio on the table. "Rabbi, I got for you tonight good news."

"I've asked you not to call me rabbi. I'm still a student."

"Your worries are finished. I have for you a first-class bride."

"Leave me in peace concerning this subject." Leo pretended lack of interest.

"The world will dance at your wedding."

"Please, Mr. Salzman, no more."

"But first must come back my strength," Salzman said weakly. He fumbled with the portfolio straps and took out of the leather case an oily paper bag, from which he extracted a hard seeded roll and a small smoked whitefish. With one motion of his hand he stripped the fish out of its skin and began ravenously to chew. "All day in a rush," he muttered.

Leo watched him eat.

"A sliced tomato you have maybe?" Salzman hesitantly inquired.

"No."

The marriage broker shut his eyes and ate. When he had finished, he carefully cleaned up the crumbs and rolled up the remains of the fish in the paper bag. His spectacled eyes roamed the room until he discovered, amid some piles of books, a one-burner gas stove. Lifting his hat, he humbly asked, "A glass of tea you got, rabbi?"

Conscience-stricken, Leo rose and brewed the tea. He served it with a chunk of lemon and two cubes of lump sugar, delighting Salzman.

After he had drunk his tea, Salzman's strength and good spirits were restored.

"So tell me, rabbi," he said amiably, "you considered any more the three clients I mentioned yesterday?"

"There was no need to consider."

"Why not?"

"None of them suits me."

"What, then, suits you?"

Leo let it pass because he could give only a confused answer.

Without waiting for a reply, Salzman asked, "You remember this girl I talked to you — the high-school teacher?"

"Age thirty-two?"

But, surprisingly, Salzman's face lit in a smile. "Age twenty-nine."

Leo shot him a look. "Reduced from thirty-two?"

"A mistake," Salzman avowed. "I talked today with the dentist. He took me to his safety deposit box and showed me the birth certificate. She was twenty-nine last August. They made her a party in the mountains where she went for her vacation. When her father spoke to me the first time, I forgot to write the age and I told you thirty-two, but now I remember this was a different client, a widow."

"The same one you told me about? I thought she was twenty-four?"

"A different. Am I responsible that the world is filled with widows?"

"No, but I'm not interested in them, nor for that matter, in schoolteachers."

Salzman passionately pulled his clasped hands to his breast. Looking at the ceiling he exclaimed, "Jewish children, what can

I say to somebody that he is not interested in high-school teachers? So what then you are interested?"

Leo flushed but controlled himself.

"In who else you will be interested," Salzman went on, "if you not interested in this fine girl that she speaks four languages and has personally in the bank ten thousand dollars? Also her father guarantees further twelve thousand. Also she has a new car, wonderful clothes, talks on all subjects, and she will give you a first-class home and children. How near do we come in our life to paradise?"

"If she's so wonderful, why wasn't she married ten years ago?"

"Why," said Salzman with a heavy laugh. " — Why? Because she is *partikler*. This is why. She wants only the *best*."

Leo was silent, amused at how he had trapped himself. But Salzman had aroused his interest in Lily H., and he began seriously to consider calling on her. When the marriage broker observed how intently Leo's mind was at work on the facts he had supplied, he felt positive they would soon come to an agreement.

Late Saturday afternoon, conscious of Salzman, Leo Finkle walked with Lily Hirschorn along Riverside Drive. He walked briskly and erectly, wearing with distinction the black fedora he had that morning taken with trepidation out of the dusty hatbox on his closet shelf, and the heavy black Saturday coat he had thoroughly whisked clean. Leo also owned a walking stick, a present from a distant relative, but had decided not to use it. Lily, petite and not unpretty, had on something signifying the approach of spring. She was *au courant*, animatedly, with all subjects, and he weighed her words and found her surprisingly sound — score another for Salzman, whom he uneasily sensed to be somewhere around, hiding perhaps high in a tree along the street, flashing the lady signals; or perhaps a cloven-hoofed Pan, piping nuptial ditties as he danced his invisible way before them, strewing wild buds on the walk and purple summer grapes in their path, symbolizing fruit of a union, of which there was yet none.

Lily startled Leo by remarking, "I was thinking of Mr. Salzman, a curious figure, wouldn't you say?"

Not certain what to answer, he nodded.

She bravely went on, blushing, "I for one am grateful for his introducing us. Aren't you?"

He courteously replied, "I am."

"I mean," she said with a little laugh — and it was all in good taste, or at least gave the effect of being not in bad — "do you mind that we came together so?"

He was not afraid of her honesty, recognizing that she meant to set the relationship aright, and understanding that it took a certain amount of experience in life, and courage, to want to do it quite that way. One had to have some sort of past to make that kind of beginning.

He said that he did not mind. Salzman's function was traditional and honorable — valuable for what it might achieve, which, he pointed out, was frequently nothing.

Lily agreed with a sigh. They walked on for a while, and she said after a long silence, again with a nervous laugh, "Would you mind if I asked you something a little bit personal? Frankly, I find the subject fascinating." Although Leo shrugged, she went on half embarrassedly, "How was it that you came to your calling? I mean, was it a sudden passionate inspiration?"

Leo, after a time, slowly replied, "I was always interested in the Law."

"You saw revealed in it the presence of the Highest?"

He nodded and changed the subject. "I understand you spent a little time in Paris, Miss Hirschorn?"

"Oh, did Mr. Salzman tell you, Rabbi Finkle?" Leo winced, but she went on, "It was ages and ages ago and almost forgotten. I remember I had to return for my sister's wedding."

But Lily would not be put off. "When," she asked in a trembly voice, "did you become enamored of God?"

He stared at her. Then it came to him that she was talking not about Leo Finkle, but a total stranger, some mystical figure, perhaps even passionate prophet that Salzman had conjured up for her — no relation to the living or dead. Leo trembled with rage and weakness. The trickster had obviously sold her a bill of goods, just as he had him, who'd expected to become acquainted with a young lady of twenty-nine, only to behold, the moment he laid eyes upon her strained and anxious face, a woman past thirty-five and aging very rapidly. Only his self-control, he thought, had kept him this long in her presence.

"I am not," he said gravely, "a talented religious person," and in seeking words to go on, found himself possessed by fear and shame. "I think," he said in a strained manner, "that I came to God not because I love Him, but because I did not."

This confession he spoke harshly because its unexpectedness shook him.

Lily wilted. Leo saw a profusion of loaves of bread sailing like ducks high over his head, not unlike the loaves by which he had counted himself to sleep last night. Mercifully, then, it snowed, which he would not put past Salzman's machinations.

He was infuriated with the marriage broker and swore he would throw him out of the room the moment he reappeared. But Salzman did not come that night, and when Leo's anger had subsided, an unaccountable despair grew in its place. At first he thought this was caused by his disappointment in Lily, but before long it became evident that he had involved himself with Salzman without a true knowledge of his own intent. He gradually realized — with an emptiness that seized him with six hands — that he had called in the broker to find him a bride because he was incapable of doing it himself. This terrifying insight he had derived as a result of his meeting and conversation with Lily Hirschorn. Her probing questions had somehow irritated him into revealing — to himself more than her — the true nature of his relationship with God, and from that it had come upon him, with shocking force, that apart from his parents, he had never loved anyone. Or perhaps it went the other way, that he did not love God so well as he might, because he had not loved man. It seemed to Leo that his whole life stood starkly revealed and he saw himself, for the first time, as he truly was — unloved and loveless. This bitter but somehow not fully unexpected revelation brought him to a point of panic controlled only by extraordinary effort. He covered his face with his hands and wept.

The week that followed was the worst of his life. He did not eat, and lost weight. His beard darkened and grew ragged. He stopped attending lectures and seminars and almost never opened a book. He seriously considered leaving the Yeshivah, although he was deeply troubled at the thought of the loss of all his years of study — saw them like pages from a book strewn over the city — and at the devastating effect of this decision upon his parents.

But he had lived without knowledge of himself, and never in the
Five Books and all the Commentaries — *mea culpa* — had the
truth been revealed to him. He did not know where to turn, and
in all this desolating loneliness there was no *to whom*, although
he often thought of Lily but not once could bring himself to go
downstairs and make the call. He became touchy and irritable,
especially with his landlady, who asked him all manner of questions; on the other hand, sensing his own disagreeableness, he
waylaid her on the stairs and apologized abjectly, until mortified,
she ran from him. Out of this, however, he drew the consolation
that he was yet a Jew and that a Jew suffered. But gradually, as
the long and terrible week drew to a close, he regained his composure and some idea of purpose in life: to go on as planned.
Although he was imperfect, the ideal was not. As for his quest
of a bride, the thought of continuing afflicted him with anxiety
and heartburn, yet perhaps with this new knowledge of himself
he would be more successful than in the past. Perhaps love would
now come to him and a bride to that love. And for this sanctified seeking who needed a Salzman?

The marriage broker, a skeleton with haunted eyes, returned
that very night. He looked, withal, the picture of frustrated expectancy — as if he had steadfastly waited the week at Miss Lily
Hirschorn's side for a telephone call that never came.

Casually coughing, Salzman came immediately to the point:
"So how did you like her?"

Leo's anger rose and he could not refrain from chiding the
matchmaker: "Why did you lie to me, Salzman?"

Salzman's pale face went dead white, as if the world had
snowed on him.

"Did you not state that she was twenty-nine?" Leo insisted.

"I give you my word — "

"She was thirty-five. *At least* thirty-five."

"Of this I would not be too sure. Her father told me — "

"Never mind. The worst of it was that you lied to her."

"How did I lie to her, tell me?"

"You told her things about me that weren't true. You made me
out to be more, consequently less than I am. She had in mind a
totally different person, a sort of semimystical Wonder Rabbi."

"All I said, you was a religious man."

"I can imagine."

Salzman sighed. "This is my weakness that I have," he confessed. "My wife says to me I shouldn't be a salesman, but when I have two fine people that they would be wonderful to be married, I am so happy that I talk too much." He smiled wanly. "This is why Salzman is a poor man."

Leo's anger went. "Well, Salzman, I'm afraid that's all."

The marriage broker fastened hungry eyes on him.

"You don't want any more a bride?"

"I do," said Leo, "but I have decided to seek her in a different way. I am no longer interested in an arranged marriage. To be frank, I now admit the necessity of premarital love. That is, I want to be in love with the one I marry."

"Love?" said Salzman, astounded. After a moment he said, "For us, our love is our life, not for the ladies. In the ghetto they — "

"I know, I know," said Leo. "I've thought of it often. Love, I have said to myself, should be a by-product of living and worship rather than its own end. Yet for myself I find it necessary to establish the level of my need and to fulfill it."

Salzman shrugged but answered, "Listen, rabbi, if you want love, this I can find for you also. I have such beautiful clients that you will love them the minute your eyes will see them."

Leo smiled unhappily. "I'm afraid you don't understand."

But Salzman hastily unstrapped his portfolio and withdrew a manila packet from it.

"Pictures," he said, quickly laying the envelope on the table.

Leo called after him to take the pictures away, but as if on the wings of the wind, Salzman had disappeared.

March came. Leo had returned to his regular routine. Although he felt not quite himself yet — lacked energy — he was making plans for a more active social life. Of course it would cost something, but he was an expert in cutting corners; and when there were no corners left he could make circles rounder. All the while Salzman's pictures had lain on the table, gathering dust. Occasionally as Leo sat studying, or enjoying a cup of tea, his eyes fell on the manila envelope, but he never opened it.

The days went by, and no social life to speak of developed with a member of the opposite sex — it was difficult, given the circumstances of his situation. One morning Leo toiled up the stairs to his room and stared out the window at the city. Although the day was bright, his view of it was dark. For some time he watched the people in the street below hurrying along and then turned with a heavy heart to his little room. On the table was the packet. With a sudden relentless gesture he tore it open. For a half-hour he stood there, in a state of excitement, examining the photographs of the ladies Salzman had included. Finally, with a deep sigh he put them down. There were six, of varying degrees of attractiveness, but look at them long enough and they all became Lily Hirschorn: all past their prime, all starved behind bright smiles, not a true personality in the lot. Life, despite their anguished struggles and frantic yoohooings, had passed them by; they were photographs in a brief case that stank of fish. After a while, however, as Leo attempted to return the pictures into the envelope, he found another in it, a small snapshot of the type taken by a machine for a quarter. He gazed at it a moment and let out a cry.

Her face deeply moved him. Why, he could at first not say. It gave him the impression of youth — all spring flowers — yet age — a sense of having been used to the bone, wasted; this all came from the eyes, which were hauntingly familiar, yet absolutely strange. He had a strong impression that he had met her before, but try as he might he could not place her, although he could almost recall her name, as if he had read it written in her own handwriting. No, this couldn't be; he would have remembered her. It was not, he affirmed, that she had an extraordinary beauty — no, although her face was attractive enough; it was that *something* about her moved him. Feature for feature, even some of the ladies of the photographs could do better; but she leaped forth to the heart — had lived, or wanted to — more than just wanted, perhaps regretted it — had somehow deeply suffered: it could be seen in the depths of those reluctant eyes, and from the way the light enclosed and shone from her, and within her, opening whole realms of possibility: this was her own. Her he desired. His head ached and eyes narrowed with the intensity of his gazing, then, as if a black fog had blown up in the mind, he experienced fear of her and was aware that he had received an impression, somehow, of filth. He shuddered, saying softly, it is thus with us all. Leo brewed some tea in a small pot and sat sipping it, without sugar, to calm himself. But before he had finished drinking, again with excitement he examined the face and found it good: good for him. Only such a one could truly understand Leo Finkle and help him to seek whatever he was seeking. How she had come to be among the discards in Salzman's barrel he could never guess, but he knew he must urgently go find her.

Leo rushed downstairs, grabbed up the Bronx telephone book, and searched for Salzman's home address. He was not listed, nor was his office. Neither was he in the Manhattan book. But Leo remembered having written down the address on a slip of paper after he had read Salzman's advertisement in the "personals" column of the *Forward*. He ran up to his room and tore through his papers, without luck. It was exasperating. Just when he needed the matchmaker he was nowhere to be found. Fortunately Leo remembered to look in his wallet. There on a card he found his name written and a Bronx address. No phone number was listed, which, Leo now recalled, was the reason he had originally communicated with Salzman by letter. He got on his coat, put a hat on over his skull cap and hurried to the subway station. All the way to the far end of the Bronx he sat on the edge of his seat. He was more than once tempted to take out the picture and see if the girl's face was as he remembered it, but he refrained, allowing the snapshot to remain in his inside coat pocket, content to have her so close. When the train pulled into the station, he was waiting at the door and bolted out. He quickly located the street Salzman had advertised.

The building he sought was less than a block from the subway, but it was not an office building, nor even a loft, nor a store in which one could rent office space. It was an old and grimy tenement. Leo found Salzman's name in pencil on a soiled tag under the bell and climbed three dark flights to his apartment. When he knocked, the door was opened by a thin, asthmatic, gray-haired woman, in felt slippers.

"Yes?" she said, expecting nothing. She listened without listening. He could have sworn he had seen her somewhere before but knew it was illusion.

"Salzman — does he live here? Pinye Salzman," he said, "the matchmaker?"

She stared at him a long time. "Of course."

He felt embarrassed. "Is he in?"

"No." Her mouth was open, but she offered nothing more.

"This is urgent. Can you tell me where his office is?"

"In the air." She pointed upward.

"You mean he has no office?" Leo said.

"In his socks."

He peered into the apartment. It was sunless and dingy, one large room divided by a half-open curtain, beyond which he could see a sagging metal bed. The nearer side of the room was crowded with rickety chairs, old bureaus, a three-legged table, racks of cooking utensils, and all the apparatus of a kitchen. But there was no sign of Salzman or his magic barrel, probably also a figment of his imagination. An odor of frying fish made Leo weak to the knees.

"Where is he?" he insisted. "I've got to see your husband."

At length she answered, "So who knows where he is? Every time he thinks a new thought he runs to a different place. Go home, he will find you."

"Tell him Leo Finkle."

She gave no sign that she had heard.

He went downstairs, deeply depressed.

But Salzman, breathless, stood waiting at his door.

Leo was overjoyed and astounded. "How did you get here before me?"

"I rushed."

"Come inside."

They entered. Leo fixed tea and a sardine sandwich for Salzman.

As they were drinking, he reached behind him for the packet of pictures and handed them to the marriage broker.

Salzman put down his glass and said expectantly, "You found maybe somebody you like?"

"Not among these."

The marriage broker turned sad eyes away.

"Here's the one I like." Leo held forth the snapshot.

Salzman slipped on his glasses and took the picture into his trembling hand. He turned ghastly and let out a miserable groan.

"What's the matter?" cried Leo.

"Excuse me. Was an accident this picture. She is not for you."

Salzman frantically shoved the manila packet into his portfolio. He thrust the snapshot into his pocket and fled down the stairs.

Leo, after momentary paralysis, gave chase and cornered the

marriage broker in the vestibule. The landlady made hysterical outcries, but neither of them listened.

"Give me back the picture, Salzman."

"No." The pain in his eyes was terrible.

"Tell me where she is then."

"This I can't tell you. Excuse me."

He made to depart, but Leo, forgetting himself, seized the matchmaker by his tight coat and shook him frenziedly.

"Please," sighed Salzman. *"Please."*

Leo ashamedly let him go. "Tell me who she is," he begged. "It's very important for me to know."

"She is not for you. She is a wild one — wild, without shame. This is not a bride for a rabbi."

"What do you mean wild?"

"Like an animal. Like a dog. For her to be poor was a sin. This is why she is dead now."

"In God's name, what do you mean?"

"Her I can't introduce to you," Salzman cried.

"Why are you so excited?"

"Why he asks," Salzman said, bursting into tears. "This is my baby, my Stella, she should burn in hell."

Leo hurried up to bed and hid under the covers. Under the covers he thought his whole life through. Although he soon fell asleep he could not sleep her out of his mind. He woke, beating his breast. Though he prayed to be rid of her, his prayers went unanswered. Through days of torment he struggled endlessly not to love her; fearing success, he escaped it. He then concluded to convert her to goodness, himself to God. The idea alternately nauseated and exalted him.

He perhaps did not know that he had come to a final decision until he encountered Salzman in a Broadway cafeteria. He was sitting alone at a rear table, sucking the bony remains of a fish. The marriage broker appeared haggard, and transparent to the point of vanishing.

Salzman looked up at first without recognizing him. Leo had grown a pointed beard, and his eyes were weighted with wisdom.

"Salzman," he said, "love has at last come to my heart."

"Who can love from a picture?" mocked the marriage broker.

"It is not impossible."

"If you can love her, then you can love anybody. Let me show you some new clients that they just sent me their photographs. One is a little doll."

"Just her I want," Leo murmured.

"Don't be a fool, doctor. Don't bother with her."

"Put me in touch with her, Salzman," Leo said humbly. "Perhaps I can do her a service."

Salzman had stopped chewing, and Leo understood with emotion that it was now arranged.

Leaving the cafeteria, he was, however, afflicted by a tormenting suspicion that Salzman had planned it all to happen this way.

Leo was informed by letter that she would meet him on a certain corner, and she was there one spring night, waiting under a street lamp. He appeared, carrying a small bouquet of violets and rosebuds. Stella stood by the lamppost, smoking. She wore white with red shoes, which fitted his expectations, although in a troubled moment he had imagined the dress red, and only the shoes white. She waited uneasily and shyly. From afar he saw that her eyes — clearly her father's — were filled with desperate innocence. He pictured, in hers, his own redemption. Violins and lit candles revolved in the sky. Leo ran forward with the flowers outthrust.

Around the corner, Salzman, leaning against a wall, chanted prayers for the dead.

SAUL BELLOW (b.1915) Bellow was born in Lachine, Quebec; when he was nine, his family moved to Chicago. He attended the University of Chicago where he is now a member of the faculty. He studied anthropology at Northwestern University and the University of Wisconsin.

In his stories and novels Bellow exhibits a great range of style and mood. A frequent hero of Bellow's fiction is a strong-willed, slightly fanatic, eloquent seeker after large philosophical truths. The rhetoric of the hero, like the subjects which concern him, ranges from highbrow to lowbrow in swift alternation. In other instances his fiction has been severely naturalistic, tightly controlled, and objective.

In addition to stories, essays, and plays, he has written six novels: *Dangling Man* (1944), *The Victim* (1947), *The Adventures of Augie March* (1953), *Seize the Day* (a novella, 1956), *Henderson the Rain King* (1959), and *Herzog* (1964). A play, *The Last Analysis,* was produced on Broadway in 1964.

LEAVING THE YELLOW HOUSE

Saul Bellow

The neighbors — there were in all six white people who lived at
Sego Desert Lake — told one another that old Hattie could no
longer make it alone. The desert life, even with a forced-air furnace in the house and butane gas brought from town in a truck,
was still too difficult for her. There were older women in the
county. Twenty miles away was Amy Walters, the gold miner's
widow. But she was a hardier old girl. Every day of the year she
took a bath in the lake. And Amy was crazy about money and
knew how to manage it, as Hattie did not. Hattie was not exactly
a drunkard, but she hit the bottle pretty hard, and now she was
in trouble and there was a limit to the help she could expect
from even the best of neighbors.

They were fond of her, though. You couldn't help being fond
of Hattie. She was big and cheerful, puffy, comic, boastful, with a
big round back and stiff, rather long legs. Before the century
began she had graduated from finishing school and studied the
organ in Paris. But now she didn't know a note from a skillet;
she had tantrums when she played canasta. And all that remained
of her fine fair hair was frizzled along her forehead in small grey
curls. Her forehead was not much wrinkled, but the skin was
bluish, the color of skim milk. She walked with long strides in
spite of the heaviness of her hips, pushing on, round-backed,
with her shoulders and showing the flat rubber bottoms of her
shoes.

Once a week, in the same cheerful, plugging but absent way,
she took off her short skirt and the dirty aviator's jacket with the
wool collar and put on a girdle, a dress and high-heeled shoes.
When she stood on these heels her fat old body trembled. She
wore a big brown Rembrandt-like tam with a ten-cent-store
brooch, eyelike, carefully centered. She drew a straight line with

lipstick on her mouth, leaving part of the upper lip pale. At the wheel of her old turret-shaped car, she drove, seemingly method-ical but speeding dangerously, across forty miles of mountainous desert to buy frozen meat pies and whiskey. She went to the Laundromat and the hairdresser, and then had lunch with two Martinis at the Arlington. Afterwards she would often visit Marian Nabot's Silvermine Hotel at Miller Street near skid row and pass the rest of the day gossiping and drinking with her cronies, old divorcées like herself who had settled in the West. Hattie never gambled any more and she didn't care for the movies, and at five o'clock she drove back at the same speed, calmly, partly blinded by the smoke of her cigarette. She was a tough-looking smoker. The fixed cigarette gave her a watering eye.

The Rolfes and the Paces were her only white neighbors at Sego Desert Lake. There was Sam Jervis too, but he was only an old gandy walker who did odd jobs in her garden, and she did not count him. Nor did she count among her neighbors Darly, the dudes' cowboy who worked for the Paces, nor Swede, the telegrapher. Pace had a guest ranch, and Rolfe and his wife were rich and had retired. Thus there were three good houses at the Lake, Hattie's yellow house, Pace's and the Rolfes'. All the rest of the population — Sam, Swede, Watchtah the section foreman, and the Mexicans and Indians and Negroes — lived in shacks and box-cars. You could count all the trees in a minute's time: cotton-woods and box elders. All the rest, down to the shores, was sage-brush and juniper. The lake was what remained of an old sea that had covered the volcanic mountains. To the north there were some tungsten mines; to the south, fifteen miles, was an Indian village built of railroad ties.

In this barren place Hattie had lived for more than twenty years. Her first summer was spent not in a house but in an Indian wikiup on the shore. She used to say that she had watched the stars from this almost roofless shelter. After her divorce she took up with a cowboy named Wicks. Neither of them had any money — it was the Depression — and they had lived on the range, trapping coyotes for a living. Once a month they would come into town and rent a room and go on a bender. Hattie told this sadly, but also gloatingly, and with many trimmings. A thing no sooner happened to her than it was transformed into something else. "We were caught in a storm," she said, "and we rode hard, down to the lake and knocked on the door of the yellow house" — now her house. "Alice Parmenter took us in and let us sleep on the floor." What had actually happened was that the wind was blowing — there had been no storm — and they were not far away from the house anyway; and Alice Parmenter, who knew that Hattie and Wicks were not married, offered them separate beds; but Hattie, swaggering, had said in a loud voice, "Why get two sets of sheets dirty?" And she and her cowboy had slept in Alice's double bed while Alice had taken the sofa.

Now Wicks was gone. There was never anybody like him in the sack; he was brought up in a whorehouse and the girls taught him everything, said Hattie. She didn't really understand what she was saying, but believed that she was being Western, and more than anything else she wanted to be thought of as a rough, experienced woman of the West. Still, she was a lady, too. She had good silver and good china and engraved stationery, but she kept canned beans and A-1 sauce and tunafish and bottles of catsup and fruit salad on the library shelves of her living room. On the night table was the Bible her pious brother Angus — her other brother was a heller — had given her; but behind the little cabinet door was a bottle of bourbon. When she awoke in the night she tippled herself back to sleep. In the glove compartment of her old car she kept little sample bottles for emergencies on the road. Old Darly found them after her accident.

The accident did not happen far out in the desert as she had always feared, but near her home. She had had a few Martinis with the Rolfes one evening and as she was driving home over the railroad crossing she lost control of the car and drove off the crossing onto the tracks. The explanation she gave was that she had sneezed, and the sneeze had blinded her and made her twist the wheel. The motor was killed and all four wheels of the car sat smack on the rails. Hattie crept down from the door, high off the roadbed. A great fear took hold of her — for the car, for the future, and not only for the future but for the past — and she began to hurry on stiff legs through the sagebrush to Pace's ranch.

Now the Paces were away on a hunting trip and had left old Darly in charge; he was tending bar in the old cabin that went back to the days of the pony express when Hattie burst in. There were two customers, a tungsten miner and his girl.

"Darly, I'm in trouble. Help me. I've had an accident," said Hattie.

How the face of a man will alter when a woman has bad news to tell him! It happened now to lean old Darly; his eyes went flat and looked unwilling, his jaw moved in and out, his wrinkled cheeks began to flush, and he said, "What's the matter — what's happened to you now?"

"I'm stuck on the tracks. I sneezed. I lost control of the car. Tow me off, Darly, with the pickup before the train comes."

Darly threw down his towel and stamped his high-heeled boots with anger. "Now what have you gone and done?" he said. "I told you to stay home after dark."

"Where's Pace? Ring the fire bell and fetch Pace."

"There's nobody on the property but me," said the lean old man. "And I'm not supposed to close the bar and you know it as well as I do."

"Please, Darly. I can't leave my car on the tracks."

"Too bad!" he said. Nevertheless he moved from behind the bar. "How did you say it happened?"

"I told you, I sneezed," said Hattie.

Everyone, as she later told it, was as drunk as sixteen thousand dollars: Darly, the miner and the miner's girl.

Darly was limping as he locked the door of the bar. A year before, a kick from one of Pace's mares had broken his ribs as he was loading her into the trailer, and he hadn't recovered from it. He was too old. But he dissembled the pain. The high-heeled narrow boots helped, and his painful bending looked like the ordinary stooping posture of a cowboy on the ground. However, Darly was not a genuine cowboy, like Pace who had grown up in the saddle. He was a late-comer from the East and until the age of forty had never been on horseback. In this respect he and Hattie were alike. They were not the Westerners they seemed to be.

Hattie hurried after him through the ranch yard.

"Damn you!" he said to her, "I got thirty bucks out of that sucker and I would have skinned him out of his whole pay check if you minded your business. Pace is going to be sore as hell."

"You've got to help me. We're neighbors," said Hattie.

"You're not fit to be living out here. You can't do it any more. Besides, you're swacked all the time."

Hattie couldn't afford to talk back to him. The thought of her car on the tracks made her frantic. If a freight came now and smashed it, her life at Sego Desert Lake would be finished. And where would she go then? She was not fit to live in this place. She had never made the grade at all; she only seemed to have made it. And Darly — why did he say such hurtful things to her? Because he himself was sixty-eight years old, and he had no other place to go, either; he took bad treatment from Pace besides. Darly stayed because his only alternative was to go to the soldier's home. Moreover, the dude women would crawl into his sack. They wanted a cowboy and they thought he was one. Why, he couldn't even raise himself out of his bunk in the morning. And where else would he get women? "After the season," she wanted to say to him, "you always have to go to the Veterans' Hospital to get yourself fixed up again." But she didn't dare offend him now.

The moon was due to rise. It appeared as they drove over the ungraded dirt road toward the crossing where Hattie's turret-shaped car was sitting on the rails. At great speed Darly wheeled the pickup around, spraying dirt on the miner and his girl who had followed in their car.

"You get behind the wheel and steer," Darly told Hattie.

She climbed into the seat. Waiting at the wheel she lifted up her face and said, "Please, God, I didn't bend the axle or crack the oil pan."

When Darly crawled under the bumper of Hattie's car the pain in his ribs suddenly cut off his breath, so instead of doubling the tow chain he fastened it at full length. He rose and trotted back to the truck on the narrow boots. Motion seemed the only remedy for the pain; not even booze did the trick any more. He put the pickup into towing gear and began to pull. One side of Hattie's car dropped into the roadbed with a heave of springs. She sat with a stormy, frightened, conscience-stricken face, racing the motor until she flooded it.

The tungsten miner yelled, "Your chain's too long."

Hattie was raised high in the air by the pitch of the wheels. She had to roll down the window to let herself out because the door handle had been jammed from the inside for years. Hattie struggled out on the uplifted side crying, "I better call the Swede. I better have him signal. There's a train due."

"Go on, then," said Darly. "You're no good here."

"Darly, be careful with my car. Be careful."

The ancient sea bed at this place was flat and low and the lights of her car and of the truck and of the tungsten miner's Chevrolet were bright and big at twenty miles. Hattie was too frightened to think of this. All she could think was that she was a procrastinating old woman, she had lived by delays; she had meant to stop drinking, she had put off the time, and now she had smashed her car — a terrible end, a terrible judgment on her. She got to the ground and, drawing up her skirt, she started to get over the tow chain. To prove that the chain didn't have to be shortened, and to get the whole thing over with, Darly threw the pickup forward again. The chain jerked up and struck Hattie in the knee and she fell forward and broke her arm.

She cried, "Darly, Darly, I'm hurt. I fell."

"The old lady tripped on the chain," said the miner. "Back up here and I'll double it for you. You're getting nowheres."

Drunkenly the miner lay down on his back in the dark, soft red cinders of the roadbed. Darly had backed up to slacken the chain.

Darly hurt the miner, too. He tore some skin from his fingers by racing ahead before the chain was secure. Uncomplainingly the miner wrapped his hand in his shirttail saying, "She'll do it now." The old car came down from the tracks and stood on the shoulder of the road.

"There's your goddam car," said Darly to Hattie.

"Is it all right?" she said. Her left side was covered with dirt, but she managed to pick herself up and stand, round-backed and heavy, on her stiff legs. "I'm hurt, Darly." She tried to convince him of it.

"Hell if you are," he said. He believed she was putting on an act to escape blame. The pain in his ribs made him especially impatient with her. "Christ, if you can't look after yourself any more you've got no business out here."

"You're old yourself," she said. "Look what you did to me. You can't hold your liquor."

This offended him greatly. He said, "I'll take you to the Rolfes. They let you tie this on in the first place, so let them worry about you. I'm tired of your bunk, Hattie."

He speeded up. Chains, spade and crowbar clashed on the sides of the truck. She was frightened and held her arm and cried.

Rolfe's dogs jumped at her to lick her when she went through the gate. She shrank from them crying, "Down, down."

"Darly," she cried in the darkness, "take care of my car. Don't leave it standing there on the road. Darly, take care of it, please."

But Darly in his ten-gallon hat, his chin-bent face wrinkled, small and angry, a furious pain in his ribs, tore away at high speed.

"Oh, God, what will I do," she said.

The Rolfes were having a last drink before dinner, sitting at their fire of pitchy railroad ties, when Hattie opened the door. Her knee was bleeding, her eyes were tiny with shock, her face grey with dust.

"I'm hurt," she said desperately. "I had an accident. I sneezed and lost control of the wheel. Jerry, look after the car. It's on the road."

They bandaged her knee and took her home and put her to bed. Helen Rolfe wrapped a heating pad around her arm.

"I can't have the pad," Hattie complained. "The switch goes on and off and every time it does it starts my generator and uses up the gas."

"Ah, now, Hattie," Rolfe said, "this is not the time to be stingy. We'll take you to town in the morning and have you looked over. Helen will phone Doctor Stroud."

Hattie wanted to say, "Stingy! Why you're the stingy ones. I just haven't got anything. You and Helen are ready to hit each other over two bits in canasta." But the Rolfes were good to her; they were her only real friends here. Darly would have let her lie in the yard all night, and Pace would sell her to the bone man if he had an offer.

So she didn't talk back to the Rolfes, but as soon as they left the yellow house and walked through the super-clear moonlight under the great skirt of branch shadows to their new car, Hattie turned off the switch and the heavy swirling and battering of the generator stopped. Presently she began to have her first real taste of the pain in her arm, and she sat rigid and warmed the injured place with her hand. It seemed to her that she could feel the bone. Before leaving, Helen Rolfe had thrown over her a comforter that had belonged to Hattie's dead friend India, from whom she had inherited the small house and everything in it. Had the comforter lain on India's bed the night she died? Hattie tried to remember, but her thoughts were mixed up. She was fairly sure the death-bed pillow was in the loft, and she believed she had put the rest of the bedding in a trunk. Then how had this comforter got out? She couldn't do anything about it now but draw it away from contact with her skin. It kept her legs warm; this she accepted, but she didn't want it any nearer.

More and more Hattie saw her own life as though from birth to the present every moment had been filmed. Her fancy was that when she died she would see the film shown. Then she would know how she appeared from the back, watering the plants, in the bathroom, asleep, playing the organ, embracing — everything, even tonight, in pain, almost the last pain, perhaps, for she couldn't take much more. How many more turns had life to show her yet? There couldn't be a lot. To lie awake and think such thoughts was the worst thing in the world. Better death than insomnia. Hattie not only loved sleep, she believed in it.

The first attempt to set the bone was not successful. "Look what they've done to me," said Hattie and showed the discolored skin on her breast. After the second operation her mind wandered. The sides of her bed had to be raised, for in her delirium she roamed the wards. She cried at the nurses when they shut her in, "You can't make people prisoners in a democracy without a trial." She cursed them fiercely.

For several weeks her mind was not clear. Asleep, her face was lifeless; her cheeks were puffed out and her mouth, no longer wide and grinning, was drawn round and small. Helen sighed when she saw her.

"Shall we get in touch with her family?" she asked the doctor. "She has a brother in Maine who is very strait-laced. And another one down in Mexico, even older than Hattie."

"No younger relations?" asked the doctor. His skin was white and thick. He had chestnut hair, abundant but very dry. He sometimes explained to his patients, "I had a tropical disease during the war."

"Cousins' children," said Helen. She tried to think who would be called to her own bedside. Rolfe would see that she was cared for. He would hire a nurse. Hattie could not afford one. She had already gone beyond her means. A trust company in Philadelphia paid her eighty dollars a month. She had a small bank account.

"I suppose it will be up to us to get her out of hock," said Rolfe. "Unless the brother down in Mexico comes across."

In the end, no relations had to be called. Hattie began to recover. At last she could recognize some of her friends, though her mind was still in disorder; much that had happened she couldn't recall.

"How much blood did they have to give me?" she kept asking. "I seem to remember five, six, eight different times. Daylight, electric light. . . ." She tried to smile, but she couldn't make a pleasant face as yet. "How am I going to pay?" she said. "At twenty-five bucks a quart. My little bit of money is just about wiped out."

Blood became her constant topic, her preoccupation. She told everyone who came to see her, " — have to replace all that blood. They poured gallons of the stuff into me. I hope it was all good." And, though very weak, she began to grin and laugh again. There was more of a hiss in her laughter than formerly; the illness had affected her chest.

"No cigarettes, no booze," the doctor told Helen.

"Doctor," Helen asked him, "do you expect her to change?"

"All the same, I am obliged to say it."

"Life may not be much of a temptation to her," said Helen.

Her husband laughed. When his laughter was intense it blinded one of his eyes and his short Irish face turned red except for the bridge of his small, sharp nose where the skin grew white. "Hattie's like me," he said. "She'll be in business till she's cleaned out. And if Sego Lake was all whiskey she'd use her last strength to knock her old yellow house down and build a raft of it. So why talk temperance to her now?"

Hattie recognized the similarity between them. When he came to see her she said, "Jerry, you're the only one I can really talk to about my troubles. What am I going to do for money? I have Hotchkiss Insurance. I paid eight dollars a month."

"That won't do you much good, Hat. No Blue Cross?"

"I let it drop ten years ago. Maybe I could sell some of my valuables."

"What have you got?" he said. His eye began to droop with laughter.

"Why," she said defiantly, "there's plenty. First there's the beautiful, precious Persian rug that India left me."

"Coals from the fireplace have been burning it for years, Hat!"

"The rug is in perfect condition," she said with an angry sway of her shoulders. "A beautiful object like that never loses its value. And the oak table from the Spanish monastery is three hundred years old."

"With luck you could get twenty bucks for it. It would cost fifty to haul it out of here. It's the house you ought to sell."

"The house?" she said. Yes, that had been in her mind. "I'd have to get twenty thousand for it."

"Eight is a fair price."

"Fifteen. . . ." She was offended, and her voice recovered its strength. "India put eight into it in two years. And don't forget that Sego Lake is one of the most beautiful places in the world."

"But where is it? Five hundred and some miles to San Francisco and two hundred to Salt Lake City. Who wants to live way out here in Utah but a few eccentrics like you and India and me?"

"There are things you can't put a price tag on. Beautiful things."

"Oh, bull, Hattie! You don't know what they are any more than I do. I live here because it figures for me, and you because India left you the house. And just in the nick of time, too. Without it you wouldn't have had a pot of your own."

His words offended Hattie; more than that, they frightened her. She was silent and then grew thoughtful, for she was fond of Jerry Rolfe and he of her. He had good sense and moreover he only spoke her own thoughts. He spoke no more than the truth about India's death and the house. But she told herself, *He doesn't know everything. You'd have to pay a San Francisco architect ten thousand just to* think *of such a house. Before he drew a line.*

"Jerry," the old woman said, "what am I going to do about replacing the blood in the blood bank?"

"Do you want a quart from me, Hat?" His eye began to fall shut.

"You won't do. You had that tumor, two years ago. I think Darly ought to give some."

"The old man?" Rolfe laughed at her. "You want to kill him?"

"Why," said Hattie with anger, lifting up her massive face with its fringe of curls which had become frayed by fever and perspiration; at the back of her head the hair had knotted and matted so that it had to be shaved, "he almost killed me. It's his fault that I'm in this condition. He must have blood in him. He runs after all the chicks — all of them — young and old."

"Come, you were drunk, too," said Rolfe.

"I've driven drunk for forty years. It was the sneeze. Oh, Jerry, I feel wrung out," said Hattie, haggard, sitting forward in bed. But her face was cleft by her nonsensically happy grin. She was not one to be miserable for long; she had the expression of a perennial survivor.

Every other day she went to the therapist. The young woman worked her arm for her; it was a pleasure and a comfort to Hattie, who would have been glad to leave the whole cure to her. However, she was given other exercises to do, and these were not so easy. They rigged a pulley for her and Hattie had to hold both ends of a rope and saw it back and forth through the scraping little wheel. She bent heavily from the hips and coughed over her cigarette. But the most important exercise of all she shirked. This required her to put the flat of her hand to the wall at the level of her hips and, by working her fingertips slowly, to make the hand ascend to the height of her shoulder. That was painful; she often forgot to do it, although the doctor warned her, "Hattie, you don't want adhesions, do you?"

A light of despair crossed Hattie's eyes. Then she said, "Oh, Dr. Stroud, buy my house from me."

"I'm a bachelor. What would I do with a house?"

"I know just the girl for you — my cousin's daughter. Perfectly charming and very brainy. Just about got her Ph.D."

"You must get quite a few proposals yourself," said the doctor.

"From crazy desert rats. They chase me. But," she said, "after I pay my bills I'll be in pretty punk shape. If at least I could replace that blood in the blood bank I'd feel easier."

"If you don't do as the therapist tells you, Hattie, you'll need another operation. Do you know what adhesions are?"

She knew. But Hattie thought, *How long must I go on taking care of myself?* It made her angry to hear him speak of another operation. She had a moment of panic, but she veiled it from him. With him, this young man whose skin was already as thick as buttermilk and whose chestnut hair was as dry as death, she always assumed the part of a small child. She said, "Yes, doctor." But her heart was in a fury.

Night and day, however, she repeated, "I was in the Valley of the Shadow. But I'm alive." She was weak, she was old, she couldn't follow a train of thought very easily, she felt faint in the head. But she was still here; here was her body, it filled space, a great body. And though she had worries and perplexities, and once in a while her arm felt as though it was about to give her the last stab of all; and though her hair was scrappy and old, like onion roots, and scattered like nothing under the comb, yet she sat and amused herself with visitors; her great grin split her face; her heart warmed with every kind word.

And she thought, "People will help me out. It never did me any good to worry. At the last minute something turned up, when I wasn't looking for it. Marian loves me. Helen and Jerry love me. Half Pint loves me. They would never let me go to the ground. And I love them. If it were the other way around, I'd never let them go down."

Above a horizon in a baggy vastness which Hattie by herself occasionally visited, the features of India, or her shade, sometimes rose. She was indignant and scolding. Not mean. Not really mean. Few people had ever been really mean to Hattie. But India was annoyed with her. "The garden is going to hell, Hattie," she said. "Those lilac bushes are all shriveled."

"But what can I do? The hose is rotten. It broke. It won't reach."

"Then dig a trench," said the phantom of India. "Have old Sam dig a trench. But save the bushes."

Am I thy servant still? said Hattie to herself. *No,* she thought, *let the dead bury their dead.*

But she didn't defy India now any more than she had done when they lived together. Hattie was supposed to keep India off the bottle, but often both of them began to get drunk after breakfast. They forgot to dress, and in their slips the two of them wandered drunkenly around the house and blundered into each other, and they were in despair at having been so weak. Late in the afternoon they would be sitting in the living room, waiting for the sun to set. It shrank, burning itself out on the crumbling edges of the mountains. When the sun passed, the fury of the daylight ended and the mountain surfaces were more blue, broken, like cliffs of coal. They no longer suggested faces. The east began to look simple, and the lake less inhuman and haughty. At last India would say, "Hattie — it's time for the lights." And Hattie would pull the switch chains of the lamps, several of them, to give the generator a good shove. She would turn on some of the wobbling eighteenth-century-style lamps whose shades stood out from their slender bodies like dragonflies' wings. The little engine in the shed would shuffle, then spit, then charge and bang, and the first weak light would rise unevenly in the bulbs.

"Hettie!" cried India. After she drank she was penitent, but her penitence too was a hardship to Hattie, and the worse her temper the more English her accent became. *"Where the hell ah you Het-tie!"* After India's death Hattie found some poems she had written in which she, Hattie, was affectionately and even touchingly mentioned. But Hattie's interest in ideas was very small, whereas India had been all over the world and was used to brilliant society. India wanted her to discuss Eastern religion, Bergson and Proust, and Hattie had no head for this, and so India blamed her drinking on Hattie. "I can't talk to you," she would say. "And I'm here because I'm not fit to be anywhere else. I can't live in New York any more. It's too dangerous for a woman my age to be drunk in the street at night."

And Hattie, talking to her Western friends about India, would say, "She is a lady," (implying that they made a pair). "She is a creative person," (this was why they found each other so congenial). "But helpless? Completely. Why she can't even get her own girdle on."

"Hettie! come here. Het-tie! Do you know what sloth is?"

Undressed, India sat on her bed and with the cigarette in her drunken, wrinkled, ringed hand she burned holes in the blankets. On Hattie's pride she left many small scars, too. She treated her like a servant.

Weeping, India begged her afterward to forgive her. *"Hattie, please, don't condemn me in your heart. Forgive me, dear, I know I am bad. But I hurt myself more in my evil than I hurt you."*

Hattie would keep a stiff bearing. She would lift up her face with its incurved nose and puffy eyes, and say, "I am a Christian person. I never bear a grudge." And by repeating this she actually brought herself to forgive India.

But of course she had no husband, no child, no skill, no savings. And what she would have done if India had not died and left her the yellow house, nobody knows.

Jerry Rolfe said privately to Marian, "Hattie can't do anything for herself. If I hadn't been around during the '44 blizzard she and India both would have starved. She's always been careless and lazy and now she can't even chase a cow out of her yard. She's too feeble. The thing for her to do is go East to her brother. Hattie would have ended at the poor farm if it hadn't been for India. But India should have left her something besides the house. Some dough. India didn't use her head."

When Hattie returned to the lake she stayed with the Rolfes. "Well, old shellback," said Jerry, "there's a little more life in you now."

Indeed, with joyous eyes, the cigarette in her mouth and her hair newly frizzed and overhanging her forehead, she seemed to have triumphed again. She was pale, but she grinned, she chuckled, and she held a bourbon Old-Fashioned with a cherry and a slice of orange in it. She was on rations; the Rolfes allowed her two a day. Her back, Helen noted, was more bent than before. Her knees went outward a little weakly; her feet, however, came close together at the ankles.

"Oh, Helen dear and Jerry dear, I am so thankful, so glad to be back at the lake. I can look after my place again, and I'm here to see the spring. It's more gorgeous than ever."

Heavy rains had fallen while Hattie was away. The Sego lilies, which bloomed only after a wet winter, came up from the loose dust, especially around the marl pit; but even on the burnt granite they seemed to grow. Desert peach was beginning to appear and in Hattie's yard the rosebushes were filling out. The roses were yellow and abundant, and the odor they gave off was like that of damp tea leaves.

"Before it gets hot enough for the rattlesnakes," said Hattie to Helen, "we ought to drive up to Marky's ranch to cut watercress."

Hattie was going to attend to lots of things, but the heat came early that year and, as there was no television to keep her awake, she slept most of the day. She was now able to dress herself, though there was little more that she could do. Sam Jervis rigged the pulley for her on the porch and she remembered once in a while to use it. Mornings when she had her strength she rambled over to her own house, examining things, behaving importantly and giving orders to Sam Jervis and Wanda Gingham. At ninety, Wanda, a Shoshone, was still an excellent seamstress and house-cleaner.

Hattie looked over the car, which was parked under a cotton-wood tree. She tested the engine. Yes, the old pot would still go. Proudly, happily, she listened to the noise of tappets; the dry old pipe shook as the smoke went out at the rear. She tried to work the shift, turn the wheel. That, as yet, she couldn't do. But it would come soon, she was confident.

At the back of the house the soil had caved in a little over the cesspool and a few of the old railroad ties over the top had rotted. Otherwise things were in good shape. Sam had looked after the garden. He had fixed a new catch for the gate after Pace's horses — maybe because he never could afford to keep them in hay — had broken in and Sam found them grazing and drove them out. Luckily they hadn't damaged many of her plants. Hattie felt a moment of wild rage against Pace. He had brought the horses into her garden, she was sure. But her anger didn't last long. It was reabsorbed into the feeling of golden pleasure that enveloped her. She had little strength, but all that she had was a pleasure to her. So she forgave even Pace, who would have liked to do her out of the house, who had always used her, em-barrassed her, cheated her at cards, passed the buck whenever he could. He was a fool about horses. They were ruining him. Breeding horses was a millionaire's amusement.

She saw the animals in the distance, feeding. Unsaddled, the mares appeared undressed; they reminded her of naked women walking with their glossy flanks in the Sego lilies which curled on the ground. The flowers were yellowish, like winter wool, but fragrant; the mares, naked and gentle, walked through them. Their strolling, their perfect beauty, the sound of their hoofs on stone touched a deep place in Hattie's nature. Her love for horses, birds and dogs was well-known. Dogs led the list. And now a piece cut from a green blanket reminded her of Richie. The blanket was one he had torn, and she had cut it into strips and placed them under the doors to keep out the draughts. In the house she found more traces of him: hair he had shed on the furniture. Hattie was going to borrow Helen's vacuum cleaner, but there wasn't really enough current to make it pull as it should. On the doorknob of India's room hung the dog collar.

Hattie had decided to have herself moved into India's bed when she lay dying. Why use two beds? A perilous look came into her eyes while her lips pressed together forbiddingly. "I follow," she said, speaking to India with an inner voice, "so never mind." Presently — before long — she would have to leave the yellow house in her turn. And as she went into the parlor thinking of the will, she sighed. Pretty soon she would have to attend to it. India's lawyer, Claiborne, helped her with such things. She had phoned him in town, while she was staying with Marian, and talked matters over with him. He had promised to try to sell the house for her. Fifteen thousand was her bottom price, she said. If he couldn't find a buyer, perhaps he could find a tenant. Two hundred dollars a month was the rental she set. Rolfe laughed. But Hattie turned toward him one of those proud, dulled looks she always took on when he angered her and said haughtily, "For summer on Sego Lake?"

"You're competing with Pace's ranch."

"Why, the food is stinking down there. He cheats the dudes," said Hattie. "He really cheats them at cards. You'll never catch me playing blackjack with him again."

And what would she do, thought Hattie, if Claiborne could neither rent nor sell the house? This question she shook off as regularly as it returned. *I don't have to be a burden on anybody,* thought Hattie. *It's looked bad many a time before, but when push came to shove, I made it. Somehow I got by.* But she argued with herself. *How many times? How long, O God — an old thing, feeble, no use to anyone?* Who said she had any right to hold a piece of property?

She was sitting on her sofa which was very old, India's sofa, eight feet long, kidney-shaped, puffy and bald. An underlying pink shone through the green; the upholstered tufts were like the pads of dogs' paws; between them rose bunches of hair. Here Hattie slouched, resting, with her knees wide apart and a cigarette in her mouth, eyes half shut but far-seeing. The mountains seemed not fifteen miles but fifteen hundred yards away, the lake a blue band; the tea-like odor of the roses, though they were still unopened, was already in the air, for Sam was watering them in the heat. Gratefully Hattie yelled, "Sam!"

Sam was very old, and all shanks. His feet looked big. His old railroad jacket was made tight across his back by his stoop. A crooked finger with its great broad nail over the mouth of the hose made the water spray and sparkle. Happy to see Hattie he turned his long jaw, empty of teeth, and his blue eyes, which seemed to penetrate his temples with their length (it was his face that turned, not his body), and he said, "Oh, there, Hattie. You've made it back today? Welcome, Hattie."

"Have a beer, Sam. Come around the back and I'll give you a beer."

She never had Sam come in, owing to his skin disease. There were raw patches on his chin and the back of his ears. Hattie feared infection from his touch. She gave him the beer can, never a glass, and she put on gloves before she used the garden tools. Since he would take no money from her — she had to pay Wanda Gingham a dollar a day — she got Marian to find old clothes for him in town and she left food for him at the door of the damp-wood-smelling boxcar where he lived.

"How's the old wing, Hat?" he said.

"It's coming. I'll be driving again before you know it," she told him. "By the first of May I'll be driving again." Every week she moved the date forward. "By Decoration Day I expect to be on my own again," she said. In mid-June however she was still unable to drive. Helen Rolfe said to her, "Hattie, Jerry and I are due in Seattle the first week of July."

"Why, you never told me that," said Hattie.

"You don't mean to tell me this is the first you heard of it," said Helen. "You've known about it from the first — since Christmas."

It wasn't easy for Hattie to meet her eyes. She presently put her head down. Her face became very dry, especially the lips. "Well, don't you worry about me. I'll be all right here," she said.

"Who's going to look after you?" said Jerry. He evaded nothing himself and tolerated very little evasion in others. Except, as Hattie knew, he always indulged her. She couldn't count on her friend Half Pint, she couldn't really count on Marian either.

Until now, this very moment, she had only the Rolfes to turn to. Helen, trying to be steady, gazed at her and made sad, involuntary movements with her head, sometimes nodding, sometimes seeming as if she disagreed. Hattie, with her inner voice, swore at her: *Bitch-eyes. I can't win because I'm old. Is that fair?* And yet she admired Helen's eyes. Even the skin about them, slightly wrinkled underneath, was touching, beautiful. There was a heaviness in her bust that went, as if by attachment, with the heaviness of her eyes. Her head, her hands and feet should have taken a more slender body. Helen, said Hattie, was the nearest thing she had on this earth to a sister. But there was no reason to go to Seattle — no genuine business. It was only idleness, only a holiday. The only reason was Hattie herself; this was their way of telling her that there was a limit to what she could expect them to do. Helen's head wavered, but her thoughts were steady; she knew what was passing through Hattie's mind. Like Hattie, she was an idle woman. Why was her right to idleness better?

Because of money? thought Hattie. Because of age? Because she has a husband? Because she had a daughter in Swarthmore College? But a funny thing occurred to her. Helen disliked being idle, whereas she herself never made any bones that an idle life was all she was ever good for. But for her it was uphill, all the way, because when Waggoner divorced her she didn't have a cent. She even had to support Wicks for seven or eight years. Except with horses, he had no sense. And then she had had to take a ton of dirt from India. *I am the one,* Hattie asserted to herself. *I would know what to do with Helen's advantages. She only suffers from them. And if she wants to stop being an idle woman why can't she start with me, her neighbor?* Her skin, for all its puffiness, burned with anger. She said to Rolfe and Helen: "Don't worry. I'll make out by myself. But if I have to leave the lake you'll be ten times more lonely than before. Now I'm going back to my house."

She lifted up her broad old face and her lips were childlike with suffering. She would never take back what she had said.

But the trouble was no ordinary trouble. Hattie was herself aware that she rambled, forgot names, and answered when no one spoke.

"We can't just take charge of her," Rolfe said. "What's more, she ought to be near a doctor. She keeps her shotgun loaded so she can fire it if anything happens to her in the house. But who knows what she'll do? I don't believe it was Jacamares who killed that Doberman of hers."

He drove into her yard the day after she returned to her house and said, "I'm going into town. I can bring you some chow if you like."

She couldn't afford to refuse his offer, angry though she was, and she said, "Yes, bring me some stuff from the Mountain Street Market. Charge it." She only had some frozen shrimp and a few cans of beer in the icebox. When Rolfe had gone she put out the shrimp to thaw.

People really used to stick by one another in the West. Hattie now saw herself as one of the pioneers. This modern race had come later. After all, she had lived on the range like an old-timer. Wicks had had to shoot their Christmas dinner and she had cooked it — venison. He killed it on the reservation, and if the Paiutes had caught them there would have been hell to pay.

The weather was hot, the clouds were heavy and calm in a large sky. The horizon was so huge that in it the lake must have seemed like a saucer of milk. *Some milk!* Hattie thought. Two thousand feet deep in the middle, so deep no body could ever be recovered. It went around with the currents, and there were rocks like eyeteeth, and hot springs, and colorless fish at the bottom which were never caught. Now that the white pelicans were nesting they patrolled the rocks for snakes and other egg thieves. They were so big and flew so slow you might imagine they were angels. Hattie no longer visited the lake shore; the walk exhausted her. She saved her strength to go to Pace's bar in the afternoon.

She took off her shoes and stockings and walked on bare feet from one end of her house to the other. On the land side she saw Wanda Gingham sitting near the tracks while her great-grandson played in the soft red gravel. Wanda wore a large purple shawl and her black head was bare. All about her was — was nothing, Hattie thought: for she had taken a drink, breaking her rule. Nothing but mountains, thrust out like men's bodies; the sagebrush was the hair on their chests.

The warm wind blew dust from the marl pit. This white powder made her sky less blue. On the water side were the pelicans, pure as spirits, slow as angels, blessing the air as they flew with great wings.

Should she or should she not have Sam do something about the vine on the chimney? Sparrows nested in it, and she was glad of that. But all summer long the king snakes were after them and she was afraid to walk in the garden. When the sparrows scratched the ground for seed they took a funny bound; they held their legs stiff and flung back the dust with both feet. Hattie sat down at her old Spanish table, watching them in the cloudy warmth of the day, clasping her hands, chuckling and sad. The bushes were crowded with yellow roses, half of them now rotted. The lizards scrambled from shadow to shadow. The water was smooth as air, gaudy as silk. The mountains succumbed, falling asleep in the heat. Drowsy, Hattie lay down on her sofa; its pads were like dogs' paws. She gave in to sleep and when she woke it was midnight; she did not want to alarm the Rolfes by putting on her lights, so took advantage of the moon to eat a few thawed shrimps and go to the bathroom. She undressed and lifted herself into bed and lay there feeling her sore arm. Now she knew how much she missed her dog. The whole matter of the dog weighed heavily on her soul; she came close to tears in thinking about him and she went to sleep, oppressed by her secret.

I suppose I had better try to pull myself together a little, thought Hattie nervously in the morning. *I can't just sleep my way through.* She knew what her difficulty was. Before any serious question her mind gave way; it became diffused. She said to herself, *I can see bright, but I feel dim. I guess I'm not so lively any more. Maybe I'm becoming a little touched in the head, as mother was.* But she was not so old as her mother was when she did those strange things. At eighty-five her mother had to be kept from going naked in the street. *I'm not as bad as that yet,* thought Hattie. *Thank God. I walked into the men's wards, but that was when I had a fever, and my nightie was on.*

She drank a cup of Nescafé and it strengthened her determination to do something for herself. In all the world she had only her brother Angus to go to. Her brother Will had led a rough life; he was an old heller, and now he drove everyone away. He was too crabby, thought Hattie. Besides he was angry because she had lived so long with Wicks. Angus would forgive her. But then he and his wife were not her kind. With them she couldn't drink, she couldn't smoke, she had to make herself small-mouthed, and she would have to wait while they read a chapter of the Bible before breakfast. Hattie could not bear to wait for meals. Besides, she had a house of her own at last; why should she have to leave it? She had never owned a thing before. And now she was not allowed to enjoy her yellow house. *But I'll keep it,* she said to herself rebelliously. *I swear to God I'll keep it. Why, I barely just got it. I haven't had time.* And she went out on the porch to work the pulley and do something about the adhesions in her arm. She was sure now that they were there. *And what will I do?* she cried to herself. *What will I do? Why did I ever go to Rolfe's that night — and why did I lose control on the crossing!* She couldn't say now "I sneezed." She couldn't even remember what had happened, except that she saw the boulders and the twisting blue rails and Darly. It was Darly's fault. He was sick and old himself, and couldn't make it. He envied her the house, and her woman's peaceful life. Since she returned from the hospital she hadn't even come to visit her. He only said, "Hell, I'm sorry for her, but it was her fault." What hurt him most was that she said he couldn't hold his liquor.

Her resolve to pull herself together did not last; she remained the same procrastinating old woman. She had a letter to answer from Hotchkiss Insurance, and it drifted out of sight. She was going to phone Claiborne the lawyer, and it slipped her mind. One morning she announced to Helen that she believed she would apply to an institution in Los Angeles that took over the property of old people and managed it for them. They gave you an apartment right on the ocean, and your meals and medical care. You had to sign over half of your estate. "It's fair enough," said Hattie. "They take a gamble. I may live to be a hundred."

"I wouldn't be surprised," said Helen.

However, Hattie never got around to sending to Los Angeles for the brochure. But Jerry Rolfe took it on himself to write a letter to her brother Angus about her condition. And he drove over also to have a talk with Amy Walters, the gold miner's widow at Fort Walters — as the ancient woman called it. One old tar-paper building was what she owned, plus the mine shafts, no longer in use since the death of her second husband. On a heap of stones near the road a crimson sign *Fort Walters* was placed, and over it a flagpole. The American flag was raised every day. Amy was working in the garden in one of dead Bill's shirts. He had brought water down from the mountains for her in a home-made aqueduct so she could raise her own peaches and vegetables.

"Amy," Rolfe said, "Hattie's back from the hospital and living all alone. You have no folks and neither has she. Not to beat around the bush about it, why don't you live together?"

Amy's face had great delicacy. Her winter baths in the lake and her soups and the waltzes she played to herself alone on the grand piano that stood beside her wood stove and the murder stories she read till darkness made her go to bed had made her remote. She looked delicate, yet her composure couldn't be touched. It was very strange.

"Hattie and me have different habits, Jerry," said Amy. "And Hattie wouldn't like my company. I can't drink with her."

"That's true," said Rolfe, recalling that Hattie referred to Amy as though she were a ghost. He couldn't speak to Amy of the solitary death that was in store for her. There was not a cloud in the arid sky today, and there was not a shadow of death on Amy. She was tranquil, she seemed to be supplied with a sort of pure fluid that would feed her life slowly for years to come.

He said, "All kinds of things could happen to a woman like Hattie in that yellow house, and nobody would know."

"That's a fact. She doesn't know how to take care of herself."

"She can't. Her arm hasn't healed."

Amy didn't say that she was sorry to hear it. In the place of those words came a silence which could have meant that. Then she said, "I might go for a few hours a day, but she would have to pay me."

"Now, Amy, you must know as well as I do that Hattie has never had any money — not much more than her pension. Just the house."

At once Amy said, no pause coming between his words and hers, "I would take care of her if she'd agree to leave the house to me."

"Leave it in your hands, you mean?" said Rolfe. "To manage?"

"In her will. To belong to me."

"Why, Amy, what would you do with Hattie's house?" he said.

"It would be my property, that's all. I'd have it."

"Maybe you would leave Fort Walters to her in your will," he said.

"Oh, no," she answered quickly. "Why should I do that? I'm not asking Hattie for her help. I don't need it. Hattie is a city woman."

Rolfe could not carry this proposal back to Hattie. He was too wise ever to mention her will to her.

But Pace was not so careful of her feelings. By mid-June Hattie had begun to visit the bar regularly. She had so many things to think about she couldn't keep herself at home. When Pace came in from the yard one day — he had been packing the axles of his horse-trailer and was wiping grease from his fingers — he said with his usual bluntness, "How would you like it if I paid you fifty bucks a month for the rest of your life, Hat?"

Hattie was holding her second Old-Fashioned of the day. At the bar she made it appear that she observed the limit; but she had started drinking at home after lunch. She began to grin, expecting Pace to make one of his jokes. But he was wearing his scoop-shaped Western hat as level as a Quaker, and he had drawn down his chin, a sign that he was not fooling. She said, "That would be nice, but what's the catch?"

"No catch," he said. "This is what we'd do. I'd give you five hundred dollars cash, and fifty bucks a month for life, and you'd let me put some dudes in the yellow house, and you'd leave the house to me in your will."

"What kind of a deal is that?" said Hattie, her look changing. "I thought we were friends."

"It's the best deal you'll ever get," he said.

The day was sultry, but Hattie till now had thought that it was nice, that she was dreamy, but comfortable, about to begin to enjoy the cool of the day; but now she felt that such cruelty and injustice had been waiting to attack her, that it would have been better to die in the hospital than be so disillusioned.

She cried, "Everybody wants to push me out. You're a cheater, Pace. God! I know you. Pick on somebody else. Why do you have to pick on me? Just because I happen to be around?"

"Why, no, Hattie," he said, trying now to be careful. "It was just a business offer."

"Why don't you give me some blood for the bank if you're such a friend of mine?"

"Well, Hattie, you drink too much, and you oughtn't have been driving anyway."

"The whole thing happened because I sneezed. Everybody knows it. I wouldn't sell you my house. I'd give it away to the lepers first. You'd let me go and then never send me a cent. You never pay anybody. You can't even buy wholesale in town any more because nobody trusts you. It looks as though I'm stuck, that's all, just stuck. I keep on saying that this is my only home in all the world, this is where my friends are, and the weather is always perfect and the lake is beautiful. I wish the whole damn empty old place were in Hell. It's not human and neither are you. But I'll be here the day the sheriff takes your horses — you never mind."

He told her then that she was drunk again, and so she was, but she was more than that, and though her head was spinning she decided to go back to the house at once and take care of some things she had been putting off. This very day she was going to write to the lawyer, Claiborne, and make sure that Pace never got her property. She wouldn't put it past him to swear in court that India had promised him the yellow house.

She sat at the table with pen and paper, trying to think how to put it.

"I want this on record," she wrote. "I could kick myself in the head when I think how he's led me on. I have been his patsy ten thousand times. As when that drunk crashed his Cub plane on the lake shore. At the coroner's jury he let me take the whole blame. He had instructed me when I was working for him never to take in any drunks. And this flier was drunk. He had nothing on but a T shirt and Bermuda shorts and he was flying from Sacramento to Salt Lake City. At the inquest Pace denied he had ever given me such instructions. The same was true when the cook went haywire. She was a tramp. He never hires decent help. He cheated her on the bar bill and blamed me and she went after me with a meat cleaver. She disliked me because I criticized her for drinking at the bar in her one-piece white bathing suit with the dude guests. But he turned her loose on me. He hints that he did certain things for India. She would never have let him. He was too common for her. It can never be said about India that she was not a lady in every way. He thinks he is the greatest sack-artist in the world. He only loves horses, as a fact. He has no claims at all, oral or written, on this yellow house. I want you to have this over my signature. He was cruel to Pickle-Tits who was his first wife, and he's no better to the charming woman who is his present one. I don't know why she takes it. It must be despair." She said to herself, *I don't suppose I'd better send that.*

She was still angry. Her heart was knocking from within: the deep pulses, as after a hot bath, beat at the back of her thighs. The air outside was dotted with transparent particles. The mountains were red as clinkers. The iris leaves were fan sticks — they stuck out like Jiggs's hair.

She always ended by looking out of the window at the desert and the lake. *They drew you from yourself. But after they had drawn you, what did they do with you? It was too late to find out. I'll never know. I wasn't meant to. I'm not the type,* Hattie reflected. *Maybe something too cruel for women or for any woman, young or old.*

So she stood up and, rising, she had the sensation that she had gradually become a container for herself. *You get old, your heart, your liver, your lungs seem to expand in size, and the walls of the body give way outward,* she thought, *and you take the shape of an old jug, wider and wider toward the top. You swell up with tears and fat.* She no longer even smelled to herself like a woman. Her face with its much-slept-upon skin was only faintly like her own — like a cloud that has changed. It was a face. It became a ball of yarn. It had drifted open. It had scattered.

I was never one single thing anyway, she thought. *Never my own. I was only loaned to myself.*

But the thing wasn't over yet. And in fact she didn't know for certain that it was ever going to be over; she had only had other people's word for it that death was such and such. *How do I know?* she asked herself challengingly. Her anger had sobered her for a little while. Now she was again drunk. *It was strange. It is strange. It may continue being strange.* She further thought, *I used to wish for death more than I do now. Because I didn't have anything at all. I changed when I got a roof of my own over me. And now? Do I have to go? I thought Marian loved me, but she has a sister. And I never thought Helen and Jerry would desert me. And now Pace insulted me. They think I'm not going to make it.*

She went to the cupboard — she kept the bourbon bottle there; she drank less if each time she had to rise and open the cupboard door. And, as if she were being watched, she poured a drink and swallowed it.

The notion that in this emptiness someone saw her was connected with the other fancy that she was being filmed from birth to death. That this was done for everyone. And afterward you could view your life.

Hattie wanted to see some of it now, and she sat down on the dogs' paw cushions of her sofa and, with her knees far apart and a smile of yearning and of fright, she bent her round back, burned a cigarette at the corner of her mouth and saw — the Church of Saint-Sulpice in Paris where her organ teacher used to bring her. It looked like country walls of stone, but rising high and leaning outward were towers. She was very young. She knew music. The sky was grey. After this she saw some entertaining things she liked to tell people about. She was a young wife. She was in Aix-les-Bains with her mother-in-law, and they played bridge in a mud bath with a British general and his aide. There were artificial waves in the swimming pool. She lost her bathing suit because it was a size too big. How did she get out? Ah, you got out of everything.

She saw her husband, James John Waggoner IV. They were snowbound together in New Hampshire. "Jimmy, Jimmy, how can you fling a wife away?" she asked him. "Have you forgotten love? Did I drink too much — did I bore you?" He had married again and had two children. He had gotten tired of her. And though he was a vain man with nothing to be vain about — no looks, not too much intelligence, nothing but an old Philadelphia family — she had loved him. She too had been a snob about her Philadelphia connections. Give up the name of Waggoner? How could she? For this reason she had never married Wicks. "How dare you," she had said to Wicks, "come without a shave in a dirty shirt and muck on you, come and ask me to marry! If you want to propose, go and clean up first." But his dirt was only a pretext. *Trade Waggoner for Wicks?* she asked herself again with a swing of her shoulders. She wouldn't think of it. Wicks was an excellent man. But he was a cowboy. He couldn't even read. But she saw this on her film. They were in Athens Canyon, in a cratelike house, and she was reading aloud to him from *The Count of Monte Cristo*. He wouldn't let her stop. While walking to stretch her legs, she read, and he followed her about to catch each word. After all, he was very dear to her. Such a man! Now she saw him jump from his horse. They were living on the range, trapping coyotes. It was just the second grey of evening, cloudy, moments after the sun had gone down. There was an animal in the trap, and he went toward it to kill it. He wouldn't waste a bullet on the creatures, but killed them with a kick of his boot. And then Hattie saw that this coyote was all white — snarling teeth, white scruff. "Wicks, he's white! White as a polar bear. You're not going to kill him, are you?" The animal flattened to the ground. He snarled and cried. He couldn't pull away because of the heavy trap. And Wicks killed him. What else could he have done? The white beast lay dead. The dust of Wicks' boots hardly showed on its head and jaws. Blood ran from the muzzle.

And now came something on Hattie's film she tried to shun. It was she herself who had killed her dog, Richie. Just as Rolfe and Pace had warned her, he was vicious, his brain was turned. She, because she was on the side of all dumb creatures, defended him when he bit the trashy woman Jacamares was living with. Perhaps if she had had Richie from a puppy he wouldn't have turned on her. When she got him he was already a year and a half old and she couldn't break him of his habits. But she thought only she understood him. And Rolfe had warned her, "You'll be sued, do you know it? The dog will take out after somebody smarter than that Jacamares' woman and you'll be in for it."

Hattie saw herself as she swayed her shoulders and said, "Nonsense."

But what fear she had felt when the dog went for her on the porch. Suddenly she could see by his skull, by his eyes that he was evil. She screamed at him, "Richie!" And what had she done to him? He had laid under the gas range all day growling and wouldn't come out. She tried to urge him out with the broom, and he snatched it in his teeth. She pulled him out and he left the stick and tore at her. Now, as the spectator of this, her eyes opened, beyond the pregnant curtain and the air wave of marl dust, summer's snow, drifting over the water. "Oh, my God! Richie!" Her thigh was snatched by his jaws. His teeth went through her skirt. She felt she would fall. Would she go down? Then the dog would rush at her throat — then black night, bad-odored mouth, the blood pouring from her torn veins. Her heart shriveled as the teeth went in her thigh, and she couldn't delay another second but took her kindling hatchet from the nail, strengthened her grip on the smooth wood and hit the dog. She saw the blow. She saw him die at once. And then in fear and shame she hid the body. And at night she buried him in the yard. Next day she accused Jacamares. On him she laid the blame for the disappearance of her dog.

She stood up; she spoke to herself in silence, as was her habit. *God, what shall I do? I have taken life. I have lied. I have borne false witness. I have stalled. And now what shall I do? Nobody will help me.*

And suddenly she made up her mind that she should go and do what she had been putting off for weeks, namely, test herself with the car, and she slipped on her shoes and went out. Lizards ran before her in the thirsty dust. She opened the hot, broad door of the car. She lifted her lame hand onto the wheel. Her right hand she reached far to the left and turned the wheel with all her might. Then she started the motor and tried to drive out of the yard. But she could not release the emergency brake with its rasplike rod. She reached with her good hand, the right, under the steering wheel and pressed her bosom on it and strained. No, she could not shift the gears and steer. She couldn't even reach the hand brake. The sweat broke out on her skin. Her efforts were too much. She was deeply wounded by the pain in her arm. The door of the car fell open again and she turned from the wheel and with her stiff legs outside the door she wept. What could she do now? And when she had wept over the ruin of her life she got out of the old car and went back to the house. She took the bottle of bourbon from the cupboard and picked up the ink bottle and a pad of paper and sat down to write her will.

My Will, she wrote, and sobbed to herself.

Since the death of India she had numberless times asked the question, To Whom? Who will get this when I die? She had un-consciously put people to the test to find out whether they were worthy. It made her more severe than before.

Now she wrote, "I, Harriet Simmons Waggoner, being of sound mind and not knowing what may be in store for me at the age of seventy-two (born 1885), living alone at Sego Desert Lake, instruct my lawyer, Harold Claiborne, Paiute County Court Building, to draw my last will and testament upon the following terms."

She sat perfectly still now to hear from within who would be the lucky one, who would inherit the yellow house. For which she had waited. Yes, waited for India's death, choking on her bread because she was a rich woman's servant and whipping girl. But who had done for her, Hattie, what she had done for India? And who, apart from India, had ever held out a hand to her? Kindness, yes. Here and there people had been kind. But the word in her head was not kindness, it was succor. And who had given her that? Only India. If at least, next best after succor, someone had given her a shake and said, "Stop stalling. Don't be such a slow, old, procrastinating sit-stiller." Again, it was only India who had done her good. She had offered her succor. *"Hettie!"* said that drunken mask. *"Do you know what sloth is? Damn your poky old life!"*

But I was waiting, Hattie realized. *I was waiting, thinking, "Youth is terrible, frightening. I will wait it out. And men? Men are cruel and strong. They want things I haven't got to give."* *There were no kids in me,* thought Hattie. *Not that I wouldn't have loved them, but such my nature was. And who can blame me for having it? My nature?*

She drank from an Old-Fashioned glass. There was no orange in it, no ice, no bitters or sugar, only the stinging, clear bourbon.

So then, she continued, looking at the dry sun-stamped dust and the last freckled flowers of red wild peach, *to live with Angus and his wife, and have to hear a chapter from the Bible before breakfast; once more in the house — not of a stranger, perhaps, but not far from it either.* In other houses, in someone else's house, to wait for mealtimes was her lifelong punishment. She always felt it in the throat and stomach. And so she would again, and to the very end. However, she must think of someone to leave the house to.

And first of all she wanted to do right by her family. None of them had ever dreamed that she, Hattie, would ever have something to bequeath. Until a few years ago it had certainly looked as if she would die a pauper. So now she could keep her head up with the proudest of them. And, as this occurred to her, she actually lifted up her face with its broad nose and victorious eyes; if her hair had become shabby as onion roots, if at the back her head was round and bald as a newel post, what did that matter? Her heart experienced a childish glory, not yet tired of it after seventy-two years. She, too, had amounted to something. *I'll do some good by going,* she thought. *Now I believe I should leave it to, to. . . .* She returned to the old point of struggle. She had decided many times and many times changed her mind. She tried to think, *Who would get the most out of it?* It was a tearing thing to go through. If it had not been the yellow house but instead some brittle thing she could hold in her hand, then the last thing she would do would be to throw and smash it, and so the thing and she herself would be demolished together. But it was vain to think such thoughts. To whom should she leave it? Her brothers? Not they. Nephews? One was a submarine commander. The other was a bachelor in the State Department. Then began the roll call of cousins. Merton? He owned an estate in Connecticut. Anna? She had a face like a hot-water bottle. That left Joyce, the orphaned daughter of her cousin Wilfred. Joyce was the most likely heiress. Hattie had already written to her and had her out to the lake at Thanksgiving, two years ago. But this Joyce was another odd one; over thirty, good, yes, but placid, running to fat, a scholar — ten years in Eugene, Oregon, working for her degree. In Hattie's opinion this was only another form of sloth. Nevertheless, Joyce yet hoped to marry. Whom? Not Dr. Stroud. He wouldn't. And still she had vague hope. Hattie knew how that could be. At least have a man she could argue with.

She was now more drunk than at any time since her accident. Again she filled her glass. *Have ye eyes and see not? Sleepers, awake!*

Knees wide apart she sat in the twilight, thinking. Marian? Marian didn't need another house. Half Pint? She wouldn't know what to do with it. Brother Louis came up for consideration next. He was an old actor who had a church for the Indians at Athens Canyon. Hollywood stars of the silent days sent him their negligées; he altered them and wore them in the pulpit. The Indians loved his show. But when Billy Shawah blew his brains out after his two-week bender, they still tore his shack down and turned it inside out to get rid of his ghost. They had their old religion. No, not Brother Louis. He'd show movies in the yellow house to the tribe or make a nursery of it.

And now she began to consider Wicks. When last heard from he was south of Bishop, California, a handy man in a saloon off toward Death Valley. It wasn't she who heard from him but Pace. Herself, she hadn't actually seen Wicks since — how low she had sunk then! — she had kept the hamburger stand on Route 158. The little lunchroom had supported them both. Wicks hung around on the end stool, rolling cigarettes (she saw it on the film). Then there was a quarrel. Things had been going from bad to worse. He'd begun to grouse now about this and now about that. He complained about the food, at last. She saw and heard him. "Hat," he said, "I'm good and tired of hamburger." "Well, what do you think I eat?" she said with that round, defiant movement of her shoulders which she herself recognized as characteristic (*me all over,* she thought). But he opened the cash register and took out thirty cents and crossed the street to the butcher's and brought back a steak. He threw it on the griddle. "Fry it," he said. She did and watched him eat.

And when he was through she could bear her rage no longer. "Now," she said, "you've had your meat. Get out. Never come back." She kept a pistol under the counter. She picked it up, cocked it, pointed it at his heart. "If you ever come in that door again, I'll kill you," she said.

She saw it all. *I couldn't bear to fall so low,* she thought, *to be slave to a shiftless cowboy.*

Wicks said, "Don't do that, Hat. Guess I went too far. You're right."

"You'll never have a chance to make it up," she cried. "Get out!"

On that cry he disappeared, and since then she had never seen him.

"Wicks, dear," she said. "Please! I'm sorry. Don't condemn me in your heart. Forgive me. I hurt myself in my evil. I always had a thick idiot head. I was born with a thick head."

Again she wept, for Wicks. She was too proud. A snob. Now they might have lived together in this house, old friends, simple and plain.

She thought, *He really was my good friend.*

But what would Wicks do with a house like this, alone, if he was alive and survived her? He was too wiry for soft beds or easy chairs.

And she was the one who had said stiffly to India, "I'm a Christian person. I do not bear a grudge."

Ah, yes, she said to herself. *I have caught myself out too often. How long can this go on?* And she began to think, or try to think of Joyce, her cousin's daughter. Joyce was like herself, a woman alone, getting on, clumsy. She would have given much, now, to succor Joyce.

But it seemed to her now that that too had been a story. First you heard the pure story. Then you heard the impure story. Both stories. She had paid out years, now to one shadow, now to another shadow.

Joyce would come here to the house. She had a little income and could manage. She would live as Hattie had lived, alone. Here she would rot, start to drink, maybe, and day after day read, day after day sleep. See how beautiful it was here? It burned you out. How empty? It turned you into ash.

"How can I doom a young person to the same life?" asked Hattie. "It's for somebody like me. When I was younger it wasn't right. But now it is. Only I fit in here. It was made for my old age, to spend my last years peacefully. If I hadn't let Jerry make me drunk that night — if I hadn't sneezed! My arm! I'll have to live with Angus. My heart will break there away from my only home."

She now was very drunk, and she said to herself, *Take what God brings. He gives no gifts unmixed. He makes loans.*

She resumed her letter of instructions to lawyer Claiborne: "Upon the following terms," she wrote a second time. "Because I have suffered much. Because I only lately received what I have to give away, I can't bear it." The drunken blood was soaring to her head. But her hand was clear enough. She wrote, "It is too soon! Too soon! Because I do not find it in my heart to care for anyone as I would wish. Being cast off and lonely, and doing no harm where I am. Why should it be? This breaks my heart. In addition to everything else, why must I worry about this, which I must leave? I am tormented out of my mind. Even though by my own fault I have put myself into this position. And I am not ready to give up on this. No, not yet. And so I'll tell you what, I leave this property, land, house, garden and water rights, to Hattie Simmons Waggoner. Me! I realize this is bad and wrong. It cannot happen. Yet it is the only thing I really wish to do, so may God have mercy on my soul."

"How can that be?" She studied what she had written and finally she acknowledged that she was drunk. "I'm drunk," she said, "and don't know what I'm doing. I'll die, and end. Like India. Dead as that lilac bush. Only tonight I can't give the house away. I'm drunk and so I need it. But I won't be selfish from the grave. I'll think again tomorrow," she promised herself.

GEORGE P. ELLIOTT (b.1918) Elliott was born in Indiana and educated at the University of California where he received an M.A. in 1941. He has taught at St. Mary's College in California, Cornell University, Barnard College, University of Iowa and is currently teaching at Syracuse University. He received a Guggenheim Fellowship and a Ford Foundation grant to write a play.

Elliott has written in a variety of literary forms and on a variety of subjects. The dominant mode of his writing, however, is narrative, whether poetry or prose, essay or fiction. Nearly all his imaginative work contains a story, be it implicit or explicit. Moreover, he commonly uses the device of combining elements from experience which normally would be incompatible. This may be done for satiric or comic ends, or as a way of opening up a situation or characters for serious exploration, or for the pleasures of fantasy alone. Perhaps the purest combination of narrative mode with fantasy occurs in the story "Among the Dangs."

His novels are *Parktilden Village* (1958), *David Knudsen* (1962), and *In the World* (1965). His works also include a short story collection *Among the Dangs* (1961) and a book of essays *A Piece of Lettuce* (1964).

AMONG THE DANGS

George P. Elliott

I graduated from Sansom University in 1937 with honors in history, having intended to study law, but I had no money and nowhere to get any; by good fortune the anthropology department, which had just been given a grant for research, decided that I could do a job for them. In idle curiosity I had taken a course in anthro, to see what I would have been like had history not catapulted my people a couple of centuries ago up into civilization, but I had not been inclined to enlarge on the sketchy knowledge I got from that course; even yet, when I think about it, I feel like a fraud teaching anthropology. What chiefly recommended me to the department, aside from a friend, was a combination of three attributes: I was a good mimic, a long-distance runner, and black.

The Dangs live in a forested valley in the eastern foothills of the Andes. The only white man to report on them (and, it was loosely gossiped, the only one to return from them alive), Sir Bewley Morehead, owed his escape in 1910 to the consternation caused by Halley's comet. Otherwise, he reported, they would certainly have sacrificed him as they were preparing to do; as it was they killed the priest who was to have killed him and then burned the temple down. However, Dr. Sorish, our most distinguished Sansom man, in the early thirties developed an interest in the Dangs which led to my research grant; he had introduced a tribe of Amazonian head-shrinkers to the idea of planting grain instead of just harvesting it, as a result of which they had fattened, taken to drinking brew by the tubful, and elevated Sorish to the rank of new god. The last time he had descended among them — it is Sansom policy to follow through on any primitives we "do" — he had found his worshipers holding a couple of young Dang men captive and preparing them for ceremonies which would end only with the processing of their heads; his godhood gave him sufficient power to defer these ceremonies while he made half-a-dozen transcriptions of the men's conversations and learned their language well enough to arouse the curiosity of his colleagues. The Dangs were handy with blowpipes; no one knew what pleased them; Halley's comet wasn't due till 1986. But among the recordings Sorish brought back was a legend strangely chanted by one of these young men, whose very head perhaps you can buy today from a natural science company for $150 to $200, and the same youth had given Sorish a sufficient demonstration of the Dang prophetic trance, previously described by Morehead, to whet his appetite.

I was black, true; but as Sorish pointed out, I looked as though I had been rolled in granite dust and the Dangs as though they had been rolled in brick dust; my hair was short and kinky, theirs long and straight; my lips were thick, theirs thin. It's like dressing a Greek up in reindeer skins, I said, and telling him to go pass himself off as a Lapp in Lapland. Maybe, they countered, but wouldn't he be more likely to get by than a naked Swahili with bones in his nose? I was a long-distance runner, true, but as I pointed out with a good deal of feeling I didn't know the principles of jungle escape and had no desire to learn them in, as they put it, the field. They would teach me to throw the javelin and wield a machete, they would teach me the elements of judo, and as for poisoned darts and sacrifices they would insure my life — that is, my return within three years — for five thousand dollars. I was a good mimic, true; I would be able to reproduce the Dang speech and especially the trance of the Dang prophets for the observation of science — "make a genuine contribution to learning." In the Sansom concept the researcher's experience is an inextricable part of anthropological study, and a good mimic provides the object for others' study as well as for his own. For doing this job I would be given round-trip transportation, an M.S. if I wrote a thesis on the material I gathered, the temporary insurance on my life, and one hundred dollars a month for the year I was expected to be gone. After I'd got them to throw in a fellowship of some sort for the following year I agreed. It would pay for filling the forty cavities in my brothers' and sisters' teeth.

Dr. Sorish and I had to wait at the nearest outstation for a thunderstorm; when it finally blew up I took off all my clothes, put on a breechcloth and leather apron, put a box of equipment on my head, and trotted after him; his people were holed in from the thunder and we were in their settlement before they saw us. They were taller than I, they no doubt found my white teeth as disagreeable as I found their stained, filed teeth, but when Sorish spoke to me in English (telling me to pretend indifference to them while they sniffed me over) and in the accents of American acquaintances rather than in the harsh tones of divinity their eyes filled with awe of me. Their taboo against touching Sorish extended itself to me; when a baby ran up to me and I lifted him up to play with him, his mother crawled, beating her head on the ground till I freed him.

The next day was devoted chiefly to selecting the man to ful-fill Sorish's formidable command to guide me to the edge of the Dang country. As for running — if those characters could be got to the next Olympics, Ecuador would take every long-distance medal on the board. I knew I had reached the brow of my valley only because I discovered that my guide, whom I had been lag-ging behind by fifty feet, at a turn in the path had disappeared into the brush.

Exhaustion allayed my terror; as I lay in the meager shade re-cuperating I remembered to execute the advice I had given my-self before coming: to act always as though I were not afraid. What would a brave man do next? Pay no attention to his aching feet, reconnoiter, and cautiously proceed. I climbed a jutting of rock and peered about. It was a wide, scrubby valley; on the banks of the river running down the valley I thought I saw a dozen mounds too regular for stones. I touched the handle of the hunting knife sheathed at my side, and trotted down the trackless hill.

The village was deserted, but the huts, though miserable, were clean and in good repair. This meant, according to the movies I had seen, that hostile eyes were watching my every gesture. I had to keep moving in order to avoid trembling. The river was clear and not deep. The corpse of a man floated by. I felt like going downstream, but my hypothesized courage drove me up.

In half a mile I came upon a toothless old woman squatting by the track. She did not stop munching when I appeared, nor did she scream, or even stand up. I greeted her in Dang according to the formula I had learned, whereupon she cackled and smiled and nodded as gleefully as though I had just passed a test. She reminded me of my grandmother, rolled in brick dust, minus a corncob pipe between her gums. Presently I heard voices ahead of me. I saw five women carrying branches and walking very slowly, I lurked behind them until they came to a small village, and watched from a bush while they set to work. They stripped the leaves off, carefully did something to them with their fingers, and then dropped them in small-throated pots. Children scrabbled around, and once a couple of them ran up and suckled at one of the women. There remained about an hour till sunset. I prowled, undetected. The women stood, like fashion models, with pelvis abnormally rocked forward; they were wiry, without fat even on their breasts; not even their thighs and hips afforded clean sweeping lines undisturbed by bunched muscles. I saw no men.

Before I began to get into a lather about the right tack to take I stepped into the clearing and uttered their word of salutation. If a strange man should walk in your wife's front door and say "How do you do" in an accent she did not recognize, simultaneously poking his middle finger at her, her consternation would be something like that of those Dang women, for unthinkingly I had nodded my head when speaking and turned my palm up as one does in the United States; to them this was a gesture of intimacy, signifying desire. They disappeared into huts, clutching children.

I went to the central clearing and sat with my back to a log, knowing they would scrutinize me. I wondered where the men were. I could think of no excuse for having my knife in my hand except to clean my toenails. So astonishing an act was unknown to the Dangs; the women and children gradually approached in silence, watching; I cleaned my fingernails. I said the word for food; no one reacted, but presently a little girl ran up to me holding a fruit in both hands. I took it, snibbed her nose between my fingers, and with a pat on the bottom sent her back to her mother. Upon this there were hostile glances, audible intakes of breath, and a huddling about the baby who did not understand any more than I did why she was being consoled. While I ate the fruit I determined to leave the next move up to them. I sheathed my knife and squatted on my hunkers, waiting. To disguise my nervousness I fixed my eyes on the ground between my feet, and grasped my ankles from behind in such a way — right ankle with right hand, left with left — as to expose the inner sides of my forearms. Now this was, as I later learned, pretty close to the initial posture taken for the prophetic trance; also I had a blue flower tattooed on my inner right arm and a blue serpent on my left (from the summer I'd gone to sea), the like of which had never been seen in this place.

At sundown I heard the men approach; they were anything but stealthy about it; I had the greatest difficulty in suppressing the shivers. In simple fear of showing my fear I did not look up when the men gathered around, I could understand just enough of what the women were telling the men to realize that they were afraid of me. Even though I was pelted with pebbles and twigs till I was angry I still did not respond, because I could not think what to do. Then something clammy was plopped onto my back from above and I leaped high, howling. Their spears were poised before I landed.

"Strangers!" I cried, my speech composed. "Far kinsmen! I come from the mountains!" I had intended to say *from the river lands,* but the excitement tangled my tongue. Their faces remained expressionless but no spears drove at me, and then to be doing something I shoved the guts under the log with my feet.

And saved my life by doing so. That I seemed to have taken, though awkwardly, the prophetic squat; that I bore visible marvels on my arm; that I was fearless and inwardly absorbed; that I came from the mountains (their enemies lived toward the river lands); that I wore their apron and spoke their language, albeit poorly, all these disposed them to wonder at this mysterious outlander. Even so they might very well have captured me, marvelous though I was, possibly useful to them, dangerous to antagonize, had I not been unblemished, which meant that I was supernaturally guarded. Finally, my scrutinizing the fish guts, daring to smile as I did so, could mean only that I was prophetic; my leap when they had been dropped onto my back was prodigious, "far higher than a man's head," and my howl had been vatic; and my deliberately kicking the guts aside, though an inscrutable act, demonstrated at least that I could touch the entrails of an eel and live.

So I was accepted to the Dangs. The trouble was they had no

ceremony for naturalizing me. For them every act had a significance, and here they were faced with a reverse problem for which
nothing had prepared them. They could not possibly just assimi-
late me without marking the event with an act (that is, a ceremony) signifying my entrance. For them nothing *just happened*,
certainly nothing that men did. Meanwhile, I was kept in a sort
of quarantine while they deliberated. I did not, to be sure, understand why I was being isolated in a hut by myself, never spoken
to except efficiently, watched but not restrained. I swam, slept,
scratched, watched, swatted, ate; I was not really alarmed because
they had not restrained me forcibly and they gave me food. I
began making friends with some of the small children, especially
while swimming, and there were two girls of fifteen or so who
found me terribly funny. I wished I had some magic, but I knew
only card tricks. The sixth day, swimming, I thought I was being
enticed around a point in the river by the two girls, but when
I began to chase them they threw good-sized stones at me, missing
me only because they were such poor shots. A corpse floated by;
when they saw it they immediately placed the sole of their right
foot on the side of their left knee and stood thus on one leg till
the corpse floated out of sight; I followed the girls' example,
teetering. I gathered from what they said that some illness was
devastating their people; I hope it was one of the diseases I had
been inoculated against. The girls' mothers found them talking
with me and cuffed them away.

I did not see them for two days, but the night of my eighth
day there the bolder of them hissed me awake at the door of my
hut in a way that meant "no danger." I recognized her when she
giggled. I was not sure what their customs were in these matters,
but while I was deliberating what my course of wisdom should
be she crawled into the hut and lay on the mat beside me. She
liked me, she was utterly devoid of reticence, I was twenty-one
and far from home; even a scabby little knotty-legged fashion
model is hard to resist under such circumstances. I learned before
falling asleep that there was a three-way debate among the men
over what to do with me: initiate me according to the prophet-
initiation rites, invent a new ceremony, or sacrifice me as propi-
tiation to the disease among them as was usually done with
captives. Each had its advantages and drawbacks; even the news
that some of the Dangs wanted to sacrifice me did not excite me as

it would have done a week before; now, I half-sympathized with their trouble. I was awakened at dawn by the outraged howl of a man at my door; he was the girl's father. The village men gathered and the girl cowered behind me. They talked for hours outside my hut, men arrived from other villages up and down the valley, and finally they agreed upon a solution to all the problems: they proposed that I should be made one of the tribe by marriage on the same night that I should be initiated into the rites of prophecy.

The new-rite men were satisfied by this arrangement because of the novelty of having a man married and initiated on the same day, but the sacrifice party was visibly unmollified. Noticing this and reflecting that the proposed arrangement would permit me to do all my trance research under optimum conditions and to accumulate a great deal of sexual data as well I agreed to it. I would of course only be going through the forms of marriage, not meaning them; as for the girl, I took this vow to myself (meaning without ceremony): "So long as I am a Dang I shall be formally a correct husband to her." More's a pity.

Fortunately a youth from down the valley already had been chosen as a novice (at least a third of the Dang men enter the novitiate at one time or another, though few make the grade), so that I had not only a companion during the four-month preparation for the vatic rites but also a control upon whom I might check my experience of the stages of the novitiate. My mimetic powers stood me in good stead; I was presumed to have a special prophetic gift and my readiness at assuming the proper stances and properly performing the ritual acts confirmed the Dangs' impressions of my gift; but also, since I was required to proceed no faster than the ritual pace in my learning, I had plenty of leisure in which to observe in the smallest detail what I did and how I, and to some extent my fellow novice, felt. If I had not had this self-observing to relieve the tedium I think I should have been unable to get through that mindless holding of the same position hour after hour, that mindless repeating of the same act day after day. The Dangs *appear* to be bored much of the time, and my early experience with them was certainly that of ennui, though never again ennui so acute as during this novitiate. Yet I doubt that it would be accurate to say they actually are bored, and I am sure that the other novice was not, as a fisherman waiting hours for a strike cannot be said to be bored. The Dangs do not sate themselves on food; the experience which they consider most worth seeking, vision, is one which cannot glut either the prophet or his auditors; they cannot imagine an alternative to living as they live or, more instantly, to preparing a novice as I was being prepared. The people endure; the prophets, as I have learned, wait for the time to come again, and though they are bitten and stung by ten thousand fears, about this they have no anxiety — the time will surely come again. Boredom implies either satiety, and they were poor and not interested in enriching themselves, or the frustration of impulse, and they were without alternatives and diversions. The intense boredom which is really a controlled anxiety, they are protected from by never doubting the worth of their vision or their power to achieve it.

I was assisted through these difficult months during which I was supposed to do nothing but train by Redadu, my betrothed. As a novice I was strictly to abstain from sexual intercourse, but as betrothed we were supposed to make sure before marriage that we satisfied one another, for adultery by either husband or wife was punishable by maiming. Naturally the theologians were much exercised by this impasse, but while they were arguing Redadu and I took the obvious course — we met more or less surreptitiously. Since my vatic training could not take place between sunrise and sundown I assumed that we could meet in the afternoon when I woke up, but when I began making plans to this effect I discovered that she did not know what I was talking about. It makes as much sense in Dang to say, "Let's blow poisoned darts at the loss of the moon," as to say, "Let's make love in broad daylight." Redadu dissolved in giggles at the absurdity. What to do? She found us a cave. Everyone must have known what I was up to, but we were respectable (the Dang term for it was harsher, *deed-liar*) so we were never disturbed. Redadu's friends would not believe her stories of my luxurious love ways, especially my biting with lips instead of teeth. At one time or another she sent four of them to the cave for me to demonstrate my prowess upon; I was glad that none of them pleased me as much as she did for I was beginning to be fond of her. My son has told me that lip-biting has become if not a customary at any rate a possible caress.

As the night of the double rite approached, a night of full

moon, a new conflict became evident: the marriage must be consummated exactly at sundown, but the initiation must begin at moonrise, less than two hours later. For some reason that was not clear to me preparing for the initiation would incapacitate me for the consummation. I refrained from pointing out that it was only technically that this marriage needed consummating and even from asking why I would not be able to do it. The solution, which displeased everyone, was to defer the rites for three nights, when the moon, though no longer perfectly round, would rise sufficiently late so that I would, by hurrying, be able to perform both of my functions. Redadu's father, who had been of the sacrifice party, waived ahead of time his claim against me; legally he was entitled to annul the marriage if I should leave the marriage hut during the bridal night. And although I in turn could legally annul it if she left the hut I waived my claim as well so that she might attend my initiation.

The wedding consisted chiefly of our being bound back to back by the elbows and being sung to and danced about all day. At sunset we were bound face to face by the elbows (most awkward) and sent into our hut. Outside the two mothers waited — a high prophet's wife took the place of my mother (my Methodist mother!) — until our orgastic cries indicated that the marriage had been consummated, and then came in to sever our bonds and bring us the bridal foods of cold stewed eel and parched seeds. We fed each other bite for bite and gave the scraps to our mothers, who by the formula with which they thanked us pronounced themselves satisfied with us. Then a falsetto voice called to me to hurry to the altar. A man in the mask of a moon slave was standing outside my hut on his left leg with the right foot against his left knee, and he continued to shake his rattle so long as I was within earshot.

The men were masked. Their voices were all disguised. I wondered whether I was supposed to speak in an altered voice; I knew every stance and gesture I was to make, but nothing of what I was to say; yet surely a prophet must employ words. I had seen some of the masks before — being repaired, being carried from one place to another — but now, faced with them alive in the failing twilight, I was impressed by them in no scientific or aesthetic way — they terrified and exalted me. I wondered if I would be given a mask. I began trying to identify such men as I could by their scars and missing fingers and crooked arms, and noticed to my distress that they too were all standing one-legged in my presence. I had thought that was the stance to be assumed in the presence of the dead! We were at the entrance to The Cleft, a dead-end ravine in one of the cliffs along the valley; my fellow novice and I were each given a gourdful of some vile-tasting drink and were then taken up to the end of The Cleft, instructed to assume the first position, and left alone. We squatted as I had been squatting by the log on my first day, except that my head was cocked in a certain way and my hands clasped my ankles from the front. The excitements of the day seemed to have addled my wits, I could concentrate on nothing and lost my impulse to observe coolly what was going on; I kept humming *St. James Infirmary* to myself, and though at first I had been thinking the words, after awhile I realized that I had nothing but the tune left in my head. At moonrise we were brought another gourd of the liquor to drink, and were then taken to the mouth of The Cleft again. I did, easily, whatever I was told. The last thing I remember seeing before taking the second position was the semicircle of masked men facing us and chanting, and behind them the women and children — all standing on the left leg. I lay on my back with my left ankle on my right and my hands crossed over my navel, rolled my eyeballs up and held the lids open without blinking, and breathed in the necessary rhythm, each breath taking four heartbeats, with an interval of ten heartbeats between each exhalation and the next inspiration. Then the drug took over. At dawn when a called command awakened me, I found myself on an islet in the river dancing with my companion a leaping dance I had not known or even seen before, and brandishing over my head a magnificent red and blue, new-made mask of my own. The shores of the river were lined with the people chanting as we leaped, and all of them were either sitting or else standing on both feet. If we had been dead the night before we were alive now.

After I had slept and returned to myself, Redadu told me that my vision was splendid, but of course she was no more permitted to tell me what I had said than I was able to remember it. The Dangs' sense of rhythm is as subtle as their ear for melody is monotonous, and for weeks I kept hearing rhythmic snatches of *St. James Infirmary* scratched on calabash drums and tapped on blocks.

Sorish honored me by rewriting my master's thesis and adding my name as co-author of the resultant essay, which he published in *JAFA* (*The Journal of American Field Anthropology*): "Techniques of Vatic Hallucinosis among the Dangs." And the twenty-minute movie I made of a streamlined performance of the rites is still widely used as an audio-visual aid.

By 1939 when I had been cured of the skin disease I had brought back with me and had finished the work for my M.S. I still had no money. I had been working as the assistant curator of the University's Pre-Columbian Museum and had developed a powerful aversion to devoting my life to cataloguing, displaying, restoring, ware-housing. But my chances of getting a research job, slight enough with a Ph.D., were nil with only an M.S. The girl I was going with said (I had not told her about Redadu) that if we married she would work as a nurse to support me while I went through law school; I was tempted by the opportunity to fulfill my original ambition, and probably I would have done it had she not pressed too hard; she wanted me to leave anthropology, she wanted me to become a lawyer, she wanted to support me, but what she did not want was to make my intentions, whatever they might be, her own. So when a new grant gave me the chance to return to the Dangs I gladly seized it; not only would I be asserting myself against Velma, but also I would be paid for doing the research for my Ph.D. thesis; besides, I was curious to see the Congo-Maryland-Dang bastard I had left in Redadu's belly.

My assignment was to make a general cultural survey but especially to discover the *content* of the vatic experience — not just the technique, not even the hallucinations and stories, but the qualities of the experience itself. The former would get me a routine degree, but the latter would, if I did it, make me a name and get me a job. After much consultation I decided against taking with me any form of magic, including medicine; the antibiotics had not been invented yet, and even if there had been a simple way to eradicate the fever endemic among the Dangs, my advisers persuaded me that it would be an error to introduce it since the Dangs were able to procure barely enough food for themselves as it was and since they might worship me for doing it, thereby making it impossible for me to do my research with the proper empathy. I arrived the second time provided only with my knife (which had not seemed to impress these stone-agers), salve to soothe my sores, and the knowledge of how to preserve fish against a lean season, innovation enough but not one likely to divinize me.

I was only slightly worried how I would be received on my return, because of the circumstances under which I had disappeared. I had become a fairly decent hunter — the women gathered grain and fruit — and I had learned to respect the Dang's tracking abilities enough to have been nervous about getting away safely. While hunting with a companion in the hills south of our valley I had run into a couple of hunters from an enemy tribe which seldom foraged so far north as this. They probably were as surprised as I and probably would have been glad to leave me unmolested; however, outnumbered and not knowing how many more were with them, I whooped for my companion; one of the hunters in turn, not knowing how many were with me, threw his spear at me. I side-stepped it and reached for my darts, and though I was not very accurate with a blowpipe I hit him in the thigh; within a minute he was writhing on the ground, for in my haste I had blown a venomous dart at him, and my comrade took his comrade prisoner by surprise. As soon as the man I had hit was dead I withdrew my dart and cut off his ear for trophy, and we returned with our captive. He told our war chief in sign language that the young man I had killed was the son and heir of their king and that my having mutilated him meant their tribe surely would seek to avenge his death. The next morning a Dang search party was sent out to recover the body so that it might be destroyed and trouble averted, but it had disappeared; war threatened. The day after that I chose to vanish; they would not think of looking for me in the direction of Sorish's tribe, north, but would assume that I had been captured by the southern tribe in retribution for their prince's death. My concern now, two years later, was how to account for not having been maimed or executed; the least I could do was to cut a finger off, but when it came to the point I could not even bring myself to have a surgeon do it, much less do it myself; I had adequate lies prepared for their other questions, but about this I was a bit nervous.

I got there at sundown. Spying, I did not see Redadu about the village. On the chance, I slipped into our hut when no one was looking; she was there, playing with our child. He was as cute a little preliterate as you ever saw suck a thumb, and it made me chuckle to think he would never be literate either. Redadu's screams when she saw me fetched the women, but when they heard a man's voice they could not intrude. In her joy she lacerated me with her fingernails (the furrows across my shoulder festered for a long time); I could do no less than bite her arm till she bled; the primal scene we treated our son to presumably scarred him for life — though I must say the scars haven't shown up yet. I can't deny I was glad to see her too, for, though I felt for her none of the tender, complex emotions I had been feeling for Velma, emotions which I more or less identified as being love, yet I was so secure with her sexually, knew so well what to do and what to expect from her in every important matter that it was an enormous, if cool, comfort to me to be with her. *Comfort* is a dangerous approximation to what I mean; being with her provided, as it were, the condition for doing; in Sansom I did not consider her my wife and here I did not recognize in myself the American emotions of love or marriage, yet it seemed to me right to be with her and our son was no bastard. *Cool* — I cannot guarantee that mine was the usual Dang emotion, for it is hard for the cool to gauge the warmth of others (in my reports I have denied any personal experience of love among the Dangs for this reason). When we emerged from the hut there was amazement and relief among the women: amazement that I had returned and relief that it had not been one of their husbands pleasuring the widow. But the men were more ambiguously pleased to see me. Redadu's scratches were not enough and they doubted my story that the enemy king made me his personal slave who must be bodily perfect. They wanted to hear me prophesy.

Redadu told me afterward, hiding her face in my arms for fear of being judged insolent, that I surpassed myself that night, that only the three high prophets had ever been so inspired. And it was true that even the men most hostile to me did not oppose my reëntry into the tribe after they had heard me prophesy; they could have swallowed the story I fed them about my two-year absence only because they believed in me the prophet. Dangs make no separation between fact and fantasy, apparent reality and visionary reality, truth and beauty. I once saw a young would-be prophet shudder away from a stick on the ground saying it was a snake, and none of the others except the impressionable was afraid of the stick; it was said of him that he was a beginner. Another time I saw a prophet scatter the whole congregation, myself included, when he screamed at the sight of a beast which he called a cougar; when sober dawn found the speared creature to be a cur it was said of the prophet that he was strong, and he was honored with an epithet, Cougar-Dog. My prophesying the first night of my return must have been of this caliber, though to my disappointment I was given no epithet, not even the nickname I'd sometimes heard before, Bush-Hair.

I knew there was a third kind of prophesying, the highest, performed only on the most important occasions in the Cave-Temple where I had never been. No such occasion had presented itself during my stay before, and when I asked one of the other prophets about that ceremony he put me off with the term Wind-Haired Child of the Sun; from another I learned that the name of this sort of prophesying was Stone is Stone. Obviously I was going to have to stay until I could make sense of these mysteries.

There was a war party that wanted my support; my slavery was presumed to have given me knowledge which would make a raid highly successful; because of this as well as because I had instigated the conflict by killing the king's son I would be made chief of the raiding party. I was uneasy about the fever, which had got rather worse among them during the previous two years, without risking my neck against savages who were said always to eat a portion of their slain enemy's liver raw and whose habitat I knew nothing of. I persuaded the Dangs, therefore, that they should not consider attacking before the rains came, because their enemies were now the stronger, having on their side their protector, the sun. They listened to me and waited. Fortunately it was a long dry season, during which I had time to find a salt deposit and to teach a few women the rudiments of drying and salting fish; and during the first week of the rains every night there were showers of falling stars to be seen in the sky; to defend against them absorbed all energies for weeks, including the warriors'. Even so, even though I was a prophet, a journeyman prophet as it were, I was never in on these rites in the Cave-Temple. I dared not ask many questions. Sir Bewley Morehead had described a temple surrounded by seventy-six poles, each topped by a human head; he could hardly have failed to mention that it was in a cave, yet he made no such mention, and I knew of no temple like the one he had described. At a time of rains and peace in the sky the war party would importune me. I did not know what to do but wait.

The rains became violent, swamping the villages in the lower valley and destroying a number of huts, yet the rainy season ended abruptly two months before its usual time. Preparations for war had already begun, and day by day as the sun's strength increased and the earth dried the war party became more impatient. The preparations in themselves lulled my objections to the raid, even to my leading the raid, and stimulated my desire to make war. But the whole project was canceled a couple of days before we were to attack because of the sudden fever of one of the high prophets; the day after he came down five others of the tribe fell sick, among them Redadu. There was nothing I could do but sit by her, fanning her and sponging her till she died. Her next older sister took our son to rear. I would allow no one to prepare her body but myself, though her mother was supposed to help; I washed it with the proper infusions of herbs, and at dawn, in the presence of her clan, I laid her body on the river. Thank heaven it floated or I should have had to spend another night preparing it further. I felt like killing someone now; I recklessly called for war now, even though the high prophet had not yet died; I was restrained, not without admiration. I went up into the eastern hills by myself and returned after a week bearing the hide of a cougar; I had left the head and claws on my trophy in a way the Dangs had never seen; when I put the skin on in play by daylight and bounded and snarled only the bravest did not run in terror. They called me Cougar-Man. Redadu's younger sister came to sleep with me; I did not want her, but she so stubbornly refused to be expelled that I kept her for the night, for the next night, for the next; it was not improper.

The high prophet did not die, but lay comatose most of the

time. The Dangs have ten master prophets, of whom the specially gifted, whether one or all ten, usually two or three, are high prophets. Fifteen days after Redadu had died, well into the abnormal dry spell, nearly all the large fish seemed to disappear from the river. A sacrifice was necessary. It was only because the old man was so sick that a high prophet was used for this occasion, otherwise a captive or a woman would have served the purpose. A new master prophet must replace him, to keep the complement up to ten. I was chosen.

The exultation I felt when I learned that the master prophets had co-opted me among them was by no means cool and anthropological, for now that I had got what I had come to get I no longer wanted it for Sansom reasons. *If the conditions of my being elevated,* I said to myself, *are the suffering of the people, Redadu's death, and the sacrifice of an old man, then I must make myself worthy of the great price. Worthy* — a value word, not a scientific one. Of course, my emotions were not the simple pride and fear of a Dang. I can't say what sort they were, but they were fierce.

At sundown all the Dangs of all the clans were assembled about the entrance to The Cleft. All the prophets, masked, emerged from The Cleft and began the dance in a great wheel. Within this wheel, rotating against it, was the smaller wheel of the nine able-bodied master prophets. At the center, facing the point at which the full moon would rise, I hopped on one leg, then the other. I had been given none of the vatic liquor, that brew which the women, when I had first come among the Dangs, had been preparing in the small-throated pots, and I hoped I should be able to remain conscious throughout the rites. However, at moonrise a moon slave brought me a gourdful to drink without ceasing to dance. I managed to allow a good deal of it to spill unnoticed down with the sweat streaming off me, so that later I was able to remember what had happened, right up to the prophesying itself. The dance continued for at least two more hours, then the drums suddenly stopped and the prophets began to file up The Cleft with me last dancing after the high prophets. We danced into an opening in the cliff from which a disguising stone had been rolled away. The people were not allowed to follow us. We entered a great cavern illuminated by ten smoking torches and circled a palisade of stakes; the only sound was the shuffle of our feet and the snorts of our breathing. There were seventy-six stakes, as Morehead had seen, but only on twenty-eight of them were heads impaled, the last few with flesh on them still, not yet skulls cleaned of all but hair. In the center was a huge stone under the middle of which a now dry stream had tunneled a narrow passage; on one side of the stone, above the passage, were two breastlike protuberances, one of which had a recognizable nipple in the suitable place. Presently the dancing file reversed so that I was the leader. I had not been taught what to do; I wove the file through the round of stakes, and spiraled inward till we were three deep about The Stone; I straddled the channel, raised my hands till they were touching the breasts, and gave a great cry. I was, for reasons I do not understand, shuddering all over; though I was conscious and though I had not been instructed, I was not worried that I might do the wrong thing next. When I touched The Stone a dread shook me without affecting my exaltation. Two moon slaves seized my arms, took off my mask, and wrapped and bound me — arms at my side and legs pressed together in a deer hide — and then laid me on my back in the channel under The Stone with my head only half out, so that I was staring up the sheer side of rock. The dancers continued, though the master prophets had disappeared. My excitement, the new unused position, being mummied tightly, the weakness of the drug, my will to observe, all kept me conscious for a long time. Gradually, however, my eyes began to roll up into my head, I strained less powerfully against the thongs that bound me, and I felt my breathing approach the vatic rhythm. At this point I seemed to break out in a new sweat, on my forehead, my throat, in my hair; I could hear a splash, groggily I licked my chin — an odd taste — I wondered if I was bleeding. Of course, it was the blood of the sick old high prophet, who had just been sacrificed on The Stone above me; well, his blood would give me strength. Wondering remotely whether his fever could be transmitted by drinking his blood I entered the trance. At dawn I emerged into consciousness while I was still prophesying; I was on a ledge in the valley above all the people, in my mask again. I listened to myself finish the story I was telling. "He was afraid. A third time a man said to him: 'You are a friend of the most high prophet.' He answered: 'Not me. I do not know that man they are sacrificing.' Then he went into a dark corner, he put his hands over his face all day." When I came to the Resurrection a sigh blew across the people. It was the best story they had ever heard. Of course. But I was not really a Christian. For several weeks I fretted over my confusion, this new, unsuspected confusion.

I was miserable without Redadu; I let her sister substitute only until I had been elevated, and then I cast her off, promising her however that she and only she might wear an anklet made of my teeth when I should die. Now that I was a master prophet I could not be a warrior; I had enough of hunting and fishing and tedious ceremonies. Hunger from the shortage of fish drove the hunters high into the foothills; there was not enough; they ate my preserved fish, suspiciously, but they ate them. When I left it was not famine that I was escaping but my confusion; I was fleeing to the classrooms and the cool museums where I should be neither a leftover Christian nor a mimic of a Dang.

My academic peace lasted for just two years, during which time I wrote five articles on my researches, publishing them this time under my name only, did some of the work for my doctorate, and married Velma. Then came World War II, in which my right hand was severed above the wrist; I was provided with an artificial hand and given enough money so that I could afford to finish my degree in style. We had two daughters and I was given a job at Sansom. There was no longer a question of my returning to the Dangs. I would become a settled anthropologist, teach, and quarrel with my colleagues in the learned journals. But by the time the Korean War came along and robbed us of a lot of our students, my situation at the university had changed considerably. Few of my theoretical and disputatious articles were printed in the journals, and I hated writing them; I was not given tenure and there were some hints to the effect that I was considered a one-shot man, a flash-in-the-pan; Velma nagged for more money and higher rank. My only recourse was further research, and when I thought of starting all over again with some other tribe — in northern Australia, along the Zambesi, on an African island — my heart sank. The gossip was not far from the mark — I was not a one hundred per cent scientist and never would be. I had just enough reputation and influential recommendations to be awarded a Guggenheim Fellowship;

supplemented by a travel grant from the university this made it possible for me to leave my family comfortably provided for and to return to the Dangs.

A former student now in Standard Oil in Venezuela arranged to have me parachuted among them from an SO plane. There was the real danger that they would kill me before they recognized me, but if I arrived in a less spectacular fashion I was pretty sure they would sacrifice me for their safety's sake. This time, being middle-aged, I left my hunting knife and brought instead at my belt a pouch filled with penicillin and salves. I had a hard time identifying the valley from the air; it took me so long that it was sunset before I jumped. I knew how the Dangs were enraged by airplanes, especially by the winking lights of night fliers, and I knew they would come for me if they saw me billowing down. Fortunately I landed in the river, for though I was nearly drowned before I disentangled my parachute harness I was also out of range of the blow-pipes. I finally identified myself to the warriors brandishing their spears along the shore; they had not quite dared to swim out after so prodigious a being; even after they knew who I said I was and allowed me to swim to shore they saw me less as myself than as a supernatural being. I was recognized by newcomers who had not seen me so closely swinging from the parachute (the cloud); on the spot my epithet became, and remained, Sky-Cougar. Even so no one dared touch me till the high prophet — there was only one now — had arrived and talked with me; my artificial hand seemed to him an extension of the snake tattooed onto my skin, he would not touch it; I suddenly struck him with it and pinched his arm. "Pinchers," I said using the word for a crayfish claw, and he laughed. He said there was no way of telling whether I was what I seemed to be until he had heard me prophesy; if I prophesied as I had done before I had disappeared I must be what I seemed to be; meanwhile, for the three weeks till full moon I was to be kept in the hut for captives.

At first I was furious at being imprisoned, and when mothers brought children from miles about to peek through the stakes at the man with the snake hand I snarled or sulked like a caged wolf. But I became conscious that one youth, squatting in a quiet place, had been watching me for hours. I demanded of him who he was. He said, "I am your son," but he did not treat me as his father. To be sure, he could not have remembered what I looked like; my very identity was doubted; even if I were myself, I was legendary, a stranger who had become a Dang and had been held by an enemy as captive slave for two years and had then become a master prophet with the most wonderful vision anyone knew. Yet he came to me every day and answered all the questions I put to him. It was, I believe, my artificial hand that finally kept him aloof from me; no amount of acquaintance could accustom him to that. By the end of the first week it was clear to me that if I wanted to survive — not to be accepted as I once had been, just to survive — I would have to prophesy the Passion again. And how could I determine what I would say when under the vatic drug? I imagined a dozen schemes for substituting colored water for the drug, but I would need an accomplice for that and I knew that not even my own son would serve me in so forbidden an act.

I called for the high prophet. I announced to him in tones all the more arrogant because of my trepidations that I would prophesy without the vatic liquor. His response to my announcement astonished me: he fell upon his knees, bowed his head, and rubbed dust into his hair. He was the most powerful man among the Dangs, except in time of war when the war chief took over, and furthermore he was an old man of personal dignity, yet here he was abasing himself before me and, worse, rubbing dust into his hair as was proper in the presence of the very sick to help them in their dying. He told me why: prophesying successfully from a voluntary trance was the test which I must pass to become a high prophet; normally a master prophet was forced to this, for the penalty for failing it was death. I dismissed him with a wave of my claw.

I had five days to wait until full moon. The thought of the risk I was running was more than I could handle consciously; to avoid the jitters I performed over and over all the techniques of preparing for the trance, though I carefully avoided entering it. I was not sure I would be able to enter it alone, but whether I could or not I knew I wanted to conserve my forces for the great test. At first during those five days I would remind myself once in a while of my scientific purpose in going into the trance consciously; at other times I would assure myself that it was for the good of the Dangs that I was doing it, since it was not wise or safe for them to have only one high prophet. Both of these reasons were true enough, but not very important. As scientist I should tell them some new myth, say the story of Abraham and Isaac or of Oedipus, so that I could compare its effect on them with that of the Passion; as master prophet I should ennoble my people if I could. However, thinking these matters over as I held my vatic squat hour after hour, visited and poked at by prying eyes, I could find no myth to satisfy me; either, as in the case of Abraham, it involved a concept of God which the Dangs could not reach, or else, as with Oedipus, it necessitated more drastic changes than I trusted myself to keep straight while prophesying — that Oedipus should mutilate himself was unthinkable to the Dangs and that the gods should be represented as able to forgive him for it was impious. Furthermore, I did not think, basically, that any story I could tell them would in fact ennoble them. I was out to save my own skin.

The story of Christ I knew by heart; it had worked for me once, perhaps more than once; it would work again. I rehearsed it over and over, from the Immaculate Conception to the Ascension. But such was the force of that story on me that by the fifth day my cynicism had disappeared along with my scientism, and I believed, not that the myth itself was true, but that relating it to my people was the best thing it was possible for me to do for them. I remember telling myself that this story would help raise them toward monotheism, a necessary stage in the evolution toward freedom. I felt a certain satisfaction in the thought that some of the skulls on the stakes in the Cave-Temple were very likely those of missionaries who had failed to convert these heathen.

At sundown of the fifth day I was taken by moon slaves to a cave near The Cleft, where I was left in peace. I fell into a troubled sleep from which I awoke in a sweat. "Where am I? What am I about to do?" It seemed to me dreadfully wrong that I should be telling these, my people, a myth in whose power, but not in whose truth, I believed. Why should I want to free them from superstition into monotheism and then into my total freedom, when I myself was half-returning, voluntarily, down the layers again? The energy for these sweating questions came, no doubt, from my anxiety about how I was going to perform that night, but I did not recognize this fact at the time. Then I thought it was my conscience speaking, and that I had no right to open to the Dangs a freedom I myself was rejecting. It was too late to alter my course; honesty required me, and I resolved courageously, not to prophesy at all.

When I was fetched out the people were in assembly at The Cleft and the wheel of master prophets was revolving against the greater wheel of dancers. I was given my cougar skin. Hung from a stake, in the center where I was to hop, was a huge, terrific mask I had never seen before. As the moon rose her slaves hung this mask on me; the thong cut into the back of my neck cruelly, and at the bottom the mask came to a point that pressed my belly; it was so wide my arms could only move laterally. It had no eye holes; I broke into a sweat wondering how I should be able to follow the prophets into the Cave-Temple. It turned out to be no problem; the two moon slaves, one on each side, guided me by prodding spears in my ribs. Once in the cave they guided me to the back side of The Stone and drove me to climb it, my feet groping for steps I could not see; once, when I lost my balance, the spears' pressure kept me from falling backward. By the time I reached the top of The Stone I was bleeding and dizzy. With one arm I kept the mask from gouging my belly while with the other I helped my aching neck support the mask. I did not know what to do next. Tears of pain and anger poured from my eyes. I began hopping. I should have been moving my arms in counterpoint to the rhythm of my hop, but I could not bear the thought of letting the mask cut into me more. I kept hopping in the same place for fear of falling off; I had not been noticing the sounds of the other prophets, but suddenly I was aware they were making no sounds at all. In my alarm I lurched to the side and cut my foot on a sharp break in the rock. Pain converted my panic to rage.

I lifted the mask and held it flat above my head. I threw my head back and howled as I had never howled in my life, through a constricted, gradually opening throat, until at the end I was roaring; when I gasped in my breath I made a barking noise. I leaped and leaped, relieved of pain, confident. I punched my knee desecratingly through the brittle hide of the mask, and threw it behind me off The Stone. I tore off my cougar skin, and holding it with my claw by the tip of its tail I whirled it around my head. The prophets, massed below me, fell onto their knees. I felt their fear. Howling, I soared the skin out over them; one of those on whom it landed screamed hideously. A commotion started; I could not see very well what was happening. I barked and they turned toward me again. I leaped three times and then, howling, jumped wide-armed off The Stone. The twelve-foot drop hurt severely my already cut foot. I rolled exhausted into the channel in the cave floor.

Moon slaves with trembling hands mummied me in the deerskin and shoved me under The Stone with only my head sticking out. They brought two spears with darts tied to the points; rolling my head to watch them do this I saw that the prophets were kneeling over and rubbing dirt into their hair. Then the slaves laid the spears alongside the base of The Stone with the poisoned pricks pointed at my temples; exactly how close they were I could not be sure, but close enough so that I dared not move my head. In all my preparations I had, as I had been trained to do, rocked and weaved at least my head; now, rigidity, live rigidity. A movement would scratch me and a scratch would kill me.

I pressed my hook into my thigh, curled my toes, and pressed my tongue against my teeth till my throat ached. I did not dare relieve myself even with a howl, for I might toss my head fatally. I strained against my thongs to the verge of apoplexy. For a while I was unable to see, for sheer rage. Fatigue collapsed me. Yet I dared not relax my vigilance over my movements. My consciousness sealed me off. Those stone protuberances up between which I had to stare in the flickering light were merely chance processes on a boulder, similes to breasts. The one thing I might not become unconscious of was the pair of darts waiting for me to err. For a long time I thought of piercing my head against them, for relief, for spite. Hours passed. I was carefully watched.

I do not know what wild scheme I had had in mind when I had earlier resolved not to prophesy, what confrontation or escape; it had had the pure magnificence of a fantasy resolution. But the reality, which I had not seriously tried to evade, was that I must prophesy or die. I kept lapsing from English into a delirium of Dang. By the greatest effort of will I looked about me rationally. I wondered whether the return of Halley's comet, at which time all the stakes should be mounted by skulls, would make the Dangs destroy the Cave-Temple and erect a new one. I observed the straight, indented seam of sandstone running slantwise up the boulder over me and wondered how many eons this rotting piece of granite had been tumbled about by water. I reflected that I was unworthy both as a Christian and as a Dang to prophesy the life of Jesus. But I convinced myself that it was a trivial matter, since to the Christians it was the telling more than the teller that counted and to the Dangs this myth would serve as a civilizing force they needed. Surely, I thought, my hypocrisy could be forgiven me, especially since I resolved to punish myself for it by leaving the Dangs forever as soon as I could. Having reached this rational solution I smiled and gestured to the high prophet with my eyes; he did not move a muscle. When I realized that nothing to do with hypocrisy would unbind me desperation swarmed in my guts and mounted toward my brain; with this question it took me over: *How can I make myself believe it is true?* I needed to catch hold of myself again. I dug my hook so hard into my leg — it was the only action I was able to take — that I gasped with pain; the pain I wanted. I did not speculate on the consequences of gouging my leg, tearing a furrow in my thigh muscle, hurting by the same act the stump of my arm to which the hook was attached; just as I knew that the prophets, the torches, the poisoned darts were there in the cave, so also I knew that far far back in my mind I had good enough reasons to be hurting myself, reasons which I could find out if I wanted to, but which it was not worth my trouble to discover; I even allowed the knowledge that I myself was causing the pain to drift back in my mind. The pain itself, only the pain, became my consciousness, purging all else. Then, as the pain subsided leaving me free and equipoised, awareness of the stone arched over me flooded my mind. Because it had been invested by the people with a great mystery, it was an incarnation; the power of their faith made it the moon, who was female; at the same time it was only a boulder. I understood Stone is Stone, and that became my consciousness.

My muscles ceased straining against the bonds, nor did they slump; they ceased aching, they were at ease, they were ready. I said nothing, I did not change the upward direction of my glance, I did not smile, yet at this moment the high prophet removed the spears and had the moon slaves unbind me. I did not feel stiff nor did my wounds bother me, and when I put on my cougar skin and leaped, pulled the head over my face and roared, all the prophets fell onto their faces before me. I began chanting and I knew I was doing it all the better for knowing what I was about; I led them back out to the waiting people, and until dawn I chanted the story of the birth, prophesying, betrayal, sacrifice, and victory of the most high prophet. I am a good mimic, I was thoroughly trained, the story is the best; what I gave them was, for them, as good as a vision. I did not know the difference myself.

But the next evening I knew the difference. While I performed my ablutions and the routine ceremonies to the full moon I thought with increasing horror of my state of mind during my conscious trance. What my state of mind actually had been I cannot with confidence now represent, for what I know of it is colored by my reaction against it the next day. I had remained conscious, in that I could recall what happened, yet that observer and commentator in myself of whose existence I had scarcely been aware, but whom I had always taken for my consciousness, had vanished. I no longer had been thinking, but had lost control so that my consciousness had become what I was doing; almost worse, when I had told the story of Christ I had done it not because I had wanted to or believed in it but because, in some obscure sense, I had had to. Thinking about it afterward I did not understand or want to understand what I was drifting toward, but I knew it was something that I feared. And I got out of there as soon as I was physically able.

Here in Sansom what I have learned has provided me with material for an honorable contribution to knowledge, has given me a tenure to a professorship — thereby pleasing my wife — whereas if I had stayed there among the Dangs much longer I would have reverted until I had become one of them, might not have minded when the time came to die under the sacrificial knife, would have taken in all ways the risk of prophecy — as my Dang son intends to do — until I had lost myself utterly.

FLANNERY O'CONNOR (*1925–1964*) Miss O'Connor was born in Savannah of an old family of Georgia Catholics. She went to parochial school, The Sacred Heart, and Georgia Women's College in Milledgeville. She was editor of the literary magazine while in school and later attended the Writer's Workshop in Iowa on a fellowship. She particularly admired Nathaniel West's *Miss Lonelyhearts,* William Faulkner's *As I Lay Dying,* and the works of Ring Lardner. In 1956 and 1963 she won first prize in the annual O. Henry short story competition.

She suffered from lupus, a disease that riddled and incapacitated her body for many years. After she became ill, she visited the bath at Lourdes. The last thirteen years of her life were spent in infirmity in a bare, austere room at the family farm, Andalusia, near Milledgeville. By her bedside she kept the Sunday missal, the breviary, and the Holy Bible.

Her dialogue is written in the country idiom, tight yet colorful; usually a sense of the grotesque pervades her stories. As Robert Fitzgerald says in his fine introduction to her last book: "They begin and end with coffin dreams"; she writes of "the skull beneath the skin." Yet in each story the possibility of some kind of personal and immediate salvation is held out to the main character.

Her books include *Wise Blood* (1952), *A Good Man Is Hard To Find* (1955), *The Violent Bear It Away* (1960), and *Everything That Rises Must Converge* (1965), published after her death. "Revelation" is included in this last volume.

REVELATION

Flannery O'Connor

The doctor's waiting room, which was very small, was almost full when the Turpins entered and Mrs. Turpin, who was very large, made it look even smaller by her presence. She stood looming at the head of the magazine table set in the center of it, a living demonstration that the room was inadequate and ridiculous. Her little bright black eyes took in all the patients as she sized up the seating situation. There was one vacant chair and a place on the sofa occupied by a blond child in a dirty blue romper who should have been told to move over and make room for the lady. He was five or six, but Mrs. Turpin saw at once that no one was going to tell him to move over. He was slumped down in the seat, his arms idle at his sides and his eyes idle in his head; his nose ran unchecked.

Mrs. Turpin put a firm hand on Claud's shoulder and said in a voice that included anyone who wanted to listen, "Claud, you sit in that chair there," and gave him a push down into the vacant one. Claud was florid and bald and sturdy, somewhat shorter than Mrs. Turpin, but he sat down as if he were accustomed to doing what she told him to.

Mrs. Turpin remained standing. The only man in the room besides Claud was a lean stringy old fellow with a rusty hand spread out on each knee, whose eyes were closed as if he were asleep or dead or pretending to be so as not to get up and offer her his seat. Her gaze settled agreeably on a well-dressed grey-haired lady whose eyes met hers and whose expression said: if that child belonged to me, he would have some manners and move over — there's plenty of room there for you and him too.

Claud looked up with a sigh and made as if to rise.

"Sit down," Mrs. Turpin said. "You know you're not supposed to stand on that leg. He has an ulcer on his leg," she explained.

Claud lifted his foot onto the magazine table and rolled his trouser leg up to reveal a purple swelling on a plump marble-white calf.

"My!" the pleasant lady said. "How did you do that?"

"A cow kicked him," Mrs. Turpin said.

"Goodness!" said the lady.

Claud rolled his trouser leg down.

"Maybe the little boy would move over," the lady suggested, but the child did not stir.

"Somebody will be leaving in a minute," Mrs. Turpin said. She could not understand why a doctor — with as much money as they made charging five dollars a day to just stick their head in the hospital door and look at you — couldn't afford a decent-sized waiting room. This one was hardly bigger than a garage. The table was cluttered with limp-looking magazines and at one end of it there was a big green glass ash tray full of cigaret butts and cotton wads with little blood spots on them. If she had had anything to do with the running of the place, that would have been emptied every so often. There were no chairs against the wall at the head of the room. It had a rectangular-shaped panel in it that permitted a view of the office where the nurse came and went and the secretary listened to the radio. A plastic fern in a gold pot sat in the opening and trailed its fronds down almost to the floor. The radio was softly playing gospel music.

Just then the inner door opened and a nurse with the highest stack of yellow hair Mrs. Turpin had ever seen put her face in the crack and called for the next patient. The woman sitting beside Claud grasped the two arms of her chair and hoisted herself up; she pulled her dress free from her legs and lumbered through the door where the nurse had disappeared.

Mrs. Turpin eased into the vacant chair, which held her tight as a corset. "I wish I could reduce," she said, and rolled her eyes and gave a comic sigh.

"Oh, *you* aren't fat," the stylish lady said.

"Ooooo I am too," Mrs. Turpin said. "Claud he eats all he wants to and never weighs over one hundred and seventy-five pounds, but me I just look at something good to eat and I gain some weight," and her stomach and shoulders shook with laughter. "You can eat all you want to, can't you, Claud?" she asked, turning to him.

Claud only grinned.

"Well, as long as you have such a good disposition," the stylish lady said, "I don't think it makes a bit of difference what size you are. You just can't beat a good disposition."

Next to her was a fat girl of eighteen or nineteen, scowling into a thick blue book which Mrs. Turpin saw was entitled *Human Development*. The girl raised her head and directed her scowl at Mrs. Turpin as if she did not like her looks. She appeared annoyed that anyone should speak while she tried to read. The poor girl's face was blue with acne and Mrs. Turpin thought how pitiful it was to have a face like that at that age. She gave the girl a friendly smile but the girl only scowled the harder. Mrs. Turpin herself was fat but she had always had good skin, and, though she was forty-seven years old, there was not a wrinkle in her face except around her eyes from laughing too much.

Next to the ugly girl was the child, still in exactly the same position, and next to him was a thin leathery old woman in a cotton print dress. She and Claud had three sacks of chicken feed in their pump house that was in the same print. She had seen from the first that the child belonged with the old woman. She could tell by the way they sat — kind of vacant and white-trashy, as if they would sit there until Doomsday if nobody called and told them to get up. And at right angles but next to the well-dressed pleasant lady was a lank-faced woman who was certainly the child's mother. She had on a yellow sweat shirt and wine-colored slacks, both gritty-looking, and the rims of her lips were stained with snuff. Her dirty yellow hair was tied behind with a little piece of red paper ribbon. Worse than niggers any day, Mrs. Turpin thought.

The gospel hymn playing was, "When I looked up and He looked down," and Mrs. Turpin, who knew it, supplied the last line mentally, "And wona these days I know I'll we-eara crown."

Without appearing to, Mrs. Turpin always noticed people's feet. The well-dressed lady had on red and grey suede shoes to match her dress. Mrs. Turpin had on her good black patent leather pumps. The ugly girl had on Girl Scout shoes and heavy socks. The old woman had on tennis shoes and the white-trashy mother had on what appeared to be bedroom slippers, black straw with gold braid threaded through them — exactly what you would have expected her to have on.

Sometimes at night when she couldn't go to sleep, Mrs. Turpin would occupy herself with the question of who she would have chosen to be if she couldn't have been herself. If Jesus had said to her before he made her, "There's only two places available for you. You can either be a nigger or white-trash," what would she have said? "Please, Jesus, please," she would have said, "just let me wait until there's another place available," and he would have said, "No, you have to go right now and I have only those two places so make up your mind." She would have wiggled and squirmed and begged and pleaded but it would have been no use and finally she would have said, "All right, make me a nigger then — but that don't mean a trashy one." And he would have made her a neat clean respectable Negro woman, herself but black.

Next to the child's mother was a red-headed youngish woman, reading one of the magazines and working a piece of chewing gum, hell for leather, as Claud would say. Mrs. Turpin could not see the woman's feet. She was not white-trash, just common. Sometimes Mrs. Turpin occupied herself at night naming the classes of people. On the bottom of the heap were most colored people, not the kind she would have been if she had been one, but most of them; then next to them — not above, just away from — were the white-trash; then above them were the home-owners, and above them the home-and-land owners, to which she and Claud belonged. Above she and Claud were people with a lot of money and much bigger houses and much more land. But here the complexity of it would begin to bear in on her, for some of the people with a lot of money were common and ought to be below she and Claud and some of the people who had good blood had lost their money and had to rent and then there were colored people who owned their homes and land as well. There was a colored dentist in town who had two red Lincolns and a swimming pool and a farm with registered white-face cattle on it. Usually by the time she had fallen asleep all the classes of people were moiling and roiling around in her head, and she would dream they were all crammed in together in a box car, being ridden off to be put in a gas oven.

"That's a beautiful clock," she said and nodded to her right. It was a big wall clock, the face encased in a brass sunburst.

"Yes, it's very pretty," the stylish lady said agreeably. "And right on the dot too," she added, glancing at her watch.

The ugly girl beside her cast an eye upward at the clock, smirked, then looked directly at Mrs. Turpin and smirked again. Then she returned her eyes to her book. She was obviously the lady's daughter because, although they didn't look anything alike as to disposition, they both had the same shape of face and the same blue eyes. On the lady they sparkled pleasantly but in the girl's seared face they appeared alternately to smolder and to blaze.

What if Jesus had said, "All right, you can be white-trash or a nigger or ugly"!

Mrs. Turpin felt an awful pity for the girl, though she thought it was one thing to be ugly and another to act ugly.

The woman with the snuff-stained lips turned around in her chair and looked up at the clock. Then she turned back and appeared to look a little to the side of Mrs. Turpin. There was a cast in one of her eyes. "You want to know wher you can get one of themther clocks?" she asked in a loud voice.

"No, I already have a nice clock," Mrs. Turpin said. Once somebody like her got a leg in the conversation, she would be all over it.

"You can get you one with green stamps," the woman said. "That's most likely wher he got hisn. Save you up enough, you can get you most anythang. I got me some joo'ry."

Ought to have got you a wash rag and some soap, Mrs. Turpin thought.

"I get contour sheets with mine," the pleasant lady said.

The daughter slammed her book shut. She looked straight in front of her, directly through Mrs. Turpin and on through the yellow curtain and the plate glass window which made the wall behind her. The girl's eyes seemed lit all of a sudden with a peculiar light, an unnatural light like night road signs give. Mrs. Turpin turned her head to see if there was anything going on outside that she should see, but she could not see anything. Figures passing cast only a pale shadow through the curtain.

There was no reason the girl should single her out for her ugly looks.

"Miss Finley," the nurse said, cracking the door. The gum-chewing woman got up and passed in front of her and Claud and went into the office. She had on red high-heeled shoes.

Directly across the table, the ugly girl's eyes were fixed on Mrs. Turpin as if she had some very special reason for disliking her.

"This is wonderful weather, isn't it?" the girl's mother said.

"It's good weather for cotton if you can get the niggers to pick it," Mrs. Turpin said, "but niggers don't want to pick cotton any more. You can't get the white folks to pick it and now you can't get the niggers — because they got to be right up there with the white folks."

"They gonna *try* anyways," the white-trash woman said, leaning forward.

"Do you have one of those cotton-picking machines?" the pleasant lady asked.

"No," Mrs. Turpin said, "they leave half the cotton in the field. We don't have much cotton anyway. If you want to make it farming now, you have to have a little of everything. We got a couple of acres of cotton and a few hogs and chickens and just enough white-face that Claud can look after them himself."

"One thang I don't want," the white-trash woman said, wiping her mouth with the back of her hand. "Hogs. Nasty stinking things, a-gruntin and a-rootin all over the place."

Mrs. Turpin gave her the merest edge of her attention. "Our hogs are not dirty and they don't stink," she said. "They're cleaner than some children I've seen. Their feet never touch the ground. We have a pig-parlor — that's where you raise them on concrete," she explained to the pleasant lady, "and Claud scoots them down with the hose every afternoon and washes off the floor." Cleaner by far than that child right there, she thought. Poor nasty little thing. He had not moved except to put the thumb of his dirty hand into his mouth.

The woman turned her face away from Mrs. Turpin. "I know I wouldn't scoot down no hog with no hose," she said to the wall.

You wouldn't have no hog to scoot down, Mrs. Turpin said to herself.

"A-gruntin and a-rootin and a-groanin," the woman muttered.

"We got a little of everything," Mrs. Turpin said to the pleasant lady. "It's no use in having more than you can handle yourself with help like it is. We found enough niggers to pick our cotton this year but Claud he has to go after them and take them home again in the evening. They can't walk that half a mile. No they can't. I tell you," she said and laughed merrily, "I sure am tired of buttering up niggers, but you got to love em if you want em to work for you. When they come in the morning, I run out and I say, 'Hi yawl this morning?' and when Claud drives them off to the field I just wave to beat the band and they just wave back." And she waved her hand rapidly to illustrate.

"Like you read out of the same book," the lady said, showing she understood perfectly.

"Child, yes," Mrs. Turpin said. "And when they come in from the field, I run out with a bucket of icewater. That's the way it's going to be from now on," she said. "You may as well face it."

"One thang I know," the white-trash woman said. "Two thangs I ain't going to do: love no niggers or scoot down no hog with no hose." And she let out a bark of contempt.

The look that Mrs. Turpin and the pleasant lady exchanged indicated they both understood that you had to *have* certain things before you could *know* certain things. But every time Mrs. Turpin exchanged a look with the lady, she was aware that the ugly girl's peculiar eyes were still on her, and she had trouble bringing her attention back to the conversation.

"When you got something," she said, "you got to look after it." And when you ain't got a thing but breath and britches, she added to herself, you can afford to come to town every morning and just sit on the Court House coping and spit.

A grotesque revolving shadow passed across the curtain behind her and was thrown palely on the opposite wall. Then a bicycle clattered down against the outside of the building. The door opened and a colored boy glided in with a tray from the drug store. It had two large red and white paper cups on it with tops on them. He was a tall, very black boy in discolored white pants and a green nylon shirt. He was chewing gum slowly, as if to music. He set the tray down in the office opening next to the fern and stuck his head through to look for the secretary. She was not in there. He rested his arms on the ledge and waited, his narrow bottom stuck out, swaying slowly to the left and right.

He raised a hand over his head and scratched the base of his skull.

"You see that button there, boy?" Mrs. Turpin said. "You can punch that and she'll come. She's probably in the back somewhere."

"Is thas right?" the boy said agreeably, as if he had never seen the button before. He leaned to the right and put his finger on it. "She sometime out," he said and twisted around to face his audience, his elbows behind him on the counter. The nurse appeared and he twisted back again. She handed him a dollar and he rooted in his pocket and made the change and counted it out to her. She gave him fifteen cents for a tip and he went out with the empty tray. The heavy door swung to slowly and closed at length with the sound of suction. For a moment no one spoke.

"They ought to send all them niggers back to Africa," the white-trash woman said. "That's wher they come from in the first place."

"Oh, I couldn't do without my good colored friends," the pleasant lady said.

"There's a heap of things worse than a nigger," Mrs. Turpin agreed. "It's all kinds of them just like it's all kinds of us."

"Yes, and it takes all kinds to make the world go round," the lady said in her musical voice.

As she said it, the raw-complexioned girl snapped her teeth together. Her lower lip turned downwards and inside out, revealing the pale pink inside of her mouth. After a second it rolled back up. It was the ugliest face Mrs. Turpin had ever seen anyone make and for a moment she was certain that the girl had made it at her. She was looking at her as if she had known and disliked her all her life — all of Mrs. Turpin's life, it seemed too, not just all the girl's life. Why, girl, I don't even know you, Mrs. Turpin said silently.

She forced her attention back to the discussion. "It wouldn't be practical to send them back to Africa," she said. "They wouldn't want to go. They got it too good here."

"Wouldn't be what they wanted — if I had anythang to do with it," the woman said.

"It wouldn't be a way in the world you could get all the niggers back over there," Mrs. Turpin said. "They'd be hiding out and lying down and turning sick on you and wailing and hollering and raring and pitching. It wouldn't be a way in the world to get them over there."

"They got over here," the trashy woman said. "Get back like they got over."

"It wasn't so many of them then," Mrs. Turpin explained.

The woman looked at Mrs. Turpin as if here was an idiot indeed but Mrs. Turpin was not bothered by the look, considering where it came from.

"Nooo," she said, "they're going to stay here where they can go to New York and marry white folks and improve their color. That's what they all want to do, every one of them, improve their color."

"You know what comes of that, don't you?" Claud asked.

"No, Claud, what?" Mrs. Turpin said.

Claud's eyes twinkled. "White-faced niggers," he said with never a smile.

Everybody in the office laughed expect the white-trash and the ugly girl. The girl gripped the book in her lap with white fingers. The trashy woman looked around her from face to face as if she thought they were all idiots. The old woman in the feed sack dress continued to gaze expressionless across the floor at the high-top shoes of the man opposite her, the one who had been pretending to be asleep when the Turpins came in. He was laughing heartily, his hands still spread out on his knees. The child had fallen to the side and was lying now almost face down in the old woman's lap.

While they recovered from their laughter, the nasal chorus on the radio kept the room from silence.

> "You go to blank blank
> And I'll go to mine
> But we'll all blank along
> To-geth-ther,
> And all along the blank
> We'll hep eachother out
> Smile-ling in any kind of
> Weath-ther!"

Mrs. Turpin didn't catch every word but she caught enough to agree with the spirit of the song and it turned her thoughts sober. To help anybody out that needed it was her philosophy of life. She never spared herself when she found somebody in need, whether they were white or black, trash or decent. And of all she had to be thankful for, she was most thankful that this was so. If Jesus had said, "You can be high society and have all the money you want and be thin and svelte-like, but you can't be a good woman with it," she would have had to say, "Well don't make me that then. Make me a good woman and it don't matter what else, how fat or how ugly or how poor!" Her heart rose. He had not made her a nigger or white-trash or ugly! He had made her herself and given her a little of everything. Jesus, thank you! she said. Thank you thank you thank you! Whenever she counted her blessings she felt as buoyant as if she weighed one hundred and twenty-five pounds instead of one hundred and eighty.

"What's wrong with your little boy?" the pleasant lady asked the white-trashy woman.

"He has a ulcer," the woman said proudly. "He ain't give me a minute's peace since he was born. Him and her are just alike," she said, nodding at the old woman, who was running her leathery fingers through the child's pale hair. "Look like I can't get nothing down them two but Co' Cola and candy."

That's all you try to get down em, Mrs. Turpin said to herself. Too lazy to light the fire. There was nothing you could tell her about people like them that she didn't know already. And it was not just that they didn't have anything. Because if you gave them everything, in two weeks it would all be broken or filthy or they would have chopped it up for lightwood. She knew all this from her own experience. Help them you must, but help them you couldn't.

All at once the ugly girl turned her lips inside out again. Her eyes were fixed like two drills on Mrs. Turpin. This time there was no mistaking that there was something urgent behind them.

Girl, Mrs. Turpin exclaimed silently, I haven't done a thing to you! The girl might be confusing her with somebody else. There was no need to sit by and let herself be intimidated. "You must be in college," she said boldly, looking directly at the girl. "I see you reading a book there."

The girl continued to stare and pointedly did not answer.

Her mother blushed at this rudeness. "The lady asked you a question, Mary Grace," she said under her breath.

"I have ears," Mary Grace said.

The poor mother blushed again. "Mary Grace goes to Wellesley College," she explained. She twisted one of the buttons on her dress. "In Massachusetts," she added with a grimace. "And in the summer she just keeps right on studying. Just reads all the time, a real book worm. She's done real well at Wellesley; she's taking English and Math and History and Psychology and Social Studies," she rattled on, "and I think it's too much. I think she ought to get out and have fun."

The girl looked as if she would like to hurl them all through the plate glass window.

"Way up north," Mrs. Turpin murmured and thought, well, it hasn't done much for her manners.

"I'd almost rather to have him sick," the white-trash woman said, wrenching the attention back to herself. "He's so mean when he ain't. Look like some children just take natural to meanness. It's some gets bad when they get sick but he was the opposite. Took sick and turned good. He don't give me no trouble now. It's me waitin to see the doctor," she said.

If I was going to send anybody back to Africa, Mrs. Turpin thought, it would be your kind, woman. "Yes, indeed," she said aloud, but looking up at the ceiling, "it's a heap of things worse than a nigger." And dirtier than a hog, she added to herself.

"I think people with bad dispositions are more to be pitied than anyone on earth," the pleasant lady said in a voice that was decidedly thin.

"I thank the Lord he has blessed me with a good one," Mrs. Turpin said. "The day has never dawned that I couldn't find something to laugh at."

"Not since she married me anyways," Claud said with a comical straight face.

Everybody laughed except the girl and the white-trash.

Mrs. Turpin's stomach shook. "He's such a caution," she said, "that I can't help but laugh at him."

The girl made a loud ugly noise through her teeth.

Her mother's mouth grew thin and tight. "I think the worst thing in the world," she said, "is an ungrateful person. To have everything and not appreciate it. I know a girl," she said, "who has parents who would give her anything, a little brother who loves her dearly, who is getting a good education, who wears the best clothes, but who can never say a kind word to anyone, who never smiles, who just criticizes and complains all day long."

"Is she too old to paddle?" Claud asked.

The girl's face was almost purple.

"Yes," the lady said, "I'm afraid there's nothing to do but leave her to her folly. Some day she'll wake up and it'll be too late."

"It never hurt anyone to smile," Mrs. Turpin said. "It just makes you feel better all over."

"Of course," the lady said sadly, "but there are just some people you can't tell anything to. They can't take criticism."

"If it's one thing I am," Mrs. Turpin said with feeling, "it's grateful. When I think who all I could have been besides myself and what all I got, a little of everything, and a good disposition besides, I just feel like shouting. 'Thank you, Jesus, for making everything the way it is!' It could have been different!" For one thing, somebody else could have got Claud. At the thought of this, she was flooded with gratitude and a terrible pang of joy ran through her. "Oh thank you, Jesus, Jesus, thank you!" she cried aloud.

The book struck her directly over her left eye. It struck almost at the same instant that she realized the girl was about to hurl it. Before she could utter a sound, the raw face came crashing across the table toward her, howling. The girl's fingers sank like clamps into the soft flesh of her neck. She heard the mother cry out and Claud shout, "Whoa!" There was an instant when she was certain that she was about to be in an earthquake.

All at once her vision narrowed and she saw everything as if it were happening in a small room far away, or as if she were looking at it through the wrong end of a telescope. Claud's face crumpled and fell out of sight. The nurse ran in, then out, then in again. Then the gangling figure of the doctor rushed out of the inner door. Magazines flew this way and that as the table turned over. The girl fell with a thud and Mrs. Turpin's vision suddenly reversed itself and she saw everything large instead of small. The eyes of the white-trashy woman were staring hugely at the floor. There the girl, held down on one side by the nurse and on the other by her mother, was wrenching and turning in their grasp. The doctor was kneeling astride her, trying to hold her arm down. He managed after a second to sink a long needle into it.

Mrs. Turpin felt entirely hollow except for her heart which swung from side to side as if it were agitated in a great empty drum of flesh.

"Somebody that's not busy call for the ambulance," the doctor said in the off-hand voice young doctors adopt for terrible occasions.

Mrs. Turpin could not have moved a finger. The old man who had been sitting next to her skipped nimbly into the office and made the call, for the secretary still seemed to be gone.

"Claud!" Mrs. Turpin called.

He was not in his chair. She knew she must jump up and find him but she felt like some one trying to catch a train in a dream, when everything moves in slow motion and the faster you try to run the slower you go.

"Here I am," a suffocated voice, very unlike Claud's, said.

He was doubled up in the corner on the floor, pale as paper, holding his leg. She wanted to get up and go to him but she could not move. Instead, her gaze was drawn slowly downward to the churning face on the floor, which she could see over the doctor's shoulder.

The girl's eyes stopped rolling and focused on her. They seemed a much lighter blue than before, as if a door that had been tightly closed behind them was now open to admit light and air.

Mrs. Turpin's head cleared and her power of motion returned. She leaned forward until she was looking directly into the fierce brilliant eyes. There was no doubt in her mind that the girl did know her, knew her in some intense and personal way, beyond time and place and condition. "What you got to say to me?" she asked hoarsely and held her breath, waiting, as for a revelation.

The girl raised her head. Her gaze locked with Mrs. Turpin's. "Go back to hell where you came from, you old wart hog," she whispered. Her voice was low but clear. Her eyes burned for a moment as if she saw with pleasure that her message had struck its target.

Mrs. Turpin sank back in her chair.

After a moment the girl's eyes closed and she turned her head wearily to the side.

The doctor rose and handed the nurse the empty syringe. He leaned over and put both hands for a moment on the mother's shoulders, which were shaking. She was sitting on the floor, her lips pressed together, holding Mary Grace's hand in her lap. The girl's fingers were gripped like a baby's around her thumb. "Go on to the hospital," he said. "I'll call and make the arrangements."

"Now let's see that neck," he said in a jovial voice to Mrs. Turpin. He began to inspect her neck with his first two fingers. Two little moon-shaped lines like pink fish bones were indented over her windpipe. There was the beginning of an angry red swelling above her eye. His fingers passed over this also.

"Lea' me be," she said thickly and shook him off. "See about Claud. She kicked him."

"I'll see about him in a minute," he said and felt her pulse. He was a thin grey-haired man, given to pleasantries. "Go home and have yourself a vacation the rest of the day," he said and patted her on the shoulder.

Quit your pattin me, Mrs. Turpin growled to herself.

"And put an ice pack over that eye," he said. Then he went and squatted down beside Claud and looked at his leg. After a moment he pulled him up and Claud limped after him into the office.

Until the ambulance came, the only sounds in the room were the tremulous moans of the girl's mother, who continued to sit on the floor. The white-trash woman did not take her eyes off the girl. Mrs. Turpin looked straight ahead at nothing. Presently the ambulance drew up, a long dark shadow, behind the curtain. The attendants came in and set the stretcher down beside the girl and lifted her expertly onto it and carried her out. The nurse helped the mother gather up her things. The shadow of the ambulance moved silently away and the nurse came back in the office.

"That ther girl is going to be a lunatic, ain't she?" the white-trash woman asked the nurse, but the nurse kept on to the back and never answered her.

"Yes, she's going to be a lunatic," the white-trash woman said to the rest of them.

"Po' critter," the old woman murmured. The child's face was still in her lap. His eyes looked idly out over her knees. He had not moved during the disturbance except to draw one leg up under him.

"I thank Gawd," the white-trash woman said fervently, "I ain't a lunatic."

Claud came limping out and the Turpins went home.

As their pick-up truck turned into their own dirt road and made the crest of the hill, Mrs. Turpin gripped the window ledge and looked out suspiciously. The land sloped gracefully down through a field dotted with lavender weeds and at the start of the rise their small yellow frame house, with its little flower beds spread out around it like a fancy apron, sat primly in its accustomed place between two giant hickory trees. She would not have been startled to see a burnt wound between two blackened chimneys.

Neither of them felt like eating so they put on their house clothes and lowered the shade in the bedroom and lay down, Claud with his leg on a pillow and herself with a damp wash-cloth over her eye. The instant she was flat on her back, the image of a razor-backed hog with warts on its face and horns coming out behind its ears snorted into her head. She moaned, a low quiet moan.

"I am not," she said tearfully, "a wart hog. From hell." But the denial had no force. The girl's eyes and her words, even the tone of her voice, low but clear, directed only to her, brooked no repudiation. She had been singled out for the message, though there was trash in the room to whom it might justly have been applied. The full force of this fact struck her only now. There was a woman there who was neglecting her own child but she had been overlooked. The message had been given to Ruby Turpin, a respectable, hard-working, church-going woman. The tears dried. Her eyes began to burn instead with wrath.

She rose on her elbow and the washcloth fell into her hand. Claud was lying on his back, snoring. She wanted to tell him what the girl had said. At the same time, she did not wish to put the image of herself as a wart hog from hell into his mind.

"Hey, Claud," she muttered and pushed his shoulder.

Claud opened one pale baby blue eye.

She looked into it warily. He did not think about anything. He just went his way.

"Wha, whasit?" he said and closed the eye again.

"Nothing," she said. "Does your leg pain you?"

"Hurts like hell," Claud said.

"It'll quit terreckly," she said and lay back down. In a moment Claud was snoring again. For the rest of the afternoon they lay there. Claud slept. She scowled at the ceiling. Occasionally she raised her fist and made a small stabbing motion over her chest as if she was defending her innocence to invisible guests who were like the comforters of Job, reasonable-seeming but wrong.

About five-thirty Claud stirred. "Got to go after those niggers," he sighed, not moving.

She was looking straight up as if there were unintelligible handwriting on the ceiling. The protuberance over her eye had turned a greenish-blue. "Listen here," she said.

"What?"

"Kiss me."

Claud leaned over and kissed her loudly on the mouth. He pinched her side and their hands interlocked. Her expression of ferocious concentration did not change. Claud got up, groaning and growling, and limped off. She continued to study the ceiling.

She did not get up until she heard the pick-up truck coming back with the Negroes. Then she rose and thrust her feet in her brown oxfords, which she did not bother to lace, and stumped out onto the back porch and got her red plastic bucket. She emptied a tray of ice cubes into in and filled it half full of water and went out into the back yard. Every afternoon after Claud brought the hands in, one of the boys helped him put out hay and the rest waited in the back of the truck until he was ready to take them home. The truck was parked in the shade under one of the hickory trees.

"Hi yawl this evening?" Mrs. Turpin asked grimly, appearing with the bucket and the dipper. There were three women and a boy in the truck.

"Us doin nicely," the oldest woman said. "Hi you doin?" and her gaze stuck immediately on the dark lump on Mrs. Turpin's forehead. "You done fell down, ain't you?" she asked in a solicitous voice. The old woman was dark and almost toothless. She had on an old felt hat of Claud's set back on her head. The other two women were younger and lighter and they both had new bright green sun hats. One of them had hers on her head; the other had taken hers off and the boy was grinning beneath it.

Mrs. Turpin set the bucket down on the floor of the truck. "Yawl hep yourselves," she said. She looked around to make sure Claud had gone. "No. I didn't fall down," she said, folding her arms. "It was something worse than that."

"Ain't nothing bad happen to you!" the old woman said. She said it as if they all knew that Mrs. Turpin was protected in some special way by Divine Providence. "You just had you a little fall."

"We were in town at the doctor's office for where the cow kicked Mr. Turpin," Mrs. Turpin said in a flat tone that indicated they could leave off their foolishness. "And there was this girl there. A big fat girl with her face all broke out. I could look at that girl and tell she was peculiar but I couldn't tell how. And me and her mama were just talking and going along and all of a sudden WHAM! She throws this big book she was reading at me and . . ."

"Naw!" the old woman cried out.

"And then she jumps over the table and commences to choke me."

"Naw!" they all exclaimed, "naw!"

"Hi come she do that?" the old woman asked. "What ail her?"

Mrs. Turpin only glared in front of her.

"Somethin ail her," the old woman said.

"They carried her off in an ambulance," Mrs. Turpin continued, "but before she went she was rolling on the floor and they were trying to hold her down to give her a shot and she said something to me." She paused. "You know what she said to me?"

"What she say?" they asked.

"She said," Mrs. Turpin began, and stopped, her face very dark and heavy. The sun was getting whiter and whiter, blanching the sky overhead so that the leaves of the hickory tree were black in the face of it. She could not bring forth the words. "Something real ugly," she muttered.

"She sho shouldn't said nothin ugly to you," the old woman said. "You so sweet. You the sweetest lady I know."

"She pretty too," the one with the hat on said.

"And stout," the other one said. "I never knowed no sweeter white lady."

"That's the truth befo' Jesus," the old woman said. "Amen! You des as sweet and pretty as you can be."

Mrs. Turpin knew just exactly how much Negro flattery was worth and it added to her rage. "She said," she began again and finished this time with a fierce rush of breath, "that I was an old wart hog from hell."

There was an astounded silence.

"Where she at?" the youngest woman cried in a piercing voice. "Lemme see her. I'll kill her!"

"I'll kill her with you!" the other one cried.

"She b'long in the sylum," the old woman said emphatically. "You the sweetest white lady I know."

"She pretty too," the other two said. "Stout as she can be and sweet. Jesus satisfied with her!"

"Deed he is," the old woman declared.

Idiots! Mrs. Turpin growled to herself. You could never say anything intelligent to a nigger. You could talk at them but not with them. "Yawl ain't drunk your water," she said shortly. "Leave the bucket in the truck when you're finished with it. I got more to do than just stand around and pass the time of day," and she moved off and into the house.

She stood for a moment in the middle of the kitchen. The dark protuberance over her eye looked like a miniature tornado cloud which might any moment sweep across the horizon of her brow. Her lower lip protruded dangerously. She squared her massive shoulders. Then she marched into the front of the house and out the side door and started down the road to the pig parlor. She had the look of a woman going single-handed, weaponless, into battle.

The sun was a deep yellow now like a harvest moon and was riding westward very fast over the far tree line as if it meant to reach the hogs before she did. The road was rutted and she kicked several good-sized stones out of her path as she strode along. The pig parlor was on a little knoll at the end of a lane that ran off from the side of the barn. It was a square of concrete as large as a small room, with a board fence about four feet high around it. The concrete floor sloped slightly so that the hog wash could drain off into a trench where it was carried to the field for fertilizer. Claud was standing on the outside, on the edge of the concrete, hanging onto the top board, hosing down the floor inside. The hose was connected to the faucet of a water trough nearby.

Mrs. Turpin climbed up beside him and glowered down at the hogs inside. There were seven long-snouted bristly shoats in it — tan with liver-colored spots — and an old sow a few weeks off from farrowing. She was lying on her side grunting. The shoats were running about shaking themselves like idiot children, their little slit pig eyes searching the floor for anything left. She had read that pigs were the most intelligent animal. She doubted it. They were supposed to be smarter than dogs. There had even been a pig astronaut. He had performed his assignment perfectly but died of a heart attack afterwards because they left him in his electric suit, sitting upright throughout his examination when naturally a hog should be on all fours.

A-gruntin and a-rootin. and a-groanin.

"Gimme that hose," she said, yanking it away from Claud. "Go on and carry them niggers home and then get off that leg."

"You look like you might have swallowed a mad dog," Claud observed, but he got down and limped off. He paid no attention to her humors.

Until he was out of earshot, Mrs. Turpin stood on the side of the pen, holding the hose and pointing the stream of water at the hind quarters of any shoat that looked as if it might try to lie down. When he had had time to get over the hill, she turned her head slightly and her wrathful eyes scanned the path. He was nowhere in sight. She turned back again and seemed to gather herself up. Her shoulders rose and she drew in her breath.

"What do you send me a message like that for?" she said in a low fierce voice, barely above a whisper but with the force of a shout in its concentrated fury. "How am I a hog and me both? How am I saved and from hell too?" Her free fist was knotted and with the other she gripped the hose, blindly pointing the stream of water in and out of the eye of the old sow whose outraged squeal she did not hear.

The pig parlor commanded a view of the back pasture where their twenty beef cows were gathered around the hay-bales Claud and the boy had put out. The freshly cut pasture sloped down to the highway. Across it was their cotton field and beyond that a dark green dusty wood which they owned as well. The sun was behind the wood, very red, looking over the paling of trees like a farmer inspecting his own hogs.

"Why me?" she rumbled. "It's no trash around here, black or white, that I haven't given to. And break my back to the bone every day working. And do for the church."

She appeared to be the right size woman to command the arena before her. "How am I a hog?" she demanded. "Exactly how am I like them?" and she jabbed the stream of water at the shoats. "There was plenty of trash there. It didn't have to be me."

"If you like trash better, go get yourself some trash then," she railed. "You could have made me trash. Or a nigger. If trash is what you wanted why didn't you make me trash?" She shook her fist with the hose in it and a watery snake appeared momentarily in the air. "I could quit working and take it easy and be filthy," she growled. "Lounge about the sidewalks all day drinking root beer. Dip snuff and spit in every puddle and have it all over my face. I could be nasty.

"Or you could have made me a nigger. It's too late for me to be a nigger," she said with deep sarcasm, "but I could act like one. Lay down in the middle of the road and stop traffic. Roll on the ground."

In the deepening light everything was taking on a mysterious hue. The pasture was growing a peculiar glassy green and the streak of highway had turned lavender. She braced herself for a final assault and this time her voice rolled out over the pasture. "Go on," she yelled, "call me a hog! Call me a hog again. From hell. Call me a wart hog from hell. Put that bottom rail on top. There'll still be a top and bottom!"

A garbled echo returned to her.

A final surge of fury shook her and she roared, "Who do you think you are?"

The color of everything, field and crimson sky, burned for a moment with a transparent intensity. The question carried over the pasture and across the highway and the cotton field and returned to her clearly like an answer from beyond the wood.

She opened her mouth but no sound came out of it.

A tiny truck, Claud's, appeared on the highway, heading rapidly out of sight. Its gears scraped thinly. It looked like a child's toy. At any moment a bigger truck might smash into it and scatter Claud's and the niggers' brains all over the road.

Mrs. Turpin stood there, her gaze fixed on the highway, all her muscles rigid, until in five or six minutes the truck reappeared, returning. She waited until it had had time to turn into their own road. Then like a monumental statue coming to life, she bent her head slowly and gazed, as if through the very heart of mystery, down into the pig parlor at the hogs. They had settled all in one corner around the old sow who was grunting softly. A red glow suffused them. They appeared to pant with a secret life.

Until the sun slipped finally behind the tree line, Mrs. Turpin remained there with her gaze bent to them as if she were absorbing some abysmal life-giving knowledge. At last she lifted her head. There was only a purple streak in the sky, cutting through a field of crimson and leading, like an extension of the highway, into the descending dusk. She raised her hands from the side of the pen in a gesture hieratic and profound. A visionary light settled in her eyes. She saw the streak as a vast swinging bridge extending upward from the earth through a field of living fire. Upon it a vast horde of souls were rumbling toward heaven. There were whole companies of white-trash, clean for the first time in their lives, and bands of black niggers in white robes, and battalions of freaks and lunatics shouting and clapping and leaping like frogs. And bringing up the end of the procession was a tribe of people whom she recognized at once as those who, like herself and Claud, had always had a little of everything and the God-given wit to use it right. She leaned forward to observe them closer. They were marching behind the others with great dignity, accountable as they had always been for good order and common sense and respectable behavior. They alone were on key. Yet she could see by their shocked and altered faces that even their virtues were being burned away. She lowered her hands and gripped the rail of the hog pen, her eyes small but fixed unblinkingly on what lay ahead. In a moment the vision faded but she remained where she was, immobile.

At length she got down and turned off the faucet and made her slow way on the darkening path to the house. In the woods around her the invisible cricket choruses had struck up, but what she heard were the voices of the souls climbing upward into the starry field and shouting hallelujah.

JOHN BARTH (b. 1930)   Barth was born in Cambridge, Maryland. He received his B.A. and M.A. degrees from Johns Hopkins University. He taught literature and writing at Pennsylvania State University and is now a member of the faculty of the State University of New York at Buffalo.

Barth has described the aim of his fiction as "farce inspired with passion — and with mystery." He has published four novels: *The Floating Opera* (1956), *The End of the Road* (1958), *The Sot-Weed Factor* (1960), and *Giles Goat-Boy* (1966). They have been praised for their comic inventiveness, as in "Night-Sea Journey," as well as for their philosophical range.

NIGHT-SEA JOURNEY

John Barth

One way or another, no matter which theory of our journey is correct, it's myself I address; to whom I rehearse as to a stranger our history and condition, and will disclose my secret hope though I sink for it.

"Is the journey my invention? Do the night, the sea, exist at all, I ask myself, apart from my experience of them? Do I myself exist, or is this a dream? Sometimes I wonder. And if I am, who am I? The Heritage I supposedly transport? But how can I be both vessel and contents? Such are the questions that beset my intervals of rest.

"My trouble is, I lack conviction. Many accounts of our situation seem plausible to me — where and what we are, why we swim and whither. But implausible ones as well, perhaps especially those, I must admit as possibly correct. Even likely. If at times, in certain humors — stroking in unison, say, with my neighbors and chanting with them 'Onwards! Upwards!' — I have supposed that we have after all a common Maker, Whose nature and motives we may not know, but Who engendered us in some mysterious wise and launched us forth toward some end known but to Him — if (for a moodslength only) I have been able to entertain such notions, very popular in certain quarters, it is because our night-sea journey partakes of their absurdity. One might even say: I can believe them *because* they are absurd.

"Has that been said before?

"Another paradox: it appears to be these recesses from swimming that sustain me in the swim. Two measures onward and upward, flailing with the rest, then I float exhausted and dispirited, brood upon the night, the sea, the journey, while the flood bears me a measure back and down: slow progress, but I live, I live, and make my way, aye, past many a drownèd com-

rade in the end, stronger, worthier than I, victims of their un-
remitting *joie de nager*. I have seen the best swimmers of my
generation go under. Numberless the number of the dead! Thousands drown as I think this thought, millions as I rest before
returning to the swim. And scores, hundreds of millions have
expired since we surged forth, brave in our innocence, upon our
dreadful way. 'Love! Love!' we sang then, a quarter-billion
strong, and churned the warm sea white with joy of swimming!
Now all are gone down — the buoyant, the sodden, leaders and
followers, all gone under, while wretched I swim on. Yet these
same reflective intervals that keep me afloat have led me into
wonder, doubt, despair — strange emotions for a swimmer! —
have led me, even, to suspect . . . that our night-sea journey is
without meaning.

"Indeed, if I have yet to join the hosts of the suicides, it is because (fatigue apart) I find it no meaningfuller to drown myself
than to go on swimming.

"I know that there are those who seem actually to enjoy the
night-sea; who claim to love swimming for its own sake, or
sincerely believe that 'reaching the Shore,' 'transmitting the
Heritage' (*Whose* Heritage, I'd like to know? And to whom?) is
worth the staggering cost. I do not. Swimming itself I find at best
not actively unpleasant, more often tiresome, not infrequently
a torment. Arguments from function and design don't impress
me: granted that we can and do swim, that in a manner of speaking our long tails and streamlined heads are 'meant for' swimming; it by no means follows — for me, at least — that we *should*
swim, or otherwise endeavor to 'fulfill our destiny.' Which is to
say, Someone Else's destiny, since ours, so far as I can see, is
merely to perish, one way or another, soon or late. The heartless
zeal of our (departed) leaders, like the blind ambition and good
cheer of my own youth, appalls me now; for the death of my
comrades I am inconsolable. If the night-sea journey has any
justification, it is not for us swimmers ever to discover it.

"Oh, to be sure, 'Love!' one heard on every side: 'Love it is
that drives and sustains us!' I translate: We don't know *what*
drives and sustains us, only that we are most miserably driven
and, imperfectly, sustained. *Love* is how we call our ignorance
of what whips us. 'To reach the Shore,' then: but what if the
Shore exists only in the fancies of us swimmers, who dream it to

account for the dreadful fact that we swim, have always and only swum, and continue swimming without respite (myself excepted) until we die? Supposing even that there *were* a Shore — that, as a cynical companion of mine once imagined, we rise from the drowned to discover that all those vulgar superstitions and exalted metaphors are literal truths: the giant Maker of us all, the Shores of Light beyond our night-sea journey! — whatever would a swimmer do there? The fact is, when we imagine the Shore, what comes to mind is just the opposite of our present condition: no more night, no more sea, no more journeying. In short, the blissful estate of the drowned.

" 'Ours not to stop and think; ours but to swim and sink. . . .' Because a moment's thought reveals the pointlessness of swimming. 'No matter,' I've heard some say, even as they gulped their last: 'The night-sea journey may be absurd, but here we swim, will-we nill-we, against the flood, onward and upward, toward a Shore that may not exist and couldn't be reached even if it did.' The thoughtful swimmer's choices, then, they say, are two: give over thrashing and go under for good, or embrace the absurdity: affirm in and for itself the night-sea journey; swim on with neither motive nor destination, for the sake of swimming, and compassionate moreover with your fellow swimmer, we being all at sea and equally in the dark. I find neither course acceptable. If not even the hypothetical Shore can justify a sea full of drowned comrades, to speak of the swim-in-itself as somehow doing so strikes me as obscene. I continue to swim — but only because blind habit, blind instinct, and blind fear of drowning are still more strong than the horror of our journey. And if on occasion I have assisted a fellow thrasher, joined in the cheers and songs, even passed along to others strokes of genius from the drownèd great, it's that I shrink by temperament from making myself conspicuous. To paddle off in one's own direction, assert one's independent right-of-way, overrun one's fellows without compunction in pursuit of selfish ends, or dedicate oneself entirely to pleasures and diversions without regard for conscience — I can't finally condemn those who journey in this wise; in half my moods I envy them and despise the weak vitality that keeps me from following their example. But in reasonabler moments I remind myself that it's their very freedom and self-responsibility I reject, as more dramatically absurd, in our senseless circumstances, than tailing along in conventional fashion. Suicides, rebels, affirmers of the paradox — nay-sayers and yea-sayers alike to our fatal journey — I finally shake my head at them. And I splash sighing past their corpses, one by one, as past a hundred sorts of others: friends, enemies, brothers, fools, sages, brutes — and nobodies, million upon million. I envy them all.

"A poor irony: that I, who find abhorrent and tautological the doctrine of survival of the fittest (*fitness* meaning, in my experience, nothing more than survival ability, a talent whose only demonstration is the fact of survival, but whose chief ingredients seem to be strength, guile, and callousness), may be the sole remaining swimmer! But the doctrine is false as well as repellent: Chance drowns the worthy with the unworthy, bears up the unfit with the fit by whatever definition, and makes the night-sea journey essentially *haphazard* as well as murderous and unjustified.

" 'You only swim once.' Why bother, then?

" 'Except ye drown, ye shall not reach the Shore of Life.' Poppycock.

"One of my late companions — that same cynic with the curious fancy, among the first to drown — entertained us with odd conjectures while we waited to begin our journey. A favorite theory of his was that the Father does exist, and did indeed make us and the sea we swim — but not a-purpose or even consciously; He made us as it were despite Himself, as we make waves with every tail thrash, and may be unaware of our existence. Another was that He knows we're here but doesn't care what happens to us, inasmuch as He creates (voluntarily or not) other seas and swimmers at more or less regular intervals. In bitterer moments, such as just before he drowned, my friend even supposed that our Maker wished us unmade; there was indeed a Shore, he'd argue, which could save at least some of us from drowning and toward which it was our function to struggle — but for reasons unknowable to us He wanted desperately to prevent our reaching that happy place and fulfilling our destiny. Our 'Father,' in short, was our adversary and would-be killer! No less outrageous, and offensive to traditional opinion, were the fellow's speculations on the nature of our Maker: That He might well be no swimmer Himself at all, but some sort of monstrosity, perhaps even tailless; that He might be stupid, malicious, insensible, perverse, or asleep and dreaming; that the end for which He created and launched us forth, and which we flagellate ourselves to fathom, was perhaps immoral, even obscene. *Et cetera, et cetera:* there was no end to the chap's conjectures, or the impoliteness of his fancy; I have reason to suspect that his early demise, whether planned by 'our Maker' or not, was expedited by certain fellow swimmers indignant at his blasphemies.

"In other moods, however (he was as given to moods as I), his theorizing would become half-serious, so it seemed to me, especially upon the subjects of Fate and Immortality, to which our youthful conversations often turned. Then his harangues, if no less fantastical, grew solemn and obscure, and if he was still baiting us, his passion undid the joke. His objection to popular opinions of the hereafter, he would declare, was their claim to general validity. Why need believers hold that *all* the drownèd rise to be judged at journey's end, and nonbelievers that drowning is final without exception? In *his* opinion (so he'd vow at least), nearly everyone's fate was permanent death; indeed he took a sour pleasure in supposing that every 'Maker' made thousands of separate seas in His creative lifetime, each populated like ours with millions of swimmers, and that in almost every instance both sea and swimmers were utterly annihilated, whether accidentally or by malevolent design. (Nothing if not pluralistical, he imagined there might be millions and billions of 'Fathers,' perhaps in some 'night-sea' of their own!) However — and here he turned infidels against him with the faithful — he professed to believe that in possibly a single night-sea per thousand, say, one of its quarter-billion swimmers (that is, one swimmer in two-hundred-fifty billions) achieved a qualified immortality. In some cases the rate might be slightly higher; in others it was vastly lower, for just as there are swimmers of every degree of proficiency, including some who drown before the journey starts, unable to swim at all, and others created drownèd, as it were, so he imagined what can only be termed impotent Creators, Makers unable to Make, as well as uncommonly fertile ones and all grades between. And it pleased him to deny any necessary relation between a Maker's productivity and His other virtues — including, even, the quality of His creatures.

"I could go on (*he* surely did) with his elaboration of these mad notions — such as that swimmers in other night-seas needn't be of our kind; that Makers themselves might belong to different *species,* so to speak; that our particular Maker mightn't Himself be immortal, or that we might be not only His emissaries but His 'immortality,' continuing His life and our own, transmogrified, beyond our individual deaths. Even this modified immortality (meaningless to me) he conceived as relative and contingent, subject to accidental or deliberate termination: his pet hypothesis was that Makers and swimmers *each generate the other* — against all odds, their number being so great — and that any given 'immortality chain' could terminate after any number of cycles, so that what was 'immortal' (still speaking relatively) was only the cyclic processs of incarnation, which itself might have a beginning and an end. Alternatively he liked to imagine cycles within cycles, either finite or infinite: for example, the 'night-sea,' as it were, in which Makers 'swam' and created night-seas and swimmers like ourselves, might be the creation of a larger Maker, Himself one of many, Who in turn, etc. Time itself he regarded as relative to our experience, like magnitude: who knew but what, with each thrash of our tails, minuscule seas and swimmers, whole eternities, came to pass — as ours, perhaps, and our Maker's Maker's, was elapsing between the strokes of some super-tail, in a slower order of time?

"Naturally I hooted with the others at this nonsense. We were young then, and had only the dimmest notion of what lay ahead; in our ignorance we imagined night-sea journeying to be a positively heroic enterprise. Its meaning and value we never questioned; to be sure, some must go down by the way, a pity no doubt, but to win a race requires that others lose, and like all my fellows I took for granted that I would be the winner. We milled and swarmed, impatient to be off, never mind where or why, only to try our youth against the realities of night and sea; if we indulged the skeptic at all it was as a droll, half-contemptible mascot. When he died in the initial slaughter, no one cared.

"And even now I don't subscribe to all his views — but I no longer scoff. The horror of our history has purged me of opinions, as of vanity, confidence, spirit, charity, hope, vitality, everything — except dull dread and a kind of melancholy, stunned persistence. What leads me to recall his fancies is my growing suspicion that I, of all swimmers, may be the sole survivor of this fell journey, tale bearer of a generation. This suspicion, together with the recent sea change, suggests to me now that nothing is impossible, not even my late companion's wildest visions, and brings me to a certain desperate resolve, the point of my chronicling.

"Very likely I have lost my senses. The carnage at our setting out; our decimation by whirlpool, poisoned cataract, and sea convulsion; the panic stampedes, mutinies, slaughters, mass suicides; the mounting evidence that none will survive the journey — add to these anguish and fatigue; it were a miracle if sanity stayed afloat. Thus I admit, with the other possibilities, that the present sweetening and calming of the sea, and what seems to be a kind of vasty presence, song, or summons from the near upstream, may be hallucinations of disordered sensibility. . . .

"Perhaps, even, I am drowned already. Surely I was never meant for the rough-and-tumble of the swim; not impossibly I perished at the outset and have only imaged the night-sea journey from some final deep. In any case I'm no longer young. For it is we spent old swimmers, disabused of every illusion, who are most vulnerable to dreams.

"Sometimes I think I am my drownèd friend.

"Out with it: I've begun to believe, not only that *She* exists, but that She lies not far ahead, and stills the sea, and draws me Herward! Aghast, I recollect his maddest notion: that our destination (which existed, mind, in but one night-sea out of hundreds and thousands) was no Shore, as commonly conceived, but a mysterious being, indescribable except by paradox and vaguest figure: wholly different from us swimmers, yet our complement; the death of us, yet our salvation and resurrection; simultaneously our journey's end, midpoint, and commencement; not membered and thrashing like us, but a motionless or hugely gliding sphere of unimaginable dimension; self-contained, yet dependent absolutely, in some wise, upon the chance (always monstrously improbable) that one of us will survive the night-sea journey and reach . . . Her! *Her,* he called it, or *She,* which is to say, Other-than-a-he. I shake my head; the thing is too preposterous; it is myself I talk to, to keep my reason in this awful darkness. There is no She! There is no You! I rave to myself; it's Death alone that hears and summons. To the drowned, all seas are calm. . . .

"Listen: my friend maintained that in every order of creation there are two sorts of creators, contrary yet complementary, one of which gives rise to seas and swimmers, the other to the Night-which-contains-the-sea and to What-waits-at-the-journey's-end: the former, in short, to destiny, the latter to destination (and both profligately, involuntarily, perhaps indifferently or unwittingly). The 'purpose' of the night-sea journey — but not necessarily of the journeyer or of either Maker! — my friend could describe only in abstractions: *consummation, transfiguration, union of contraries, transcension of categories.* When we laughed he would shrug and admit that he understood the business no better than we, and thought it ridiculous, dreary, possibly obscene. 'But one of you,' he'd add with his wry smile, 'may be the Hero destined to complete the night-sea journey and be one with Her. Chances are, of course, you won't make it.' He himself, he declared, was not even going to try; the whole idea repelled him; if we chose to dismiss it as an ugly fiction, so much the better for us; thrash, splash, and be merry, we were soon enough drowned. But there it was, he could not say how he knew or why he bothered to tell us, any more than he could say what would happen after She and the Hero, Shore and Swimmer, 'merged identities' to become something both and neither. He quite agreed with me that if the issue of that magical union had no memory of the night-sea journey, for example, it enjoyed a poor sort of immortality; even poorer if, as he rather imagined, a swimmer-hero plus a She equalled or became merely another Maker of future night-seas and the rest, at such incredible expense of life. This being the case — he was persuaded it was — the merciful thing to do was refuse to participate; the genuine heroes, in his opinion, were the suicides, and the hero of heroes would be the swimmer who, in the very presence of the Other, refused Her proffered 'immortality' and thus put an end to at least one cycle of catastrophes.

"How we mocked him! Our moment came, we hurtled forth, pretending to glory in the adventure, thrashing, singing, cursing, strangling, rationalizing, rescuing, killing, inventing rules and stories and relationships, giving up, struggling on, but dying all, and still in darkness, until only a battered remnant was left to croak 'Onward, upward,' like a bitter echo. Then they too fell silent — victims, I can only presume, of the last frightful wave — and the moment came when I also, utterly desolate and spent, thrashed my last and gave myself over to the current, to sink or float as might be, but swim no more. Whereupon, marvelous to tell, in an instant the sea grew still! Then warmly, gently, the great tide turned, began to bear me, as it does now, onwards and upwards will-I nill-I, like a flood of joy — and I recalled with dismay my dead friend's teaching.

"I am not deceived. This new emotion is Her doing; the desire that possesses me is Her bewitchment. Lucidity passes from me; in a moment I'll cry 'Love!', bury myself in Her side, and be 'transfigured.' Which is to say, I die already; this fellow transported by passion is not I; *I am he who abjures and rejects the night-sea journey! I. . . .*

"I am all love. 'Come!' She whispers, and I have no will.

"You and I may be about to become, whatever You are: with the last twitch of my real self I beg You to listen. It is *not* love that sustains me! No; though Her magic makes me burn to sing the contrary, and though I drown even now for the blasphemy, I will say the truth. What has fetched me across this dreadful sea is a single hope, gift of my poor dead comrade: that You may be stronger-willed than I, and that by sheer force of concentration I may transmit to You, along with Your official Heritage, a private legacy of awful recollection and negative resolve. Mad as it may be, my dream is that some unimaginable embodiment of myself (or myself plus Her if that's how it must be) will come to find itself expressing, in however garbled or radical a translation, some reflection of these reflections. If against all odds this comes to pass, may You to whom, through whom I speak, do what I cannot: terminate this aimless, brutal business! Stop Your hearing against Her song! Hate love!

"Still alive, afloat, afire. Farewell then my penultimate hope: that one may be sunk for direst blasphemy on the very shore of the Shore. Can it be (my old friend would smile) that only utterest nay-sayers survive the night? But even that were Sense, and there is no sense, only senseless love, senseless death. Whoever echoes these reflections: be more courageous than their author! An end to night-sea journeys! Make no more! And forswear me when I shall forswear myself, deny myself, plunge into Her who summons, singing . . .

" 'Love! Love! Love!' "